I0754307

[illegible]

[illegible]

WILD SOUTHERN SCENES.

A TALE OF

DISUNION! AND BORDER WAR!

BY J. B. JONES, ESQ.,

AUTHOR OF "WILD WESTERN SCENES," "WAR PATH," "THE RIVAL BELLES," "LIFE OF COLONEL VANDERBOMB," "LIFE AND ADVENTURES OF NED LORN," ETC., ETC.

Complete in one large vol., neatly bound in cloth, for One Dollar and Twenty-five Cents; or another edition, in two vols., paper cover, for One Dollar.

READ THE FOLLOWING OPINIONS OF THE PRESS.

From the "New York Leader."

"We have found a decided and most irresistible sensation in 'Wild Southern Scenes,' and don't care who knows it. That sensation is not by any means one of entire content, but it *is* one of fully developed surprise—such as a quiet and well-disposed young lady, sitting cosily in her boudoir, might be supposed to feel at the sudden dropping down through the ceiling of a full-grown Cossack, booted to the knees, moustached to the ears, and armed with a whole arsenal of cosmopolitan weapons. The sensation might not be one of fright, exactly—but so mingled with curiosity that the gaze of the occupant might express quite as much of interest as of apprehension. We are a little at a loss for a class under which to rate this new volume. Perhaps it comes nearer to a political Allegory than any thing else; and yet it is so free from the ineffable stupidities which generally characterize allegorical works, and has so much of the brilliant action and stirring interest of the Military Novel, that we cannot well avoid appending it to the latter class. Upon still more mature reflection, we are compelled to range it under that still larger class—the Nondescript, which every body reads, which nearly every body admires, but which nobody quite understands. As may be supposed from the title, the author has taken an entirely new field for his romance. His is a bold thought; and yet, the field once marked out, many will wonder that it has never before been thought of; and it is easy to predict that—the egg once broken—there will be found many more to try their hand at it. To say that the author has fulfilled his task ably—would be but giving the book a very negative recommendation. He has done more: he has written with startling vigor, and with a naturalness absolutely astounding, when it is remembered that the ground he is treading is entirely imaginary, and ground, too, the exact like of which has never been trodden in the world of literature or in history. There is much of personal interest in the book—much of that 'stream of human happiness' which 'glides on,' as Bulwer says, 'through plots and counterplots, through gain and loss, through glory and disgrace, along the plains where passionate Discord rears eternal Babel.' But this, with the vigorous character sketching which embodies and accompanies it, we must leave to that legion of readers who will probably peruse it. We have already, in the length of this notice, gone beyond the possibility of any extended extracts, but must make room for two—graphic and weird as the book itself."

From the Philadelphia "City Item."

"We have received from T. B. Peterson & Brothers, 'Wild Southern Scenes,' by J. B. Jones, author of 'Wild Western Scenes' and other works of great popularity and excellence. 'Wild Western Scenes' had a sale of 100,000 copies, and 5000 are now sold annually, though the work was published twenty years ago. 'Wild Southern Scenes' is written in the same vein, and cannot fail to create a deep sensation among all classes of the community, both on account of its topics generally, and the thrilling interest that makes the reader reluctant to lay it down till he has read it quite through. The work is duodecimo, of upwards of 500 pages, well got up, with good paper and handsome cloth binding. Its style is peculiarly happy, and pleasingly reminds one of the 'Wild Western Scenes,' to which this is, if possible, a superior work. The stirring events, and hair-breadth escapes—the ups and downs—the scenes full of joy, sorrow, hope, fear, love, hatred, and in short, all the emotions of the mind—take full possession of the reader and enchain him; while the author, like a potent magician, is perfect master of the passions by one single wave of his enchanting wand. The work will have an immense sale. Every body will read it, and the effect it will have will be of the most salutary kind, and by showing the ill effects of Disunion, draw the bands of Union yet closer midst the various sections of our great Republic. Everything in the work is of an elevating character in a moral sense, and abounding in passages of rare merit and extraordinary beauty, it does credit to the head and heart of the author, with whom we have had the pleasure of being acquainted for some time. We cordially recommend the work to the public in general, and our friends in particular. It will be found a rich treat, and will not fail to improve the reader. Booksellers need not be afraid of ordering this volume in quantities, as the popularity of the author's other book, will produce a large sale for the new one."

From the "Portland Argus."

"The publishers of 'Wild Western Scenes,' by J. B. Jones, Esq., the author of this volume, have sold One Hundred Thousand copies of that captivating book. If we are not much mistaken, 'Wild Southern Scenes' will obtain as wide a circulation. It is a capital tale—full of love incidents, patriotism, statesmanship and generalship. The book is one of the most intensely interesting that we have read for many a day, and it is amusing and patriotically instructive as well. Its influence cannot fail to be good. We heartily commend it to every body. No one will commence to read and not finish it."

From the "Richmond (Va.) Enquirer."

"We have ventured the prediction that this work is destined to achieve a success. We hope half a million copies may be disseminated among the people North and South, and we are glad that it has fallen into the hands of the fortunate publishers of it."

From the "New York Observer."

"A very remarkable and novel book. * * * * The scenes that follow are portrayed with great skill and effect, with a love story running through, and amusing scenes introduced, making the tale entertaining, and holding the reader's attention to the close."

From the "New York Day Book."

"The author of 'Wild Western Scenes' has given us another very entertaining book. The terrible results that will follow the inevitable climax of sectional madness and folly are made the subject of the story. The author takes a south side view of the quarrel, but the book ought not to be of less interest to northern readers on that account. They may read and profit thereby. The tale is of intense interest. There is much humor running throughout it. The President's daughter, Capt. Bim, and General Crook, are well drawn characters. We can confidently recommend the work as one of absorbing and peculiar interest."

From the Philadelphia "Pennsylvanian."

"We have been informed that certain critics and Republican publishers and booksellers have agreed to *freeze* this book to death. This we think impracticable—there is too much fire in it. The work will reach the hands of the people."

From the New York "Daily Times."

"Mr. J. B. Jones, who once wrote a book called '*Wild Western Scenes*,' has just favored us with a romance of American life, which is a fiction, pure and simple, and in which no small degree of imaginative power is exhibited. The theme is really a very admirable one. There is a good deal of ingenuity in his narrative, and no small amount of invention, in sustaining the interest of the story. The scene opens on the eve of a wedding at the Capitol, when Alice Randolph, the President's daughter, was to be the principal bridesmaid to Edith Langdon, the daughter of Senator Langdon. To compose a narrative of this character so that it can be read at all, is no small triumph, and we must admit that he has given us a book which may be read with interest, for the subject has been so often discussed that there are very few men who will not be interested in reading the supposititious history of an event, the contemplation of which puzzles and terrifies the strongest minds."

From the Philadelphia "Christian Chronicle."

"The author of this work is well known to the public, and already enjoys a large measure of popularity. This work will prove of equal popularity, and be eagerly sought after by the thousands who have read 'Wild Western Scenes.' It contains 502 pages."

From the "Troy (N. Y.) Whig."

"It is an amusing, readable book, in which the interest is kept up, and the incidents are so well told as to make one almost believe they are real. The author made a happy hit in a previous work, 'Wild Western Scenes,' and we should not wonder if 'Wild Southern Scenes' was equally well received by the public."

From the "Detroit (Mich.) Advertiser."

"This is a book that Western people will read. The reputation which the author acquired as a graphic writer in 'Wild Western Scenes,' a book that has reached an immense sale, and acquired a universal popularity, especially among the young, will insure for it a welcome reception and large sale. It contains many thrilling scenes, and many remarkable and laughable incidents. As popular as his previous work has proved, this cannot prove less so."

From the "New York Courier and Inquirer."

"Mr. Jones is known as the author of 'Wild Western Scenes,' and in the present tale he pictures an attempt to dissever the Union, which only terminates in defeat. The volume is issued with good taste."

From the Philadelphia "Inquirer."

"This is a powerful story from the pen of J. B. Jones, author of 'Wild Western Scenes.' It abounds in vigorous sketches, strong delineation of character, and telling incidents. The style of writing is bold and forcible."

From the Boston "Ledger."

"The above novel makes a bulky book, of nearly seventy chapters. The scenes are laid principally in Virginia and the South. It is exciting in a high degree, and has lots of love sprinkled over its pages. The publishers get it out in their usual fine style."

Price for the complete work, in two volumes, in paper cover, One Dollar only; or another edition, handsomely bound in one volume, cloth, gilt, is published for One Dollar and Twenty-five cents.

Copies of either edition of the work will be sent to any person, to any part of the United States, *free of postage*, on remitting the price of the edition they may wish, to the publishers in a letter.

Published and for Sale by

T. B. PETERSON & BROTHERS,

No. 306 Chestnut Street, Philadelphia,

To whom all Orders should be addressed, post-paid.

LORD SLYSIR AND WIRY WILLY IN THE LIBRARY

WILD SOUTHERN SCENES.

A TALE OF

DISUNION! AND BORDER WAR!

BY

J. B. JONES, ESQ.,

AUTHOR OF "WILD WESTERN SCENES," "THE RIVAL BELLES," "WAR PATH," ETC., ETC.

"We have ventured the prediction that this work is destined to achieve a success. We hope half a million copies may be disseminated among the people North and South, and we are glad that it has fallen into the hands of the fortunate publishers of it." —*Richmond Enquirer.*

"A very remarkable and novel book. * * * * The scenes that follow are portrayed with great skill and effect, with a love story running through, and amusing scenes introduced, making the tale entertaining, and holding the reader's attention to the close."—*New York Observer.*

"A capital tale of love incidents, patriotism, and statesmanship. The book is one of the most intensely interesting that we have read for many a day, and it is amusing and patriotically instructive as well. Its influence cannot fail to be good. We heartily commend it to everybody. No one will commence to read and not finish it."—*Portland Argus.*

Philadelphia:

T. B. PETERSON & BROTHERS,

306 CHESTNUT STREET.

CONTENTS.

———o———

WILD SOUTHERN SCENES.

CHAPTER I.

THE EVE OF THE WEDDING.

OLD MAUD CLUSKY, the cook, had repeatedly looked out from the basement of a stately mansion, in the Federal City, impatiently awaiting her master's return from the Capitol. The hour for dinner had struck, and the punctual Senator Langdon had not taken his seat at the table. And, that day, of all others, the President's daughter, Alice Randolph, was to dine with Miss Edith Langdon; and the day following, Miss Randolph was to be Miss Langdon's principal bridesmaid. The Honorable Henry Blount—for he was a member of the House of Representatives, whilst his venerable father occupied a seat in the Senate—was on that day to espouse the beautiful Edith in St. John's Holy Church. And the daughter of the President of the United States was now with the affianced maiden in her boudoir.

To say nothing of the honor of preparing a dinner for the President's daughter, it was very natural for Maud to evince some impatience to have it served precisely at the appointed time. Her son Dick, the coachman and gardener, had been despatched to the Capitol at the usual hour—and now it was full twenty minutes past the ordinary time of serving the first course!

"The bad boy!" she exclaimed, vainly peering through the iron railing, and evidently disposed to vent her wrath on her innocent son. "He's got a watch," she continued, her face red with vexation, "and he ought to know the things 'll be spoilt." And, just as she was in the act of re-entering the door under the marble steps, her ear caught the sound of wheels; and, pausing, she beheld the gold band on the hat of her boy. But he was driving most furiously. "You Dick!" she exclaimed, "the Senator 'll kill you for such conduct. Stop, I say!" Dick did not stop. He kept up an incessant fusillade with his whip on the spirited horses, and, turning the corner, vanished from sight. "Crazy as a loon!" cried Maud, staring wildly. "What is the matter? He's gone to the stable, and I'll run through and catch him there." She did attempt it; but being extremely corpulent and short-winded, by the time she was ready to enter the door of the coach-house Dick emerged from it into the garden. His face was very pale, and all his limbs were trembling.

"You Dick!" cried his mother, seizing him by the collar, "where's Senator Langdon?"

"He's at the Capitol, in concus."

"In what?"

"In the Vice-President's room, in 'portant consulteration. He told me to come home and put up the horses quietly. He'll come in a hack when he's done in concus. He said I musn't 'larm Miss Edith—and she and Miss Randolph is to dine together alone without him. And they musn't know what's the matter yet awhile. Then I'm to give this note, and—"

"You Dick!" cried his mother, seizing him with both hands, "what *is* the matter?"

"Let go, or I can't speak! You choke me! Oh Lord! I'll faint! I'm frightened half to death! Give me some brandy, mother."

"Not a drop till you tell me! What's happened? Come, now!"

"They've dissolved the Union!"

"Hey! How! What's that?"

"These United States are all knocked into flinders!"

"Who done it?"

"Both sides. Mr. Langdon's no Senator now. Mr. Randolph's no President, and Miss Alice is no President's daughter."

"That's a lie, Dick! Mr. Langdon's elected for six years,

and his grandfather made the Constitution! 'Taint so. I know better. There's the bell—run!" Dick darted forward, leaving his mother to follow.

Alice and Edith, unconscious of the flight of time, held consultation over the rich *trousseau* displayed before them. Satins, and laces, and flowers, and jewels, have still their attractions for the sex, even while governments may be crumbling into their original elements. And yet Edith and Alice were not of that giddy and flippant class which deem the vanities of worldly fashion paramount to the other objects of existence. They had been schoolmates at St. Mary's Hall, New Jersey, where the duties as well as the adornments of American ladies were inculcated. The bride of the morrow was rather above the medium height, though not robust in form. Her pale and expressive face was regular in its features, though perhaps not sufficiently oval for the prevailing taste. But her brilliant dark eyes, with their long silken lashes, betrayed the happy emotions of an innocent heart to the beholder. With a similar stature, and equal loveliness, Alice's light flaxen hair and sky-blue eyes, contrasted pleasantly with the opposite hues of those of her friend.

"To-morrow, Edith, oh, to-morrow!" she exclaimed, as she again surveyed the magnificent vestments spread out before them. "One short day, and then—why are you so sad, and so suddenly?"

"Ah, Alice! you remember what the Bishop used to say of the anticipations of to-morrow! But this to-morrow may come as well as any morrow. You know I am not fearful; indeed they call me brave; and yet, I don't know why it was—but when you mentioned that word, a pang seemed to shoot across my breast, and there was a sensible check of respiration. If I should know no morrow, I would be incapable of lamentation. As for Harry, I know his truth and constancy. If he lives, he will come with the morrow!"

"It is not to be doubted. And yet—"

"Alice, speak on. Our thoughts have ever been freely shared. We are alone."

"I was saying—and yet the times are perilous. Those fearful resolves, so fiercely discussed, both in the country and in the Capitol; the menacing action of the State Legislatures; the thunders of the journals and the threats of the Senators; these, Edith, when considered in connexion with the measured step of my father in the chamber directly over my own, sometimes till early morn, induce the belief that we may be upon the eve of some great political convulsion."

"And what would be the fate of the President?"

"He apprehends no perils for himself. Nor do I believe he could be made very unhappy by any of the events which have been prognosticated."

"Why do you not believe so?"

"Because, once, when I supposed him ill, and rushed into his presence, at the hour of two in the morning, he turned quickly round, gazed a moment at my ghostly habiliments, and then merely vented hearty peals of laughter. There were no traces of vexation on his brow. He kissed me, said he was never in better health or spirits, and that I might slumber *securely*, never dreaming of loss of *position*. He emphasized the words. And there was meaning in them, Edith."

"What could he mean?"

"I could only conjecture, for I durst not interrogate him. But he who has wrought so boldly and so successfully hitherto is not likely to be a loser in the political game hereafter. He is not troubled, else I should see it, and I *do* feel tolerably secure. The clock strikes."

Edith started.

"And father is not here," said she. "He should have arrived fifteen minutes ago. I hear the carriage now. No; it is not his. He is never driven so furiously. But some one rings," she added soon after. The ring was repeated several times before Dick, released from the grasp of his mother, could reach the door.

Dick, however, presently made his appearance, with two notes and a card on a silver salver.

"Who left this?" asked Alice, recognising her father's handwriting.

"The gentleman's name is on the card," said Dick, stammering, bowing, and then withdrawing.

Edith read as follows:—"My dear child, be not impatient for my return. Dine with Alice, and be of good cheer. I have had a lunch brought me. We have voted on the 'Abstraction Resolution,' and there is some commotion in consequence of the result, requiring consultation. Henry's father and I voted differently. I will see you in an hour. Your affectionate father," etc.

"Now listen to mine," said Alice:—"*Be marble. Great events are about to transpire. Edith could furnish an example of imperturbability if it were not for her approaching nuptials and the variance between Blount and her father, which may involve a temporary estrangement. Tell her it will be only temporary; and beseech her to impart a portion of her native courage to her friend Alice. I send this by Wiry Will, my trusty messenger. When he returns from the Capitol, you may accompany him home.* ALL GOES WELL!"

A brief pause ensued.

"You sigh, Edith," said Alice, taking the hand of her pale companion.

"I did; but that is past. And the tear is not followed by another. The President—your father, foresees correctly. His words were designed partly for me. His eagle glance penetrates hearts, and his great mind comprehends characters. If a wife, I must obey my husband—I am sure I shall love him! A daughter, my father shall command. They must decide my course; and once decided, Alice, your friend, if not indeed marble, will not be fearful and vacillating. Even you, Alice, the President's daughter, may lean upon me amidst the direst convulsions that can happen."

"Dear Edith, I know it well!" said Alice, throwing herself in the arms of her friend.

"And there may be horrors to try us all. We may suffer many pangs: but let us not forget we are capable of much suffering. There is Maud. Let us dine, if not for the sake of our appetites, to please the cook, you know. Come."

They repaired to the dining-room, and tasted the viands and delicacies prepared with such great care and solicitude, and moistened their lips with the generous wine.

"Who is this Mr. William Wire?" asked Edith, gazing at the enamelled card which had accompanied the notes.

"They call him Wiry Willy; and many suppose him half-witted. But my father employs not, trusts not, half-witted men. I have seen, from my chamber window, this tall, pale, cadaverous youth, stride across the lawn in the rear of the mansion, at late and solemn hours of the night; and he obtained ready access to my father. Once I alluded, inquiringly, to these mysterious visits. My father smiled, and said the youth was in *love.* And immediately after added that the object of his affection was the beautiful Mary Penford. She had repulsed him, in obedience to the command of her grandfather, the old clerk about whom the papers have said so much. And, strangely enough, it was Wiry Will who obtained from the President a peremptory order for the old man's restoration to the desk from which the Secretary had removed him."

"And then, of course, there was gratitude, and a removal of the cruel ——"

"No, Edith. Do you not know there is no such thing as gratitude in politics? You should read some of the letters to the President. Nor yet is it the want of gratitude on the old man's part. He deems himself an important dignitary, and has determined to bestow the hand of Mary on the Hon. Mr. Ruffleton, who is some day to be President, and then the superannuated clerk is to be promoted —to be the chief of a bureau, if not the head of a department. But why should you listen to this idle prattle?"

"It interested me. I know Mary, and have never believed the stories malignantly circulated concerning her. But if we, who have parents possessing wealth and power, shrink from the dark future, whose shadows are upon us, what must be the meditations and the fate of poor Mary, pursued, as I believe her to be, by one incapable of a good design?"

"You speak thus of General Ruffleton!"

Just then a carriage stopped at the door, and Mr. Langdon and the two Blounts, the father and son, entered the mansion. They proceeded into the parlor, whither the young ladies awaited in vain a summons to join them. Without such summons they would not present themselves. The gentlemen, however, had hardly been seated, before Alice was called for by Wiry Willy, and departed for the Presidential Mansion.

We will introduce the reader to the gentlemen. Mr. Langdon was corpulent, and presented an imposing appearance, as he stood with his hands behind him, hidden under the skirts of his coat. His features, full and handsome, and his head surmounted by a wig of very dark grey hair, one might have supposed him a vigorous gentleman of fifty, whereas he was not less than seventy years of age. The elder Blount, facing the Northern Senator, was his junior by several years, and his antipodes in almost every thing. He was tall and thin: his long hair was very white: his face was pale, and his clothes evinced his contempt for the prevailing fashion. Henry, his son, who sat apart on a sofa, was a perfect model in stature and manly beauty. He had served four years in Congress, having been elected the first time a few weeks before he became eligible, according to the Constitution. He was now in his twenty-ninth year.

"I tell you, sir," said Mr. Langdon, with much emphasis, "this is a very serious, if not an irremediable rupture. A majority of the Representatives and Senators of thirteen States to abandon their places, and then solemnly resolve never to resume them! And it was this, as might have been foreseen, when the animosity was mutual, for it is irresistibly contagious, Mr. Blount, led to the withdrawal of an equal number of Republicans!"

"And for my part," responded the Southern Senator, with *sang froid*, "I am not sure that I shall ever regret the occurrence. You would not pass the resolution declaratory of our right to erect additional slave States; and of course we could not look for any other guarantee. In the Union all must be equals; equality denied, the Union ends. My son and myself were among the first to relinquish our seats. I glory in it."

"But, sir, it was a mere abstraction!" rejoined Mr. Langdon. "I would have voted for the admission of a new slave State, being satisfied a majority of its inhabitants desired the institution of slavery; but I voted nay on this measure. It was one of supererogation, and of no practical use whatever; and history will condemn you for the step you have taken."

"Sir," said Mr. Blount, "when my judgment and my conscience tell me I am right, history may say what it pleases. The historians, however, often utter falsehoods, like irresponsible editors and reckless orators!"

"Gentlemen," said the younger Blount, who rose from

the sofa, and promenaded to and fro in front of the excited Senators, "you forget that you are no longer in the Senate Chamber, and that the Federal Senate has ceased to exist. That is past. The object of this meeting——"

"True, Harry," said the elder Blount. "If the political confederacy be dissolved, as I believe it is, and for ever, that may be no sufficient reason why domestic ties should be severed, and no more matrimonial unions be contracted. Edith's mother was a daughter of the South, and yours a native of the North. The match has my cordial approbation. Still, it may be a question whether the nuptials ought not, under existing circumstances, to be postponed."

"I, too, most heartily approve the alliance," said Mr. Langdon; "and I agree with your father, that it might, perhaps, be well to postpone the ceremony until a more quiet time."

"Your apparent accord, gentlemen," said Henry, with the faintest shadow of a smile, as he recollected that for them to agree on any subject was an almost unprecedented occurrence, "is, I confess, greatly adverse to my hopes. If you differed, as usual, on the point of time, I might have some weight in the decision. But should we not consult Edith, the other party interested? We know not, we cannot know, what storms and convulsions the inflammable elements may engender; and what may be deemed a postponement for merely a short space of time, might prove an eternal separation."

"True, sir," said Mr. Langdon. "And if I may credit the assurances of divers members from your section, it is not unlikely, if the union be consummated now, the youthful bride may very soon be a young widow. They tell me that you will be made a military chieftain; that war will be declared; and much other nonsense."

"How, sir! how nonsense?" asked the elder Blount, quickly. "Can any man in his senses suppose our differences may be adjusted without the intervention of the sword? I tell you our negroes will be at work on our fortifications in forty-eight hours."

"Would they not join us?" asked Mr. Langdon, imprudently.

"No, sir!" was the reply, in almost startling tones, while the usually pale forehead of the aged Senator was momentarily flushed with crimson. "The lying Abolitionists have propagated that idea. They will be undeceived. The slaves will defend their masters, and when opportunity serves, will avenge them. The time at length has arrived, when the fanatics of the North——"

"Remember," said Mr. Langdon, interrupting him, "that all the Northern people are not fanatics. I am not one, though opposed to slavery. Nor am I a Republican, but——"

"Gentlemen," again interposed the younger Blount, "recollect the Senatorial debate is concluded. It is *my* affair, now, upon the tapis. And pray let us confine ourselves to the question, for time presses."

"Very well, Harry," said Mr. Langdon, slightly annoyed at the interruption, though conceding its justice—"you are right, no doubt. And as there are some matters I would confer about with your father—not at all political—I suggest that you find Edith, and confer with her. Whatever conclusion you may arrive at—since the matter has gone to this extremity—will be ratified, I trust, by both your father and myself."

"Go, Harry, and with plenary powers," added the elder Blount.

Harry, heartily concurring in the proposition, withdrew immediately, and in the space of fifteen minutes reappeared, conducting Edith, who had promptly acquiesced in his desire that their fates should be united at the altar on the morrow. Their opportune presence also served to suppress an incipient renewal of the debate which had been brought to so abrupt a conclusion in the Senate.

CHAPTER II.

A MIDNIGHT CONSPIRACY.

On the left bank of the Potomac, a few miles distant from the Federal City, at the still hour of midnight, some two hundred men were assembled under a gigantic sycamore.

They were all armed. Save the low hum of earnest voices, a profound silence brooded over the scene. The canopy above was radiant with stars, and ever and anon a shooting meteor traversed the heavens with its dissolving light.

"Gentlemen," said one of the watchers, who seemed to be the leader, "if we succeed in this enterprise we shall be the fixed lights of the age, like the stars; if we fail, we shall be merely ephemeral scintillations, fading into utter darkness, leaving no enduring rays of glory behind. If there be one present, therefore, whose heart is not decided, let him depart."

No one moved during the pause that ensued. Then a simultaneous clapping of hands followed, in token of the unanimity of sentiment and purpose which prevailed.

"We will succeed or die," was uttered by nearly all present.

"SUCCESS OR DEATH, shall be the watchword," said the first speaker.

"But, General," said the Hon. Mr. Steel, who stood on the General's left, enveloped in a cloak, "do you think there will be serious resistance on the part of the President? He is a Southern man."

"Unquestionably! It is true he is a Southern man—but he is also the PRESIDENT."

"Not of the United States!" said the honorable gentleman.

"Not now—not by a great deal!" responded many voices.

"That's to be tested, gentlemen," said General Crook, the leader of the band. "I know Randolph's character. He is Southern by birth, and cannot be Northern by inclination or interest. He believes the Constitution a sufficient protection for both sections, and he does not intend to relinquish it. Without regarding him either as a friend or an enemy, our purpose is to possess ourselves of that portion of the archives, and of the arms and treasure, to which our section is justly entitled, at all hazards, and at any sacrifice. You have chosen me your leader, and I have undertaken to perform the service. The only regret I feel is, that the men I am to command are not all Southerners. One half are from the North, as I learn, and many of them have been the followers of General W. The difficulty will be in restraining them. They are brave, no doubt; but it is to be feared they are actuated too much by the hope of immediate reward, and too little by considerations of patriotic devotion. But no matter. I am an Alabamian, and this is an enterprise in behalf of the South. The paramount object is, to *strike a blow*—a terrible blow—which will be retorted by the other side, and render compromise, reconciliation, and reunion impracticable. For many years I have longed for an opportunity such as this. The South will throw off her degrading vassalage. We shall have great cities and fleets, and factories of our own."

"But *we* are almost naked, and will soon be hungry," said a swarthy and gigantic individual, named Bim, a New Yorker, and a leader of a club of one hundred, whose arrival was momentarily expected. "I bargained for a share of defunct Uncle Sam's treasure."

"Your services shall be recompensed, Jack Bim, according to contract. You shall have everything promised; but you must receive it from the paymaster, not seize it. And everything, you know, was to depend upon success."

"Success is certain," observed the Hon. Mr. Steel.

"I hope so," replied the General. "Nevertheless, we should not expect a triumph without blows given and received. The steamer now nearly due, will land eight hundred men, and six or eight pieces of artillery. We shall have one thousand against I know not how many on the side of the President. Small detachments of troops and marines have been daily arriving in Washington from different quarters. Such is my information. But I hope he can have no intelligence of this expedition. We will fall upon him suddenly—by ten o'clock to-morrow, at the latest—and in the consternation of the moment, our purpose must be accomplished. Who goes there?—stop that man!"

A tall individual enveloped in a long frock coat, was observed gliding out from under the branches of the tree.

"Who are you?" demanded the General, when the person was brought before him.

"Wiry Willy," was the response.

"And pray who is Wiry Willy? Be careful what you say. If I deem you a spy, I shall order a bowie-knife to your throat, to avoid the report of gunpowder."

"Willy's a friend—Willy's everybody's friend. Why,

General, Willy was only going out yonder on the grass to get you a horse. Generals ought to have horses, and white ones too."

"It is a half-witted fellow; I know him very well," said the Hon. Mr. Steel. "He used to bore me in behalf of an old clerk who had been removed, and with whose daughter he was in love."

"Mary Penford," said Wiry Willy, turning towards the ex-member, "is old John Penford's grand-daughter. If you'll listen, I'll tell you the whole story, and all about General Ruffleton's conduct, too. General Ruffleton's a villain; and as he's to be the general on the other side, of course I'll fight under General Crook."

"Enough," said the General. "I will trust you. General Ruffleton, I learn, intends really to organize a rabble army in the North, on his own responsibility, and, I presume, for his own aggrandizement; and, truly, I see a white horse yonder. Secure him for me, Willy."

Wiry Willy vanished instantly, and in a few brief moments returned, leading the horse.

"General," said he, "may I have leave of absence till I can find you a saddle and bridle?"

"Yes, Willy." Then turning and addressing the gentlemen nearest him, the leader said: "President Randolph possesses the greatest mind and the bravest heart in America. He was born on Southern soil, and when the Federal Chair is engulfed in destruction, he will join us, and be our commander-in-chief. Therefore, I desire it to be made known to every man who shall march with me to-morrow, that under no circumstances is the President to be slain. A magnificent reward will be paid those who may capture him; but he who kills him shall be hung. Does this proposition meet your approbation, gentlemen?"

"It does," was the unanimous reply.

A moment after the steamer hove in sight, and the whole party moved down to the brink of the water.

As for Wiry Willy, instead of approaching any of the country houses to obtain a bridle and saddle for the General, he glided through the bushes in the vicinity, until his ear was saluted by a low whinny, and turning to the left, he placed his hand on a black pony, which he mounted. He proceeded at an easy pace until he emerged into a well beaten road, and then, plying his hickory switch, seemed to fly upon the wings of the wind.

During the same solemn hour of midnight, the great east room of the presidential mansion was as brilliantly illuminated as it had ever been on any former occasion. President Randolph, with folded arms, promenaded slowly to and fro with measured and deliberate step. His cabinet ministers sat round a table, under the full glare of an immense chandelier. Other groups were scattered in different parts of the large saloon, either silent or conversing in suppressed tones, as if awed by the majestic brow of the chief executive. The President, though slightly stricken in years, betrayed none of the infirmities of age. Of middle stature, and erect frame—an eye that seemed to penetrate the thoughts of all—a commanding mien, and features indicating firmness of purpose and decision of character, no one living, perhaps, was better qualified to inspire the respect and win the confidence of mankind. Vigilant and indefatigable in his incessant labors—endowed by his Creator with the highest gifts of genius, and his mind improved by the attainment of every species of knowledge imparted by books, or derived from association with the best intellects of his country, he had merited and received the suffrages of a majority of his fellow-citizens for the high position he then occupied, *and he resolved not to abandon it until satisfied that such was the will of those who had exalted him.*

The folding-doors were thrown open, and there entered from the great hall, the diplomatic representatives of all the nations, followed by some forty Senators and members of the House, who still lingered in the Federal City.

"My Lords and Gentlemen of the Diplomatic Corps, and Senators and Representatives of the States and the People," said the President, when encircled by that distinguished auditory, "I have desired your presence for a brief interval, at this unseasonable hour, because I felt quite certain that the request would be granted with alacrity, and that the extraordinary event which has just transpired would render any apology unnecessary for the temporary inconvenience to which you would be subjected. And yet, my Lords and Gentlemen, I should not have imposed this trouble upon you, if I had not been advised of the destruction of the telegraphic wires leading from the different points of the country to this city. I understand that many of you have it in contemplation to depart presently from this seat of government, and I have deemed it my duty to see that you shall be provided with authentic information of a portion, at least, of the purposes of the Chief Executive. It is, then, to be distinctly understood, that, although the Legislative Department has seen proper to indulge in an abrupt and an irregular abandonment of its duties, the Executive and Judicial Functionaries will remain intact, and endeavor to fulfil the obligations imposed by the solemn oath they have taken to support the Constitution of the United States. On my part, there shall be no recognition of a dissolution of the Union. The means at my command, to maintain the position I have indicated, will be apparent when the emergency shall arise for their employment. My Lords and Gentlemen of the Diplomatic Corps, you are aware that the Constitution forbids any State making treaties, or maintaining direct diplomatic correspondence with foreign powers. You will therefore excuse me when I say, that in pursuance of my duty as the Chief Magistrate of the Federal Union, I shall hold to a strict accountability any parties that may attempt an infraction of that provision of the fundamental instrument of this government. This information, my Lords and Gentlemen, I deemed it necessary to impart in this informal manner, because of the peculiar exigencies existing at the present moment."

The President having been bowed to repeatedly during the delivery of his speech, made, at its termination, a very emphatic bow himself.

But the Lords and Gentlemen were not quite satisfied to be dismissed in so summary a manner; and, to prolong the audience, which seemed fraught with much interest to them, they lingered for many minutes, and stammered out numerous protestations of respect for the distinguished functionary, whom they really supposed to have been effectually despoiled of his power, and diplomatic assurances of high consideration, etc., etc.

And when the foreign gentlemen had finally taken their departure, the President, resuming the frank and social demeanor among his own countrymen, for which he was so justly celebrated, mingled cheerfully and even gaily among his personal friends, precisely as he had been in the habit of doing when no cause of alarm existed.

"I think," said he, "that those agents of the great monarchical powers, instead of enjoying a scramble for the fragments of a shattered empire, may find that we have still a government, both *de facto* and *de jure.* My friends," he continued, in a more serious tone, "and my enemies—if there be any such present—I would impress upon your minds, before you return to your respective homes, that I still regard the Federal Constitution as the paramount authority. I have sworn to defend it—*and I do not doubt my ability to do so.* I could not prevent a dissolution of Congress, and perhaps, my proclamations, calling the members together again, may long be disregarded. I believe I have no legal power of forcing a compliance. But what then? Cannot the government exist in the absence of Congress? Has it not done so, at least one half the time, since its creation? Depend upon it, gentlemen, it will continue to exist, whatever the disorganizers and traitors may do. *I shall collect the revenue.* I may not disburse it without appropriations by Congress; but I will keep it in safety, and issue audited certificates of dues. If I cannot increase the army, I may call out the militia. I shall make appointments and removals, as usual, in the civil service. In short, gentlemen, I doubt not I shall administer the affairs of the people quite satisfactorily. Therefore, I beg that it may be made known to the Quixotic Disunionists, North and South, that the Federal Government does not intend to succumb until its abandonment is decreed by the people. Whenever a majority of all the voters of the United States shall demand a relinquishment of my functions, I will then be absolved from my oath—and not till then. A moment, gentlemen," he added, stepping aside, on beholding Wiry Willy standing a few paces apart. Glancing over the few lines handed him by Wiry Willy, his eagle eye sparkled with animation, and a joyous smile, for an instant, illuminated his expressive features. "Breathe it to no one, sir," said he, in a whisper.

"Not even to Mary, sir? She would listen to that, and it might save her grandfather's life."

"To no one before nine o'clock. There!" he continued, writing two words with his pencil on Willy's scrap of paper, "take this to General Valiant, and then go to bed."

"My friends," he continued, resuming his position, "I have, I believe, communicated everything I had intended to say. There are other matters of great moment, I must not reveal. Those who shall adhere to me, will, I think, be on the side of the people. But enough of this. I have only to add, that those who do not intend to abide permanently at the Capital, would do well to leave it immediately —even by the trains that depart before the dawn of day—else, from the information in my possession, they may be liable to molestation on the road."

These words produced a most wonderful commotion. They were hardly uttered before a general dispersion commenced. Many rushed away without even taking leave of the President; but others, with tears, assured him that they would, if necessary, perish in the maintenance of his cause.

The President's brow, however, exhibited a most terrible expression upon witnessing the withdrawal of the Secretary of State, from the North, and of the Postmaster General, from the South.

"I desire not one word of explanation, gentlemen. Go! I am not at all surprised. Yesterday you professed to be my friends. I doubted it, but could not deny it. If you should become my enemies, all I ask is a candid avowal of it at the time of the decision." Saying this, he not only bowed them out, but closed the door behind them with his own hands.

All had departed but five faithful confidential advisers of the President, the two Blounts, and Mr. Langdon. The President taking each of the Senators by the arm, and beckoning Henry Blount to follow, led them into the embrasure of one of the Southern windows, where the lawn and the distant river were made visible by the rising moon.

"How peaceful the scene!" said he, "but, alas! how soon the scene may be changed!"

"That does not seem so peaceful," remarked the younger Blount, perceiving some workmen not far distant, throwing up the earth with spades. "And there are cannon," he added, "commanding the avenue."

"A precaution," said the President. "The whole country may be one battle-field; and there must be many bloody conflicts here before the Federal Government can be overthrown."

"It is already destroyed, sir," said the elder Blount, "and no one can reconstruct it. Come with us South, and you may be our President still."

"Better come North," said Mr. Langdon, "for the most ultra fire-eaters have denounced you."

"Neither North nor South, gentlemen, until sufficient force can be brought to drive me from my constitutional entrenchment."

"And that might not be so difficult a matter," rejoined Mr. Langdon. "More than once I have heard Crook, from Alabama, declare that with one thousand men he would take possession of the government, capture the President, and bear away the arms and munitions from the arsenal."

The President, after a momentary but penetrating glance at the speaker, turned to the younger Blount, and asked his opinion.

"You will be safe. You have a heavy purse—it is said twenty millions—and that will command the sword. I know of no place of greater security. It may be the only *neutral* ground. And if Mr. Langdon persists in his objections———"

"I do, Henry. I will not consent for Edith to go South, until it is first ascertained that she may do so with safety."

"Gentlemen," interposed the President, "it was in relation to this very thing that I desired to see you. For the sake of gratifying the dearest wish of my daughter Alice, if you are not permitted, politically, to accord any favor to the President, I have to beg that you will permit Edith to be a cherished guest in this mansion until the dangers we all anticipate shall have passed away. It will not be a great many months before the tempest will have expended itself, and then there will be a resuscitation of the Union——"

"Never!" said the elder Blount.

"I fear the broken bowl can never be mended," said Mr. Langdon.

"I think differently," pursued the President. "It will

be like the rupture of lovers. Men do not sometimes appreciate a blessing until it is apparently lost, or at least in peril. The glorious traditions of the past, wherein a common ancestry mingled their tears and blood in a common cause; the fame of Washington, and Jefferson, and Adams, and Hancock; the renown achieved at Bunker Hill, at Princeton, at Trenton, and Yorktown; our gigantic dimensions as a nation of thirty millions of freemen and the consideration we inspire throughout the civilized world—can all these be sacrificed at the demand of the ephemeral factions always incident to a republic? No. Believe it not."

"But I do not admit them to be factions," said the elder Blount. "They are *sections*, and the difference irreconcilable."

"You err, sir," continued the President. "The immediate pretext for the dissolution of your co-ordinate branch of the government, was merely the refusal of one section to comply with a capricious, if not an arbitrary demand of the other. And what was the resolution but an abstraction? It might have been observed by a succeeding Congress and it might have been repudiated. Sir, the CONSTITUTION is a sufficient guarantee for both sections, and that I had sworn to support. If a State had been repulsed from the Union because a majority of its inhabitants desired to possess slave property, that would have been the proper time for action. If the Supreme Law had been violated, in defiance of the intervention of the Executive and the Judiciary, and the infraction had been sanctioned by the people of the stronger section, then I should have been false to every principle of honor and justice, if I had not cast my weight in the scale of the weakest party, not only because it was the section of my nativity, but because it was in the right, and menaced with oppression. But such was not the case."

"Would to God you had spoken thus in the Senate!" exclaimed Mr. Langdon. "But now it is too late. The majority of the Northern members have solemnly asseverated that they will never permit the Southern people to add another slave State to the Union."

"I crave your pardon, gentlemen," said the younger Blount, interposing. "It was not the purpose, I believe, either to discuss or to lament the past——"

"True, sir," said the President. "In brief, then, is it

determined that these nuptials shall be celebrated to-morrow?"

"Quite," said the younger Blount.

"And it is likewise decided that my daughter is not to go Southward at present," said Mr. Langdon.

"Neither must she go to the North," said Henry Blount.

"Then she will remain here," added the President, "and, after the lapse of a few days, it will be a place of security. As bride or maiden, you may trust her in my keeping. Nevertheless, gentlemen, let the ceremony be despatched as early in the morning as possible. I have a reason for it."

"Harry," said Mr. Langdon, "do you acquiesce?"

"I do, sir. And, having consigned her to the protection of the President, I shall, an hour afterwards, be on my way to the Sunny South. If we meet no more, one, at least, who knew me well, will mourn my fate. Sir," he continued, grasping the tendered hand of the President, "will you not be present?"

"If possible—but it may not be possible. My daughter will be with you. Let me see you again before you depart from the city. Farewell!" The two Senators and Harry withdrew immediately.

CHAPTER III.

THE EVE OF BATTLE.

The sun resembled a great blood-red ball of fire as seen through the vapor that curtained the Eastern horizon. But the air was motionless, and the booming of the morning gun at the arsenal, reverberated far up the valley of the Potomac; and the screams of peacocks could be distinctly heard from the villas on the surrounding heights, betokening, as was believed by the curious villagers, the speedy advent of foul weather.

At that early hour an individual rode along the main street of Georgetown, whose long drab coat, reaching down to his heels when standing on terra firma, now, by reason of the diminutive stature of the animal he bestrode, nearly brushed the earth. And the pony being very black, the contrast was so distinct, if not ludicrous, as to attract the attention and elicit the gibes of the servant girls who awaited the baker and milkman at the doors of the dwellings. But Wiry Will was not disturbed by such exhibitions of innocent curiosity. He proceeded on his way, without looking to the right or the left, until he turned a corner and dismounted in front of an humble wooden tenement, inclosed with whitewashed palings, and scented with every variety of bud and blossom and creeper that gladden the senses in the balmy month of May. We need not premise that one of the inhabitants of that lowly abode was a tasteful maiden. But we can testify that the heart of Willy palpitated most violently when he beheld the mistress of that paradise in the little front area, watering the flowers, for she had already discovered that no dew that night had fallen from heaven.

"Mary," said Wiry Willy, throwing the reins over a post at the gate, "I have not come to annoy you with the old story. It is business with your grandpa—business of the utmost importance—a matter of life and death."

"Oh, the scene of yesterday! It is concerning that. But enter, Willy. Grandpa told me not to disturb him until breakfast was served. He is examining some papers which the new Secretary permitted him to bring home. And, Willy, I said the old story was not annoying to me—but to him. I have promised obedience, as was my duty, and—must perform it—while he lives. And when he is gone, I shall have no one on earth to—"

"Mary, I am yours till death. Your grandfather may command you to wed General Ruffleton—and you may be his—but I am thine. I will watch over you, protect you, die for you—for I well know that Ruffleton will not be your friend!"

"I fear he will not, and he knows I fear it. His jewels and fine coaches and mansions, would have no attractions for me, equal to the humble dwelling of my grandpa—or—I will say it, Willy—the plain farm-house of your grandma, near the Brandywine." And it needed not the pearls that stood on the long, black lashes of the beautiful girl, to bear witness to the sincerity of her declaration. "But, Willy," she asked, placing her little hand on his arm, "what is this about life and death?"

"Oh, Mary, I had forgotten it! I must be brief, and return to my duty. I must hasten away. There is danger, Mary, and that is all I am permitted to say, for the greatest calamity would be a panic among the people. Your grandfather calls. Let us go together."

They entered a small parlor, where the gaunt, grey, and palsied old John Penford sat before a table covered with tape-tied files of papers brought from the War Department, where his duties as a lower class clerk had been diligently performed, with a single brief intermission, for the space of fifty years. Peering through his spectacles a moment at the visitor, he arose abruptly and extended his hand, which was heartily grasped.

"Mary, bring hither my journal," he said, turning to his daughter. "It was for that I called you. I want to see if I made any note of Mr. Grubb's claim against the United States. Now, sit you down, William Wire," addressing the visitor upon the withdrawal of Mary. "You are my kinsman. Your mother and I were second cousins—"

"My grandmother, you mean," said Willy.

"Yes—your father's mother. How the time passes! And yet I recollect everything. Your father and mother died of the epidemic. And your grandmother—does she still live?"

"Certainly, sir. You were her guest last winter, when they removed you from office."

"True, true! I had forgotten it. But occurrences of fifty years ago seem as recent as yesterday. Well, William Wire, you may live to see your kinsman a Cabinet Minister! General Ruffleton will surely be President! Be a good boy, and you shall have the post I now hold. Ha! ha! ha! Family connexions, in our Republic, as in other governments, sometimes wield a vast influence."

"But, sir, I have come to announce the certain and instant dissolution of the Union."

"Impossible! I tell you it is a nonsensical impossibility! It is a mere scarecrow! A humbug, sir! I have heard such threats before. Don't name it, sir! It is a treason, and I am a sworn officer of the Government. I have taken an oath to support the Constitution, as well as the President,

3

and we *will* support it, sir. Disunion! Impossible, sir! And now, William, I have a great secret for you. In two or three days you will again see my name in the papers. I am on the eve of a discovery which would do any officer honor. I am going to produce such documents as will establish the claim of Grubb against the Government for cannon furnished the army seventy or eighty years ago! These papers were sent up to Little Falls, when the British came, and have never been untied since then, until I overhauled them! I have calculated the amount of the claim with interest—and it must be paid. So much for the vigilance of a faithful officer."

"But, sir, I fear the establishment of such a claim *against* the Government, may not be considered meritorious conduct."

"What do you mean? Can figures lie? These figures, and facts, and the records, prove this demand to be just. What difference can it make whether it is for or against the government? Does it not prove in either case the capability of the officer?"

"Very true, sir; but merit is not always followed by promotion, else you would have been at the top of the ladder long ago."

"That is a verity, William," said the old man, rubbing his hands with delight. "But family influence can accomplish anything. I shall mount up—never fear! And you, William Wire, where are you? Before this strange malady seized you—and all about my Mary—they sent you to the Legislature. Foolish boy! why did you fall in love, go mad, and resign. You might have come to Congress, been Governor, a Cabinet Minister, and finally President! I wish I were a young man again!"

"My dear, sir," said Willy, looking up, his head having fallen on his breast, "this is no time for such speculations. I came to request that you would not go to the Department this morning. The President himself says there will probably be disturbance and danger."

"Does he say so officially? Does he order the Departments to be closed? It is not in the official organ."

"No, sir. But he told me so."

"Impossible. All folly. They may threaten—and that is all. Abandon my post without official orders? Not I.

Why the most essential document in the Grubb case is in a pigeon-hole of my office! I have been in pursuit of it for twenty years. To-day my eyes will be gladdened by the consummation of my great achievement."

"I beg that you will stay away till noon—if no longer."

"I shall do no such thing!"

"Sir, you will be in danger. You may lose your life."

"Impossible. But I must not lose my claim for the cannon which won our liberty."

"Your papers cannot be molested, but—"

"How do you know that? If the enemy would destroy the officer, of course they would take possession of the office. I shall not permit my duties to be interfered with."

"My dear sir, the rabble that may attempt to carry away the archives, would not respect the Secretary, or the President himself, much less an old and faithful officer like yourself."

"Seizing the archives! Good heaven! Mary! Mary! Hurry breakfast. Carry off the archives! Not while breath is in the body of John Penford! He'll die at his post. Sit down, sir!"

"No. I must depart immediately. Think of what I have said." And Willy, seeing Mary again among the flowers, rejoined her there. "Farewell, Mary," said he, sadly. "But be sure and keep your grandpa at home till noon."

"Oh, Willy, they would not injure him!"

"Not intentionally. But a bullet or a cannon ball is no respecter of persons."

"God can direct the course of a cannon ball, as well as avert the lightning. In him we put our trust! I will dissuade him, Willy, if possible; but if not, I will accompany him!"

"No! Do not, I beseech you, Mary! Breathe it not to any one—but there will be a battle—and oh, keep beyond the reach of destruction."

"And, Willy, where shall such a place be found! Yes, it is in heaven—and only there. Adieu!"

Willy mounted his pony, with moistened eyes, and sped away. He had scarcely passed the last house in the town before a clatter of hoofs attracted his attention. Lifting his eyes he beheld a horseman under whip and spur riding towards him. It was a young man he had seen more than once at the White House. "Halt!" he cried.

The young man reined in his steed and grasped the pistol half hidden in his side-pocket.

"Don't shoot me," said Willy; "I'm a friend."

"Then make it known," said the other.

"Oh, I'm on the right side—that is, I'm in the centre, with the President."

"Then make it known, sir! I have no time for jesting."

"I forgot. THE UNION FOR EVER!"

"That will do," replied the young man, relinquishing the pistol and extending his hand. "Now what have you to say?"

"You go to Col. Carleton in the valley?"

"Yes. He has two hundred and fifty dragoons concealed there."

"Is he to move immediately?"

"I am not to know the order. But orders have been dispatched to all troops, in every direction, to concentrate in the President's grounds behind the Treasury building. Adieu."

"Farewell, sir," said Willy, "and may God prosper the right!" And as Willy proceeded on his way, he observed, on the opposite side of the river, a body of infantry, perhaps one hundred and fifty in number, slowly approaching the southern end of the bridge.

Every preparation had been completed by the President to repel any assault on the Executive Departments; and so skilfully had the arrangements been made under the immediate superintendence of Gen. Valiant, that none of the inhabitants of the city had the remotest idea that within an hour an army of 4,000 well-drilled men could be mustered in their defence. The President himself had a caparisoned steed in readiness, resolved, in the capacity of Commander-in-Chief, to take the field. None of his predecessors had practically illustrated that prerogative conferred by the Constitution. But Randolph acted from his convictions of duty, irrespective of precedents, and none doubted his qualifications to become a great military commander.

CHAPTER IV.

THE ATTACK AND REPULSE.

At the appointed hour the bridal company had assembled in St. John's Church. If the military preparations for battle had been kept a secret from the inhabitants of the city, it was very different with the hymeneal preparations. For weeks the contemplated wedding had been the theme of Washington correspondents for the press, and the nuptial day had been repeatedly announced in the newspapers, from Boston to New Orleans. From her glossy black hair to the very hem of her garment, the vigilant reporters had omitted nothing in the descriptions of the charming bride; and the fact that the President's daughter was to be present on the occasion, in the capacity of bridesmaid, had likewise been ascertained and duly promulgated. It was no wonder, then, that the church contained quite a congregation of witnesses.

The bridal party, upon descending from the carriages, lost no time in proceeding to the altar, where they were met by the priest in the vestments of his office. The holy man, after seeing that all were in their appropriate places, cast his eyes down on the book in his hand, and his lips began to move, when they were all startled by the report of musketry, at no great distance from the church; and during the pause which ensued, the rush of horsemen was distinctly heard. Turning his eyes towards the door, Henry Blount recognised the well known form of General Crook, followed by a company of mounted men, dashing furiously in the direction of the White House.

"Pray be brief, sir!" exclaimed the bridegroom, addressing the minister, who stood pale and trembling, whilst the occupants of the pews had all risen to their feet.

Again the priest cast his eyes on the page, and advanced a step in the chancel,—when all were amazed by the shrill cry of Maud Clusky in the gallery.

"Laws a' mercy!" she screamed, "they're shooting real balls and bullets! Yonder's some people killed in the street!"

Alice, instead of supporting the bride, took refuge on the breast of her friend. Edith alone was composed, but very pale. The two Senators stood like marble statues, looking at each other.

"Is this your work?" asked Mr. Langdon.

"No, sir; nor Harry's."

"Proceed!" once more said the younger Blount to the minister, in an urgent tone, which attested his anxiety; for now the vibrations of rapid discharges of cannon, in the vicinity, were causing the glass to fall from the windows.

"They're fighting!" exclaimed Dick Clusky, springing in at the door, and rushing quite up to the altar.

"Where is the carriage?" demanded Henry.

"Near the door, sir. I was afraid to stay there, sir. Gen. Crook told me to tell you all you shouldn't be hurt—but he can't stop the cannon balls, and they're flying everywhere. His foot soldiers have left the Avenue, and now they're shooting right past the church at the White House. Boo!" and the frightened youth gave vent to sobs and tears.

"Return to your horses, or I will take your life!" said Henry, with so ferocious an aspect, that poor Dick, believing death imminent anywhere, resolved to die at his post, and so withdrew, without paying the slightest attention to his mother, who vehemently forbade his departure.

"Now, sir!" said Henry, once more turning to the priest. But at that moment an eight-pound projectile struck the roof of the church, ploughing through the arch of the ceiling, and precipitating a quantity of lime and clouds of dust.

"God save us!" ejaculated the priest, the book falling from his hands. Henry sprang forward and restored it.

"It must be postponed!" said Mr. Langdon, drawing his daughter's arm through his own.

"'Tis well, perhaps," said the elder Blount to his son.

"And *you*, Edith! Do you renounce me at the altar?"

"No, Harry," said she, in a voice singularly distinct and calm; "I shall never renounce you anywhere; but my father commands on the present fearful occasion. We must submit."

"Come with me to the mansion," said Alice, still clinging to her friend, and vainly striving to emulate her composure.

A moment after the minister had vanished, and the people were rushing out and dispersing in all directions. The bridal party were the last to reach the door, half suffocated by the dust which still descended from the breach made by the ball; and before they had all ascended the steps of the President's coach, which Dick had driven on the occasion, General Crook came thundering back, discomfited, at the head of his diminished troop. His brow was dark with rage and disappointment, and he spurred forward without glancing to the right or the left. He was followed immediately by some dragoons, led by Col. Carleton; and galloping at his side was the President himself, in full military costume, and with a sword in his hand, stained with blood.

"Give them no opportunity to rally, Colonel!" said he, as he drew rein at the window of the coach.

"Oh! father!" exclaimed Alice, in tears.

"What! tears, Alice?" he rejoined, smiling blandly. "The danger is over. A few discharges swept them out of the Avenue! Why, daughter, we are victorious. It is an exhilarating triumph; and henceforth remember you are a soldier's daughter."

"True!" whispered Henry to Edith, as he regarded the animated features of the President.

"Joy, Edith!" continued the President, kissing his hand. Then addressing Dick, he said: "Drive to the mansion. Gentlemen, by your leave, the bridal festivity shall be under my roof."

"There has been no wedding, sir!" said Mr. Langdon. "I forbade it. But we will accept your hospitality and protection. I still hear the discharges of cannon."

"They have one battery yet," said the President. And just then several branches of one of the trees in front of the Church fell to the earth; "but Carleton will soon silence that. Come!" And saying this he led the way through the grounds to the mansion. As they alighted at the portico, the gentlemen were surprised to see the premises abounding with soldiers.

"This resembles a regular encampment!" said Henry, lingering and looking round, after the ladies had entered.

"They are mostly regulars," said the President, indifferently.

"I was not aware that such a force was in the vicinity of the Capitol," said the elder Blount.

"Not exceeding four thousand," said the President, with a significant look.

"I understand!" said Mr. Langdon. "And this, after all, Randolph, may be the most congenial pursuit. I have had such intimations. And *you* have been a calm spectator during *our* extraordinary proceedings!"

"It was incumbent on the Chief Executive to provide for any emergency," said the President, with determination. "And, gentlemen," he added, with a flashing eye and a contracted brow, "rely upon it, the Federal authority will be maintained, if forty, or even eighty thousand troops will suffice."

The elder Blount shook his head as he followed the President, who led the way into the hall. Harry, in silence, his lip slightly compressed, was the last to follow.

CHAPTER V.

WIRY WILLY'S PLEDGE.

Mary Penford used her utmost endeavors to prevent her grandfather from repairing to his office as usual that morning. The claim of Mr. Grubb, a most respectable and worthy iron-master of the preceding century, which he was resurrecting, was deemed of vital importance, not only to the cause of justice and patriotism, but to his own fame as an officer of the government. In vain, therefore, were the exertions of Mary; and so, when the omnibus came, she resolved to accompany her aged relative to the post of danger.

"Everything is in its place!" exclaimed the old man, when they had ascended to his narrow and dingy office in the Department. "Not a paper has been molested," he continued, unlocking the case and surveying with delight the formidable array of paper-stuffed pigeon-holes.

"And, grandpa," said Mary, brushing away the dust with her handkerchief, "if an enemy of the government should determine to destroy these precious papers, how could you prevent it?"

"Prevent it? I would die at my post in defence of the charge committed to my custody!"

"You might die, grandpa; but would that save the papers? Oh, mercy!" she cried, seizing the old man's hand, as the discharge of firearms was heard.

"It is nothing, child," said the old man, intently perusing a letter which a messenger had placed on his table.

"Nothing, grandpa! It is a battle!"

"Impossible! A battle in the Capital of the Federal Union! Don't interrupt me, child—this letter concerns you—and, indeed, *he* seems to think a disturbance is probable——"

"Oh, grandpa!" ejaculated Mary.

The sound of cannon now shook the building to its foundations, and yet old John Penford paid not the slightest heed to it. The voices of men, the rattle of iron ramrods, and the tramp of horses in the immediate vicinity, did not seem to attract his attention.

"Mary, my child, we will determine about this letter when we get home," said the old man, folding it and placing it in his pocket. "You shall now witness the consummation of my labors in the Grubb case. The remaining voucher, the copy of the receipt given for the cannon, completes the establishment of the claim."

"Oh, grandpa!" cried Mary, convulsively clinging to his hand, as the stunning discharges of artillery assailed the ear in rapid succession. "Do not go in front of that window, dear grandpa! It is a dreadful battle."

"It is impossible, child! They are merely practising. It is the flying artillery. Tut, Mary! do you suppose they would *dare* to fire balls at the War Department? They would be cashiered, every one of them."

"Don't you hear the crash among the trees and fences?"

"No, no! Release my hand, and let me get the voucher."

Mary struggled to prevent him, and her guardian angel assisted. For, a moment after, a cannon ball shattered the window and buried itself in the opposite wall. The concussion prostrated them both.

* * * * * * *

Col. Carleton succeeded in silencing the small battery which had thrown so many balls into the city, but without capturing the guns. General Crook, who had certainly conducted the assault with skill and bravery, but had been met with equal address and by superior numbers, superintended the retreat. His men retired in pretty good order towards the steamer; and more than one well directed shower of grape made frightful chasms in the ranks of Col. Carleton's pursuing dragoons. It was during this pursuit Wiry Willy was despatched with a message to General Valiant, who remained in the city, and was to dine, by invitation, with the President; so confidently and correctly had the result been calculated.

Wiry Willy dashed into the Avenue, at its extremity near the foot of Capitol Hill, and glided along with wonderful swiftness on his black pony, whilst his long white skirts streamed out behind on the wind. And now, for the first time, he beheld the scene of death wrought by the President's cannon. More than three hundred of the assailants had been swept down in the broad street leading to the executive mansion. The screams and groans of the wounded assailed his ears as he sped past, and many a cold corpse was spurned by the feet of his pony.

Willy, on reaching the White House, delayed not a moment in delivering his note, for the doorkeeper had orders to admit him at all times.

"Sit down and lunch with us," said the President. "The day's work is finished, Willy, and I desire to make known your meritorious conduct to this company. He certainly saved me from being taken prisoner by that audacious General Crook. I was completely surrounded, and somewhat pressed, for a moment, by three or four of the enemy, when Willy cried out, 'Here's the President!' and pointed towards the garden. Crook sprang in that direction, not recognising me in my uniform, and the next moment my ambushed guards were with me, and then the odds were on my side. You saw what followed from the church, Alice."

Alice cast a grateful look at Willy's modest face, and pointed to a chair beside her own. But Willy begged to be excused, and was permitted to retire.

He hastened away towards the War Department; and his heart palpitated painfully when, on casting his eyes in the direction of old John Penford's office, he beheld the condition of the window. He rushed up the deserted stairway and entered the office just as Mary was recovering animation. Her first movement was to throw her arms around the neck of her aged grandfather, who sat amidst fragments of glass, bricks, lime and papers, staring as if suddenly awakened from sleep.

"Oh, grandpa!" exclaimed Mary, "God saved us, when one step more would have brought us directly before the cannon ball!"

"Before what?" asked he.

"A cannon ball," said Wiry Willy, who stepped forward for the purpose of assisting him to rise.

"Impossible!" was the emphatic denial. "Don't tell me they would dare to fire at the War Department."

"But they *did*, sir!" said Mary. "Rise and see for yourself."

"Im—" The word was suppressed by a gasp of agony, when the old man, on turning his eyes towards the wall that had been perforated, beheld the scene of destruction. He sprang to his feet, and with both hands raised, stared in silence at the pulverized debris of his dear papers.

"Impossible!" he uttered at length, unconsciously. "My vouchers, my duplicate receipt, my all, in the claim of Grubb for cannon, swept away by a cannon ball!"

The ball had first passed through the papers on the table, and then demolished the pigeon-hole containing the copy of the receipt referred to so often by the faithful old clerk.

"Perhaps, sir," said Willy, "they may be found uninjured."

"William Wire," said the old man, "you will bear witness that it was no act of mine: that it was not for lack of fidelity on my part, that this destruction occurred."

"Very freely, sir," said Willy; "if necessary I will testify on oath to it. But if you had taken my advice this morning——"

"Reproach him not, Willy!" said Mary, interposing; "the past cannot be recalled, and sufficient for the present is his misery."

"Pardon, Mary," said Willy, rebuked; "and believe me that rather than inflict an additional pang, I would cheerfully, if possible, bear all his sufferings."

During these remarks the old man continued to stare at the demolished pigeon-hole.

"Grandpa!" said Mary, endeavoring to divert him from the grievous contemplation, "let us leave this place." Not replying to the request, the poor girl took his hand, and gently led him away from the scene of his sorrow. "You know, grandpa," she continued, "you have not told me the contents of the letter, which you said had something concerning me."

"True, child," said he, with unwonted animation. "I forgot it. Yes, that is of most importance. And here is William Wire to take you to his mother's house."

"His mother's house?" asked Mary, astonished.

"He meant my grandmother's," said Willy, delighted at the suggestion.

"True—his grandmother's," said the old man. "The letter was written by General Ruffleton ——"

"Ah!" gasped Willy, and his head sank dejectedly on his breast.

"What means that?" asked the old man. "He says there may be danger here, and that Grandma Wire's farm-house would be a place of safety. Is that not considerate?"

"It is cool impudence, sir," said Willy.

"Do not fret him, Willy," whispered Mary.

"What have you to say against it, William Wire?" pursued the old man. "Will your grandmother, think you, decline receiving the granddaughter of her own blood relation?"

"No, sir, no!" said Willy. "And if you desire it, I will conduct Mary thither this night, for I shall return home immediately. I have been too long away, and——"

"I cannot go," said Mary.

"Why not?" asked the old man.

"I will not leave you."

"And I hardly know what I should do without my Mary," said he.

"Then," said Willy, "I propose that you both accompany me."

"Impossible!" said the old man. "The General says that he will soon be in Washington, and will desire to have the benefit of my experience in certain matters connected with this department."

"The villain!" said Willy, in a low tone, which, however,

reached the ear of Mary; but she made no remark upon it. She merely exerted her ingenuity to convince her aged relative that it would be utterly impossible for him to dwell in Georgetown without his granddaughter, and succeeded.

Willy accompanied them home, and, on the way thither, riveted the attention of the faithful old public servant by a recital of the thrilling incidents of the day. And John Penford, when listening to the details of the battle, was forced to admit that such a thing as an assault on the Federal authorities was by no means "impossible."

And during the brief hours before Willy bade them adieu that day, not knowing when, if ever, they would meet again, it was not strange that he should repeat his warning to Mary to beware of the insidious wiles of General Ruffleton.

When Willy returned to the President's mansion, he was met near the entrance by the Blounts, who had just taken leave of their friends within, and were on the eve of departure for the sunny South.

"Come here, Willy," said Henry; "I have heard your history, and shall remember your meritorious conduct to-day. Here is something which may be of service to you in the scenes that will probably occur hereafter."

"Money, sir?" asked Willy, somewhat haughtily.

"No, Willy. But if that were needed, my purse would be at your service," said Henry, folding a piece of paper on which he had written a few lines with his pencil. "Take this, and keep it, till you hear of me again, and then you may know its value."

"Sir," said Willy, "if you should lead a Southern army against the President——"

"Think not of that, Willy," said Henry; "my object is to serve you, even if we should be enemies. And now I would request a favor. It may not be in your power to serve me, in the matter I refer to, but if it should be, I think you would not hesitate to perform the generous office."

"Name it," said Willy.

"Edith!"

"God bless her!" said Willy, clasping Henry's extended hand. "She has been Mary's friend. Rely on me! Farewell." Henry wrung his hand, and hastened to overtake his father.

CHAPTER VI.

HORRORS OF CIVIL WAR.

ALL the State Legislatures, north and south, east and west, were immediately convened; and the first measure brought forward in most of them was an act ordering the election of delegates to meet in State Conventions, or in Conventions of Southern and Northern Confederated States. Public meetings abounded everywhere, and the press sounded its thunders. In the large cities ungovernable mobs swept through the streets by day and by night, committing every species of violence, and often indiscriminately, on friend and foe. The Demon of Faction was unchained, and in many places ruled supreme. In the North, the Republicans demanded the utter subjugation of the Southern people, and an unconditional enfranchisement of the slaves. In the South, many of the Democracy urged the invasion of the North; and, incited by British agents, proposed the destruction of factories, the razing of cities, and the conflagration of shipping at the wharves.

Nevertheless, the bold and dashing conduct of the President in the repulse of General Crook, speedily engendered a formidable party in almost every State, favorable to the maintenance of the Federal authority. The brave always inspire confidence; and President Randolph seemed to know exactly what he was fighting for. In the North, the strictly conservative men of substance, who deprecated a violent collision of the opposing sections, embraced every opportunity of manifesting their approbation of the action of the Executive, and of indicating their design of adhesion to his cause. In the South, likewise, the less excitable citizens who desired peace, and an amicable adjustment of the differences between the sections, in the event, now pretty generally conceded, of a perpetual separation, instinctively regarded the President as a mediator and protector.

Meanwhile the President's policy had been perfectly

conceived, and his measures, in some respects, indubitably indicated. He had issued several proclamations, which were disseminated throughout the country. In these, without in the slightest degree identifying himself with either of the parties to the disruption, he labored to demonstrate the advantage to be reaped by a general acquiescence in the Federal authority—as a *pis aller*, at least, for a Provisional Government—and which seemed to be demanded for the convenience, if not for the security of the whole American family, distracted by internal dissension. And in response to his suggestions, it was almost universally agreed that the operations of the Post Office and Revenue systems should not be interrupted. As for the collection and safe-keeping of the public money, President Randolph had made ample provision by the powers conferred on him as the Chief Magistrate. With inconceivable promptitude, he had secured the fidelity of the best officers of the Army and Navy to the Government from which their commissions had been derived. It was even conjectured by some that he had sounded these commanders long before the occurrences at the Capital. But if such were really the case, it could only be cited as one of the many evidences of his superior judgment and foresight. It was certain, however, that not a ship or a regiment refused to obey his orders; and besides having an ample naval force stationed off the principal ports of entry, to insure the collection of duties, it was immediately apparent that notwithstanding the troops concentrated in Washington, there were ample military forces likewise in all the cities, to guard the Federal treasure. In New York and Philadelphia mobs were foiled in their attempts to pillage the mint, the custom-houses, and post-offices. Cannon, charged to the muzzle, commanded every avenue of approach to the public edifices, and the duty of defending them had been confided to officers of fidelity, skill, and determination.

It was different in the country. Predatory bands crossed the borders from both sides, and maintained a guerilla warfare for plunder. In the North, strangers and sojourners, natives of the South, as well as citizens suspected or known to sympathize with the pro-slavery party, were subjected to many cruelties and sacrifices. Nor was it the guilty alone that comprised the victims. Advantage was taken of the prevailing exasperation by profligate, revengeful, and grasping wretches, to consummate the ruin of the rich, the exalted, and the purest members of society, who had unconsciously incurred their envy or hatred. The gutters ran with blood, and the waysides were strewn with the dead. Banks were pillaged, daring burglaries and remorseless assassinations were of frequent occurrence, and the vault of heaven was every night illuminated with the glare of conflagrations. And such frightful scenes were not confined to the North. They were, if possible, excelled by the retaliatory measures adopted in the South. If there were no ungovernable mobs, and no instances of indiscriminate destruction of great magnitude, it was owing to the fact that no large cities existed to harbor any formidable number of the degraded class of population, ever infesting dense communities, whose demoniac delight consists in the misfortunes of others. But there were not wanting the "suspected," or even the guilty, among them. For the first, it was sufficient to have been born on Northern soil; for the last, any former expression of aversion to slavery was conclusive against them. Confiscations, executions, imprisonments, and every conceivable mode of punishment or annoyance seemed to be employed.

Not many days after the occurrences described at the Capital, Mr. Langdon received an account of the ravage of one of his estates in the country by his own neighbors and constituents. The reason alleged was his alliance with the "slave-driving" Blounts of the South. In disregard to the entreaties of Edith and Alice, and the earnest solicitations of the President himself, the indignant Senator resolved to set out immediately for the North; and, when the hour was fixed for his departure, Edith announced her purpose of accompanying him. No opposition could avail, whatever her reluctance might be to a separation from her dearest female friend. She had a presentiment of danger menacing her father, and it was her duty to attend him, through evil as well as good report.

There were but two cars in the train that conveyed them away from the Federal City, and these were not half filled with passengers, and but few of these were destined to cross the border—the line separating Delaware from Pennsylvania. Although "little Delaware" had long been regarded as almost a free State, and for many years the chief managers of what was known as the "underground railroad" had an office in Wilmington, yet it was a singular fact, that this diminutive State, exposed as she was to the first fury of the insane and fanatical invaders, had adopted the most decided position of hostility to the North. Her Senators and Representatives had been among the first to abandon their seats in Congress, and her Legislature, the first assembled, had immediately passed resolutions inviting her sisters of the South to send an unlimited number of volunteers within her limits, to hurl back the anticipated hordes of Northern invaders. Already thousands from Maryland and Virginia were on their march to occupy the Northern line of brave "little Delaware." And a majority of the passengers in the cars, it was observed by Edith, were either in military uniform or bore some of the instruments of deadly warfare.

It was not without reason, therefore, that the daughter indulged forebodings of evil in crossing the line separating two hostile sections; or that the parent should muse in painful abstraction, when vainly striving to penetrate the future through the tempest of civil war so insanely inaugurated by the unfaithful agents of the people.

The sun had set in a cloudless sky, golden and gorgeous, and the silver stars twinkled in joyous mockery of the fantastic tricks of wicked man, making an earthly paradise a hideous spectacle. The fields were deserted, the fences thrown down, and here and there small parties of men were seen with various implements of destruction in their hands.

At the first stopping-place after passing through Wilmington, several persons warned the conductor of danger ahead, and advised him to remain where he was until the enemy should retire. To this the conductor turned a deaf ear, and jestingly remarked that he would like to "see a fight." He added that if "the d—d Abolitionists" got in his way, he would charge through them on his iron horse. This might have inspired confidence, had not the remark of the bar-tender of the inn been overheard. It was to the effect that when he had once crossed the line, he would say to the Abolitionists that he *had* charged through the d—d slave drivers on his iron horse.

"Father," said Edith in a whisper, "had we not better get out and endeavor to reach the city some other way?"

"No, child," said he. "Fear nothing. We are natives of the North returning home. They will not molest us. Besides, the mails are transported in these cars, and both parties have agreed to let them pass. We shall be in Philadelphia in an hour. It is but little over twenty miles."

The whistle sounded, and the locomotive was soon careering at full speed. But they had not proceeded more than ten minutes in this manner, when discharges of firearms were heard, and the train suddenly slackened its speed, and soon after stood perfectly still. The conductor, upon being questioned by Mr. Langdon, said the track was obstructed by a breastwork of fence rails, behind which one of the parties, probably the Northern, was posted. Meanwhile, the fire, now perceived as well by the flashes as by the reports, seemed to be slackened, and finally ceased altogether. There was a rush of both parties to the train, and after a hand-to-hand contest, which continued for several minutes, around the cars and within them, the tide flowing to and fro, sometimes one party expelling the other, Edith became separated from her father in the melée, and being run against by a large man, was precipitated down a gravel embankment among the rank weeds on the road side.

Recovering from the concussion of the fall, the poor girl, bewildered, and partly blinded by the dust, essayed to climb the steep embankment, but in vain, and fell back again to the bottom of the ditch, fortunately, at that time, quite dry.

"Father! father!" she cried. But no one answered. The cars were gone; and Edith supposed she must have lain some time in a swoon. The moon had risen, and cast a flood of light over the now silent scene. She arose once more, and ran along the margin of the ditch until she came to where the rails were level with the plain. She stood upon the track and strained her eyes in both directions. Neither cars nor living beings were seen. But several dead bodies, weltering in their gore, were left upon the ground. The wounded had been taken away. The horror-stricken girl, summoning all her resolution, approached with breathless haste and palpitating heart the fallen victims. A single glance sufficed. Her father was not there; and she uttered thanks to heaven that he had, in all probability, escaped with his life. But where was he? Had he been taken away in the cars, or was he, like herself, a wanderer on the heath? She had no means of solving the question, and knew not where to go or what to do. In the confusion of the scene she had become unconscious of the direction in which they had been travelling, and was unable to decide which course led towards the city. Long and motionless she stood uttering fervent prayers to heaven for guidance in that hour of dread dismay.

"Father!" she at length cried aloud, hoping her parent might be in hearing; but no response was made, save the barking of a watch-dog in the distance. "Oh, merciful God!" she exclaimed, "what will become of me!" and stooping down, she buried her face in her hands. How long she remained in this attitude, she could not tell; but when she again lifted her tearful eyes, the form of a tall man was before her. "Oh!" cried she, "have pity on a dutiful daughter, cruelly separated from her father, who may be wounded or even dead—"

"No! heaven forbid!" said the stranger. "But come with me, and you shall find a friendly shelter, no matter whether you be Southern or Northern-born. We are all brothers and sisters in the eyes of the Heavenly Parent."

"Oh, sir! will you not aid me, then?" said Edith, emboldened by the words she had heard, and the tone of the voice, which seemed to be not altogether strange to her ear.

"To the utmost of my ability," said the stranger. "But who are you? Have we not met before?"

"I do not know; until this morning I have been residing in Washington, with my father, for many months."

"Miss Edith Langdon! The constant friend of one dearer to me than life itself, Mary Penford!"

"And you are Wiry Willy! Yes, Willy, I will trust to your guidance, believing that heaven sent you hither as my deliverer."

"And if I prove unfaithful, may heaven smite me with its scathing lightnings. Besides, I am solemnly pledged to serve you." He then related the promise which Henry Blount had exacted from him, and she believed in the overruling Providence that shapes our actions.

"I will go with you, Willy," said she, taking his arm and leaning on it for support. "You say your grandmother lives near this place."

"That was the friendly shelter I meant, before I knew the one to whom it was tendered. But now you will be doubly welcome, for Mary, when a sojourner beneath our humble roof, often described her friend and protector to my aged grandma, and made her love you."

"And it was there that Mary culled the beautiful wild flowers for me? Oh, if my father were only with me, or if I could only know he was unharmed and in safety, how contented could I be to dwell in the peaceful little vale so fondly painted by the truthful Mary!"

Wiry Willy led the way across a meadow, and by a narrow path through a dense growth of sapling oaks; and there they beheld the humble cottage by a winding brook. Passing through a wicker gate, they approached the tenement between trellises of grape-vines which scented the air with their blossoms. They were met by a large black Newfoundland dog, whose baying Edith had heard, but which now seemed to welcome her with manifestations of friendship.

Lifting the latch, Willy conducted his charge into a capacious room, illuminated with a lamp on a plain table, and warmed by a bright blaze in the broad fire-place. Mrs. Wire was knitting, seated on a low chair at the corner of the hearth. She was in her ninety-seventh year, small of stature, thin, and her face a mass of wrinkles. Yet her features were regular, and must have been handsome. She rose up without difficulty on perceiving the entrance of her grandson and the stranger.

"Who is this, Willy?" she asked, with curiosity, but not displeasure, and perhaps the secret of her longevity consisted in the uniform amiability of her nature.

"It is Miss Edith Langdon, grandma, that Mary Penford used to speak so much about."

"I am sure she will have a hearty welcome, then," said the old lady, approaching Edith, and gently taking her hand. "Come, sit down before the fire, my sweet child; the night is chill and damp. You seem distressed, and no wonder, for the times are stormy, as in the days of the Revolution, when I, too, was young. Give me your bonnet and mantilla, and warm your feet. Then you shall have tea, or milk, and such bread and butter as the poor house affords."

"I leave you, grandma, for a short time," said Willy; "I must saddle my pony, and—"

"And what, Willy? Whither are you going?"

"I will explain everything before I depart. I will see you again before I mount."

"It is right and proper, no doubt," said the old lady, gazing at the door which the young man had closed behind him.

Edith, while partaking moderately of the repast set before her, explained the circumstances of her condition to the attentive old lady, who retained not only the faculty of hearing, but of seeing without the use of glasses.

"Now I know Willy's purpose without another word from him," said the grandame. "He will leave us under the protection of Bruce, the faithful dog, and seek information regarding your parent."

"Bless him! And may heaven prosper his endeavors!" exclaimed Edith.

"Oh, he is a blessed boy—and yet he has been stricken with affliction. His love for Mary Penford has unsettled his reason a little, at times; but he is not a lunatic, as some have said. The boy was well educated, for we own a hundred acres of good land, which have been well tilled, and yielded their profits. He was even elected to the Legislature, but resigned his seat, when he received the terrible announcement that General Ruffleton was an accepted suitor for the hand of Mary."

"And does General Ruffleton really propose to marry Mary?" asked Edith.

"That is the point. He makes John Penford believe so; but Willy is convinced that he has no such intention. That thought has robbed him of sleep, and at times almost bereft him of reason. The neighbors call him a poor harmless demented young man. But he is not demented on any subject but the one. It is true that, living here on the line between the free and the slave states, Willy, being once a politician, takes sometimes one side and sometimes the other; but in whatever he does, I can see a good motive, and both parties have become accustomed to his eccentricities, and permit him to pass and repass at pleasure. Oh, he can serve you better than any of the violent partisans. And he will do it. You may have the most perfect reliance on his honor and his judgment!"

"I certainly have!" said Edith. "He came to me as if in answer to my prayer for aid!"

"God sent him—depend upon it! I am now nearly one hundred years old, and when I look back through the long vista of time, I can recognise the hand of a special Providence in a thousand fortunate occurrences. Have faith in God, my daughter, and He will not desert you. He will lead thee forth, by such instruments as He may be pleased to select, out of every difficulty, if you trust implicitly in his goodness and wisdom."

"I will endeavor to do so, to the utmost of my ability!"

"And that is a right kind of resolution, for we cannot be sure what temptations may beset us. But, as for Willy, although in politics, and in these civil strifes, there may be no seeming consistency in his words or acts (for he appears very willing that they should deem him but half-witted), you will find all his promises and engagements in your behalf will be redeemed, if human wit and exertion, with approbation from above, can accomplish them."

"Now!" said Willy, throwing open the door, "farewell grandma—farewell, Miss Langdon. I am going in quest of the Senator. Slumber peacefully, both of you. The night is fair, my pony eager for a race, and I could not rest on my pillow, if I sought it, knowing that the father is separated from the daughter, and that daughter the friend and protector of Mary! I will see Mary's approving smile as she flits through the air before me. Do not fear for me. None will molest Wiry Willy; and none durst disturb the last surviving matron of the Revolution, who dressed the wounds of both friends and enemies brought hither from Chadds' Ford. Farewell. In three hours I will be in Philadelphia. And you may look for me back in the morning. I will leave the pony at the Black Bear, and return in the cars." He then closed the door, and a moment after the clatter of the pony's hoofs was heard.

"He will do all he says, my child," said the grandame, proudly. "And I see he has removed a load of anxiety from you."

"He has, indeed! He cannot fail to get some tidings of

my father, for many in the city know him well, and his reputation for moderation in all things, together with his vote against the Declaratory Resolution, will surely shield him from harm in a Northern city. Oh, yes; I shall slumber sweetly, dreaming all the time that Willy has returned with my father, or with good news of him. But, grandame, did you really dress the wounds of the sufferers at the battle of Brandywine?"

"Indeed I did, my child. The battle-ground was not far from this place." She then entertained Edith with the recital of the incidents of that terrible day; and among the rest mentioned the fact that at the urgent solicitation of Washington, La Fayette dismounted, and rested a few moments in her humble domicil. But he had not time to permit her to dress his wound. The British were in pursuit; and so, drinking a cup of fresh milk, and taking a few biscuits in his pocket, the wounded General remounted his horse and sped away, until faint with the loss of blood, they placed him in a carriage. She described the sufferings of the officers and men of both armies left wounded on the field; and the gratitude they expressed for the kindness and care bestowed on them. Yet, she added, that a great many people in Delaware, at that day, were reluctant to give up their King. But God had so willed it, and the country had prospered ever since, until the coming of the present troubles, the issue of which was in the hands of One mightier than any earthly King.

And thus the hours sped. The grandame smoking her pipe in the chimney corner, relating anecdotes of a past generation; the listening maiden transported in fancy to scenes of the dim and distant past, while the cricket chirped upon the hearth, until the demands of nature admonished them of the arrival of the hour for repose.

CHAPTER VII.

EDITH'S DISGUISE AND FLIGHT.

WIRY WILLY was familiar with the highways and cross-roads between Chadd's Ford and Philadelphia; but more than once he found it prudent to diverge from the direction he was pursuing to avoid an encounter with the predatory parties prowling at such unseasonable hours. On one occasion he was hailed by several ill-looking men; and, not choosing to waste his precious time in nocturnal conferences with strangers, he was fired upon and pursued. He merely laughed at the fruitless efforts to arrest his progress, knowing his pony could distance pursuit, and that there were a thousand chances to one he would escape the bullets.

As he drew near the Schuylkill, however, he was confronted by a man who stepped into the road before him and presented a bayoneted musket at his breast.

"Who goes there?" demanded the man.

"Wiry Willy," was the prompt reply, the pony halting suddenly.

"On which side?"

"Sometimes one, sometimes the other."

"Well, on which side now?"

"On *your* side, I think," said Willy, perceiving himself surrounded by armed men rising up on all sides, and emboldened by the conviction flashing upon him that these were men in the service of the President, although not in martial uniform. He suspected correctly; for it was a convoy of specie. The President did not suffer the public funds to accumulate in places where riots prevailed; and every day considerable amounts of the precious metals, guarded by trusty agents, arrived at Washington.

"We must know that," said the commander of the detachment, stepping forward, "or else you will have to return with us towards Wilmington."

"Strike a light!" said Willy, "and I'll convince you;" and drawing a paper from the lining of his boot-leg, placed it in the hands of the officer. It was brief, and a single match sufficed for its perusal.

"Enough!" said the officer, returning the paper, "Pass on. And yet, if you have not been ordered thither, I would advice you to keep out of the city. There are fifty thousand rioters in the streets. Houses have been burnt, and horrible murders are committed."

"Did you see or hear anything of Senator Langdon?" asked Willy.

"Yes. He is a prisoner of the Abolitionists. They condemn him as a Doughface for having permitted his daughter to marry a Southerner. But I do not think they will kill him, because he voted in opposition to the Blounts."

"Where is he confined?"

"Nowhere as yet. The prisons have been broken open and blown up. They keep their prisoners in their midst as they move about the city."

"Thank you. Farewell." And saying this, Willy urged his pony towards the city, the glare of whose burning dwellings was now plainly perceptible.

He proceeded through the very heart of the city, avoiding the mob on one or two occasions, by cutting through an alley and emerging again into the same street in the rear of the multitude. At the Black Bear he was well known, and his panting pony was placed in safe hands.

Willy, on foot, plunged into the first mob he could find, and this was in Chestnut street. Some thousands of men, armed with every conceivable weapon, from the blunderbuss to a brickbat, were pushing forward those before them towards the Custom House.

"Down with the President!" cried many.

"D——n Uncle Sam!" shouted others.

"Hurrah for General Ruffleton!" screeched one just at Willy's elbow. And this was responded to by deafening cheers.

"Where is General Ruffleton?" asked Willy, in a low, familiar voice, of the one who had named him.

"Don't you know? Where have you been all day? In Southwark?"

"South," said Willy.

"I thought so, or else you wouldn't have asked the question, because he made a great speech in Independence

Square, and we all heard him. Didn't he give it to the South? And we're all going to march under him to Washington, and seize the government."

"Good!" said Willy. "But when do you march?"

"In a few days; as soon as we can get arms enough. The General's rich, and we won't have to wait long. He is to go before, and we are to join him at the Delaware line. We're going to wipe out all the niggers as we go! Won't you join?"

"Yes, by George! But how many are to go?"

"At least a hundred thousand. They're coming from the free States every hour. But what's your name? I'm a recruiting sergeant."

"William Wire," said Willy, after some hesitation, and concluding that it might be policy to give his true name.

"That's recorded," said the other, writing in a small book, with a pencil, by lamplight, the moon having gone down.

"Now, *your* name, sergeant—the higher officers, I suppose, are to be elected, and if we improve on acquaintance, I may desire to nominate you for captain."

"True, Wire, and I shall be much obliged to you. Recollect my name is Punt."

"I won't forget it. Can you tell me where I'll find the General?"

"He goes down to the Delaware line in the morning—and may be on his way there now."

"Then can you tell me what they have done with the Hon. Mr. Langdon?"

"I can. They've got him in a cage hereabouts somewhere. It's on wheels. They exhibit him as a Doughface, according to the request of the Rev. Mr. Fire, who has been preaching so long against slavery. They don't intend to hurt him, though; it's just to make an example for the benefit of some other public men who have been too fond of Southern associates."

About this time a number of pistol shots were fired from the head of the dense throng, without the word of command, and by whom no one could tell, at the soldiers guarding the Custom House. The officer in command ordered a company to disperse the assailants by a discharge of musketry at their feet. More than forty fell, and ten thousand were put to flight. Willy seized this opportunity to abandon his sergeant for the purpose of seeking Mr. Langdon. Directing his course towards the square in the rear of Independence Hall, always a common centre in times of commotion, his diligence was soon rewarded with a sight of the Honorable Senator's cage, at the head of a long row of similar impromptu contrivances made of wood, in imitation of a menagerie. There were several persons acting as showmen, and their language and manners as they goaded the animals or fed them, produced immense laughter.

Willy recognised in the keeper of Mr. Langdon the same Jack Bim who had volunteered under General Crook to seize the Federal treasure, and he was not quite certain whether it would be prudent to make himself known to him.

"Now, gentlemen and ladies," said Jack Bim, and by the glare of the torches it could be seen that hundreds, if not thousands, of females were on the ground, "let me exhibit this wonderful nondescript *han*imal when he's *h*eating. You shall see that he's carnivorous, herbivorous, and granivorous. Now, sir," he continued, addressing Mr. Langdon, "I desire that you will eat this leg of a chicken." The grave Senator, thinking submission the best line of conduct, under the circumstances, complied with the request. "Very good, sir," said Bim. "Now you will oblige me by masticating a few ground nuts. Very good. Now take a bite of the celery. Done most meekly." That was the appropriate word, and it struck a sympathetic chord in the breasts of even that hardened mob.

"Shame!" said one of the better costumed women, who had seen the dignified Senator at Washington. "Shame!" repeated many voices.

"What do you mean?" asked Jack Bim, who looked for plaudits instead of reproaches.

"I say it's a great mistake to put such an indignity upon a great man," exclaimed a portly gentleman, in a dress coat with metal buttons, urging his way through the crowd.

"Who are you?" demanded Bim.

"I, sir, am D—— P—— B——!" And a hundred voices cheered him. "Do you know the name, sir?"

"I do."

"Then release that man!" Several persons sprang forward and tore off the wooden slats of the cage.

"I thank you, sir," said Mr. Langdon, addressing his deliverer. "But I do not think it was their design to injure me, and I doubt if they can be induced to release me yet. I see thousands of copies of the *Censor* in their hands, and that sheet contains a most villanous calumny on me. I had intended to address the multitude the first opportunity; but their fury was not sufficiently modified. May I retire with this friend?" This was addressed to Bim.

"No, by ——!" was the response. Bim had just received information that some forty of the rioters had been shot down in front of the Custom House. "If I were to release you now, they would tear me to pieces. But if your friend, who seems to be a pet of the sovereign people, will pledge his word that you will not escape, he may conduct you into the room of the 'Signers' yonder, where you may enjoy such comforts as your purse can command. I have no money, *as yet*," he added, between his teeth. Mr. B—— without hesitation, complied with the condition; and taking the arm of the Senator, led him into the sacred chamber where the Declaration of Independence had been signed, and where the Convention which framed the Constitution, over which Washington himself presided, and of which an ancestor of Mr. Langdon had been a member, had assembled in the first days of the Republic! Willy had whispered to Mr. B—— that the Senator's daughter was safe.

"Do you not remember me?" asked Willy, turning and addressing Bim, when Mr. Langdon was led away.

"By George, I do!" said Jack, fixing his fierce grey eyes on him. "I thought I had seen that long-tailed coat somewhere. Why, you were one of us at Washington! I thought they had peppered you. Only fifteen of my club escaped—and we had to walk back—didn't get enough money to buy railroad tickets, and we were too few to seize the train. Well, how goes it, old fellow?"

"I've not received a dime, either. General Crook either had no money, or else he gave it only to his *Southern* men."

"I suppose that is exactly what he did. But, my friend, What's-your-name, the less we say about having fought under Crook, in this crowd, the better."

"I understand," said Willy. Then giving way to an impulse which seemed irresistible, he continued: "It's a pity, Jack, that we brave fellows should fight and bleed, and get no pay. I think I know where there is some treasure; but then it may be the property of friends."

"D——n the friends!" said Bim. "Where is it? I can easily make them enemies. I don't care who they are—all I have to do is to whisper a few words in the ears of my brother leaders, and there will be ten thousand men at our backs."

"But I mean the Rev. Mr. Fire. It is in the basement of his church. He has the safe-keeping of the plate of many of his congregation—and he has much treasure of his own."

"Why he's an infernal Puritan. And it was him who made them attack the Custom House, before—no, that won't do. But, I have it! Come on. I'll swear he's hiding the plate of the Southerners in the city. That'll do. Come on!" And Bim led the way in quest of his brother chieftains. But Willy embraced the first opportunity of losing himself in the dense crowd. He was impelled down the avenue in front of the line of cages where there was the most brilliant glare of torches, and the loudest laughter. A man seated on a three-legged stool, in the largest cage, attracted his attention. He was a fine-looking individual, of large dimensions, and upon inquiry, Willy learned he was the publisher of a Democratic journal which had always been very bitter in its strictures against the Abolitionists. And the Rev. Mr. Fire, with a torch in one hand and a newspaper in the other, was reading an article advising the incarceration of clerical fanatics, who were denounced as traitors.

"Thus," said the parson, "is the chalice commended to your own lips," and the crowd applauded, and asked the prisoner how he liked the taste of his own prescriptions.

"I didn't write a line of it," said he.

"But you know who did; and you published it," said the Rev. Mr. Fire.

"Who wrote it? Make him tell!" cried several.

"I'll see you d——d first, Dick Dodge!" replied the gigantic publisher, foaming with rage; and recognising one of his persecutors.

"He's pluck, any how," said several.

"That infernal rascal," said the publisher, pointing at Dick, "was one of my compositors, and set up the manuscript. If I was the publisher, he was the printer."

"That's enough!" cried the keeper. "Get in, Dick! You set up the type. Is it a sentence, fellow-citizens?" This was decided affirmatively, and Dick was no sooner thrust into the cage than the publisher fell upon him with his tremendous fists, amidst the delighted shouts of the populace.

In the next cage was a lawyer, of similar politics, and one supposed to be a contributor to the journal so obnoxious to the partizans of the reverend gentlemen which seemed then to preponderate, although amongst these a large number were never Republicans or Abolitionists, and had really no conscientious scruples with regard to African slavery. The greatest annoyance perpetrated on the lawyer was the compelling him to chew tobacco, for which he had a mortal aversion. And what added to the poignancy of this exaction was, that the suggestion came, very innocently, from the publisher, who had asked one of the bystanders for a "chew."

Another cage contained a jackass eating hay, with an imprisoned politician brushing the flies from its ears with his handkerchief. It was a most singular freak of the mob. The politician had been either born in the South, or had been a very noisy advocate of the fire-eating doctrines. He had been a candidate for Congress, and seemed to have been made half crazy by defeat. He was very profane, cursing the ass, an ill-natured, kicking, and biting animal, and the mob. But just in proportion to the excess of his profanity, was the laughter of the spectators.

Next to the politician's cage was one containing the editor of the ——— ———. He had been caught early the morning before, and now exhibited evidences of loss of rest. His hands were tied behind him, and although forced to stand, his eyes frequently closed involuntarily, and his head fell down in fitful naps on his breast.

"Brighten up dar!" said the negro boy who attended him, pulling an end of the rope violently. "Now, gemmen!" said he, "I offers a likely sound fellow, ob de Caucus tribe, to the highest bidder. How much you bid?

Give a bid, gemmen! He is a great worker, and can see without specks, sir, and dat's what his age is. Only please him, and he'll sarve you well. But don't show him blood, and den he's not dang'rous. He never hurt a mortal living crittur, 'less dey tried to hurt him fust. He's been shot at, and worked de next minute same as ever."

"What sort of work?" asked one of the spectators.

"You're too hard for me, dar!" said the auctioneer. "I don't understand it—but 'spose de man who buys him will make de most he kin off of him. How much? Bid for him, gemmen!" There being no bidders, the exhausted editor sank down on the straw and fell asleep.

It was now early dawn, and Willy, alarmed at the news of General Ruffleton's presence in the vicinity of his mother's cottage, hastened his preparations for departure. He considered Mr. Langdon's condition one of safety, but he had fearful misgivings as to the fate of Edith, if she should be seen at his mother's humble dwelling by the profligate Ruffleton. The latter, no doubt, supposed Mary Penford had been sent thither in compliance with his request; and his disappointment and rage on finding the contrary, might augur ill for the security of Edith. And he learned that measures had been taken to subject every one passing into the city to a strict scrutiny. To obviate this difficulty, and to insure the meeting of the daughter with her father, it occurred to Willy that it would be proper for the former to assume some sort of disguise. Therefore, after taking some food at the Black Bear, he wandered up Market street, and entered the first clothing store he found open at that early hour. He then lost no time in haggling, but selected a suit of boy's apparel, such as he supposed would suit the height and shape of Edith. Then, hastening away to the depôt, he was soon flying at railroad speed towards the Delaware line.

At the station nearest his grandmother's residence, and just when, having descended from the car, he was in the act of starting across the country, Willy heard his name uttered by some one at the inn. He paused, and beheld General Ruffleton approaching.

"Willy," said the general, "I am about to be at the head of a great army. The whole country will be under my command. I believe you have never taken any part in these sectional quarrels. It is well. I can trust you. Old Penford has given me his daughter, and you love her. Serve me well, and you shall have her. Do you understand? Why don't you answer? Do you not want riches? Stupid fellow! But how fares Mary? She is now at your grandame's?"

"She is not, sir," said Willy.

"If you lie, sir," said the general, "you shall be confined in a dungeon! But why not be frank with me?" he added, in a lower tone, for many of his staff were standing near. "You must know that if she has been there recently I will find it out, and that neither she nor you could possibly escape me."

"I tell the truth, sir. Her grandfather desired her to come, but she would not leave him."

"That seems probable," said Ruffleton. "The old incumbrance must be put out of the way," he continued, aside, but Willy heard it. "Well, sir," added the general, turning once more to Willy, "see that you do not attempt to deceive me, or to thwart my plans. Go—but remember my eyes are upon you!"

Willy did go. And when an orchard hid him from view he mended his pace, and never paused until he reached the door of his own domicil; then he stopped on the outside to take breath and to compose his features, for the considerate young man did not desire to alarm the friend of Mary, or his good grandame, by any symptoms of peril or panic in his physiognomy.

So, when Willy entered the cottage there was a pleasant smile on his lip, and this was instantly interpreted aright by Edith.

"He is safe, Willy?" she cried.

"Quite safe," said Willy.

"And I can see him—go to him?"

"I hope so," said Willy, seriously; "but you will have to be very careful." He then detailed enough of that which he had seen and heard, to make both Edith and his grandmother fully comprehend the condition of affairs.

"I must go!" said Edith. "My father can neither eat nor sleep until he knows of my safety."

"He knows you are safe," said Willy, "if Mr. B—— told him what I whispered in his ear."

"Then," said the grandame, "I think this is the best place for Edith. I know how it was travelling in 1777. In such troublous times it is best for maidens to keep under shelter."

"I cannot answer for Miss Edith's safety here," said Willy.

"And why not, Willy?" asked the grandame, while Edith was all attention. Willy described what had passed in his interview with General Ruffleton, and Edith grew very pale. She knew Ruffleton quite well enough, and had once repulsed his marked advances as a lover.

"Yes, I must go," said she; "and the sooner the better. He is a bold bad man, and I shall not be happy until removed beyond the atmosphere in which he breathes. But how can I go?"

"Willy will go with you, if you must leave our house," said the grandame.

"I will, with pleasure," responded Willy; "but the next train will not pass for some hours; and I learn that the army under Ruffleton is collecting in great numbers on this side of the Schuylkill. There might be difficulty in passing. The men are rude, and many of them utterly without scruples."

"I will disguise myself, and travel as a servant," said Edith.

"No, my child," said the old lady, "that would be the worst thing you could do. As the daughter of Senator Langdon, some of the officers might be respectful; but as a chambermaid, none would hesitate to insult you."

"I have provided this disguise," said Willy, exhibiting the apparel he had brought home in his handkerchief; "and I do sincerely believe it would be the most effectual that Miss Edith could adopt."

Edith expressed her reluctance to assume any disguise whatever, and above all, that of male attire; nevertheless, she would submit to any ordeal in the performance of a duty. And this determination was strengthened when Bruce, the faithful dog, gave notice of the approach of strangers.

"There are two young men," said the grandame, looking out of the window.

"And they are armed," said Willy, "with swords and pistols, and ——"

"What else?" asked Edith.

"They are the aides of General Ruffleton! Could you not keep out of their view?"

"It is too late," said Edith, joining the others at the window. "They have seen me. But they do not seem to be meditating evil."

Willy called back the dog, and stepped forward to meet the strangers, who had entered the gate.

"We are merely walking for exercise and amusement," said one of them, "and being thirsty, we ventured hither to crave a little water."

Without uttering any reply, Willy stepped back and presented them a pitcher and glasses. They drank slowly, casting glances towards the window from which Edith had retired. After lingering a few moments they withdrew.

"Now, for heaven's sake!" said Willy, re-entering and addressing Edith, "let us depart as soon as possible. These men have been sent hither by Ruffleton. He did not believe me when I told him Mary had not arrived at the cottage in obedience to his request; and these men, not knowing you from Mary, will confirm his suspicions."

Edith snatched up the male attire, and hastened into the chamber where she had slept the preceding night, and hastily donned the clothes, which, thanks to Willy's judgment, were of the proper dimensions. Then tying up her hair on the summit of her head, and surmounting it with a cloth cap, the transformation was complete. She had worn her heavy travelling shoes on the journey, and these being the only essential articles that Willy had omitted, she now felt convinced that her sex was in no danger of discovery.

"Upon my word, I don't think they'll find you out," said the grandame, when Edith re-entered, confident and self-possessed, but without the slightest shadow of merriment.

"Now, grandame," said she, "give me pen, ink, and paper. I will leave a note addressed to you, expressing my thanks for your kind hospitality, and intimating the cause of my unexpected sojourn under your roof, &c., which must be left on this table; so that General Ruffleton, if he comes, may see it."

"There is woman's wit in that," said the grandame, while Edith was writing.

"Yes, grandma," said Willy, "it will serve as a protection to you, and may also shield me from harm."

The note was written, and Edith then announced herself in readiness to depart. They set out, after brief but sincere adieus to the helpless one they left behind. But she said she trusted in the strength of the Lord.

Our travellers arrived at the depôt without encountering any one on the way. But when they were seated in the car, they were startled by the voice of General Ruffleton himself, who thrust his head in the side door and gazed very steadily for an instant at Edith. She had the sagacity not to attempt to conceal her face.

"So, Willy," said he, averting his eyes, "you have a great deal of running backwards and forwards to do?"

"I forgot my grandma's coffee," said Willy.

"Ha, ha! and perhaps that was the very thing she sent you for. Silly fellow!"

"Euripides! General! Wasn't it enough to knock coffee out of any one's head?"

"There were some striking scenes, it is true, and there may be more of them. But then, I don't see why you should return to them so soon."

"I'm afraid to go to Wilmington, sir. They say the Southerners are getting as thick as hops there."

"And that's true. You prefer, then, to take your chances among the free state men? But what pretty boy is that?"

"A young friend from College."

"He seems to be a very delicate lad. See that you take good care of him. And be sure you told me the truth this morning—else when you return, you may be called to an account. Good bye!" and glancing once more at Edith, he withdrew his head. Soon after the whistle was sounded, and the cars rattled away towards the city.

"Willy," said Edith, after sitting some time in silence, "that man doubted your story. His eyes were full of suspicion. He did not recognise me, however, and he knew it was not Mary. He will see my note, and then the mystery will be explained. He cannot, I think, sate his vengeance on you. For anything done by me, he surely would not hold you accountable."

"Do not fear for me," said Willy. "Half-witted as they

deem me, I shall outwit them all. I feel no apprehension on my own account. But here we are at the bridge."

"That is cannon," remarked a stranger, sitting just behind our travellers, as several rumbling reports, in quick succession, were heard in the direction of the city.

"That is one of the men to whom you gave the water," whispered Edith, recognising the voice, and looking round.

"It is so!" said Willy, "and there may be some danger going the usual way in the omnibus."

"Perhaps we had better hire a coach," said the stranger.

"Would that diminish the danger?" asked Edith.

"We could go a circuitous route," said he, and then, after a little hesitation, and addressing Willy, he continued: "You were kind enough to give me a glass of delicious water this morning. A friend and myself were walking through the country. I am familiar with the city, and will conduct you and your young friend to any part of it, without the slightest danger of encountering a cannon ball."

Willy thanked him, but remarked that he was well acquainted with the streets himself, neither declining nor accepting the tender. And when they arrived at the depôt the stranger hastened to employ a hackney coach, which drew up near the place where Willy and Edith were standing. Most fortunately Willy happened to be acquainted with the driver, and urging Edith to enter, and then whispering a word in the ear of his old acquaintance, sprang in himself and closed the door. The driver cracked his whip, and the horses bounded away, leaving the gentleman in semi-military costume standing like a fool looking after them.

Not really apprehending any danger from the cannon, which indeed had now ceased to be heard, Willy, with the concurrence of Edith, told the driver to go by the shortest way to the Black Bear, a place, as Willy observed, to which he would not have taken Edith in any other costume than that she was then in. Although, in its line, the inn was quite respectable, as a place of resort for farmers from the neighborhood; yet it was not quite up to the fashionable hotels to which Edith had been accustomed. The chief recommendation was, that General Ruffleton would not be likely to think of such a place, if he were determined to pursue her; and pursuit seemed very probable, since one of his aides had evidently been directed to accompany them to the city.

Arrived without accident at the Black Bear, Edith strode into the parlor and sat among the few market women and the rosy daughters of honest farmers, awaiting the return of their husbands and parents who had ventured out to transact business among the shop-keepers. It was deemed best for Willy to go forth alone, and endeavor to obtain tidings of Mr. Langdon. The city was terribly agitated; and the landlord said nearly a thousand men had been killed since sunrise, in fruitless attempts to storm the Mint and the Custom House. But he could give no information of Mr. Langdon, having heard nothing of him whatever. This, negative as it was, nevertheless afforded some comfort to Edith; for, thought she, if anything dreadful had happened to him, it would certainly have been bruited over the city. She therefore promised to await the report of Willy, and requested him not to precipitate his return on her account, unless, indeed, his inquiries were quickly crowned with success.

Willy, therefore, after seeing that his pony had not been molested by any of the roving recruiting sergeants, set out alone. But he had not gone twenty paces before he observed with some concern that he was followed by the gentleman whom he had so unceremoniously abandoned at the depot! At first he resolved to stride on very briskly, and thus shake off this persistent companionship. But finding his follower likewise quickened his steps, Willy slackened his pace, and resolutely awaited the result.

"That was rather a shabby trick you served me, comrade," said the stranger, coming up; "but we'll say nothing more about it. I was a stranger, and in times like these one cannot be too prudent in selecting his companions. But where is the lady?"

"Lady!" uttered Willy, pausing abruptly.

"I meant boy! The youth's complexion being as fair as a lady's, made me say *lady*. But where is he?"

"It would be difficult for me to say. I parted with him at a place where he wished to be, and did not ask him where he was going."

"And it is no business of mine, you might add. And indeed I ought not to be so inquisitive."

They were now in front of the State House, which had been made a hospital for the wounded. Surgeons, and the nursing wives and sisters of the mutilated rioters, were seen in the hall and in the rooms on either hand above and below. A glance sufficed to convince Willy that Mr. Langdon had been conveyed to some other place; and then, striving to elude his unpleasant companion, he directed his steps towards the mansion of Mr. B——. But before he had gone fifty paces he was seized by two strong men, and dragged into a house in Sixth street, fronting Independence Square. The building was occupied by the recruiting officers of General Ruffleton, and all the lower rooms were filled with boisterous men, mostly armed. Willy, glancing back as he was hurried up the marble steps, beheld the stranger, who had followed him, smiling significantly, if not tauntingly; and then poor Willy's heart experienced a painful sensation. His captors, imposing silence with menacing gestures, led him up several winding stairways and turned him into an attic room.

"What is this done for?" asked Willy, when the men were about to leave him.

"Don't know," said one of them.

"We're only obeying orders," said the other.

"Whose orders?" continued Willy.

"Major Trapp's," was the reply. They then withdrew, locking the door behind them.

CHAPTER VIII.

A MOB OF DESTRUCTIVES.

Returning to Senator Langdon, it is necessary that the reader should be apprised of some of the changing scenes of the awful panorama. Jack Bim, in pursuance of the hint he had received from Wiry Willy, lost not a moment in organizing a select party for a demonstration on the Rev. Mr. Fire's church. The assault was completely successful. More than $100,000 in plate and coin had been deposited in the safe-keeping of the clerical party leader, and the assailants were not only no respecters of persons, but had, in reality, no party predilections. This predatory expedition, and its remunerative result, when made known, produced a wonderful effect upon the desperate rioters throughout the city, as well as on the revengeful instigators of the mob. It was perceived that the reckless sword of popular violence, bloody and ungovernable, was liable to be turned in any direction, and that those who wielded it one hour might become its victims the next.

The Abolitionists were astounded. They beheld the wind they had sown converted already into a whirlwind, and directed against themselves. Tens of thousands of rioters, incapable of comprehending a principle, floated with every capricious current, or turned with every circling eddy. Hundreds of free negroes, who had but a few hours before participated freely in the demoniacal saturnalia, were now lying dead and gory in the gutters, while the survivors of that miserable race were flying for refuge into the forests of New Jersey.

No doubt this great change in the popular sentiment was partly owing to the vast numbers of desperate free-soil recruits withdrawn from the city by General Ruffleton, for his Southern invasion; and it was, in some degree, superinduced by a spontaneous concert of action on the part of the wealthy citizens and men of business for the protection of their property; but the controlling causes were terror and cupidity—apprehension that the party so audaciously and so successfully despoiling the leaders of the Abolitionists, might be the preponderating power, and if so, an irresistible impulse to participate in its gains.

Meetings of the more substantial and respectable citizens were held in every ward—but in such hurricanes of popular phrensy, whatever may be the wisdom of the measures recommended, it is often difficult to realize their adoption. One thing, however, was quite apparent to all. The insane populace had been taught by experience a proper respect for the resolution and military skill of the adherents of the President, guarding the Federal buildings. No less than seven assaults of the mob had been promptly repulsed by the comparatively small numbers of troops detailed for this service; and all the bitter denunciations of the "tyrant" at Washington uttered in mass meetings and in the streets, had as yet amounted to nothing more than the expenditure of so much idle breath. On the other hand, it was remarked that the better classes, who desired the prevalence of law and order in the city, however much they might be exasperated against the Secessionists of the South, seemed to regard with approbation the firm and resolute stand so courageously maintained by the Federal Executive.

During the progress of this reaction and of these events Mr. B—— had been called away from the State House to make speeches to the people in different quarters of the city, and to exert his eloquence for the purpose of calming the surges of the wild ocean of human passions. He had been the friend of the colored man, and he boldly avowed it; but, at the same time, he implored the mob to refrain from acts of unlawful violence. All, except the colored people themselves, listened with patience, and some with favor. And it was on one of these occasions that the great champion of the Africans endured the bitter penalty of their native inferiority and ingratitude. Some five hundred of this degraded class, who had on one occasion assembled before his door, in Locust street, and made themselves hoarse with cheers, because he had succeeded in the liberation of a fugitive, now surrounded him with an intent to inflict summary punishment for an alleged abandonment of their cause, which merely consisted in his condemnation of pillage, conflagration, and murder! And it was this very act which caused the massacre of the free negroes.

Mr. B—— returned to his charge, the unhappy Senator, whom he found seated in the chair of Washington, a victim of deep dejection. He thought of the illustrious men who had once congregated in that hall to found a glorious Republic—and such was the result! He, a descendant of one of the worthies who had ushered into existence the inappreciable boon of constitutional liberty, was now the captive of an unfettered mob, composed of the offscouring of all the nations!

"You are now at liberty, sir," said Mr. B——. "None are guarding the door. All are gone."

"Then what means that uproar in the square?" asked Mr. Langdon.

"It is a new set entirely—and mostly Democrats. The

reign of the fanatics is over; at least for the time being. They are dispersed by enlistments, frightened away, or preparing for another attack on the custom-house. But this new brood now in possession of the Square, although they belong to your party, have been quite as sanguinary as their predecessors. They have been robbing churches and cutting the throats of the free negroes. I have been requested to address them; but it occurs to me that one of their own politics could be more effective."

"Mr. B——, my politics never sanctioned the burning of churches and the cutting of throats. No; I cannot make a speech! But I will go among them, hoping to hear something of my daughter."

They passed through the rear door of the State House, and were in the midst of some ten thousand boisterous men, cursing, laughing, hallooing, and disputing, while several hundred carpenters were completing an immense row of cages. The huge publisher had broken his bars, and was now vowing vengeance; the profane politician had turned his ass's heels to the front of his cage, and made him kick off the timbers. And, when liberated, the first thing he did was to cut the poor ass's throat! The editor of the —— —— had gone to his office, followed by his negro keeper, who begged his protection, and promised to serve him. All the world might come to an end, but the paper must go to press at the appointed time.

Large handbills were posted on the trees and walls, informing the public that there would be a grand "gratis exhibition" in the Square that night. And the incensed publisher and profane politician were appointed to act as the master showmen. The latter, indeed, could hardly be restrained from thrusting the benevolent Mr. B—— into one of the half-finished cages—accused him of being a Know Nothing, half Abolitionist, and cheek by jowl with the infernal rowdies who had put him in the cage. But the fact, which had really occurred in the presence of this irascible Democrat, of Mr. B——'s interposition in behalf of Senator Langdon, saved him.

Not being able to learn anything in relation to his daughter in the Square, and being convinced that no good could be accomplished by making speeches to the multitude before him, Mr. L—— proceeded to the Musical Fund

Hall, where a large meeting of merchants and capitalists had assembled. Mr. Langdon, the distinguished Senator from a State still further north, was well known to many of them, and he was requested to occupy a seat on the stand. This he acceded to, and soon after, his name being called by many who desired to hear him speak, he rose to his feet, and announced his inability to comply fully with the request, incapacitated as he was by the grief of being separated from his daughter. He then narrated the manner of the separation, and invoked the aid of his friends. This was promised him, for his narrative excited their sympathy.

But nearly every one present had met with bereavements, and all seemed to deplore the calamity which had befallen the country. The jobbers estimated that not less than fifty million of dollars were owing them in the South and Southwest, a greater sum than the capital invested in their business. They were ruined irrevocably in the event of continued separation and civil war.

The commission merchants said their "Bills Receivable" consisted of the notes of the jobbers, and they, too, must be ruined if payments were not made.

The manufacturers said the goods sold by the commission merchants to the jobbers had been consigned by them, and they, too, would be hopeless losers.

The presidents of the banks said their "Bills Discounted" consisted of notes of these three classes, and the stockholders would be sacrified.

Several millionaires and lesser capitalists declared that their collaterals consisted of the notes of country merchants, mostly Southern and Western, which would be so much worthless paper. All—all would be involved in a common ruin!

And many individuals among these lamenting citizens had encouraged the abolition lecturers and newspapers by expending large sums of money in their behalf—and such were a few of the bitter fruits of sectional agitation and alienation of one portion of the people against the rest!

"But what remedy is proposed, gentlemen?" asked Mr. Langdon.

"Do you suggest one," cried several; "for we are unable to propose anything whatever."

"I doubt," he continued, "whether anything effectual can be accomplished in the present excited condition of the country. Elections have been ordered by the Legislatures for delegates to conventions to devise a remedy; but I learn that but few of the people are disposed to vote. I take it that public sentiment is not yet formed, and therefore the wishes of the States, either North or South, cannot now be ascertained. I think it well, however, that we should, at least for the present, regard the existing Federal authority as neutral between the contending parties. Randolph is a man of ample mind, and it cannot be his policy to promote the destruction of our interests. I think it his design to hold the balance of power between the sections, and I can see no objection to it." Here there was a hum of approbation, followed a moment after by decided applause. "But, above all things," continued Mr. Langdon, "I consider it our duty to frown upon all military expeditions against the Southern States."

"Will our frowns prevent them?" asked a millionaire.

"You can refuse them money."

"That we have already done. Nevertheless, Ruffleton finds men."

"True. And the object is to find money by plundering the enemy, or the people who will thus be made our eternal enemies! It is a sad business, gentlemen! Both sections should have paid more regard to the warnings of Washington. Commerce, trade, all employments will cease, if this separation continues, and millions will have nothing to do but to engage in deadly conflict! But I must find my daughter. And, alas! gentlemen, how many thousands of happy families must be cruelly divided!"

The distressed Senator retired from the meeting, still attended by Mr. B——, who dispatched every one he met, over whom he had sufficient influence, in quest of Edith Langdon. They visited many collections of people, in the usual places of public meetings, in the streets and in the squares, and still nothing was heard of the missing one. At the depôts and at the wharves no satisfactory intelligence could be obtained. All they knew of her was that some one, the preceding night, had whispered in Mr. B——'s ear that she was in safety. And there was some consolation in this—for how could the individual have known that a daughter existed, or that she had been separated from her father, without likewise knowing that she was in some place of security? There could be no motive for imparting incorrect information on such a subject and under such circumstances; and this was the comforting deduction of Mr. Langdon, although he would not for a moment abandon the search.

Having made the round of the hotels, they entered the Exchange just when the chandeliers were lighted in the evening. There was an immense crowd within and around the building. With a doleful countenance an auctioneer was selling stocks and real estate, and Jews, mostly, were the purchasers. They seemed like greedy vultures, snatching, scrambling for the scattered fragments of ruined fortunes. They were incessantly bargaining, chaffering, quarrelling. Buying one moment and selling the next, on an advance or a decline, there was something in the scene that reminded one of the gaming-house.

Dwellings and stores had already fallen fifty per cent. in value. Federal securities were at an awful discount. City Sixes brought only $40. State Fives, but $30. Pennsylvania Railroad, $20. Reading, $5; and even the Camden and Amboy shares were sold for $21. Bank stocks could find no purchasers, even among the Jews, for several of them had been pillaged.

Turning from this wretched spectacle, Mr. Langdon descended the broad stairs, and on Third street found his way impeded by a dense throng of rioters.

"These are desperate fellows," said Mr. B——, reading the mottoes on several of their illuminated transparencies, "and there will be sad work. They will attack the party now in Independence Square. I had intimations that they were rallying for that purpose."

"What party do they belong to?" asked Mr. Langdon.

"The party of demons," was the whispered reply. "They never had any principles, only impulses; sometimes they voted on one side, and as often on the other. Such is and must be the history of the very lowest class of citizens in all Republics. If they are not rewarded for their work, whatever it may be, they will pay themselves. Their gains are the losses of others. They create nothing. Such is the profligate rabble of the great cities."

Women were with them in great numbers, some on foot, bearing loaves of bread on poles, and others drawn in open carriages, covered with fantastic decorations. Mr. Langdon gazed at the frightful procession, and sickened at the thought that his own delicate Edith might possibly be forced to participate in some such terrible pageant. Taking the arm of his friend, he turned away. And his abhorrence of the scene was increased, if possible, by hearing the piteous cry of a child in quest of its parent. "Poor boy! take him home!" said the senator, placing a purse in the hand of a plain man of honest countenance, into whose arms the fainting youth had fallen. And even little girls, not five years old, were seen wandering about at such an hour and in such a place, in search of parents perhaps no more among the living.

CHAPTER IX.

EDITH AT THE BLACK BEAR.

SEVERAL hours had passed, and yet Wiry Willy had not returned. Edith, strong in mind and bold in heart, endeavored to repress the perturbations natural to one in her forlorn condition; and for a long time she struggled bravely against the approaches of despair. She read the papers, or rather the extras, issued from the newspaper offices in narrow slips; for there had ceased to be any regular editions, inasmuch as a vast number of printers had abandoned their cases. But in these slips, which she purchased from the newsboys as they ran screaming past the window, she learned much that had occurred, and was occurring in the city, as well as something of the political and warlike news at a distance. The President had detached a thousand men to guard the telegraphic wires, now repaired, running north and south from Washington. And she read, with throbbing heart, the proceedings of the Convention in Richmond. Pale and trembling, but with her cap obscuring as much of her face as possible, she learned that her own affianced lord had been appointed Commander-in-Chief of the Southern armies! But—and she perused it with joy—the Convention had resolved that the Southern people, while prepared to repel aggression, did not design immediately to act on the offensive against the North. The attempt of General Crook at Washington was disavowed; nevertheless, he was not punished for it. There was, indeed, considerable hesitation on the part of the Convention to adopt extreme measures; for the reason, as it was alleged, that the Southern, like the Northern people, had manifested a reluctance to vote for Delegates, and it was apparent that a large majority had neglected or refused to exercise the elective franchise.

"Here's a later slip, sir," said a handsome, smiling lass, seeing Edith's abstraction after finishing the perusal of the extra *Ledger* that lay upon her knee.

"Thank you," said Edith, and then eagerly devoured the contents. This bulletin referred exclusively to incidents within the city. It contained an account of the captivity of the editor of the —— by a party of Abolitionists, and his confinement in a wooden cage. It likewise dwelt to some extent on a sad mistake committed by the same party. It appeared that they had burned down a very large printing establishment west of the Square, supposing it to be the property of the editor, when, in fact, it was the property of one belonging to the Anti-slavery party. Edith could not avoid smiling at this blunder; and the hearty maiden, whose brilliant dark eyes had long been riveted on her, moved closer and said:—

"I'm glad to see any one smile in such times as these. It is a great comfort to me; and, indeed, I was afraid to let my father go out alone; but he said I must stay here till he came back. I don't know a single soul in this room, but I suppose they all live in the neighborhood of the city, as we do, and are waiting for their fathers, or brothers, or husbands. I have no brother nor—"

"Husband?"

"Fy, no!" said she, blushing. "I never thought of such a thing. But really, it makes me melancholy to see you looking out of the window so often, and sighing so—"

"Have you seen that?"

"I thought so; but I might 've been mistaken. And I couldn't help thinking that perhaps your friends were killed, or your home destroyed, and there might be no place for you to go to in such dreadful times; and if such were the case, I'm sure my good-natured father would be glad if you would go home with him. We live only five miles from Camden. We have a good house, and one of the finest farms in the State."

"I'm sure I feel very grateful," said Edith, somewhat vexed at the impetuous earnestness of the damsel, who was probably inclined to fall in love with her, a complication she by no means desired; "but I have a friend, whose return I am looking for every moment."

And when the maiden was, soon after, departing with her father, she found an opportunity to indicate precisely where she dwelt, and to intimate that the supposed young man would at any time be a welcome visitor.

Another bulletin, purchased by Edith, contained the joyful intelligence that Senator Langdon had appeared at the meeting of merchants and others in the Musical Fund Hall, and the few remarks he uttered on the occasion were printed in the extra. A weight was removed from Edith's heart, and she felt greatly relieved. But her impatience for the return of Wiry Willy increased. She strode backwards and forwards in the parlor, repressing as much as possible her eagerness to fly to her father, and innocently exerting, at the same time, her powers of imitation in acting the part of one of the opposite sex. And she did this with decided success, for no one seemed to suspect her presentment might be a counterfeit.

It was during this promenade that Edith, on turning, was confronted by Major Trapp, the stranger who had begged a glass of water in the country, and subsequently appeared in the cars. He bowed to her, and, in return, had a haughty and scarcely perceptible nod.

"Pardon me," said he, advancing to Edith's side, who strove in vain to elude him; "but your friend parted from me very abruptly at the depôt." He did not add that he had been revenged.

"That may be, sir," said Edith, with a cold averted look; "but I presume he can make a satisfactory explanation."

"But he is not here," said he, "and I am very desirous of having an explanation."

"And I have none to offer!" said Edith, courageously turning on her heel and walking away. He followed.

"You must know, most valiant youth," continued he, "that I am Major Trapp, and aide-de-camp to the General-in-Chief of the army of invasion."

"And what then, sir?" said Edith, almost fiercely. "Do you hold me responsible for the act of my friend? If so, sir, according to etiquette, any further conferences should be maintained by our mutual friends."

"Exactly; that is precisely what I wish. And I desired only an opportunity of intimating that the address I am to place in the possession of my friend, has not yet been communicated to me."

This not only embarrassed Edith, but diverted her. She had not thought of an assumed name; and the idea of being engaged in an affair of honor, and with one of the military profession, was, in her case, anything but a grave matter.

"You seem to hesitate," said the officer; "and, to be sure, in times like these, one may have a motive for concealing his real name. But any cognomen will answer—pray choose any that may suit your fancy; one is just as good as another to fight under."

"Sir," said Edith, weary of his presence, "you say you are an officer; an officer ought to be a gentleman—and——"

"I will finish the sentence," said he, in a low voice, "a gentleman should not quarrel with a lady!"

Edith's face was now crimsoned with anger.

"Sir," said she, "if what you seem to suspect be true, and the sentence be correctly concluded, what am I to think of the one who, admitting such conclusions, and supposing he addresses a lady, still persists in his offensive demeanor?"

"Excuse me, I pray, Miss Langdon," said he, with apparent seriousness; "but fearing one in your unprotected condition might, in a time like the present, be subjected to rudeness, if not liable to injury, I have been sent here for the purpose of warding off any danger that might menace the daughter of the friend of my General."

"I am to suppose, then, that your General detached you on this service?"

"You have rightly conjectured," said he, bowing; "and

I am happy to inform you that the General himself is now entering the door."

This was true. Edith turned, and cast an offended look at the General.

"I saw your note at the old grandame's," said Ruffleton, bowing familiarly, "and I deemed it my duty to assist in restoring you to your father. These are perilous times, Miss Langdon," said he, in an under tone; "and I should have been censurable if I had not taken some pains to mitigate your unhappiness."

"I know not what thanks to express, sir, for the *pains* thus endured on my account—and will not attempt any, since I should consider myself meriting any disparaging estimate you might be pleased to form of my understanding, or sense of maidenly behavior, if I did not resent the unworthy stratagem resorted to for the production of this interview. Sir, can you be ignorant that my father is at this moment in my immediate vicinity?"

"You do me great injustice, Edith, by such suspicions. I am aware that your father is in the city. He has just requested me to conduct you to his hotel."

"General Ruffleton! Is this so?"

"Upon my honor."

Edith mused in silence. The hope that Ruffleton's words were true, had but a momentary existence. The design he had conceived, must have been antecedent to the interview with her father, if indeed they had met at all. Believing herself now reduced to a desperate strait, she resolved to dissemble.

"General," said she, with an assumed gladness, "I will go to my father immediately. But I must see the landlord first. He is now in the hall. Excuse me a moment." Then approaching the host, she asked him if he was not Willy's friend.

"Yes, indeed, to the death!" said he. "I owe him more than I'll mention—but enough to——"

"Did he not say he was my friend?"

"He did. And I promised to do anything you desired."

"Then show me how I may get away from those men in the parlor."

"If you can run fast, you might slip round the corner into Market street. It is getting dark, and you could hide.

I will go in where they are and lock the door after me. I'll drop the key, and be long enough finding it to let you run a whole square. Go!"

And poor Edith sprang into the street, and ran, she knew not whither.

CHAPTER X.

EDITH'S ADVENTURES.

Poor Edith sped into Market street, and turning to the right, ran down towards the river until her course was obstructed by a dense crowd of men and women in the market-house. Some were dancing, some singing, and most of them laughing. The contents of a large confectionery store, recently rifled, were spread out before them, and the contributions of a neighboring wine establishment were being added to the entertainment. No man's property was any longer his own. "Everything," said the mob, was "free."

Edith was seized by a gaudily-dressed young woman and held securely by the wrist.

"Whither away so fast, fair sir?" said she.

"Release me! exclaimed the poor girl, for an instant forgetful of the part she was acting. This attracted much notice, and produced a great deal of merriment.

"Why, where did this bird come from?" continued the young woman. "He's neither a specimen of nature or philosophy. He really trembles like some poor frightened maiden. What sort of boy are you? Where did you come from? You must take courage. Here! Swallow this. It is good. You must drink it!"

She presented a glass of wine to Edith's lips, and poor Edith, exhausted and thirsty, drank of it, and soon felt renewed courage and strength.

"Now, wont you be my partner?" asked the young woman. "We will waltz down between the rows. Music!"

"No—not now!" said Edith, with a decision which inspired respect. "I am on an errand of life and death, and you must await my return. if indeed I shall ever return."

"He's in earnest," said the young woman, "and we must let him go. Can I assist you? If I say the word, a hundred men will back you! And if that won't do, I have but to see General Ruffleton, and you shall have a thousand!"

"No—thank you," said Edith, shivering at the mention of the hated name. "That would spoil all—I mean I must go alone, or else my plan will be defeated."

"Go, then; but come back when your errand is done. Remember Flora Summers. If I am not here, ask for me. Oho! yonder comes the General, now; and he, too, seems on some hasty errand!"

Edith, released, did not pause to behold her pursuer. But it occurred to her that she must soon be overtaken, if Flora Summers's men should be sent in pursuit, a thing by no means improbable. And therefore, when she supposed no one observed her, she stooped down and concealed herself under one of the counters used by the butchers. And this was most fortunate; for, not many moments after, General Ruffleton, Major Trapp, and several others came running past. They did not pause, and poor Edith breathed freer. There were fragments of old carpets under the counter, and her position was not uncomfortable. Knowing the necessity of bearing her ills with all the resolution she could command, whilst hiding thus, she eat heartily of the store of sweetmeats the liberal Flora had forced upon her. For many minutes she remained in this situation, and never ventured to peep out until, from the comparative silence in the vicinity, she became aware that the market-house had been deserted. Then she ventured to thrust forth her head and reconnoitre. All was silent and still, and she resolved to abandon her hiding-place. But her cap had fallen off, and that being indispensable, she crawled back in quest of it. At the farthest extremity of the shelter, whilst groping in the dark, and after having just recovered the cap, her hand was seized by another fugitive.

"In the name of God!" said a tremulous voice, "have pity on a poor old man!"

This speech served to dispel the affright at first experienced by Edith.

"What can I do for you?" she asked.

"You are a boy, and will not hurt me," said the old man, for such it was, still grasping Edith's hand, and leading her into the centre of the deserted market-place, where the rays of the distant lamp enabled him to see her features. "And you are not one of the *bad* boys, who prowl about of nights. You are lost, or have been driven into the streets. That's well. And I am an old man who has not tasted food for forty hours. Thank you! thank you!" he cried, eagerly seizing and devouring the cakes and candy tendered him by Edith, whose pity was excited in his behalf. He was indeed an old man, but yet not so tall as Edith. His small face was sharp and cadaverous, and his bent neck and narrow shoulders were enveloped in an old blue cloth cloak.

"Now I must leave you, sir," said Edith, preparing to resume her flight.

"No! no!" said he, in piteous tones. "Don't leave me. I shall be robbed and ruined. There is one, Moses Abra hams, over yonder, in the upper story, where I will be safe. I will pay you to help me—how much will you charge?"

"I want no reward," said Edith.

"Not want money? Good boy! Don't leave me."

"I *must* leave you, sir. I could not protect you."

"No! no! Don't go. Good boy! You can help me carry my little trunk."

"Where is it, sir?"

"Wait a minute." Saying this the diminutive old man crept under the counter, and dragged forth a small trunk, which, however, seemed weighty. "There now!" said he, breathing rapidly from exhaustion, as he rose. "Do you take one end and I will the other. It's some old scraps I can sell for bread. Just help me into the alley and this silver coin shall be yours." He exhibited a half dime!

Edith knew not what to do. But the idea occurring that she, who required assistance, ought not, perhaps, to refuse her aid to this trembling old man, she stooped down and raised one end of the trunk. It was very heavy, and both staggered under the burden while crossing the street. The old man indicated the course in fearful whispers—but to no purpose; for just when they were gliding round the corner they were suddenly met by a number of ill-looking men running rapidly. The trunk was knocked from the feeble hands that held it, and breaking to pieces, a large amount of gold coins rolled out, glittering and ringing upon the pavement. The men threw themselves upon the treasure, while the old Jew begged, and struggled, and cursed in vain. He called upon Edith to save his treasure, and reproached her for not fulfilling her bargain.

Edith ran away as fast as possible, and never cast a look behind until she entered Second street. Here the massacre of the negroes had commenced, and many of the victims still lay where they had fallen. It was a horrible spectacle, and the poor girl averted her eyes and hastened past. In Walnut street she encountered an immense mob, vowing vengeance against the "pro-slavery" Democracy. She was irresistibly swept onward by the throng. In vain were her endeavors to extricate herself; and in addition to a natural aversion for such companions, she thought she might be dragged in this manner to some bloody battle-field. But suddenly her eyes rested upon the revered features of her father! Not anticipating so joyful a realization of her hopes in such a place, the revulsion was too much for the poor girl. It was impossible to repress her pent up feelings; and she sprang forward, struggling with all her might, and called aloud, "Father! father!" He heard the voice, and his heart was smitten with a tender pang; but on beholding merely a boy fainting in the arms of a bystander, he gave him some money, and requested that the lad might be tenderly cared for. A moment after, and the father and child were pursuing different directions!

"What is the matter, boy?" asked the man who bore the fainting Edith, when he perceived symptoms of returning animation.

"Where is my father?" asked she, springing from his arms, and looking wildly.

"That is more than I can tell," said the man.

"Was it a dream then? or merely the imagination?"

"I cannot tell that, either," was the reply.

The head of the dense column soon came in view of the rear of Independence Square—the conflict commenced. The assailants had no shelter, and suffered the most. The other party fired briskly from behind the wall, with small-arms, and Edith could see that they were likewise preparing to discharge cannon. People were falling around her, and yet she could not retrace her steps, or escape to the right or the left. She therefore took refuge in the ruins of the block of houses that had been burned. Several voices warned her against seeking such a refuge, and it was supposed she would be suffocated or burnt to death. She heeded them not, but sprang down and ran under an archway of brick, where she found a clearer atmosphere than that she had abandoned, and where she suffered no inconvenience from the heat. The only source of alarm was the many rats running about, seeking egress from the ruins. But they did not molest her, except with their cries.

Meanwhile the cannon made such havoc that the attack was soon repulsed. But Edith remained until the firing ceased and the crowd dispersed. She then abandoned the arch, and directed her steps towards the square, where all was joy and hilarity. She learned, as she followed some men towards the State House, that many speakers were expected to address the meeting that night, and among the rest Senator Langdon! Her first impulse was to proclaim herself the Senator's daughter. But this was overcome by a reluctance to attract attention to her disguise, and by the rational conclusion that when her father should appear there would be no necessity for the aid of any of his friends. And if he did not come, circumstances might render a preservation of her incognito still necessary.

She was borne by the dense throng slowly up the main avenue, and in front of the row of cages which had been prepared for retaliating on the Abolitionists the outrages of the preceding evening. The profane politician and the fat publisher were the managers.

"Take care, boy!" said the former, addressing Edith. "Don't venture too near these animals." Poor Edith was so hemmed in that she could neither advance nor retire but with the crowd. But she lifted her eyes and gazed at the contents of the cage. Her astonishment was great on beholding a middle-aged Quaker, of low stature, but large calves, reached by the ample skirts of his coat, standing in front of Frederick Douglas, who was seated in a barber's chair. The Quaker was an apothecary who had come from a town in New Jersey, where his sect greatly abounded, to rescue the negroes from the avenging hands of their enemies.

He was now forced by the goad of the profane politician to read W——'s poems to Frederick, an unmixed African!

As she gazed, Edith did not think the warning of the profane politician at all necessary. The Quaker was one of the class of conscientious Abolitionists, like the poet himself; and so far from being angry at the indignities to which he was subjected, he seemed to read, with much feeling, the finest passages the volume contained, with the faintest hope it might be, but yet with hope, that the hearts of his enemies would be touched. But Fred. sat uneasily in his chair, whilst large drops of perspiration ran down his dusky cheeks. Nevertheless, he had the address to beseech his keeper to permit him to resign his seat to the Quaker. This, at last, was granted; and then the profane politician cited the voluntary exchange as a proper demonstration of the relative positions of the two races.

The next cage contained a huge monster frightful to behold. Edith gazed long before she could be convinced that the being before her was really of the human race. But he too was a Quaker. It was the same who had been incarcerated for his complicity with a gang of ruffians in depriving a Southern citizen of his slaves. His corporeal dimensions filled the cage. He had been immersed several times in tar, and overwhelmed with feathers.

Another cage held a colored specimen from Bristol, named Purvis, and three white men from the same town, his constant admirers. The Abolitionists were required to kiss the negro every third minute by the State House clock. This was a great torture to them all, and it would have been difficult to decide which was the most disgusted, the negro or the white men.

There was also a literary cage, containing several ex-judges, anti-slavery biographers, editors, and publishers, upon whom no greater severity was inflicted than the forced exhibition of their faces to the prying multitude.

And next to this was the cynosure of all eyes—a cage of mammoth dimensions, from which there proceeded a medley of discordant sounds, and before which the crowd, ever and anon, fell suddenly back as if in fear of the claws or fangs of wild beasts. It was, therefore, with no slight trepidation that Edith found herself impelled in that direction. But the matter was soon explained. The cage contained at least a dozen distinguished women, Abby K., Lucy S., L M., Mrs. S., etc., etc. No wonder there was a Babel of voices! These prisoners gesticulated most frantically, and uttered every conceivable defiance. To each of the questions the keeper or spectators propounded there were a dozen answers, in every key of the gamut; and in every controversy that arose they invariably assumed the offensive. And when they ceased to speak from very weariness, the keeper had the inhumanity to sprinkle them with vinegar, using a large watering pot and sponge. And it was on such occasions as these that the tempest of invectives produced an involuntary falling back of the spectators.

One more surge of that multitudinous sea of human beings brought Edith in front of the stand erected for the speakers who were to address the meeting. Not less than fifty were seated on it, but their faces could not all be seen. Among these Edith did not recognise her father. Nor could she change her position to be enabled to survey the rest. She could only hear the announcement of his name, and that he was certainly to address the meeting.

The first who rose to address the multitude was the son of a distinguished Southern statesman who had occupied the highest position in the government. This popular orator was hailed with repeated and prolonged applause, for in addition to the elevated rank of his family, he was possessed of a high order of genius, and endowed with a power of eloquence that never failed to captivate the masses. And when he resumed his seat, cries were heard for many of the distinguished men then in the city, and among the rest, Senator Langdon.

Edith held her breath and gazed in painful suspense. The calls for speakers continued, and, as it seemed it had not been exactly arranged who should be the second orator, there ensued a competition among the audience which of several names should be demanded by the greatest number. And while this incertitude prevailed, poor Edith swooned again! One who stood near bore her away from the crowd, room being made for him to pass. And when he had extricated himself, he conveyed his burden towards the iron gate on the western side of the enclosure.

CHAPTER XI.

WIRY WILLY AND JACK BIM.

When Wiry Willy found himself alone in the attic, a prisoner, and thought of the painful anxiety of Edith for his return, her disappointment, and her probable fate, if she fell into the hands of the creatures of Ruffleton, a result to be anticipated, he became a victim of the most excruciating misery. His first impulse was to burst open the door, when he reflected that every passage was strictly guarded. His next was to throw up the window opening on the roof; but his escape by day seemed impossible. He threw himself on a bed in the corner of the room to rally his energies and concentrate his wits for the emergency. He remained perfectly motionless for many minutes, when he remembered what Edith had done in her extremity. Springing from the bed he fell down on his knees, and uttered a long and fervent prayer for the intervention of Divine assistance in behalf of Edith—the Edith who had already been once delivered by Providence.

When Willy arose his eyes rested on the partly opened door of a closet beside the window. He gazed steadfastly, for he thought he had seen it move on its hinges; he recollected that he had once essayed unsuccessfully to open it. He strode forward, and thrusting it wide open, beheld a man seated on the floor within, presenting a pistol at his breast.

"Why should you kill me?" said the young man, in amazement, but not endeavoring to elude the aim.

"I don't exactly know," said the other. "But if I must kill you I will. No! You're my friend. It's Wiry Willy!" Saying this he thrust the pistol in his belt and sprang out of the dark hole.

"Jack Bim!" exclaimed Willy. "And you heard my prayer!"

"Heard it, and *felt* it too! I never had such queer feelings in my life."

"Still, you were ready to shoot me."

"That was after you were done, and my natural feelings returned."

"But why were you hiding there, Jack? What have you done?"

"I've done just what you advised."

"What I advised?" asked Willy, forgetful of his advice.

"Yes. We've done it. The church was a perfect mint. All sorts of plate, as well as chests of gold eagles. The parson prayed—but it was no go. He didn't pray to God, like you, but to *us*, and we were pretty much devils. There were casks of wine, also, and we helped ourselves."

"And what did you do with the money?"

"It made a big pile, and each of us are pretty well off, if we can only keep from being robbed. I have not slept a wink since this business was done. Where will you put your share?"

"My share?"

"Yes. It is with mine in the closet. I demanded an equal share for you—"

"I will not touch it!" said Willy.

"You can do as you please. And I confess my part has not made me feel better. I have been hiding with it, and starving over it. I have been afraid to leave it, and it's too heavy to carry with me. My pockets and belt are filled, and yet they don't hold a quarter of my share."

"Why did you come here?"

"Oh, I *live* here, at present. I'm a captain in General Ruffleton's army, on leave; but he says we'll have fighting to do in about a week. Then, suppose I should be *killed?* What's to become of this confounded gold?"

"But, Jack, Ruffleton's army is not here."

"But his headquarters are. He's had doors cut through the walls, so he can go from one end of this block to the other. This whole square was reserved."

"And I suppose I'm his prisoner."

"You may be quite sure of it! But what have you done?"

"Nothing except strive to protect a young lady—"

"That's it. I thought so. But why should I be only

a captain? Hang me if I will! I've got enough money to rise. I'll get you off from here, Willy, when it's a little darker."

"Do, Jack, and you may have my share of the money."

"No, *sir!* I have had trouble enough with my own. If you take your share, it'll be some comfort to me. I won't have all the care and trouble myself. So make up your mind to stay here, or else to take the money."

"I'll do anything, almost, to be released from this confinement."

"Willy, all you have to do is to say SOUTH, and they'll let you pass."

"But how am I to get out of this room?"

"Do you ask such a question? See here!" and with his bowie knife Jack removed the lock in a few minutes. "But you'd better not venture down just now. Wait till this battle's over, and if the Democrats whip the others, our folks won't like to be kicking up rows. Just listen! That's pretty smart fighting." It was the battle in which Edith became involved.

"It's a bad business!" said Willy.

"I like it!" responded Bim, looking out of the window at the flashes. "They've got a cannon in the Square, and when it's rigged up and fired, the others will run. A big noise frightens the men. 'Twas so at Washington. As soon as the batteries opened upon us, we couldn't keep the men in the Avenue. I cut down some cowards for running away. Wiry Willy, where were you?"

"I was running about with messages."

"For the General, I suppose. Crook is brave—but he ought not to 've divided his forces. It was wrong to mount some on horses, and think to carry off the President. But there goes the cannon! and yonder run the cowards. How they are getting pinked in their backs! Fools! They don't know anything about war. It's always best to go right through and take the cannon. If they turn tail and run they're sure to suffer more. It was so at Lodi. If the little Corporal and his men hadn't crossed the bridge, after getting on it, they'd have suffered more than they did. I've been reading, Wiry Willy, and I've seen some service, too. It's all over now, and I'm as hungry as a shark. Do you stay here, Willy, and watch the money, till I can snatch a loaf and a bottle; and when I come back you can go."

"I will remain if you desire it, Jack; but I would rather go with you. Why not leave the gold where it is? It is not probable, after all your care and watching, it will be lost? Why not be content with what you have about your person, and aid me in restoring a poor distressed daughter to her father?"

"What daughter? What father?"

Willy told him everything connected with the misfortunes of Edith. Jack was strangely agitated. He had read of the heroic gallantry of soldiers, and all at once conceived the idea of becoming a champion of the beautiful maiden. And when he turned again towards the treasure, as if his conscience smote him for the manner in which he had obtained it, he justified himself by condemning the crime of ministers preaching politics, and philanthropic Abolitionists stealing slave property from the Southerners. The treasure being wrested from these two classes, it seemed a just retribution.

"I am with you, Willy!" said he, grasping the young man's hand, "and now we will hunt in couples, and will be too much for all the Trapps."

Jack boldly led the way down stairs, and at every turning jested with the sentinel that hailed him. But when they were passing through the hall, Willy's blood ran cold on recognising the angry voice of General Ruffleton in the parlor, and before the open door of which it was necessary to pass in order to reach the street.

"Jack Bim! come here, sir!" cried the General. Willy held his breath and paused.

"When I sneeze you must pass," whispered Jack

"Captain Bim," continued the General, when Jack entered and made the military salute, "I request that you will take a trusty man and scour the city for me. I want you to find a slender boy, with black eyes, about fifteen years of age, in black pantaloons and roundabout, with a blue cap on his head. Call him Langdon, and if he starts, bring him hither. I have sworn to have him, and rather than be balked, I would see this whole city in flames."

Jack sneezed. Willy passed the parlor door, gave the word to the sentry in the vestibule, and descended to the street.

"All right!" said Bim, overtaking him: "when I sneezed the General's back was towards you. I managed to get round him. Now let us go into the Square."

Having entered the western gate, and proceeded a few steps, Willy paused and listened an instant to the one who then addressed the people.

"That's Senator Langdon," said he.

"But who is this?" cried Jack Bim, seeing a boy answering the General's description, struggling in the arms of Major Trapp, under one of the trees.

"Merciful Heaven!" said Willy, "it is Edith!"

"Then we'll have her, Willy," said Bim: "but that's Major Trapp! He's my superior officer, and I don't want him to recognise me, unless it's to be my luck to kill him!"

"And Jack," said Willy, "I *want* him to recognise me. I want him to see the man he so deeply offended." And Willy approached the tree where the Major was striving to pacify the now recovered Edith.

"Oh, Willy!" cried she. "Heaven sends you to be my deliverer. Save me! save me!" and she held out her hands towards him.

"I will, or die!" said Willy, springing forward.

"Then die!" said the Major, presenting a pistol. He fired, and Willy fell.

"Now or never!" cried Bim, springing forward, with his bowie-knife. He plunged it into the Major's breast, who fell without a groan.

Edith, without pausing to witness the whole of the fearful tragedy, ran towards the stand. She pushed forward with the determination not to be bereft of consciousness again. Having reached the front of the stand, and recognised both her father's voice and features, she uttered no word—no shriek escaped her; she did not even strive to attract his attention; but working diligently round to the opposite side, where there were steps leading to the summit, she mounted them, and struggling through the chairs occupied by the distinguished citizens, she reached the goal which had so often baffled her, and throwing her arms around the surprised Senator's neck, said, "Oh, father, I am Edith!"

Recognising the beautiful features of his child, the happy

father folded her to his heart, and announced to the astonished multitude that he had found his daughter. The cap had fallen from Edith's head, and her long dark hair rolled down in waves over her shoulders.

Senator Langdon, of course, could speak no more; but he was succeeded by Mr. B——.

The Senator descended with Edith, and conducted her to his hotel, nearly opposite, in Chestnut street. But even before Edith had reached her chamber, she had related the manner of her deliverance, and almost frantically insisted that poor Willy, stunned, not fatally wounded, whose fall she had witnessed, should be removed from the Square, and taken to his aged grandmother. Soon after the poor girl succumbed to her many trials. A fever seized her, and delirium ensued.

CHAPTER XII.

INSURRECTION OF THE SLAVES.

The excitement and consternation in all sections of the country increased in intensity. One-fourth of the great city of New York was in ashes, and Boston was the scene of a Reign of Terror never surpassed in Paris. The Unitarians had assailed the Catholics; and after a number of sanguinary battles, the city fell completely into the hands of the foreign population. The Rev. T——e P——r, W——ll P——s, Wm. Lloyd G——n, Senators S——r and W——n, and the chivalrous B——e, with sundry masculine women, and lesser clerical abolition lecturers, including Mr. K—ll—h, had been shipped on a vessel, chartered for the purpose, to Liberia. Nevertheless, the Northern States, with some show of concert of action, if not unanimity of sentiment, proceeded to appoint delegates to a Northern Convention, and Philadelphia was designated as the place for the sessions. Senator Langdon was chosen one of the delegates, whilst nursing his sick daughter. But he accepted the honor, if such it might be called, that had been conferred on him. He deemed it a duty to contribute his energies for the public good in such an exigency.

In the South, while all were ready to defend the soil, there was a manifest reluctance on the part of the people to adopt final measures. The Convention, in which all the Southern States were represented, had assembled at Richmond, and appointed Henry Blount commander-in-chief of the armies to be raised for their defence. Blount was the possessor of vast wealth, of distinguished extraction, endowed with genius of a high order, and had been educated in one of the best military schools in the country. But there was no military organization, and months would be required to place a well-appointed army in the field. Money, arms, ammunition would have to be procured, and contributions exacted from the people. There were, however, some forty or fifty thousand volunteers, recognising General Crook as their leader, composed in part of enthusiastic patriots, who defrayed their own expenses, and as many destitute adventurers, who deemed anything they could lay their hands on fair prize. This promiscuous army was concentrating in Delaware to oppose the progress of General Ruffleton. Neither of these generals was acting in pursuance of authority derived from the sections or people they professed to represent; but there existed no means, for the time being, in either section, of controlling their operations or of annulling their action. It was supposed, however, that a few engagements, the fatigues of a short campaign, and, above all, the absence of a military chest, would render them subservient to the civil authority.

At all the important points the agents of the central government at Washington were surrounded and protected by the soldiers of the United States; and so far, in every instance, the picked men of the President had vindicated his wisdom and foresight. Not a dollar of the Federal money had been lost. Not a cargo had been landed without paying duty; and all the forts, and arsenals, and ships, with a few exceptions in the South, were still held by Randolph. Several incumbents, in the civil service, who sympathized with the sectional factions, were summarily removed, and even then no difficulty was experienced in finding other men to take their places. Nor were these the most extraordinary achievements of the President. In the very teeth of the disruption of the sections, and in despite of the contempt of law and order that prevailed, this great man had issued a proclamation, calling out a certain portion of the militia of all the States for the "suppression of domestic violence;" and *every State in some degree responded*, or, at all events, more or less of the militia promptly joined the Federal standard. Missouri, Illinois, Kentucky, and Indiana furnished seventy thousand men and fifteen thousand horses. In those great Western States the sentiment against disunion was nearly unanimous, and Southern Fire-eaters and Northern Abolitionists were seized alike in any of them and incarcerated in the same prison.

Alabama, and all the cotton States, were in a perfect blaze; and no wonder, for a vast conspiracy for the enfranchisement of the slaves and the massacre of the white population had been discovered, and the accomplishment of the fiendish purpose had been prevented with difficulty, and not till after the effusion of much blood. Several thousand of the whites fell victims to the servile insurrection, and a still greater number of the deluded slaves paid the penalty of following the evil counsels of their worst foes in the disguise of friends. But the slaughter was not confined to the master and slave. More than three hundred fanatics, or the rash agents of fanatics, were arrested, tried, condemned, and executed on the scaffold.

So great was the indignation in these States, that their journals teemed with the most urgent appeals to the Convention at Richmond to cut the Gordian knot, and sever all intercourse, of whatever nature, with the North. They likewise demanded the appointment of General Crook to the head of the Southern armies. And when it was announced that the appointment had been conferred on Henry Blount, and that a subordinate position had been tendered Crook, then at the head of the only Southern army in the field, there arose a very great outburst of dissatisfaction.

Under such circumstances, the controlling spirits in the Convention advised a postponement of decisive action, until events should unite the Southern people in opinion, in policy, and in destiny.

CHAPTER XIII.

A DEATH SCENE.

THE President was sitting in one of the offices of the executive mansion, smiling affectionately on his daughter, whose arm encircled his neck. It was at a late hour of the night, and all seemed still and silent without, save the measured tramp of the sentinels.

"And so, you would go with me on the field of battle?" asked the President. "What a change from the timid and fearful Alice of a few short weeks ago! And this, too, after reading an account of the painful adventures of Edith!"

"True, father, I am changed," said she, distinctly and seriously. "And this, too, after reading the thrilling recital of poor Edith."

"I really believe you have become more courageous, or, it may be, reckless of your safety, than you were formerly. And what has produced the change? It cannot be a desire for such *night*-errantry as Edith's?"

"No—no!"

"And yet it must proceed from some extraordinary cause. Can it be love?"

"Would that be extraordinary?" she responded, with a sad smile, while the color entirely faded from her cheeks.

This was too apparent to escape the notice of Randolph. He rose up and confronted his daughter, and gazed upon her pale forehead for several moments in silence. Her eyes were cast down, and she stood motionless before him, with folded arms.

"Without my knowledge, Alice," said he, his voice slightly tremulous, "or without my concurrence, it *would* be extraordinary. In the field, in the closet, on my pillow, Alice, the only unpleasant thought ever connected with my destiny, was the vision, or the fear,—"

"Fear not, father!" said she. "The man does not live who will be the husband or the lover of Alice." This was said in a low and almost plaintive voice. "And yet, father, I love."

"And this is an enigma. Alice! the day may come when kings and emperors will sue at thy feet! How, then, can you love, and not be loved in turn?"

"I did not say so, father."

"You said you loved."

"Father," said she, again twining her arm round his neck, "I LOVE MY COUNTRY!"

Randolph, disengaging himself, strode rapidly backwards and forwards across the room, his forehead pale, his lips compressed, and his eye gleaming with unwonted fierceness.

"You love your country?" he reiterated, after a silence of many moments, and pausing abruptly in front of his pale daughter.

"AND WOULD SAVE IT!" said she.

"And would save it! Why, what nonsense is this?"

"It is not nonsense, father."

"Then, pray, how could *you* save your country?"

"By invoking the aid of heaven to touch my father's heart."

"Alice! Nay, start not, my child—although it was harshly uttered, it was not in anger. But, my pure Alice, you will tell me who has been whispering an insinuation that I would either destroy the country, or would not strive to save it?"

"No one, father."

"An angel from heaven, Alice, could not be more truthful than my daughter. I need not say I believe you. And so you discovered it yourself?"

"I feared so, father. And now will you not tell me I was mistaken?"

"Have I not served the country," said he, again walking rapidly to and fro, "all the best years of my life? My labors by day, and my thoughts by night, have all been devoted to the welfare of the country. And what is the result? What do we behold? The intrigues of factions, sectional animosities, disruption of the Legislature, destruction of property, civil war, and the contempt of nations less in magnitude, in population, in prowess, wealth, and intelligence. Not strive to save such a country as this? I WILL save it, Alice—ay, in spite of itself! The Union SHALL be preserved!"

"And the REPUBLIC, father? The glorious REPUBLIC OF WASHINGTON?" cried Alice, running to the President and seizing both his hands.

"Why, certainly, Alice, if it be possible," said he gravely.

"But if it be *not* possible?"

"Ha, ha, ha! Would you have me promise impossibilities? We will sit down," he continued, leading her to the chair beside his own, "and argue this matter. We can confide in each other. I fear our people—any people—are, after all, incapable of self-government. Where, under heaven, has a larger liberty been enjoyed? Have we not prospered by land and by sea abundantly? All religions have been tolerated. Churches in every village; colleges in the cities; newspapers, with infinite license, everywhere. From thirteen, we have expanded to thirty odd States, and from three millions of inhabitants to thirty millions. Our fields have been cultivated, and no famine ever cursed the land. Our commerce has spread its sails in every sea. We have a monopoly of the greatest staple the earth produces; inexhaustible mines; scores of thousands of miles of railroads; immense cities, factories, and all the comforts and luxuries known to civilized man;—and yet, what is the condition of the people? Survey them now, Alice. Must I permit them to be divided into petty States, independent of and hostile to each other? Shall the people be suffered to inflict irremediable evil on themselves—to degenerate into semi-barbarism, and become the easy, if not the willing, prey of the effeminate monarchs of Europe? That is the question. Are we, Republicans, worthy of the Republic of Washington?"

"We will be, father! Why not!" exclaimed Alice, with great animation, and with recovered color. "Are we not the descendants of the people for whom Washington fought and prayed? Are we spoiled children? Then chastise, but do not destroy. We will see our folly, and reform. The North will confess that they had no right to meddle either with the consciences of the Southern people, or the property of the South; and the South will acknowledge that the North is indispensable for the consummation of the national destiny."

"That is very fine in theory, Alice; but we behold the body politic desperately, if not fatally, diseased. It must be phlebotomized!"

"Be it so—but may that not effect a cure? Doubtless the people have transgressed, and must be punished. Men in arms with angry passions, will certainly fight. The fall of thousands is inevitable. But oh, father! is not death, a speedy death, the lot of all? If *we* must die, still our country may survive. Dust returns to dust, but the glorious actions of the good and great are imperishable. Father! I would have you live in bronze and marble, like the immortal Washington!"

"And would you not survive to see it? Or, Alice, is it FAME with which you are in love? Fy, daughter, that none of the gallant sons of our great country could inflame thy cold fancy!"

"Father!"

"Well? Have you a secret? Silent! Who is he? Where is he?"

"He lives not for me!" said Alice, again as pale as monumental marble.

"Does he live at all? Did he die?"

"Father! think that once a bright object flitted for a moment athwart the vision of your daughter—and—when he crossed it again another claimed him; he another. But likewise think he never knew, could never know——"

"Enough, my child! What! pale and in tears!"

"Before none but you and my Heavenly Parent. Father, do you not remember the note you sent me on that eventful day? You said, '*Be marble.*' And now I can be. There is not a living thing I hate; and but two objects to love—you and my country. But, father, is it not probable these Conventions may decree an irrevocable separation?"

"No—it is not probable. I have partisans in both."

"I might have known it!"

"And I have still more adherents out of them, and in both sections."

"But not in these armies about to engage?"

"No. They are more like mobs than armies, and cannot be restrained by their respective sections. It may be different when they shall have weakened each other. This spasmodic patriotism will be mitigated when the hardships and dangers of a campaign are experienced. Both promiscuous hosts are maintained by private contributions, or enforced levies. This will not last long; but in the meantime much may be accomplished. There will be a battle."

"And, father, why should you take part in it? On which side will you fight?"

"Perhaps neither. It may not be *meant* as an insurrection: but it would be domestic violence, and it is my duty to suppress it. I shall forbid the collision; then when they engage, the aggressor must be punished."

A servant entered and announced a messenger from Delaware. It was Wiry Willy, recovered from his wound.

"Willy!" exclaimed Alice, running to the faithful messenger and receiving a letter from his hand. "But speak!" said she. "Just one word of Edith, before you proceed to business."

"She has entirely recovered."

"That is sufficient," said the President. "Read your letter, daughter. Now, Willy, I see important news in your face. Ruffleton has not destroyed your little farm, I hope?"

"No, sir. He turned to the right and avoided Delaware."

"Ah, indeed!"

"He has crossed the Susquehanna, sir."

"That menaces us in this district! But he will find the Caudine forks between the Chesapeake and the Potomac!"

"He intends to enter Virginia, sir, by crossing the Long Bridge."

"How do you know that?"

"He told me so himself. We are friends again."

"I understand. The fool! But enough of him. What of Crook? I have not received intelligence from him since he permitted the wires to be demolished."

"Two hours after I left General Ruffleton, I was in the camp of General Crook!"

"Then there was a night march—or else Crook was an ignoramus."

"There was, sir. He marched all night, and is now between this city and the Northern army. But he is retreating, sir. They say, and my own eyes confirmed it, that the Eastern recruits or volunteers received within the last week by Ruffleton, amount to 100,000 men. His army is 150,000 strong, sir."

"His rabble, you mean. Still, they must make a very formidable appearance, and might even penetrate the Old Dominion. Crook has not one-third the number of his opponent, but he has better men—men, who if they do not know how to fight, will be willing to die in defence of their native soil. Go to Mary Penford, Willy, she is in distress. You may conduct her hither if she desires it." Willy's eyes were dilated with surprise, but he did not pause for further information.

"Poor old man!" said Alice, after Willy had departed; "I fear it is over with him. But Mary will find protection here."

The President had General Valiant summoned; and then Alice, having kissed her father again, retired for the night.

When the General entered, he found the President absorbed in study, with a map spread out before him.

"I have sent for you, General," said the President, "to impart some rather alarming news."

"I doubt very much, sir, whether there is any necessity for alarm, although I do not question the accuracy of your information."

Valiant was a young general, in whose genius and fidelity the President had great confidence.

"We may not be in danger, General," pursued the President, his finger resting on the map; "but here are two armies, at this moment probably within twenty miles of us. Crook is retreating in this direction, followed by Ruffleton with 150,000 men."

"Men and boys, sir—all novices. It is just as I predicted. And both armies are hemmed in between the Chesapeake and the Potomac. We might destroy them both."

"No! that is not our policy. But ought Ruffleton to be permitted to pass through the District of Columbia? That's the question. I know he would be overwhelmed by Blount before he could penetrate far into Virginia. But is it not my duty to arrest the invasion?"

"You may do so very easily. The whole District is now a military encampment. Sixty thousand infantry, twenty thousand cavalry, and six hundred cannon. And they have been drilled day and night by the very best officers in the service. Why the d—l don't Crook select a good position and give Ruffleton battle?"

"He is not deficient in courage, or he would never have made his bold dash at me. I like him, Valiant. He is the soul of honor, when his word is plighted. And, between us, I have some overtures from him. If he can cut the Gordian knot, he will—but you know he can't—and if not, he will co-operate with us, if we give him an opportunity to beat the Northern people, whom he hates so heartily. But he is not to fight a pitched battle without apprising me of his purpose. I desire to ascertain, General, if we could not so manœuvre as to give Crook a victory without being directly implicated ourselves."

"I can easily make Ruffleton attack us, and then, in our own defence, you know, we can destroy him."

"I should be reluctant—very reluctant to be the instrument of the destruction of such a host of Northern people, whose ostensible purpose was not an assault on the Federal authority. Crook must do it! There is a messenger."

An aide came in with a sealed letter.

"This is from Crook!" said the President. "He asks an interview, and I will grant it. Let the one who brought this be conducted hither. I must interrogate him. My position, Valiant," he continued, "is certainly an anomalous one. It is an exceedingly difficult game."

"But you are a good player," said the General.

"That must be proven by the event. But whom have we here?" said he, starting up on beholding the entrance of the supposed messenger from General Crook. He was enveloped in a cloak, and wore a broad-brimmed hat, such as is used in a Southern clime. Randolph gazed a moment at the clear grey eye of the stranger, and then advanced and grasped his hand. "Throw off your disguise, General," said he. "This is General Valiant, who will not betray us."

"I am in your hands, gentlemen," said General Crook, declining to sit. "But I am now about defending the Capital instead of attacking it. It is your policy, Randolph, either as President, Usurper, Emperor—or whatever it may be—to see that the invaders be rolled back from the Federal City. All I ask is a battery of fifty pieces of artillery and a few thousand horse—the last merely for show, and not to fight. I want them to appear on an eminence and menace the enemy's flank and rear. That is all. I will do the rest."

"And so you intend to offer battle?" asked the President.

"Ay, I intend to give it, and that too before we enter your exclusive territory of some seven miles square. We will fight at Bladensburg."

"Provided you have a few thousand of my cavalry, and the battery?"

"Ay, the former only for show; and the latter can be transported under cover of the darkness, so that the country will never know whence I obtained them. I pledge my honor that it shall never be known, contrary to your wishes, how they were obtained."

"Enough, General. Valiant will furnish the cannon. The horse I will lead myself. Where will you make a stand?"

"At Bladensburg."

"Then I know the eminence for the horse. You need take no further thought about the matter. I will be there at the critical moment. And if Ruffleton should be determined to beat you in spite of your artillery, I will interpose and require him to retrace his steps. It *is* my duty to prevent one section from invading the other, and that duty shall be performed!"

"But, sir!" said Crook, with much earnestness, "I hope you will not deprive me of the opportunity of beating him. Don't interpose unless you see the day about to be lost."

"Very well. If you can vanquish him, I shall be content. But, recollect, the victor must not cross the line in pursuit. You must not invade them in turn."

Crook smiled, and, turning, followed General Valiant to his quarters. The President then reclined on a sofa, and was soon steeped in quiet slumber.

* * * * * *

Wiry Willy hastened away at that late hour to Georgetown. He bore the infatuated old clerk a letter from General Ruffleton, who, believing Willy little better than a mere simpleton, had not destroyed him.

Perceiving lights in several of the rooms, Willy knew that Mary was watching, and that he could obtain admittance. The servant girl who answered the bell, conducted him into the little parlor, where he beheld Mary, pale, and with traces of recent tears on her lovely face. She was sitting beside the physician, but immediately arose, and taking the hand of Willy, conducted him in silence to a chair. The doctor, after a few brief words, departed.

"Willy," said Mary, "my poor grandpa is about to leave me."

"Let us hope not, Mary," said he. "But if it must be so, we should not be unprepared for the event. He has been spared to an extreme old age, and his life has been without guile."

"That is true, Willy. I do not think it was ever his design to inflict injury on any human being. And he is now about to be at rest."

"Is it so certain, Mary?"

"The doctor has just told me that his pulse is failing, and that he cannot possibly survive more than a few hours."

"And you, Mary—what will be your condition?"

"The neighbors are kind, and we have many good friends. There are two nurses with him now. Oh, Willy—that dreadful day! It was a fatal blow, the loss of those papers! But come with me—he will know you. He is more rational as he approaches his end."

"I have a letter for him, Mary—shall I deliver it?"

"From Ruffleton?"

"Yes."

"I do not know. Oh, Willy, I fear him more than ever, since his abominable conduct to Edith! She has written me all—and warned me against his machinations. But still the letter may do no harm."

They ascended to the chamber of the dying man. He recognised Willy.

"William Wire," said he, "what news do you bring of General Ruffleton?"

Willy presented the letter. At a signal from Mary the kind women who had been watching, withdrew into an adjoining chamber. With difficulty the old man broke the seal, but his vision was too dim to see.

"Read it for me, William Wire," said he.

The letter announced that the General would, in two or three days, be in possession of the Capital, and occupy the Executive Mansion.

"Impossible!" exclaimed the old man. "He has not

been elected. Randolph's term has not expired. Impossible!"

The letter went on to say that Mary would be made the mistress of the Presidential Mansion.

"Oh, grandpa!" said Mary, observing that the old man did not manifest as much interest in this communication as in preceding ones from the same source, "now, when it may be God's will that you must abandon all earthly pursuits, I beseech you to revoke that frightful pledge exacted from the lone companion of your declining years, that she would unite her destiny with the one, above all others, she could not help most disliking."

The old man gazed a moment at her sweet face, and then succeeded by a violent effort in turning on his pillow. He caught her hand and kissed it, and then placed it tenderly in Willy's.

"William Wire!" said he, "she is thine. Guard her well. Defend her if I should die. But if I survive, and consummate that claim for cannon—"

"Alas, grandpa!" said Mary, "you forget the destruction of the papers!"

"True, my cherub! And if they should be mad enough really to dissolve the Union, what a universal destruction of papers will ensue. My eyes grow dim when I think of it, and I pray God not to let me see it. But President Randolph is a great man—have faith in him, adhere to his fortunes. Call in the women and light the lamps. I feel better. To-morrow I will endeavor to see the President."

"Oh, grandpa!" said the weeping Mary, who, with the rest, observed the fearful change rapidly spreading over his features, "to-morrow you may be called into the presence of your heavenly father!"

"God is my judge and my savior," said he. "But what says the doctor?"

"He says the end is near," said Willy; for Mary was incapable of utterance.

"Impossible!" said the old man, and instantly expired.

* * * * * *

Pale, though composed, Mary sat at one end of the breakfast table, and Willy occupied the other. During the repast they were startled by the sound of cannon in the distance.

"That is the commencement of the battle!" said Willy.

"And when will battles end, Willy?"

"God knows. But I have faith in the President. And, Mary, last night he said you must remove to the Mansion, after the obsequies of your grandfather."

"Alice was here yesterday, and said the same thing. And I will go there."

The thunder of the distant cannon increased. And soon the clatter of the hoofs of horses was heard. To the utter consternation of both Mary and Willy, the door was thrown violently open, and several armed men rushed in.

"There she is," said the leader, who was instantly recognised by Willy as one of the aides of Ruffleton, Major Snare.

"Pray what is your business with me, sir?" demanded Mary, confronting the red-faced and apparently inebriated Major.

"My orders are to remove you to a place of security."

"Am I not secure here?"

"No—not by a great deal! But I am to be gentle and careful, and all that. You need not be alarmed."

"I cannot leave this place, sir. My grandfather—"

"Never mind him. We must obey orders."

"Her grandfather is dead!" said Willy, approaching the officer. "His corpse is now up-stairs."

"The d—l! That's something we didn't look for. But such things in time of war are not novelties. The neighbors will bury the old man. Come, Miss, I must execute the order of my superior or be executed. We have a light carriage, and the road is not rough. You can remain, Willy."

"But if you mean to take Mary, I would prefer going."

"As you please. But you must find your own horse. You can't go in the carriage. Come, Miss; my orders are to use expedition."

"I must see my grandpa, first!" said Mary, weeping, and passing up-stairs. She ran forward, and seizing the cold hand of her dead parent, fell upon her knees. The few neighbors who were present, endeavored to assuage her grief. But as the voice of Major Snare was heard below, demanding the return of the aggrieved girl, she clung the closer to the corpse.

"I can wait no longer!" said the Major, ascending the stairs, and entering the chamber of death. "Come!" he continued, "there is a crowd collecting in the street, and we may have to kill some of the good people. The d—l!" said he, on perceiving the body of John Penford. "That's more than I expected—and it's a spectacle not to my taste. Still, orders must be obeyed. Come!"

"Oh, sir!" said Mary, "you cannot be so hard-hearted as to drag me away from my grandpa—now so cold and still."

"It is not to my taste, Miss Mary; but I must execute the order, or I shall be dead myself."

"Then I obey. I would not have a worm suffer death on my account," said she, rising. "Excuse me but a few moments, sir, until I can get some additional apparel, and then I will attend you."

"Oh, very well!" said the Major, "I will wait two minutes."

When the neighbors learned the nature of the Major's mission, they were very indignant, and would have resisted the execution of the inhuman order, if they had possessed the ability.

Mary appeared before the Major, and in the presence of the people declared her departure was in obedience to a demand which she possessed no ability to resist. She then requested to see Wiry Willy—but he could nowhere be found. Then they led her to the light carriage, and having thrust her in, drove away at a furious rate.

CHAPTER XIV.

THE BATTLE OF BLADENSBURG.

General Crook began the cannonade at sunrise, and when the two armies were yet some twelve or fifteen hundred yards apart. This was quite an unexpected occurrence to Ruffleton. That some fifty thousand men would make a stand against three times their number, seemed the very madness of temerity. When informed that morning that the Southern army was drawn up in battle array, his own forces were much scattered. They had encamped in a line extending some six miles in length, and the van and rear were now that distance apart, while the flanks were, as usual, in much disorder, for about one-fourth of his men were robbing hen-houses, killing pigs, and hunting forage. Crook had his troops in good position, and well concentrated; his left extending to a steep hill, and his right defended by a stream of water, then considerably swollen by the recent rains.

President Randolph, at the head of five thousand horse, was hidden from view by the crest of a hill, in readiness to appear on the field at any moment, if it should be requisite for him to take any active part in the engagement. And Alice was at the side of her father, mounted on a spirited charger. She wore a velvet cap, and her riding dress was confined by a silken scarf, *en militaire.*

"We have a fine view, here," said Randolph, as his steed and Alice's stood on the summit of the hill, whence they could behold the greater portion of both armies.

"And General Crook is firing his cannon! See the white smoke!" said Alice. "There!" she continued, when their thunder was heard; "how long between the smoke and report! And, father, it is not so frightful as I supposed. See! Sir Archy merely curves his neck and snuffs the breeze. He did not lift a hoof to paw the earth. Brave Sir Archy!"

"I have had him trained, Alice. But there is a different scene over yonder. Take my glass and view the meadow to the left of the grove."

Alice did so—and uttered no more points of admiration. Some forty thousand of Ruffleton's rabble were crowded in a meadow of about five acres in extent, and through these the cannon balls were ploughing fearfully. The commotion was indescribable; and in a few minutes the place was almost entirely deserted.

"Father!" said Alice, returning the glass, "you are the President of the United States!"

"I understand, daughter," said Randolph, again surveying the field. "It is my duty, if possible, to prevent domestic violence and suppress insurrection. These men will not regard my authority, and I would, if possible, avoid shedding their blood. But you shall be my witness that I strove to prevent the collision." He then beckoned an officer, stationed some twenty paces in the rear, to advance.

"Take a flag, sir, and go to Ruffleton. Deliver this note, and return with an answer." The officer spurred down the hill in view of both armies, regardless of the cannon balls and bombs now discharged from both sides, the distance separating them being still too great for the effective use of small arms. The flag was respected, and the officer passed the lines in safety. The message was delivered, and an answer promptly returned.

"What does he say, father?" inquired Alice, when the officer had retired to his original position.

"He is impudent and defiant!" said Randolph, in tones of anger. "He says the Federal Government has ceased to exist, and that I have no more authority to require him to retire and dismiss his forces than he has to demand my abandonment of the city and the functions of the Presidency."

"Alas! I know you will not brook such language."

"I can smile at him, Alice, until forced to act. But if I should pounce upon him, he will find it a different matter than merely withstanding this lazy assault of Crook. Not so slothful either, by Jupiter!" he exclaimed, again looking through his glass. "Well done, and worthy a military genius!"

General Crook, while attracting attention to his batteries in the centre, had detached ten thousand men from his right wing; they marched by a circuitous route, and were entirely unperceived, until they fell perpendicularly upon the left flank of the enemy. The effect was tremendous. One-half the invading army fell back instantly, panic-stricken, while the other half was impelled forward. The ten thousand Southern men were between them, and, for a time, did great execution. That portion of the Northern army precipitated forward, was, for a considerable length of time, subjected to two fires, in front and rear, and much slaughter was the result. The field seemed lost, and doubtless would have been with disciplined armies. But it has occurred more than once, that novices in war, unable to appreciate the advantages of a superior position, or the fatal effects of a blundering movement, have failed to realize success with victory in their grasp, or refused to retire, when completely beaten, according to all the precepts of military science. Men inexperienced in battle, are unable to conceive how an army can be defeated until all the soldiers are killed! And Ruffleton's army, although cut in twain, still presented two mighty hosts, each more formidable in numbers than the enemy. Ruffleton, perceiving this, soon rallied his forces, and then the detachment of ten thousand, which had performed so great a manœuvre, was subjected in turn to a fire both in front and rear. There was no alternative but for the Hon. Mr.—now General—Steel, to retrace his steps, and endeavor to reunite his column with the main body of the army, now menaced by overwhelming numbers.

Ruffleton had contrived to secure the services of a number of experienced officers, always to be found in New York, travellers, or exiles from many nations. These gentlemen, who at one time supposed everything lost, now disposed their columns with alacrity as for certain victory. But they were deficient in artillery, and almost destitute of horse.

Crook stood his ground manfully, and continued to make frightful chasms in the ranks of the foe, both with his well-served cannon and with one thousand minie rifles he had borrowed from General Valiant. But still the mighty wave of invaders continued to roll on, threatening to inundate or sweep away every opposing obstacle.

"Now, father!" exclaimed Alice. "If you do not interpose, that multitude will annihilate the little army of the defenders of the South!"

"The moment has not yet arrived, my daughter," said the President, calmly and deliberately, a distinguishing trait of his character, always evinced in moments of peril, and whenever any species of panic seized upon those by whom he was surrounded. "But how is it, Alice, that you manifest so sudden and so decided a sympathy for Crook and his followers? Is it your Southern blood instinctively pulsating in behalf of your countrymen?"

"No, father!" said Alice, resuming her statue-like patriotism. "The South is but an integral portion of the Union. Maine and Texas are alike my country. To you I confess the cause of the solicitude I felt and expressed. It was a *woman's* pity for the weaker party. But now I am MARBLE. Call me, if you please, a statue of LIBERTY, or of AMERICA. All I ask, father, is that you will preserve the whole Union, as one country, one Republic, as Washington and his compatriots formed it. If it be necessary that yonder little army, now struggling in defence of their native soil, should perish a few years before their allotted time in the course of nature, that the GREAT REPUBLIC may survive for generations, be it so! Man cannot live beyond a limited term—but the republic may be immortal."

"It is not necessary, Alice. Now gentlemen!" he continued, in a loud voice, to his aides, awaiting his commands a few paces apart, "sound the charge! Blow all your bugles! We will rush down like a torrent towards the plain. But not a shot must be fired, not a sword bathed in blood. I will lead the van myself, as soon as we shall have attracted the attention of Ruffleton."

But this was not accomplished in a moment, although a vast number of bugles and kettle-drums did their utmost. The reason was that General Steel, whether from accident or design, in executing the *detour* which was to accomplish a junction with the main body of the army, fell somewhat short of the contemplated march, and was once more precipitated on the left flank of the advancing enemy. This time he did not attempt to sever the van from the rear, but his well-directed fire, now that his men had recovered from the first trepidation of the battle, did much havoc, and created great consternation. Ruffleton himself spurred towards the menaced point, and in the confusion of sounds the charge of the bugles did not reach his ear. With difficulty he succeeded in restoring some degree of order, and in impelling forward the columns whose progress had been arrested.

It was at this moment that he received intelligence of the demonstration on his right. Several of his most experienced generals despatched very urgent messages to him to the effect that if the formation of squares were delayed a moment all would be lost. That a charge of 5,000 cavalry, at such a juncture, on their right, would be fraught with the most fatal consequences. He then spurred to the other side of the field, and assisted in the vain endeavor to form his undisciplined rabble into hollow and solid squares.

Meanwhile, Steel kept up an incessant fire from the fine position so fortunately occupied, while Crook's batteries in front, like so many volcanoes, belched forth destruction. And President Randolph, placing himself at the head of his glittering cavalry, thundered down the hill on the right. The effect was complete. More than 100,000 men, deaf to the commands of their officers, simultaneously wheeled and fled away. Randolph, infinitely diverted at the scene, inclined to the right, and swept along in the opposite direction to that pursued by the fugitives; and as none of them turned their eyes behind, they naturally supposed the cavalry were cutting down their comrades, who had been the farthest advanced on the bloody field. But Randolph led his horse without striking a blow, into the first valley he encountered, and wheeling once more, conducted his entire column back to the position they had occupied early in the morning, and where his daughter, guarded by a select troop, awaited the result.

"I witnessed everything, father," said Alice. "The invaders are routed. But, see! The terrible Crook pursues! What slaughter! And yonder dark mass of horse! Father, they are yours! Was that right?"

"The horses are mine, Alice, but not the men. Valiant, it seems, has loaned General Crook some 8,000 animals, and Crook has mounted his own followers on their backs. No doubt I shall be charged with having fought this battle in conjunction with the Southerners. But to-morrow, or next week, the South may accuse me of throwing my weight into the Northern scale. My duty is to prevent aggression, to punish offences, and support the Constitution. But who comes hither from the woods? It is Wiry Willy!"

This was true. Willy emerged in view, urging his pony to the top of his speed, while his long coat floated out on the breeze.

"What news now, Willy?" demanded the President, as the young man halted in his presence.

Willy, with mingled pain and consternation, by speech and gesture succeeded in making known the catastrophe which had befallen Mary.

"Father!" exclaimed Alice, "let me be her rescuer!"

"Then be my Knight of the Velvet Cap!" said the President, drawing his sword and striking her gently on the shoulder. "Colonel Carleton," he added, "consider yourself under the command of the Knight of the Velvet Cap. Take one hundred of your best dragoons—hereafter let them be known as the Blue Caps—and rescue this fair maiden. Willy will show you the way to intercept Major Snare. Do not kill him; merely *ensnare* him. I must shed no blood, unless compelled to do so to preserve, protect, and defend the Constitution, in obedience to my oath. I entrust my daughter to you, sir!" he added, in a lower tone.

Alice touched her noble steed with her whip. He sprang forward proudly, with curved neck, distended nostrils, and flashing eye, as if eager for the service demanded of him.

"I want one hundred volunteers!" said she. Three hundred came forward. It was necessary to select every third man, and the fortunate ones were heartily cheered by the rest.

Wiry Willy indicated the road by which Major Snare would be likely to attempt to form a junction with the main body of Ruffleton's army, then in full retreat, with Crook thundering in the rear. The squadron set off at a rapid pace, in a line parallel with the flying army. They continued in this manner for several miles, when the carriage containing the captive, and the escort under the command of Major Snare, were discovered at some distance to the left, making almost superhuman exertions to join the rear guard of their Northern friends. Alice and Carleton, perceiving the object, made every effort to intercept them; and this they certainly should have done, if they had not been unexpectedly confronted by a deep chasm, over which it was deemed impossible or hazardous to leap the horses. Thus their career was momentarily checked, but only momentarily, for Alice, supposing it might be solicitude for her safety which deterred the Colonel from attempting the passage, spoke the word to Sir Archy, and with a bound he cleared the ditch. The rest followed, of course, excepting poor Wiry Willy, whose pony fell short of the opposite side, and rolled down to the bottom, landing, however, without injury to horse or rider, in a bed of leaves.

Carleton, placing Alice in the centre of the troop, renewed the chase, and reached the extreme left flank of the now fugitive army just in time to prevent Snare from dashing into it. There was no alternative but to surrender, and

Major Snare yielded to the summons; and this, too, within sixty paces of the Northern army! But the poor infantry, defeated, fatigued, hacked, and pelted, had no disposition to pause and turn aside for the relief of the abducting party of horsemen.

Alice, giving the reins to her attending servant, sprang into the carriage beside the half-fainting Mary, who uttered many heartfelt thanks for the timely interposition. Carleton, embarrassed by the presence of his prisoners, for it was not known by what authority he could detain them, lost no time in separating his charge and his men from the line of march of the armies, for General Steel was roaring in pursuit like a tornado. Finding that Snare and his men still followed, though guarded very loosely, Carleton, after having proceeded about a mile on the way back to the position occupied by the President, liberated his prisoners.

When the Blue Caps, for by this name were they to be afterwards known, returned to their disappointed if not envious comrades, the President was holding a conference with General Crook, who had sent General Steel in pursuit of the fugitives.

"Very well done, Sir Velvet Cap!" said Randolph, when the result was made known to him. "Perhaps, in time, you may win a regiment. But where is Willy?" he continued, observing that Mary, notwithstanding his congratulations, was very pale, and ever and anon looked round in quest of some one evidently not then present.

"Willy! and true enough, where is he?" exclaimed Alice.

"He is not here—nor was he present when you released me," said Mary; and surely she must have looked for him.

"He must be found," said the President, in a confident tone to Mary. "I would send a thousand men to bring him back, if it were necessary. Therefore be not uneasy. Return with Alice. The battle is over, and no further dangers can menace us." Then, kissing his hand to the ladies as they departed, he resumed his conversation with Crook.

"General," said he, "you should not have taken so many prisoners."

"If you advise it," said the General, very coolly, "I'll have every —— rascal of them shot!"

"No, sir, that is not what I mean. Too many have already fallen, and, I fear, are falling still. But you might have released them on parole. You can do so yet."

"Do you know how many abolition members of Congress and editors we have taken?"

"No; I have not heard the *quality* of any of your prisoners; but the *quantity* is enormous. It cannot be short of thirty thousand."

"On the contrary, it is rather longer than that. But these gentlemen alluded to put in a plea that they are non-combatants, and claim both an exemption from duress and from a forfeiture of the horses and other property taken with them."

"Were they taken with arms in their hands?"

"No—they had thrown them away."

"How many of this non-combating class have you?"

"Four hundred."

"Four hundred members of Congress, abolition preachers, and editors?"

"Such is the report to me. If they are non-combatants—and I must confess they were captured when huddled together where bullets could not reach them, and where it would have been impossible for them to inflict injury on us—I would like to know what they were doing in the midst of Ruffleton's invading army, and on the slave-soil of the South?"

"Oh, merely missionaries and reporters. Political and spiritual guides, and inoffensive chroniclers of the events of the campaign for the delectation of the world, at three cents per copy. I suppose you mean to dismiss them as the Roman Emperor's Proconsul did the first vagabond Christians—with pity and contempt?"

"If I do, may I be ——! Why, sir, these miscreants have produced all the mischiefs which have afflicted the country, or are likely to afflict it. If it had not been for them, I should have been a peaceful citizen on my cotton plantation, in the midst of my family, instead of skulking about of nights, forming plots to seize the archives and carry off the President. Yes, sir, these same —— rascals are the originators of all the slaughter and destruction now cursing the land, and likely to scourge it hereafter. Dismiss them with pity and contempt! Why, sir, if I were to let one of these scoundrels escape, I would be denounced from the Gulf to the Potomac!"

"But what can be done with them?"

"That's the difficulty. I don't know. I won't kill them; and, besides, according to the military code, if not the code of honor, perhaps I have no authority."

"But you have authority, General Crook, it seems," said the President, with irony, "to wage war without the sanction of either the Federal or the State governments?"

"In a case of emergency. The people are the source of all authority. We were invaded, and ——"

"Self-defence is the first law of nature," said the President. "We will say nothing more about these agitators and *non-combatants!* Do nothing cruel or unjustifiable—nothing that may not be sanctioned hereafter—and whatever you do, let me know nothing about it until it be done. But now, General Crook, that you have repelled the invaders,—"

"Mr. President," said the General, interrupting him, "a very large share of the glory belongs to you."

"You are welcome to all. And, I assure you, it will be inscribed in our annals as a very great victory. But the thing I desire to impress upon you is this—that if it was a duty to hurl back an invader, the merit of the achievement may be easily extinguished by becoming, in turn, an invader yourself. You understand me. Whoever becomes the aggressor must be defeated. To-day I have assisted you in driving Ruffleton out of Maryland. To-morrow it might be my duty to assist Ruffleton in driving you out of Pennsylvania."

"Who could have thus misrepresented me to your Excellency?" exclaimed Crook, in apparent earnestness; for he well knew that Randolph was a man of his word, and possessed the ability to perform all his promises, and to execute all his threats. "I give you my word, sir, that when our men reach the Pennsylvania line they will relinquish the pursuit. But Blount, who is now advancing with another Southern army, spontaneously levied since the announcement of this invasion, will not find many laurels to reap, unless your Excellency should prove a partial mediator, and permit him to cross over the border."

"No—I shall not prove a partial mediator; nor shall I

approve an invasion of the North, under any circumstances likely to arise—never, unless the North, in a confederated capacity, should declare war against the South. But this will not be done, General Crook, if the South, in the same capacity, does not first set the example."

"And why not?"

"Because it would be wrong?"

"Wrong! And which section has suffered the most wrong? Have not the Southern people been despoiled of their property to the amount of fifty millions of dollars? Have they not been denied the equal rights of citizens, and precluded from taking their lawful private property into territories won by the common blood and treasure of the Union? When have the Southern people ever pillaged the North of her property? When have they ever decreed that Northern citizens should be deprived of their right to settle on the public domain, carrying with them every description of property they possessed, or might choose to possess?"

"These are grievances, sir, I admit, demanding a remedy; and if nothing else sufficed, I would not be averse to the arbitrament of the sword. The first has grown out of the forbearance of the Executive power, which will forbear no longer; the last is a mere menace of these very gentlemen you have now in captivity, whose fate it is so difficult to determine. No, sir; I am satisfied that a large majority of the Northern people are quite willing to accord the South all the rights and privileges guaranteed by the Constitution. Let us afford them a fair opportunity of manifesting it. The Union is necessary to them—to us—to all."

"The Union!" said General Crook, sighing deeply. "May Heaven forgive me if I err—but I shall deem it the happiest day of my life when I can see the last link of it severed. *You*, Randolph, are that link!"

"If that be so, sir," said the President, with an erect form and noble expression of face, "the last link was made of stubborn metal. But, General, I have detained you long enough. Restrain the sanguinary steel. I shall rely on your pledge not to cross over the line. Farewell!"

They separated, the President returning to the head of his splendid cavalry, and the General spurring his steed over the bloody plain.

CHAPTER XV.

WIRY WILLY'S STRANGE ADVENTURE.

When Wiry Willy and his pony fell into the chasm, they were so completely buried in the leaves which had been wafted thither by the winds of autumn, that neither were perceived by the hundred horsemen who passed over their prostrate bodies. And when Willy, extricating himself from his pony, endeavored to rise on his feet, he was clasped in the arms of a powerful man, aud all attempts at resistance were utterly vain.

"I've got him, Sergeant," said the gigantic man who had seized Willy. "Now do you hug the horse, so's not to make any noise."

"I'm on him, Captain," said the Sergeant, embracing the neck of the pony as he lay in the leaves; "but he bites like the ——!"

"Never mind that—but hold him. My man here is as gentle as a lamb."

"I make no resistance, gentlemen," said Wiry Willy, "because I feel you have me in your power. But why am I thus used? I don't think I ever injured either of you. I am no man's enemy."

"And he asks why he's thus used in battle! And then he says he's no man's enemy, when he's fighting! Lord, if our powder hadn't given out! Stranger, my sword flew off its handle the very first blow, and I've nothing left to fight with but my hands, and nobody to follow me but the Sergeant. They peppered every man of my company, of upwards of a hundred, except the Sergeant, there. And so we two retreated into this place, resolved to sell our lives as dearly as we could."

"But, gentlemen, as I don't want your lives, I think you might release me."

"No, sir! We want to surrender to you, and save our own lives."

"Surrender to me!" said Willy in amazement.

"Yes, sir! And if we were to let you escape, the next squad of the enemy might blow our brains out."

"But which army do you belong to?" demanded Willy.

"We fought under General Ruffleton, because he pledged us there should be plenty of fighting."

"And for my part," said the Sergeant, "I have had about enough. And many others are sick enough of it."

"Oh, if you come to that," said the Captain, "there are plenty of 'em *dead* of it. But see here, stranger, which side are you on?"

"I'm a private in General Ruffleton's army," said Willy.

"Then our cake's all dough," said the Captain, in disappointment.

"He may be lying," said the Sergeant. "Question him."

"In whose company, sir?"

"Captain Bim's."

"What? Well, that *must* be a lie!"

"Stop!" cried the Sergeant, springing up from the pony. "What's your name? Here's my book. I saved *it*, Captain, though all the men in it's lost."

"William Wire."

"By the smoking nostrils of the dragon!" cried Captain Bim, "it *is* Wiry Willy!" and he turned Willy around and embraced him.

"And give me your hand, comrade!" cried the Sergeant, joining them. "Don't you recollect Sergeant Punt? See, here's your name writ in my book by gas-light. But how can we surrender to you?"

"I'll arrange it," said Willy. "I belong to all three of the armies. Jack Bim, have you spent your money?"

"Every coin in the world, except that—you know where."

"Then here, take mine. It was this gold that pitched me into the ditch. It was the last feather that broke my pony's back."

"I'll take a few pieces, Willy—but not all. If it was unfortunate for you, it was lucky for us. I got you out of prison, and you're bound to clear me of this scrape."

"That's true, Jack. Follow me. I'll walk with you and lead the pony. Come along, Sergeant Punt."

They succeeded, after some labor, in extricating the pony,

and then Willy directed his steps towards the eminence lately in possession of the President and his fine cavalry. But they had not proceeded more than a mile before Sergeant Punt, who had been silent while the others conversed incessantly, came to a sudden halt.

"Gentlemen," said he, "I intend to give up fighting, and go to work. I'm a ship carpenter by trade. I've got a wife and three children in Philadelphia, and I'm getting home-sick. If I go any further with you, I may fall into the hands of General Crook, and what'll become of me then?"

"You're a fool, Punt!" said Bim, contemptuously. "He'd release you on parole, and then you might join your wife. But if you were to go to her without binding yourself not to serve again, what'd become of you if you fell into the hands of Ruffleton? Why, he'd shoot you as a deserter."

"That would be worse than all," said the Sergeant, going forward again. "But, Willy, wouldn't General Crook take me into his service?"

"General Crook will not enlist Northern men," said Willy.

"That's a mistake," said Bim, "for I fought under him once."

"Then," said the Sergeant, "won't he shoot you as a deserter?"

"I never thought of that!" said Bim, pausing.

"Never fear," said Willy. "I'll arrange everything for you both. On my recommendation the President will take you into his service. He has a *regular* army, and millions of money."

"Do you think there'll be any fighting?" asked Bim.

"After a while—abundance of it."

"Then I'm *in*, if he wants a real man! And when we have the first battle, I can say I've fought on all sides. And you, Willy, who have been on all sides, have fought on none."

"The Bible says thou shalt not kill," said Willy.

"But ain't there a sight of fighting in the Bible?" asked Bim.

Willy acknowledged there was. He believed the President was right, however, in his endeavors to save the Union.

"But where are all the niggers?" asked Punt, suddenly, after being silent again for many minutes.

"They have been taken to the other side of the Potomac," said Willy. "They make them work on the fortifications."

"Ruffleton deceived me," said Punt. "He said I might get rich catching niggers, and that they were as plenty as crows in Jersey, and every one I caught would sell for a thousand dollars."

"Punt, they called you an abolitionist at home," said Bim.

"I know it. I said I was one. But I was electioneering for votes. I confess I never knew anything about the right or wrong of holding such property; and I made up my mind to catch a few and sell 'em for a thousand dollars apiece."

In this manner they discussed their own affairs and the affairs of the nation, until they arrived before the President, in the great East Room of the Executive Mansion.

"Whom have you here, Will?" demanded the President.

"Two prisoners, sir."

"Prisoners? You had no authority to take prisoners. I want no prisoners."

"He'll put us to the sword, I'm afraid," whispered Punt.

"But he couldn't help taking us, sir," said Bim, "because we seized him, and——

"Seized *him*, and became his prisoners. Explain this matter, Will," said the President, with impatience.

Willy easily made him comprehend everything.

"Bim," said the President, "will you enrol among the militia? I have no authority to increase the regular army, in the absence of Congress."

"Wiry Willy," said Bim, casting a ferocious glance at the one addressed, "you have deceived me. You said I could get into the *regular* army. No, sir, I can't join the militia —I want to be where *fighting* is done."

"Is that it?" said the President, smiling.

"Yes, sir, that's *it*. And I thought from the looks of your soldiers as we came here, that you had been increasing the regular army."

"Militia, nearly all militia, Bim. But they are trained to fight, and no doubt there will be abundance of fighting."

"That's enough, sir," said Bim, comprehending the Pre

sident. "I'll enrol, sir. And if fighting can bring promotion, I'll *rise*."

"And *you*, sir," said the President, turning to Punt.

"I'm a ship carpenter by trade, sir; and from what I've seen in this campaign, I think I'd rather work with my adze."

"Very good, sir. I must have a *militia* navy as well as a *militia* army. Conduct them to General Valiant, Will, and then hasten to Georgetown." Saying this, the President turned away and resumed his contemplative exercises.

"By George, Willy!" said Bim, as they withdrew, "I didn't think you were on such intimate terms with the President. His eyes command as well as his words. He's the leader for me! I'll never change sides again."

CHAPTER XVI.

MEETING OF BLOUNT AND ALICE.

The battle of Bladensburg, and the events which succeeded it, produced intense excitement both in the South and in the North. The fact that the soil of Maryland had been invaded by a Northern army, although that army had met with defeat, removed much of the repugnance to decisive measures in the Convention at Richmond. From Mason and Dixon's Line to Texas, there were rejoicings and illuminations in honor of the victory; while the victor, General Crook, was hailed as a hero and a deliverer. Nevertheless, the Convention still adhered to the general of their choice, and Blount was invested with almost dictatorial powers. He might, at discretion, retaliate on the enemy by an invasion of the North.

In the North, although Ruffleton had not acted with the sanction of the representatives of the people, yet something more than fifty thousand Northern men, under his command, had been either killed or taken prisoners on the plains of Bladensburg. The cruelties alleged to have been inflicted by the Southerners, seemed to shock the sensibilities and rouse the indignation of the population. And it was under the influence of this state of public feeling, that the Convention in Philadelphia decreed the establishment of a vast military organization, and placed the distinguished General Hudson at its head. Ruffleton was commissioned as his second in command.

But, perhaps, the greatest sensation succeeding the astounding disaster at Bladensburg, was caused by the singular conduct of General Crook, in regard to his prisoners. He marched them to Annapolis, and separating the three or four abolition members of Congress, the many political parsons, and the editors and reporters, from the rest, the larger number, consisting of many thousands, were confined in Maryland and Delaware; while the others, in imitation of the mob at Boston, were shipped to Liberia in one of the emigrant vessels sailing from the Chesapeake. The members of Congress attempted in vain an escape under the plea of privilege; the preachers prayed to no purpose; and the editors and reporters drew up fruitless remonstrances. General Crook was inexorable; and he became more implacable still when it was ascertained that W——ll P——s, who had escaped from the Boston mob, instead of being on his way to Liberia, was among the prisoners. The Rev. Mr. Blood, Rev. Mr. Carp, Rev. Mr. F——e, Rev. Mr. Cleaver, and Rev. Mr. Aaron, were among the hundreds of clergymen taken on the field of battle. Among the editors and reporters were some of the ablest journalists and scholars of the North. All were banished by the inflexible Crook to the distant coast of Africa, where, as he remarked, when they were about to sail, they might be satiated with the "negro without annoying decent white people."

Having disposed of his captives, General Crook marched up the country to Havre de Grace, where General Steel was resting after having thrust the invaders out of Maryland. True to his promise, Crook did not follow Ruffleton into Pennsylvania; but he wheeled to the right, and marched through the northern part of Delaware and occupied the town of Newcastle. Here it was not long before his intentions became known. Blount, whose army had been transported across the Chesapeake, to the eastern shore of Virginia, was marching up the country through eastern Maryland and Delaware, to form a junction and assume the chief command. And from the vast number of boats which had been collected, no one could doubt the purpose to enter New Jersey. And this seemed the more manifest from the fact that an army from New York and New England was landing at Amboy, on the opposite side of the same State.

Simultaneously with the junction of the Southern armies at Newcastle, was the arrival in the same vicinity of President Randolph, at the head of seventy-five thousand men, one-third of whom were superb cavalry. He had likewise one hundred and fifty cannon, with ammunition and provisions in abundance, and all the equipments of a regular army for a protracted campaign.

It was a pleasant moonlight night in June. The President, having established his headquarters at an ancient farmhouse a few miles from Newcastle, awaited the arrival of General Blount, who had solicited an interview. The only guards in the immediate vicinity were the troop of Blue Caps, and among these fighting Jack Bim had been incorporated by the President, at the desire of Alice, upon learning from Wiry Willy the generous conduct of the Captain in Philadelphia.

"Alice," said Randolph, striding to and fro across the apartment, while his daughter sat in silence at the window, her cheek resting on her hand, and the gold tassel of her velvet cap touching her shoulder, "Alice, why are you so pensive? Whence this dejection? There can be no necessity for painful forebodings. From the day that the Executive Power was left to take care of the Government, I have never been so strong as at the present moment, and never had more confidence in my ability to accomplish my purpose."

"And that purpose, father?"

"Have not my words and actions manifested sufficiently my intention to fulfil my oath? Did I not swear to preserve, protect, and defend the Constitution?"

"But, father, what if that Constitution should cease to exist. What would be that purpose then, father?"

"Alice, how could I be prepared for such a catechism as this? You imagine impossible, or at least improbable events, and then demand what will be my course in such and such a contingency. Is it dutiful conduct on your part?"

"Father!" cried she, running to him and seizing his hand, "forgive me! It did really seem like impertinence, but it was not meant so."

"I know it, Alice. And I knew it at the time, and should not have expressed any doubt of the motive. But how can I penetrate the dim and distant future? How foretell what may be my thoughts and actions if this rupture becomes incurable?"

"Will it not cure itself, if the hostile armies be kept asunder?"

"I will endeavor to keep them asunder. Have I not commanded the peace between the sections, or when an invasion was accomplished, secured the defeat of the invader? The only way to effect a cure is to punish every aggressor. They will soon abandon such enterprises when only disaster attends them. Both sections will grow weary of the strife, so unprofitable and exhausting, and then—"

"And *then*, father? You pause."

"The Executive Power will be vindicated. We are interrupted. Here is Wiry Willy."

The faithful messenger entered at that moment, wearing a serious visage.

"And Edith, Willy!" exclaimed Alice; "where is she?"

"In Philadelphia."

"Well? Is she well?"

"Quite well."

"And would not come?" asked the President, pausing in his walk.

"This letter, sir, to Miss Alice, will probably explain everything," said Willy, delivering the letter.

"But why are you so sad, sir?" continued the President.

"Because, sir, when I called at Mr. Langdon's hotel, I met General Ruffleton there."

"And that produced unpleasant feelings, did it?"

"Miss Edith took his arm, sir, when they descended to dinner."

"Ha! ha! And that grieved you? What would have been your feelings, Will, if it had been Mary instead of Edith?"

"God knows, sir! But I do not think I could have been

more surprised, knowing as I do Miss Edith's recent aversion."

"There seems to have been a mistake, Willy," said Alice, "and it is fitting that you should know it. Edith writes that the General has produced letters, signed by Major Trapp, in which it is confessed it was the purpose of the Major himself to abduct her. And she says the General has offered a mass of testimony to prove he could have had no other object than her preservation. Why do you smile, father?"

"I was thinking what an intricate web all this will be for Blount to unravel! And no doubt he expects to see his affianced here, while she is dining with his enemy! Oh, woman! Utterly enigmatical! And Edith knows that Blount is near this place, and a meeting would be not at all impracticable."

"You did not hear all," said Alice. "She adds that it would be impossible to esteem the character of General Ruffleton, however innocent he might be of any complicity in the designs against herself; but that, in obedience to her father's desire, it is necessary to evince some show of respect for the General, who, she says, was slightly wounded in the battle, and for whom much sympathy is felt by the public. Nor is that all. She says that her father, like a great many others in the North, cannot applaud the President's partiality for the Southern side on the occasion referred to; and, for that reason, she has failed to obtain permission to meet me here."

"Does she say anything of Blount? Willy, see who has just arrived."

"Yes, sir. She laments that he has not responded to any of her recent letters—"

"Ha! The deputy postmaster at Philadelphia then, as I have had reason to suspect, has joined the Northern party. But I know the remedy!"

"And she implores me, if I can exert any influence over General Blount, to dissuade him from a career of warfare against her native country. She prays for him, and that's all!"

"No—not all. She loves him, and he her, and they are worthy of each other. They shall be reconciled. Never fear, Alice. It is a *great* achievement on your part, my child, to rise superior to your own woe, and feel only solicitude for the happiness of your friend. Fie! be not so pale—or is it the MARBLE again? I have spared you the confession of the name. I will not demand it. Let it pass. You shall see Edith in Philadelphia. And so they do not applaud me for standing by Crook when the South was invaded? That was foreseen. And I foresee that the South will not applaud me for standing by General Hudson, when the North is invaded. But no matter. I will be just!"

"And so may heaven prosper you, my dearest father!" exclaimed Alice.

"Yes, I will be just, and fear not. And all my ends shall be my country's—and that, too, Alice, whether the Constitution stands or falls. But of this I am sure—when the present Constitution is destroyed, there will never be another securing a larger liberty to the people. Enough of that. Willy, who is it?" he asked, seeing his faithful messenger at the door, awaiting permission to announce some one.

"Commodore Stout and Captain Early, with some prisoners," said Willy.

"What can this mean? Alice, if Blount arrives, you must detain him while I am engaged with these gentlemen."

Alice retired, and the visitors were admitted.

The President welcomed his faithful officers, but stared in astonishment at Lord Slysir, accompanied by several of the attachés of the British Legation.

"Pray be seated, gentlemen," said he. "And now, Commodore, can it be true, as my messenger informs me, that his Lordship and these gentlemen are your prisoners?"

"It is so, sir!" responded the officer.

"But, Commodore," continued the President, "are you not aware that the representatives of foreign nations are exempted from arrest?"

"But this is an extraordinary case, sir," said Captain Early.

"To cut the matter short, Mr. President," said the Commodore, "we took him on our own responsibility. If we have done wrong, we can very easily be dropped from the service, you know."

"But what is the case, gentlemen?" demanded the President.

"Making overtures to the South, sir, for an alliance, offensive and defensive!" said the Commodore.

"And that is a violation of the Constitution, Mr. President," said the Captain.

"What proof have you of this, gentlemen?"

"They need not produce any, sir," said his Lordship, with an air of unconcern. "I have no hesitation in saying that my government, in view of the probable separation of the sections of this Union, is desirous of cultivating friendly relations with the governments of both the new confederacies."

"That may be the diplomatic mode of expressing it," said the Commodore; "but we have intercepted messengers from the British fleet in the bay with dispatches to the Commander-in-chief of the Southern army, tendering assistance, &c."

"Of course we can have no aversion to an alliance," said his Lordship, "since the Northern politicians have been in communication with some of Her Majesty's turbulent subjects in Canada."

"These are very grave matters, gentlemen," said the President, glancing at the papers. "You have done well, my friends," he continued, addressing the officers.

"We know our duty, sir," said the old Commodore.

"And we shall endeavor to perform it," added the Captain.

"My Lord, you will excuse me for a brief space," said the President. Then rising, he led the naval officers into a private closet, where they remained some time in confidential consultation.

Alice sat alone in the parlor, the large glass doors of which, at the southern extremity, opened on a narrow vine-clad piazza. The moon floated in a cloudless sky, and streamed her vestal light across the rich carpet at the maiden's feet. She gazed out upon the lawn, with a forehead as pale, if not as cold, as the marble vase at her elbow redolent of flowers.

"They come!" said Wiry Willy, who sat in the piazza.

"He does not come alone then?" asked Aliee.

"There are three horses," said Willy. "But I can see

that his two attendants are not officers of high rank—perhaps they are common soldiers."

"Admit *him*, Willy," said Alice, adjusting the ample folds of satin at her feet.

Willy walked out upon the lawn. Blount gave the reins to one of his attendants and dismounted. The next moment his tall form was seen by Alice advancing alone. Willy met him, and was recognised. Blount, with a pale, and almost haggard countenance, received his proffered hand in silence, and they proceeded several paces together before a word was uttered.

"Willy," at length said the lofty son of the South, "your pledge was nobly fulfilled. I have had an account of your magnanimous exertions in my—in *her* behalf, up to the time of your departure from the city. I thank you, and will not forget your meritorious conduct."

"I was in the city to-day, sir," said Willy.

"To-day! Is Edith here, or does she remain in the city?"

"Her father detains her in the city."

"Her father! But no matter. Tell President Randolph I am here, with the two attendants stipulated."

"He is at this moment engaged on business of importance with— "

"Proceed, without naming those with whom he is engaged."

"He desired Miss Alice to receive you in the southern parlor, yonder. You enter from the piazza. When he can dismiss his company he will join you there."

"Enough, Willy," said Blount, striding on alone. When he ascended the steps of the piazza, his glance caught the glitter of a diamond on the alabaster forehead of Alice. She arose and offered her hand, which was almost cold to his touch. But her words expressed a warmer greeting. And Blount, with the respectful demeanor of the high-toned gentleman, occupied the chair to which she pointed.

"General," said Alice, "the field does not seem so congenial as the halls of legislation. You are paler, and seem older, than formerly."

"I *am* older, Alice—and may be paler. I have learned more of evil, and that itself might blanch a ruddier cheek than mine."

"The world is full of evil. But a knowledge of its existence does not often appal the military chieftain. A failure to consummate the projects of ambition—ambition, which is too often itself an evil—would be more likely to cast a sickly hue over the face of a leader, than the mere knowledge of the wickedness of the world. It was not that, sir."

"No—not that, in the sense you put it. Not the general infidelity of mankind, but the—"

"Let me end the sentence—but the infidelity of one woman. Is it not so?"

"I fear so!"

"You are mistaken."

"Did she authorize you to say that?"

"No. But I say it on my own responsibility. Here is a letter which I received this morning. Read it by moonlight."

And as Blount did so, the eyes of Alice were steadily fixed on his noble features. Having completed the perusal, Henry's hand holding the letter sank down at his side, and he gazed some moments in silence at the stars.

"I am incapable of doubting her words," said he, mournfully. "But, before heaven, she does me injustice. I have written her many pages—"

"They were intercepted!" said Alice, quickly. "My father intimated as much. He seems to suspect the fidelity of the deputy postmaster, and I think has decreed his dismissal."

"He, I mean your father, would be incapable of winking at official misconduct. But what could be his motive?"

"To serve General Ruffleton."

"Ruffleton! What need has he of the service of a third party? Alice, I have correspondents in Philadelphia whose letters have not been intercepted; and they inform me that Ruffleton, once so repugnant to her, and so recently defeated on Southern soil, is an almost inseparable companion of Edith! Alice, you know we stood together at the holy altar. You were present and a witness—and now you behold the change!"

"I have not beheld a change of Edith's heart, General Blount, if it be that you mean. And oh! be careful that you do not cast a priceless jewel away, and become yourself poor indeed. Think that although the words were not uttered at the holy altar, your espousals were registered in heaven where angels were the witnesses. Edith false! Oh! speak not the word, conceive not the thought! We were as sisters--but I the least worthy. Henry Blount, Edith Langdon is true, if truth ever abideth in woman! She is worthy of you, you of her, if you prove incapable of wrong. For my part, I have often envied her—her superiority—but if that were wrong, I could never—"

"Enough, Alice. The fates have severed us; and if it be the will of heaven that we shall never meet again, then heaven will be my witness how I loved!"

"You love her still! Else whence that pallid cheek, that mournful tone, that sunken eye?"

"Alas! I love my country, and there is enough in the ills it suffers, and is likely to suffer, to make her sons weep tears of blood."

"Henry! You have touched a sympathetic chord in this poor breast of mine! Save my father, there remains no object on earth for me to love, but my country. And oh, I love it with all a fond woman's devotion! Henry, save our country!"

"Would I had the power! But why not address your father?"

"I have—and the answer, though satisfactory to the ear, is still oracular to the sense. But great as he is—and good —may not he be mistaken or unable—"

"No, Alice. Such men as your father do not commit mistakes, though both friends and enemies may censure them. They may be overcome by circumstances, but their fall must involve the engineers of the ruin. May God protect and guide that man of destiny! How willingly, were he not President, would I, and all the South, glory in following his triumphant banner."

"Oh, man—thou Sphynx-like riddle! You tell me this, and yet you are upon the eve of inflicting an incurable wound on the bosom of your country! What greater triumph than the reign of peace, and yet you are panting to become an invader."

"Have we not been invaded?"

"But that is past, and the aggressor punished."

"The North is arming again. In war, the State which

awaits the enemy's blow is both ignominious and doomed. We shall probably strike them on their own soil, and thus avert many blows in future."

"No—no! Every battle is but another dividing wedge driven into the Union. The cruelties of war must inevitably inflame the already excited animosities of the opposing sections. Why not stand on the defensive?"

"And leave unavenged the ignominy perpetrated in Maryland. The track of the invaders resembles the pathway of a hurricane. The only way to prevent a recurrence of such scenes, is to return the chalice to their own lips. And then the time may come when both sections will realize the conviction that they are too terrible and destructive to remain apart and in hostility. Then they may be reconciled. But, in the meantime, the sovereignty of the people, so wantonly trifled with by their unfaithful agents, may vanish for ever."

"That is what I fear," said Alice, half abstractedly, and through her tears. "And if strong men deem such a result inevitable, what can weak woman do? We might suffer—ay, woman can vie with man in that—but it is not those who suffer, who accomplish most. My father comes. Promise me that *you* will not cross over into the enemy's country."

"For my part, I had no such design," said Blount, just as the President entered the parlor, a lighted candle in one hand, and a map in the other.

"General," said the President, after a frank and hearty salutation, "I hope I have not detained you long. I am now entirely at your service."

"I have sought this interview," said Blount, as Alice withdrew, "for the purpose of a free and friendly consultation with you. You cannot be inimical to your native South, and I know you are my friend. Your partisans in the Convention proposed my name for the position to which I have been exalted, and for this I must be grateful."

"I am your friend, and of course I love my native land. But the whole Union, as it was, and as it must be again, is my country—" and seeing Blount startled at this phraseology, he added—"my native land. You are quite correct in attributing your nomination to my friends, and I will have the candor to say that one motive was the apprehension that another, more inimical, might be chosen, if they did not unite on you. But in regard to this qualification they have attached to your command,—what is your determination about it? I learn they desire Crook to retaliate on the North. If he chooses to invade New Jersey, and unless you see proper to accompany him, he is not to be under your authority."

"Your advice in relation to this matter is the object of this interview."

"Without your aid, Crook cannot cross the Delaware, or rather he would not venture to do so. Therefore you can prevent it."

"Shall I prevent it?"

"I cannot answer," said the President, after a pause. "But I would counsel you not to accompany him. Your men are all true Southerners, and ought not to leave this barrier defenceless. Crook's army is composed of men of all the nations of the earth."

"And yours?" asked Blount.

"Mine are pretty equally divided between the North and the South, and I assure you they agree very well together, just as all the sections would have remained harmoniously united, if the Executive Power had been exerted for other purposes than the distribution of patronage. I mean the Executive Power antecedent to my election."

"*Subsequently* to that event," said Blount, with a faint smile, "the Executive has not been distinguished for maidenly timidity."

"And it is not likely to be," added the President. "Let Crook lose his laurels in the sands of New Jersey if he sees proper. You will not be reproached. Ruffleton is collecting the remains of his rabble army for the purpose of cutting off his retreat. He will menace this position, and may invade Delaware."

"Would *you* permit it?"

"*My* time has not yet come. But, if you remain on this side of the river, I think you will be strong enough to measure swords with him—provided you have any disposition for the encounter."

"Disposition! Let me once have an opportunity!"

"I think you will some day meet this Bombastes face to face. But, Blount, how is this matter with the British envoy? Take care you do not go too far!"

"In the event of an irrevocable separation, sir, we should certainly cultivate friendly relations with England. By consuming her manufactures we would be aiming a blow at the North."

"But the separation is not to be irrevocable, sir. And Great Britain, at all events, must take no part in our domestic quarrels. She must wait until she can treat with independent sovereignties. But it seems she is not willing to be an idle spectator. Before many days, perhaps, I may find some employment for her!"

"I do not understand you, sir," said Blount.

"True. I acquit you of any complicity. I intercepted the overtures. Here they are."

Blount read them. They were addressed to him. He then said:

"I should have responded to them in a friendly manner, because I believe it would be in accordance with Southern sentiment."

"It is premature. But I do not wonder at the impatience of England. She would have, for a time, at least, a monopoly of the great staple, as well as of manufactures and commerce. But the project has been defeated. My Lord Slysir, with quite a number of his attachés, has fallen into the hands of the old Commodore. They have just departed for *our* ships, and not Her Majesty's fleet, at anchor down the bay. The old Commodore says they shall be his *guests*, and you are not likely to receive any communication from his lordship while Stout is treating him."

Here the President was interrupted by the unceremonious entrance of Wiry Willy. He panted for breath, and had evidently been running.

"What is the matter?" demanded Randolph.

"As I was walking, sir, about a mile hence, to the left of the encampment, I heard the approach of a body of horse. I concealed myself in a hedge, and presently overheard the guide who rode with the commander of the party, promise to lead it *hither*, sir, without encountering any of the sentinels of the army, provided no pistols were fired. The guide was Samuel Carlisle, who brought General Blount's letter to you, sir." The President's quarters were a mile distant from the army, and only one hundred of the Blue Caps were on duty at the farm-house.

"What number of men followed?"

"Not less than eight hundred, sir," answered Willy.

"Ho, there!" said the President, throwing open an opposite window, and addressing a sentinel. "Inform Carleton that we are about to be assailed by a detachment of General Ruffleton's army—say they will be upon us in a few minutes!"

Immediately the Blue Caps were in the saddle, and the commotion having been observed by Alice, she re-entered the parlor.

"Had we not better fly, father?" she asked, upon learning the great superiority of the approaching force.

"It is me they seek," said General Blount. "That Quaker guide has betrayed me. They told me he was a descendant of the Carlisle of the Revolution, a tory, who was hung. But I will not fly."

"We shall ensnare this Major," said the President, Willy having added that the leader of the party was the same Major Snare who had abducted Mary Penford. He then wrote a few words to General Valiant, and despatched them by Willy, who proceeded thither under cover of the hedges.

"We must surrender, General," he added, smiling, "and you may be *marble*, Alice, in perfect safety. Here is Col. Carleton. Colonel, do you hear them yet?"

"Distinctly, sir."

"They are eight to one."

"But the Blue Caps will give them a hearty reception."

"I will assist at the ceremony, Colonel," said Blount.

"No—nor you, father!" said Alice, with great energy. "Why should your lives be put in jeopardy with such odds against you? Neither duty nor honor can require the hazard. If the object be the possession of the person of General Blount, it cannot be the design to destroy his life. Then why should he rush upon certain death? You, father, are not in arms against the North, and they durst not molest you."

"My brave little Knight of the Velvet Cap, General, has the better part of valor."

"Her discretion, sir, is by no means preposterous, when we consider the odds. Still I do not despair. I see my attendants approaching. I will mount."

"No!" exclaimed Alice, interposing. "Rely upon my father. His eye is too calm now for imminent danger to be encompassing us."

"What say you, Colonel?" demanded the President.

"If you, sir," said the Colonel, "and Alice, and General Blount, will permit me to encompass you with the Blue Caps, I'll answer for your safety until we are in the lines of our army."

"No, Colonel; it is a mere foray led hither by a treacherous guide—and led into a labyrinth from which there can be no extrication. We will remain until forced to yield ourselves prisoners to superior numbers. They come! If we surrender, mark me! our captors will soon after sue for mercy! Carleton, surround the house with your Blue Caps, and await the result. They may deem it prudent to retire without striking a blow."

Major Snare, deficient in military experience, but proud of his epaulettes, without pausing a moment to ascertain what might be the effect of a peremptory summons, dashed into the midst of the little band of defenders. Carleton's men, better instructed in the use of the sword, soon cut down several of the assailants. But they were borne aside at last by the irresistible weight of numbers. The assailants then formed a circle round the house, and facing outward, became in turn the assailed, for the Blue Caps, rallying, charged them repeatedly at several points, but nothing less than superhuman power seemed capable of penetrating so dense a mass of horses and men. And that power appeared to be possessed by one—Jack Bim—who, in several charges, never failed to cut his way through the writhing mass; and he emerged as often unscathed on the opposite side.

"Cease this strife! Forbear!" cried President Randolph, from a window. It was the tone of command, and Carleton's men obeyed the order.

"Now, what is your purpose, sir?" continued the President, addressing Major Snare.

"We demand the surrender of General Blount and Colonel Carleton, sir," said Snare.

"The Blue Caps never surrender!" said Colonel Carleton.

"Not unless it be my pleasure, Colonel," said the President.

"We shall obey you, sir," said the Colonel.

"It is my will and pleasure, then, that the Blue Caps sheathe their swords. Now, sir," he continued, again addressing Major Snare, "since we have a cessation of hostilities, we can confer more deliberately. In whose name is this demand made?"

"In the name of the People of the North, the demand for General Blount. The demand for Colonel Carleton is my own."

"Will you ride with me to the end of the lawn, and assert your manhood, point to point, sir—or do you still prefer encountering helpless women?" said Carleton.

"Silence!" said the President.

"Is my demand to be complied with? I cannot delay," said Snare.

"Major Snare," said the President, "General Blount is my guest. If you take him you must likewise take me, and all who are with me, else an ineffaceable stigma will sully my honor. Will you assume that responsibility, sir?"

"I will. My orders were to capture General Blount, regardless of consequences."

"Very well, sir. We shall attend you presently."

And in a brief space of time the President, his daughter, and General Blount, were mounted on horseback. They were surrounded, however, according to stipulation, by the faithful Blue Caps; and in this manner they were conducted in a north-western direction towards the Pennsylvania line. But they had not proceeded far before the solution of the President's "calm eye" and perfect equanimity became apparent.

The word was given to halt, when they had advanced about two miles. On the moonlit plain, and directly before him, Major Snare beheld a dark line of horsemen, extending as far as the eye could reach to the right and the left. The Major, panic-stricken, wheeled to the right, and in a few minutes the same spectacle of an interminable line of cavalry confronted his vision. Again he paused, and wheeling about, proceeded at a brisk pace to the south, and lo! the same barrier of sabres arrested his progress.

"Turn back, Major!" said the President, with one of his taunting smiles, so well understood by Alice, who rode at his side. "Dismiss us with proper apologies and you may escape. Are you prepared to pronounce our liberation?"

"No, sir! There is one course left." He then attempted to retrace his steps towards the farm-house, from which there was a road leading up the river. But here, too, an impenetrable hedge of horsemen hemmed him in!

The President, calling a bugler of the Blue Caps to his side, ordered him to sound a charge. This was answered by more than a hundred bugles. Then was heard the rush of thousands of horses, coming from all directions towards a common centre. In vain Major Snare galloped round his men, seeking some avenue of escape. He was environed on every side, and finally reined up his steed in despair.

"Now, Major," said the President, "will you relinquish your prisoners?"

"I submit, sir," said the discomfited officer. "Here is my sword."

"Throw it away, sir, and buy a lath. This is the second time you have been disarmed, and in both instances your expeditions involved the liberty of a woman. If you must be a warrior, learn to cope with men. Colonel Carleton, send him under an escort to Georgetown, where he will be tried by the civil authority for the abduction of Mary Penford."

"A just decision," said General Blount. "Nevertheless the same exemption does not embrace the people of foreign nations."

"You allude to my Lord Slysir," said Alice. "But remember he is only a *guest* of the Commodore."

"A guest under restraint. And I am a guest."

"But under no such restraint, sir," said Alice, "else we had not shared your captivity."

"General Valiant," said the President, addressing his faithful lieutenant, who commanded the splendid cavalry, "you have convinced these gentlemen, I trust," turning to the followers of Snare, "that the Executive power of the Federal Union is neither extinct, nor likely to be circumvented. Take them beyond our lines, and dismiss them unharmed. Then send a detachment of surgeons to my head-quarters to heal the wounded which my mad caps——"

"Blue Caps, father!" said Alice.

"Blue and mad—left lying on the ground. But see that

no more expeditions of this nature pass between me and the army."

"And now, Mr. President," said Blount, when the mighty host had vanished, "I will take my leave of you here. I see the camp fires of the Southern army, and they are burning low. I shall be looked for at early dawn. Farewell."

"I cannot detain you, sir," said Randolph, grasping the proffered hand.

"What shall I say to Edith?" demanded Alice when the General turned to her.

"I do not know. Pray tell me—what should I say?"

"Have you a heart, and it does not prompt you?"

"I have a heart, but it is very sad. Take this ring. You know the reason it was not placed upon her finger. Perhaps the deed should have been accomplished amidst the roar of cannon. It was not done—and lamentation cannot avail. Say to her—Oh, Alice! what shall I say?"

"The ring!"

"Yes; if you *know*—if you *see* she is unchanged, and has been wronged by me—give it her. If she wears it on the finger I would have encircled with it, it will, at least—I mean it might, if she desires it, signify—Alice, are you ill?" he asked, seeing her lean forward and clasp her forehead.

"A slight pain, produced by the excitement," said she. "Proceed, I pray you. The ring!"

"Be you the judge. Give it, or retain it, as you deem her worthy or unworthy. Tell her what your discretion may suggest, and forbear what may seem imprudent. But say I daily and nightly invoke heaven's blessings on her—whether she be true or—Adieu. God bless you!"

And when Alice lifted her head he was gone, and the hoofs of his steed, madly spurning the earth, were dying away in the direction of the camp-fires, near the river.

"Ah, Willy," said Alice, seeing the faithful messenger of her father approaching on his pony, "I hope this Northern General has ceased to mar your happiness."

"No, Miss Alice. Mary only detests and fears him, it is true; but I cannot be happy whilst he has access to any whom I esteem. And when you go to the city, he will appear before even you with many flattering speeches and professions of profound respect for Edith, for Mary, and for General Blount, against whom he doubtless planned this base attack."

"That may be, Willy—but I shall not be uneasy or annoyed. He can grieve no one by his flatteries to me, Willy, and I shall know their value."

They were now in front of the farm-house, where several of the wounded were still groaning in pain. Alice's sympathies were excited, and the greatest part of the night was devoted to the alleviation of the sufferings of those who might have been considered her enemies.

CHAPTER XVII.

RESCUE OF WIRY WILLY.

It was just as the first streaks of morning appeared in the East that Wiry Willy rode along the highway near the Delaware river. The place was at no great distance from New Castle, and his destination seemed a few miles below the encampment of General Crook, where the naval officers, who were with the President the preceding evening, had been landed.

Willy, supposing he had passed the last sentinels in that direction, which he desired to avoid merely because he might be temporarily detained by them, and not that he apprehended serious molestation from the Southerners, began to whistle a lively tune, for his affairs seemed in a prosperous condition. Mary was at his grandame's, and he had seen her the day before, on his return from Philadelphia; and, if nothing untoward occurred to disappoint his expectation, he would be likely to see her again the day following. He was bearing a despatch from the President to Commodore Stout, which he had been told was of an important character, as it related to a matter of startling moment just communicated to the President by an express from Washington.

But just when Willy was passing a dilapidated barn on the wayside, four men, armed with muskets, rushed out and seized his pony, which strove in vain to elude their grasp by dint of kicking and biting.

"Dismount, sir!" said one of the men.

"Willy hasn't time," said Willy.

"Willy! Wiry Willy! The very man we want. Come, sir!" And the soldiers led him in the direction of the Southern encampment.

"Gentlemen!" said Willy, "I hope you will not detain me. I am on important business for the President."

"No doubt of it!" said the other. "And we are on important business for General Crook."

"Very well," rejoined Willy; "and is General Crook an enemy of the President? Did we not assist him at Bladensburg?"

"Very true—but now we're afraid you'll assist the other side. You say you are now on the President's business. Well, what business can he have in this direction?"

"His fleet is down yonder."

"And the British fleet is only a little lower down. We are just returning from *it*. The British are our friends, and the President is their enemy. Admiral Bang says the President has taken Lord Slysir prisoner."

"Can I see General Crook?"

"Most assuredly, if you have the use of your eyes. He is in yonder mansion, and we shall conduct you into his presence."

In the course of fifteen or twenty minutes they arrived at the mansion indicated, the orchard and out-houses around it being filled with soldiers preparing their breakfast. But no sooner was Willy recognised by several of the subordinate officers, who recollected having seen him at Bladensburg, than they began to express sorrow for his fate.

"Gentlemen," said Willy, "I cannot see why you should be so very sorry for me, since I am sure General Crook will order my release immediately."

"I hope so," said one of the officers, "but I doubt it very much, for within the last half hour we have received news of the attempt to capture General Blount."

"Well—did I not assist in his escape?" said Willy.

"Carlisle tells quite a different story. He says you were in the city yesterday and gave information of the intended interview between the President and the General to the infamous Snare."

"Yes, sir!" said General Crook himself, approaching from the house, "that is the story, and an ugly one it is. I fear you are a spy, Wiry Willy. You vanished very mysteriously the night before my attack on the Federal Departments; and several of my wounded men left on the ground have testified that they saw you enter the White House after the engagement."

"That is true, sir; I do not deny it," said Willy; "but did I not serve you afterwards, when the President was not your enemy?"

"He did, gentlemen," said Crook, turning to the officers that had collected around them. "Nevertheless this last act merits death. Willy, you shall have a fair trial, but it must necessarily be a brief one."

"General, I hope you will not credit the story of Carlisle. He has always been my enemy, because Mary Penford disliked his attentions. Let him be brought before me, face to face."

"That shall be done. You shall confront the witness, and if innocent, I shall be truly rejoiced. But if guilty, Willy, I cannot save you."

"If I could see General Blount himself," said Willy, apprehensive of the effect of Carlisle's testimony, "I am sure he would acquit me."

"No, Willy; he might pardon you, but how could he acquit you? How could he know that you did not betray him? No—no! He has released several under the death sentence already, who proved ungrateful afterwards, and wrought us injury; and, when informed of the evil effects of his ill-judged clemency, he requested that no more such cases might be referred to him. Let us enter, and Carlisle shall be brought in."

A drum-head court-martial was summoned, before whom Carlisle testified, with great circumstantiality, to the guilt of Willy. It was in vain that the prisoner solemnly protested his innocence, and asserted that every material particle of the testimony was without foundation in truth. Although accused of deliberate perjury, Carlisle affected to maintain an even and amiable temper, theeing and thouing his victim with imperturbable gravity. Poor Willy was condemned to die upon the gallows within the space of three hours!

"General," said he, "will you permit me to send a note to General Blount? I have served him likewise."

"I cannot, Willy."

"Or to the President?"

"Impracticable. His authority would not be acknowledged. Besides, it is doubtful whether the messenger could return before the hour of execution. I would pardon you myself, had I not declared that all such sentences as these should be executed. And I must say, though reluctantly, I cannot avoid believing you guilty."

"Mary! Oh, sir! it will break her heart! And she could save me!"

"How, sir?"

"She possesses a paper, which I left in her keeping, written by General Blount, in which he desires any one friendly to him to render me protection."

"The validity of such a document would be acknowledged," said the General. "Look round and select any one to go on this errand for you. If he can return before the expiration of the third hour, with the paper you mention, you will be saved."

Willy selected the one most familiar with the country, by whom he sent a few lines, written with a pencil. In the meantime the gallows was erected, and every preparation made for the execution; for no one supposed that such a paper as Willy had mentioned could be produced.

It was during these hours of agonizing suspense that several communications were received by General Crook from Admiral Bang; and these, if anything, operated greatly to the prejudice of the prisoner, who had intimated that his destination, when taken, was the American fleet, which the British, anxious to co-operate with Crook, desired to have removed.

"Wiry Willy," said General Crook, "you must deliver into my hands the despatches for Commodore Stout."

"Pardon me, General," said Wiry Willy. "If it were true that I have such despatches, they would not, I think, be subject to your inspection. They would be from the President, with whom you are not at war."

"In times of Revolution the strongest arm is the highest authority, and the will of every commander is the law. Search him, gentlemen," he continued, addressing those who attended him. This was done carefully and thoroughly, but without success.

"Willy," said the general, "I cannot break my word by pardoning you. But deliver up the despatch, or tell where it can be found, and you may regain your liberty."

"General," said Willy, his eyes steadily fixed on the floor, "I have neither destroyed any despatch, nor thrown it away since my arrest. And you have searched me in vain. If I were to say that none had been sent by me, would you credit my word?"

"Will you say so?"

"I say I am innocent of the charge for which I am condemned to die."

"This is trifling with me! But if the messenger returns not with the paper from Mary Penford, Commodore Stout will behold you swinging between heaven and earth near the brink of the water."

Saying this, the General shook Willy's hand, and mounting his horse, rode away after the troops, all of whom, with the exception of a small party, were now marching towards the main body of the army in the immediate vicinity of New Castle.

The scaffold was near the water, in full view of the American frigates.

"There are no signs of salvation, Willy," said the Sergeant, "and only five minutes remain. I would give this hand to save you, but I fear it is impossible."

"Must you be punctual to the moment, Sergeant?" asked Willy, casting down his eyes on the watch in the Sergeant's hand.

"I must obey the order or take the consequences. You must forgive me, Willy."

"As freely as I hope to be forgiven. I can reproach no one but Carlisle, who bore false testimony against me."

"You still deny the charge. Remember, Willy, that although I may delay the execution a few minutes, there is no probability that you will escape the death penalty. Learn, Willy, that the messenger was intercepted on the way and captured by some of General Ruffleton's men. This news I did not intend to impart, for I thought I would

10

spare you as much pain as possible. But such is the fact. Now, when there is no hope, do you still persist in asserting your innocence?"

"Before God, I do! I would as soon have betrayed the President himself as General Blount!"

"It is strange. And will you deny having been a spy in General Crook's camp the night before his attack on the Government?"

"That I will not deny, Sergeant. But then it was not war, but a conspiracy. The President sanctioned my act. And since then I have rendered good service in General Crook's behalf."

"True!"

"Your reluctance to take my life, Sergeant, and pity for my condition," said Willy, "is some alleviation. And the messenger did not reach his destination?"

"No—Ruffleton's men intercepted him."

"Did you learn where this happened?"

"It was near the railroad station. If he had not been taken, there would have been ample time for him to have returned ere now." As the Sergeant said this he held the watch before Willy's face. The hour had arrived.

"A few minutes more, Sergeant," said Willy.

"Five more, Willy; but hope not."

They were standing under the gallows, and the Sergeant beckoned one of the men to adjust the rope.

"Hangman ahoy!" cried one from under the river bank, a little below. "Stay your tackle. What are you going to hoist that man for?" And the next moment a midshipman sprang up and approached the party.

"What right have you to know, sir?" was the Sergeant's reply.

"The Commodore's orders," said the youthful officer, pausing.

"What right has he to order?" continued the Sergeant, motioning his men, just eight in number, to present arms.

"That's a matter I've never thought about once," said the young man. "All I have to do is to execute his orders. Why, it's Wiry Willy!" cried the midshipman, recognising Willy. "Sergeant!" he added, "if he were even guilty of the assassination of General Crook, you should not hang him!"

"That's brave language, sir," said the Sergeant, "but my duty must be done, however irksome it may be. Therefore, men, take hold of the rope, and when my hat falls, hoist him up." The Sergeant took off his hat and held out his arm.

The midshipman gave a signal, and twelve marines sprang up the bank and presented their Minié rifles.

"Sergeant," said the young man, "will this force suffice?"

"I think not, sir. It may prevent the execution at the present time, but not save the prisoner. But if you attack us, we'll fight!"

"I like that fellow!" said the old Commodore himself, scrambling up the bank a short distance above, followed by some half-dozen more men. "You're a brave lad, Sergeant," he continued, advancing, "but we are too many for you."

"I will surrender now, Commodore, if you demand it," said the Sergeant.

"You must surrender the prisoner—that's all we demand. Throw off that tackle, Willy," he said, turning to the prisoner. But Willy's hands were tied, and the Commodore dashed off the halter himself, and then cut the cord that bound his hands. "Now, sir, you are free. But what brought you here?"

"I have a dispatch for you, sir."

"Let me have it! I have been waiting for it."

"Pardon me, Commodore," said Willy; "but the Sergeant and his men saw the search ordered by General Crook—"

"They searched you, and found it?"

"No, sir; they did not find it. But if they were now to see where I conceal it, at some future day they might——"

"I understand. Come on board. Sergeant, give the old Commodore's respects to General Crook, and say the guest on the flag-ship expects his company soon."

The boats, for there were two, returned to the ship, while the Sergeant, not at all distressed at the occurrence, gazed after them.

"Now, sir," said the Commodore, when Willy was conducted into the cabin, "let me see how you contrived to conceal the despatch, so that the land-lubbers couldn't find it."

Willy ran his fingers through his hair, and touching some hidden springs, removed the scalp from his crown. Between that and the shaven skin the paper was concealed.

"Oh, you wear a wig!" said the Commodore. "But how the —— could one so young have——"

"I had it shaved off, sir, by a barber," said Willy, "expressly for the purpose of carrying despatches."

"And you were going to let them run you up to the yard-arm, when the production of these few lines would have saved your life! They are very important. Up anchor!" he continued to the first Lieutenant. "I must run up to the city. The rest of the squadron is to remain."

The Commodore, after making signals, got under way and steamed up the Delaware. He passed through a fleet of barges and small boats engaged in the transportation of Southern troops across the river. He had no orders to interfere with these; but his eye flashed every time he gazed in the direction of the British ships anchored down the river.

CHAPTER XVIII.

ALICE AND EDITH.

President Randolph, at the head of an army of 80,000 men, entered the city of Philadelphia. There were no demonstrations of hostility on the part of the citizens. On the contrary, it resembled a grand parade in celebration of the anniversary of the Declaration of Independence, for it occurred on the Fourth of July. Every regiment that defiled through Chestnut street, uttered enthusiastic cheers when opposite Independence Hall. They marched down to the river, and were transported into New Jersey, receiving a national salute from the Commodore.

The President himself remained in the city, retaining the Blue Caps, some battalions of horse, and a few pieces of artillery. But the city was quite calm, and he learned that New York was in the same condition. The deportation of a few members of Congress, and some hundreds of political parsons and newspaper scribblers, had acted like a charm, and the effect was wonderful.

Although General Ruffleton remained in the city, the fragments of his broken army were concentrating at a point on the Pennsylvania border, west of the Delaware line.

Meantime the Convention held its regular sittings in the old Independence Hall, and Senator Langdon had been elected its President, so that in this official capacity he now occupied the chair into which he had been thrust as a prisoner and fugitive but a few weeks before. It was the same that had been occupied by Washington, and had ever been regarded with patriotic reverence. Although this body of the representatives of the Northern States and people labored diligently in the organization of a military force commensurate with the population and the great interests involved, they had hitherto refrained, like the representatives of the Southern people assembled at Richmond, from any formal declaration of war, or an unconditional purpose of erecting a separate confederacy. And until this final step should be taken, neither of the sections was prepared to aim a blow at the Federal Government; and the position of armed neutrality, maintained by the President, and his invincible reluctance to embark in offensive operations against either of the sections, seemed to have the approbation of vast numbers of both Northern and Southern people, whilst in the far West, his adherents comprised an overwhelming majority of all classes of the population.

When the carriage containing President Randolph and Alice arrived in front of the hotel in which lodgings had been taken, the street was so much thronged that it was with difficulty an avenue could be made by the Blue Caps, to pass to the entrance of the house. There was cheering and some hissing. While the conservative classes applauded, there were many others, who had lost friends and relatives on the fatal field of Bladensburg, uttered only curses. Nevertheless, in response to the calls, the President re-appeared at the window of the parlor, and made a short speech, which was followed by hearty applause, for he was an orator. And, besides, Senator Langdon, the President of the Convention, that body having adjourned to witness the reception, was standing at the President's side, and seemed to pay him every honor.

After the speech, thousands rushed in and took the President by the hand. Among these Randolph recognised many of his adherents.

Alice had no sooner entered the hotel than she was clasped in the arms of Edith. Without delay they repaired to a private apartment, and unbosomed themselves without restraint.

"Edith," said Alice, "you do not even look pale after your perilous adventures."

"And during the progress of them, Alice, so far from being pale, I assure you I could sometimes feel the scalding blood that must have crimsoned my cheeks. But you seem strangely composed after the perils of that dreadful night, when the infamous Major bore you off a prisoner."

"Edith," said Alice sadly, "I have indeed experienced a change; your friend is no longer the timid hare. She has become enamored of her country, and vehemently longs for its salvation, as the most cherished object of devoted woman. My father and my country, now are all that remain for me. With you it is different. You have your father, your country, and still another object."

"I *had!*" said Edith.

"You *have.* It cannot be that vows registered in heaven, and almost repeated at the altar, may be annihilated by the machinations of wicked man, or the caprices of—"

"Foolish woman, you would say. No, Alice, it is no caprice of mine. Do you not remember my words on that eve when we spoke of the eventful morrow? As wife, I would obey my husband; as daughter, obedience should be rendered my father. And now, Alice, my father demands an indefinite suspension, if not, indeed, a total cancellation of the engagement."

"Why, Edith?"

"Because Henry is invading the North. Such, Alice, is the prudence of the parent, and resignation is the duty of the child. Henry and I may meet no more!"

"But Henry—General Blount is *not* invading the North.

He remains at New Castle, and I am very sure he will not pass over the river."

"That may be so—and I said as much to my father. But he replied it was a mere device, or subterfuge, or something else unworthy the husband of his daughter. He assured me that he had reliable authority for saying that although Henry himself remained on the Southern territory, yet the greater portion of his men had joined the army of invasion under General Crook."

"And even that might not be with his consent, or within his control."

"Still, my father is inexorable. But you know, even were this obstacle removed, Henry himself has interposed another. Oh, Alice, he distrusts my plighted faith!"

"Believe it rather the intensity of his love, which cannot brook the approach of another—and especially of an enemy. Edith, I did not write you all. He was pale and worn with care. His words faltered on his lips. A tear! You cannot eradicate him from your heart. Well! by every obligation, human and divine, you are his and he yours. Whatever trials may be in reserve for you, bear them with a brave heart, Edith; and never hesitate to throw yourself on your constant friend for sympathy. Yes, Edith, I *am* changed. The words of my father were the words of Fate: 'Be marble,' said he. Edith, I AM MARBLE! Nay, start not. As unyielding, as unchangeable as a statue, I am still thy friend. But the trivial alarms of life, which are wont to banish the blood from the timid maiden's cheek, can never again obstruct or quicken the pulsations of this poor heart of mine. On earth, my father, my country, the friend of my girlhood, are all that may claim the thoughts and sympathy of Alice."

"Oh, Alice!" cried her friend, "this is a change, indeed. I will not ask, nor even conjecture, what has produced it."

"Nay, it were bootless, Edith; I am calm. If sympathy, or aught else within thy power could avail, surely I would seek it. You have confided in me, and I in you. And I do so still, when I declare to you that the veil must not be lifted. Think of me as ever your constant friend—to others, save my father and my country, as MARBLE. Prophetic word! And long ere that the petrifying alembic had encompassed me. But the process of crystallization was imperceptible.

Now the work is done! No more of this, Edith! There is the ring!"

"That ring! It is the same!"

"The same. He bade me give it thee, if I deemed thee constant."

"Constant! And you deem me so?"

"Come to my arms! Now take the ring!"

"No! not yet! Keep it till *he* too deems me worthy. And he spurred away in desperation. No! When he renews the tender, if ever, it must be done with deliberation and confidence. No, I must not take it—not now—it would be disobedience to my father."

And thus the meeting of the friends was characterized until evening, when they were summoned to appear in the saloon.

The President was the centre of attraction; but Mr. Langdon also occupied a high place in the public estimation. And but few of that throng of visitors retired without paying their respects to Alice and Edith. Among these, the gallant old Commodore was by no means the least conspicuous; and he was followed by Wiry Willy, who had just landed from the frigate, under the protection of whose guns the President's army was crossing over to Camden.

As soon as the young ladies perceived Willy, they distinguished him above all others by the cordiality of their reception.

"That is a heartier welcome," said the old Commodore, "than any of us old salts could look for; or than any one could expect after having seen the predicament in which I found Willy this morning."

"And pray what was that?" asked Alice.

"With a halter round his neck, standing under the gallows."

The astonishment of the young ladies was natural. And when all the circumstances were made known, they overwhelmed the modest young man with expressions of sympathy, and earnest congratulations on his escape.

"They would have swung him the next minute," said the Commodore, "if I had not interfered. But I should have brought young May, the middy, along. I see how it is."

"Good, great Commodore!" said Alice.

"Now I will sail to leeward," said he, passing on. "Here

comes a General, some forty years my junior, and this is not the place I would choose to encounter him. But I leave with you the gallows-bird. I must look after my gulls."

And Willy shrank back on turning his head and recognising General Ruffleton. His purpose was, instinctively, to avoid him; but it was too late. The General's hand was on his shoulder before he could extricate himself from the crowd.

"Willy," said the General, a mocking smile playing on his broad features, "you told me the truth. Mary Penford was not there. But you might have told me the *whole* truth, and saved Miss Edith a world of painful apprehension. But Trapp was a bad man, and deserved his fate. Never conceal anything from me again, Willy. And *now*, where is Mary? At your grandmother's?"

"She—she *was* there, sir—but——"

"Is there no longer. How do you *know* that, Willy?" asked the General.

"I do not know it, sir. I have not been there myself since Major Snare——"

"Oho! Never mind. It is of no consequence. She is safe. And Snare was another fool to be meddling in matters above his comprehension. You did perfectly right to ensnare him."

"I, sir?"

"Yes—you did your share. You see I have a little bird that tells me everything. Never attempt to deceive me, Willy, and you may have your Mary." The General then strode forward towards the ladies, who awaited his inevitable presence.

"Ah! Miss Alice, it has been long since I had the pleasure of seeing you! And the vicissitudes of the country have wrought no change in your appearance. I congratulate you."

"General," said she, "you will permit me to reciprocate the compliment. Vicissitude has not effected the slightest alteration in your bearing. Nevertheless, it might not be a reciprocity of compliments to congratulate you!"

"There it is! There, Edith! A sharp wit is to finish what the sword left undone."

"Edith!" muttered Wiry Willy, who overheard the familiar term.

"I think not, sir," said Edith. "I cannot believe that woman's wit will pursue the vanquished."

"Ah, me! I must be a victor, Miss Alice; I see it plainly. And when we meet again, perhaps the fortune of war will have made amends."

"I am sure I wish you no misfortune, sir, unless you should stand against the right. With right and merit on your side, if you should be unfortunate, it would be unlucky indeed. But they say fortune favors the bold—and——"

"No more of that, I beseech you. But where is Blount? I expected to meet him here; and I am sure that Edith would have hailed the chief who advanced too late for the triumph."

"He relinquishes the laurels to his second in command," said Alice, seeing the embarrassment of Edith; "and I can assure you he does it very cheerfully. I saw him but recently, and he did not express a word of regret."

"No. Blount does not regret that he was absent. I should have been most happy to have met him on this joyous occasion. But, no matter; I shall see him where he is, and will be happy to deliver any message Edith may intrust me with."

"If Edith has none to send, pray say to him that the Knight of the Velvet Cap requires a fulfilment of his pledge, and that the laurels he is to wear must be gathered on Southern soil. He will understand me, sir. And say to him that I chose this mode of transmitting the message, since he is aware that the post-office has become an insecure medium of communication."

"It shall be done!" said the General, in some confusion. But instantly recovering his impudence, he added, "The postmaster was my friend; and, since the arrival of your father, he has been suspended! I have besought the President to restore him, and pledged myself to produce testimony——"

"It is in vain, General," said Alice. "My father, first convinced of the sufficiency of the evidence against an unfaithful agent, acts with decision—and the case is then decided."

"So it seems. However, all this is merely temporary. When the great event of separation is completed, my friend will be replaced. Adieu." And the General moved on.

"Come here, Willy!" said Edith, in a low voice. "Fly! Say that he meditates an attack——"

"Pray, go on, Miss Edith," said Willy.

"Do you not understand?"

"Not clearly," said he, for he did not hear the words which had alarmed Edith.

"General Ruffleton intends to surprise General Blount at New Castle."

"That I can, and will prevent, by informing General Blount of his purpose. And when he demands my authority, I will say my information comes from Miss Edith."

"Stay! No. I fear——"

"Say, then, it comes from Alice," said Edith's friend. "But why did you hesitate, Edith?" continued Alice, when Willy had departed.

"Alas, Alice! I did not know how he might construe it —whether as a friendly warning, or a hostile menace."

"Be composed. All will be well. Your good father and mine are coming this way."

The President and Mr. Langdon approached, attended by Mr. B., when an ill-featured man sprang forward, and uttering a curse on the President for permitting his soldiers to fire on the mob at the Custom House, drew a pistol and aimed it at his breast. But the President's steady eye unnerved the miscreant, and the contents of the weapon did no farther mischief than shattering a chandelier. And before he could repeat the fire, the revolver was wrested from his hand by one of the Blue Caps that mingled in the crowd. A moment after, the assassin sank down lifeless, for the stalwart arm that held the pistol had crushed in his skull with it. It was Jack Bim.

"Do not slay him, Bim!" said the President.

"It's too late, your Excellency," said Bim. "If you had only given the order a moment sooner——"

"Remove him," said the President. It was done.

"Oh, father!" cried Alice, recovering from the shock, and throwing her arms around her parent's neck.

"Be not alarmed. There is no danger, and was none. I saw his hand tremble when I caught his eye. Be MARBLE, Alice!" he whispered, smiling calmly.

And Alice, resuming her composure, returned to her place at the side of the frightened Edith. The saloon was soon after filled with the Blue Caps, and if there had been twenty assassins present, the infamous attempt would not have been repeated.

Without paying further heed to the occurrence, the President led his daughter and Edith round the room, avoiding the spot where the man had fallen, which was stained with blood. He assured them that he felt quite as secure in Philadelphia as in Washington. He then rallied Edith on her flight from General Ruffleton, who had subsequently fled before her Southern avengers.

"Rely on your Southern champions, Edith," said he, in conclusion.

"Alas, sir!" said she, "how can I, if the reliance be not mutual?"

"There are risks," he added, "it is true; but I think, with patience, prudence, and forbearance, you may both be guaranteed against loss. I have hopes of your father. You understand. I am for the *Union!*" Then bidding them good-night, at the door, the young ladies, being the last of their sex remaining, retired to rest.

CHAPTER XIX.

GOLD, GLITTERING GOLD.

Wiry Willy made preparations to set out immediately on his mission.

The first person he encountered in the street, when looking for a hack, was the tall form of Sergeant Bim, who had just been relieved from duty at the President's lodgings.

"Oh, it's you, Sergeant!" said Willy. "I am glad to meet you. What is this rumor about some one attempting to kill the President?"

"It's no rumor, Wiry Willy," said the Sergeant, throwing an arm round his friend's neck, for he was in excellent humor, having repeatedly drunk the President's health after saving his life. He detailed the particulars of the occurrence in the greedy ears of Willy. "Now, Willy," he continued, "can you spare another half-eagle or so?"

"Gladly, Sergeant! Here, take the whole belt."

"No, indeed. I've just borrowed an X or so. It'd be stealing to rob you. I had my share and lost it at—in one of the hells. But I'm going to rummage the old closet for the rest. If I find it still there, you shall take your share of it, or I'll serve your head like an egg! But what are you after? Where are you going?"

"On important business to General Blount."

"Speed and good luck to you! Manage things, Willy, so I shall never be obliged to fight against him. I like his eagle eye. And, besides, you know, I cracked some skulls in defending him. Good-bye!"

Sergeant Bim plunged into one of those gambling establishments where so much of his money had gravitated; and in less than fifteen minutes all that he had obtained from Wiry Willy passed the same inexorable bourn. Without drinking any more, Bim turned away and left the place, uttering no word of malediction. He directed his steps towards Independence Square. Entering the inclosure, he sat down on a stool near the spot where Major Trapp had fallen, and gazed at the row of buildings opposite. They seemed dark and deserted, although it was known that General Ruffleton and his staff resorted thither. Fixing in his mind the locality of the treasure he had abandoned, Bim could perceive no evidences of present occupation.

"I'll try it, any how!" said he, rising and directing his steps in that direction. Having ascended to the hall door of a tenement, he placed his shoulder against it. The frail barrier yielded, and he stepped in. Closing the door behind him, he stood in such impenetrable darkness that before advancing another step he struck a light with a match, and ignited the wick of a sperm candle with which he had provided himself. This done, he ascended the stairway.

"Go to the d—l!" he muttered, at the second turning, when a large rat attempted to pass between his feet. He kicked the squeaking animal down to the bottom of the stairs, where it still continued its cries. "But it's a sign," he continued, "that no person's in the house." Nevertheless, at every turning he reconnoitred somewhat carefully, for the walls between the houses had been cut through at each of the landings.

Meeting no one to dispute his progress, the Sergeant soon arrived at the attic room, where he had concealed his treasure. The door was fast, although the lock did not seem to have been repaired. "It is fastened on the inside," he muttered, "and that looks like some one might be within. Hallo, there! open the door!" Saying this he stooped down and listened. He thought he could distinguish a slight noise, made by one moving lightly across the floor, but he was not certain. "If there is mortal man or woman in here, I demand admittance," said Bim. "I have business in this room, and must enter. I don't fear flesh and blood, and my trade is fighting. My name is Sergeant Bim, and you may have heard it--because I've sent more than one man to his long account, and one of them this very night. But if you are a ghost, just say so, and I'll retire." He was awfully afraid of ghosts. But no one responding, Bim placed his knee against the door and it flew open, sending the bolt into the middle of the room. "Who was that?" he exclaimed, when his light was suddenly extinguished. Receiving no answer, he stooped down and rasped a match on the sole of his shoe, and relighted the candle. "Now face me!" he said, standing erect, and gazing round, not aware that the rush of wind had blown out the light. No one met his view. The place seemed quite deserted. The bed, the fractured chairs, and the old table, appeared to have been unmolested since he and Wiry Willy abandoned the premises. And there was the same closet with its low door shut quite closely, as he had left it.

Placing the candle in the neck of a bottle on the table, the Sergeant approached the place where he had concealed the treasure. But when he applied his fingers to the door, it resisted his endeavors to open it. It had neither lock nor bolt, and it seemed most extraordinary that it should refuse to turn on its hinges. At length the mystery was solved. The sleeve of an old shirt was wedged tightly between it and the floor. Seizing this with his fingers, the door yielded to his strength. It was dark within, and he arose from his stooping posture to fetch the light; but his impatience to clutch the treasure overcame his purpose, and so he stooped down and crawled in. Groping to the extremity of the closet over the fragments of old clothes, cast-off boots, and stove-pipes, he reached the corner where he remembered to have deposited the gold. Here his hand encountered a substance like the hair of a man's head; and the next moment a most awful groan assailed his ear. He fell back, rolled over, and retreated precipitately until he attained the centre of the room, when he sprung up and faced the closet, with a pistol in one hand, and his sword in the other.

"If you are flesh and blood, come out and have a fair fight! If you are the devil, my time hasn't come yet. If you are a ghost, just make it known, and I'll give you a wide birth. But if you don't give me some sort of satisfaction, I'll send a few bullets in there after you."

"In the name of heaven, have pity on a poor old man, who has not tasted bread for forty-eight hours," was the response, and in such squeaking tones that Bim believed his tale.

"Then come out, old Tuppenny, and let me see your phiz. If you're actually hungry, I'll get you something to eat. Let me see your phiz, I say."

"As God is my judge it is true," said the little old man, who made his appearance.

"Why, you are that infernal little, old, bill-broking sharp-faced, screw-flint Jew, Solomon Mouser! What the d—l are you doing here!"

"Oh, brave captain!" said the Jew, crawling to the Sergeant's feet, "if you will listen, you shall learn my sad history since these terrible times began. I was rich, but now I am poor indeed—robbed of my last dollar—on that dreadful night—and ruined by a boy I hired to carry my trunk to Moses Abrahams. He ran away with it, and I have not put eyes on him since."

"That's a lie, Solomon. I know all about it. Wiry Willy related to me what Miss—I mean the boy—said had happened. I knew it was you, from the description, and I was glad to hear you had lost your money—no, not *your* money, but the earnings of poor men and women you had shaved from them. Begone, you lying varmint! Go, I say, or I'll make mince meat for the rats, and that's all you are fit for!"

"Let me die, then, in the place I have chosen. Leave me to my miserable fate, and I will be a trouble to no one!" Saying this, he was about to re-enter the closet; but the

Sergeant, catching his heel, threw him to the opposite side of the room.

"No, you don't!" said Bim. "Tell me, is my money safe?"

"It is my treasure!" said the Jew. "I have been watching and starving over it for days and nights! Oh, father Abraham!"

"You are welcome to all the aid you can get from any of the Abrahams in this city—and the Moseses too. But if you really have been watching my gold for me, I'll pay you fair wages. How much can you make a day committing usury for the religious misers and millionaires?"

"As God is my judge—"

"If you must lie, don't call upon God to judge you. Stay there, till I see if all's safe."

The Sergeant re-entered the closet and ascertained that the treasure had not been removed. It was in an old coffee bag, which he dragged to the door, backing out like a crab. But just as he emerged from the closet, his quick eye caught the glitter of descending steel, and throwing up his left hand, he seized the wrist of the Jew, and arrested the murderous blow.

"See here, old Tuppenny!" he exclaimed, rising, but still holding the Jew by the wrist, "do you think my back was made to be stung by such a weak Israelitish wasp as you? How much will you pay me for every stab I'll let you have at my back? If you'll take the job at fair wages, I'll stand with my face to the wall and let you cut away all day. You caricature of London Punch, do you think there's no difference between bleeding hard-up merchants, run-down editors, and distressed widows, and a six-feet-seven man, whose trade is war? Hold on, sir—I don't want your knife. Clasp it tight, and you shall have blood." Saying this, Bim so turned the Jew's wrist that the point of the steel was opposite the assassin's own breast. But before he could plunge it in, the Jew straightened his fingers and the weapon fell to the floor.

"Mercy! mercy!" cried the Jew. "Let me live, and I will serve you faithfully as——"

"Well, live. I should be ashamed to kill such a specimen as you. Solomon Mouser, I'll trust you. If you deceive me, you know very well that I can kill you. Will you take care of my money for me?"

"It shall be sacred in my keeping."

"I don't believe your words, old fellow, but I know your instincts. You nosed out my treasure just as naturally as a buzzard finds carrion. Not to eat, like the sensible buzzard, but to watch and starve over it for others. What a fool you are, old Tuppenny! You can lie in rags all your life and hug a pile of gold, and when you die you can't even take it to the devil with you. But here—I'll leave the greater part of the money. I'm not afraid you'll spend it; but remember, if you hide it when I want it, or refuse to honor any order I may send for any portion of it, less than one-half the sum before I filled my belt this time——"

"Twenty-eight thousand, nine hundred and fourteen dollars and nineteen cents——"

"No doubt you've counted it a thousand times, and I'll take your word for it. But stay—I see you have writing tools, and here is a sheet of paper on which you have been compounding interest for several hundred years ahead, until the amount is many tons beyond my arithmetic. Now sign me a receipt for the deposit."

"But I don't know how much you have taken out of the bag."

"No matter; guess at it. Say two or three thousand dollars."

"Three thousand and fourteen."

"Well, give me a receipt for the balance. By George, but you can write! Stick to the pen, Shylock, and let the dagger alone. You can wound enough with your tongue. Let me read it—I'm no lawyer; but I think that'll do. I haven't time to calculate whether you've subtracted it right; but I know you'll never spend anything. If you steal a portion you'll hide it—not spend it, and so I'm safe. And if you don't pay me, I shan't take the law of you—I'll cut your throat! Harkee, though—take a few dollars and buy enough bread and ham——"

"I don't eat pork."

"True! you're too religious for that. Then buy what you please, so as to keep life in you—and take care of my gold. I'm off!" and Bim strode out of the room and descended the stairway. But when he reached the hall, it occurred that it might be good policy not to be seen issuing from the same door he had entered. He had no bodily fear; but some one might discover his hidden treasure. Therefore, he turned to the right and passed through the hole cut in the partition wall, and here the same reason moved him to continue on some distance down the block. When he had reached the sixth house he was brought abruptly to a pause. The sound of voices was heard in the parlor where he was about to plunge. He extinguished the light in his hand, and then the rays of a chandelier within illuminated the opening through which he had been on the eve of passing.

The persons speaking were females, and two in number. The Sergeant peeped in cautiously from his hiding-place, and beheld a lovely dark-haired maiden, and a woman of middle age, who seemed to exercise some control over her young companion.

"Why did they bring me here?" asked the beautiful girl, while tears stood on her long, black eyelashes.

"It was to save you, they said," replied the other.

"Save me from whom?"

"Why, from the Southerners, of course. Didn't they take a man prisoner who was going after you? That was the way they found you out. When they showed the paper to the General, he ordered some of his men to bring you to the city, where none of the Southerners come. I have the paper, and you may see it."

"Oh, good woman! Oh, madam!" exclaimed the young girl, on perusing the writing, "these lines were written to me by a dear friend, for a paper he left in my keeping. No doubt he was in trouble. Oh, pray assist me to return! You are a woman, and no doubt feel the duty a wife owes her husband. I am his affianced bride——"

"I'm a widow, Miss, not a wife. My husband must go to the wars! He was killed at Bladensburg. And he left three poor little children for me to support!" And the widow seemed to weep.

"I sympathize with you, madam. Oh, that man's inhumanity to man——"

"Yes, though he's gone, he *was* inhuman to leave me alone in such dreadful times as these! And if it hadn't been for the kindness and nobleness of General Ruffleton, in making me his housekeeper——"

"General Ruffleton's housekeeper! Is this his house?"

"He comes here every now and then. He leaves all his fine things in my keeping, and supplies me with money, which Sergeant Punt left me without."

"But, oh, assist me to return to my home! Poor Willy may lose his life for the want of the paper!"

"Who? Wiry Willy? I didn't read his name."

"Yes, madam."

"Then you needn't give yourself any more trouble about him. He's dead. They hung him this morning as a spy. I heard the General say so."

"Oh, my God!" exclaimed poor Mary, clasping her hands and falling prostrate at the feet of the woman.

"It's a lie! It's an infernal lie!" said Sergeant Bim, stalking into the room. Mrs. Punt, unheeding Mary, began to scream with ear-splitting intensity; but Bim seized her by the waist with one arm, and employed the other in stopping her mouth. "Be easy!" said he, "and bring the girl to life. Willy escaped, and I saw him not two hours ago. I'm no burglar, and so you needn't be frightened; and, besides, I have good news for you, too. I'm—I mean I was Captain Bim, and Sergeant Punt was my Sergeant. They said we were both killed. Punt has joined the President, and is now working on a ship. So behave yourself, and help me to bring this beautiful maiden to life again."

Bim released the woman after delivering himself of his speech, and taking Mary in his arms, sprinkled her face with some water he found in a pitcher.

Meantime, Mrs. Punt, recovering her speech, cried:

"It's *not* good news, sir. He's never been worth a cent to me since he took to politics. And here I'm left to support the family! And they've put up sugar to twenty cents, and rice to fifteen. Levy shirting is now a quarter of a dollar; and they say it'll soon be fifty cents, because they can't make it in the North, and the Southerners won't let us have any more!"

During this tirade Mary revived.

"Oh, sir!" said she, "who are you?"

"Wiry Willy's friend—and no friend of General Ruffleton."

"Then you'd better be getting away from here," said Mrs. Punt.

"I'm Jack Bim. You can't marry again."

"Pray release me, sir. I am stronger now, I thank you

I have heard him speak of your bravery and generosity. But did not some one say poor Willy was dead?"

"Yes, Miss, that h—l cat did say so, but it's a lie! Wiry Willy was in this city, alive and well, this very night. He loaned me twenty dollars not more than two hours ago."

"Thank heaven! Oh, Sergeant Bim, please take me where I can see him."

"That can't be done immediately, because Miss Edith sent him to New Castle with a message——"

"Miss Edith? Oh, yes! She's in the city. Take me to her!"

"I will, in spite of a whole regiment of Ruffletons!"

"No, you won't!" cried Mrs. Punt. "That's the General's walk in the hall. I thought I heard a deadlatch key! Now, down on your marrow-bones, for you haven't got two minutes to live!"

Bim listened an instant, and distinguishing voices, and the tread of several men approaching hurriedly, he cast a glance of inquiry at Mary. The response was satisfactory, aud lifting her in his arms again, he vanished through the aperture in the wall. He could not expect to find his way readily from one aperture to another, and he knew pursuit would be made, therefore when he had passed the second wall, he turned aside one step, and stood perfectly still in the darkness.

"Breathe easy!" said he in a whisper to Mary, "and they will pass us."

"Then place me on my feet. If we must fly again, I can keep pace with you. I will hold your hand. There."

"Take my other—the left. They come!"

There was just sufficient light from the distant chandelier for Bim to see the forms of the pursuers. The foremost of the party, from his portly dimensions, he supposed to be the General. He awaited, in perfect composure, his arrival.

"These holes must be made larger or closed up entirely," said Ruffleton, making an effort to squeeze through. "Ah!" he cried, and fell back at full length on the floor, from the effect of a tremendous blow, dealt by the Sergeant.

"Alas, why did you not suffer them to pass?" whispered Mary.

"Just to make 'em cautious," was Bim's reply; and then he prostrated the second, and the third, as they successively filled the orifice. "Now," said he, "let us retreat behind the next wall." This was accomplished, and just in time, for a moment after the pursuers fired their pistols through the aperture.

"Can we not get into the street?" asked Mary.

"Oh, yes—but that might be falling out of the frying-pan into the fire."

"Could we not escape through the yard?"

"Possibly. Are you willing to risk it?"

"Oh, yes! There can be no more danger than to remain here."

Bim found the back door locked, but the key was in it. This he turned, and the door came open. They now stood in the diminutive yard, in the brilliant light of the moon. Locking the door behind him, the Sergeant led the way to a dingy gate opening into a narrow alley. This likewise, on being unbolted, turned on its rusty hinges. They proceeded along the alley, and were about to emerge into the street, when the sounds of feet and voices arrested their progress.

"Do you watch up that way and I'll look this," said one.

"But didn't he say we must not use our pistols?"

"Yes. The report of fire-arms might bring upon us the President's men. Besides, we won't need the shooting irons. There is but one of the enemy, and a single sword or dagger will do for him."

"I'd like to know how many there are of *you?*" said the Sergeant, stooping down and peeping out. In doing this, some of the spangles with which he had decorated his velvet cap, sparkled in the moonbeams.

"What's that?" cried one of the men in the street. "It moves, and there must be life in it. Let's see." And he approached.

"Stand back against the wall, Miss!" said Bim, drawing his sword. "They've found me out, and I must fight. I've got a keen appetite, and I won't detain you long. Ahem!" he continued aloud, and then stepped forth.

"Yield or die!" exclaimed the foremost of the men.

"I'll be —— if I do!" said Bim. "So come on." He was assailed by them both, but he was a capital fencer. "I don't murmur, gentlemen," he continued, "at having two against me, so long as you keep in front, and I'll try to take care of my back. This is mere child's play, and I can talk and fence with such as you. There, sir! Pick it up again. Now for yours," he added to the other, whose sword flew into the middle of the street. "So, if you beg for quarter, I'll let you go. No? Very well! And here comes another. Two to one was the bargain, and the third's an interloper. However, he's fresh, and I'll give him one of your places." As he said this, Bim thrust one of the combatants between the ribs. He staggered off a few steps and fell. "Now, gentlemen, it's only two to one again," said he, "and if there are any more recruits on the way, let 'em come—but for every fresh one that appears, an old one must disappear."

"Oh, sir!" said Mary, "do not shed blood on my account."

"Very well!" said Bim, and the next moment the swords of both his antagonists flew out of their hands. "Now, gentlemen," said he, "you may retire. My blood is getting warm, and you might find me dangerous. If you will take a friend's advice, stay where you are, and keep your points down. If I were not in somewhat of a hurry, and had no precious charge in my keeping, it would afford me considerable amusement to play till morning. Come, Miss Mary." He lifted her with his left arm, and holding his sword in his right hand, walked briskly away. But, hearing the approach of many footsteps, and finding himself pursued by his two antagonists, he paused a moment with the resolution to dispatch them—but they hesitated to trust themselves within his reach. And now, seeing he must soon be overwhelmed by numbers, if he remained on the ground, the Sergeant again lifted his burden and fled away.

CHAPTER XX.

NOCTURNAL VISITORS.

The hotel in which the President had taken lodgings was opposite old Independence Hall.

After the guests in the great saloon had retired, the

attempted assassination induced General Valiant to adopt a measure of precaution likely to deter others from venturing on so hazardous an experiment. In the streets surrounding the hotel, opposite its front, and in the square behind the State House, he silently posted some 5,000 picked men, of very quiet demeanor, but of reliable fidelity.

The President himself retired to his private parlor for *the transaction of business.* His hours for rest were usually between 3 and 10 o'clock A. M. After perusing a great number of letters with inconceivable rapidity, and noting briefly the replies to be written by his Secretary the next day, he rose from the table, and with folded arms promenaded backwards and forwards as was his custom when plunged in profound meditation. But he had not been thus engaged many moments, before he heard the signal of the doorkeeper announcing a visitor. He glanced at his watch which lay upon the table, and seemed surprised that any one should be approaching. Beside the watch was a memorandum in pencil marks of his appointments; but full twenty minutes remained before the time for the admission of the first visitor.

"Ah! It is your fairy foot then!" said he, turning, and seeing his daughter glide in.

"Light fantastic toe, father," said Alice, pausing and beckoning Edith, who lingered behind and hesitated to enter.

"Come in—come one, come all!" said the President, in his blandest tone and manner. "I have some minutes on my hands for idle gossip," he continued, giving each of the girls an arm, and promenading round the room.

"Idle gossip!" said Edith. "What a word! But we will not criticise it, for we did not mean to tarry."

"Ay, you have no time to waste on one who never has any leisure, save in such unseasonable hours as these. But your errand. Is it to pardon the assassin? Freely he has my forgiveness!"

"No, no, father!" said Alice. "We merely came to wish you a hearty good-night, and to receive the kiss you neglected in the saloon."

"True, God bless you both"—said he, kissing them—"and he will bless you. But stay. It may be necessary for you, one or both, to see a certain visitor, who shall be nameless, before the dawn of morning. Nay, do not stare so, nor plead with mute lips for a solution of the mystery. The individual—male or female, I say not which—may not come, or, coming, may not demand—mind, I say *demand* —an interview. I think, now, when summoned—if summoned—you will be found with wakeful eyes. Adieu."

The girls withdrew, wondering who this visitor could be, and they had but just disappeared, when some one else was announced by the doorkeeper. He came with a heavy tread, and when the door was opened, the President beheld his faithful Blue Cap, fighting Jack Bim, bearing in his arms the almost inanimate Mary Penford.

"Bim! What is this? Why are you here?" demanded the President, gazing at the poor girl, and at the bloody hands and garments of the Sergeant.

"This is Miss Mary Penford, sir, that I've rescued from General Ruffleton's people."

"Is it possible? Poor child! That bold bad man— "

"I have not seen General Ruffleton, sir—it was his people. They had just brought me to the city, when this brave man rescued me."

"I am glad it is no worse, Mary," said the President, ringing a bell. "Take this young lady to your mistress," he continued, to the chambermaid, a mulatto slave. "Relate your story to Alice, Mary. You are now in perfect security."

"But poor Wiry Willy, when he finds out that they have taken her away from his grandmother's," said Bim, "will be perfectly miserable."

"That is probable," said the President, "but it will not last long. Do you be at the wharf, some two hours hence, when the Wabash comes up the river——"

"Pardon me, sir, but the Wabash is now anchored——"

"The Wabash *was* anchored there, and will be again—but at this moment she is down the river. Be there at the time I have indicated, and you will see Willy, to whom you can deliver your glad tidings. But, Jack, I'm afraid this *night*errantry of yours will prove fatal on some desperate occasion, and I shall lose a stout-hearted and strong-armed guardsman. There are gashes on you now, and some of them have bled pretty freely. Dress your wounds and change your clothing before morning. Here is my purse."

"Forgive me, Mr. President. It ain't pay-day—and I have plenty of money."

"Very well, sir. I will not question you as to the manner in which your treasure was obtained——"

"From the wine vault of the roaring Rev. Mr. Fire's abolition church, sir."

"I have heard of no such robbery, Jack; and, remember, I do not intend to learn anything in relation to it. But have your wounds attended to."

"Mere scratches, sir—only flea-bites."

"And change your clothes."

"I'd change my skin, sir, to please you!" responded Jack, bowing and departing.

The President glanced again at his watch, and then put the written list of expected visitors in his pocket. This had hardly been done before the door opened, and Mr. Langdon entered.

"Well, Langdon," said the President, "it appears that your Committee are averse to a Northern Confederacy."

"And partial to the present Federal Executive. Every one is surprised that you should have so many partisans in the Convention."

"None can be more gratified than myself to learn it," said the President.

"And the wonder is, how you should have contrived it."

"Contrived it! No matter. You are convinced, then, that I have a majority—no, perhaps not a majority——"

"I think a majority, Randolph; and my desire is to know what you intend they shall do."

"Nothing—nothing decisive. Be not precipitate. Try the effect of a little 'masterly inactivity.' There must be a season of painful apprehension, and some suffering, or else a rupture of the sections might be repeated. The second revolt would be final and fatal."

"But we are invaded! What remedy do you propose for that?"

"It will cure itself. Crook and Steel have thrown themselves between the Delaware and the Hudson, as Ruffleton threw himself between the Susquehanna and the Potomac. They will return to their own country with greater precipitation than they left it."

"I hope so. Then you would have no extreme measures

on the part of the Convention? But why need I ask? I see plainly that whatever may be done will be in accordance with your will."

"That is conceding a great deal. But do we understand each other? There are to be no separate Confederacies, at least for the present, and until other remedies fail."

"We agree in that. But shall we go on under the old Constitution? And if not, what kind of an Executive are we to have?

"Let us first save the Union. And that reminds me of Edith. Blount will rise to the head of affairs some day——"

"When another's head lies low," said Langdon, smiling.

"I am younger than you by twenty years. But why not have this knot tied at once? Blount is a mere shadow, and the great spirit within him cannot be roused."

"It must be delayed."

"Do you object to a meeting, and a reconciliation?"

"I would not desire it—nor would I oppose it."

"Then Edith herself must decide."

"Is Blount in the city?"

"No, sir."

"Adieu." Langdon, suffering from loss of rest, repaired to his apartment.

The next visitor was a man in the prime of physical and intellectual vigor, medium stature, dark hair mixed with gray, and a lustrous, clear, and calm black eye. This was General Hudson.

"Hudson, you are punctual to the minute," said the President, exhibiting his watch to his visitor.

"I was impatient, sir, to express my thanks to the one to whom I was indebted for the distinction bestowed on me by the Convention. Your friends—"

"No more of that, Hudson. You, I supposed, were an adherent of the Union—"

"Supposed! You must have known it, Randolph."

"Well. And I supposed you would remain so with the sword in your hand."

"It was a safe supposition. But I must fight this hotspur Crook."

"Yes—but not yet. Let him pass to the Hudson river—"

"And intercept my communications?"

"Will you not intercept his? Will you not fall upon his rear? And will he not be in an enemy's country?"

"You would have me, then, retire up the Hudson river, or fall back towards the mountains, as Washington did, when Cornwallis or Clinton invaded New Jersey?"

"Precisely. The example of Washington shall be cited in the newspapers."

"Crook's army and mine are nearly equal in numbers, but his has the advantage of experience on the field of battle, and the prestige of success."

"I understand. But he is in an enemy's country, and danger lurks in every bush. You must not destroy him—only demoralize his army as he did Ruffleton's; and when I interpose, you must cease the pursuit."

"That is presupposing a victory, which would be ample retaliation for the drubbing he dealt us at Bladensburg."

"Exactly. It would be balancing accounts between the North and the South. Both would be losers, and that, you know, for *you* understand me, would be a striking argument against dissolution."

"But why let him penetrate so far as the Hudson?"

"I have Crook's pledge that he will not wreak his vengeance on any but the Abolitionists, and it will do no harm to demonstrate to these fanatics that they are liable to be called to an account for the mischief they have wrought. Hudson, you have often confessed that the North was the aggressor in this quarrel of the sections. The Southern people, besides the abuse and indignities they have long endured, have been robbed by these *pious* philanthropists of some $50,000,000. Such things should not pass with impunity, and then they would cease. The South does not even criticise the domestic policy of the Northern people, much less attempt to deprive them of any portion of their inheritance. The mischievous and wicked meddling has been altogether on the part of the North. Not the whole Northern people, or the case would be hopeless; but a class of fools and traitors of just sufficient numbers and influence to engender deadly prejudices between the sections. A rebuke to these meddlesome fanatics will afford as much gratification to the conservative and patriotic citizens of the free States as any others."

"That is true, sir! And if Crook would confine his

blows to them, I would rather assist than oppose him—were it not indispensable that a Southern invader should be driven from our soil."

"Oh, you shall have a crop of laurels! But where are your head-quarters?"

"At Trenton."

"Very well. Keep your army out of his way for the present, and let him dash forward."

"But where is he now?"

"He is *now* marching towards the Raritan, and will march all night. He will make a push for Jersey City—"

"What! And assail New York?"

"No matter what his design may be. I'll answer for it that he does not cross over into the city. Were it not for me, he would be revelling *here*."

General Hudson looked at his watch, rose rather hastily, and saying that he must be at his head-quarters before the dawn, took leave of the President.

The next arrival was one not in the President's programme. It was Mr. B——, the good friend of Senator Langdon; and he had been permitted to pass the sentry on the ground of having some very important intelligence to communicate to the President.

"Excuse me, Mr. President," said he, "for this unseasonable visit. But I have received what I deem an important letter from Burlington, which I will read to you. It is from my friend, Mrs. Kinsey." The letter stated that the head of General Crook's army was passing through the town of Burlington, New Jersey, in the direction of New York; that the General had seized a train of burden cars, thrown off the freight and put in its place his mortars and cannon; that quite a number of Abolitionists had been made prisoners; and finally, pursuit had been made after one of the Banks, which escaped in a Tuckerton oyster wagon.

The President, of course, appreciated his zeal for the service, and thanked Mr. B—— very cordially. He had not the heart to seem to have been already apprised of General Crook's movement.

When Mr. B—— retired, General Ruffleton was admitted.

"So, General, you are determined to try your fortune again?" said the President, with a slight smile.

"I must retrieve my reputation, sir."

"And you think that can be done on Southern soil? Very well."

"All I ask is that you will not interfere again, Mr. President."

"I struck no blow at Bladensburg."

"No; but we could not tell what moment you might strike. Your manœuvre amounted to the same thing. It was that which decided the day."

"I will not be at Newcastle."

"Nor any of your horses and cannon?"

"Neither."

"Then I'll throw Blount into the river, or be food for worms myself."

"That is a matter, General, for your own consideration. But why not unite your forces with Hudson's, and be revenged on Crook and Steel?"

"I will not be the subordinate of Hudson."

"That, then, is the reason. General, there is blood on your ruffles. I hope no assassin has been trying experiments on you."

"I have been assailed in my own house, and by one of Blount's creatures——"

"No, General."

"Yes, Mr. President."

"An assassin?"

"What else?"

"I will tell you what else, General Ruffleton!" said Randolph, fixing his eagle gaze on the visitor, who quailed under it. "It was one of my Blue Caps, sir, engaged in the commendable duty of rescuing poor Mary Penford from your infamous harem!"

"By George, then, it was one of *your* men!"

"Well."

"Oh, you have learned the story. But the girl herself will tell you that she had not seen me at all. I have no harem, sir; and this assailant was altogether mistaken." Then with an awkward inclination of the head he departed.

A carriage rolled through the street, and stopped in front of the hotel. Words were uttered which gave those within it the privilege of access to the President; and soon after two gentlemen, one very tall and erect, the other low and corpulent, enveloped in cloaks, were admitted.

"I am glad to see you, gentlemen," said Randolph, shaking each of them by the hand. "But," he continued, when they were seated, "we must be brief, else the stars may desert their posts. I rejoice, my lord, that you acceded to my request; and you, Blount, have again ventured within my power."

"Go, where I will," said General Blount, the slow Englishman having no response in readiness, "it seems that I cannot escape your power. It is almost without limit."

"As for unlimited power, General," said the President, "none but women may wield it; and if you will enter yonder anteroom, my daughter will, I think, at your request, summon a divinity who can impose fetters on the stoutest general."

Blount entered the room indicated without a moment's delay.

"I see there is partiality in your American hospitality," said his Lordship, looking after Blount. But the instant the door closed, his manner changed. "And now, Mr. President," he continued, in a low, earnest, and rather hurried voice, "I desire to make the utmost use of my time. My overtures to the South were based upon a contingency which I am apprehensive is not destined to happen. But I have plenary powers to treat with *you;* and I am prepared to stipulate for a loan of £20,000,000, a fleet of twenty-five ships, and the junction with your forces of fifteen thousand men from Canada."

"And then, my Lord, what equivalent do you require?"

"Only some minor commercial advantages, and a government of greater stability."

"The head of which, no doubt, to be a British Prince?"

"No matter where the prince comes from, so the monarch be of our race. We would be perfectly willing to maintain the President on a throne. The object is to arrest the progress of Republicanism, which menaces all the kingdoms of the earth! Assume the crown, sir, and all the monarchies will support you. You will be acknowledged by every civilized government immediately. You can create a peerage, making the Senators and their descendants and other distinguished individuals, the Patrician order, and——"

"Enough, sir," said the President, emphatically. "If I were desirous of wielding a sceptre, I should not seek the approbation of the present crowned heads of Europe. That would not be the way to retain it. Their intervention would be of no benefit whatever. Therefore, my Lord, I would urge you, by every consideration of policy, to refrain from diplomatic correspondence with the contending sections, as well as with the mediatorial central power, until our internal difficulties are adjusted. These matters which now engage our attention must be settled exclusively by ourselves. They are affairs with which your government can have no concern. As for myself—if I were capable of betraying the trust reposed in me, I have millions of money and arms, and men and ships in abundance. Therefore, my Lord, our conference is ended."

"Certainly, sir, on that subject. But, Mr. President, I hope it will not be deemed unreasonable for me to demand a release from this restraint imposed for obeying the instructions of my government in tendering the alliance of Great Britain to the Cotton States of the——"

"*Union*, you were about to say; and it would have been a diplomatic blunder. But, my Lord, the demand would be both unreasonable and impolitic."

"If so, it is beyond my comprehension. Nevertheless, Admiral Bang has found means to communicate with me, and hostilities will certainly ensue unless you set me at liberty immediately!"

"My Lord, you may easily perceive that the menace does not affect my nerves. The means the Admiral found to communicate with you, and you with him, were supplied by myself. Moreover, an American ship will transmit the tidings across the ocean to your government. My Lord, a war with England is an alternative which I most particularly desire; and I have taken the means to prevent our commercial people from suffering by it. The vessels of our merchant marine will be converted into vessels of war. For your orders in council we will be prepared to retaliate with our Berlin and Milan decrees. Your Lordship seems incredulous. It is a case of necessity. I am sorry, however, to be compelled to use a diplomatist of your distinction, when any other subject of Her Majesty might have answered the purpose. Our interview is at an end. General Blount is returning. Your Lordship will oblige me by becoming the guest of my daughter for a brief interval. Be seated, General," said the President, when his Lordship closed the door of the anteroom, and vanished from view.

CHAPTER XXI.

INTERVIEW BETWEEN GENERAL BLOUNT AND EDITH.

The hour struck for Sergeant Bim to go on duty, and Wiry Willy, parting from his friend, was met by Mary in the passage between the President's and Mr. Langdon's suites of apartments. Intelligence of his arrival had been communicated by General Blount, and hence Mary's vigilance. The meeting was, without doubt, a happy one. Once more they were together in spite of the obstacles and dangers interposed by capricious fortune, and the evil machinations of man.

At the same hour, and during the interview between the President and Lord Slysir, Blount was standing at the south end of a long drawing-room, holding the hand of Edith. The single jet of gas which illuminated the centre of the room, paled before the flood of moonbeams that came in at the extremity.

Alice, attired magnificently, moved to and fro with folded arms, at some distance from the lovers; and whenever a stream of light fell upon her pale forehead, the lustrous diamond on her brow radiated a thousand prismatic hues.

"And now, Edith," said Blount, "I am convinced that Ruffleton—we are both convinced—has been exerting his evil ingenuity to estrange us from each other. These are the intrigues of city life, the stratagems of civilization, the artifices of superior society. Oh, Edith, honor, purity, religion, happiness, may be found only in the rural districts. Abandon the dense population of the North, and cast your lot at once with mine. Among my people, there will be no

Ruffletons, nor Trapps, nor Snares. All is quiet now in the South——"

"To-day all may be quiet—but to-morrow?"

"You would be ever safe. No invasion or civil tumult would subject you to such distressing ordeals as you have passed through in this city. Here, even the presence of your father was not sufficient to exempt you from insult. There, every true son of the South would be a champion and a protector."

"Harry, I know you could not approve infidelity on the part of a daughter to a father, any more than you could applaud the falsehood of a wife to her husband."

"The words trembled on our lips at the altar, which if once uttered, our union would have been indissoluble. Why were they not pronounced? Was it destiny? Oh, Edith, I should have seized the priest, and, perforce, extorted from him a performance of his duty. And yet, the solemn pledge, the sacred vow, what are they but merely words?—and why should not their sanctity be the same, when we repeat them to each other, and call heaven, everywhere above us, to attest the obligation voluntarily assumed?"

"You forget the Church. Authority is given its ministers, which must not be disregarded."

"Certainly not, when it is available. There are ministers now present in this city——"

"Nay, Harry, cease. In God's time, if it be His will, every impediment will be removed. There must be peace between the North and the South before my father will consent to our union. We can pray for a speedy reconciliation of the differences which now distract our country——"

"Ay, and *fight* to end them. Edith, I fear many a sword will be bathed in fratricidal blood before these differences can be adjusted. And fate, which has thrown us together again, if we neglect the opportunity, may sever us for ever hereafter."

"Not if we live, and be faithful. The vows you spoke of, disunited though we be, might suffice for us. United, even according to all the forms and ceremonies of the Church, the present scenes of peril and destruction would sever us. I could not dwell in camps, nor could I be with my father, whose lot it might be to war against my husband. No, Harry—it is better thus; but if it were not better, still it is a duty. Only let us confide in each other. Let us blame the post-masters, or censure the negligence of messengers, but never reproach each other, when communications are not received; and, above all, let us never harbor the thought that other attachments can be engendered."

"I stand rebuked—self-condemned, Edith—but it was not the thought that you could possibly listen to the serpent-hisses of Ruffleton. It was his presumption, his unchastised impudence—but I will meet him yet. No, Edith, it was not jealousy, or fear of rivalry, but an ardor of affection that would engross all the thoughts, all the time and attention of the object upon which it is lavished."

"And you supposed," responded Edith, smiling, "it might not be possible for me to listen to the flatteries of Ruffleton and think of you at the same time?"

"No. But I would not have him present when you think of me! He contaminates the atmosphere in which he breathes; a moral leprosy follows him wherever he goes——"

"A monster, truly! And in truth I would willingly expel him from my presence if it might be done without disobedience to my father. Think not of him!"

"Your father, Edith, I fear——"

"Nay, do not blame him. Let us quarrel with each other, rather."

"Well. And where is the ring I sent you?"

"It was the fatal wedding ring."

"Why say *fatal?* But where is it? Why not wear it on this finger?"

"Because you did not place it there."

"But I sent it by Alice."

"And Alice keeps it."

"Keeps it? What does that mean?"

"It means that she keeps the ring you gave her."

"I gave it her for you. Did she not say so?"

"She did. And, faithful to her trust, she offered it to me."

"And you refused it?"

"It was when I was offended at your apparent suspicions."

"Oh, Edith, a world in arms could not unman me as you have the power to do. To you I must seem as a capricious child, or an enthusiast without mental ballast. I am now very angry—but you, too, were offended?"

"Very much—and I am not yet appeased. Such gifts as that should be presented by the donor."

"I will get it now, and place it on your finger."

"No. Not yet. The probation is not ended. Alice is a safe depository. Let us call her hither. See how incessantly she glides to and fro. How beautiful!"

"It is too late! I have lingered too long!" said Blount, as the clock struck four. "Farewell! but come with me to Alice and take the ring."

"No; not till you have done sufficient penance. You frown! But go—go in anger, if you will! I will not wear the ring until you are worthy, and——"

"Forbear, Edith! Adieu!" And pressing her hand to his lips he hastened to Alice.

"Here is the ring!" said she, the light falling at the same time on her pallid brow, where the diamond sparkled like a star.

"You are very pale, Alice, and grave," said Blount, taking her hand. "What a change! But I must be brief. I have quarrelled with Edith about this ring. I leave you as my mediator. Tell her it is the excess of my love which makes me capricious, exacting, impatient, jealous. Tell her I love——"

"Nay, say that or write it yourself. Take back the ring."

"No, no, no! keep it!" and he forced it on her finger. "Adieu, now!—one word with your imperial—I mean imperious—father, and then away. If I linger a moment longer my word will be broken——"

"Your word broken?"

"His Lordship and myself pledged——"

"True; adieu!"

Blount a moment after was alone with the President.

"General," said the latter, "his Lordship will bear no order of release to Commodore Stout, and we shall probably have some rather startling reports from Admiral Bang before long."

"That is a matter for your Excellency's consideration. My business is with Ruffleton."

"My advices convince me that he is preparing to beat you up in your quarters."

"I desire nothing better. Only one word. You will not interpose?"

"You have *carte blanche*."

"Enough! Let him come! Farewell, sir."

The President, observing the excited condition of the General, and attributing it to the right cause, did not seek to prolong the interview.

CHAPTER XXII.

THE INVASION OF THE NORTH.

General Crook, with augmented forces, his army amounting to over 100,000 men, rapidly traversed the State of New Jersey. Much to his astonishment and gratification, at least one-third of his regiments were made up of recruits from Philadelphia and its vicinity; and it was observed that in most localities in the country, where the anti-slavery party had triumphed at the polls, a vast proportion of the defeated Democrats seemed strongly inclined to espouse the cause of the Southern people. It was quite the reverse in the South. There, when the soil was invaded by a Northern army, all classes and parties, without exception, united for the expulsion of the enemy.

As might have been expected, great consternation prevailed along the line of march; and this was some miles in breadth. Nor were there wanting guides and informers in the several counties through which the sweeping host pursued its devastating course. General Crook, though naturally disposed to clemency, became, when the question of slavery was on the tapis, perfectly inflexible. His first thought was to send out parties to capture all the fugitive slaves they could find, and his next was to inflict a fearful retribution on all who had participated in stealing or harboring that species of property. And in this category he included, rather indiscriminately, the people called Quakers, and they fared very badly. Forage for the horses, and bread and meat for the men, under a compulsory process, were furnished by them without charge. And whenever one peculiarly obnoxious was taken, everything movable in his possession was confiscated, and everything combustible was consumed. He was painted black, tarred and feathered, and then turned loose in the woods.

At Burlington, the General was anxious to cash a draft, for several of his own negroes that had escaped from Alabama, at one of the banks, of which a Republican was the president. But this bank, as Mrs. K. had written to Mr. B., had escaped to Tuckerton. With the rich men of the town, who were either Democrats or Constitutionalists, General Crook had no quarrel; but from others, he was determined to get what indemnity he could for the fifty million dollars' worth of slave property the South had been despoiled of since the formation of the Federal Union.

In many places the militia had been called out by the Governor; but such defenders never assembled in sufficient strength to make the slightest resistance. Besides, it was known that General Hudson was concentrating his army in the neighborhood of Trenton, where it was supposed the tide of invasion would be arrested.

But General Hudson, contrary to the wishes and anticipations of many of the inhabitants, who had ridiculed the idea of a Southern army penetrating the free States, seemed to avoid encountering General Crook, and fell back on the Delaware River.

Without turning to the left for the purpose of offering battle, General Crook pushed forward with expedition, seeming more intent upon intercepting the communications of Hudson with his base of operations, than upon preserving his own. During the heat of the day he permitted his men to rest and refresh themselves; but at night the march was continued. As he approached the Hudson River, he received many accessions to his ranks. From these he obtained such information in relation to the defences of the metropolis, as induced him, by forced marches, to fall upon Jersey City without delay. Not the least resistance was made. On the contrary, a sufficient number of boats were procured to have transported the entire army to the opposite side of the river in a few hours. But this was not deemed expedient. Captain S., of the Navy, forbade it. More than one hundred thousand men had arrived in the city of New York within forty-eight hours, and preparations were in progress for a resolute defence. Therefore General Crook contented himself by erecting batteries which menaced the city. More than one hundred and fifty guns and mortars were in readiness for the destruction of the great commercial emporium, when a deputation of Councilmen, bearing a flag of truce, waited upon the General.

"Gentlemen," said Crook, "at the expiration of three hours send me four millions of dollars, and I will retrace my steps, and fight Hudson. You have some thirty millions in your banks, and you can easily produce the amount I demand. It is less than one-tenth the value of the slaves your negro-stealers have deprived us of. It is a moderate quota for New York."

"It is a large sum, sir," said the President, "and we might not be able to negotiate the loan."

"Seize it, then, and tax the citizens to pay it! Two millions for our stolen slaves, and two millions for harboring the political parsons and Abolition editors who have produced the separation of the States and civil war. I would have demanded the surrender of the preachers, had I not shipped them to Liberia. And as for your fanatical editors, I think you will punish them sufficiently yourselves for having subjected your city to such enormous sacrifices. Go, gentlemen, and send me the money at the time specified, else be prepared for the consequences. The injury I can inflict would be not less than a million an hour—and I should not cease at the fourth hour. I have one hundred thousand red hot balls in my furnaces, and as many bombs in the boats. If my demand be not complied with, you will, of course, see that the women and children are removed beyond the reach of my projectiles."

At the time mentioned the money was delivered. Then Crook, learning that General Hudson had intercepted his communications, made preparations for battle, with a desperate resolve to preserve his treasure.

On the night succeeding the day of General Crook's financial coup de main, the Southern army was encamped upon the magnificent lands of the anti-slavery Quakers, and feasted abundantly without expense. But the camp-fires of General Hudson gleamed in a few miles of them, and in the line of their retreat. Crook and Steel were seated together in the best parlor of a neat Quaker mansion, the messuage of a noted Abolitionist, condemned to the flames the next morning. In war fire either follows or precedes the sword.

The Generals were interrupted in the examination of the maps spread out before them, by the entrance of Samuel C———, the Quaker proprietor of the mansion.

"Well, Samuel," said General Crook, "thee is still here. I am bound to tar and feather thee, thee knows."

"No, General, thee will not tar and feather me."

"That is saying a great deal, Samuel, and saying it positively."

"I am positive. I tell thee that I will not be tarred or feathered—but I may be plucked."

"Plucked? Samuel, this is facetious, and I like thee none the worse for it. But be brief."

"Then, in a word, what will be an equivalent in money for omitting the tar and feathers, and for sparing my house?"

"Now I understand thee. How much did thy house cost?"

"Eight thousand dollars."

"Very good. No doubt you have a heavy purse. Next, how many negroes have you assisted to escape from their masters; how many have you harbored, hidden, stolen? How many pamphlets have you circulated in the South inciting servile insurrections? How many anti-slavery newspapers have you supported? Ah, Samuel! You see how painful a thing it is, when the iron enters your own soul! How bitter the draught you have been concocting, when the chalice is commended to your own lips! We have been robbed of property to the amount of fifty million dollars; and, until this moment, no recompense has been demanded. We have borne much and long without retribution, until, at last, the cup is overflowing! You must acknowledge that the Southern people never interfered with any of your domestic arrangements; they never despoiled you of any of your property; and, above all, they never placed torches and knives in the hands of the debased among you to consume your dwellings and to cut the throats of your wives and children!"

"Name the sum that will content thee, General, and then I will tell thee a secret."

"Ten thousand dollars. Now the secret."

"I am a hypocrite."

"That is no secret, Samuel!"

"But I was a slave-trader, and made my money in Brazil There are papers at Washington, sent thither by our Minister at Rio, which establish the fact that one of the most successful traders between the coast of Africa and the Brazilian empire was a New Jersey Quaker. I am that man."

"I remember it. And here, at home, you will consume only 'free' sugar, 'free' rice, and 'free' coffee. Ah, Samuel, the devil will make you dance on red-hot-dollars!"

"And, near Trenton, if thee should meet with one George K——, do not molest him. He is a Democrat, and preaches against interference with slavery."

"Very well. Thee shall drink the health of King Cotton. But thy money, Samuel! If thee had not been a hypocrite, I would have remitted everything. The money shall be judiciously expended in halters."

"Thee shall have thy money in an hour."

"If not, thy house will be a bonfire, Samuel."

The two Generals then resumed the examination of the maps.

"Let us commence the battle before daylight," said Steel.

"No, General."

"Then, perhaps, we had better await Hudson's attack; our position is a good one for defence——Who is that?

A tumult arose among the sentinels without, and shortly after a Sergeant appeared at the door conducting a prisoner.

"Here is a spy of the enemy, General," said the Sergeant.

"Make short shrift of him! We have no time for court-martials now."

"He's been condemned already, sir. He's the same man that was rescued from under the gallows by Commodore Stout's men."

"Indeed!" exclaimed General Crook. "Willy, I'm sorry to see you in my clutches again. There is now no appeal to Blount."

"General, I have this for you," said Willy, delivering a diminutive scrap of paper.

"Ha!" cried Crook, springing to his feet. "Go, Sergeant," said he, "we have been mistaken. Wiry Willy is not an enemy. Let that be made known. Willy," he continued, shaking the hand of the faithful messenger, "I'm glad we didn't hang you!"

"So am I, General," said Willy, with a very serious countenance.

"Steel," said Crook, "see all the Generals. We must be under full march in an hour. There will be no battle to-morrow."

"Does he say so?"

"No—the assurance is from S——, who knows what he says. We will, at all events, leave the enemy behind us. If he desires a battle, of course he will follow. Wiry Willy," he continued, "can you tell me what Blount was doing?"

"He was preparing to fight General Ruffleton, whose attack was looked for daily."

"And the fleets? Did they remain in the same positions? Hudson being in our rear, we have had no advices."

"Both had moved further up the river, and it was rumored that the British Admiral would attack the American ships, unless Lord Slysir were given up."

"I don't wonder at it. But does the President remain in the city?"

"No, sir; he has joined the army which is encamped near the old battle-field at Red Bank."

"Mount and ride with me, Willy; I have more to say to you. Come."

Within the hour specified, the Southern army was in motion; and, as anticipated by Crook, there was no attempt on the part of Hudson to arrest his march. By sunrise the former had passed several miles beyond the dim camp-fires of the latter, and was now in full retreat, but with flying colors and laden with treasure.

But many of the ardent volunteers under General Crook began to murmur at his inglorious retrograde movement, and demanded a battle. Sufficiently versed in military affairs to be aware that in the event of defeat, with a broad river to pass before he could evacuate the enemy's country, his army might be exposed to total destruction, the General would have been content to retire in good order with his booty; but still he was not prepared to resist the demands and reproaches of his chivalrous followers. Therefore, when he had crossed the bridge of the marshy creek on the east of the town of Burlington, he faced about on the common, and resolved to await the attack of his pursuers.

Hudson was not slow in making his dispositions. A battery was established on a neck of land near the river, which raked the invading host in that direction; and one was erected on the Mount Holly road, which assailed them on the right. These two concentric fires were replied to by divergent batteries with spirit, but not with the same fatal effect.

For a long time the combatants remained so far asunder, that the few thousand Minié rifles in their possession were the only small arms employed. But the terrible batteries of round shot and bomb-shells dealt destruction in their ranks, and went crashing among the houses in the vicinity. The building near the bridge, used as a Catholic church, was perforated in so many places that the east end of the house fell down, and the priest, who had been devoutly praying, fled away with the candlesticks. The building next to the church, occupied by a spiritualist, was blown to pieces by a bomb, and it was said that screams were uttered by invisible beings in the air.

But the iron projectiles flew through every portion of the town, and most of the citizens hastened out of their range. Many took refuge in St. Mary's Church, whose massive walls were cannon proof; and these were saved. Mr. W. stood in the street and pointed with his cane to the places where he said the population would be in perfect safety; and he assured the panic-stricken, with vehemence and gesticulation, that in dodging in the alleys they were liable to run into the "jaws of destruction." The Bishop, mindful of the precious charge committed to his parental protection, conveyed the three hundred girls at the Hall over to Bristol, beyond the possibility of injury; and then he returned, scatheless, amidst the roar of cannon and the whistling of balls, to that portion of his flock which had taken sanctuary in St. Mary's holy church. A solemn service was performed, during which angelic voices floated on the air.

Ever and anon the wind hurled clouds of smoke from the battle-field through the streets, and the sun was completely darkened. And, to add to the horror of the scene, a bomb burst in the apothecary shop of Friend Alison, among the gallipots and gums and essences, and the suffocating effluvia drove hundreds from the walls, where they had taken shelter, in obedience to the commands of Mr. W. The banks were broken to pieces, but the officers escaped unhurt; and several of the tallest houses on Main street were damaged in their upper stories. The host of a hotel stood his ground manfully on a balcony at the corner, and escaped unhurt. But, while there, a cannon ball struck the neck of a lame free negro, who attempted to limp across the street. His head flew a great distance up in the air, and curving over the flag-staff in front of the hotel, descended to the balcony, and remained crown up, snapping its eyelashes in astonishment, but apparently not in pain.

In the meantime, General Hudson was projecting a terrible charge on Crook's centre at the bridge. For this purpose he had obtained a locomotive from the outer depôt, and generating a full head of steam, set it in motion without engineer or conductor. It rushed down the track and passed the bridge in spite of the shells and balls aimed for the purpose of disabling it. It thundered onward, and the lines opened as it rushed through the Southern army. It passed through the town of Burlington, whizzed by Beverly, over the Rancocas bridge, and on to Camden, at the rate of a mile a minute, smashing every opposing obstacle, and finally plunged into the river, just as the steamer "State Rights" had left the landing.

It was during the commotion produced by the charge of this novel engine of war, that Hudson led forward the attack at the bridge. A column of forty thousand men advanced, while the fire of all the batteries converged to the same point; and in return, Crook concentrated all his fire on the head of the assailing column. The bravery was equal on both sides. The dark mass of advancing men made no perceptible progress, after the head of the column had reached within a hundred paces of the guns of the enemy. At that point, every discharge swept down scores of the foremost; and although those in the rear continued to push forward, the front melted away at the point indicated. At length the heaps of slain were converted into breastworks, and the mangled remains of the dead were used as protecting shelters for the living. On both sides the slaughter was frightful; but the assailants, as usual, suffered the most, being more fully exposed to the aim of the infantry, and incapable, from the compact order of their approach, of returning the fire.

For a long time this immense sacrifice of human life continued; but the attack was repulsed, for it seemed a physical impossibility, under such a murderous volcano as that belched forth by the Southern army, for any number of living men to pass the bridge. Hudson, leaving one-fourth of the column on the ground, drew off the rest. But he was not dismayed, and immediately organized a second assaulting column, to be preceded by eighty pieces of cannon. Under cover of these field-pieces, hurling cannister and grape, another corps was pushed forward, but not in so dense a mass as to prevent the use of their arms.

Crook now in turn suffered the most severely. He was assailed by superior numbers in the centre, and perceived with some uneasiness, that a strong detachment had passed over the Mount Holly bridge for the purpose of turning his right wing. To provide against such a contingency as ultimate defeat, he started off a locomotive and one car with his specie.

The battle continued until after sunset, when an immense force, supposed to be not less than fifty thousand horse and infantry, was observed descending Gallows Hill, on the right, and in the rear of the Southern army. This produced great confusion.

"Give me a glass," cried Crook. "It's Randolph," he exclaimed, after intently regarding the menacing host. "He will not attack us."

"True," said Steel. "Neither did he attack Gen. Ruffleton. But his presence decided the battle."

"And I fear it will decide this," said Crook. "Gentlemen," he continued, addressing several of the Generals standing near, "if we can only persuade our men that Randolph will not assault us, I think Hudson will be beaten yet."

"But they cannot be persuaded," was the reply. And, indeed, many of the regiments were already retreating precipitately.

Crook exerted himself, but in vain, to inspire confidence. His line gave way at all points, and the only thing he could do was to cover the retreat with his artillery. This he did with such promptitude and resolution, that Hudson was for a long time kept at bay. Then, burning the bridge, and compelling his pursuers to make the circuit of the marshes on the south, the rear-guard of the defeated host reluctantly abandoned the town.

President Randolph disappeared mysteriously. None of his men were seen from the time that the Southern army was in full retreat. Some conjectured that he had withdrawn behind the hills, to reappear somewhere on the line of march between Burlington and Red Bank. But Crook had no apprehension of being intercepted by the Federal troops; and vented his chagrin at the manœuvre of the President, with an ill grace, since, on Southern soil, a similar manœuvre had enabled him to gain a great victory.

CHAPTER XXIII.

EXCITEMENT IN THE CONVENTION.

On the same day of the battle of Burlington, General Ruffleton had attacked General Blount in the neighborhood of New Castle. The forces were about equal in numbers, but the Generals and the men engaged were unequal in the qualities of skill and bravery. Blount's volunteers were mostly the sons of Southern planters who fought for glory, whilst those against whom they contended, in many instances, struggled mainly for plunder. Blount gained a victory over his assailant, at the expense of some five thousand men on either side; and Ruffleton retired towards Philadelphia, chagrined at the consciousness of a second defeat, but boiling with rage, and intent on direful revenge. Blount did not pursue the enemy, contenting himself with a successful defence of Southern soil.

His army being encamped near Gray's Ferry, some two or three miles from the city, General Ruffleton proceeded with one or two attendants to his head-quarters opposite Independence Square. The first thing that arrested his attention on entering the city, was the illumination of a great many buildings in the vicinity of Independence Hall, where he learned the Convention was still in session. It could not be popular exultation over his defeat, in a Northern city—nor in celebration of Hudson's victory, for the citizens of Pennsylvania had not been characterized for their zeal in behalf of that General. But Ruffleton was not long in doubt. He had many partisans and agents in the city, who usually kept him advised of every occurrence likely to be of interest. They filled his apartments as soon as it was known he had arrived in the city; and then he learned that the rejoicing was produced by the news from Richmond. The Southern Convention had made a formal rejection of the overtures of the British Government, and had passed a resolution recalling General Crook from New Jersey, and proposing terms of reconciliation with the North.

Ruffleton was thrown into a great rage, and foamed at the mouth. His friends could not pacify him, or mitigate his fury, until, at length, he received information of the arrival of Lord Slysir, whom Commodore Stout had embraced the first opportunity—and for which he had long been impatient—to set at liberty.

His Lordship, at the special request of Ruffleton, waited upon the General at his lodgings.

"My Lord," said Ruffleton, "the play of Disunion is not ended yet!"

"The play, General? Why not say farce?"

"Because I prefer tragedy, my Lord. It *would* be a farce, indeed, if it were brought to so lame and impotent a conclusion as the adherents of Randolph in the two—yes, in *both* of the Conventions—would have it. But I shall say nay to that!"

"I would say nay, myself, if it would avail anything."

"It would avail much. Aid us in dethroning King Cotton, and we will share his dominions. If you do not uncrown him, he will subjugate the world. Why not unite with us?"

"I am prepared to do so whenever you are united among yourselves. But the demonstrations in this city, on the receipt of the news from Richmond, would lead one to suppose that the North was languishing to be reunited with the South."

"Your Lordship will soon think differently. This infernal city and State, and perhaps New Jersey, which runs down beyond the Southern border, always have sympathized with the slave States, and always will. Philadelphia is jealous of New York, and New Jersey is fed by Southern travel. We shall have the Convention in New York, and then its action will be different."

"But it will be too late! They tell me the Convention will respond to the Richmond movement this very night."

"Let them tell you what they please! *They shall not respond!*"

"That is decisive language, at all events!"

"And it will be followed by decisive action! North of the river Hudson, the whole country will soon be in a blaze of indignation, that Crook should have been permitted to transport his specie in safety to the Delaware shore. No, my Lord! There will be no reconciliation! General Hudson will be removed. *I* shall be the commander-in-chief. And the Convention will be under *my* influence, instead of this intriguing President's!"

"Convince me of this, and I will treat with you on such a basis as will effectually prevent a readjustment of the difficulties. I will stipulate to furnish in money ten millions sterling, twenty steam frigates, and, if needed, fifty thousand men. The equivalents—"

"Will be granted, if territory in a Southern clime, and the emancipation of the slaves, will embrace all your demands."

"These will be quite sufficient, provided a stronger Government or Governments, guaranteeing greater stability in policy, be added."

"Oh, if you will stand by me, the Government shall be strong enough! My Lord, I have said enough. With the aid of Great Britain, I will undertake to put an end to this Republican Government!"

"Satisfy us of that, and most assuredly our aid will not be withheld."

"Then be patient, my Lord, and await events."

"Very well, General. But there is not much time now for patience. If the resolutions should pass the Convention, our negotiations will be nipped in the bud."

"They will not pass, my Lord."

"Then, General, I take my leave, so that your time for counteraction may not be interfered with. Adieu, till morning."

When his lordship had gone, General Ruffleton rose up, and gazed steadfastly at a large mirror.

"I see no change," said he, "in the expression of my face; and yet I am thinking of a bloody deed. My cheeks have still their color, my brows are not knit together, and my lips do not press against my teeth, as those are painted who deliberately resolve to cut the thread of life! No; it is all a lie! Blood is merely a highly colored fluid, whether it flows from a calf or a man. The color is the same, and so is the temperature. Then why should we be more horrified at the one than the other? Popoli!" said he, rapping at a closet door. "Signor," he continued, when a dark-visaged Italian came forth and confronted him, "the time we looked for has arrived. You heard the promise made me. It was his Lordship, the Envoy Extraordinary and Minister Plenipotentiary of her Britannic Majesty."

"Ten millions sterling," said the Italian.

"Yes. And it is nearly equal to fifty millions of dollars."

"How much, General, shall Popoli and Cardini have?"

"When I receive it, you shall have ten thousand dollars each—in addition to the sum originally named. Go then! Lose not a moment. An hour going, an hour to ——, and an hour to return. Three hours hence I shall be master of the new world. Go!"

"Three hours hence, and you may look for one of us, with good news." Saying this the dark Italian turned and glided out of the door.

"Ha!" exclaimed Ruffleton, starting back on again beholding his features in the glass. "I was premature! The devil himself could not have presented a more savage scowl! But the hue! Why so dark? It is the same blood and the same surface. It must have been the impression of the Italian's countenance daguerreotyped on the retina. No matter! Summers," he continued, throwing open a door in the rear of the room, "come in. I want you." A fair-faced youth glided in at the door, and threw his arm familiarly on the General's shoulder.

"I thought you had forgotten me, General," said the youth, almost reproachfully. "Here have I been caged like some neglected bird, and fearful every moment of hearing bad tidings from the battle-field! You must take me with you next time."

"Perhaps. But I am busy now. Go to Brigadier Balatrum in the next building, and say I desire to see him immediately. You need not return. But tell Mrs. Punt to have refreshments in readiness when the clock strikes twelve."

Summers withdrew, and soon after General Balatrum came in through the door cut in the partition wall.

"Balatrum," said Ruffleton, "has your brigade arrived in the city?"

"Yes, sir. The companies are dispersed so as not to attract attention and create alarm. In ten minutes they could be concentrated in the Square."

"That is well. I may not have need of them; but if I should desire to use them, can I rely upon their fidelity?"

"I will answer it with my head. They are your partisans to a man."

"I have treated them well, and hereafter will be more liberal still. Let one of your officers attend me at Independence Hall to-night, to receive and transmit the order, if I find it necessary to issue it. Balatrum, you are bold, I know. Nevertheless, the consequences of the action I have in contemplation may be serious——"

"Fear me not, my General! If you should require it, I would throw President Langdon out of the window!"

"I may require something of the kind, if nothing less will suffice. Go, General, and promenade the Square. Have with you one hundred men, in citizens' attire; and when any members of the Convention go out among them, let them not return."

"You shall be obeyed. Shall they be despatched?"

"No—not necessarily—that is, if they be not refractory. It is a dreadful thing to shed human blood! Nothing but the most urgent necessity may justify it. And yet the best of men, when treason stalks abroad, and the fate of millions is suspended by a hair, may destroy a few lives to save a great many. This would be patriotism. Remember my words, Balatrum. Can you tell me why those rockets are so continually sent up from the river?"

"The President's ships are rejoicing over the news from Richmond. The rockets are answered by others at Randolph's head-quarters. The President, they say, as well as Hudson, and Crook, and Steel, are in high spirits. They will visit the city to-morrow, and be received by the Convention."

"Balatrum, you know the old adage?"

"A great many, General. But which do you allude to?"

"This—The best laid schemes of men and mice aft gang awry."

"Ha! ha! Adieu, General."

Ruffleton followed soon after, attended by a retinue of aides. At the moment of his appearance in the Convention, the members were considering a series of resolutions which had just been reported. The speakers seemed to be all in favor of an amicable response to the sentiments transmitted by telegraph from Richmond, and Ruffleton began to despair of the practicability of his scheme. Turning his head aside, and whispering to a member from Massachusetts, he asked if Crook had restored the money taken from the city of New York. As if startled from a dream, the member sprang to his feet, and put the question to the chairman of the committee, who had the floor, and was urging a prompt adoption of his resolutions. He seemed embarrassed, and replied that he had no information on the subject. And then a general awakening from the apparent lethargy seemed to ensue among the most Northern members, and a great deal of bitterness was expressed. Then an amendment was proposed to the resolutions, and a vote demanded, as a test question, and it was found that the report and resolutions of the committee would probably be adopted by a very small majority. When this was ascertained, General Ruffleton had risen and gone into the lobby, where he was surrounded by a number of his friends. A moment after it was observed that several of the leading friends of

President Randolph, and among them the chairman of the committee, were beckoned aside, and led out of the Hall, on pretence of business, or important intelligence, by urgent messengers. This produced a pause in the proceedings of the Convention, supposed to be but momentary. But these gentlemen did not return, as was expected. They were sent for, but could nowhere be found.

In the meantime, Ruffleton resumed his seat, and the opponents of the measure of the Committee on Federal Relations renewed their opposition to the report and resolutions with increased zeal and determination. They read despatches from the New England States, to the effect that any yielding on the part of the committee, or amicable arrangement with the slave States, which did not make the return of the money taken from New York by General Crook a *sine quâ non*, would be repudiated with scorn by the people.

At the end of the boldest speech of this character, the member having the floor moved the *previous question*. Great excitement ensued, and pages were seen running in different directions in quest of the absent members. But they did not return, and the measure of conciliation was lost.

It was during this scene that a member from Boston rose in his place and demanded a vote on a resolution he had offered in the morning, expressing the thanks of the Convention to General Ruffleton for his zeal and bravery in the cause of the Northern States. There being no opposition to it, the resolution was adopted *nemine contradicente.*

Then the General himself, by the permission of the Convention, rose up, and briefly, though with honied words, returned his thanks for the expressions of confidence and approbation contained in the resolution.

The applause that followed the speech could not be stifled until the General rose to withdraw. But just when he was on the eve of retiring from the Hall, a prodigious uproar was heard in the street. Men were seen moving hastily to and fro with consternation on their faces.

"What is the matter?" asked the President, turning to a member.

"I have not heard," was the reply. The member was one of the partisans of Ruffleton.

"Move to adjourn," pursued the President.

"No," said the other. "It may be business reqairing action. And, Mr. President," he continued in a whisper, "if it be a matter demanded by the North, however distasteful to your *Blount* ears, it will be best not to throw any obstacle in the way."

"You are impertinent, sir," said Mr. Langdon, re-adjusting himself in his chair.

CHAPTER XXIV.

SUSPENSION OF HOSTILITIES.

The President's head-quarters in New Jersey were in a country mansion near Red Bank, between the Northern and Southern encampments. Randolph was in high spirits, surrounded not only by his own Generals and Commodores, but by several of the most distinguished officers of the hostile armies. Hudson, Crook and Steel were present.

"Commodore," said the President, addressing his senior naval officer, "will not Blount unite with us in a toast to the Union?"

"Yes, sir. He'll be here."

"He makes it a point to go round with the surgeons," said Commodore Early. "Three thousand of his men were wounded, and he nurses them like brothers."

"And they will be as brothers to him hereafter!" said the President. "But can it be true that Ruffleton abandoned his wounded on the field?"

"I am sorry to say the information is correct," remarked General Hudson. "He did not even propose a suspension of hostilities after the battle, for the purpose of burying his dead."

"He suspended hostilities himself," said General Crook, "by abandoning the field. Still the fellow fought for more than an hour like a lion."

"Who," said Commodore Stout, "wouldn't fight like a lion for four millions of dollars?"

'But it was not solely in defence of the treasure that Blount achieved his victory," said the President.

"Nor was it necessary," said General Hudson. "Your Excellency, will, I think, award a restitution of the money. On no other terms will the North lay aside her arms."

"We will pass it to your credit," said General Crook.

"But, General," said Hudson, "this contribution was levied on friend and foe alike."

"The Richmond Convention says nothing concerning the money."

"The Cotton States would not sanction its restitution," said General Steel.

"Then, it is probable, the North will require an equivalent," said Hudson, with a smile.

"And what would that be?' asked the President.

"Metal for metal. Iron for gold."

"I understand," said Crook. "It is my cannon and mortars they want. They may have the bombs and balls, but not the tubes."

"Gentlemen," said the President, "let us not discuss these matters too closely. Recollect, no unpleasant words are to be uttered this night; or if any should escape us, they are to be promptly retracted. How now, Willy?" he continued, directing the attention of his company to Willy. "The wonder is, or rather would be with any other, why you should have the temerity to present yourself before so many of the recently opposing Generals."

"They have defeated the resolutions, sir," whispered Willy.

"Ah!" responded the President, with gravity. A moment after the approach of General Blount was announced.

"PEACE and UNION!" cried Alice on the porch, as Blount ascended the steps.

"And happiness!" was his response, as he cordially kissed the fair hand of the President's daughter. "If I may exert any influence over the councils of the nation, Alice, you may be certain it will be for peace, union, and happiness."

"Go on, then, and may Heaven aid you!"

"But here is still my ring!" said Blount, lingering, and detaining her hand.

"She will not take it yet—from me," said Alice, the diamond on her forehead again twinkling like a star in the firmament.

"Nor from me, it seems. But where is she? Is she not here?"

"No—but will be to-morrow. Ruffleton has returned to the city."

"True! And I do not think he will pay me another visit soon. But you think Edith will leave the city because he has returned to it?"

"Partly because of his presence, and partly——"

"Because I am here? I hope so!"

"But your business here is with the sterner sex. There lies your way. But yonder is one of the Generals beckoned out. Merciful God!"

This was uttered upon beholding some one spring from a dark corner and aim a blow at the General who had been called out of the apartment.

The one stricken fell heavily on the porch. There was a rush to the place with many lights.

"General!" cried the President, "are you wounded?"

"To the death, Randolph!" said General Hudson, as the arterial blood issued in jets from his neck.

"Who did this dastardly act?" demanded the President, endeavoring to raise the wounded General.

"The Italian," said General Hudson, in a feeble voice.

"The Italian! Seize the Italian!" cried the President to the Blue Caps, then arriving from all directions.

"Here's one!" cried Sergeant Bim, dragging Popoli forward. Popoli had been standing near the General.

"Not him—he was talking to me—and the other—another Italian, struck the blow—it was one of your Blue Caps, Randolph, a traitor—ah!" General Hudson, uttering these words with difficulty, sank back, and died in the arms of the President.

"He's gone!" said the President.

"Secure the assassin," cried General Blount, "or we shall be branded as murderers! Where are his aids? Where are the officers who attended him?"

"Fled!" said Crook.

"The rascals were capable of supposing we could do such an infamous deed!" said the old Commodore.

"Where is Sergeant Bim?" asked the President.

"Gone in pursuit of Cardini," said Col. Carleton. "No doubt he was the assassin. To-night he begged to be on duty an extra term. And now he is missing!"

"Colonel!" said the President, "send others in pursuit! Hasten! or Bim will slay the wretch! There may be papers in his possession—he might confess—you understand! Some one else had the motive—he was but the hireling slave—dispatch!" Then addressing the people crowding round, he continued, "Bear Hudson into the house, my friends. He was brave, and noble, and patriotic. Alas, Blount! the country has met with an irreparable loss!"

"Do not be distressed, sir," said Blount. "It is over. No one can censure you."

"Censure me! Certainly not. I fear not the breath of calumny. He was my friend and I his. The success of my most cherished designs depended, in some measure, on the preservation of his life. So far from desiring his destruction, I here declare that the one who caused this deed to be perpetrated was my worst enemy."

"Here is a paper which fell from his hand as we bore him in," said General Steel. "It was probably delivered just as the blow was struck."

It was from Ruffleton, and ran as follows:—

"Dear General—I think it probable the Resolutions will not pass the Convention. Be upon your guard. It may not be safe to leave your own lines. An attempt has been made on my life. Be careful, General. I will join you in a few days, and shall be happy to serve, the second in command, under the first General and the first man of the country. These, by my honest and faithful messenger, Signor Popoli. "RUFFLETON."

"I am Popoli, gentlemen," said the Italian, when the note was read, "and I hope you will believe me innocent."

"Who admitted you within the yard, sir?" demanded the President.

"One of the guards, sir. I said I had a letter for the General."

"Willy," said the President, "come to my closet for letters as soon as you are in readiness to start for the city.

I will send a communication to President Langdon, and inclose the note from Ruffleton."

When the President withdrew, General Blount sought Alice, who promenaded a balcony on the side of the house opposite to that where the assassination had been committed.

"I am glad," said he, "to find you calm on such a night as this."

"I am calm, General Blount," she replied; "but ill at ease. I cannot conceive why the attendants of Hudson fled so precipitately, unless they apprehended danger themselves from the hand that struck down their leader. And if this be so, they must suppose my father had some complicity in the guilt, and such a supposition—Oh, it is too dreadful to think that half the people should believe him guilty!"

"Nay; it is too absurd. Why should they not be quite as likely to suppose Crook or myself planned the infamous butchery?"

"Alas! they may! At all events there will not be wanting accusers of the South, who will make use of this occurrence for the accomplishment of their pecuniary or political purposes. But here is my father. He, too, is calm."

"Alice," said he, taking his daughter's hand tenderly, "be not distressed at this event. It will, in time, be manifest who was the guilty party. I can derive no benefit, nor you, General, nor the South, from General Hudson's fall?"

"On the contrary," said Blount, "if my suspicions prove well founded, it may result in evil to us all."

"Who is suspected?" asked Alice.

"I suspect Ruffleton," said Blount.

"If it should be Ruffleton," continued Alice, "what would become of Edith? And poor Mary is with her!"

"I have written Langdon," said Randolph, "in the event of insecurity in the city, to send Edith and Mary hither."

"And I," said Blount, "if the truce be ruptured, will transport my army hither, and share the fate of brave Crook!"

"Nay, mine also," said the President. "If the truce be broken, I shall no longer forbear to resist the aggressor.

But let us return to the parlor. I have ordered the removal of poor Hudson to his own head-quarters. They will hardly run away from their General—and he lifeless."

They descended from the balcony, and rejoined the company in the parlor, where intelligence was impatiently awaited from the city.

CHAPTER XXV.

THE TREASURE.

JACK BIM distanced all other pursuers. But Cardini sprang into a boat and pushed out from shore, just when Bim had arrived in hailing and pistol-shot distance. Bim, abandoning his horse, plunged into the water, firing at every step, until his pistols were empty. Then he was under the necessity of retracing his steps, for he could not swim. He soon found another skiff, however, and without demanding permission of the owner, took possession and rowed after the fugitive. It was too late. But still the Sergeant rowed on, resolved to overtake the dastardly assassin.

When Jack landed, he proceeded to the head-quarters of General Ruffleton. Bold as a lion, he disdained any disguise, notwithstanding his recent exploit in Sixth street must have constituted him a marked man. He recharged his revolvers under a tree in Independence Square and escaped the observation of General Balatrum's brigade, then dispersed in groups in the grounds of the Square.

Watching an opportunity, he crossed over, and obtained easy access, for the lock had not been repaired. Closing the door behind him, he had recourse to his match and candle, implements always in his possession. But he had not proceeded many steps before it struck him that instead of finding the object of his search with a lighted candle in his hand, he might be exposed to discovery himself.

"Out you go!" said he, blowing out the candle. "I know every foot of the way by heart. Gad, this is a lucky affair! I'm out of money!"

He turned to the left and felt for the orifice in the wall.

Having passed it, stepping cautiously, he pursued his way through several others, until he came to the apartment where he had found the imprisoned Mary. Here there was a dim light burning, and, sitting in a great chair near the centre table, he beheld the murderer panting from the effects of his recent exertions. Mrs. Punt was moving about the room.

Three times the Sergeant raised his pistol and aimed it steadily at the assassin's breast; but finally replaced it in his belt, unable to reconcile his conscience to the idea of taking life without giving his victim a chance to defend himself. And besides, he did not like to make a disturbance with the report of fire-arms. So he remained perfectly still in his place of concealment, to reconnoitre and await a more favorable opportunity of securing an equal combat with the assassin.

"Where is the General?" asked Cardini.

"At the State House," said Mrs. Punt. "If you want to see the General, why not go to Independence Hall?"

"I have reasons, Mrs. Punt."

"And you know my name. I never saw you before. But it must be all right. You got the card of admission from Signor Popoli?"

"Yes."

"You know I must be careful in admitting strangers. They threatened to confine me in the General's underground chamber because a great desperado and vagabond, named Jack Bim, once got in and carried off a crying girl."

"Has no one inquired for me?"

"Yes. General Balatrum asked if any one had come from the camp of General Hudson."

"How long since?"

"Not two minutes before you scratched at the front door."

"He will return soon. Give me some wine."

"What sort?"

"Let it be brandy. That's stronger."

"La's a mercy!" said Mrs. Punt, seeing blood on the hand and garments of the Italian, when placing the brandy on the table.

"What's the matter?" cried Cardini, springing up, and placing his hand on his dagger.

"The blood! You're covered with blood!"

"Is that all! A little water will wash it off. Show me to a basin, and then give me one of the General's shirts."

"La! How you order! But you do it in such a commanding way, I'm afraid to refuse. I hope, sir, the blood ain't—"

"Yes, it is. Ask no questions."

"The water's in the next house, in the hall, to the left of that opening. Shall I light the gas?"

"No; I can wash in the dark. Have the shirt ready." Saying this, he rose from the chair and passed through the aperture in the wall.

"Be easy, and don't make a fuss," said Bim, encircling the slight form of the Italian with one of his gigantic arms, and gagging him with the other. Not the slightest noise ensued. Cardini trembled in submission when Bim whispered his name in his ear.

The Sergeant lifted up his victim, and bore him to a room at the northern end of the row. Here he paused, and stood the little man on his feet.

"Now, Signor," said he, "I'm going to strike a light; but while I'm doing it, you might stab me in the dark. So, I'll just hold both your hands in one of mine, and with the other take your pistols and dagger." This accomplished, Jack drew his match and ignited his candle.

"Sergeant, what are you going to do with me?" asked Cardini.

"Signor, the first thing I must do is to take an oath that I won't kill you—at this time. If I don't, I can't answer for the consequences. Before this looking-glass, I do solemnly swear that I will not kill Signor Cardini this night, unless I'm compelled, to save my own life, or to prevent his escape—so help me ——! Signor, now you're safe. One of the Blue Caps to be a traitor! D—— you! it's well I took that oath. But I'll forget you ever were a Blue Cap;" he continued, snatching the cap from the Italian's head and throwing it into a corner. "Let it be a bed for rats! And you have the devilish impudence to look me in the face and ask what I intend to do with you!—you, who have been pretending to serve two masters!"

"Sergeant," said the Italian, "you did the same thing. You served both Ruffleton and the President."

"But not at the same time, Signor. That makes all the

difference in the world. But why did Ruffleton hire you to kill General Hudson?"

"I haven't said he did, Sergeant."

"But you *will* say so, because it *is* so."

"I will say nothing about it."

"But you shall! Confess the whole truth in a minute, or I'll strangle you."

"Remember your oath, Sergeant."

"I ought not to have sworn aloud! Very well; I can put you where nobody will find you till this night is past. Can you tell me whether anybody's down there?" pointing at the hearth.

"Down where?"

"Oh, you don't know anything about it. Luckily, I am one who helped to dig the dungeon, and know all about its twistings and turnings." Saying this, Bim touched a spring in the fireplace and the hearth-stone flew up in front, turning on hidden hinges, and disclosed a dark and dismal vault, in which there was a ladder. "Go down first," said Bim. "Obey me, or I'll pitch you down, and that won't be breaking my oath; if you die it will be killing yourself."

Cardini descended very reluctantly. When they reached the bottom, Bim, with the candle in his hand, led the way until they entered a dry chamber, supposed to be under the centre of the street. This room was walled round with massive stone, to which there was an iron door that could only be fastened and unfastened on the outside. It was perforated at the top for the admission of air, but no particle of the light of heaven penetrated it. Bim ignited the wick of an iron lamp suspended from the ceiling, and pointed to a barrel of crackers and a keg of smoked herrings.

"There, Cardini," said he, "is provision for two months. In the corner you will find a leaden pipe that will supply water. Here are some old clothes. There is a stool to sit on and meditate. Think of your crimes and repent."

"Sergeant," said Cardini, "have you not taken the lives of many men?"

"In fair fight, I grant you; but never one in any other way. I confess I killed Major Trapp without giving him a chance to shoot me. But he had a revolver in his hand, and had just scaled the temple of my friend. And now, good night, Cardini. You will not need a jailor. There is some straw in one of the corners, and there would have been a bible if the general had permitted." Saying this, Bim fastened the door and departed.

"And now," said he, as he closed the trap-stone at the hearth, "I must replenish my finances. I have only three cents remaining." He proceeded without delay to the attic room where he had left Solomon Mouser to watch his gold. And having some curiosity to see how the old Jew passed his time, he endeavored to make his appearance before him without any premonition of his approach. It was in vain, for when he burst into the room he saw the closet door close quickly after the retreating Jew.

"Come out, old Tuppenny!" said he—"it's nobody but me. I thought I'd just slip up softly to see how my affairs were attended to in my absence. Come out, I say—it's *me*—Jack Bim."

"As I am a mortal man," said the Jew, coming forth. "I feared it was a burglar!"

"I suppose the Bank is all right?"

"No—no—no! We made an error."

"What? See here—Tuppenny! If any of my money is gone—"

"Gone? All that is gone you took away yourself, except a few cents—I mean dimes—I bought bread and cheese with, and a pitchfork to fight off the rats."

"Oh d— the dimes! I don't care for even a few dollars. But what did you mean by 'no! no! no!' and 'an error?'" demanded Bim, imitating the Jew's voice.

"I'll show you," said the Jew, exhibiting several scraps of paper covered with figures. "If you will sit down and go through these calculations, you will see that we failed to carry one, and that it made a difference of one hundred dollars. So you have my receipt for that amount over and above the actual sum in my custody."

"Figures and calculations! Why, it would take me a whole day. I won't look at them. But I'll correct the error."

"I thought you would! I knew you would give me back ten eagles."

"You didn't know any such thing. But I will do this: I'll credit you on the receipt with a hundred dollars more than I take this time."

"Mercy on me! And is all that gold gone?"

"Shell out!" said Bim.

"It stabs me to the heart—but you must have your will."

"Of course I'll have my will, and it's my will to have my money. But what difference does it make to you?"

"What difference? I'll tell you. I charge the slightest commission for the safe custody of the treasure, and the more the sum is diminished the less will be my compensation. Don't you understand?"

"Not very clearly. But was that in the bargain?"

"It was the same thing."

"I don't remember it. But what do you call the slightest commission?"

"Only the one-tenth of one per cent., *per diem*."

"One-tenth of one per cent! That's only ten cents on the hundred dollars."

"Exactly."

"How many hundred years would it take, at that rate, to eat up the whole?"

"Thrifty Jacob! Would you wait till I made the calculation?"

"No—and I've no time to spare—so shell out! I'll take care that you don't get it all."

"How much will you take from me?"

"Take from *you*. I don't like the word, old Tuppenny. It's too soon to talk that way. Wait till *my* capital is consumed, and when I come to borrow *your* money——"

"I'll lend you as much as you want! I'll accommodate you now! You shall have thousands! And without usury!"

"Well, there is warm blood in a Jew, after all!"

"We are a persecuted race! Borrow of me, sir, and then your deposit won't be diminished at all—and you won't have to alter the receipt you hold. You will just sign me a little note, and that will be all. No security will be demanded——"

"That sounds like nonsense to me, Tuppenny—*security*, when you have my gold! But no matter—I'll try it for a thousand. Shell out, for, I repeat, I'm in a hurry!"

This was done with alacrity, very much apparently to their mutual satisfaction. But Bim, pausing suddenly when departing, as if struck by a new idea, asked the Jew if the thousand dollars were not taken from the gold deposited in the coffee bag. The Jew confessed they were, but reminded the Sergeant that the receipt in his possession was for the whole sum, and not minus the amount subtracted. He said he would replace the thousand dollars immediately from his funds deposited with Moses Abrahams. This, although it puzzled the rather obtuse Bim, seemed to satisfy him, and he strode away with a grave physiognomy.

CHAPTER XXVI.

HUDSON'S SUCCESSOR.

THE uproar in the vicinity of Independence Hall arose from a rumor that General Hudson had been assassinated in the camp of President Randolph. It soon reached the Convention, and produced, as was natural, a very great commotion. Colonel Maller, an officer who had accompanied General Hudson to the quarters of President Randolph, came in, and beckoned to General Ruffleton, then surrounded by many of his friends and partisans. And about the same time Wiry Willy obtained admission, and placed a communication from President Randolph in the hand of the President of the Convention.

For several minutes the proceedings of the Convention were completely interrupted. President Langdon was observed to change color, and to clasp his forehead with his hand. But a moment after his composure was recovered, and despatching a brief note by Willy to Edith, his official demeanor was resumed with dignity. Calling the Convention to order, he stood up and read a brief narrative of the melancholy occurrence at Red Bank, as written by President Randolph, as well as the letter found in the hand of the dying General.

During the reading of these papers General Ruffleton returned to his seat, followed by several of his partisans,

A pause ensued, and for a long time no one seemed bold enough to make a motion, or to suggest any action.

At length Mr. Monmouth, a delegate from New Jersey, moved an adjournment. This was followed by an extraordinary ebullition of derisive opposition, and the motion was lost by a majority of five votes.

"Mr. President," said Monmouth, "I move an adjournment, because I see no disposition to institute any action."

"You *will* see a disposition to act!" said Mr. Virus, a zealous partisan of General Ruffleton. "I can well understand why the partisans of the Southern Randolph in this body should desire an adjournment——"

"Sir!" said Monmouth, "do not insinuate that this foul deed had the privity and sanction of President Randolph!"

"I judge him by the evidences of his guilt! Of that hereafter."

"The gentlemen will confine themselves to the business before the Convention," said President Langdon.

"Mr. President," said Mr. V., "that business will come legitimately before us. But, in the meantime, let us proceed to the nomination of General Hudson's successor. I propose General Ruffleton."

"Mr. President," said Monmouth, "I again move an adjournment."

"No! no!" cried many voices, and nearly half the members sprang to their feet.

"Then let there be a call of the house," said Monmouth. "Several of my friends are absent—*mysteriously* absent."

"Whom do *you* accuse," asked Mr. Virus, at the instigation of General Ruffleton.

"I accuse General Ruffleton!" cried Mr. Carbon, one of the members whose absence had been alluded to, rushing forward with torn garments. "Yes, I accuse *you*, sir!" he continued, pointing to Ruffleton, whose face was red with anger. "It was *your* messenger that summoned me away, and it was *your* soldiers who withheld me, and who now prevent my colleagues from returning to their seats."

Here the President's hammer imposed order.

"Gentlemen," said he, "let us remember that we assume to be the representatives of virtuous freemen. The motion now pending is for an adjournment, and it must have precedence. But before I put the question, I would remark, in view of the proposition to nominate a General-in-Chief in place of the one who has just fallen, that it is not clear to my mind, nor was it at the time of General Hudson's selection, that any power has been conferred upon us to appoint military officers. I think we were sent here merely to represent public opinion. At all events, let us not act with precipitation."

"I demand the vote on my question," said Monmouth.

It was decided in the negative by a majority of four.

"I ask a vote on the nomination of General Hudson's successor," said Mr. Virus.

"Excuse me," said the President. "I would rather not put it to the vote—at least to-night, and in any other than a full house. I know this proceeding is not in accordance with parliamentary rules; but if I cannot be gratified, I will resign."

"It is not in accordance with your duty, sir," said Col. Maller. "You are the tool of Randolph——"

"Order! order!" cried many.

"Remove that man!" said the President to the doorkeeper.

"At your peril!" said the Colonel, drawing his sword.

"The chair is unoccupied," said President Langdon, rising, and retiring from the chamber with dignity. A moment after, all the members who coincided with Langdon rose up, and were about to follow their President, when General Ruffleton stamped violently on the floor, and this was immediately followed by the entrance of a body of soldiers, with fixed bayonets, led by General Balatrum.

"And *you* would be the Commander-in-Chief?" said Monmouth, turning to Ruffleton. "Say, Dictator or Tyrant!"

"I am a true Northern man," said Ruffleton, smiling in his blandest manner; "and will not see the people sold to the Southern assassin, Randolph!"

"It is false!" cried Monmouth. "Randolph is no assassin. But you ——"

"Die, d—d traitor!" cried Maller, rushing forward and stabbing Monmouth to the heart. He fell and expired beside his chair, while consternation seized the rest.

"The vote! The vote!" cried Virus. "All in favor of General Ruffleton succeeding to the chief command, say aye!"

14

This was responded to unanimously by all who voted.

"Gentlemen," said Ruffleton, "I thank you. I will immediately repair to the head-quarters of my murdered predecessor, and either avenge his death or share his fate."

"I move, next," said Virus, "that this Convention do now adjourn, to meet again as soon as practicable, in the city of New York." This, too, was carried by a similar vote.

CHAPTER XXVII.

IMPENDING PERILS.

It was high tide. A skiff containing three persons lay upon the water at the Chestnut street wharf. A cloud of inky hue was rising in the west, and the lightning ever and anon revealed the sad and pallid countenances of the occupants of the boat.

"Father," said Edith, for the three consisted of Langdon, his daughter, and Mary Penford, "I fear they will not permit Willy to return." Mr. Langdon had sent him to the State House for intelligence.

"They might not, Edith, if they knew him; but he will escape observation."

"I do not fear for Willy," said Mary, "for his Maker, in whom we trust, will guard him."

"Mercy! oh, what terrific lightning!" exclaimed Edith, as several brilliant flashes, in quick succession, illuminated the scene.

"Pray let me have the oars," said Mary, "and I will row out a few yards from the shore. I saw several ill-looking men near the bow of yonder ship." And while she did so, a loud peal of thunder smote upon her ears, and poor Edith took refuge in the arms of her father.

"Edith," said he, "where is your courage? My brave child, now is the trying time. Brace yourself to withstand the worst possible alarms of anarchy on earth and of tempests in the sky."

"I will, father," said she.

"There they are!" said some one, in a full, manly voice.

"Who was that?" whispered Mary, peering in vain towards the shore, now obscured in darkness.

"No matter," said Langdon. "It could not have had reference to us. Probably it was a fisherman."

Another flash of lightning, while their eyes were directed towards the shore, did not reveal any human being.

"Here we are," said the same voice, and the next instant the prow of another skiff touched their boat at the stern.

"Willy!" exclaimed Mary. "How you frightened us!"

"Who is that with you?" asked Mr. Langdon, another flash of lightning showing the herculean form that accompanied Willy.

"It is Sergeant Bim," said Willy, "as true a friend as ever lived."

"Or died," said Bim; "and I would die to save or serve any here."

"We thought we were watched and followed," said Willy; "and so we determined not to come down Chestnut street. At the Arch street wharf we found this boat, which is larger and stronger than the one you are in."

"You did well," said Langdon, "and we will get into it. Our baggage can remain in this, and we will tow it over. Let us go to the shore—and do you keep watch, Bim, whilst the transfer is made."

"I'll answer for your safety," said Bim. "I have two revolvers, a sword and a bowie knife."

"They are assaulting the Federal troops at the Mint and Custom House," said Willy, in reply to an interrogatory of Mr. Langdon, upon hearing discharges of fire-arms.

The party was soon bounding out from the shore, under the impulsion of the strong arms of Bim and Willy. The tide was on a stand, and the water smooth and motionless. The dark cloud loomed up nearer the zenith, and its forked lightnings were succeeded by stunning explosions of thunder at shorter intervals. But yet there was no wind to ruffle the surface of the river.

And in such a moment Wiry Willy narrated the occurrences in the Convention, subsequently to the abandonment of the chair by Mr. Langdon. He said that Ruffleton had dispatched a file of soldiers to the hotel for the purpose of seizing him, and that his escape had been effected just in time to avoid, perhaps, the fate of Mr. Monmouth.

"Alas! what would have been your lot, father," said Edith, "if you had remained in the city?"

"I know not, my child. But I would have remained in the city, if you had not been there. If you were only in some place of security I should not care much what my fate might be, since I behold the people bent on the destruction of the finest Government that ever existed under heaven."

"And now we are wanderers, fugitives from our own countrymen!" said Edith. "We, father, around whom so many friends and flatterers used to throng! A Senator of the United States, and his daughter, flying in the night from the people who once delighted to honor them! Oh, my country!"

"May heaven save it and us!" said Mary.

"Yes, fugitives, on the waste of waters, without shelter, and exposed to the pitiless storm!" continued Edith.

"I will be revenged on 'em!" said Bim.

"Do you not think, sir," asked Willy, addressing Mr. Langdon, "that we had better row to the Jersey shore before the heavy rain comes on?"

"No, Willy," said he, "we might fall into the hands of Ruffleton's myrmidons, far more cruel than the raging elements!"

"We'll do our best, sir," said Bim, exerting his gigantic powers, "to row you down before the worst of the storm reaches us."

"Oh, yes—never mind the rain," said Edith.

"It may not rain at all—or very little," said Mary. "I have often seen such dark clouds expend themselves before they spread over the sky."

Soon after a few large drops pattered on the surface of the river; and as they fell, the incessant flashes of lightning caused them to resemble showers of sparkling diamonds.

"Father," said Edith, "if our lot would have been uncertain, remaining in the city, is it not equally dubious flying to the army menaced by General Ruffleton?"

"We are not flying to the Southern army, my child. It is the camp of President Randolph we are approaching. I will not be identified with either section. I have determined upon my course. I shall adhere to the Government of the United States."

"But will not Ruffleton attack the President himself?"

"It may be so—but all the Northern people are not fanatics. If they were we should be ruined irretrievably. Ruffleton may attack the President, but Randolph will triumph in the end."

"Amen!" said Bim. "And all I ask is to have an opportunity to strike his enemies."

"We are approaching the landing," said Willy; "and I saw a boat push out from shore, rowed by sailors. There it is again. I saw the uniform of the Commodores. We might go with them to one of the United States steamers."

"No," said Mr. Langdon. "Mary was right. The cloud is passing round the horizon, and we shall have no rain. Keep straight on unless they hail us." These words had hardly been uttered before they were hailed, and a few moments after the Commodores were near them, and demanded the news from the city.

"D—n me," said the old Commodore, "if Ruffleton is not acting in concert with the British! We'll soon have work enough on our hands. That explains the motions of John Bull down yonder."

"They have signalled us," said Commodore Early to Mr. Langdon, "that the British ships seem preparing for action, and hence our return to the fleet at this hour."

The tars resumed their labor, and the boats were immediately flying asunder. The fugitives soon after landed in safety. They proceeded without delay to the house occupied by the President, situated midway between the hostile armies. An officer of the guard dispatched information in advance, so that when the fugitives arrived, Randolph, Alice, Blount, and Crook, came forth and received them on the porch, and conducted them into the parlor. Alice and Edith long remained locked in each other's arms, and the poor orphan, Mary, was not less cordially received.

"Langdon," said the President, after hearing a recital of the transactions in the city, "you have done well to abandon the conspirators. Twelve months will not elapse before a large majority of the Northern people will condemn them, precisely as the conservative citizens of the South withhold their approbation from the invasion of the North by our friend Crook."

"I'm a fire-eater," said Crook, "and represent fire-eaters alone. Blount represents the majority. I am satisfied with what I have accomplished, and am now willing to abandon this free soil for ever, according to my instructions and the stipulations with Hudson."

"You will not be *permitted* to retire peaceably," said Blount. "Ruffleton will not let you off on such terms."

"Then I'll fight!" said Crook.

"I fear there is no other alternative," continued Blount. "Ah! do you not hear the shouts in the Northern camp? Doubtless General Ruffleton, their usurping leader, has arrived! The war is only about to begin. And, Crook, when he ruptures the truce, I am with you!"

"Before me, General!" said Crook. "I will follow and obey you!"

"And I cannot be an idle spectator!" said the President. "I have been a mediator between the sections, and if pledges be violated by either of them, I shall be absolved from my neutrality. I will either keep the peace, or endeavor to repel the aggressor!"

"Mr. President," said Blount, "Ruffleton's purpose cannot be doubtful. Before the expiration of twenty-four hours, he will commence the attack upon us all. His numerical force is superior to ours combined, and every hour will bring him accessions. The calumny in relation to the death of Hudson will be used to precipitate upon us all the prejudiced combatants in the North. And neither you nor Crook can evacuate Jersey with impunity. I will set out immediately and transport my army hither. I will relieve you, or die with you!"

"And what will become of you, Alice, Edith, and Mary?" said the President. "I have decided what must be done. Langdon, I confide my daughter to your care. Take her with Edith and Mary to the District of Columbia. You can occupy the Presidential mansion, or your own, whichever you may prefer."

"Father," said Alice, "you have commanded, and I obey.

But I should have been content to partake of your perils and successes."

"I know it, Alice. But you could be of no service in the scenes about to ensue. Blount will see that you are landed in safety on the Southern shore of the Delaware, and one hundred of the Blue Caps shall accompany you, and remain under your command."

Not many hours afterwards Blount and Langdon conducted the ladies to the barge provided for their reception; and they were landed in safety on the friendly soil of the South just as the first rosy streaks of morning gilded the sky.

Mr. Langdon, at the solicitation of Alice, determined to occupy the country mansion, which had been the President's head-quarters. The purpose was two-fold; first, to recover from the effects of the recent fatigues, loss of rest, and painful excitement; and second, to await the issue of the fearful collision in New Jersey.

Having first embarked his forces on the immense flotilla which he had long been accumulating, either for the purpose of facilitating the withdrawal of General Crook from New Jersey, or promptly to fly to his relief, General Blount mounted his horse, with an intention of making a hasty visit to the mansion, before leaving, perhaps for ever, the friendly soil of his nativity. And it was likewise his purpose, if circumstances should favor his suit, to renew the proposition for an immediate union with Edith. But just when he was setting out, a messenger arrived from Red Bank, with demands for his immediate presence. He turned the head of his war-horse towards the steamer in waiting, and with a sigh relinquished the new-born hope that had just sprung into existence. And before the boat had pushed out from land, Sergeant Bim came galloping from the mansion, flourishing Alice's leave of absence for five days, during which he had a presentiment that there would be a harvest of fighting.

CHAPTER XXVIII.

NEGOTIATIONS.

President Randolph sat alone in his chamber at the farm-house. He was in the act of breaking the seal of a letter just received from a friendly correspondent in the camp of the enemy. This was Major S——, an aide-de-camp of the late General Hudson. Major S—— resolved to dissemble for the purpose of serving his benefactor and his country, and Ruffleton besought the Major to retain his position in the staff. The letter ran as follows:

"*Ruffleton has conspired with the British Government for the overthrow of the Republic. The latter has stipulated to furnish money, ships, and men, if need be. But time will be required to consummate the treaty. More British ships are daily expected. Ruffleton will temporize with you. He must gain time. Many thousands of fanatics are on the way hither to join him. Although he will be apparently reasonable in his demands, he has no intention to permit either Crook or yourself to withdraw without a battle. His purpose is to destroy you both, and he will be in readiness at any hour to begin the assault. He has sent agents to charter or seize the shipping at the wharves, and the steam ferry boats.*"

This was written in characters, for which the President alone had the key.

"General Valiant," said the President, in a low voice. A door opened, and the General entered from an adjoining room. "General," continued the President, with his usual calm smile, "I want a spy or deserter."

"Wiry Willy?" asked the General.

"Did he not go with Mary Penford and the rest?"

"No, sir. He said you did not name him as one of the party."

"I did not; but I thought he would go. Yes; he will answer."

"I will have him sent immediately."

The General returned to his apartment. The Proclamations had been struck off in the camp, a press being kept by Randolph for such purposes. The President, having been applied to by the Governor of New Jersey, who was conservative in his politics, and it being impracticable to assemble the Legislature, for aid in the suppression of domestic violence, now required all insurgents to return to their homes, and to abstain from the commission of unlawful acts, or else they would be declared the enemies of the country, and proceeded against in accordance with the powers conferred on him by the Constitution of the United States.

And in a supplementary notification, the country was informed that in pursuance of the decree of the Richmond Convention, General Crook was upon the eve of retiring from the State of New Jersey; and, through the mediation of the Federal Executive, General Hudson had agreed upon a basis for an armistice, having that object in view, when an assassin, supposed to have been employed by some one averse to measures of pacification, put an end to his existence.

"Willy," said the President, when the faithful messenger appeared, "can you go, without risk, into Ruffleton's camp?"

"Oh, yes, sir. A friend of mine in his army has told him how near they came to hanging me at New Castle."

"And that event, that lucky event, will serve you now?"

"I think so, sir. I am willing to make the venture."

"Very well. You can give Ruffleton some intelligence that will please him, and inspire his confidence. Say to him the 30,000 prisoners taken in Maryland are now in Sussex county, Delaware, loosely guarded, and with the slightest assistance from the British fleet they could be landed in a few hours on the Jersey side of the water. Why do you stare, Will?"

"Because, sir, what you have said is precisely so!"

"Certainly. My diplomacy is without falsehood. I have two objects, Willy. One to get rid of a troublesome mob of useless vagabonds; the other, to tempt the British to commit an act of intervention. And, further, it will serve to convince the Northern people that the prisoners have not been massacred, as the newspapers report."

"I will start immediately, sir," responded Willy, withdrawing.

A moment after, General Valiant returned, accompanied by General Crook.

"Well, General," said Randolph, "everything conspires to convince me that we are on the eve of a battle. In the course of two or three days more, Ruffleton will have an immense force—perhaps 300,000 men!"

"We shall beat them," said Valiant.

"Certainly we shall," said Crook, "with the aid of Randolph's horse and artillery. But Hudson's men fought like the d—l! My killed and wounded, disabled and missing, amounted to 25,000."

"And Hudson's loss was equally as great," said the President.

"I should have beaten him, Randolph, if it had not been for you."

"His apparition!" said Valiant. "He struck not a blow—fired not a gun."

"Neither did he strike at Bladensburg."

"Crook," said the President, "I interposed, partly, to save you from destruction. If you had beaten Hudson that day, the next week you would have been enveloped by half a million of Northern avengers, and then I should not have been able to save you. *Now*, the conservative men of the North, who approved my conduct, will be influenced by me. They will regard my proclamations, and keep aloof. Nine-tenths of Ruffleton's host of warriors are desperate fanatics, but they will fight like demons."

"All except the Quakers," said Crook. "I have five hundred of them prisoners, and all the morning we have been trying to organize them into a regiment; but in vain. They would die first."

"Have you tried to make them work on the entrenchments?" asked the President.

"No, sir, I didn't think of that. Excuse me a few minutes." Saying this, Crook hastened out.

"The cotton lords," said Randolph, "can never forgive the Quakers. And the Quakers of New Jersey will remember Crook. But here is Wiry Willy, returned already. Well? They did not hang you?"

"No, sir," said Willy. "General Ruffleton was in too fine a humor for that. He has sent off an express to the British Admiral; and he said, *in my hearing*, that in a day or two he would withdraw the Northern army from New Jersey, and confirm the agreement subscribed by General Hudson."

"Enough!" said the President. "Here is a note for General Blount. Lose no time, Willy, in placing it in his hands, and he will not delay in coming to our aid. We must be prepared to fight like lions," he added, as Crook returned and Willy departed.

CHAPTER XXIX.

NEGOTIATIONS WITH RANDOLPH.

General Ruffleton's head-quarters were not more than two miles distant from Randolph's. He was now in possession of the chief command of the Northern army—the largest body of armed men ever before collected on the Continent, and its volume was swelling every hour by the arrival of the enemies of the South and of slavery, from the densely populated New England States.

The General-in-Chief was seated in a magnificent tent, comprising many apartments. He was reading one of the proclamations of the President. These documents were nailed to the trees, the walls, and the telegraph posts. But Ruffleton had no fear of the patriotic people.

"Summers," said he, when his fair attendant appeared before him, "say to his lordship that I have received important intelligence, and would be glad to see him." Summers drew aside a gorgeous curtain and vanished. A moment after Lord Slysir entered.

"I attend you, General," said his Lordship, occupying the seat at the table pointed to by Ruffleton.

"I have just learned," said the General, with a triumphant smile, "that all the prisoners taken by Crook at Bladensburg are on the coast of Sussex county, Delaware, and within sight of the British fleet. Now, your Lordship can permit me to dispatch an order to Admiral Bang, for their transference across the bay."

"My dear sir," said his Lordship, much startled, "have you reflected that such a step would rupture our web of diplomacy? Is it not determined that the release of these prisoners is to be a *conditio sine quâ non* in the prolongation of the armistice? And as it would be impossible for the demand to be granted, you know the retention of the prisoners is to be the pretext and justification for a renewal of hostilities."

"That is all very true, my Lord, as it regards the negotiations; but in point of *fact*, the escape of the prisoners will not only be a personal triumph for myself, and gratifying to the country, but it will serve as an indubitable manifestation of the co-operation of Great Britain."

"Unquestionably. It would be a most palpable demonstration; a deliberate laying aside of the mask; it would be, in short, a very bold initiative, and henceforth the identification of Her Britannic Majesty with your cause would be apparent to the whole world."

"True. And does your Lordship hesitate to make it so?"

"By no means! But what would become of the requisition for a release of the prisoners, after their escape had been effected?"

"Neither Randolph nor Crook will know anything about their escape until after the battle. If your lordship will co-operate in this matter, well; if not——"

"I will write the order immediately. In two minutes your messenger shall have it." Saying this Lord Slysir, overruled by the General, withdrew to his own apartment.

When this business was disposed of, Summers again glided in, and announced the presence of a deputation of Quakers. The committee was introduced, at the head of which appeared the victim of General Crook, Samuel C——.

"Now, gentlemen," said Ruffleton, "I have not a moment to spare."

"Thee should remember," said Samuel, "that it is in answer to the prayers of good philanthropists that this mighty host has been gathered together for the liberation of the enslaved."

"Very well—grant all that. What next?"

"The Lord will surely prosper thee according to thy merits. We have to say the spirit mourns over the vi lent death of John Monmouth."

"This is nonsense. Can you allege that I ordered or sanctioned the act?"

"Thee still keeps Colonel Maller in thy employ. John was one of our most worthy citizens, and his murder is causing many people to slacken their zeal."

"This is ill-timed, gentlemen, when, perhaps, we are on the eve of a decisive battle. But why have you said nothing about the assassination of General Hudson?"

"The hand which dealt the fatal blow on that good man, has not been made manifest, as in the case of thy officer; but still the spirit grieves. Yet other matters brought us hither. We ask protection from thy soldiers. Wherever they have passed over the land it is a waste—a desolation. Our farms are destroyed, our smoke houses pillaged, and our animals driven off."

"The soldiers of Liberty must eat," said Ruffleton.

"They have burned our fences—"

"And they must cook their victuals," continued the General. "But have they not receipted for everything? All will be paid for."

"And so they told our fathers during the revolutionary war."

"The country was poor then—it is rich now. Send us your horses; and if you will not fight yourselves, your shot guns."

"Another grievance we have to complain to thee about," pursued Samuel, "is the tyrannical conduct of thy General Balatrum, who forces our young people into the ranks of his brigade, and swears, in vile language, that they shall fight against the slave-driving Southerners, when our people never did and never will lift a deadly weapon in mortal strife."

"Have not your people repeatedly said," asked Ruffleton, "that even if blood should cover the face of the earth, the enslaved must be set free?"

"Thee quotes us correctly."

"Then how is blood to flow without fighting? You say the negro slave must be set at liberty, even if it costs oceans of blood; but when the moment comes to strike for the freedom of the slave, you are not willing to fight! Fools! do you not know that slavery itself is the conclusion of conquest, and that only those who fight can ever be masters?

Having stimulated a civil war, if you will not fight, depend upon it, you will become the slaves of the uncompunctious combatants!"

"Thee cannot terrify us. We may suffer, but we cannot be made afraid. Another grievance is the conduct of thy Colonel Maller in organizing a regiment of the free colored people—"

"What! and you object to that, too?"

"Thee must know that these people, having been liberated by our agents, are under our training, to become members of our society."

"But *they* are eager enough to fight! Come with me," said the General; "this is the hour I was to review them. Colonel Maller will put them through their paces."

Saying this he led the Quakers into a meadow where there were a thousand negroes on parade.

The sun shone down from a cloudless sky, and the day was the hottest of summer. The effects of the heat were soon visible on the countenances of the General and the deputation of Quakers; and the *effluvium* in the vicinity of the negroes was so dense that they involuntarily retreated a distance from the regiment.

"And such are the specimens of humanity," said Ruffleton to Samuel, "that you would put on an equal footing with the white man! It was not their masters, but their Maker that made them thus."

"I agree with thee, General," said Samuel, in a low voice, turning aside his face.

"The d—l you do! And yet—"

"Pray do not speak so loud, General. But I tell thee that I differ with our people about the equality of races."

And as they gazed at the sooty regiment, performing their military exercises, several crows, that were flying over the meadow, upon entering the deleterious atmosphere, flapped their wings wildly, and fell to the earth quite dead.

"Thee is not aware, perhaps, General," said Samuel, "that the odor of the negro is fatal to crows. I have seen them die from that cause several times."

"I hope it may prove equally fatal to the enemy," said Ruffleton, abruptly dismissing the deputation and returning to his tent.

He had Mr. Virus summoned. Mr. V. was his protegé and dependent, an oleaginous lawyer, who, with the helping hand of his patron, had graduated in all the courts, from the lowest to the highest, making money, and finally achieving that species of influence and importance which the notoriety of success never fails to confer in large cities. He was now the General's chief diplomatist—his Talleyrand—and his services were to be immediately put in requisition.

"Virus," said Ruffleton, "we understand each other. I am to be the master of this new world, and you my chief minister."

"You will succeed, sir," said Virus.

"If so, you will be the first in my confidence, and my second in power. The service now required will test your diplomacy. You will have to cope with Randolph, a man of universal genius. The grand object of your mission is *to keep the Southern army on this side of the river until I am ready to annihilate it, and all its allies and defenders.* For this purpose it will be necessary to meet Randolph, Crook, and Blount, and disavow any authority to treat with either of them separately. The demand for the restitution of the specie must be urged, and restitution of the prisoners taken at Bladensburg must be insisted on. The first, you know, is impracticable, and the last will be obviated in a few hours. Nevertheless these are secrets of which they are not to suppose you can have any knowledge. The object is to protract the truce until my arrangements are completed. If, however, Randolph can be detached from his Southern friends, we shall make speedy work of the latter. He has now 25,000 splendid horse, and 75,000 well drilled infantry, besides many cannon! Bring him and Crook in collision. Why not? It seems to me that a skilful diplomatist might produce a quarrel between Randolph and Crook. What do you think?"

"With any other than Randolph, success would be certain. Crook would quarrel, but—"

"Do your utmost. Blount is a listener—but terrible in the field. Be plausible and *conciliatory.* We must not forget the *public*, with whom Randolph has still some influence. You may intimate to Randolph, that nothing less than the total annihilation of the Southern armies, will be likely to avert an alliance between the North and Great

Britain, which would result in universal emancipation and the adoption of another form of Government. Tell him that I, alone, have the ability to adjust amicably the affair of the capture and detention of the British Minister. And whatever they propose, whatever may be agreed on, remember *nothing is to be consummated.*. The object is to protract the negotiations until I am in readiness to act."

Virus, bearing a flag, was, an hour afterwards, conducted to the head-quarters of Randolph, where Blount and Crook joined the Conference.

"Well, sir," said Randolph, "I see your General is not inclined to pay attention to the President's Proclamation."

"I assure you," responded Virus, "he was attentively perusing it when I left the head-quarters."

"Oh, yes," said Crook, "the President's messages are read everywhere."

"But who regards them?" added the President. "Let us proceed to business, gentlemen; and, as you seem to desire it, I will open the case. Here are we, the Southern and the Federal armies, some two hundred thousand strong, facing the Northern army of three, and perhaps soon to be four hundred thousand men; and, what is worse, perhaps, the parties of the first part have a broad river in their rear, to attempt a passage of which, without the forbearance or permission of the party of the second part, might subject them to great sacrifices. In the next place, the parties of the first part are desirous of withdrawing beyond the river, and they await the announcement of the conditions imposed by the party of the second part, to wit:"

"Now proceed, Virus," said Crook, laughing heartily.

"By your leave, gentlemen," said Blount, "I would ask the negotiator, whether it is the purpose of his principal to disavow the agreement signed by his predecessor."

"I am glad the question is propounded," said Virus: "and am happy to say that General Ruffleton has not the slightest purpose to annul any of the stipulations agreed to by his lamented predecessor. But—"

"I thought there would be a *but*," said Crook.

"But the Convention was not completed. It was not ratified."

"Are you prepared, then," asked the President, "to re-affirm the stipulations?"

"So far as I know them, I am."

"It was mutually agreed," said Randolph, "that the Southern troops should be withdrawn from the free States, and they were to be exempted from molestation by the Northern army."

"Very true," said Virus; "and it remained only for the Convention to ratify the agreement."

"The Southern Convention," said Blount, "had already agreed to it, and actually instructed General Crook to retire from New Jersey."

"And," said Crook, "the Northern Convention would have responded affirmatively had it not been for the lobby influence."

"In the course of a day or two," said Virus, "the Northern Convention, now assembling in New York, will express their sentiments. If I am not misinformed, however, it was the expectation of the Convention that the contribution levied in New York would be reimbursed."

"To that I should make no objection," said the President.

"We deem it but fair reprisal for a portion of the slave property of which the South has been despoiled by the abolitionists who have been harbored in New York," said Blount.

"And," said Crook, "as that point has been deferred to me; as I levied the fine and collected it; and have it in my possession; all I have to say is, if it be made an ultimatum, hostilities must recommence immediately."

"I have not said—nor am I prepared to say—it is an ultimatum," responded Virus.

"If you should be prepared to say it," said Crook, "you ought also to be prepared to fight."

"Enough blood has been shed already," said Virus; "and I trust my mission is to be one of peace. Nevertheless I must report the answer to my principal. The next thing demanded is the liberation of the prisoners taken at Bladensburg."

"That matter, too," said Crook, "is placed exclusively in my hands. The Governors of Maryland and Delaware did not make a requisition on the Federal Executive to repel an invasion, or to suppress domestic violence—but gave me authority to do it. I did it, then, in the name of

Maryland, and have received a commission from her Legislature, in addition to the one conferred by the Convention. Therefore, the prisoners are in the custody of Maryland and Delaware. Without a violation of the principle of State-Rights, as enunciated in the resolutions of '98 and '99, the President cannot interfere; and with all proper respect for General Ruffleton, I'll see him —— before I do."

"But, my dear General," said Virus, "what will you do with them?"

"I have counted the cost," said Crook, "and have drawn the funds from New York. But that money, I think, had better be expended for powder and ball. The prisoners shall support themselves. I can incorporate them with the niggers and make them work on our plantations. The sun will tan them, and, in time, no doubt they will be absorbed. They say a nigger is as good as a white man—and I intend to demonstrate that such white men are no better than niggers. At all events, if we must lose our slaves, it will be well to teach these political economists how to grow cotton, sugar, and rice."

Virus laughed very heartily at this sally.

"How long, Virus," said the President, "will it be before we may expect your attack?"

"I hope there will be no necessity for expecting it at all."

"There may be a necessity for this evasion. But you should not be ignorant that we are quite as well prepared to receive it now as we will be at any future time."

"Mr. President," responded Virus, "we are upon Northern soil, which has been invaded by a Southern army."

"In retaliation for an invasion of Southern soil, and, fortunately, planned and executed by your present Commander-in-Chief," replied Randolph.

"But, on that occasion, the Federal Executive did not deem it incumbent to participate directly in the strife. And if he should do so on this occasion, will he not be charged with partiality? Will it not be said that he abandoned the functions of President of the United States to become the champion of a mere section, and at a moment, too, when that section was an aggressor and an invader?"

"No, sir!" responded the President. "The Executive of the sovereign State of New Jersey has officially invoked my intervention. The Southern army has signified its willingness to yield to my authority, and retire beyond the limits of the State. But its commanders say, what is apparent to every one, that to attempt an evacuation under the fire of an enemy would be certain destruction. Hence it was that I issued my proclamation, commanding the peace; and hence I have resolved to repel any assault with all the military force I can bring into the field."

"And that there may be no possible misconception," said Blount, "on the part of General Ruffleton, and no misrepresentation to the Northern people, I, as Commander-in-Chief of the Southern armies, have determined, in the contingency of a recommencement of hostilities, to place all the troops at the disposal of the President, as a *posse comitatus* to vindicate the laws and preserve the public peace."

"And for my part," said General Crook, "while submitting to my superiors in rank, I disclaim and despise the whole vocabulary of diplomacy. And, according to a presentiment I cannot repress, I am quite sure there will be but small regard for the laws, and d—— little public peace preserved after the next gun is fired!"

Blount and Crook then withdrew to prosecute the work going on with spades preparatory to resist the storm now daily anticipated.

"Virus," said Randolph, "have you no secret overtures for me?"

"I am authorized to say if the Federal troops be withdrawn from this contest, the British government will overlook the detention of Lord Slysir, and ——"

"Pause there. If I do not forbear to defend the weaker party, and if I shall identify myself with the section to be assailed, then Great Britain will unite with Ruffleton. England, if not jealous, is fearful of us. The example of a successful Republic is inimical to monarchies; and Ruffleton would gladly achieve power, and hold it by a more stable tenure than the mere caprice of the multitude. Let the war come. Let England unite with Ruffleton to overthrow the Republic, and to subjugate the South. They will fail. But our shipping, owned exclusively in the North, will escape destruction. Say to Ruffleton that I am not at all chagrined at his alliance with the old enemy of his country, because the merchant marine of the United States will be preserved. The navy is with me. Tell him, moreover, that I am well aware of the design to rescue Crook's prisoners. I understand his motive. It is his purpose to become a popular military chieftain. He may succeed in this; but it will be at a fearful price. He may accumulate such overwhelming numbers as to insure a victory—but it will be a bloody one. By this time to-morrow, when we shall all know—and it will not improve the amiability of Crook's temper—that the prisoners are at liberty, I trust you will be prepared to announce Ruffleton's final determination. We shall not embark till then. If we do not hear from him, it will be regarded as the signal for action. And let it be distinctly understood that not a shot can be fired at the Southern army without first passing through mine. One-fourth of my troops consist of horse; and I have marked the ground for them to occupy. They shall not be circumscribed. Any intrusion on the prescribed limits will be war on the United States. Adieu, sir."

Virus, much astonished at the result of his first interview with the President, and altogether unable to felicitate himself on any achievement in the field of diplomacy, returned somewhat crest-fallen to his patron.

"There is but one other mode of treating with Randolph!" exclaimed Ruffleton, upon learning the result of the mission. "Where is Popoli?"

"He attends at the entrance of the tent," said Virus. "I will send him in," and, glad to escape the gathering storm, he embraced the opportunity to retire.

"Popoli," said Ruffleton, "I have use for Cardini. "Where is he?"

"It is a mystery, sir. Mrs. Punt left him but for a few minutes, and when she returned to the parlor he was gone. He has not since been heard of."

"The craven dog! But you shall have his reward. If I could be assured he had departed, never to return—you understand—I would be satisfied. You must ascertain where he is, and what became of him. If alive, bring him to me—if dead, furnish me evidence of it. Popoli, could you not find access to Randolph?"

"He fixed his eagle eye on me, sir, for more than a minute without speaking. Then he warned me never to appear in his presence again."

"Could you not approach him in the dark? When he is asleep? But are there no disguises? If you can serve me, I shall hear of it—if not, call to-morrow or the next day for the reward due for services already rendered."

The Italian, bowing, withdrew from the presence of his taskmaster.

CHAPTER XXX.

THE EVE OF BATTLE.

It was the night preceding the battle. General Blount, attended only by Wiry Willy, had left the camp as soon as the troops were steeped in slumber, and embarked on a small steamer of great swiftness. They had landed opposite the mansion occupied by Mr. Langdon and the ladies under his charge, where horses awaited them. Arrived in front of the mansion, they found the vigilant Blue Caps faithfully guarding the premises. Upon dismounting, Willy, familiar with all the entrances, abandoned the General to the guidance of Alice, who received him on the vine-clad porch at the southern extremity of the house. Again she was arrayed in great magnificence, and the star of diamonds sparkled brilliantly on her smooth, pale forehead.

"It is before the hour," said Alice, "and Edith is not here."

"And you, alone, looked for my coming?"

"I heard the hoofs of your horse, as I sat alone in the parlor. Edith will come soon. She is with her father, striving to alleviate his distress, and prognosticating victory to-morrow. And alas! who can tell whether victory or defeat would be the greater misfortune for the country!"

"Which, Alice, would be the greater misfortune for you and Edith?"

"Our sympathies—our prayers—are for you; and my father. Oh! that he too had come! and if I should never see him again!"

"Fear it not. The fearless are never in danger. Such a

contingency as defeat or death never seems to cross his mind."

"Still, it may be his destiny to fall on this great field. And you, Henry, by this time to-morrow night, may be among the slain. Does not the thought sometimes appal you?"

"Perhaps it should—but it does not. I can only think of the victory, the plaudits of the world, and the security of the South."

"Henry, if it should be the will of heaven for my father to fall on this bloody field, and you should survive, will you not recall the sunny days when we were children together—when we followed the corses of our sainted mothers to the same peaceful churchyard—and when we addressed each other as brother and sister?"

"Alice," said he, taking the maiden's hand, "I never see you that I do not recall those early days. If God spares me and not your father, I will be your brother."

"And I your sister. But promise, in any event, that you will preserve the Union."

"Most assuredly I will do all in my power to preserve it; but these are themes too grave and melancholy. Your great father bears a charmed life—Providence designs him to be the preserver of his country. He bade me convey to you his blessing, and with his accustomed smile, he said at parting, 'Alice must be *marble* until this battle be fought and won.'"

"Marble!" said Alice, placing her hand upon her breast. "Statues have not aching hearts. Go, Henry—I have detained you too long."

"No, Alice," said he, "I will await her coming. I supposed she would be the first to greet me."

"Beware, Henry. Do not accuse her. Remember the injustice you have done her. Where, now, are the images of the rivals your fruitful imagination once conjured into existence?"

"How can I know," said he, smiling, "that some one, more favored than myself, does not at this moment withhold her from me?"

"By believing me. Her father is ill, and requires her constant attendance."

"That has escaped my memory—and I fear he would not

be disposed to second the request I had in contemplation. On you I am sure I can rely."

"What is it?"

"I did purpose imploring your aid in obtaining his consent to the performance of the marriage ceremony this night, for, Alice, it may be my fate to fall to-morrow."

"Oh, do not urge it!. If you should fall, indeed, what avail would it be? A mourning widow! Think you she would not mourn as well without the mockery of an empty ceremonial? Or is man so selfish, that, dying, he would have certain survivors under obligations, signed and sealed, to lament him? Without a solemn pledge, would no one be inclined to mourn your loss? You turn aside, Harry—be not offended. Believe me, there are those who would shed bitter tears over your corse."

"Yes, Alice, you, for one, I am sure, would mourn the death of a brother." He kissed her hand, and started. "Why, Alice!" he continued, "you are ill. Your hand is cold, your face is pale. I will call some one."

"No, Harry, I beseech you. I am *not* ill—it was a mere passing cloud—a spectre, now vanished—it was a mere fancy—and now it's gone. I will, if you desire it, speak to Mr. Langdon. I will not advise you or Edith. I shall not, will not, be responsible for any omission or commission. Edith and I are sisters in all but blood. I would not have her reproach me—nor incur your censure for opposing your will."

"You will not. Ah, Alice, if I might have aspired to this hand——"

"Did you not hear some one?"

"No."

"I thought it was the step of Edith, and the rustle of satin."

"No; but still she does not come, and the minutes fly. Alice, there can be but few remaining for me. The Commodore, whom I saw in coming hither, warned me against what he called a protracted dalliance here, and said that when the time arrived for my departure, he would make a signal. I fear her father is worse."

"I will go to him, and send Edith hither."

Alice sped through the dimly lighted apartments, and Blount promenaded the veranda, where he was joined by Wiry Willy.

"Are you ready to return, Willy?" he asked, with a sad tone.

"Quite ready, sir."

"There is the signal," said Blount.

"It was a blue rocket from the Commodore's ship, sir."

"And the signal for our departure. Mount, Willy—I will overtake you."

Willy had hardly passed out of view when Alice returned, agitated and almost breathless.

"She is not there. Mr. Langdon sleeps. The maid says Edith descended some few minutes after your arrival. I am alarmed at her absence. Where can she be?"

"Certainly no evil could have befallen her. Ah, Alice, can it be mere caprice?"

"No, no."

"Farewell!" He kissed her hand, and her fair forehead.

"Oh, do not go until you have seen her," said Alice.

"Did you not see the signal? It illuminated the heavens. I cannot delay. Tell her all, and utter my adieus. Farewell, and may heaven bless you both."

Alice gazed after him, and never turned her straining eyes away until the last echoes of the hoofs of his steed died upon the ear. Then she felt the breath of Edith on her cheek, and the next moment her friend was sobbing in her arms.

CHAPTER XXXI.

THE BATTLE.

THE signal of battle was given by Ruffleton. Supposing himself able, from his overwhelming and hourly-increasing numbers, to destroy all his opponents, and afterwards to assume the supreme military and civil authority of the nation, he ordered the attack to be commenced.

More than five hundred field-pieces were discharged almost simultaneously by Ruffleton, and not a single ball reached the Southern columns. The President alone had to bear the brunt, and this he did with calmness. His horses suffered a great deal from the first discharges. The men were dismounted, and partially sheltered by the breastwork of sand and turf covering the entire position.

For a considerable length of time, Randolph bore the infliction, whilst his impatient generals surrounded him, awaiting his orders.

"General," said he, addressing the recently-promoted Carleton, "will your column go into the jaws of that volcano?"

"They await the order, sir."

"The slaughter of horses, then, does not appal them?"

"It inspires them with a desire of revenge."

"Revenge, I suppose, is desired by many. But we want only victory, so we can put an end to the strife, by withdrawing from the field. I desire it to be understood that I have no projects of conquest, and am engaged only in a defensive war. I would this day, and on this field, unite with Ruffleton, if he desired peace, and acted on the defensive against Blount and Crook."

"And I," said Blount, "as the commander-in-chief of the Southern armies, have never contemplated offensive measures; and the States represented by me would be content merely to repel aggression. But since I am not permitted to withdraw in peace, no other alternative remains but to accept the gage of battle."

"D—— it, let us give as well as receive," said General Crook. "They have killed a thousand horses and five hundred men, and we have not fired a shot."

"The matter demonstrated, then," said Randolph, "is, that my army *can stand fire;* but they have stood it long enought. Valiant, let all our batteries fire twice towards the centre, then once at the wings. Under the smoke, Carleton, charge upon the enemy's centre with your ten thousand men, and let me see how many of their guns you can take or silence."

A few minutes afterwards the earth was shaken by a terrific discharge, and General Carleton issued from behind the breastworks, and charged the enemy's batteries. These not being protected by any sort of breastwork, were immediately carried. But the fanatics, whom Ruffleton had posted in front, could stand fire as well as the Federal troops. All of them seemed to expect death or victory; and they were of course prepared to die, in the event of defeat. Therefore, although they were swept down by hundreds, still the survivors would not run away. Carleton seeing this, seized some forty guns, and wheeling them round, struck down whole multitudes of Abolitionists with their own engines. Then, dividing his column, he swept along the right and left from the centre, *in the rear of the enemy's batteries*, sabreing the gunners and spiking the cannon. With the enemy on either hand, the contest was for many minutes maintained with the sword and the bayonet. Neither musketry nor cannon could be used by Ruffleton, who was prompt to afford succor to his menaced divisions; and it was the celerity of Carleton's movements which saved him from immediate destruction.

Sergeant Jack Bim distinguished himself as usual in this charge. Northern born as he was, he had a mortal aversion for the negro; and so, when he encountered the Black Regiment, he could not forbear. He plunged in their midst, parying their thrusts, and laid about him with such terrible effect, that his horse was soon knee deep in the slain, and his progress so much obstructed, that the witnesses of his exploit began to fear he would never be able to extricate himself from the labyrinth of his own creation. Nevertheless, General Carleton, who had paused scarcely a moment in his furious career, was gratified to see Bim leaping his fiery steed after him in the avenue made by the irresistible charge of the squadrons. Bim had sheathed his sword, and was clasping his nose!

Carleton, having executed his charge in accordance with the orders of Randolph, returned with the forty cannon which he had taken. But this was at the expense of nearly a thousand men, and there was but little effect produced on the determined front of the enemy. A great many had fallen, but these were the zealous enthusiasts in the cause of negro emancipation, whom Ruffleton had thrust forward to be killed.

The ordnance taken and spiked by Carleton was soon replaced from the vast supply in Ruffleton's rear, brought from New York and New England. They not only continued to thunder along the whole extent of the line, but advanced, unsheltered as they were, in the face of the incessant fire of more than three hundred guns, discharging round shot, grape, and canister.

The tide continued to roll onward, and it became necessary for Randolph's artillery to withdraw behind the second line of defences thrown up by Blount and Crook. This was done without the loss of a gun, under the superintendence of General Valiant. When this was completed, Randolph, placing himself at the head of twenty thousand horse, kept in readiness under the river bank, charged the rear of the right wing of the enemy. Nothing could oppose a force of such magnitude. It swept over the plain like a tornado. The scene was appalling. Thousands upon thousands fell, and were trampled in the dust, but none fled away, for the reason that the interminable host behind, still advancing, prevented the escape of fugitives. Many who attempted to fly were cut down by their own friends, in obedience to the orders of Ruffleton. Twice he had been defeated by the Southern Generals, and now he was resolved to be revenged upon them both, or perish in the most horrible conflict known in the annals of warfare.

The President several times cut his way through the dense ranks, and severed the right wing from the main body of the enemy. With regular troops, according to the science of war, this would have been decisive; but here, as at Bladensburg, the enemy remained unconscious of the danger of defeat, and when the destroying cavalry passed away, the amputated wing was immediately re-united to the advancing trunk; and perceiving that nothing could be accomplished by this mode of assault, Randolph drew off his column, now blown and bathed in blood, and occupied a position in the rear of the Southern encampment.

Several times the enemy charged to the very muzzles of the cannon, and were swept down rather than driven back. This murderous and appalling spectacle continued until night, when the Northern host diverged a little to the east, where a depression in the earth sheltered them, and encamped upon the field of battle.

As soon as the enemy ceased to menace the position of the combined armies, the batteries, which had so long been vomiting their destructive fires, became suddenly silent, and their recent startling explosions were succeeded by sounds still more horrible to the human ear. These were the groans of the wounded, and the shrieks of the dying.

* * * * * *

Generals Blount and Crook met in the tent of President Randolph. Steel, and many other officers of high rank, on both sides, had fallen.

"Gentlemen," said Randolph, "I desire your opinion in the present emergency. I know Ruffleton's purpose. He is determined to crush us by his physical superiority. Never were men so imperturbable. But such is the idiosyncrasy of fanatics. A month hence, when the people shall have reflected on the horrors of this monstrous field, they will not be so resolute to plunge into the jaws of destruction. Shall we retire?"

"It would be madness to attempt an embarkation in the presence of such an enemy," said Blount.

"Certainly," replied Randolph, "that is out of the question. But we might retire a few hours before day, and succeed, with the aid of the fleet, in regaining a footing on Southern soil."

"And Ruffleton, then, would claim the victory," said Crook.

"Oh, he has done that already," said Randolph. "Here is a note brought me by a deserter. It was written by a friend of mine in Ruffleton's camp, in whom I have confidence." The note stated that Ruffleton had telegraphed the Convention in New York, that he had beaten the President's army, which had taken refuge in the camp of the invaders, and that in the course of a few hours more he would overwhelm all opposition. A subsequent despatch indicated that Ruffleton's intrigues and machinations had been far more extensive in their ramifications than had been suspected. His partisans in the Convention had seized the occasion to move and carry some extraordinary measures. They invested him with almost unlimited power *for five years.* The assassination of Monmouth, in Philadelphia, had induced many of the conservative members of the Convention to resign their seats, and that body was now under the control of Ruffleton, whose creatures comprised a vast majority.

"There will be a reaction, gentlemen," said Randolph. "This thing of popular sentiment ebbs and flows, like the ocean. But we must await the subsidence of the waters; we cannot oppose them. How now?" he added, upon the introduction of a messenger. This was followed by the unexpected appearance of Virus, Ruffleton's negotiator. "You are welcome, sir," said Randolph, "if your mission be one of peace."

"That is the object of my coming," said Virus, and his pale visage indicated that he might be in earnest.

"Then unfold your propositions," said Randolph. "One of Ruffleton's propositions has been obviated by the escape of the prisoners taken at Bladensburg and——"

"Is that so?" demanded Crook, springing up from a corner of the tent, where he had been reclining.

"It is true," said Blount.

"No matter," said Crook. "I shall take twice the number to-morrow."

"Then a renewal of the terrific butchery," said Virus, "seems a foregone conclusion."

"Certainly," said Crook.

"Your proposal, sir," said Randolph, addressing Virus.

"Either a surrender as prisoners of war, or the restitution of the money taken from New York, an abandonment of all arms, and an immediate evacuation of New Jersey, Delaware, and Maryland."

"D—— me, if I subscribe to any one of the stipulations," said Crook, his face crimsoned with rage.

"Return to your principal, Virus," said Randolph, "and say that we regard his demands as the vauntings of a too confident adventurer."

"To-morrow," said Blount, "the fortune of war may make Ruffleton a suppliant, and in that event we shall not mock him with preposterous demands."

"General," said Virus, "I assure you, since this battle commenced, the recruits we have received, exceed the amount of our slain. If the contest be prolonged, your destruction is inevitable."

"That is an unwarrantable assumption," said Blount.

"Nothing short of demonstration, however," said Randolph, "will convince Ruffleton. Crook is right. We must fight it out. When the fanatics are all destroyed, the rest will not be insensible to fear. Virus, we were anxious to avoid the effusion of blood, as Ruffleton knows, and as the whole country will soon know, notwithstanding the efforts to suppress my proclamation; and we proposed to abandon the soil of the free States, stipulating never to invade them again. But this was not a sufficient humiliation to satisfy your *Imperator*. He desired revenge, and the eclat of a great victory, for his personal gratification, or his individual aggrandizement. The result is before him. If he is not satisfied with it, of course he will gratify his inclination in the prosecution of the war; but he must be accountable for the blood unnecessarily expended. We act on the defensive."

Virus withdrew without another word, accompanied by an officer to the outposts. Both Blount and Crook advanced to the President, each taking one of his hands.

"Sir," said Blount, "we would rather die with you than surrender to that man."

"My friends, we will not surrender, nor will we die on this field. But we must retire further down the river, and find another strong position for defence. I will send a messenger to Commodore Stout, and we may embark under cover of his batteries. I have fifteen ships in the river——"

"And," said Crook, "the British have eighteen."

"True, but the metal and men are nearly equal. Let your flotilla glide quietly down the tide, gentlemen, and it is possible we may get away without serious damage. If the British Admiral has no order to assail us, we can manage Ruffleton."

This was agreed to, and at midnight the march commenced. The groans of the wounded lying between the armies prevented the trampling of horses and the creaking of the artillery carriages from being heard. Nevertheless, information of the movement was soon conveyed to Ruffleton by his spies, and before the combined armies had proceeded two miles, the enemy was in full pursuit. At this distance apart, they continued to march with all the rapidity of which they were capable, until about four o'clock in the morning, when the guides announced to Randolph that a swampy creek, over which they were crossing, would be impassable for man or horse, if the several bridges were destroyed. The creek ran in a semicircular line, its base being the river, and the tide ebbed and flowed through it. The extent of country enclosed was sufficiently ample as a defensive position for the retreating armies, but not for the operations of cavalry. And here they were met by a messenger from the Commodore, with the information that below this point, for many miles, there would not be a sufficient depth of water for the frigates to approach them.

At this point Randolph made dispositions to receive the enemy. An embankment of turf was hastily thrown up along the entire length of the creek; and just before daybreak, the bridges were blown up, as the heads of the hostile columns were beginning to pass over them.

CHAPTER XXXII.

ATTEMPTED ASSASSINATION.

During the whole of the succeeding day the battle raged without intermission, but it was mostly a battle of artillery. The Northern army, destitute of pontoon trains, were unable to pass the creek in sufficient numbers to effect a lodgment on the opposite side. But the cannon did awful execution on both sides, and an incessant flight of bombs wrought a dreadful carnage in all directions.

Towards evening the attention of General Crook was attracted by a cloud of dust in the South; this body of men, he learned, upon inquiry, were the escaped prisoners, and he found it difficult to resist the temptation to recapture them. He suggested the idea to Randolph.

"I will undertake to drive them across the creek and within our lines, with 5,000 horse."

"And Ruffleton's fanatics might come in with them," said Randolph. "No, General—let them alone. They would consume our rations, and we have not a superabundance. Let them prey upon the enemy."

"Very well," said Crook. "But I shall give them a parting salute when they reach the meadow in their line of march." He had a battery of ten guns erected to sweep the meadow; and when the dark mass reached the designated point, he played upon them with a vengeance! *They* were not all fanatics, and by no means insensible to fear. Abandoning their guides, they fled in all directions, and very soon produced a panic, for such is the influence of example, in the left wing of Ruffleton's army, where they fled for shelter. And Randolph, perceiving this, seized the opportunity to throw bridges (he possessed an excellent pontoon train) over the lower end of the creek, and dashed out with 5,000 horse. Before the extremity of the left wing of the adverse army could recover from the confusion produced by the presence of the panic-stricken fugitives, he was upon them, dealing right and left. This time they threw down their arms and fell back upon the rear guard, where they rallied again. Then, without exposing his men unnecessarily, and after having administered a salutary chastisement on the fanatics, Randolph returned to his friends, who greeted him with hearty cheers.

Sergeant Bim, who of course had been one of this party, and had performed his share of the execution, as if he had grown weary of slaying the enemy, resolved to make a prisoner. So he snatched a man from his horse and placed him before him on his own; and in that manner conveyed him into camp.

"Whom have you there, Bim?" demanded President Randolph, when they repassed the bridge, attracted by the novelty of the burden.

"It's Popoli, sir," said Bim. "I found him aiming a rifle at you, sir. I killed a Colonel near him, and then the monkey mounted his horse, and tried to get away. It was an old plough horse with a Quaker-looking face. Popoli begged me to spare his life and I brought him in as a show. I've found a blank passport in his pocket signed by General Ruffleton, which I will fill up with my own name."

"Did you find any other papers, Bim?"

"No, sir."

"But I have more, Mr. President."

Popoli produced several dispatches from Admiral Bang, which he was bearing to the camp of Ruffleton, when taken by Bim.

They were important, and Randolph perused them with interest as he rode towards his head-quarters, unmindful of the cannon balls ever and anon ploughing up the earth near the feet of his horse.

"Gentlemen," said Randolph, when Blount and Crook joined him in his tent, "here is some interesting information. A British cruiser, it seems, boarded the Boston vessel on the coast of Africa, supposing it to be a slaver, when they found only a cargo of Abolitionists! The officers and crew were put in irons, and the vessel sent back to Boston."

"That is bad news!" said Crook.

"But not the worst," continued the President. "Your ship from Annapolis was intercepted by the same cruiser, and, returning, has landed its contents in New York."

"Then there will be no peace on this mundane sphere!" said Crook. "All the devils in —— could not foment so much discord and strife on earth, as those two cargoes of wicked preachers, fanatics, and fools!"

"You must be merciful, if you would obtain mercy," said Randolph. "But I have another project for the delectation of Ruffleton. I think some impression was made by this last charge, and that another, on a larger scale, will make the enemy more respectful, at least more circumspect." What this was, the following events will sufficiently indicate.

Commodore Stout, leading with the Wabash, steamed along the shore as near the right wing of the enemy as the depth of water would permit, and poured broadside after broadside into the flank and rear of them. This demonstration swept away almost every man in the hostile ranks within a half mile of the river; and under the rolling clouds of smoke, Randolph, throwing his bridges over the creek, sallied out at the head of nearly twenty thousand horse, and fell like an avalanche on their disordered columns. The charge was irresistible. And so many terrible examples of the fatality of these quadrupedal apparitions in their midst, had begun to produce their natural effect upon all who looked forward to any other object in this life besides the abolition of African slavery. The entire right wing of Ruffleton's army was soon folded against the centre, where, perforce, its retrograde movement was arrested by the impenetrable wall of steel. Having penetrated to the very centre of the enemy's camp, Randolph turned upon them all the cannon he had taken, some eighty in number, and fired one round of their own missiles into their ranks! Then spiking the guns, he led back his cavalry without serious diminution, just as the dusk of eve fell upon the scene.

"What sort of a burden is that?" asked Randolph, when returning to his tent, and observing an enormous object, enveloped in a coarse canvas, which Bim carried before him on his horse.

"I don't know exactly, sir," said Bim; "but I hope it's General Ruffleton himself. This is part of his tent, I know. We swept over his head-quarters, and I saw this thing rolling itself in the canvas, and snatched it up. I think it must be General Ruffleton, for it's pot-bellied like him, and heavy as lead."

"Bring him to my tent," said Randolph.

It was Lord Slysir.

"My bones are broken!" said his lordship, when Bim unrolled him from his mummy-like covering. "I am bruised to a jelly! Mr. President, I demand the punishment of your ill-mannered dragoon!"

"Your lordship forgets that my dragoon was merely discharging his duty."

"Duty! Is cruelty to prisoners—if you regard me such—a duty?"

"I declare, sir," said Bim, addressing the President, "when I first saw the canvas move, I thought it was a pig, and wrapped him up so he couldn't bite me."

"Begone! you unmannered hound!—you untutored boor!" said Slysir.

"If I'm to be mistaken for a pig, sir," said Bim, stepping back, "let it be a boar pig. But I'm no manner of a hound, sir! I repel the imputation. And if your rank would only permit you to fight a Sergeant of dragoons, I think I could give you abundant satisfaction."

"My Lord," said Randolph, when Bim withdrew, "I trust you will be immediately restored to health and usefulness."

"Health and usefulness! and from an enemy!"

"I am perfectly aware of that, my lord. And, really, I am delighted at your alliance with Ruffleton, for it will guarantee the security of our merchant marine, belonging almost exclusively to the free States. But, instead of annexing New England to the British crown, be careful that Canada is not annexed to New England."

"Your Excellency seems to possess a vast amount of information."

"Would your Lordship be prepared to listen to a proposition—"

"I am not at liberty—I mean I am a prisoner, Mr. President, and any negotiations—"

"Would be an infraction of the convention with the military, if not the civil, head of the Northern confederacy!"

"That is not what I desired to say, Mr. President. But a stroke of your pen would restore me my liberty, and then—"

"And then the words of warning I uttered on the night of the dissolution of Congress, would prove to have been without meaning. My lord, whatever others may do, I always mean what I say. You have espoused the cause of a traitor, and we are enemies. My war with England will rally, sooner or later, all the patriotism and republicanism of the Union under my standard. I repeat, that a war with England is regarded by me as a most fortunate event. Therefore, there need be no hesitation on your part to begin hostilities. And, indeed, your cruisers have already taken the initiative—"

"How? When?" asked Slysir.

"These papers will enlighten your Lordship," said Randolph, placing in his hands the intercepted dispatches.

"Ah! these were intercepted," said his lordship. "But were these all? Was nothing said about—"

"About what?"

"If your Excellency has in your possession other dispatches—"

"I have no other."

"Then, of course, there were no others, and I cannot imagine—"

His Lordship was interrupted by the entrance of a messenger, who placed a letter in the President's hand. By the light of a lamp, Randolph recognised the characters of Major S——.

"Who brought this?" he demanded.

"A deserter, sir," said the messenger.

While the President was reading, Popoli, who had been lying concealed among a number of flags taken by the cavalry, sprang up and aimed a blow with his dagger at the heart of the President. The President stumbled backwards, and fell into the chair from which he had risen. And Bim, who stood near the entrance, seeing Popoli glide out into the darkness, ran in pursuit of him.

"That was an assassin, with whom I protest I had no complicity!" said Slysir. "I hope your Excellency is not seriously wounded."

The President pressed one hand against his heart, and without replying to his lordship, waved him away with the other. The officer having his Lordship in custody hurried him off towards the river.

The guards in the immediate vicinity of the President's tent having informed Generals Blount and Crook of the occurrence, they repaired instantly to Randolph's quarters, where, to their joyful surprise, they found him quietly perusing a communication from Major S——, his dissembling partisan in the camp of the enemy.

"Not dead, by Jupiter!" cried Crook.

"No, thank heaven!" said Blount, pale and fearfully excited.

"Not even scratched," said Randolph. "It was well aimed, but Providence interposed my heavy-cased hunting watch. Now, gentlemen, that little matter blown over, we enter upon affairs of the greatest magnitude. My correspondent, on whose information you are aware we may always rely, says that Ruffleton and Bang have determined to make a simultaneous attack on us by land and by water. Our flotilla cannot be reached by the enemy at low tide; and it seems to me that the time has arrived for us to take our departure from this shore, provided we succeed in repulsing the attack by land."

"I concur fully," said Blount.

"Good! So long as there is no such word as surrender," said Crook. "And," he continued, with an uplifted hand, "when that alternative is contemplated, I desire it to be understood that I am not to be consulted. I will *never* surrender. I will escape in the old Roman manner."

"My brave brother in arms!" said Randolph, taking the General's hand, "your life is too valuable to be lost in that way. Such an alternative as a surrender is certainly not to be contemplated; but if it were, of what avail would be self-destruction? Think not of it. And remember I have Lord Slysir, whose equivalent in an exchange would be at least a General."

"Your last charge," said Blount to Randolph, "must have been seriously felt by the enemy, and was a great relief to us. There is a very perceptible diminution of projectiles thrown into our camp. But in accordance with the information derived from your correspondent, the fire had not ceased at nightfall."

"Let us double the guard at those places on the creek where they will be most likely to attempt a passage; and at the same time we will redouble the fire from our mortars," said the President.

"Yes," said Blount; "and the amount of metal thus expended, will be a diminution to that extent of the burden to be transported in the flotilla." And at the same time that these measures were put in execution, every preparation was made to embark.

CHAPTER XXXIII.

PROMOTION.

Bim never lost sight of the flying Italian until the latter plunged into the river and dived beneath the surface. The Sergeant sprang into a light skiff and awaited the rising of his victim.

"By George!" said he, after sitting some time in silence, "I believe he's drowned himself. No mortal man could hold his breath this long, unless he was first cousin to a maremaid. And this fellow may be a pollywog—or at most a man muskrat. Hello! what's that!" said he, leaping up and rubbing his back. Popoli had risen softly under the stern of the boat, with the design of despatching the Sergeant with the same dagger used against the President. But he proved too weak to execute his purpose. "You infernal water-mosquito!" cried Bim, seizing the wrist of Popoli as he attempted to strike a second blow, "or gally-nipper, or craw-fish! You're done biting now! I don't believe you brought blood, but you are a double murderer, although you've killed nobody, and—"

"Sergeant," said Popoli, "is President Randolph not dead?"

"Can a flea-bite kill? If not, how could such a contemptible toad as you kill such an exalted and glorious genius as President Randolph? Why, the point of your dagger didn't go through the gold case of his watch!"

"I thought so," said the Italian, with a low malediction. "But it broke the point off, and that's the reason I could not——"

"Stick me, I suppose you meant to say," added Bim; and at the same time lifting Popoli, like a fish, into the boat, and forcing him to lie down on his back. "Popoli," he continued, "if you had killed the President, or even bled him pretty freely, do you suppose I'd be merciful enough to be indulging you in this way? No, indeed! I could not have restrained my hand. Now, listen to me and bear witness all the stars: I do hereby solemnly swear that I will not kill this Mr. Signor Popoli, this night, unless he attempts again to kill me, tries to escape, or I am ordered to do so by a superior officer."

"Then what do you intend to do with me, Sergeant?" asked the culprit.

"I intend to introduce you to the society of your loving friend, Cardini."

"Cardini? Oh, Sergeant, he's the one I wish to see! Take me to him, and you'll bind me to you for life! Give me the name and location of any enemy, and he will cease to live!"

"Thank you, Popoli,—but I'd prefer to do my own killing."

"But where is he?"

"He's—I don't know that I'm under obligations to tell you—thought I should have done so, no doubt, if you hadn't been so eager to find it out."

"But, Sergeant, is he alive?"

"Oh, yes, I suppose so—at least he was quite well when I saw him last, and I haven't heard of his being taken ill since."

"Sergeant! if you'll only take me to him, I'll give you—"

"Silence, fool! or I'll forget my oath, perhaps. I'm out of money again, it is true; but I know where more is to be had. I prefer glory to the filthy lucre; and now I'm in a fair way of being promoted. By to-morrow, if President Randolph and I both live, I think I'll be a live captain in the Blue Caps, the most magnificent body of men in these United States—or, perhaps, just about this hour, I should say, disunited States."

Bim, hearing his name called, rowed to the shore, where he was met by General Carleton, who announced that the President had promoted him to the rank of Captain, in consideration of his gallant conduct on divers recent occasions, but especially for his meritorious service in the capture of Lord Slysir. The General further stated that the President desired Captain Bim to proceed with four rowers, having his Lordship in custody, to the flag-ship of Commodore Stout.

"General," said Bim, "is there to be no more fighting?"

"Quite enough, I apprehend, Captain," said Carleton. "But the probability is that the most desperate conflict will be between the fleets."

"Then I'm *in*, that is, General, if I may be allowed to fight in a ship!"

"You may fight anywhere for your country and your President."

Captain Bim, having first conducted Lord Slysir into the boat which was to convey him to the ship, next ordered the men, for he now appreciated the importance attached to a commissioned officer, to transfer Popoli to the same boat. This accomplished, the crew rowed briskly away from the shore, whilst Bim voluntarily performed the lighter duty of helmsman.

"Bim!" said his Lordship, as they glided out into the current.

"*Captain* Bim, at your Lordship's service, sir," said the Captain.

"You have served me a cruel turn—you have done my business, sir, I fear. I shall not recover from my bruises for a month, if I get over them at all!"

"My Lord, I was doing a little business of my own, at the same time, and you answered the purpose exactly. It was that feat which brought promotion."

"Well, I suppose I ought to congratulate you; but I do

so in great agony of body. However, you have done a good service for your employers. In this game they are playing, they have obtained by your blundering luck a very high trump card."

"Sir—your Lordship—that reminds me of the game I had last night. I had two bullets and a bragger, when a bomb scattered the cards and the money, and all the men but myself, to the d——l. Wasn't that an unlucky blunder?"

"I desire none of your familiarity, sir," said his Lordship.

"Then don't speak to me, sir!" said Bim, assuming an erect posture.

"I hope your Lordship," said Popoli, lying in the bottom of the boat, "will report my conduct to the General."

"Who are you?" demanded his lordship.

"I am Popoli."

"As —— a rascal as ever went unhung!" said Bim.

"Ah, the assassin!" said Slysir. "Yes, I will report your conduct, and if I have any influence, you shall swing on the nearest tree. To attack the President in such a ruffianly manner, and in my presence!"

"Oh, he has no manners, sir," said Bim.

"Captain Bim," resumed his Lordship, "I agree with you in abhorrence of the dastardly crime of assassination, and particularly when perpetrated on persons of rank and distinction."

"The rascal tried his hand on me," said Bim.

"You! Nonsense. But here we are under the ship. I hope they can contrive some means of hoisting me, for I cannot climb up the ladder. Ah, Commodore," he continued, seeing that officer above, "I'm not a guest this time."

"No, sir," said Bim; "he's a prisoner of war."

"Commodore," continued Slysir, "is there not some way of getting up besides ascending these steep steps?"

"Yes, my Lord," said the Commodore. "I will have a rope thrown over, which you can pass under your arms, and be lifted up." This was done.

CHAPTER XXXIV.

LORD SLYSIR'S CAPTIVITY.

SUDDENLY a great consternation prevailed at the head quarters of Ruffleton. Lord Slysir could nowhere be found, and the rumor that he had been captured by Randolph was credited by the Commander-in-Chief. All at once the batteries of the Northern army were silenced. This, of course, induced a corresponding cessation of the fire from the besieged.

"Balatrum!" said Ruffleton, "they have taken the British minister! Everything depends upon his recovery. Without his orders, we shall have no assistance from the British forces, unless, indeed, Admiral Bang should act on his previous instructions. And Slysir alone can commit his government to our cause. Call Virus!" And when that astute diplomat made his appearance, Ruffleton continued thus: "Go, Virus, into the camp of the enemy, with a flag, and propose a conference. Let Randolph send hither his chief General, Valiant, and I will send him mine, Balatrum. Haste, Virus!" To this Balatrum made no objection, and Virus departed without loss of time.

* * * * * * *

"General," said Randolph, when Valiant reported the very singular conduct of the besiegers, "we can only await an elucidation."

"I hope their Commander-in-Chief has been nipped in the bud!" said Crook.

"No; it is not that," said Randolph. "He keeps a bank of sand bags, ten feet through, on the south side of his tent."

"We have been in a desperate strait," said Randolph. "At present, however, we may congratulate ourselves on this grateful respite, after the hard pounding we have endured."

As this speech was concluded, Virus, blindfolded, was ushered into the tent.

"Now," said the President, "for the elucidation. Virus, has your ammunition given out?"

"It has not even been diminished, sir."

"What brings you hither?"

"General Ruffleton proposes an exchange of prisoners."

"An exchange of prisoners!" cried Crook. "He has no prisoners, if it be true, as the deserters allege, that all our wounded taken by him are summarily killed."

"That is not true," said Virus.

"Then will he return *my* prisoners?" This question of Crook produced a burst of laughter.

"If you mean the 30,000 transported across the bay by the British fleet," said Virus, "I have to say that the number was seriously diminished by your batteries, in the meadow on our left, and that the remainder have dispersed themselves in so many directions it would be impossible to restore them."

"We have several of your men," said the President, willing to protract the cessation of hostilities, while his horses were being quietly taken on board the flotilla, "which we do not think can be matched by any captives in your possession. We do not think we had any assassins in our camp; but one of the prisoners taken in yours aimed a dagger at my heart. It was Popoli. Next, we have a Lord ——"

"Is he living? We understood he died!" It was thus Virus endeavored to mask the interest he felt in the announcement.

"So far he has escaped death," said Randolph. "But several shells have exploded in his presence, and it is a miracle that he lives."

"In a word, then, would any consideration induce your Excellency to restore his Lordship to liberty? If so, General Ruffleton will send you his chief officer as a hostage for the safe return of General Valiant, whom he would desire to be bearer of your conditions, etc."

"I think I may be induced to set his Lordship at liberty, since I am not clear that the circumstances warrant his detention. This you may say to Ruffleton; and further—if General Valiant should not make his appearance in the space of an hour, he may recommence hostilities."

Virus was conducted back within the lines of the Northern army; and Randolph, resolved to make the best possible use of the time, retained Valiant until the hour specified had nearly expired. And when the General was at length conducted into the presence of Ruffleton, every art was employed to compass the restitution of Slysir.

"The only difficulty likely to arise," said Valiant, "is the matter of time. Randolph has no disposition to use his Lordship ill, and is quite willing to liberate him when the last of our forces shall be safely embarked, to-morrow or the next day."

"And why not immediately? General Balatrum will remain with you, if it be desired, as a guarantee of the fulfilment of the stipulation that not another gun will be fired from our side of the quicksand creek—the creek which, Valiant, was all that saved you from destruction."

"And now, with the addition of Her Britannic Majesty's Envoy Extraordinary and Minister Plenipotentiary interposed between us, we deem ourselves doubly safe. I do not think Randolph will consent to yield up his Lordship until we shall be prepared to begin the evacuation."

Ruffleton saw that Valiant was conscious of his advantage; but he never suspected the evacuation was already in progress, or that Lord Slysir had been conveyed to the Commodore's ship. He was quite willing, then, to treat for the restoration of his Lordship on the basis suggested by Valiant; and it was agreed that the convention should be signed at sunrise the next morning; that the Generals should return to their respective armies; and that hostili ties were not to be resumed by either party, before the landing of the troops on the Delaware side of the river, unless there should occur an infraction of the articles or agreement.

To these stipulations Randolph and his colleagues heartily agreed; and, moreover, it was their purpose to fulfil the main stipulation, the rendition of his Lordship, to the letter. But they were not aware of the fact that Virus had overheard, though blindfolded very securely, as he returned to his General's head-quarters, some one say that Lord Slysir had been sent away, and that all President Randolph's cavalry, under the command of General Carleton, had been landed on the opposite shore of the broad river!

CHAPTER XXXV.

CESSATION OF THE BOMBARDMENT.

Mr. Langdon was suffering with a severe fit of the gout, but had been wheeled in a great chair out on the balcony, where, with his telescope, he watched the progress of the protracted battle.

Willy had just arrived from the battle-field.

"Miss Edith!" said he, "General Blount has not been wounded, and his health is perfect—and his spirits good."

"I am rejoiced to hear of his health, Willy," said Edith; "and if his good spirits may be indicative of a speedy termination of this horrible strife, I shall be happy indeed. He did not write?"

"No, Miss; but he sent his heartiest greeting. President Randolph did not write—I mean to Miss Alice—but here is a large packet for Mr. Langdon."

"Wheel me back into the chamber," said Mr. Langdon, "and bring a candle."

This was done by the tender hands of Edith and Mary, who had been his constant nurses. He broke the seal and read the letter aloud, while the rest stood around.

Randolph's lines were in the bold legible hand of calm deliberation, and, as usual, without blot or interlineation. The President announced the startling intelligence that a free-soil army was approaching from the West through the State of Pennsylvania, for the purpose, probably, of cutting off the retreat of the Southern and Federal forces in New Jersey. But this project would probably be defeated in the course of a few hours—but if not, Mr. Langdon, if sufficiently recovered to travel, was advised to set out in the course of two or three days, with the ladies under his care, for Washington city. Randolph, however, assured him and his daughter that they need be under no apprehension for his safety, and for his own part, he had not at all lost confidence in the virtue and patriotism of the American people.

"But *I* have," said the heart-stricken statesman, the letter falling from his relaxed grasp, and his head sinking down in dejection.

"Oh, sir!" said Alice, "let us have faith in the wisdom and energy of my father."

"I fear I shall not have the heart, even if I have the strength," said Langdon, "to fly from my countrymen. I would be content now to take refuge in a peaceful grave! My daughter! and my young friends! if it were not a duty incumbent on us to take thought for the Government, it would be far better to dwell in humble obscurity, in peace and plenty, than mount the topmost round of ambition's ladder. Willy, when the fratricidal strife is over, do thou never emerge from the peaceful vale where my daughter found a hospitable shelter, on the purling Brandywine!"

"The firing has ceased!" exclaimed Mary, with hands uplifted.

"Wheel me out again!" said Mr. Langdon, with a more cheerful expression of countenance.

When they were re-assembled on the balcony, a solemn silence brooded over the scene, where so lately the earth vibrated with the continual discharges of great guns, and the frequent explosions of shells.

On the lawn surrounding the mansion, there were groups of Blue Caps, conjecturing the probable causes of such an unexpected occurrence.

"It cannot be a surrender!" said Alice.

"No—not that," said Mr. Langdon, "after the confident letter he wrote me."

"Nor his fall—nor the fall of any of the Generals," said Mary, "if my prayers have been heard."

"It may be the fall of Ruffleton himself," said Edith.

"No, daughter!" said Mr. Langdon; "and even that would not put an end to the strife. There are others eager always to succeed in the chief command. If he were a king, it might be different."

"No doubt he aspires to be king," said Alice.

For a long time, on that summer's night, they sat on the balcony and gazed at the darkened scene which had succeeded the fires of furious warfare.

CHAPTER XXXVI.

PREPARATIONS FOR A NAVAL BATTLE.

Just about the time of the suspension of the fire between the land forces, Commodore Stout perceived evidences of an intention on the part of Admiral Bang, to intercept the flotilla. Already an immense fleet of transports had succeeded in landing on the Delaware flats the President's superb corps of cavalry; but the positions assumed by the British ships, if maintained, would enable them to interfere with the passage of the artillery and infantry.

Under these circumstances the Commodore sent an officer to the Admiral with the announcement that his menacing attitude would, if persisted in, be construed as the signal of battle. To this message, the Admiral, a Shakespearian wag, returned no other response than "I bite my thumb, sir!"

"Then I'll powder it with saltpetre, brimstone, and charcoal!" said the Commodore, and he ordered an immediate preparation for action.

"Commodore—Commodore!" said Lord Slysir, limping up to the old officer, "are you going to fight?"

"My Lord, there will be a fight or a foot race, and you may judge how likely the last is in seven fathom water."

"But, Commodore, this is no place for me! It is my province to make war—not to expose myself in battle. I swore, when that herculean Bim was jolting me to death in the bag, that I would never be caught in such a predicament again—and now I find myself about to be exposed to the furious fire of Her Majesty's ship Vesuvius! I protest against it, Commodore!"

"Then protest to Bang, and not to me! I don't intend to shoot you. But I mean to see which can vomit the hottest fire, the Wabash or the Vesuvius!"

"But, Commodore, I must not stay here!"

"Then go below."

"Will I be safe there?"

"Tolerably, under the water-line. A horizontal ball can't reach you. A perpendicular one, going through the decks, might crack your head. A bomb descending to the bottom would make mince meat for the rats; if the ship sinks, you will go down first, being nearest the bottom; and if the magazine should explode, of course we would all be pulverized in a twinkling."

"Can't you put me ashore?"

"Then Ruffleton, when rested, and his guns cooled, may resume the cannonade, and you might be pounded to a jelly. So you see if it be a pleasant amusement to make war, it is no pastime to be in it."

"Commodore, why can't you send me to the Delaware shore?"

"Bim wants to fight on my ship. He is your custodian."

"I could be back in fifteen minutes," said Bim. "And even if the battle begins before that time, I'll be sure to board you. I hope you will permit me to place his Lordship in the custody of the Blue Caps, sir, as I have a special reason for it."

"I am disposed to accommodate you, Bim," said the Commodore; "but do you think his Lordship can be trusted with the ladies?"

"Miss Alice's guards will protect them, sir. But my special reason, sir, is that I wish to place Signor Popoli in a secure place. He might be killed here, and that would be too mild a punishment."

"Go—but see that neither of the prisoners escapes."

"I'll answer for that, sir!" said Bim; and a few moments after a boat put out from the ship, containing Slysir, Bim, and Popoli, the latter still in chains.

CHAPTER XXXVII.

LORD SLYSIR IN CAPTIVITY.

While the party at the mansion were still sitting on the balcony, Captain Bim made his appearance in the lawn below, reporting what he had done, as in duty bound, to his superior officer, Major Milnor, and to Alice.

"I propose," said Lord Slysir, "being the captive of the President's daughter. And if she will permit me to repose my bruised body in a soft chair beside Mr. Langdon's, I pledge my word not to escape."

"And I think you may trust him, Miss Alice," said Bim, "for I have been obliged to help him along every step since we left the boat."

"Assist him up the stairway, Sergeant ——"

"Captain, if you please, Miss Alice," said Bim. "The President, your father, promoted me on the field of battle."

"Then I am sure it was for meritorious conduct, and I am rejoiced at it."

"Thank you, Miss," said Bim, bowing rather awkwardly, but it was too dark to perceive it. "Now, fellow Blue Caps," said he, addressing his comrades standing near, "guard Popoli till I return." Then encircling his Lordship with his gigantic arms, he lifted him with perfect ease, and carried him to the balcony. A chair being in readiness, he placed him in it tenderly. "Good-bye, sir!" said he, shaking hands with his Lordship; "you will be safe in this place."

"Farewell, my friend!" said Slysir, heartily. "You are a little rough, sometimes, but really a true man. I am much indebted to you for your generous care. Wear my watch in token of my gratitude."

"No, sir—I mean my Lord. I might lose it—it might get sunk with my body. And, besides, officers of the United States, it seems to me, are not allowed to accept presents from foreign powers. Good night—I must hurry back!"

"Do you return, Captain?" asked Alice.

"Oh, yes; my leave's not up yet. You promised me five days."

"Then say to my father——"

"Pardon me for interrupting you, Miss, but I do not return to Jersey. They will all be here soon, if the British don't whip us. Your father's magnificent cavalry are all over, and browsing in the flats down yonder; and they are as ravenous as wolves. Not a spear of grass could they get in Jersey—it was all dry sand, except where the blood moistened it. Farewell! I'm in for another fight before morning!"

"Another battle?"

"Yes, indeed. I've promised the Commodore. I've fought every sort of an enemy but the British. The battle will begin very soon, by starlight. But the Commodore says there will be plenty of light—for he intends to pour hot shot into the Vesuvius——"

"What's that?" exclaimed Lord Slysir.

"All the furnaces are in full blast, and we intend to shoot red-hot balls."

"Tell Commodore Stout that such a mode of warfare is not tolerated among Christian nations. I protest against it!"

"I'll tell him, sir; but I don't think he'll hear me. I thought all was fair in war. We fight on our own grounds, sir—or rather in our own waters; and if Admiral Bang—bang! there goes the signal gun! don't like it, why don't he turn tail and run away?" A few minutes after, and Bim was rowing towards the Wabash. Popoli, in chains, was confined in the barracks.

CHAPTER XXXVIII.

THE CANNONADE RESUMED.

Virus did not fail to inform his patron of the remarks he heard in the camp of the enemy regarding the disposition that had been made of Lord Slysir; but for a long time he paid no heed to it, supposing the words to have been uttered by some one for the purpose of misleading him. After the departure of Valiant, however, and the return of Balatrum, although the latter did not confirm the suspicions which Virus might have excited, several messengers from the Western outpost reported the departure of many transports from the Southern camp, having horses on board, supposed to be cavalry, and several deserters were brought in who confirmed the statement that his Lordship had been sent on board the flag-ship of the Commodore.

"Then," said Ruffleton, "there can be no danger of killing him by resuming the cannonade! See to it, Balatrum. Let our batteries re-open on them. What is that?" he continued, as the booming of distant guns struck upon his ear.

"By St. George, General!" said Balatrum, "it comes from the fleet! It is Bang's cannon! And there goes a broadside from the Wabash! They are at it, General, at last!"

"And we are idle! They have discovered the attempt of these Southern heroes to steal away! Sound the alarm! Fly to arms! Let all the batteries re-open upon the encampment of the enemy. Balatrum, suppose you attempt once more to penetrate their lines with a column of infantry?"

"I shall be happy to do so, General, and will set about it without delay."

In a very few minutes the roar of cannon was again resounding through the forests of New Jersey, and the heavens were illuminated with the incessant bursting of bombs.

But Balatrum was unfortunate in his attempt to lead a column of infantry across the creek. His hastily constructed bridges were immediately destroyed, and he found himself, and nearly half his men, suddenly struggling in the treacherous sand and mud, an easy prey to the foe. Many sank never to rise again; and those that succeeded in extricating themselves were in no condition to resume the offensive. They fled back, numbers falling by the way, the victims of their own batteries.

CHAPTER XXXIX.

THE NAVAL BATTLE.

"God bless us!" said Mr. Langdon, upon beholding the fire of the American ships of war illuminating the heavens, the earth, and the water. A great crashing of timbers followed, and was succeeded by a deafening detonation. This was replied to by the British ships, and then the fire became general, and without intermission; and, save the partial obscurity, fitfully produced by the rolling volumes of smoke, the whole scene, by reason of the streams of fire belched forth, was painfully visible.

"Father!" said Edith, "it's the British with whom the brave Commodore is contending. And he is defending our soil, our homes, and liberties, assaulted by a foreign enemy. God *will* bless us, as he has ever done when our cause was just."

"There goes another broadside from the old Vesuvius!" said Lord Slysir, leaning forward with intense interest. "And there falls the old Commodore's flag! And he would have kept me on board with him."

"*Our flag is still there!*" cried Alice. "It was shot down, but the Commodore has replaced it."

"Oh, merciful Parent!" said Mary, "save their lives and put an end to this strife."

"Nonsense, child!" said Slysir. "It is in this way the fate of empires is determined. Diplomacy first—that is thought, calculation; action next—that is demonstration, and then follow the results. Regard it as merely a game of chess, and those who fall, the pawns, knights, rooks, etc., removed. The fruits of victory are reaped by many generations—as for instance, that of Hastings; but those who win them, or those who fall in the game, could not, under any circumstances, survive their allotted three score and ten years. Such is the importance of diplomacy—such the necessity of thinking men devoting themselves to the affairs of the world. By St. George! there goes the Persia! Down, head foremost!"

This was true.

"They have recommenced the cannonade on the land," said Wiry Willy.

"Alas!" said Alice, "how can my father and his friends return to this side of the river, while thus assailed on land by the fanatics, and intercepted by a hostile fleet on the water!"

"President Randolph is a great player," said Lord Slysir: "he is bold, and boldness is greatness both in war and diplomacy. There is always danger of checkmate, playing with such men."

"Look!" exclaimed Edith.

One of the ships of the enemy had taken fire, and bright flames were leaping from its hatches.

"That is the Combustible," said his Lordship. "It is the farthest off, too, and seems to be aground. Ah! your infernal Commodore is firing red-hot shot, sure enough. I thought he was not in earnest."

"Not in earnest!" exclaimed Alice; "and when the hostile fleet of England presumes to menace the Chief Magistrate of this country! And that, too, in our own waters. Brave and glorious Commodore! Long may the Star-Spangled Banner wave triumphantly over your venerable head!"

"The British are retiring," said Edith, seeing the distance widening between the fleets.

"No!" said Lord Slysir. "It is only a manœuvre. Admiral Bang is brave; and besides, he is aware I am a witness of his conduct. It must be those red-hot balls. He could not suppose such barbarous missiles would be used by a civilized and Christian nation."

"And can any species of carnage be consistent with civilization and Christianity?" asked Mary.

"All the great improvements in the art of war, as well as in the other arts," said his Lordship, "have kept pace with the progress of civilization. As to the amicable effect Christianity should produce upon the nations, it is true its mission is alleged to be one of peace and love; but, it cannot be denied, if history be credited, that more wars and bloodshed have been produced by the disputes of religionists than by any other causes."

"And, my Lord," said Mr. Langdon, "the very wars you allude to were mostly the work of designing diplomacy. But war is the history of man—peace is the dream of the wise."

"See!" exclaimed Edith, "there are two more ships on fire! And one on our side."

"Alas, it is true!" said Alice. "But the British flag has been lowered, while the American Stars and Stripes are still flying."

"The fire has ceased on both," said Willy, "and I can see the small boats plying between them and the other ships. They are saving the crews."

This was true. And there seemed to be a diminution of the work of destruction. Nevertheless, this flagging of the strife was only of short duration. Some of the steamships had drawn off to repair damaged machinery, and others to turn, or to tow into better position the ships that had no propelling power. These arrangements completed, the battle was renewed with desperate resolution.

The Wabash continued to belch forth its red-hot balls; and the Vesuvius, although a large number of the men were constantly employed extinguishing the flames, that burst forth in many places, fired broadside after broadside with surprising rapidity. And, over all, and in the height of the conflict, there arose a dark cloud in the sultry south, emitting brilliant flashes from heaven, and stunning the earth with its jarring thunders. Above and below, the slaughter of man by man, and the war of the elements, presented a spectacle that awed the beholders into silence. It seemed as if the hour of doom, the era of universal destruction, had arrived. Ship after ship either burst into flames, or went down beneath the wreck-covered waters. The lightning flashed, the thunder pealed, and the rain fell in fitful showers.

And during this awful scene, two frightful calamities occurred. The magazine of the Vesuvius became ignited by a red-hot ball, and the ship was blown to atoms. Men, and bombs, and cannon, were hurled a great distance in the air, and were distinctly visible by the lightnings in the heavens. One of the guns, it was afterwards asserted, exploded in the clouds; and it was declared that human beings, at the height of a thousand fathoms, gesticulated frantically.

This catastrophe put an end to the naval battle. A solitary British ship, the Antelope, escaped. The rest were either destroyed or captured.

CHAPTER XL.

RETURN OF THE CHIEFTAINS.

TEN of the American ships had sustained but little injury, and not half of the red-hot balls of the Wabash had been expended. Therefore in obedience to an order from the

President, who had witnessed the triumph of the stars and stripes, the old Commodore led his fleet, flushed with victory, to the assistance of the besieged. Again the ships poured a destructive fire into the camp of the enemy, and this time the besiegers were to experience the consternation of having red-hot shot hurled amongst their ranks. The effect produced surpassed all expectations. Ruffleton was under the necessity of drawing back his men and batteries beyond the range of the insupportable missiles thrown from the fleet, which, sailing up and down the river, discharged larboard and starboard broadsides without intermission.

It was under cover of this bombardment that Randolph and the Southern Generals urged forward the work of embarkation; and by the dawn of day the evacuation was completed.

"Run, Willy!" exclaimed Alice, upon learning the armies had landed on the Delaware shore—for the party at the mansion watched through the night—"and if my father and his friends, I mean our friends, the several commanders, have escaped unharmed, give us a signal—let it be the prolonged blast of a bugle."

"But Ruffleton's word is law in New Jersey," said Lord Slysir, musing. "He is absolute there. And if this is the case in New Jersey, notwithstanding the Governor invoked and obtained the aid of the Federal Government, backed by two Southern armies, what resistance can be looked for in any other free State without such auxiliaries?"

"Oh, land of Washington!" said Alice.

"Where are the guardian spirits of the Revolution?" exclaimed Edith.

"God will preserve us!" said Mary.

"Nonsense!" pursued his Lordship. "It will be only a change of form. A monarchy is the Anglo-Saxon's hereditary government. If the first Cromwell had lived a year longer he would have been king. This second Cromwell will either be king himself, or make one of somebody else. Then you will be united again, like England and Scotland. You will have Lords and Ladies—and a magnificent Court. It was from such civil and military convulsions as these, that my ancestor derived his patent of nobility." Turning his eyes on Edith, he then added, "What a magnificent countess you would make!"

"A Senator's daughter would be sufficient distinction for me," said she.

"You might be both the one and the other. Your father, by espousing the cause of his native North, would unquestionably have an elevated seat assigned him in Parlia ment——"

"I pray your Lordship not to amuse my daughter with any such illusory sketches of the imagination!" said Mr. Langdon.

"They are merely fancy sketches, father," said Edith.

"Fancy sketches! I am a bachelor, and, by St. George, ——"

They were interrupted by the bugle-blast announcing the arrival in safety of the chieftains.

"Saved! all saved!" cried Alice—and the next moment she and Edith were locked in each other's arms.

"They are coming!" said Mary.

Alice and Edith hastened below to greet them at the threshhold.

"My MARBLE!" said Randolph, embracing his child.

"No--father—say your daughter. Not marble, now!"

"Edith! dearest Edith!" said Blount, folding the unresisting maiden in his arms.

"Good!" said Crook. "I have a wife and nine children at home; but since such greeting is the reward of valor, I don't see why I may not claim my share of it!" and before the young ladies could escape, he had embraced and kissed them both.

They repaired without delay to the apartment above, in which lights were gleaming, and into which Mr. Langdon had been wheeled, upon the announcement of the arrival of the President and the Generals.

"I congratulate you, Randolph," said the venerable Senator, "and you, Generals, on your escape from the toils of the arch-fiend, who supposed he had compassed your destruction!"

"And will no one congratulate me on my victory over the British?" said the President, affectionately taking the hand of Mary.

"That would I do, were I not an Englishman," said Lord Slysir. "And if I may not congratulate you, nevertheless I do not hesitate to say that your iron-sided—perhaps I should say infernal—Commodore, has gained a great naval victory over my countrymen. The only advantage he had was superior pilots and his inexcusable red-hot balls."

"Oh, we'll excuse them, my Lord," said Randolph, "since it was Bang's good fortune to escape."

"To escape?" cried his Lordship. "Can it be possible that Admiral Bang escaped from the blowing up of the Vesuvius?"

"Such is the fact," said the President; "and not only the Admiral, but nearly all his officers and crew. They took refuge in the small boats, or sprang overboard into the river, and were saved by the Commodore. The Commodore and the Admiral are now decapitating champagne bottles in the cabin of the Wabash."

"Ay, and Bang can beat him at that," said Slysir.

"And now, my Lord," said Randolph, "I have joyful news for you."

"I stand in need of something to cheer me," said his Lordship.

"You are free. You were to be liberated upon our evacuation; and I am not prepared to forfeit my word. You can go at any moment, sir, under the safe conduct of two of Alice's Blue Caps."

"I must crave your permission, Mr. President," replied his Lordship, "to remain where I am until I am somewhat recovered. Miss Edith has fed me and nursed me kindly during the few hours I have enjoyed the hospitality of this mansion; but I am not yet in a fit condition to walk, to ride, or to swim. And, therefore, I beg to be detained a little longer."

"Edith," said Blount, "like any American lady, makes no distinction between friend and foe, in healing the wounds received in battle."

"But for the kind offices I have experienced, I shall ever protest, although it may not be permitted to aspire to be classed among the former, that I am not, and never can become, one of the latter."

"I am sure I cannot perceive why we may not be friends," said Edith.

"I trust you may never perceive it," said his Lordship.

"My Lord," said Blount, "are you not the enemy of

her country? Have you not caused Her Majesty's ships to assail those of her Government?"

"By no means, General," said his Lordship, with vivacity. "Her country, according to my interpretation, is the North, against which Her Majesty's forces do not meditate any hostile enterprises."

"No politics!" said Alice, interposing.

"See here," said Crook, standing before a mirror. "Come, Randolph—come, Blount, behold yourselves in this glass. For my part, I confess I resemble my own Pompey, an African I purchased on Pearl river."

The Generals and Randolph were much blackened by the smoke of gunpowder; and some merriment was caused by the detection of sooty marks on the faces of the young ladies.

"Let us all seek the repose we so much need," said Mr. Langdon. "For my part, although I have been distant from the scene of conflict, I have slumbered as little as any of the combatants. Ah, Randolph," he continued, when the President held him by the hand, and bade him adieu before retiring to his chamber, "although you have performed the great feat of regaining a friendly soil after so many perils, yet, believe me, the Rubicon has been crossed! I may not live to see the end of this business——"

"Oh, father!" said Edith, "be not so desponding."

"Nay, be cheerful, my dear friend," said Randolph. "There may be more disasters in store for us; but we shall yet have brilliant days. The darkest clouds must pass away. Believe me, there are clear blue skies beyond."

"Oh, yes—and may God permit me to be an inhabitant of them! Nevertheless, go on, Randolph! You are right. Save the country, and posterity will bless you."

During the forenoon all the slumberers rose much refreshed, with the exception of Mr. Langdon and Lord Slysir. The former was too ill to leave his couch. The latter was stiff and sore from the exercises and bruises of the preceding day and night.

Alice and Edith, arrayed in spotless white, were traversing the parterres of the garden among the refreshing roses, when Bim appeared on the opposite side of the hedge, mounted on a spirited steed the President had given him. His military salute attracted the attention of the ladies, and, walking in that direction, Alice accosted him.

"Captain Bim," said she, "whither are you going?"

"With your permission, Miss, to Philadelphia."

"To Philadelphia! That might be hazardous. But, I believe, danger is your delight." She alluded to the motto worked with threads of gold on Bim's cap. It was, "Danger is my delight."

"In a good cause I do love it, Miss Alice. But fearing my leave of absence might expire before I could get back, I thought it my duty to beg another day or two, in case of accident."

"What good cause takes you to the city, Captain? An affair of honor, or of love?"

"Everything in the service of President Randolph, Miss, is an affair of honor."

"Very well answered," said Edith, "as to the point of honor; but the other point of the interrogatory is evaded."

"Postponed is the word. I am determined not to be a lover until I am a General."

"There, Edith," said Alice. "It is answered, now. But he can hardly be serious."

"I am, upon my word," said Bim. "I don't know but one woman in Philadelphia, and she's a Tartar. Oh, she's more terrible than a hundred batteries!"

"Indeed! Will you tell us her name, Captain?"

"Certainly. It's Mrs. Punt. Miss Mary knows her. She was the hag I rescued her from."

"Then it is not likely you will again venture in reach of such a terrible creature. You have my permission to go, Captain."

"Then, with your permission I will retire. I see the President and at least a dozen Generals approaching." And gathering up the reins, which had been loosened to permit his steed to crop the luxuriant grass, Bim turned and rode briskly away. The young ladies, not caring to confront the Generals in their peripatetic Council of War, vanished under cover of a row of altheas, and returned by another avenue to the mansion.

CHAPTER XLI.

THE UNDERGROUND BRIDAL CHAMBER.

CAPTAIN BIM conducted Popoli down to the river side, and through the encampment of the combined armies.

Entering a light boat, Bim took the helm, and Popoli unfurled the sail to the breeze, he being an expert sailor, and they were soon going at the rate of four miles an hour.

"Popoli," said Bim, "it would be unfortunate for you if any of the enemy's boats should board us."

"Why, Captain?" asked the Italian, whose eyes had been fixed on the various sail crossing above.

"Because, Signor, my oath expired last night: and I don't intend to renew it till we are where I mean to leave you, according to promise, with your friend Cardini."

"I shall be glad to see him, Captain. I wouldn't escape if I had an opportunity; it would prevent my meeting with my friend."

"Only be patient, Signor, and you shall see him, if he still lives."

"Was he not well?"

"Oh, quite well, but not in very good spirits. Confound the fish!" Bim made this exclamation when a large sturgeon leaped over his head and splashed a quantity of water into the boat. "That fellow, Signor," he continued, "was heavy enough to have knocked a man overboard. If he had struck me in the breast, you might have been free."

"Can't you swim?" asked Popoli, eagerly.

"Suppose you try me, Signor?" was Bim's response, not choosing to confess the truth. "If you have any curiosity that way, just flap the boat over with the sail at the next tack, and we'll see who can dive the longest. Speaking of diving, I thought you were gone last night when you didn't come up where I was looking; and all the time your nose was above water behind me. I shall say nothing about your attempt to stab me, because I don't wish to lose my temper, and miss the satisfaction of witnessing your meeting with Cardini. You asked me where Cardini was, I think, and I believe I'll tell you."

"If you please, Captain."

"He's at General Ruffleton's head-quarters."

"How can that be, Captain, since the General has sent messengers in all directions to find him?"

"Oh, they didn't look in the right chamber."

"But don't you think he's gone by this time?"

"Never fear it. I'll answer for it he remains till he gets my permission to leave. And you must do the same. Will you not promise?"

"Yes, Captain, if you insist."

"I won't insist, Signor. So you see what a kind captor you have. And yet you determined to kill me! But I won't think of that. There goes another fish. Take care!" The warning was too late; for the sturgeon striking the Italian's shoulder, carried him overboard. But Popoli rose immediately, and without difficulty clambered into the boat again. "They must be curious to see what's going on out of the water," continued Bim, seeing a great many sturgeons leaping above the surface, "and I don't wonder at it, after all the bombarding and bombursting we have had in this neighborhood."

In this familiar manner the captor and the captive approached the city, and landed in one of the slips just after nightfall. Having secured the boat to one of the rings at the wharf, Bim, taking the right arm of Popoli, led the way cautiously in a westerly direction.

Not half the lamps were burning, the shops were closed as on a Sunday night, and but few persons were seen promenading the streets.

Having thrown off his military costume it was not difficult for Bim, with his free and easy bearing, and familiar speech, to pass without hindrance to the Square in the rear of Independence Hall. Here there were several thousand loungers around the platform under the trees, whence the news from all quarters were promulgated by a committee appointed for that purpose.

Bim did not wait to hear any more news of the operations of the Dictator, but proceeded without further delay to the row of buildings on Sixth street, which he had so often resorted to previously. He found but slight impediment to his entrance at the same door he had forced on several occasions. Closing this carefully behind him, he struck a light. Then turning to Popoli, he said, with uplifted hand:

"I do hereby swear that I will not kill you, Signor Popoli, this night, provided you do not attempt to escape, don't try to give any alarm, don't try to kill me, and don't give me more provocation than common flesh and blood can bear—so help me——! Now, Signor, you are entirely safe, as it concerns the things you have committed heretofore; and you have only to be governed by the conditions of my oath to-night, to preserve your body in a whole skin."

"Take me to Cardini, Captain. Where is he?"

"Don't be impatient! You will find him soon enough. Did you ever hear of the Underground Bridal Chamber in these parts?"

"Never. It would be strange, indeed, to put a bride underground anywhere."

"But it might be convenient, sometimes; and particularly when a man has more brides than he can manage conveniently, or a single one that annoys him. This Underground Bridal Chamber was ordered to be constructed by a certain very powerful man, whose name it would do no one in this company any good to use, for the purpose, as it was thought, of holding one or more of his troublesome wives—"

"Is it a prison—a dungeon, Captain Bim?"

"What's the use of inquiring so particularly about your lodgings after you have engaged them, and when you will be occupying them in a few minutes?"

"And can it be possible, Captain Bim, that Cardini is confined in this locality."

"It is not only possible, Signor, but exactly so. Of course the General would go from home to look for a lost child. Of all the places in the world, it was the most secure one for Cardini's concealment. I will not say I had the genius to perceive this at first. But I see it now. Come, Signor, take a full breath of the upper air, and then we'll descend." Saying this Bim touched the spring, and the hearth-stone flew up. Popoli started back. "Oh! you mustn't flinch at that," said Bim; "it's nothing to the other sights you must see. Go down, Signor—there's the ladder—and I'll bring up the rear. Remember my oath. If you break it, it won't be my fault. Reflect one moment—it's the last I'll allow you. If you go down quietly, and do everything I order obediently, it will be an easier and more comfortable way to meet Cardini, than to be knocked down and dragged in—won't it?"

"Yes, Captain!" said Popoli, convinced there was no other alternative. He descended, and was followed by Bim with the light. And in this manner they proceeded to the iron door of the chamber.

"The bars and bolts are just as I left them," said Bim, "black and rusty. Signor Cardini!" he continued, rapping with the hilt of his bowie knife. "Wake up! I've brought you an agreeable companion. Why don't you answer? I've got Signor Popoli here for you—and if you don't give me a signal of approbation, I'll take him somewhere else!"

"No! no!" cried Cardini.

"That is his voice!" said Popoli.

"To be sure it is," said Bim. He opened the door, and the Italians rushed into each other's arms.

"Oh, Signor!" cried Cardini. "Do you come to set me free, or as a fellow prisoner?"

"The latter, Signor!" said Popoli.

"Stop a moment!" cried Bim, gazing at Cardini. "Stand apart! Are you the *same* Signor Cardini I put in here for murdering General Hudson?"

"The same, Sergeant—"

"Stop! Say Captain. I've been promoted."

"Then, noble Captain, I am the same unhappy man. But do not call me a murderer. It was only a blow of policy, to serve—"

"Never mind who it served. I know all about it. But the reason I didn't know you was that your hair has changed. It was black when I chucked you in this place, and now it's white!"

"Captain!" said Popoli, "you have a generous heart!"

"Not a bit! Don't believe it!" said Bim, gazing at the prisoners, who again embraced each other.

"Captain!" said Popoli—"I will make a confession to you! Signor Cardini is my father!"

"He is? But it may be a lie. Then what if he is? It only goes to show that assassination is hereditary."

"Will you not release him?"

"Release the d——l! What mercy did he show to General Hudson? And what mercy did you show to the President?"

"I ask no favor for myself, Captain. But you know the man my father slew was at the head of the army which you have been fighting. Would you not kill the head of that same hostile army now, if you could?"

"In fair fight. But I would not stab the d——l himself in the dark. No, Signor; you must both remain in this Underground Bridal Chamber until called for. But you shan't starve. I'll roll in another barrel of crackers, and more smoked fish. You have abundance of water. All I can say is to advise you to put yourselves on short allowance, and pray morning, noon, and night; for I can't say when I shall be able to see you again." Saying this, Bim threw in the food he promised, and fastening the door securely, returned to the upper region.

All was perfectly still and silent in the chambers. Not even a rat was heard; and Bim really felt lonely after the separation from his Italian captive. Nothing, however, could frighten him but a ghost. He slowly ascended the stairs. When he approached the door of the attic chamber containing his treasure, he was surprised to find the door partly open, and a light in the room.

"Hello! Old Tuppenny," said he, "I'm afraid you're getting extravagant. How could you afford to buy a candle? Where are you?" he continued, stepping in, and turning his face towards the closet, which was closed, and no Jew Mouser appearing before him. But behind him, in a corner, there was an awful spectacle. The Jew, having heard Bim confess his horror of ghosts, and his quick ear having warned him of his arrival, he resolved to put in execution a plan he had conceived of personating a spectre. The difficulty was how to present a resemblance of a ghost, Solomon having never seen one himself. Nevertheless, presuming it must have a frightful aspect, old Mouser had put on a mask, representing the face of a corpse, and enveloping himself in a sheet that reached the floor, notwithstanding he was mounted on a high stool, he awaited the result.

"Don't you hear?" continued Bim, stooping down before

the closet. "Answer me, or I'll get mad. You won't? Then I'll go in after you!"

He pulled the door open and entered, taking his candle with him.

"By George, he's not here!" said he. "But here's the coffee-bag, and the gold jingles in it. The old dog is getting negligent. I thought he would die with his eyes set on the gold, rather than live and go to heaven without it. So, my old Mouser, I will not trust you any longer with my purse—and I won't pay you, either, for deserting your post. I'll take the whole concern along with me, and let him nose it out again if he can. So, come along!"

This time he left the closet head foremost, dragging the bag after him. And when he rose, his eyes rested on the chalky face of the apparition.

"What's that?" said he, letting the coffee-bag fall with a great crash. "By George! I'm afraid I've met with my match at last! I never heard my teeth clatter this way before. I'll run." He did so; but before he had descended many steps, he paused and looked back. "I don't like to leave my gold," said he, "nor do I fancy showing the white feather before I'm hurt. I wouldn't mind killing, if that would be the last of it; but who can tell what an infernal spirit might do with one after death? Still, I ought to be satisfied that it *is* a ghost. It's not human, I think; neither flesh, fish, nor common red herring; but still it may not be a ghost. Suppose it's a mere trick? A corpse some one has been propping there to frighten me? or to frighten the Jew? I'll go back! I never was, and never will be, a coward!"

The Captain, turning about, retraced his steps. And when he re-entered the room, the ghost was still there; but the sheet which enveloped it had been evidently readjusted since his exit.

"It's alive anyhow," said Bim, staring with his great round eyes. "It's moved its covering, and I see the leg of the stool. That's queer. I thought a ghost could stand on nothing. By George! I think I see the toe of a boot! I never heard of ghosts wearing boots. See here, Mr. Ghost, or hobgoblin, or whatever you are, I want an explanation. You've injured me cruelly. You've made my blood run cold; you've made my cap too little for my head;

you've made my teeth bite my tongue; and you've caused my knee bones to smite each other as if they were not twins, but enemies. I'm a badly used man! Now, let me hear your explanation for such malignities and aggressions!"

The lips of the mask seemed to move, but no sound issued from them.

"Speak louder," said Bim; and speak English—for I don't understand the lingoes of the infernal regions."

The only response to this was a motion of the arm, which pointed to the door.

"That, I suppose, said Bim, "is meant for a polite way of ordering me out!"

To this the ghost nodded assent.

"By George! he understands English, if he can't speak it. I believe I'll go. But I'll take the bag." He cast his eyes down at the sack, and then looked again at the ghost. The ghost shook his head violently in dissent.

"That's singular," said Bim. "What can it want with money? It begins to shake my belief iu ghosts—or in this one anyhow. Suppose I try him? If it's only the ghost of the Jew, who may be dead, I don't wonder at its love for money, and I oughtn't to be afraid of it. See here, sir! Everybody who ever saw a ghost, says neither steel nor lead can hurt it. What do you say?"

The ghost, who had been looking over its right shoulder, turned its face quickly in front, for Bim had placed his hand on one of the pistols in his belt.

"If you have any objection to my trying the experiment, signify it by saying no. The ball's lead, as you well know, if you are a true ghost. No answer? By George! his knees are knocking together like mine did! Why, a ghost can't be afraid! No matter; I'll make a bull's eye of his nose!"

"Don't shoot!" said the ghost.

"Ha!" said Bim, lowering the muzzle of the pistol, and stepping back against the wall. "That was good enough English! But if he's afraid of a bullet, how can he be a ghost?"

"I was only amusing myself!" said Solomon, throwing off the mask and sheet, and stepping down from the stool.

Bim, placing his arms akimbo, gazed for a long time in silence and with perfect gravity at the Jew.

"It was only a little fun," said Solomon.

Bim continued to stare in silence.

"A little innocent amusement!" continued Solomon.

"Mr. Solomon Mouser," said Bim at length, "you have done that which mortal humanity never did before. You have made my strong joints tremble, and my hot blood turn cold like a frog's. I would certainly kill you, if I didn't think I might be ashamed of it afterwards. Perhaps it's a good thing for me. It may cure my fear of ghosts. I'll certainly fire at the next I see before I run. You may live, if you'll get down on your knees and swear never to tell anybody that you frightened Jack Bim."

He did so without the least hesitation.

"And, Captain," said Mouser, "I swear I will never be a ghost again."

"No. You needn't swear to that. If you have any taste for the fun, I shan't object to it. Now to business. Come, Old Tuppenny, I dreamt the other night you were cheating me."

"Cheating you! I'll show you the figures!"

"No doubt. And I know figures can't lie—but those who make them can. I've seen it done at elections. You have some $26,000—"

"No, sir! Here's the sum, on this paper. It is only $25,900 19."

"Well, what's the difference?"

"Why ninety-nine dollars and eighty-one cents!"

"Say twenty-five thousand, then, to make it even——"

"Very good! I'll alter it."

"You are a skinflint—and you won't gain by your avariciousness!" said Bim, snatching the pen out of the Jew's hand. "One tenth of one per cent. for keeping the deposit, would be some twenty-five dollars a day! That's more than the pay of a member of Congress, whose board costs him as much in one week as yours does in twelve months. Twenty-five dollars was too much to ask, old Tuppenny—"

"You agreed to it! You agreed to it! It was a fair bargain! And it's upwards of twenty-five dollars and ninety cents—"

"I shan't dispute about the cents, Solomon, nor fly from my contract, either, because I've found out how you intended to swindle me in time to prevent it. You know well enough that I had no idea of the amount it would come to. It was unjust, and if you had been a Christian instead of a Jew, you would not have accepted an unfair compensation for your service. But that was not all. You loaned me a thousand dollars, at I don't know what rate of interest, to keep from lessening the deposit, and of course the commission. So I am paying you a dollar a day commission for keeping *my* thousand dollars, and you are charging me interest on yours. That's the true statement of the case, Solo mon!"

"It was a contract—a fair contract!" said the Jew.

"But I did not bind myself to let the deposit remain any particular length of time."

"That's true. But the law requires notice—"

"The law! Don't name it, Jew. This right arm is my law in such times as these—beware it does not become your executioner! Count out the amount due to you up to this minute, and take your pay."

"Oh, Captain—don't remove the deposit. In these lawless times it will be lost."

"Take your pay, Tuppenny! Then, perhaps, I'll make another bargain with you."

"Well! I will do so!" and Solomon counted out his money.

"Now, Tuppenny," said Bim, "I'm going to leave just twenty thousand with you, and will allow you no commission except on the sums I draw out. You shall have ten per cent. on all payments. Don't object, or I'll take it all, and you shall have nothing!"

"Captain, won't you allow me commission on the six thousand—"

"Six thousand! Why Solomon, you said yourself it was only $25,900 19—then deducting the thousand I borrowed, only twenty-four thousand nine hundred remained. Surely it must be a pleasure for you to cheat, besides the love of gain! No—I will not pay you a cent for nothing. If you asked it as charity—"

"I'm no beggar, Captain!"

"I know that, well enough—but I came near saying you were a robber. However, I'm not afraid to trust you; and you can make some sort of calculation of your gains by our new contract. But I'm going to make a will—so if I die, or if you hire any one to murder me, you needn't think to get my money."

The Jew durst not demur to Bim's dictation. And the Captain, after settling with his banker, and leaving in his custody an unincumbered deposit of $20,000, departed with the remainder of the treasure.

Bim could not resist an inclination to explore the buildings further down the row, where he had already met with so many adventures; and so he passed through the several apertures until he came to the parlor in which he had found Mary Penford, and, subsequently, captured the assassin Cardini. Again he found the parlor illuminated; and, sitting in the large luxuriously-cushioned chair, was Mrs. Punt. She was reading the New York ——, in which were published the proceedings of the Convention, and General Ruffleton appeared in almost every paragraph.

The Captain strode in and stood before the astonished woman. She let the paper fall to the floor, rose up, and was just opening her mouth to utter a piercing scream, when Bim stepped forward and placed his hand on it.

"Don't scream, Mrs. Punt," said he; "there's no occasion for it. You know me, and I know you. And I know your husband. Now will you be quiet if I release you?"

She nodded assent, and Bim replaced her in the chair. Then sitting down beside her, he coolly inquired after her health since his last visit.

"I've been well enough," said she.

"But what are you in mourning for?'

"I'm sure there's enough to mourn for in this wicked world. I thought Punt had been killed at Bladensburg—"

"But you were disappointed."

"He might as well be dead, for I haven't got a cent from him yet."

"There has been no one to send it by. I merely called to let you know I'm going to Washington soon, and will deliver any message you may wish to send."

"All the message I have to send is, that I'd like to have the money he earns to support his children with. I don't know when I'm to see the General again, and he's left nobody here to pay me my wages. He's left plenty of wines, cigars, and such things——"

"Mrs. Punt," said Bim, interrupting her, "I'm thirsty. Get me some wine and cake, or anything else that's convenient, if you please."

"It's not mine, and I don't care who drinks it," said she, rising and producing a waiter and decanters from a closet. Bim helped himself, and invited Mrs. Punt to drink, which she accepted.

"Now a cigar," said he, "and I'll be in good condition to travel." This, likewise, was produced; and the Captain igniting it, shook hands with the hostess and departed.

CHAPTER XLII.

YOUNG SUMMERS.

When Randolph returned from the garden, he found a despatch awaiting him from Major S——. It was borne by a smooth-visaged messenger, as the Major wrote, who had been employed by Ruffleton in the capacity of confidential messenger, but now, from some pique, had resolved to abandon the service of the tyrant. He had volunteered to deliver any message in writing or otherwise to President Randolph; and hoped that his success in doing so might recommend him to a situation in the President's family.

The letter informed the President, that although Ruffleton's absence from the army might be of some duration, as he was engaged in the stupendous work of organizing a military despotism, yet there would be no pause in the preparations for an invasion of the South. It was Ruffleton's design, after retaining just sufficient forces to keep any species of opposition in subjection, to concentrate the anti-slavery hosts on the border; and it was probable half a million combatants would soon be in readiness to pass the southern line of Pennsylvania.

At dinner it was announced that both Mr. Langdon and Lord Slysir were too unwell to leave their chambers; and the former at that hour required the presence and constant attention of Edith.

A long table was set in the capacious hall of the old mansion, at which many of the highest officers of the Federal and Southern armies, as well as several captains of the Navy, were present. It was the only really good dinner most of them had partaken of for several days; and for a considerable length of time the viands were discussed almost exclusively. But, as the wine flowed freely, and the ladies seemed diverted, the time soon came for the flow of conversation.

"General," said Randolph, to Blount, who sat on his left, "I was on the eve of observing that this company had completely succeeded in dismissing from their thoughts all matters of serious import, or profound gravity, when my eye chanced to catch the melancholy expression of your countenance."

Blount looked up, and most of the guests in the immediate vicinity of the speaker were attentive during the deliberate utterance of this speech; and when it was ended, Blount himself, as well as the rest, gave vent to hearty laughter.

"And even that, Mr. President, it seems," said Blount, "was provocative of mirth."

"Be merry, then, General," said Valiant, "and we will cease to laugh at your expense."

"What say you, Crook?" demanded the President.

"I say, he who wins may laugh—and he who carves may eat." The General had been active with the carver in filling the plates of the ladies.

"Help yourself, General," said Alice.

"I will," said he; and he did. "But do you know that it is a most ungrateful and cruel speech? After heaping favors on others, to be told by them to help myself?"

Alice drew the attention of Mary to the smooth-faced young man, the messenger from the Northern camp, sitting beside Willy.

"Did you ever see him before?" asked Alice.

"Never, to my recollection."

"Nor I. But Edith, on seeing him from the balcony, was quite sure she had met him somewhere."

"They may have met," continued Mary, again looking at the stranger; "but I have no recollection—"

"Why do you pause?"

"It does seem to me now that I have seen his face somewhere. It must have been in the city; and, I think, it was on that terrible night—yes! I am sure of it. But where, I cannot remember."

"It must be so. And he, too, I think, has some recollection of it. Several times he has paused in his conversation with Willy, and looked steadily at you. Father," continued she, in a whisper, "what is the name of this new messenger?"

"Summers—Charley, they call him. Why?"

"Nothing—merely curiosity. We shall not fall in love with him. Has he entered your service?"

"He proposes to do so. But he is a mere boy. I'm afraid he's too young."

"He may not be so young as he seems. There are marks of mature decision on his face."

"And beauty?"

"No, sir. General," she continued, addressing Blount, the dialogue having become audible, "what do you think of his beauty?"

"Really I do not see any to think about," was the reply, after glancing in the direction indicated.

The President, accompanied by several of the Generals, soon after retired to the chamber used as an office, to learn the contents of certain despatches, which proved to be, in several instances, official communications from the Governors of States. Indiana, Illinois, Iowa, and Wisconsin, were still attached to the Federal Union, though many of the inhabitants had embraced the cause of the Abolitionists. On the other hand, resolutions were transmitted by a majority of the Governors of the Southern states (adopted since the interposition of the President in New Jersey, by the respective Legislatures), sanctioning the action of the Southern Generals in placing their forces at the disposal of the Chief Magistrate, as a *posse comitatus*, for the purpose of suppressing domestic violence.

But startling intelligence was mingled with the good. The van of the great Western army of fanatics, led by General Line, had reached Cumberland, Maryland, and that town had yielded without resistance, having no means of defence.

CHAPTER XLIII.

THE SOIRÉE.

There was a splendid reception in the evening. Many of the officers had been joined by their wives, and several belles from the city were present. The eye of Randolph was calm and clear; a benign dignity seemed enthroned on his brow, and a placid smile rested on his lips. And Alice stood beside him, pale though beautiful. Majestic in stature, graceful in attitude, animated in expression; her eye vying in cerulian with the cloudless sky, and her crescent forehead illuminated with its star-like diamond; the daughter of the President, in the Executive palace, never inspired greater admiration. And Edith, who stood beside her, shared the homage lavished by the multitude. Nor was the unassuming Mary, the gentle and cherished companion of the high-born maidens, obscured by the glitter of fashion.

Blount, himself the centre of a group of admirers, when the saloons were filled, nevertheless could not wholly withdraw his eyes from his affianced bride; and Edith, and even Alice observed it.

And Lord Slysir, unable either to walk or to stand without pain, was borne in by two of his servants, who had been permitted to join him, seated in a great chair that moved on rollers. He, too, seemed to gaze at Edith, as one under the spell of an irresistible fascination.

Blount, having long been waiting an opportunity to utter all he felt in the ear of Edith, embraced the earliest moment to seek a *tête-à-tête*. But when he approached, unperceived by Edith, young Summers appeared at her elbow on the opposite side. Twice before he had attracted her notice in the same manner; and this time he seemed disposed to linger.

"Have we not met somewhere?" asked Edith, unable any longer to resist an utterance of the interrogatory which rose so often to her lips.

"Yes, lady," said Summers.

"Where?"

"I ought not, perhaps, to say, if other ears might hear me," was the very mysterious reply.

"I am quite certain, sir, I should have no objection to hear it mentioned in the presence of any auditor. But we will go into yonder corner, now partially deserted."

As they moved away, Blount joined the circle round the President and Alice.

"Who is that?" asked he, after exchanging renewed greetings with Alice, and at the same time indicating by a nod, and perhaps rather an imperious one, the individual who had walked aside with Edith.

"Were I not MARBLE, General, the manner and tone of your demand might have startled me."

"Was it startling? Forgive me."

"Was it not? But you were not conscious of it. That is one of the President's clerks."

"One of the President's clerks?"

"One of the President's clerks! Is that so very remarkable?"

"No. Perhaps not," said he, half abstractedly. "I can wait—"

"General Blount!"

"Nay, fear me not. We have been reconciled."

"Ha! ha! How often, Harry?"

"Upon my word I do not remember," said he, partaking of Alice's merriment.

"General!" said the President, placing his hand on Blount's shoulder, and whispering in his ear, "follow me presently into the office. Let your eyes cease to follow that provoking magnet. She is her own mistress yet, and competent to take care care of herself. Be not uneasy or suspicious, or—what you will—"

"I am all attention, sir," said Blount. "Pray go on."

"Lead Alice round once or twice, and give me an opportunity to escape. I have important despatches." Saying this, Randolph offered his arm to one of the glittering dames from the city, and led the promenade. But, before the circle of the saloon was completed, he had uttered his apologies, and vanished through a door communicating with the library, then occupied as his office.

"You still have the ring," said Blount, looking down at the fair hand of Alice, reposing on his arm.

"Yes. Here, let me return it."

"No."

"Edith will never receive it from me."

"Nor from me, except at the altar."

"Where else should she receive it?"

"I cannot tell. Keep it until *then*. What better repository could we have? And, Alice, the day may be distant when the transfer can be made at the altar."

"Is it not your purpose to urge the completion—?"

"Not now."

"And why not? Her father has abandoned the position he held, if not, indeed, the cause of those with whom he was identified, and—and—he might consent."

"It were bootless!" said Blount, mournfully. "I could not now, consistently with my regard for Edith, ask her to brave with me the dark and terrible future looming up in the horizon. If I survive—if the cloud should be riven, and a single ray of sunshine beam upon our pathway, then—"

"Harry, you believe, then, that this storm, instead of speedily abating, is destined to increase?"

"Frankly, I do."

"And so does my father. Alas, for the Republic!"

"It will survive—though the heads of many of its defenders and champions may lie low."

"But think not Edith would be appalled. Woman can be true even when the strongest man proves false; can share the ills of life, its fearful tempests, as well as its peaceful sunshine, with the one she loves. Has she not confessed as much?"

"I have not questioned her."

"And why not? Her father might signify his approbation, and she might consent. Then all this suspense, these fearful forebodings, these cruel doubts——"

"Nay—I would not link my uncertain fate, in such a moment, with the one I have loved and cherished. Not only the pang of separation, but the fear of disaster and death, would be too much to add to her present cares. Her venerable father will require her undivided attention."

"How weak and fragile we are, in the estimation of the stern lords of creation! Will she not care for you absent, though unwedded, and fear disaster and death? Harry, the thought of an absent husband, battling for his country and achieving glory in the path of duty, would be a sustaining thought, rather than a source of additional unhappiness, whilst she watched beside her parent's couch!"

"It might be so. But the thought that I had irrevocably bound her, and left her, would rankle in my breast. But what in the name of woman's caprice can so enchain her to the side of that stripling?" he continued, momentarily pausing, and casting a glance at the corner where Edith and Summers still remained in earnest conversation.

CHAPTER XLIV.

EDITH AND SUMMERS.

When Edith and Charles Summers were separated from the company, the former demanded a reply to her question.

"I am sure I cannot be mistaken," said he; "for Wiry Willy has informed me of the incidents in the city, wherein you were an involuntary actor. It was in the market-place I saw you. You were then flying from an implacable enemy—from the most hideous and remorseless of monsters that the earth has produced!"

"Surely you mean General Ruffleton! And it was there I beheld you—it must be so. I recollect your features distinctly—but—"

"You have difficulty in recalling the part I bore, and I do not wonder at it. You, then, were in male attire, and I in the habiliments of my sex. I supposed it a boy I addressed, and now you suppose one is addressing you."

"Indeed! And is it not so? Now I remember, perfectly! Summers—the same name! And you are a woman!"

"Even so. And, like yourself, a fugitive from the same demon! I could not do much in your behalf—but your condition inspired only feelings of kindness. May I hope that in you I will find a protector?"

"Certainly. But—were you not a voluntary participant in the scene—a jovial companion of the lawless mob?"

"True. Alas! I have only to confess my errors and lament the sad fate which that man—oh, have pity!"

"I do pity you. And that man was your enemy?"

"The worst that ever an unprotected maiden had. My mother, the only parent I could ever remember, sank into the grave. I was left alone."

"Yes! I pity you! And you fled the first opportunity?"

"After I learned his wickedness—I mean the duplicity and wickedness of which he was capable. Yes, I have abandoned him for ever! *You* must hate him as——"

"No. I hate no one, because it may not be justifiable. But I would avoid him as some venomous reptile, and guard others against his fangs."

"And you will not betray my secret?"

"No—unless I deem it a duty."

"Oh, I could tell you much—but not now. I hope it may not be sinful to hate so great a monster! I have even longed for an opportunity to be revenged—to see him expire—"

"Vengeance belongs not to us. Forgive, that you may be forgiven."

"Forgive Ruffleton?"

"Even him, if—but I am beckoned away." And Edith hastened to Alice, who had just separated from Blount at the door of the President's office.

CHAPTER XLV.

THE COUNCIL BOARD AT MIDNIGHT.

Without an interruption of the festivities of the occasion, the President, several members of his cabinet, and the Generals, had quietly withdrawn from the saloon and met in council.

"Here, gentlemen," said Randolph, seated at the head of

an oval table, round which the rest were ranged, and upon which lay numerous letters, "is matter for business. In this little conclave, affairs of such gigantic importance as were never before paralleled in this country, must be determined, and determined quickly. I will state the present condition of our affairs. General Line, instead of prosecuting the contemplated invasion, is resting at Cumberland, and has fortified the place. Next, and which is the solution of Line's change of purpose, we have information of the approach, by way of the lakes, of an army of 50,000 British troops, under Sir Charles Hunt, the object being a junction with General Line; and then the two armies will be united with the Northern host under Ruffleton, perhaps in this vicinity, or at Harford, or Havre de Grace. So, although we may leave some garrisons in Delaware and Maryland, we can have no tenable positions in either."

"And so my field of victory is to be captured by the enemy!" said General Crook.

"Not only that, General," said Valiant, "but Baltimore must surrender. It is indefensible."

"The Federal Capital, also, will fall into their hands!" said Blount.

"Inevitably," said Randolph. "But, gentlemen, let me proceed. The wire of the Ocean Telegraph has been re-united, and my correspondent at Halifax informs me that the British Cabinet have not only sanctioned the stipulations of Lord Slysir, but have resolved even to exceed them. They have ordered a large fleet to sail immediately. I have, in regard to this matter, for the exigency admitted no delay, ordered a concentration of our naval forces at Hampton Roads—"

Here the President was interrupted by a simultaneous clapping of hands.

"It was the only alternative, gentlemen," said Randolph, "Our policy is to save, the security of that which we possess, when circumstances prevent us from embarking in enterprises of acquisition. I felt no scruples in directing the concentration in a Southern harbor, of all the armed ships of the United States, since it is the avowed purpose of a foreign enemy to attempt their capture. But, remember, I save the Navy, not for the South, not for the North, but for the United States. It is in that capacity I am tc co-operate with the South. I will add, however, that my instructions to the Commanders embraced the privilege of capturing British vessels in any of our ports."

Here there was another demonstration of applause.

"But when shall *we* make a demonstration?" asked Crook.

"The first great battle," said Randolph, slowly, "will probably be—and Blount coincides with me in opinion—"

"Where? where?" cried several, impatient to hear the announcement, for all regarded the President's opinions as prophecies.

"At Weldon, beyond the Roanoke, in North Carolina; the second, if we fail on that field—"

"Weldon!" cried several. "And the second?"

"Beyond the Pedee!"

"My God!" exclaimed Crook.

"Be not cast down, brave Crook!" said Randolph. "There will be a reflux of the tide. But, I fear it is to be even as I have predicted. With fifty British ships of war on our Southern coast, and a Northern army of perhaps half, and it may be three-quarters of a million men surging over our Northern barriers, there can be no alternative but to retire before them. But there must be a termination of their march, and then——"

"And then!" cried several.

"And then their backs will be exposed to our blows. In the meantime, while we should be prepared to look such a picture steadily in the face, it is no less a duty to leave no stone unturned in the endeavor to avert it. I have therefore directed messengers to be in readiness to distribute proclamations in every county, warning the people to provide for the emergency. A certain portion of the militia will conduct the slaves to places of security, and keep them in subjection; and engineers will be dispatched to superintend the construction of fortifications at such places as may be fixed upon. These great works can be done by the able-bodied slaves. I do not think the fanatics will accomplish a great deal towards emancipation."

To this the assent was unanimous. And Randolph next intimated what was to be his policy in regard to the loyal people of the North. Ruffleton and his Convention had decreed that no more proclamations of the Federal Executive should be printed or circulated in the Free States, under certain pains and penalties; but Randolph had prepared a secret circular for distribution amongst his friends, and the friends of the Union in all the Northern States. It was marked, "strictly confidential," and was to be placed in the possession of none but those whose fidelity was unimpeachable.

Everything the President had done, and all he proposed to do, seemed to meet the entire concurrence of the Council of advisers. Such is the unanimity sometimes produced by imminent peril!

But the difficulty was to find the means of disseminating the President's circulars among the partisans of the Union in the North.

"Wheel in Lord Slysir!" at length exclaimed the President.

"What!" said the Secretary of State, "admit the British Diplomatist to our Council Board?"

"Why not? It seems to me that the most effectual mode of deceiving his Lordship, is to utter nothing but verities in his presence. He will, of course, believe them to be falsehoods, or rather diplomatic deceptions, and thus deceive himself. I know he is desirous of communicating with Ruffleton, and hitherto all his couriers have been intercepted. My plan is to procure passports from him for my messenger with the circulars."

His Lordship, who was at that moment uttering his never-ceasing acknowledgments to Edith for her kind attentions in his helpless condition, obeyed the summons with some show of reluctance, as it ruptured the agreeable interview with his "guardian angel," as he was constantly calling Edith.

"My Lord," said the President, when the Diplomatist was placed in the midst of the Council, "we have some important intelligence for you."

"I am glad to hear it, Mr. President; for although I am no longer a prisoner, I am incapable of departing from your camp; and no doubt everything sent me is intercepted, and I admit, justifiably, by your Excellency's agents. You have permitted some of my servants to attend me, I must confess; but certainly a most skilful discrimination has been exercised in admitting none but stupid loons."

"My Lord," said Crook, "if you dismiss your white servants, and have a few smart black nigger slaves, it would save us the annoyance of instituting a scrutiny the next time."

"Well! If I ever fall into your hands again, General, I will take your advice."

"I have a presentiment that we shall capture you again."

"I have sent for you, my Lord," said Randolph, "for the purpose of placing in your possession all the despatches we have intercepted——"

"Ah, your Excellency! You mean to be merry at my expense."

"By no means. My object is a little convention with the enemy. You will desire, when you shall have examined the advices I am about to deliver into your hands, to communicate with your ally, General Ruffleton. I propose to furnish the messenger. Your despatches will be in plain English, and my messenger will be provided by you and Ruffleton with passports and protection."

"Conceded. I agree to everything."

"You are not to intimate—that is for twenty days—that the messenger was furnished by me."

"I will agree to that, also—although I do not comprehend its import."

"Then, my Lord, Willy will wait on you and receive, and faithfully deliver, any letters you may prepare this night. Here are the despatches superscribed with your address."

The President placed sundry documents in the hands of his Lordship; and among these was a despatch from Canada, informing him of the concurrence of his Government in his agreement with Ruffleton, and advices of the sailing of the fleet; also letters from General Sir Charles Hunt, who was approaching by way of the lakes, the rendezvous appointed for the allied armies; and quite a number of notes from General Ruffleton.

His Lordship was wheeled back into the saloon and thence borne, without delay, to his own apartment, whither Wiry Willy was summoned to attend him at a late hour of the night.

After this, the President, with a placid countenance, appeared again among the guests in the saloons, surrounded by his Generals.

CHAPTER XLVI.

WIRY WILLY IN NEW YORK.

Wiry Willy, having changed his coat, which had become known in the several armies, set out from the President's head-quarters, early in the morning, on his double mission.

As he passed through Philadelphia, poor Willy beheld, with a sad heart, the evidences of desolation produced by civil war. Not half the stores were open, and these had but few customers. Many of the mansions were deserted, and grass was springing up between the bricks of the unfrequented pavements.

Upon landing in Camden, Willy was under the necessity of exhibiting his passport; and it was frequently inspected in the cars. New Jersey, from the Hudson to the Delaware, and along the left side of that river down to Red Bank, was one military encampment. The sounds of the drum and fife and bugle; the creaking of artillery carriages, the rattle of sabres, and the tramp of armed men, prevailed everywhere.

Upon landing at the Battery in New York, the first spectacle which greeted the vision of Willy, was the glitter of innumerable bayonets. The city seemed in possession of the military followers of Ruffleton.

Willy, in obedience to the instructions of Randolph, proceeded first in quest of Mr. Lex, a gentleman of fortune, a patriot, but one of the friends of the President.

At the stately mansion of Mr. Lex, Willy was confronted by a grey-haired negro porter.

"I desire to see Mr. Lex," said Willy.

"What business have you with him?"

"Important business. I come from the President."

"Follow me!" said the aged servant, closing the door and leading the way into the library, where Mr. L. was sitting amidst his books and papers.

This patriot was then past the middle age, but still in the

zenith of physical and intellectual vigor. When it was announced that the messenger came from the President, he rose with alacrity, and taking Willy's hand between his own, in silence, led him to a chair. Then turning his benevolent countenance full upon him, awaited the communication he had to deliver.

Willy removed the scalp from his head and placed two documents in the hands of the patriot. One was a manuscript copy of the secret circular, to which allusion has been made, and the other a letter of instructions in regard to the mode of distribution. Being deemed hazardous to send any of the printed copies by Willy, the President requested Mr. Lex to have a certain number printed in the city, and to furnish Willy with a list of names of faithful friends in the Northern States to whom they might be delivered.

"Come again at midnight," said Mr. Lex, after perusing the President's letter, "and you shall have a few circulars and the names of the persons to whom they are to be delivered. You have dispatches from Lord Slysir to General Ruffleton, and the latter will probably furnish you with new passports. You will then be facilitated in the discharge of the perilous duty you have assumed. I need not warn you of the dangers on every hand. You will perceive that the Reign of Terror has commenced. Already one of the faithful friends of the President is doomed to death. Major S——'s blood has been demanded by the TRIBUNAL OF THREE, a Court created by the Convention to try and condemn without appeal those whom they call the enemies of Liberty. Endeavor to see the Major after your interview with Ruffleton, and deliver him this." Mr. Lex placed a bank note in Willy's hand.

The TRIBUNAL OF THREE, to which Mr. Lex alluded, and which had sentenced Major S——, was the most monstrous and fearful engine ever erected in any country, for the purpose of striking terror in the hearts of the people. The Convention had decreed that one of these courts should hold its sessions in every county twice a moth. They were to investigate alleged offences against the NORTH; and therefore all who sympathized with slavery or slaveholders; gave aid and comfort to the enemy; held secret or open correspondence with the Southern or Federal armies; opposed the acts of the Northern Convention, or conspired against the authority of General Ruffleton, who was entitled THE PROTECTOR—were to be adjudged guilty of treason, and condemned to die. A majority of the three judges could condemn or acquit. There was no appeal for the condemned, nor preliminary investigation before trial; and execution was to follow sentence almost immediately. These courts were to be surrounded and protected by the military creatures of Ruffleton; and so, in an inconceivably brief space of time, the Usurper had become absolute; for all power, civil and military, reposed in his hands.

Wiry Willy, after leaving the mansion of Mr. Lex, proceeded to the City Hall, now jocularly called the Lion's Den. In it the Convention held its sessions, and there the Protector issued his decrees. As he was passing near the Park, Willy's eyes were almost blinded by an object glittering in the sun; and this, when he drew nearer, he discovered to be the polished blade of a guillotine just erected. There were hundreds standing round, gazing at the new instrument of death, the first of the kind ever erected in this country. Willy shivered with dread, and passed on through the Guards which surrounded the Hall. He demanded access to the General or Protector, avowing that he was the bearer of despatches from the British Minister, and no one sought to impede his progress. He was conducted into an anteroom where many were in attendance, waiting to be admitted. Ruffleton, now, was the disposer of fortune and honor, as well as the arbiter of life; and if he had been the d—l himself, he would have been surrounded with flatterers.

Upon the announcement of the arrival of despatches from the British Minister, Ruffleton dismissed every one from his presence and ordered the messenger to be admitted without delay.

"Willy!" he exclaimed, on beholding his old acquaintance. "Is it possible? Can you have deserted Randolph, or Crook, or Blount? No! You care not a fig for any of us. But is it true that you have brought me letters from Slysir?"

"Let the letters speak for themselves, if you won't believe Wiry Willy!" and, having said this in his former simple manner, he placed the letters in Ruffleton's hand, and turned aside and sat down, while the abstracted General hastily perused them.

"Good! Capital!" exclaimed Ruffleton, quivering with delight. "Willy!" he cried, "what reward do you demand? Here, take my purse, and call again to-morrow."

Willy was afraid to refuse the gold; but he declared that he demanded no additional recompense, except a passport to go wherever he pleased.

"You shall have it! Here!" said Ruffleton, writing with great rapidity. "But do you intend returning immediately?"

"Wiry Willy is not fool enough for that! General Crook was going to hang him once! The next time they might do it! They know I was with Lord Slysir."

"Ay—they would suspect something. And his Lordship is not yet able to travel?"

"Lord! no, sir! He's all black and blue from the rough usage of fighting Jack Bim."

"Bim! I'll Bim him! But how did it happen that you offered to come hither?"

"I wanted to travel."

"And leave Mary?"

"She won't be married now, when there's nobody to object."

"A quarrel. She's a pretty girl, Willy—but I have other matters to think about now. I suppose you met with Summers at Randolph's head-quarters?"

"Oh, yes."

"He's a skilful penman, but an unfaithful clerk! Tell Randolph not to trust him. Is he much in Randolph's presence?"

"A great deal. He's writing almost all the time."

"He did the same for me, and then ran away the first chance he had. But if you do not return immediately, where are you going?"

"To get out of these troubles. Wiry Willy is resolved to see Niagara, Saratoga, Newport, and Boston. But he saw one thing yonder in the Court-house yard such as he never laid eyes on before. It shines like a looking-glass!"

"You mean the guillotine. But the blade will be red with the blood of a traitor before sunset?"

"Oh! It's the machine they cut heads off with in France, ain't it?"

"The same kind. If you linger in the Park an hour or so,

Willy, you may see the operation, and then you can tell the people all about it in your travels."

"I will, by jingo! But, General, how I would like to see the traitor first, and notice how he looks, and hear what he says!"

"Well, you may. You see I can be in a good humor. Take this line to the keeper of the prison—the Tombs—and you will see the prisoner. Your hand—good-by, Willy."

And Willy hastened away.

Ruffleton opened a door communicating with a capacious room in which were seated Virus, General Balatrum, Smiley, the new President of the Convention, and several politicians, who followed the rising fortunes of the Protector.

"Gentlemen," said Ruffleton, as all rose to their feet, "here is cheering intelligence from Lord Slysir. The destination of the British army under Sir Charles Hunt, is the Federal Capital! Sir Charles is to form a junction with us, and to be under my command. Nor is that all. A large number of ships of war have sailed from England to coöperate with us against the South. The Ministry have ratified the conditions agreed upon, and no doubt the money has been sent by the fleet!"

"Then, sir!" said Virus, exultingly, "you are not only our Protector, but our LORD PROTECTOR!"

"There is one thing, gentlemen, one thing wanting, before I can feel that I stand on firm ground; and that thing I am sure you might procure."

"Name it!" cried they.

"A sanction by the people, of the powers vested in me by the Convention."

"It shall be done!" said Virus.

"If the people could be induced to vote at all," said Smiley, "they would not dare to vote against you."

"They *shall* vote!" said Virus.

"I cannot conceive why they are so averse to voting," said Ruffleton, walking to and fro, and musing. "They are hostile to the Slave Democracy, and to the South, and I propose to liberate the slaves, and to exterminate the Democracy!"

"Recollect, General," said Virus, "that an immense number have joined the army; and that accounts for the diminutive vote polled for the delegates. Besides, the candidates nominated by your friends, rarely have any opposition."

"But not a day passes that we do not have *resignations.* This must be checked. Smiley, the delegate who abandons his post, unless under urgent necessity, must be denounced as an enemy. Let one or two of them be condemned and decapitated! That will put an end to resignations!"

"It shall be done," said Smiley.

"And, General," said Virus, "within ten days I undertake to say, the authority conferred on you by the Convention, shall be ratified by a unanimous vote of the people."

"Let that be done, Virus," said Ruffleton, "and then we shall all be secure in the positions we have assumed."

"All I require is a little work from the instrument put up in the Park."

"Let it work!" said Ruffleton, stamping the floor.

"And let a few gentlemen of the press be among the first victims."

"Are they not condemned? Why delay?" continued Ruffleton.

The General then returned to his Cabinet.

CHAPTER XLVII.

THE EXECUTIONS.

In front of the sombre prison-house Willy beheld a vast multitude of men, women, and children, impatiently awaiting the hour for the prisoners to be led forth to execution.

Willy urged his way through the crowd. Presenting the card with the awful autograph of Ruffleton, iron gates and triple-nailed doors flew open before him.

The room in which Major S—— was confined, likewise contained other persons condemned to die for political offences. The Major was sitting at the extremity of the room, in deep abstraction, and did not observe the entrance of Willy. The other prisoners were not so quiescent One of them, an editor, although he certainly did not look like a man of letters, sobbed convulsively, and blubbered like a great school boy.

"Has it come to this?" he cried. "Keeper!" he continued, "you know I have labored for the North against the slave-driving South?"

"Yes, I know it," said the attendant.

"Then why should I be a victim?"

"It's a hard case, I own; but then they say you were opposed to making General Ruffleton Protector."

"Because it conferred civil authority as well as military. I never dreamed of a despotism, or an absolutism—"

"Excuse me—but it may not be safe to listen to such things. I don't intend to meddle in politics, so long as there are guillotines about!"

"The guillotine! And must *I* die, and by the guillotine?"

"The time's been fixed, and the people outside are getting impatient to see it."

"And my friends; where are they?"

"Most of them are *non est* in times of danger. I thought, when they brought you here, your friends would soon have you out again. But it was no go. I have a brother stationed at the door of the Protector's office, and he says not even one of your 'prentices has ventured to beg your life."

"They abandon me; because to interfere in behalf of the condemned might seem to involve them in his guilt. But I am *not* guilty. My good friend, can I not write to General Ruffleton?"

"You are allowed pen, ink, and paper."

"But will you not have the letter conveyed to him?"

"If possible. But it may not be possible before it's too late. My brother says he has bushels of letters, received several days ago, not yet opened."

"I'll put my name on the envelope! He *must* see it."

"It'll do no good. The bit is in the horse's mouth, and his master bestrides him, booted and spurred. That's what I heard the Reverend Mr. Blood say."

"And *he?* Why is *he* not here?"

"He? He's too smart for that! He's joined the Protector, and says he shall be a lord, if not a king. Oh, he goes the whole thing, guillotine and all. And he makes out lists of the suspected, to be arrested hereafter."

"I will do the same! Run to General Ruffleton! Say I will support him in everything. I can rally the masses."

"That's exactly what my brother heard Mr. Virus say. But the Protector said the man who could do the most good might also be able to do the greatest injury. He said the good had been done already, and all they had to guard against was the injury. In short, he said you had been used quite enough in getting up the animosity, and that there was no further use for you."

Hearing this the editor set up a sort of howling lamentation, and went about wringing his hands distractedly.

Willy proceeded to the corner where Major S—— remained, unmindful of everything said and done by his fellow-prisoners.

"Major," said Willy, placing his hand on the prisoner's shoulder, and speaking in a low tone, "do you not know me?"

"Wiry Willy!" said the Major, starting up. "Yes, I know you—and I am glad to see you, for I feared I should never see another friend in this world. Oh, will you not hear the words of a dying man? One who, although the acts for which his life is forfeited may be termed an ignominious crime, performed only what he supposed a duty to his country. I regarded Ruffleton as a traitor, and the duplicity I practised was meant to benefit the Republic. As God is my judge, I expected not, desired not, any other recompense but to witness the salvation of the Union. Willy, repeat my words to President Randolph."

"I will faithfully, Major," said Willy.

"I have seen Mr. Lex," continued Willy, "and he sent you this." He placed the note in the Major's hand. It was a one thousand dollar bank note.

"Return it, Willy. I understand his meaning. But my guards prefer life to money. I have tried them. There is no escape for me. The Reign of Terror, so long predicted, has been inaugurated."

Willy repaired to the Park, when the prisoners were taken thither, and, by exhibiting the signature of the dreaded General, was permitted to stand at the side of the Major, who promptly announced his readiness to submit to his fate.

"I thank heaven," said he, as he surveyed the glittering

instrument of death, "that the guillotine, and not the ignominious rope, is to terminate my existence. Willy, say to the President that I did not shrink from my fate; and that I died believing my death would contribute, sooner or later, to rescue the country from the hands of the usurping despots and traitors. Say that I died with the consoling consciousness that the guillotine has often put a period to the existence of patriots and Christians; and that I go to my God, believing in the efficacy of the merits of our Redeemer. Now, headsman! Why do you hesitate?"

"We have sent to know which is to be served first, you or the editor," said one of the masked executioners.

"I would prefer to be first," said S——.

"Oh, let me not be first!" cried the editor.

"You're a fool!" said the second executioner. "It will be twice as bad after seeing his head fall."

"But General Ruffleton may spare my life, when he gets the proposition I have sent him," said the editor.

"No doubt he will. But he will not get it on this side of Jordan. The General is up yonder at the window of the hotel, looking on with an opera-glass. The messenger has gone to the Tribunal of Three, in the Court-room. The Judges will decide who must die first; but they dare not spare your life. The Protector has too many soldiers here to have his pleasure interfered with. Here comes our messenger."

The President of The Three sent back word that the condemned might settle the question of precedence among themselves, by lot or otherwise.

"Do you contest the Major's claim to precedence?" demanded the chief executioner.

"No-o-o!" cried the editor.

The Major, after giving his watch to Wiry Willy, and clasping his hand briefly while he whispered something in his ear, ascended the platform with a steady step. It was not necessary to pull him down forcibly. He adjusted himself in the necessary position, and the knife descended. His head fell into a basket, and his blood was absorbed by a profusion of sawdust.

"Now it is your turn," said the executioner, placing his hand on the editor's shoulder.

"No-o-o!" said the editor, "there's another."

This was Samuel ———, the Quaker, who was to suffer death because General Crook had spared his house. That fact had been sufficient for his condemnation by THE THREE.

"Very well," said the second executioner; "but you are the politest man I ever saw. Come, Samuel, thee must stand on the Republican platform."

Placed on the platform, Samuel was bereft of the power of speech. But he resisted with desperation, and it required the exertions of four men to drag him forward and place his neck under the dripping steel, which, descending quickly, relieved him of his terrors.

"Now!" said the first of the masked executioners, whispering in the ear of the editor, "you must ascend; the platform is of your own construction. The engines projected for the unjust destruction of others, have never yet failed to torment their inventors. I have assumed this disguise for the purpose of putting an end to one of the world's mischief-makers. I am not only your enemy, but the deadly foe of the Tyrant, and the next time I don these habiliments, it will be for the purpose of beheading *him*. You know me—my name is ——."

The editor sank to the earth in a swoon. Before he had time to revive, he was dragged upon the platform, and his head was severed from his body. Then, all too late, he seemed to recover his consciousness. His legs began to play with wonderful rapidity, as if running away. He kicked himself off the platform, and bounced about with such violence that the headsmen had to hold him. And even then, for nearly a minute, the motion of the legs continued, and no doubt the poor fellow imagined he had escaped, and was flying from his enemies.

Willy, by the exhibition of the Protector's signature—and but few took the pains to read further—had no difficulty in obtaining possession of the remains of the ill-fated Major. He had them conducted to an undertaker's establishment, and contracted for their deposit in one of the cemeteries.

More than once, Willy, in passing that night the groups of armed men—and but few others then ventured into the streets—at the crossings, was compelled to show his passport. And in every instance the beholder started back in awe at the consciousness of the high authority under which the pedestrian moved.

He was admitted without words or delay by the ancient porter, and was conducted into the presence of the patriotic friend of the President.

"And poor S—— could not escape?" said Mr. Lex, after inviting Willy to be seated.

"No, sir, it was impossible," said Willy. "I have had his remains deposited in a vault in ——— cemetery. Here is the bank note, sir, for which he thanked you, but which he could not use. He had, besides, a considerable sum of his own. He had deposited funds, likewise, with the humane keeper of the prison, to meet the expenses of his burial."

"Will you not have use for money? If so, keep it."

"No, sir; I am well provided."

"If you should need funds, by reason of accident or robbery, apply to me. You have seen Ruffleton?"

"Yes, sir, and here is the passport he gave me."

"It is well," said Mr. Lex, reading it. "It will serve you perfectly, provided it does not expose you to assassination. But there is a sign by which the patriots may know each other; and the third man, whose name is on the list I am to give you presently, will initiate you. There are the circulars on the table. They are printed on bank-note paper, and in such characters that none but the initiated can render into intelligible English. The contents cannot be made known to the enemy through any medium but a traitor to the cause."

Provided with the necessary instructions, Willy lost no time in setting out on his journey. In the cars, where there were always the secret spies of Ruffleton, Willy ceased to be the subject of suspicious scrutiny whenever he produced the awful signature of the Protector. But when he ceased to meet the military and other partisans of Ruffleton, in the less frequented lines of travel, the secret sign of the patriots availed him most. Nor was it long before he discovered to his great joy, that even in New England, a majority of the population had become inimical to the designs of those who now usurped the direction of public affairs in the North. Still, the work of the despot had been too effectually done for resistance, and it was necessary for the friends of the Union to dissemble. All the arms, public and private, were in the hands of the Protector's partisans; and there was a military organization in every county, ordered and paid by the Convention. And now the THREE—the most terrible tribunal ever created —had its ramifications in every neighborhood, and its instrument of death in every town of any magnitude!

At Boston, Garrott, Phipps, and Palter were the THREE. They had returned from the Liberian voyage breathing vengeance against their enemies. The first victims were the Catholics; and not satisfied with cutting off their heads, the awful Tribunal stretched its authority even to the tearing down of the churches. Willy lingered several days in the city, for there were many patriots there who sighed for the restoration of the Union and re-establishment of the Federal authority. But they had to conceal their sentiments.

The prosecutor before the Tribunal of THREE, was a lawyer in desperate circumstances, but who subsequently became affluent. He was accessible to the bribes of the guilty, and his cupidity induced the fabrication of charges against the innocent. The terrors of the guillotine were successfully wielded against the rich in the exaction of large sums of money; and the poor, rather than die, enrolled themselves in the army.

It was not deemed necessary for the members of the terrible Tribunal of THREE to be versed in the law; and perhaps half the judges in the New England States had not been lawyers; but they were very frequently parsons of the dissenting sects, famous for their abolition propensities, and admirably qualified to try and execute the Catholics and Episcopalians. During the sojourn of Willy in Boston a Catholic bishop was condemned to die. The charge against him was that he had enjoined upon his clergy the duty of abstaining from participation in discussions on the subject of slavery. The prelate admitted without hesitation that he delivered such a charge; but pleaded in justification that both himself and clergy had taken solemn vows to devote themselves exclusively to the service of their God. Such a reply confused, momentarily, both the prosecutor and the Court. In the printed instructions sent them by Virus, the offence of serving one's God exclusively, had been omitted. Nevertheless the Prelate had been marked for destruction; and upon being questioned as to his fellowship with Southern slave-owners, he frankly admitted that he fraternized with all pious Catholics in the Southern, as well as in the Northern States, and that the tenure by which they held their man-servants or their maid-servants was never made the subject of investigation. This, too, might have confounded his accusers, if he had been content to stop there. But he added a quotation from Scripture, viz. "Thou shalt not covet thy neighbor's wife, nor his servant, nor his maid, nor his ox, nor his ass," etc.; and this was construed both as a personal affront—for the Three had all been notorious servant stealers—and a confession of the crime of justifying slavery. He was therefore sentenced to be decapitated.

When returning from the scene of his execution, Willy felt the weight of some one's hand on his shoulder. Turning, he was thunderstruck on beholding the sharp and swarthy features of Phipps, one of the Three!

"What are you doing here, young man?" he asked.

"I—I am on business for the—the—" He paused, having almost divulged the secret of his mission before recovering his wits.

"Business for whom? Whose business?"

"That's Willy's business—and none of yours!" replied he, fortified with the recollection that he bore none of the circulars or other documents about his person.

"I saw you in Maryland with General Crook," said Phipps, "and that is *primâ facie* evidence of your guilt. The court is about to assemble again. Withhold your reply to my question, if you see proper. You are not bound to criminate yourself," Saying this Phipps strode on, while two of the secret officers of the Inquisition, who seemed to have been standing near in readiness, seized Willy and dragged him along, unmindful of his protestations of innocence, and of the assertion that he bore a passport from the Protector himself.

Arriving before the Three, Willy gazed at the accuser and the judges with an indifferent calmness, which only seemed to increase their thirst for his blood.

The prosecutor recapitulated all that Phipps had alleged; and then Willy was called upon to answer the charges of identification with the slave-driving enemy, and of being a spy.

Willy stood up, and very deliberately unfolding the passport, read it aloud to the court. For more than a minute a profound silence ensued.

"Will you allow me, Mr. Wire," at length said the prosecutor, "to look at that remarkable document?"

"Certainly, sir," said Willy, imitating the attorney's politeness.

The attorney, having satisfied himself of the authenticity of the signature, handed the passport to the judges, when both the signature and the lines to which it was appended were recognised. The passport was returned to Willy. Its validity was not only acknowledged, but its bearer was invited to dinner; an honor he declined.

Willy attended diligently to the objects of his mission, and hastened from point to point making a faithful distribution of the secret circulars. At Hartford, they were just putting up the guillotine, amidst a crowd of men and boys—the women always appearing on the scene when blood was to flow. But Willy was astonished to meet a familiar face on the ground, superintending the erection of the engine of death. This was Mr. Rook, formerly an agent of the Post Office Department, and subsequently the deputy postmaster at Hartford. Willy had seen him in the ante-rooms of the President and of the Postmaster General, at Washington; and it was somewhat notorious that he contrived to hold office under different administrations of different politics. But whatever might have been his principles, he had certainly professed to be an admirer of President Randolph, and a supporter of his administration up to the period of the rupture of the sections; and, therefore, Willy's amazement was great on beholding this politician directing the construction of one of the Protector's guillotines on Hartford common. Upon inquiry he learned that Rook had abandoned the Federal cause immediately after the battle of Burlington, and being among the first applicants for office under the new *regime*, he had obtained a commission from the Northern Convention when it re-assembled in New York, and so congratulated himself on his ability to retain his position. He had gone further, and opened a correspondence with Virus, as soon as he learned he was high in the favor of Ruffleton, and proposed to furnish the names of such of his neighbors as had sympathized with the Democracy. That he had acted with the same party himself, he admitted; but he asseverated very vehemently that he was never sincere in his professions of sympathy with the Slave Power, but used a justifiable deceit for the purpose of injuring the party. To him, therefore, the guillotine was consigned, and also the commissions for the members of the Tribunal of THREE, and for the prosecutor. These commissions were still retained in his office unopened, and he did not doubt the ones he recommended had been appointed, and from whom it was his intention to exact a large bonus for the effectual exertion of his influence in the procuration of such lucrative appointments.

"Mr. Rook," said Willy, when the former recognised him, and grasped his hand in a friendly manner, "have you turned against the President?"

"Pooh! Don't you know the jig's up? If you can't go the whole for Ruffleton and the North, don't name politics here, or your head'll be off before you can wink twice."

"But are you not a Democrat?"

"Demo-devil! I'm a Northerner, and dead against slavery! Come! I'm going to deliver the commissions, and a Court will be held and some heads cut off in an hour. They want me to say who's to be judges and prosecutor, before the package is broken open, but—you understand—I wunt do't! I want a little private chat with some on 'em first. Come! a large crowd will meet at my office to learn who's got the appointments." Willy followed, and observed that Rook called aside the men who he supposed were to be commissioned, with whom, doubtless, satisfactory agreements were made in relation to the bonuses or commissions; and then, at the hour appointed by Virus, the seals were broken in the midst of the assembled politicians.

But the Judges—THE THREE—were very different men from those designated by Rook; and the Prosecutor was his most bitter enemy. A death-like silence prevailed, and was only interrupted by one of the Judges, who read from his instructions, that he was required to repair immediately to the Court-room, and being first sworn in by any magistrate, the Tribunal was to proceed instantly to arrest and try certain individuals whose names were in the possession of the Prosecutor!

All eyes were directed towards the Prosecutor. With a pale face, and globules of perspiration projecting from his forehead, he stared at the paper clutched convulsively in his hand.

"Come, Rook!" said he, at length, placing his hand on the Postmaster's shoulder.

"What for? Where to?" asked the time-serving functionary.

"To the Court."

"What for?"

"To be tried. Your name is first on the list. Come!"

"I wunt! I'm Mr. Virus's confidential correspondent."

'But, unfortunately for you, he has other correspondents here whose statements are better worthy of belief. So *he* thinks."

"I know better! No one's written him from Hartford but myself. No letter has been mailed—— "

"True, at Hartford. But they were sent to Norwich. You are caught, Rook! Come along."

"I wunt!"

"Gentlemen!" said the Prosecutor, "I call upon you to aid me in dragging this offender to justice. You can now prove whether you are the friends or the enemies of the new Government! Mr. Virus says that Rook has attempted a deception. He has recommended only traitors to the North for exalted positions, and marked none but its friends for destruction. The three Judges and myself were proscribed by him. We see, now, how dangerous a thing it is to practise any species of deception!"

Within an hour the Three had condemned Rook to die. He was the first to suffer by the instrument he had erected for the destruction of others. And even when they dragged him upon the platform, and placed his neck beneath the glittering steel, he did nothing but repeat the words, "I wunt! I wunt!"

Amidst such scenes of summary punishment and terror, there could be no open manifestations of patriotism in New England; and Willy did not linger long in it. But he observed with many painful forebodings that the lives and the fortunes of the entire population were completely at the disposal of the despot, Ruffleton, who would use them for the destruction of the Republic and the subjugation of the South.

Upon his return to New York, Willy hastened to Mr. Lex and reported all he had seen and done. His mission had been performed with judgment and effect, and elicited the encomiums of the patriot.

Willy next repaired to the City Hall.

"Well, sir," said Ruffleton, "have you finished your travels? I suppose you have seen all the sights?"

"Wiry Willy has seen a great many; and he's tired of seeing men's heads chopped off."

"Ay—that appalled you. And did it not others?"

"Yes, indeed! There ain't a man between here and Boston fool enough to wag his tongue against General Ruffleton."

"Aha! And it will soon be the same thing between here and New Orleans, and between the Atlantic and the Pacific."

"Are there to be guillotines in the South, too?"

"Yes, and bayonets! Do you intend returning to the South?"

"Yes, sir, right off—for I'm getting homesick, and sick of the guillotine. It's a horrible thing, sir!"

"Just the reverse, Willy," said Ruffleton, laughing heartily. "It is a capital invention to keep men in order. Since I had the editor's head cut off, not a newspaper has printed a word against my government, or an offensive allusion to myself. Tell Mary I shall not have the time, if I had the disposition to annoy her more. All the pretty women in the city are attendants at my levees. Be my friend, Willy, and I will take care of you. All power is in my hands; all patronage is at my disposal; and all fortunes at my feet."

"All I ask, General," said Willy, "is to be permitted to live in peace with my good grandame on the Brandywine."

"And with Mary! Tell her, if she don't marry you immediately, I'll give her away to one of my officers."

"And your soldiers will never trouble us on the Brandywine?"

"No. Or if they do they shall die for it. Hold! I will write a protection for you that will suffice. They tell me that my signature is regarded with reverence everywhere."

"Awful reverence!" said Willy. And, while the Pro

tector was about to write, Willy described the looks and actions of those to whom he had exhibited the Dictator's autograph; and the despot seemed pleased and amused.

"There, Willy! That will be ample protection for you and Mary. Exhibit this to any one, and you'll acknowledge that Ruffleton is truly a Protector. But, in return, you must do me a favor. I cannot hear from Lord Slysir, and perhaps my despatches to him are intercepted. Can you go to him?"

"Certainly, sir; nobody troubles Willy, since General Crook was going to hang him. I can go where I please and come when I please. I'll take any letter to Lord Slysir, for you; and, if he asks me, I'll bring back here to you his answer."

"Thank you, Willy; but it will not be necessary to come this far back. I shall move closer to him in a few days."

"And will you put up a guillotine in Philadelphia, too?" asked Willy, quickly.

"No, I think not. The Philadelphians have agreed to let the army pass through the city; and I have promised not to disarm their military. I shall not molest them immediately, if they do not oppose my measures. Call again an hour hence, Willy, when my letters will be ready. But will they not search you?"

"Search Wiry Willy? No indeed. If they search me, I won't take any letters for them when they want me."

"True—you serve all."

"I do so—and that's the reason nobody hurts me. If I don't deliver your letter safely into Lord Slysir's hand, you may cut off Wiry Willy's head, and he'll never think hard of it. That is, if his Lordship is still there—at the mansion."

"No doubt he's there. Besides his bruises, I'm inclined to think he has a wound of the heart, from one of his expressions."

"Won't that kill him, sir?"

"No—no! Call an hour hence."

Willy withdrew, and loitered an hour in the Park, where he witnessed the decapitation of eleven victims.

Returning to the Protector's closet at the time appointed, the heart-sick messenger received the letters directed to Lord Slysir with trembling hands, and then hurried away from the terrible city.

In New Jersey Willy experienced no diminution of his terrors. The railroads and canals had been seized for the use of the Protector, and in his name; and the freight transported southward consisted exclusively of military stores, arms, and ammunition.

Willy hastened to the head-quarters of Randolph. He was admitted into the office, where he found Summers writing, and the President dictating. The clerk seemed startled on beholding Willy; and a moment after, by permission, he withdrew.

"This day, Willy," said Randolph, "I looked for your return. You need not tell me what you have seen and heard. I have been apprised of everything—even to the heroism of poor S——. But you have rendered good service in distributing the circulars."

"You certainly could not have heard what Major S—— whispered in my ear just before he suffered," said Willy.

"No. But it was observed by my correspondent. Was it a message for me?"

"It was a warning, sir—he told me to say that he doubted the fidelity of Summers."

"Summers! He is the most expeditious penman I ever saw."

"Therefore, it was supposed he might find employment near your person. The Major died believing he had been betrayed by Summers. Still General Ruffleton denounces him, and likewise warns you against trusting him."

"Indeed! Well. Deliver your letters, Willy. You will find Lord Slysir in his chamber, not yet quite recovered."

"Will you not inspect them, sir? General Ruffleton never hesitates to break your seals."

"No. I care not what they contain."

The President resumed his labors, calling in another Secretary, while Willy repaired to his Lordship's chamber. As he was about to enter the door, he was met by Summers, and his suspicions were confirmed.

"Summers," said he, pausing, when the Secretary had closed the door behind him, "you do not seem curious to hear tidings from the Lord Protector."

"The Lord protect us from such a Protector! No. If I could only be deprived of the power of thinking of such a monster I would be happier."

"And do you know, Charley, that he swears vengeance against you, if it should ever be in his power to——"

"You frighten me to death! But, Willy, he shall never have me in his power again! I will die first!"

"I suppose, Charley, you have heard of the death of Major S——?"

"No!" said Summers, starting back, in apparent amazement. "I am sorry. I am sorry, because he was the President's friend, and my friend, and a patriot. Was he guillotined?"

"He was."

"Another victim! What punishment will be adequate for the crimes of the tyrant! And, Willy, it may be possible that poor S—— supposed I had some agency in precipitating his doom! But the letter he gave me for the President was perused by nobody before it was delivered to the one to whom it was directed."

Willy mused in doubt. And then abruptly entered the apartment of Lord Slysir.

"Ah! I was expecting you!" said his Lordship, eagerly seizing the sealed packet. "This has not been opened, I think! Has it, Willy?"

"No, sir, upon my honor. The President declined perusing it."

"He is a most extraordinary man! And the most important dispatches from my government intercepted by his agents, after perusal, nevertheless, are punctually delivered. By St. George! it is well for me to have my residence in the camp of the enemy. Such documents would not come into my possession at all, if I dwelt elsewhere. Stay, Willy. How does the General look? Does he seem in health and spirits?"

"Yes, sir! The guillotine has made him complete master of all the Northern people. He is Protector, and some call him Lord Protector."

"That is as good a name as any. But if I had been with him, I should have protested against that Frenchified instrument. It will not do for Anglo-Saxons. Cromwell had nothing of the sort. But he seemed determined to prosecute the war, did he?"

"Oh, yes, sir! And he has the largest army, so they say, in the world. New Jersey is alive with soldiers. And I heard a Quaker declare it would be a desert when they left it with their trains of provisions."

"That is likely."

"Every horse and waggon; every ox, cow, pig; and all the poultry, the Quaker said, had been taken. Not even the vegetables are spared! And there is not a fence standing between Amboy and Camden."

"What have they done with the fences? Could they eat them?"

"No, sir—but they burnt them—burnt them as firewood. In the encampments they can't use coal—and there are thousands of bakers making biscuits for the army."

"Incidents—the mere incidents of war! Come to me again, Willy, for your reward."

"I desire none, sir," said Willy, withdrawing.

CHAPTER XLVIII.

STARTLING INTELLIGENCE.

It was late at night, and the company which usually assembled at the mansion occupied by the President, had departed. But Randolph was still laboring in his office, alone, for one after another the secretaries had retired exhausted to their couches.

At length he threw down the pen, and rising erect, strode backwards and forwards, pausing occasionally at the different windows and gazing out at the moonlit lawn, redolent of the perfume of roses. The scene was silent and peaceful.

"How calm and quiet, now!" said he, while a melancholy smile rested on his manly lip. "But soon the incessant tramping of armed men, and the rumbling of artillery carriages, will frighten peace from the land! I did my utmost to avert it. When the tempest is expended, the trees that are not riven rise again. Our young Republic is flexible: and it is the mission of our race to rule the world. We have too much intelligence to destroy ourselves. Yes—this hurricane will expend itself, and only sweep away the noxious plants among us. We will rise again! Ha!" he continued, hearing footsteps behind him, and on turning he was confronted by Alice and Edith. "Come, fairies!" said he, taking each by the hand, "my labor for the day, or night, is at an end. Give me your smiles, as a guerdon—I have been working for you and for all. But your father, Edith—how is he?"

"Much better, sir. The doctor thinks he may venture to travel in a day or two."

"It is well. For we must all abandon this place before many days."

"Ah, father, I feared so!" said Alice. "But I had conceived a project in the event of the prolonged illness of Mr. Langdon——"

"What project was that?"

"Oh, merely to defend him with my troop!"

"A project that, for the commander of the Caps!" said Randolph, smiling. "Why, Alice, this place—I mean our encampment—would be untenable with three hundred thousand men to defend it."

"But would they molest Mr. Langdon?"

"It would not be well to tempt them."

"Tempt them!" said Edith.

"Ay, you baggage!" said Randolph. "And who would not be tempted that saw you?"

"Edith!" said Alice, "that is the first gallant speech I have heard my father utter for a whole week. But do not fear him!"

"Fear him. I love him!"

"Then I will be your father, while my friend is ill. And you must obey me."

"Oh, I will be as obedient as a daughter!"

"Then follow my example," said Alice.

"No," said Randolph, "not exactly. This is the first injunction—weigh well the arguments that may be advanced by a certain General, who loyally acknowledges the authority of the Chief Magistrate of his country, in favor of a speedy union."

"I am very attentive," said Edith.

"The difficulty, father," said Alice, "may be this: the loyal General does not——"

"Peace!" cried Edith, placing her hand on the lips of

her friend. "I shall remember all you have said, sir; and will certainly listen very respectfully to whatever he may have to allege on his own motion. But pray do not *incite* him to anything!"

"No. Let him fight his own battles, say I!" was the mocking response of Randolph.

"But, father," said Alice, very gravely, "we come to impart a very serious matter. The words whispered in the ear of Wiry Willy by Major S——"

"And so you have learned that secret. But did not Willy say he had previously imparted it to me? So you see it is no secret at all."

"But there *is* a secret, father, of which you have had no intimation."

"I doubt it. Listen to me. I am perfectly aware of the treasonable purposes of Summers on coming hither. I have intercepted all his secret despatches for the despot, which I have here in my private drawer," he continued, taking a key from his vest pocket and exhibiting the papers. "Nevertheless, I have continued to employ him, for he is an intelligent and expeditious penman. But I had another object, which I confess has not been attained. I cannot understand his real character. He will not look at the future. I cannot tempt him by the glittering inducements of a lofty career."

"The secret, father, which we came to impart, will elucidate the mystery."

"Then what is this secret?"

"Summers is a woman?"

"A woman! That, then, is the solution! I thought it remarkable that I should be so baffled in the discovery of the motives of a man. A woman!"

"Yes, father—he confessed the secret to Edith."

"And I promised not to divulge it," said Edith, "unless it should seem to be demanded as an imperative duty. The words of Major S—— at the guillotine have convinced me that I ought not to withhold it longer. And since you have incontestable evidence of his treachery, I unburden my bosom without the slightest remorse."

"A woman! Ha! ha!" continued the President, laughing heartily. "I confess she was more than a match for me!"

"And, father," said Alice, "you have been keeping her in your employ when you had proof of her guilt! Every day you were exposed to her murderous steel, or still more diabolical poison!"

"I was interested in my experiment! But I was never in danger. Her purpose of mischief was circumvented. Our old friend Dr. Durnell confederated with me, and after administering chloroform, her pockets were searched, and the poison discovered—"

"The wicked creature!" said Alice.

"The infamous wretch!" exclaimed Edith. "And to make me a confidante!"

"For what purpose she carried the poison," continued the President, "we could not know; and you can do nothing more than conjecture. It might be her intention to commit suicide. No matter. It was certain the poison could do no one any possible good; and so our wag of a doctor emptied the vial of its deleterious contents, and substituted a very innocent powder. Nevertheless, she is a woman! I will dismiss her immediately. There shall be no women, no *such* women, about my offices. Let her be sent for."

The doorkeeper, answering the bell, was despatched to the clerk's apartment with a peremptory summons, and soon after Summers came in, and seemed surprised to find the young ladies with the President.

"Summers," said the President, handing him the intercepted notes, "make me a copy of these in intelligible English."

"Sir—your Excellency—these—are in characters, invented for the purpose of baffling all not in possession of the key."

"I will furnish the key," said Randolph, which he did, in a moment, with his pen.

Then Summers felt that her perfidy was exposed. Unable to utter another word, she folded her arms on her breast and fixed her eyes on the floor.

"I know not what to say, Summers," continued Randolph. "That you are my enemy, may be proof of your fidelity to Ruffleton; and fidelity is a quality I admire. I have known your purpose to betray me for some time, and was content to forestall your attempts, still hoping that interest, if not inclination, would produce a change. It was without avail. Your life is forfeited, but I pardon you on account of your sex."

At the last word Summers started, and fixed her eyes reproachfully, if not fiercely, on Edith.

"I have kept your secret," said Edith, "as long as I could do so without self-reproach."

"Your pocket-book—give me your pocket-book, Summers!" demanded the President.

It was delivered promptly, while a half contemptuous scowl seemed to animate the features of the culprit.

"Oh, don't suppose I mean to deprive you of your money," said Randolph, smiling. "You shall have your wages. I am in quest of something else," he continued, examining the book. "But I find nothing here. Yes! what is this in the vial? Silent! I will find out!" Turning to the salver, Randolph emptied the contents of the vial into a glass, and pouring in some water, raised the tumbler to his lips and swallowed the mixture.

"Dead! dead!" cried Summers. "Nothing on earth can save him! You may kill me—but I have destroyed the enemy of the man I love! Yes! I love Ruffleton!" she continued, confronting Edith. "You may betray that secret also! And if he should love others, no other can serve him so well as the lost Flora has done! Call in the guards! Let me die—I fear not death. Edith Langdon! once I thought *you* were the cause of Ruffleton's coldness. If it had been so, ere this you would have been cold in the grave. But the first hour convinced me of the mistake——"

"I am obliged to you!" said Edith. "Your keen penetration was not at fault. Without at all meaning to put an estimate on your standard of appreciation, you will allow me to say that I would much rather be cold in my grave than to have my affections centred on Ruffleton—the diabolical monster!"

"Enough of this!" said the President. "Summers, the venom was extracted by the good Dr. Durnel. I have swallowed only a dose of sugar. Return to your room. In the morning I will send you beyond the lines, so that you may go in safety to your paramour. Tell him my time has not yet come, if, indeed, he counselled my assassination."

The young ladies lingered some time after the departure

of Summers, promenading with the President, when suddenly the hoofs of approaching horses were heard.

"At this hour," said Randolph, pausing and listening, "the approach of horsemen is a little extraordinary. It must be some of the Generals."

"It may be an attack," said Alice. "It was here that Major Snare perpetrated his attempt. We will remain, father, with your permission."

"Which predominates—fear or curiosity? Answer me that, before I respond to your very ingenuous petition."

"The former," said Alice.

"For my part, the latter," said Edith.

A moment after the door was thrown open, and Generals Blount, Crook, and Valiant entered.

"I hope your Excellency, and the fairest of the fair," said Crook, "will pardon our intrusion. This is the second time we have gallopped up to the mansion to-night."

"General Crook," said Alice, "was never yet accused of an intrusion by any fair lady. He may scourge the Abolitionists, quarter himself upon the hypocritical Quakers, or demand millions of indemnity from a city that harbors clerical negro-stealers and licentious editors; but, in war, all this is very fair!"

"Cease, parrot!" said the President. "Now, General, the news!" he added, turning to Blount, who, with less gallantry than gravity, remained mute under the fire of Edith's eyes, beaming now with curiosity.

"Messengers have arrived with intelligence that a junction of the Western armies has been formed at Cumberland: and that the combined British and Abolition forces are marching eastward along the Pennsylvania line. They are, at this moment, nearer to Washington than ourselves."

"Where are they?" asked the President.

"General Line was at Emmitsburg, some fifteen hours ago, when the express started."

"How far is that?" asked Edith.

"Nearly a hundred miles," said Blount.

"They will hardly reach us to-night," said the President. "General," he continued, "this movement indicates that Ruffleton intends to put his army in motion immediately. Sir Charles Hunt and General Line would not expose themselves to our blows without an assurance of succor from the main army of fanatics. Never! We might beat them, it is true, before the succor could arrive; but then Ruffleton would interpose between us and the Capital."

"Do you hear?" said Valiant, addressing Crook, "we shall be overruled!"

Valiant and Crook had been decidedly in favor of an attack upon Sir Charles Hunt and General Line, without awaiting the motions of Ruffleton.

"I do not say, gentlemen," continued Randolph, "that we will not fight these Western foes; they may begin the attack, and then, with anything like equal numbers, it would not do to yield them the prestige of success. My opinion is, that you should march away with all expedition, and occupy Westminster. That position will be a temporary defence of the Capital. I will retain 50,000 men with which to watch Ruffleton."

"I concur fully with your Excellency," said Blount. "Not a moment must be lost, Generals. Brief adieus and then away."

"I'll begin here," said Crook, kissing both the maidens, and then hurrying up stairs to take leave of Mr. Langdon. He was followed by Valiant, while Blount remained with the President.

"General," said the President, "prompt action is quite as imperative now as prompt decision. I had, however, anticipated such an exigency in the event of this manœuvre. In ten minutes I will have the necessary orders signed; and in the meantime you can utter your adieus to the ladies." Saying this, Randolph turned to his papers.

Blount, giving an arm to each of the ladies, led them into the great saloon, then silent and deserted, but illuminated by the silver rays of the moon, streaming in from several windows.

"Is it to be a sad or merry parting?" asked Alice. "If the former, pray take leave of us singly, that we may not witness each other's tears."

"You are in a merry mood," said Edith.

"And you?" said Blount.

"My equanimity remains. There have been so many partings and meetings during the hurly-burly of the last few weeks, that I am becoming accustomed to them. I doubt not we shall meet again."

"And in sunshine, I trust."

"I predict in thunder, lightning, and in rain," said Alice. "Ruffleton is on the other side of an impassable gulf, but on this side of it we have still a formidable suitor."

"His Lordship?" asked Blount.

"Yes—his Lordship!" said Edith; "he has proposed to open negotiations for my hand. My heart is not thought of. He has intimated a disposition to treat on the basis of an alliance of *interests.* Imprimis: My father is to throw his weight in the Northern scale, and I am to relinquish all predilections for the Republic. The equivalent is to have conferred on me the title of her Ladyship immediately, with the presumptive reversion of her Grace, if a certain uncle over the wide water should happen to die without heirs. Think of that, Master Brook!"

"Oh, that is only half the story!" said Alice. "His Lordship's Machiavelism is infinite in resources. He has tempted me with a glimpse of one of the most magnificent phantoms that ever flitted athwart the dreams of an American maiden. If I will bring *my* father to the relief of the crumbling monarchies, he shall not only reign himself, but my liege Lord, who is to be one of the heavy-cheeked Princes of England, will succeed! Think of that and tremble, ye champions of American liberty! The insensate fool!" she continued, her lip trembling with momentary passion. "But with him, as with others, diplomacy is a game, and all the objects of life are made subsidiary. Armies, people, states, and even poor simple maidens, are coldly advanced on the board, or remorselessly removed from it, like so many pawns and rooks. I told his Lordship as much; and I said he had confronted one American lady at least, who could not be *moved* in that manner!"

"And did he not say that you were not the *only* one?" asked Edith.

"Oh, yes! He called you, too, incorrigible, Edith. But mind you, he made no accusation against the *sensibility* of either of us. He attributed everything to our *education.* He charged the Bishop with making heroines, Republican matrons, Spartan dames, and everything else which *we* had been taught to consider grand and glorious."

"Nor did he slander him," said Edith.

"Farewell—farewell!" said Blount, upon hearing Crook

and Valiant promenading impatiently on the porch. "The President calls. We shall meet again before the lapse of many days. But not here. Yes, let us be merry, if we can, in the midst of disasters, if they must come."

"And come they must," said Alice.

"But they will pass away," said Edith, "and we shall then have a clearer atmosphere."

"God grant it!" said Blount. "And I think he will. And you will be the priestesses at the altar of Patriotism, to keep alive the holy flame. Adieu!"

The ladies retired to their apartments, and the General returned to the President's cabinet.

"Be seated a moment, General," said Randolph, upon placing in his hands the documents he had been preparing. "I understand that you fully approve the policy of occupying Westminster?"

"I regard it as a necessity," said Blount. "Without doing so our retreat would be cut off."

"True, General," said Randolph. "And by getting in the rear of Ruffleton, we could not intercept his communications so long as he has fleets in the bays and along the ocean coast. He would be rejoiced to leave us behind, on the deserted Pennsylvania line! He would proceed southward, conquering and to conquer! The North expects it of him; and the South looks for us to face the invader. We might, I think we would, gain one or two victories, by suddenly marching against Sir Charles and Line; but then before we could reap the fruits of them, Ruffleton would be thundering in our rear! He would be but a single march behind us. No! we are not prepared to meet the foe in a decisive battle this far North, and particularly when there is such a disparity of numbers. Our new levies are in the depôts, drilling for the campaign; and if we can have 100,000 recruits in the District of Columbia, a week hence, my expectations will be more than realized."

"In everything we agree!" said Blount. "It would be madness to seek an engagement here with at least four to one against us. A defeat would dampen the spirits of our brave men, and might lead to a long train of disasters. It is bad enough at best. I see no other alternative but to retire before a foe of such numerical superiority. When Ruffleton shall have followed us into our country, and departed far from his own, we shall be better able to strike him a fatal blow. The Capital must fall into his hands!"

"It fell into the hands of the British. Rome, Paris, Vienna, Berlin, Naples, Moscow, Lisbon, and Madrid have shared the same fate. Abandoned by the Government, the Capital is no more than any other untenable city. But Ruffleton cannot hold it long, and we must not provoke him to destroy it—or Baltimore. Go, General. I think Hunt and Line will pause at Emmitsburg."

"I do not think they will attack me at Westminster. But if they do, you will, of course, keep Ruffleton at bay long enough to give me an opportunity to repel the assault. Adieu."

Blount was soon after gallopping away.

CHAPTER XLIX.

ADVANCE OF THE INVADING ARMY.

Blount, and Crook, and Valiant led their columns, by forced marches, to Westminster, Maryland; and Sir Charles Hunt and General Line being indisposed to risk a battle before uniting with the host under Ruffleton, although they had advanced several miles east of Emmitsburg, fell back on that town. The Southern generals did not pursue.

But the very next day after the departure of Blount from Newcastle, the Northern army of New Jersey was put in motion, and crossed the Delaware to Philadelphia.

President Randolph having no means of arresting the advance of such overwhelming numbers, retired across the Susquehanna at Havre de Grace.

Lord Slysir, still alleging that he was sore and stiff from the jolting inflicted by the hard-trotting horse of Captain Bim, pleaded inability to travel, and Randolph left him in possession of the mansion, at liberty to remain or to join his ally. Senator Langdon, nearly recovered from his recent indisposition, had proceeded, with Edith, on the railroad to

Washington. Wiry Willy and Mary were married by one of the chaplains of the army; and, after the ceremony, proceeded immediately to the peaceful cottage of Willy's grandame on the Brandywine. Alice had prevailed on her father to permit her to remain at his head-quarters, at least until there should be a probability of a serious engagement.

The most commodious mansion in the vicinity had been tendered the President as his head-quarters—the proprietor alleging his purpose to set fire to it whenever the invaders succeeded in crossing the Susquehanna.

At a late hour, but while the President still prosecuted his labors, Captain Bim made his appearance at the door. Alice, who was the first to perceive the presence of the embarrassed and bashful Captain, beckoned him to advance.

"Captain Bim," said Randolph, "I am glad to see you, because there is a very dangerous service to be performed."

"I thank your Excellency," said the hearty Captain.

"I shall thank *you* if you perform this service well."

"If it is to die, sir—"

"No—no! If you die you cannot serve me."

"I mean, your Excellency," stammered Bim.

"He intended to say," observed Alice, "that he would be willing to die to serve you. And he certainly would die rather than refuse any service."

"That's it," said Bim, mentally blessing Alice. "I would die with the greatest pleasure—"

"Not a word now about dying," said the President, smiling. "But the service is this: I desire you to take a hundred picked men to act as scouts, and give me the earliest information of the enemy's purpose to cross the river. If you can defeat or frustrate the pioneers, the crossing of the army will be retarded, and the delay may be of vast benefit to the country."

"If you will only permit me to fight—"

"To fight! Oh, you may have *carte blanche* as it regards that."

"A cart, your Excellency—?"

"Captain, he means full liberty to do your utmost. I believe you are not conversant with the French language."

"No—I confess I have no sort of education in the languages. I thank you, Miss Alice! Then, your Excellency, I will do my best! But the errand I have come on—"

"True, I had not sent for you, although I intended doing so. What was your errand, Captain?"

"It was to ask permission to introduce, at his own special request, Captain Fink?"

"Captain Fink! Valiant declares I know the names of all the commissioned officers in the army—but of this one I confess I have no recollection. Have you, Alice?"

"Captain Fink! Fink! No—I don't recollect hearing the name before."

"I'm sure you never did, either of you," said Bim, "because he's just arrived."

"Just arrived? And where from?" demanded the President.

"From the Lamine, sir."

"The Lamine? Where is that?"

"In Missouri, sir."

"In Missouri? And do you intend to say that Captain Fink has come all the way from Missouri to serve his country under my banner?"

"I do, by—jing! And *I* would go to the devil to serve you! Oh, pardon me, Miss—I didn't think what I was saying!"

"Show him in, Bim!"

"If this be so, father!" said Alice, "I hope you will convince him that you appreciate such devotion!"

Bim re-entered, but Captain Fink still lingered outside.

"Where is he?" asked the President.

"He wants me just to say, before he comes in," said Bim, "that he's almost ashamed to appear without some kind of uniform worn by other Captains, and he hopes you'll excuse his wild Western shirt."

"Shirt?" said Alice.

"Yes, Miss. His coat's a shirt; and he says his men all wear the same—I beg your pardon, Miss,"—stammered Bim, and at the same time blushing—"I didn't mean to allude to his under-shirt—I mean the shirt under his other clothes—but—"

"You mean a hunting-shirt," said Randolph. "Call him in."

"Yes, your Excellency," said Bim, retiring again, "a buckskin hunting-shirt."

At last Captain Fink was ushered in. He was full six feet four inches in height, erect in stature, and although not encumbered with flesh, was broad-shouldered and muscular. His hunting-shirt of dressed buckskin was encircled by an old leather belt, in which was stuck a butcher knife. He wore a coonskin cap with the tail of the animal standing up in front, and his feet were enclosed in moccasins. The face of the Captain was benevolent—but in the centre of his right eye-brow there was a *white* spot.

"Captain Fink," said Randolph, "I understand you come from Missouri."

"From the Lamine, in Missouri, an hour's trot above Boonville. Here is a letter for you, sir."

The President broke the seal, and recognised the hand of a friend—the member of Congress representing the district. He spoke in favorable terms of Captain Fink, and of the men composing his company.

"Captain," said Randolph, "it appears that you have a company of volunteers in Missouri."

"No, sir!" said the Captain. "They are here, and true men, sir, as ever drew a tomahawk."

"Tomahawk?" asked Alice.

"That means the same in Missouri," said Fink, "that drawing the sword does in these parts."

"What is your company called, Captain?"

"Called? Oh, the Boonvillians used to call us the 'Wild Western Scouts.'"

"The name will do very well, Captain," said the President, "and you are the very man I want at this particular juncture!"

"How many men have you?"

"Ninety-eight besides Lieutenant Click. I make up the hundred."

"Go with them, Captain Bim, when they are refreshed, on the service I have indicated. Two hundred men will not be superfluous."

"We're not tired, or hungry, or sleepy," said Captain Fink.

"Then set out immediately."

"That's what I like!" said Fink.

"And send me word of all the movements of the enemy," said Randolph.

The two Captains then departed.

CHAPTER L.

BATTLE AT THE BRIDGES.

At sunrise, Bim and his men, and the Wild Western Scouts, were posted up the river, watching every point where the enemy would be likely to appear. Nor did they wait long before parties of the Northern army made their appearance on the opposite shore. These were mounted on horses, and rode backwards and forwards along the margin of the river, until they decided upon the place of passage.

The place once chosen, operations began immediately. More than fifty thousand men were soon upon the bank engaged in putting together the bridges which Ruffleton had provided. The first section (and three distinct bridges were commenced at the same time) being launched and held fast by stakes and anchors, the subsequent sections were taken over them and thrust forth from the ends furthest out in the stream, and secured in a similar manner.

This occurred some ten miles above Havre de Grace, and Bim dispatched a messenger with the intelligence to the President. Then he and Fink concentrated their men on the southern shore, among the trees and bushes. As had been foreseen, it was necessary to send a number of pioneers to the southern shore, where the current was the swiftest and the deepest, to make fast the cables or chains and to provide a landing-place. And soon a number of small boats, brought thither in wagons, containing two or three hundred men, approached the grove where the Scouts lay in ambush.

"Captain Bim," said Fink, "my Scouts are all beef-winning marksmen, and we have Minié rifles. Those handsomely dressed enemies are about nigh enough for us to pink 'em over. Shall we begin the fun?"

"No, Captain," said Bim, who felt proud of his superior knowledge of the military art. "Don't you see the battery?"

"Yes—that is a battery!" replied Fink, gazing at a formidable array of artillery carriages on the summit of the opposite bank.

"Well, then, Captain," said Bim, "if we fire on this party coming over to us before they land, we shall have a salute or two from that row of cannon. But if we suffer these gentlemen to land before we give them a welcome, then the artillery can't fire on us without firing into them also. Do you see?"

"Exactly, Captain Bim! I have had no experience fighting with the big guns. But now I see how it's to be done. We must use our tomahawks and knives; and we must meet them out there in the grass." Between the grove and the water there was a patch of high grass.

"But how can we get there without being seen?" asked Bim.

"How? I'll give the order. Scouts!" said he, "Squat! Snake!"

His order was promptly obeyed, and the Wild Western Scouts sank out of sight, and the tall grass was moved but slightly as they glided through it like so many snakes.

"I and my men can't do that!" said Bim. "And they wouldn't if they could. No, by George! But we'll join you when the battle begins. We'll dash in with our swords. But you must excuse us if we can't approach the enemy like snakes."

"Do as you like, Captain Bim," said Fink; "But I'd rather be taking Abolition scalps than talking here." Saying this, Fink joined his men in the grass, where they awaited the arrival of the unconscious foe.

The Northern Pioneers and Engineers were soon landed on the Southern shore. But they had not proceeded many paces in the tall grass before Captain Fink yelled out "Into 'em Scouts, and give 'em ——" A moment after a hundred tomahawks had stricken down that number of men. Bim rushed forward at the head of his company and completed the work begun by the Scouts. A few pistol shots only were fired; and Ruffleton, who sat upon his white horse, telescope in hand, could hardly distinguish the nature

14*

of the commotion in the grass. But the boats which had brought over the detachment, pushed out immediately and returned with all possible expedition to the bridges.

"Captain Fink," said Bim, standing amid the slain, "I'm afraid I shall be sick of this business! What is that they are doing with the enemy's heads?"

"Scalping 'em!" said Fink. "And it aint right! Scouts! stop that! They've been used to fighting Indians."

But the order was too late. The Scouts had completed the work effectually. They had, however, only shaved off a small particle of skin, about an inch in diameter, from the crown of each head.

This terrible blow had, unfortunately, fallen upon men of science, and artisans, many of whom had not sympathized with the project of invasion, but were constrained by Ruffleton's officers, in fear of the guillotine, to act as pioneers, architects, etc. Among these was a gentleman of Southern birth, who designed flying to the President's standard. He had been the publisher of an Exploring Expedition, and the ignorant multitude supposed he would make a good explorer himself in the enemy's country! He was accordingly seized, and forced to accompany the pioneers. He fell before he could make known his condition. But the Scout that killed him, got a barren scalp—for he was quite bald.

It was not long before the fate of the detachment was known on the opposite shore, and the keen eye of Bim soon perceived that the battery was about to open its fire.

"Gopher!" cried Captain Fink to his Scouts, which meant that they should disappear as the prairie animal of that name is in the habit of doing when danger menaces. In a twinkling the Scouts, and they were imitated this time by Bim's men, had glided through the grass and the grove, and found a shelter in a depression of the earth.

Then came a shower of cannon balls crashing through the trees, followed quickly by such a stunning report as the Wild Western Scouts had never heard before. For some time there was no intermission of the fire, but battery after battery was drawn up on the opposite bank and discharged in quick succession. The very heavens seemed rent with the explosions, and the poor Scouts, had they not been possessed with more than ordinary courage, might have supposed the destruction of the world was at hand. None of them, however, having fallen, they soon recovered their presence of mind—they lifted their heads and ventured to survey the scene. The opposite side of the river was enveloped in a cloud of smoke so dense, that it resembled a thick fog. Not a man or a gun could be seen. But the fire soon ceased. Not a shot being returned, the Protector supposed the enemy had been either completely demolished or had taken to flight.

Nevertheless there had been no relaxation in the work of pushing forward the sections of the floating bridges; and Bim and Fink were a little surprised to behold the proximity of the platforms to the Southern shore.

"Screw sights to four hundred yards!" said Fink. "Every one of us can hit a button that distance." The order was obeyed, and the sharp reports of the Miniés rang through the valley, and all the foremost workmen, at the end of the wooden structures, fell upon the platforms of their own construction. Others took their places, but shared a similar fate. Thus, for many minutes, the work of thousands was arrested by two hundred marksmen; and Ruffleton, upon learning the state of affairs, was thrown into an ungovernable rage, and ordered forward a thousand sharp-shooters to fire upon the Scouts from the ends of the bridges.

"Gopher!" said Fink, when he saw the enemy raise their muskets to fire. "Wait till they're tired of shooting; as long as they waste powder and ball at us, the bridge can't grow, and when they stop firing, we'll begin."

"That's right, Captain!" said Bim. "And it won't be long before we hear from the President."

But the Scouts were surprised to see that an expedient had been adopted which would be likely to baffle their attempts to stop the operations of the bridge builders. Temporary defences of planks were erected on the extremity of each section, and the menacing platforms recommenced growing in length.

"Captain Bim," said Fink, who had been some time adjusting the sights of his rifle, as the wind swept the cloud of smoke away, "I'm going to risk my reputation."

"Well, Captain Fink," responded Bim, "what does that mean?"

"It means exactly this—I'm going to fire at that head

chief over the river yonder on the white horse, hit or miss."

"Then you'd better not fire, Captain," said Bim, "for you will miss to a certainty. That man is at least one thousand yards off."

"I have gauged my rifle for a thousand yards, and, hit or miss, I must fire. There's something urging me to do it."

"Stop a moment, Captain!" said Bim. "Here's a messenger. What's the news, comrade? Do you come from the President?" The Lieutenant answered in the affirmative, and then placed a note in the Captain's hand. It was from Randolph, directing the detachment under Bim and Fink to oppose every obstacle to the landing of the enemy, and promising speedy succor.

Fink drew up his rifle, but after a prolonged and steady aim, lowered the breech with a sigh. "It's a monstrous risk!" said he. "But I'll do it presently. If I didn't, the Scouts would tell the Indians I was afraid of missing. But what's that?" This question was occasioned by the deep detonation of distant artillery.

"Hush!" cried Bim, listening attentively. "It is, by thunder!" cried he. "Hasten back, Lieutenant, and say to the President that Captain Bim has heard the roar of battle far up the river. It must be Generals Blount and Crook fighting Sir Charles Hunt and General Line. Now fire away, Captain Fink!" he continued, when the Lieutenant put spurs to his horse.

Captain Fink raised his rifle steadily, and aimed at the distant target.

CHAPTER LI.

RUFFLETON'S GENERALSHIP.

General Ruffleton, the Protector and Commander-in-Chief of the Northern armies, surrounded by his staff, sat upon his magnificent white steed on the Northern bank of the Susquehanna. Recovered from his recent fit of passion, he witnessed with satisfaction the now uninterrupted elongation of his bridges. The idea of shielding the workmen by a movable breastwork had originated in his own prolific brain, and he now beheld its successful operation with an air of triumph.

"General Maller," said he, addressing his newly-promoted friend, "I think the world is destined, after all, to give me the credit of possessing as much military genius as Randolph. I have fought as many battles as he."

"Yes, General," said Maller, "and gained as many victories. The only victory Randolph can claim, was the repulse of Crook. Crook had some 1,200 men, and Randolph 4,000."

"Generalship, however," pursued Ruffleton, "does not consist alone in fighting. Randolph with his pontoon train, fifteen ships of war, and an immense flotilla, was for many days cooped up in a contracted nook on the Delaware river. Now I shall not be delayed six hours in crossing the Susquehanna. What do *you* say, General?" he continued, turning to Balatrum.

"If we are to meet with no further obstruction than the few sharp-shooters over there," said Balatrum, "we shall not only cross without serious delay, but we will gain a decisive victory. The orders you dispatched last night to Emmitsburg, if obeyed with promptitude, will enable us to interpose between the Ex-President and the main body of his army."

"Very true!" said Ruffleton, "such was the purpose—and, by Jove! it will be accomplished! Do you not hear the cannon of Hunt and Line? I knew they would be followed by Blount. Now, ——" His speech was cut short. Fink's bullet perforated his white steed's forehead, and the animal fell head-foremost to the earth, precipitating his rider down the embankment into the impalpable quicksand. Nothing but the General's heels was visible a moment after; but he was immediately rescued, puffing and blowing through the mud which plastered over his mouth and nose. His eyes were closed, and his ears stopped. His fine dress, of which he was ever punctiliously careful, was utterly marred.

"Wash me! Wash me!" were his first words. "Give me my pistols!" said he, when his face was washed; "I will shoot the horse, and hang the swindling caitiff who cheated me!"

"General," said Balatrum, "the horse is dead."

"Dead? Who killed him without my order?"

"One of the enemy, General. A Minié ball perforated his head, and that caused him to fall."

"That explains all! By Jove, I'm thankful it was no worse! If the marksman had aimed a few inches higher, he might have put an end to the war; and then some of Ruffleton's friends might have been the sufferers! I cannot stand with this load on my garments! Bear me to my tent. I hear the artillery of Sir Charles and General Line! Moments are precious! Push forward the bridges! Bring another horse. If we can interpose between Blount and Randolph, the South will be compelled to submit."

The General was borne to his tent, where his ablutions were repeated, and a new suit substituted for the coat of mud. During the process an express arrived from Sir Charles, confirming the conjectures of Ruffleton. Blount and Crook had followed the Western armies along the Pennsylvania line. But in obedience to orders, Hunt and Line had declined giving battle, and manœuvred to entice their pursuers as far northward as possible.

"By Jove!" cried Ruffleton, his good-humor restored, "everything has gone prosperously, with the exception of that unlucky fall, which hurt nobody! Run out batteries on the bridges, and sweep the opposite shore with a few rounds of grape. The tide is ebbing. If the cannon should be an obstruction to the passage of the cavalry, after a few discharges, throw them overboard. We have abundance of heavy metal—and if we gain a footing over there, we'll soon have still more!" His order was promptly obeyed; and soon after he was mounted on another steed of spotless white, elegantly caparisoned.

CHAPTER LII.

THE JUNCTION.

"HUZZA!" cried Captain Bim, when he saw Ruffleton precipitated down the bank. "He's dead, by Jupiter! And I'm afraid the fighting's all over."

"The line was true," said Bim gravely, "and the aim a steady one, I own; but there was a mistake in the distance, or else the horse raised his head after I pulled trigger."

"But I tell you the centre's been driven!" continued Bim. "The Tyrant has fallen!"

"Not a bit of it!" replied Fink. "You are too quick on the trigger, and apt to go off at half-cock."

"Don't you see 'em carrying him on a litter?" asked Bim.

"Yes, I see that. And I've seen a mud-turtle carried in a wheelbarrow, and the varmint wasn't dead. Now, I'll put a question to you. Where's the General's horse?"

"His horse? By George! he fell in his tracks! I see him now."

"That's so. *He's* dead enough—and I hadn't any grudge against the poor beast. Don't you see how it is? I've killed the horse, and given the rider a ducking. That's all. The shot will save my credit among the Indians; but it might have been better."

"You are right, Captain," said Bim. "The horse gave way at the knees first, and the pot-bellied rider rolled over his head. The bullet couldn't have killed them both. We shall have plenty of fighting yet. What's that for? Oh, I see! They're bringing some cannon out on the platforms, and we shall have to 'squat' again."

And before the men could avail themselves of the friendly shelter of the intervening earth, the batteries were discharged, and the innumerable missiles seemed to strike the surface of every tangible object exposed to view. Several of the Scouts were killed and wounded.

But when the torrent of grape ceased, and the workmen recommenced their operations, the Scouts resumed their vigilance, and rarely missed any mark that tempted their fatal aim. But still, the screen being replaced, the bridges grew rapidly; and as the tide ran down, the width of the stream was materially diminished. It became apparent that the completion of the communication with the Southern shore could not long be delayed.

While such thoughts occupied the minds of Bim and Fink, another messenger arrived from the President. Randolph directed the Scouts to hold out at all hazards, until his arrival, which would be in twenty minutes.

"Fire at the planks, Scouts!" said Fink.

"Will your bullets go through?" asked Bim.

"Yes—that distance. Don't you see?"

Bim perceived the effect of the last fire of the Miniés. A great commotion ensued among the workmen; and soon after the nailing on of additional planks was heard distinctly.

"Go back and tell the President," said Bim, "that we will defend this shore for twenty minutes; but without cannon, we shall not be able to keep them off much longer."

Bim and Fink, conscious of the responsibility imposed on them, and aware of the importance of the service they were performing, exerted all their powers to retard the completion of the bridges.

The last sections were about being thrust forward, where the ends would fall in shallow water, and a thousand riflemen stood on each of the bridges in readiness to rush out and be avenged on the handful of Scouts.

"We can't stand our ground against such a number," said Bim. "But there's one thing we can do!" he added.

"What's that, Captain?" asked Fink, as he discharged his rifle, and brought down a Colonel. He picked out the officers.

"We can die in our tracks! And I'd rather do it than disappoint President Randolph!"

"Never say die!" returned Fink. "We can pick 'em off as they land, and we can hang upon their flanks and rear as they march. But hist!" he continued, stooping down, and placing his ear near the earth. "I hear 'em! I mean I feel 'em! They jar the ground!"

"Who?" asked Bim.

"I can't tell who. But there are horses and carriages."

"Perhaps artillery!"

"Shouldn't be surprised," said Fink.

But they *were* surprised a moment after. For Randolph had come up, and ranged a brass battery in position a short distance below. The fire of twenty guns, screened by a light curtain of bushes, startled friend and foe.

The three regiments of sharp-shooters were in the act of rushing out on the shore when the first discharge burst upon the car. The bridges were broken behind them, and cut off their retreat. A second discharge demolished many other sections, and soon the surface of the river was covered with the wreck of the bridges. The three regiments laid down their arms.

Randolph, galloping forward, ordered the captives to be removed immediately; and then hastened to the aid of Blount, whose artillery could be distinctly heard responding to the fire of Hunt and Line, several miles further up the river.

But when the President was in readiness to succor his brave Generals, it was observed that Ruffleton had likewise marched to the assistance of his Western and British allies. With the utmost expedition he arranged a battery of 500 heavy field pieces, which swept the battle-ground beyond the lines of the Western armies.

Seeing no possibility of preventing the invasion, Randolph concentrated all his forces and retreated Southward in good order.

CHAPTER LIII.

HEAD-QUARTERS AT HAVRE DE GRACE.

As the shades of evening fell upon the earth, Randolph re-entered the village of Havre de Grace, and was met with joyful smiles by his daughter at the mansion occupied as his head-quarters.

"The Scouts did good service," said he, in reply to Alice's inquiry, "they certainly defeated Ruffleton's design to interpose between me and Blount, which, if it had been accomplished, would have prevented us from resting here one more night."

"One more night!" said Alice.

"This one night is all that is vouchsafed us, Alice. To-morrow we must resume the journey, and where our travels will end, who knows? I know they will end—but not where, or when. Some one said Wiry Willy had arrived. Where is he?"

"He awaits permission to enter. I will send him in. None of our officers were killed or wounded, father?"

"None, I believe. Blount had a horse killed under him. The animal's head was carried completely away by a round shot. And it may be as well to apprise you that the General is as bloody as a butcher."

"Well, Willy," said the President, presenting his hand in a familiar manner, but without rising, for he was fatigued after the exercises of the day. "You find me retreating before the enemy; but you have not abandoned what is deemed by many a sinking cause."

"Oh—no, sir! It cannot last. And when Ruffleton falls, it will be like the fall of Lucifer! Virus will be sent to you."

"For what purpose?"

"I think it will be in regard to Baltimore. A number of Northern men, doing business in that city, have arrived in the Protector's camp, no doubt to negotiate."

"No doubt, Willy. Well—perhaps it is the best thing they can do. Ruffleton, then, has no misgivings as to the result of the campaign?"

"None, sir. He is certain of capturing Washington, and is already importuned by the fanatics to destroy it. He has given them no answer yet, I think, from their grumbling."

"Grumbling? Do they grumble already?"

"Not much yet, sir—but they will. Not only Washing ton, but Richmond, Raleigh, and Charleston are to be taken, before vengeance can be satisfied."

"It will be satisfied then, Willy!"

"They are in earnest, sir, and speak of the capture of those cities as altogether practicable and probable."

"Three-quarters of a million of armed men may penetrate to Charleston, with the co-operation of the British fleets in the Chesapeake, in Albemarle and Pamlico Sounds, and on the ocean coast. They may penetrate that far before the impetus is expended. *Then*—but, Willy, I will not anticipate events."

"It was in relation to the very fleets you mention, chiefly, that I desired to speak. Lord Slysir ran over the whole programme in my hearing, when forgetful of my presence. I was waiting for a letter he was preparing to be delivered to Miss Edith Langdon. Ruffleton came in, and his Lordship thrust me behind a screen—and—sir—"

"What?"

"He had previously thrust a person there as I entered the room."

"And that person, Willy, was probably no man."

"You are right, sir."

"And, at the same time, he was writing to Edith! You must tell her everything, Willy. Has his Lordship recovered?"

"He is quite well, sir; and I am inclined to believe he was entirely recovered before you left New Castle."

"Dr. Durnell intimated as much. How long do you propose staying with us, Willy?"

"As long as I can do anything to serve the cause. Such was my compact with Mary; and my grandame is patriotic, and insists upon the fulfilment of my duty. I need not add, I hope, that it is both my will and my pleasure to discharge every obligation of a loyal citizen. Is there anything you would have me do now, sir?"

"I think you ought to go to Yorktown, and remove the effects of the late Mr. Penford to a place of security. And, Willy, by whispering into the ear of Mr. A——, the words, '*Randolph and the Union*,' he will conduct you to a place of safety where you may deposit them. I have authorized Mr. A—— to have the exclusive custody of the ARCHIVES, and none besides himself, you, and me, will have any knowledge of the place of their deposit."

Willy bowed with reverence, and lost not a moment in departing on his important mission.

"Don't be alarmed! It's horse-blood! He has not received a scratch!" said General Crook, without, upon seeing Alice staring at the soiled vest of Blount, as they entered the hall. A moment after the Generals were ushered in by Alice.

"Mr. President," said Crook, "I am as hungry as a shark. I have eaten nothing since dawn. But now I can distinguish a savory odor proceeding from your kitchen."

"Father, why don't you invite the General to dine with you?" said Alice.

"I will, as soon as I can find an opportunity."

"Oh, don't take the trouble," said Crook. "Just consider it done! I shall have my fill, I hope, once more—and it may be the last time. But we shall all have leisure to eat to-night."

"That is very true," said Blount; "for Ruffleton's forces have encamped. The heavens are illuminated with their fires, and no doubt many of them are as hungry as Crook. They burn the fences; but have not, I believe, destroyed any of the farm-houses."

"They have reserved them for their own accommodations," said Crook, "when they return in the winter, a pack of fugitives in need of shelter."

A moment after, dinner was announced.

CHAPTER LIV.

AFFAIRS AT THE CAPITAL.

WHEN Wiry Willy reached Washington and whispered the mysterious words into the ear of Mr. A —— that gentleman's face was wreathed in smiles. And, late as it was, he accompanied Willy up to the Little Falls of the Potomac, where, among the immense wilderness of mossy rocks strewn about by some convulsion of nature, the place of deposit was revealed.

Returning to the Capital, Willy perceived with interest that all the hotels were still open, and many men, in excited conversation, were passing in and out, and alternately filling and emptying the saloons. The ensuing day was the one appointed weeks before, by the President, in one of his proclamations, for the reassembling of Congress; but no one expected that any considerable number of members would arrive.

But, at a late hour of the night, to the agreeable surprise

of the friends of the Union, it was ascertained that a *large number* of members had arrived within the last few hours.

The work of computation was instituted, and a rumor ran through the city that *a quorum would in all probability be present.* This produced great rejoicing. Thousands who had retired in quest of the oblivion of slumber, abandoned their couches and repaired to the hotels. Willy, upon hearing the news, hastened to the mansion of Senator Langdon, and succeeded in rousing Dick Clusky.

"Now what do you want with me?" said Dick. "Who are you, that knows so well that I sleep in the vestibule?"

"I am Wiry Willy," said Willy.

"Wiry Willy? Hey? Why, you're a friend."

"To be sure I am."

"And you were here when the scary times began?"

"Yes, Dick. I remember the day when the cannon balls whizzed by the ears of the horses as you drove them from the church."

"That's so! But where do you come from, now? What do you want?"

"I have news for Miss Edith and Senator Langdon."

"They've been in bed for hours, though I don't believe they can sleep much. Are the British and Northerners coming? Ah, Lord! I'm afraid they'll catch Mr. Senator Langdon and his daughter, and kill me and mother—"

"Never fear; I have *good* news."

"Good news? Then I'll wake 'em up."

"Do so, Dick. Say Wiry Willy has arrived, with good news."

"I will. Come in!"

Willy stepped into the vestibule, then faintly illuminated by a jet of gas kept constantly burning in the hall; and Dick sped up-stairs to the chambers occupied by the Senator and his daughter.

Edith was the first to appear. She met Willy with her usual frank cordiality, and led him into the parlor, which was soon brilliantly illuminated.

"Your news, Willy," said she; "I am all impatience. My father will be down in a few moments. He seems entirely recovered."

"I am rejoiced to hear that!" said Willy, "for, I believe,

he will soon occupy the Chair in the Senate, the Vice-President being still incapacitated."

"The Chair of the Senate! That would, indeed, be good news."

"And I have brought this letter for you," said Willy, "in accordance with my promise. If it should displease you, you will not, I am sure, reproach me with being its bearer."

"No," said she, taking the letter. "It bears Lord Slysir's seal. I will not break it, Willy; but will merely certify to its faithful delivery with my pencil, and then, if you should see him again, you must return it into his own hand. But here comes my father."

"Well, Willy," said the Senator, entering, and taking the hand of the messenger. "What does Randolph say? We have heard of his junction with Blount, and—"

"I have not a word from him, sir," said Willy. "But he will arrive in the Capital, I think, before many hours. Only one or two more members are wanting to make up a quorum."

"Is that so, sir? When I retired to my couch it was supposed more than forty were wanting."

"They have been arriving every hour, sir; and I heard a Senator say there would certainly be a quorum. The hotels are alive with people; and many are hoping that you will be well enough to take your place in the Senate."

"I am perfectly well! Run to the hotels, Willy, and say so. Say I will repair to the Capitol, immediately. It is past the hour of midnight, and the day appointed has arrived. Perhaps not a moment should be lost. The President—"

"He's been sent for, sir. They have telegraphed for him."

"That was well. The tidings will be joyfully received by Randolph. Dick!" said he, turning to his coachman, who, in disregard of all decorum, had been standing at the parlor door with eyes, ears, and mouth open, "have the coach in readiness immediately. But first see who knocks, knocking and ringing both! What urgent messengers!"

A moment after Dick ushered in several members of Congress, and among them the elder Blount, who had just reached the city.

Edith flew into his arms, for she had long regarded him

as a second father. And Langdon embraced him. Tears were shed by every one present.

"We meet again, Langdon," said the white-haired Southern Senator, "contrary to my expectations and predictions; but we are embarked in a common cause. The despatch I received, and which caused my return to the Capital, assured me that the first business of the two houses, in the event of a quorum assembling, would be a re-consideration of the resolution ——"

"Oh, yes—anything for harmony!" said Langdon. "I will vote your abstraction, if you insist on it; and I will vote in as many more Slave States as you wish, provided the inhabitants of them have freely and fairly ratified their Constitutions."

"Enough! Nevertheless, Langdon, the resolution was something more than an abstraction. Its rejection would have the effect to deter slave-holders from taking their property into new territories——but—God forgive me! We will not discuss it here. I see a tear swelling in the eye of my Edith!"

"Nor elsewhere, Blount!" said Langdon. "It will pass *nem. con.* to avoid the consumption of time."

"Now brush away the tear!" said the aged Senator to Edith.

"You must let me weep for my country," said Edith. "Still, I shall be ready to perish with it, if it must be so."

"It will not perish, my daughter. Randolph will save it. I thought otherwise once—but now I am prepared to sustain him. My son, too, follows his fortunes, and you, daughter of the North, must be wedded to the fortunes of my son. The North and the South, the East and the West, must unite in the expulsion of the British, and then there will be a season of fraternal concord."

"But, alas!" said Edith, "before the dawn of that happy era, many a field, now quiet and peaceful, will be ensanguined with fratricidal blood!"

"True! True! But the world will then see that our slaves did not augment our danger, or even embarrass us, when the enemy came into our country. More than two hundred thousand of our negroes are at this moment doing valuable service in the construction of fortifications, and in collecting provisions and materials for our armies. And this they do most cheerfully, and even beg to fight for us!"

"Come, gentlemen," said Langdon. "Enter my coach, and we will repair to the Capitol. Let us remain there and eat and sleep, and, if needs be, die in our chairs, like Roman Senators!" They departed immediately.

CHAPTER LV.

RECEPTION AT THE WHITE HOUSE.

LIGHTS were gleaming in the Capitol, and the greater portion of the population of the city had left their dwellings and repaired, at that unseasonable hour, to the Halls of Legislation. The rotunda, the galleries, the porticos, and even the grounds surrounding the building, were crowded with anxious citizens.

When it was ascertained that a quorum had assembled in each House, the manifestations of joy could not be controlled. In the Senate, Mr. Langdon was chosen to preside, and soon after a mighty uproar without announced the arrival of President Randolph. Deafening huzzas hailed his approach to the Capitol. He and Blount were met at the threshold by the President of the Senate and the Speaker of the House of Representatives, and conducted into the Great Hall, where they were received by the members of both Houses, standing.

When the plaudits had subsided, the President addressed the Senators and Representatives, face to face, as Washington had done in the beginning. He described the extraordinary condition of affairs briefly, but comprehensively, and recommended such measures for their adoption as the exigencies of the crisis seemed to demand. He then retired to the Vice-President's room, accompanied by Blount, where Alice and Edith awaited them.

"Tell me," said Edith, while Blount grasped her hand and gazed upon her lovely countenance, "shall we be compelled to fly from the Capital?"

"It cannot be successfully defended against such an overwhelming multitude as Ruffleton is leading," was the grave reply.

"But *when* will he be here?"

"It may be a week. It might be longer—but the President inclines to the policy of non-resistance so far as the Capital is concerned. If they destroy it, all the patriotism in the nation will be outraged. If they spare it, we shall re-possess it when the reflux of the tide wafts us back."

"And there *will* be such a tide in our affairs!" said Alice.

"Certainly," said the President. "And we shall see such unanimity in the views and acts of this Congress as was never witnessed before! The country will be saved!"

"The Republic, father?" asked Alice, in a low tone.

"Unquestionably, my MARBLE, if it be susceptible of enduring vitality!"

"And now," said Blount, "farewell, until we meet again!"

"Whither do you go?" asked Edith. "You have but just arrived, and now you announce your departure."

"There is a quorum without me, and my presence will be required in the field. The glorious Crook is much better in a charge than in a retreat. Every retrograde step is a mortification to him. My resignation as a member of Congress is in the hands of the Speaker. My father awaits me in the committee-room. Farewell—brief adieus must suffice in times like the present." And he hurried away to the interview with his father.

The departure of Blount was followed by the entrance of the Secretary of the Senate and the Clerk of the House, bearing Joint Resolutions, and sundry Bills, already passed by both Houses of Congress—the rules having been modified so as to dispense with the usual ceremony and delay.

Almost dictatorial powers were conferred on President Randolph: and all his previous acts were sanctioned. Direct taxes were to be levied for revenue, and appropriations were made to defray the expenses of the war for two years, the duration of the term specified for the exercise of the extraordinary power given the Executive. All citizens found in arms, and waging war against the United States, were required to disperse and to return to their homes in obedience to the command of the Federal Executive, on or before a day to be specified in a Proclamation, under penalty of being pronounced traitors, &c. The privilege of the writ of *Habeas Corpus* might be suspended at the discretion of the President. *War was declared against Great Britain.*

A few nights after the assembling of Congress, the doors of the White House were thrown open for the reception of visitors. The President, his Cabinet Ministers, his daughter Alice, and her friend Edith, were standing in the room where the visitors were usually received. The porter then opened the door, and—not twenty persons entered! Congress had not adjourned. The heads of bureaus, with a few exceptions, and a vast majority of their subordinates, had left the city.

"Be not so lugubrious, my MARBLE," said Randolph, in a whisper to his daughter.

"I will not, father!" said she, "I could laugh, gentlemen," she continued, addressing several members of the Cabinet, men distinguished for their learning and administrative abilities, "you are the more distinguished by the desertion of others in the hour of peril. The historian will record the incidents of this hour. The names, the attitudes, and the very words of those who had the courage and fidelity to stand by the Chief Magistrate when the enemy was approaching the Capital, will be recorded, remembered, and admired!"

"Among the faithless, faithful only these!" said the President, smiling. "But be of good cheer. We shall see them back again when I have patronage to bestow. Now, none so poor to do me reverence! It is well. Why should they remain here, when I am flying and the enemy advancing? In truth, my friends, many have left the city not only by permission of their superiors in office, but in consequence of my advice. Indeed, indeed, ladies, the man has as many friends as the office."

The young ladies laughed outright, for the scene was ludicrous enough.

"We are not even regaled with music, Mr. President," said Edith.

"No. Valiant would not leave me the band! And

Blount, too, deserted me! And Senator Langdon, although proscribed by Ruffleton, is not here to dignify this mirthful occasion."

"But the Senator, you know, is engaged in the performance of his duty, and, for that matter, the General—"

"Go on. Why do you pause?"

"You said my father had been proscribed!" was the reply of the maiden, now pale and agitated.

"And for that matter," continued the President, "I, and Blount, and all who have been *particeps criminis* in resistance to his treasonable usurpation, are in the same category."

"And you see I am not alarmed, Edith," said Alice.

"Nor will I be," said Edith. "The tyrant will meet a traitor's doom!"

"Bravely spoken," said the President. "But here comes more company."

Congress having adjourned, the White House was soon thronged with the patriotic Representatives of the States and the People. They encircled the President, and renewed their vows to sustain him in his endeavor to preserve the Republic.

The President thanked them for their promptitude in enacting the laws he had recommended, and he declared his purpose to devote his energies to the salvation of his country and the overthrow of the enemies of the people. He then led the way towards the East Room, walking between Alice and Edith, and followed by his Cabinet, and the members. The folding doors were thrown open, and, to the astonishment of many, a magnificent banqueting-board greeted their vision.

The President sat down at one end of the table and Senator Langdon at the other. The ladies, and there were but two, Alice and Edith, occupied seats respectively beside their parents.

"Fall to, gentlemen, and help yourselves," said Randolph. "For a sufficient number of waiters could not be obtained, to use a common phrase, for love or money; and so, perforce, we must be content with the cooks."

Randolph was obeyed with alacrity, for many present had not enjoyed a good dinner for several days, and this was truly an imperial feast.

And, in process of time, when a clatter of knife-handles imposed silence, the President rose up with a brimming glass in his hand, and his example was followed by all the guests.

"THE UNION!" said he, "but no cheers, gentlemen. Let us drink it in silence, if we drink it at all, with the secret resolve in our hearts too sacred for utterance." This was done. But many a tear flowed down the manly cheeks of the company.

The next toast was offered by Senator Langdon.

"RE-UNION of the North with the South!" said he. "And that too, in mute resolve, gentlemen!" It was done.

"Now, Alice!" said Randolph.

"The DAUGHTERS of the Republic!" said she; "May they prove worthy of the patriotic sires who created it."

"Now, Edith!" said Langdon.

"And worthy the heroes who would preserve it!" was the response. And then the silence was ruptured. Cheers and plaudits resounded from the basement to the gables of the Federal Palace. Randolph rose again, his penetrating eye fixed on the Senator's Daughter, and proposed "The Hero Blount!" This was rapturously cheered, mingled with some merriment, while Edith blushed under the many glances directed towards her end of the table.

"And the Hero of Bladensburg, the brave Crook!" said Langdon. And this was responded to as heartily as the other.

"I propose the Knight of the Velvet Cap!" said the elder Blount; and then, if she had not been MARBLE, it was Alice's turn to blush. But she only turned paler, while acknowledging the compliment.

Soon after this the company, and particularly the ladies, were startled by the appearance of Crazy Charlotte at the door. This poor woman, not yet thirty years of age, was well known in various sections of the country, for she travelled much, but always re-appeared at Washington at the assembling of Congress. She was tall and majestic in stature, and her pale oval face, retaining traces of former beauty, and piercing eyes, usually inspired pity rather than aversion in the beholder. But now her aspect was most extraordinary. She had been to the theatre and obtained a tinselled cuirass, and a painted helmet which she wore with the ease of familiarity, and in her hand she waved a light spear of tin culled from the same armory.

"Fly! Fly!" said she in a loud but mournful voice. "Fly to the mountains, or dive under the sea, for the destroyer cometh. And who is the destroyer? Man! inhuman man!"

"Sit down, dame Charlotte," said Randolph, "and feast with us. It will be time enough to fly after we have eaten."

"'Two women shall be grinding at the mill—one shall be taken and the other left.' Nay, ladies," continued Charlotte, advancing a step and then pausing, "I do not mean either of you. You are the daughters of the Republic, and will never die. But beware—beware of the perils menacing your great sires! Beware! beware!"

"We will try and guard against them, ourselves, Charlotte," said Randolph.

"How! can the eye of the eagle penetrate the earth and detect the secret mine? Can the breast of the proud lion be mailed against the venomous fangs of the hidden serpent? Fly! Fly! I looked, and lo, the flag of my country fell from the dome of the Capitol. The stars and stripes, the symbols of glory, have vanished from the breeze, and the wolves of oppression will lap our blood, and howl in the sacred precincts of Freedom. Fly! Fly!"

"That will do, Charlotte!" said Randolph. "Come! if you will not eat with us, let me pour you some wine!"

"Throw it to the earth! pour libations on the ground, and bow your head at the desecrated Altar of Freedom! I will neither eat, nor drink, nor sleep, while the Republic is perishing. Fly! Fly! and return victors—or remain and die."

"Our army is between us and the enemy, Charlotte," said Alice.

"Alas!" cried the crazy woman, striding forward and standing at the back of Alice's chair, "we know not who are our most deadly enemies. We often eat with them and drink with them. Your great father, it is said, will be the last to leave the Capital. Hear me!" she continued in a deep voice, "let him be the first—see that he is surrounded by a wall of spears! Oh, I would die to save him. The hopes of his country are centred on his head—"

"That is flattery, dame Charlotte," said Randolph.

"Flattery! and from a woman. No! No! Flattery that kills is uttered only by man. Beware of the warning! Fly!"

"What have you heard, what do you know of danger menacing my father?" demanded Alice.

"Be not incredulous, daughter of the President!" said Charlotte, "nor haughty, nor scornful. I go—but will return to repeat the warning. Once more I will enter the Presidential mansion before you leave it. Farewell! Farewell!" And she hurried out as abruptly as she had entered.

CHAPTER LVI.

A DARK CONSPIRACY.

It was the night of the evacuation. For hours the Federal troops, for all that now defended the South and the Government of the United States, were thus denominated, had been defiling over the Long Bridge into Virginia. Baltimore had fallen into the hands of the invaders by capitulation. Delaware and Maryland were subjugated provinces!

Propositions of a similar character had been made the President, in regard to the District of Columbia and the Federal city. But the only response was that the Federal forces, unable to resist the approach of the invaders, would retire, at a time specified, across the Potomac river. But, until the time named, the President would resist any attempts of the enemy to enter the capital.

In the meantime not only the army, but all the civilians inimical to the invaders, were, day and night, crossing the Potomac and taking refuge in Virginia. But it was remarked that a very large proportion of the employés of the Government had disappeared mysteriously, and that many of them had not taken leave of the President, or heads of their respective Departments. The White House had suddenly lost its charm.

The public treasure, of course, was with the army; and Crook's four millions were safe in his military chest, to be scrupulously divided among the brave soldiers who had captured it.

In one of the offices of the deserted Treasury Building, two men were conversing in low tones. It was quite dark, and they did not invite observation. One was Mr. Windvane, holding an important position under the Government. The other individual was Virus, the Protector's confidential negotiator.

"Windvane," said the latter, "I would not have this spy of yours play us falsely, for all the money in the President's flying Treasury!"

"Be under no concern. For several years he has furnished me information of the President's most secret interviews. To sweep the floor, to replenish the grate, to announce dinner, he has had access at all hours. He has long been in my power. If he played me falsely, or even failed to communicate intelligence, he has been aware that a word of mine would crush him!"

"And he is still at the White House?"

"Still there, in obedience to my command, with an assurance that he will be promoted by General Ruffleton."

"The promise will be fulfilled, if he serves us."

"He will, assuredly. The coach is now standing at the door of the mansion, and Abel (he was a freed mulatto) will be here immediately after Randolph and his daughter enter it. They will cross the canal, where your men are in ambush, after the last soldier of the retiring army has passed over. Randolph has said repeatedly that he would be the last to abandon the Capital, and it is a point of honor to comply literally with his word."

"His capture will be an important blow. And I do not see how he can escape us."

"He cannot fail to fall into your hands, if you have men enough concealed in the boats to rush out and stop his horses."

"There are nearly a hundred. And they will stop the carriage on the bridge."

"That is right. If he passes over, he could never be overtaken. But then, Virus, you think *my* affairs will prosper?"

"You will merit the Protector's unlimited confidence That much he has authorized me to say. He remarked, moreover, that your long experience in the Departments of the Government, would be of invaluable benefit to him. If he should determine to make this city the Capital of his Empire, I think I am justifiable in saying you will be placed at the head of one of the Executive Departments."

"Virus, I possess the qualifications to discharge the duties. But what is that?" he asked, as a rushing sound was heard.

"It is the cavalry of Valiant, the rear guard of the army, abandoning the city. Within an hour the Protector will occupy the Capital!"

"And will he occupy the White House?"

"Will he not? Of course he will! And Randolph—where will he be?"

"In the power of the Protector! But what will he do with him?"

"I have not heard him say, Windvane; and, really, I cannot conjecture what disposition will be made of him. But where are his Blue Caps?"

"His Blue Caps? True? Where are they? I do not know! It is strange they should be absent at a time like the present. It is their peculiar province to guard the persons of the President and his romantic daughter. And Randolph does not commit blunders!"

"What is that!" Virus asked this question, upon being startled by a shuffling of feet and a tapping of the marble floor in the hall between the rows of offices.

"Fly! Fly! Romans! Fly to the mountains! The deluge is here! The Goths and Vandals!" Such were the words which greeted their ears.

"That is crazy Charlotte!" said Windvane. "Every day for the last week she has passed our doors uttering such unmeaning words. Everybody here has long been accustomed to her senseless jargon. But how the d—l she contrived to get into the building is past my comprehension. I saw that the doors were closed and fastened myself."

"Perhaps she remained in the building as well as yourself. I hope she has not been listening to our conversation!"

"No fear of that. Or if she had, she could never retain

it in her memory. And if she could repeat it word for word, no one would heed her. The other day she entered the East Room when the President and his adherents were striving to keep their spirits up at the magnificent banquet, and uttered her maniacal incantations. Abel says the President merely smiled, and invited her to eat and drink with the rest."

"And has she not gone to the President now?"

"It is not improbable; for she goes and comes as she pleases, and at all hours. But no one heeds her. She was here, with me, before she went to the banquet. But Abel says she did not allude to me at all."

"Very well. I suppose you know all about her. Hear how she slams the door! She has certainly gone towards the President's mansion."

"She has not done so clandestinely, at all events," said Windvane.

"The cavalry," said Virus, "must have nearly all gone by. The sounds are diminishing."

"True. I think I hear the wheels of the artillery carriage—the last batteries. It cannot be long before the President and his daughter will enter the carriage. Then we shall have Abel!"

"And then the signal! The rocket is prepared—"

"Yes. Three of them. All cannot possibly fail to ascend. Our cigars are lighted, and if *they* fail I have lucifer matches."

"And they are well named. The devil himself, they say, is on our side! But suppose that mad woman discovered the rockets in the rear as she passed out, and removed or destroyed them?"

"I will see!" said Windvane, groping his way out. "They have not been molested!" said he, returning a few moments after.

"Windvane, the Protector will reward you. Did you not hear the wheels of the coach?"

"No. But the cavalry and artillery have gone by, and all is silent in the deserted streets. Abel's appearance will be the first intimation of the departure of Randolph. The wheels of his coach will not be heard on the fine gravel of the lawn. It cannot be many moments before his arrival. He knows where we are, and will come directly to us, accompanied by one or two of the servants he has won over. Hist!" Footsteps were heard approaching.

CHAPTER LVII.

THE SCOUTS.

"Captain Fink! Captain Fink!" said Captain Bim, "I can't see the men, and I've turned round so much that I don't know where to look for them."

"That's exactly what I wanted," replied Fink. "If *we* can't see 'em or hear 'em, of course the enemy can't. They've squatted."

"But the ground's wet, here! Now, I'd have no objections in the world to stand chin deep in a slimy frog-pond to serve President Randolph or his daughter; but, for the life of me, I can't see what we are posted among these bulrushes for."

"To be hid, I suppose, from the enemy," said Fink.

"But, by George!" said Bim, "I don't *want* to be hid from the enemy. I want to meet him face to face."

"They'll want us," said Lieutenant Click. "Fighting's our trade, and our commanders know it. When they want us they'll send for us."

"Captain Bim," said Fink, "that is the opinion of my silent Lieutenant; and I've noticed that when he does speak his opinion, it's worth listening to."

"Very true, Captain," said Bim. "I was too impatient, and Click is right. A great French General once said the army obeys and never deliberates. We are machines. We act, and have no business to be thinking. The President thinks for the Generals, the Generals for the Colonels, the Colonels for the Majors, the Majors for the Captains—and Major Milnor thought proper to place us here, under the exclusive command of Miss Alice. Still I can't help thinking that this will be rather a queer place for Miss Alice to command in person. The tide is rising, and we'll soon have to take to the boats."

"Hist!" said Fink, in a whisper. "Some one approaches."

And a few moments after they could distinguish the outlines of a man walking boldly towards them.

"There's only one," said Fink.

"Then I'll hail him," said Bim. "Who goes there?"

"A friend," was the response.

"Give the word."

"The Stars and Stripes," said the stranger.

"Right. Advance," said Bim.

"I come from Miss Alice, Captain Bim," said Willy.

"Wiry Willy!" said Bim. "Now I *know* it's all right."

"She wants you, Captain Bim, and five of your best and discreetest men to follow me."

"To follow you? But I beg her pardon, I have no right to ask questions. I'll be her Italian greyhound's corporal, if she orders me to follow him. But she meant nothing derogatory, I know! Go on. I'll follow."

"Captain Fink," continued Willy, "Miss Alice desires that you will wait further orders."

"Tell her I'm comfortable."

Willy returned, followed by Bim and five of his men.

CHAPTER LVIII.

LAST SCENE AT THE WHITE HOUSE.

"Father," said Alice, "you have sent away your friends, so that none may witness and report the humiliating spectacle of the Chief Magistrate driven from the Capital."

"But I am not melancholy," said the President with one of his most confident smiles, as he stood in the glare of the brilliant chandelier that illuminated the room. "I am the last to leave, and will be the first to return. I might keep this Northern horde of fanatics at bay, and even prevent their entrance into the Capital; but it would be at the expense of many loyal lives, and might involve the ultimate destruction of the city and the Union. Hereafter I shall be economical of the blood of the patriots. But these blind followers of evil teachers—woe to them! And you! my Marble! You weep not—sorrow not—at the absence of the crowd of flatterers, or at the thought of departing from the scene of your many triumphs. Be of good cheer. The worst of your trials are over."

"Unless, father, we should become the captives of Ruffleton in our native South—or even here, before we can escape! Why do we tarry?"

"It is not the hour," said Randolph, looking at his watch. "The vanguard of the invaders have been taught the necessity of circumspection, and when they do enter the city it will be with fear and trembling."

"Fly! Fly! The precious moments are ebbing for ever!" shouted Crazy Charlotte, striding in and confronting the President and his daughter.

"I would not recall one of the precious moments, Charlotte," said Randolph. "They have been counted, and each has its allotted function."

"But is there any lurking danger?" asked Alice, placing her hand on the arm of the woman, and gazing steadily in her face.

"Lurking danger? Death lurks at every corner, and the owls are hooting from every tree. The snake is gliding through the grass that was warmed into life: the dog is whetting his teeth to bite the hand that fed him! Why not fly? But do not go in the carriage!"

"It was never my purpose to depart in the carriage," said the President.

"Indeed!" said Alice.

"I am glad of that!" said Charlotte.

"Why are you glad? I thought you were the friend of Ruffleton."

"He thought so, too! I will now convince you that I am your friend. Call your servant hither—your freed-man Abel!"

"Abel!" said Randolph, beckoning the man who stood in the hall, holding a portmanteau. "Now," he continued, when Abel approached, "what, Charlotte, can you prove by Abel?"

"Down on your knees, you traitor! or I will turn you into a spider and crush you beneath my heel!"

Abel, terrified, fell upon his knees, while his limbs trembled violently. He, like many others, believed Charlotte a witch, or in league with the Evil One.

"Now confess your sins! Confess, and ask pardon! Where's your evil genius, Windvane?"

At that word Abel fell prostrate at Randolph's feet.

"Windvane!" said the President. "He, no doubt, is a traitor!"

Abel confessed everything; and Wiry Willy arriving during the recital of the plan for the seizure of the President, was dispatched by Alice to summon Bim.

"But, Man of Destiny!" said Charlotte, "why do you keep your carriage waiting at the door?"

"You have gained my whole heart, Charlotte," said Randolph, "and I will withhold no secrets from you. My purpose is merely to deceive my enemies. Being the last to depart, they cannot conceive any other mode of departure than that."

"Great and Gifted! You would have been saved without my interposition!"

"But that does not detract from your merits, Charlotte, and when I return to the Capital, I shall remember your fidelity."

"You WILL return! It is recorded by Destiny! But, now, fly! Depart while you can do so in safety!"

"No, not yet. These conspirators in the Treasury building must be arrested. And then I will, with my own hand, give the signal. I have rockets here."

"And will the carriage depart, father?" asked Alice.

"Certainly. They will not injure the driver."

Bim and his five men arrived shortly after. They were sent to the Treasury building to apprehend Windvane and Virus, with instructions to conduct them, bound, to the boats.

"Now, Charlotte," said the President, "the time has come for my departure. Do you hasten to welcome the Despot. He will not remain as long, nor, probably, be so hospitable to the friendless Charlotte, as Randolph. You have evinced your gratitude and fidelity, Charlotte—your hand."

Crazy Charlotte shed tears when she grasped the President's hand; then turning to Alice, she embraced and kissed her.

"God bless you both!" said she. "To think that poor Crazy Charlotte, only, should be present to take leave of the President and his daughter! I am not always so wild! And, please God, I'll be of service to you!" She then rushed away.

"Abel," said the President, "get into the carriage. Willy, see the driver and tell him when the rocket ascends to start, but to proceed very slowly. He must make no resistance at the bridge, and he need not endeavor to escape."

The President, then, after promenading the halls a moment longer in perfect composure, stepped out on the balcony in the rear, and ignited a rocket. It ascended high in the air, and burst into innumerable brilliant stars.

"Now, Alice! Come Willy!" said he. "A race for the boats!" And the three hastened through the lawn towards the margin of the river.

CHAPTER LIX.

TEMPTATION.

"What is that?" demanded Virus, as a flash of light illuminated the sky seen through the half-closed windows.

"It must be a rocket?" said Windvane.

"Will it not mislead the men at the bridge?"

"How can it? They can do nothing before the carriage arrives. Have they been instructed how to act in the event of Randolph making resistance?"

"Oh, yes. They are merely to capture him."

"Between us, I think they ought to put an end to him. If they do not, I fear the business will not end here. Perhaps a lucky shot or thrust may settle it—but if not, it is too late to give other orders. Hark! That is Abel! From the footsteps several others must be with him. Let us ignite fresh cigars and meet them in the hall. Not a moment should be lost!"

And while Windvane was scratching his lucifer match against the floor, Bim, just outside of the door, was doing the same thing on the sole of his shoe, and was the first to succeed in obtaining a light.

"Now, gentlemen conspirators," said he, thrusting open the door, "by your leave we'll enter and take possession."

"Who are you?" demanded Virus, drawing a pistol, and the action was imitated by Windvane, who turned very pale.

"I am Captain Bim, of the Blue Caps," said Bim. "And unless you are prepared to kill six of us, you can't fail to see at a glance how much the odds are against you."

"We have no intention to assault you, Captain Bim," said Virus. "It was our purpose merely to defend ourselves, not knowing who you were, or what your purpose."

"That is a very satisfactory explanation. And now, as we have no intention to injure a hair of your heads, and as there can be no possible use for your pistols, we will very gently relieve you of the burden!"

This said, Bim, without further parley, wrenched the weapons from their hands.

"What does this mean?" demanded Windvane. "I am an officer of the Government!"

"And I," said Bim, "am an officer of the army. I don't think, I merely obey. And I have no time even to talk. So come along!"

"Captain Bim!" said Virus, "do you not know me?"

"It is possible I may have had the pleasure of your acquaintance, Mr. Virus; but it was in times gone by. At present I am not instructed to know anybody or anything but my duty."

"I think it your duty, Captain Bim," said Virus, "and likewise your *interest*, to make a friend of the Protector's chief officer of State. I am Virus—one whose recommendation can make any man's fortune. General Ruffleton, the Protector of his country, will be here in an hour, and Captain Bim might be Colonel Bim."

"Captain Bim means to be General Bim, under President Randolph!" was the response. "So Mr. Virus, you didn't bid high enough. But, once for all, I'd rather step back and be only a Sergeant again, under Randolph, than to be a Major General in the bogus army of the d—d infernal despot, Ruffleton! Now—if you think you can tamper with my fidelity after that, you are at liberty to try it!"

Virus was silent. There was no room for diplomacy on that barren heath. And soon after they came to where the

President and Alice were seated in a boat, in readiness to depart for the opposite shore of the Potomac.

"Bim," said Randolph, who evinced no recognition of the prisoners, "your company has gone with Captain Fink's to the Canal Bridge, to bring away some traitors lying there in ambush. You have permission to join them in the expedition."

"I thank your excellency," said Bim, "and—and, if Miss Alice—"

"Oh yes—it has my concurrence, Captain," said Alice.

"Then I'll lose no time!" said Bim, vanishing immediately, and leaving the prisoners in charge of his subaltern, who was to await further orders.

"Mr. President!" said Virus, "am I a prisoner?"

"You! who are you? Is it possible? Why, Virus, I thought you had returned to Ruffleton with my ultimatum! A prisoner? No, sir. Negotiators with flags are not made prisoners. And Presidents are not to be made prisoners. So we have a mutual understanding, and you may put it in a protocol. Excuse me, sir; I am in haste, for the dew is falling. Rowers! bend to your oars!"

"Mr. President! Mr. President!" cried Windvane, striding through the mud in his endeavors to keep pace with the boat as it moved down the outlet.

"Who are you? What do you want?" asked the President.

"I am—Mr. Windvane, your—"

"Windvane? Really I don't know you, Sir. But this I know, the wind does not blow in the right direction!"

"Gone!" said Windvane."

"Never mind, Windvane!" said Virus. "But we are in a most uncomfortable predicament! The mud is half way up my legs. And must we wait, Sergeant, until an order be transmitted from the other side of the river?"

"You must wait till doomsday, sir, unless an order comes. But there is a boat, which you might sit in, if you didn't prefer standing."

"Prefer standing!" said Virus, leading the way into the boat, where Wiry Willy, and four oarsmen, seemed to be awaiting him.

"I hope there is room for both of us?" said Windvane, crowding in.

"Oh, yes," said Willy, "it was designed to hold us all."

"Designed?" said Virus.

"Yes, sir; an hour ago it was determined that you would be here exactly at this time."

"Do you hear that, Windvane? Randolph had information."

"He knows everything!" said Windvane.

"Gad, he didn't seem to know *you*, Windvane."

"That was the unkindest cut of all. I had a speech in readiness, but forgot all about it!"

"A strange man! But where are we going? Rowers, who told you to follow the other boat?"

"They are obeying orders, sir," said Willy, as the boat glided out into the river; "but we are not to follow the President far."

"Not to follow him far? Then what is to become of us? We are pursuing the same direction. Is it the design to pitch us out in the middle of the river? If so, we shall resist!"

"Such is not the order, sir," said Willy; "but if it were, resistance would be vain. The rowers are dragoons, well-armed, and the strongest men in the Blue Caps."

"But they are certainly rowing out into the middle of the stream!" said Windvane.

"To the island," said Willy.

"But the tide is rising," said Windvane, "and the water will be over it."

"Not more than knee deep," said Willy.

There was no alternative but submission; and the two conspirators were under the necessity of stepping out of the boat into the slime among the spatterdocks in the middle of the river. And soon after a whole fleet of little boats glided out of the canal, bearing the entire detachment that had been ordered to capture the President.

"Is that you, Wiry Willy?" said Bim, who was at the head of the aquatic procession.

"Yes, Captain," said Willy, "and I see that you have executed the President's orders—"

"Miss Alice's, sir—yes, executed them to the letter, without the loss of a man—I mean with the loss of but one man, and that couldn't be prevented. It was the nigger in the carriage, and he jumped into the canal and drowned himself."

"And what became of the carriage, Captain?"

"It went over the long bridge."

Soon after all the captives were landed in the mud, and abandoned to their fate.

CHAPTER LX.

RUFFLETON IN THE WHITE HOUSE.

The day after the evacuation of Washington City by the President and the Federal army, Ruffleton promenaded the saloons of the Presidential Mansion, now crowded with exultant partisans. And it was observed that several of the heads of bureaus and clerks of the departments, that had vanished a few days before, were present on that interesting occasion mingling their congratulations with the rest, and urging the Despot to assume the functions of the Chief Magistracy of the Union north of the Potomac river. And Ruffleton yielded to the solicitations of his friends. He issued a proclamation, requiring the Representatives of the People to convene at Washington on the 1st of the ensuing November. Then he selected Cabinet Ministers, and reorganized the Departments on the old basis, with the difference that none of his appointments were to be subject to the advice and consent of the Senate.

"But where is Virus?" was the question continually on the lips of Ruffleton.

"Willy knows," was responded in the crowd.

"Willy!" said Ruffleton, his quick ear catching the words. "Ah!" he continued, when his eye detected the very demure face of Willy, "now I shall learn all about him. Come, sir; unfold!"

"General," said Willy, "if you will promise not to guillotine me, I'll show you Mr. Virus, and also his friend Windvane."

"Still in terror of the guillotine, eh? It is a glorious auxiliary, and will be erected to-day on the common. But I promise, Willy. Now where are they?"

"General, if you'll get a telescope, and come with me to the window, you shall see them."

The instrument was procured, and they were followed to the window by a large number of officers.

"They are boys," said Ruffleton, looking at the distant island.

"No, sir!" said Willy. "They are up to their knees in the mud and spatterdocks."

This announcement produced some merriment.

"Mud and spatterdocks!" said Ruffleton. "Who placed them there?"

"I did," said Willy, "and you've promised not to punish me."

"You placed them there? *You*, Willy?"

"I did, sir, upon my honor! But it was because the President ordered me."

"The President! Ha! ha! ha! Gentlemen," said Ruffleton, turning to his Generals, "Virus and Windvane were engaged in an enterprise for the capture of Randolph; but instead of placing the last of the Presidents in my hands, the last of the Presidents—and by George! he was about the best of them—has placed them in the mud and spatterdocks!"

An explosion of laughter followed.

"I thought at first," said Balatrum, "they were geese, and came near firing on them!"

"But the impudence of the thing!" continued Ruffleton. "To place them in full view of the White House! Still I admire the fellow's humor—and a flying President should be allowed a little insolence. Nevertheless, the thing does not look like despair. To place my Secretary of State in the mud and spatterdocks!"

"He ordered Willy to do it," repeated Willy, upon perceiving the rising anger of Ruffleton, the more he dwelt on the practical joke of Randolph.

"I am not condemning you, Will! General, order them to be rescued from their ludicrous position with as little delay as possible."

"There will be no delay at all, General," said Balatrum; "and I am happy to inform you that the enemy will interpose no obstacle. Randolph has withdrawn from the river, without even destroying the bridges."

"He knew very well that we could leap over at the Little Falls. We shall soon be upon his track."

This announcement was followed by applause.

"Yes, gentlemen," continued Ruffleton, elated with his success, and the fancied popularity of a prosecution of the invasion, "we shall track him like a wolf to his lair, and he cannot escape. He will not *fight*, it seems, even on his own dunghill, else he would show his teeth now, with three hundred thousand men at his back. No! these Southerners, who have achieved such a terrible reputation for contempt of danger and life, are arrant cowards after all!"

This was followed by a prodigious burst of applause. And, indeed, successive messengers brought intelligence of the retreat of the Federal forces towards Alexandria, and the abandonment of several inviting positions, and particularly one at Four Mile Run, where a superior force might have been checked in its career by inferior numbers.

CHAPTER LXI.

MOUNT VERNON.

The President, well informed of the movements of the enemy, encamped his army in the vicinity of Alexandria, and then repaired to Mount Vernon, where his head-quarters were established. Alice and Edith, and Senator Langdon had preceded him thither; and as the dusk of evening fell upon the scene, Randolph, ever punctual to a minute in all his appointments, alighted from his horse.

"Everything reposes in quiet here," said the aged Senator, clasping the hand of the President as he stepped upon the long piazza.

"And the twilight of this summer evening," said Edith, presenting the President a rich bouquet, "is scented with the perfume of roses."

"And you, my Marble," said Randolph, turning to his pale and silent daughter, "have nothing to utter, nothing to give me?"

"Have I not, father?" said Alice, throwing her arms around her parent's neck and kissing him.

"But why these tears?"

"I thought, father, that on this consecrated ground, and in the precincts of the sacred dust of the Father of his Country, LIBERTY might be taking her flight from earth for ever! That the last of the Presidents, on the last day of the Republic, might be a fugitive from the despot, and vainly seeking an asylum under the roof of Washington!"

"No. Neither my fortunes, nor the fortunes of the Republic, have arrived at such a desperate ebb. This is not the last night, perhaps, that a President, or a President's daughter will tread the halls of Mount Vernon. But let us in to tea."

And when they were seated around the table within, the weather being sultry and the windows raised, the cry of a solitary whippoorwill was heard in the distance, and Alice's melancholy threatened to return.

"I do not think I ever laughed more heartily in my life," said the President, during the repast, "than I have done this evening."

"Then I am sure I need not be sad," said Alice, "because if there were not some promising enterprise afoot I think you would at least have repressed the inclination to laugh."

"He may laugh who wins," said Edith.

"Then I am quite certain," said Langdon, relaxing his usually grave visage, "that Randolph's chief general may laugh."

"That is as much as to say he has won. And yet who knows how often it may be his fate to lose? But, Mr. President, I have a woman's curiosity to learn the provocation of your laughter."

"It was caused by the visage of my general, the valiant Crook! He came to me with tears in his eyes, begging to have a fight with the British before we retreated down the Potomac. He said his heart was breaking, and that he would rather die and be buried in sight of the dome of the Capitol, than retire without a blow out of sight of it."

"The brave Crook!" exclaimed Alice. "And, father, may we know the response you gave him?"

"I looked very grave, and merely pressed his hand. Sir

Charles Hunt will know my determination before the hour for his next breakfast. My wild western scouts have proved invaluable auxiliaries. Those Missourians are as true men as the Boons, and Kentons, and Shelbys of the last century! Captain Fink keeps me as well informed of the movements of the enemy as if I were in his camp."

"And it is the purpose, then," said Langdon, "to fall upon Sir Charles?"

"Yes. Sir Charles leads the van, and is encamping on this side the river, separated from the main army, and never dreaming of the possibility of an enemy in full retreat suddenly retracing his steps."

"I am glad," said Edith, "that the first battle south of the Potomac will be with the British. It will serve to rouse into activity all the patriotism in the country."

"True!" said Randolph, "whether we win or lose. But we shall win, of course—that is, at *first*, and until overwhelming succors are sent to the relief of Hunt. It will be rather a check than a battle. Then we must resume our journey. And the probability is that they will destroy Mount Vernon, and desecrate the tomb of Washington."

"God forbid!" exclaimed Langdon.

"God's will be done!" said Randolph. "If, however, such a thing should happen, it will be worth a dozen victories to the South. The SPIRIT of Washington, roused from its repose, will animate every manly breast, and there will be such a popular outburst throughout the country as has never yet been known." After these words a pause ensued.

"Again the plaintive cry of the whippoorwill is heard," said Alice.

"It seems to come from the direction of the TOMB," said Edith, "as if bewailing the sad destiny of the country loved and served so well by its founder and father."

"Father," said Alice, "let us go to the tomb of Washington. This may be the last opportunity."

"You have anticipated me. It was my purpose to take you thither," he continued, glancing at his watch; "and it is the hour. And you, my friend," said he, addressing Langdon, "will accompany us. We will find Dr. Love, our chaplain, awaiting us near the vault. And there you will find your Blue Caps, Alice."

"Indeed! I have been on the eve of asking why the Blue Caps were not here."

"They are in the vicinity, with muffled drums and trailing carbines, to bury a hero with the honors of war."

"To bury some one with the honors of war?" asked Edith, in surprise. "Who has fallen?"

"It is General Steel, whose remains have been faithfully transported by Crook, in obedience to the request of the dying soldier, to Southern ground; and we shall inter them in the vicinity of the tomb of Washington. Hark! It is the signal." The drum was heard, and the party of four hastened forth to witness the burial.

Near the tomb of Washington the Blue Caps were drawn up in hollow square, every fifth man bearing a torch. In the centre was the newly dug grave, and beside it the coffin. When the President, Mr. Langdon, and the maidens arrived on the ground, they were conducted by Major Milnor and Captain Bim within the enclosure, keeping step to the solemn march played by the band. When the plaintive strain had ceased, the grey-haired clergyman, Dr. Love, read the burial service. And he took occasion to descant on the merits of the fallen hero they were consigning to his final rest. He was a native of the same State, and had known General Steel from his infancy. He was impetuous, ardent, honorable, brave, and patriotic—and if sometimes too hasty in his resentments, he never failed to make amends for any apparent injustice, in his moments of cool reflection. The Dr. had baptized the General, when a boy, and the Bishop had confirmed him. Whatever his errors, God was merciful! The voice of the aged divine, as he uttered the last sentences, was broken by his emotions, and tears ran down his cheeks.

After the "dust to dust," Bim led forward a file of soldiers, who fired their carabines over the grave.

"Away! Away!" cried one, after the last round was fired, and when the gravediggers were throwing in the earth.

All eyes were turned in the direction of the speaker, and a moment after Crazy Charlotte emerged from the clump of trees in the vicinity.

"Who is that?" asked Mr. Langdon.

"It is a poor demented—but nevertheless a faithful

friend," said Randolph, stepping aside, and clasping the proffered hand of Charlotte, who still wore the theatrical cuirass and helmet, and brandished the green spear with its bright point of tin.

"And why is the tear in your eye, Man of Destiny?" exclaimed Charlotte. "Why weep over the dust of Washington, when there may be a living Washington, aye, and more than one, in the South! Rouse, O spirit of Freedom! and dart like an eagle upon the foe! The British lion again pollutes the soil of the Old Dominion, the mother of States! Away! Away! Strike him in his lair! The sons of the South cannot be restrained. They must fight, or else never hold up their heads again! Randolph, away! I invoke you, at the dread hour of midnight, in the sacred presence of Washington, whose spirit pervades the atmosphere, to fall upon the British foe. Remember Yorktown! If Washington had delayed until succor had come to his rescue, think you Cornwallis would have laid down his arms? Then rush with all your banners upon the Baronet, who has detached himself so temptingly from the main body of his traitorous allies!"

"Charlotte," said the President, "who has been telling you these things?"

"No one. I have looked with my own eyes."

"But who taught you the art of war—or how to know when an enemy was temptingly exposed?"

"Who? Common sense!"

"Do you hear, Langdon? and you, ladies? The triumph of art is merely the triumph of common sense! All the great achievements of man, by whatever process accomplished, are but the rational conclusions of adequate causes. You should have been a man, Charlotte, and then you would have made a General. Sir Charles will be beaten up in his quarters before the dawn of day. Come with us, Charlotte, and remain with the girls until this battle be won."

"Willingly, if they will permit me!" said she, "for I am weary and hungry, and my heart is sick from the scenes I have witnessed on the green! They have erected the guillotine near the Washington Monument!"

"What!" exclaimed Alice, "have they begun the bloody work already, and in the precincts of the Monument?"

"Eleven members of Congress were beheaded as the sun went down!"

"Is it possible!" said Langdon.

"Charlotte never speaks falsely," said Randolph.

"No. I utter only what these eyes have beheld!" said she, weeping. "One of the victims was my friend. *He* never spurned the unfortunate Charlotte from his presence."

"Who was it, Charlotte?" demanded Edith.

"A good old man. A noble Senator!"

"A Senator?" exclaimed Langdon. "Surely none remained in the city—although I recollect several declared they would stay—but surely, surely, they did not mean to expose themselves—and, of all men, the one who—"

"Who, father?" demanded Edith.

"Charlotte!" said Randolph—"come with me!" and leading her apart, he continued, "is Langdon right? Did the one he means, persist in remaining? And was he slain?"

"He did! He was!"

"Then, Ruffleton, may an avenging God launch His thunders at thy head! Follow, Charlotte—but do not tell them the worst. Leave that to me!"

Randolph, abandoning Charlotte to the interrogations of the young ladies, who did not even suspect the one to whom Langdon alluded, grasped the aged Senator's arm and led him along the silent dale.

"Oh! Randolph," said the Senator, in broken tones, "has the despot dared—"

"The worst, Langdon! He has dared and done the worst!"

"And Blount?"

"Yes, Blount! but do not speak so loud!"

They uttered not another word until they reached the long piazza of the mansion, where Langdon sank in a chair, and by the light of the moon Randolph beheld the tears streaming down his aged cheeks.

"Father," said Edith, coming up soon after, "what is that I heard you say about General Blount?"

"Nothing, my child."

"But what has happened? Why are you so cast down?"

"Alice" said Randolph, turning to his daughter, "exert

your art to prepare Edith to hear a terrible announcement."

"Ah!" said Edith, "I am now prepared! But he was here only a short time since, and I do not think anything could have—"

"Nothing unfortunate has happened to General Blount," said Randolph.

"I thought not!" exclaimed Alice. "Oh, yes! we can hear it, father!"

"Senator Blount—his father."

"He!" cried Edith—"my second father, and what has happened to him?"

"The worst—the worst thing in the world!" cried Charlotte. "Brace your nerves—steel your heart, bonny bride of the Southern hero. Resolve to bear it!"

"He has been taken, then!" said Edith. "But that would not distress my father so deeply. Dead! he must be dead! Oh, they have guillotined him! Still, still, I can bear it! But God will avenge it!"

"Yes, my dear child," said Randolph, taking her hand, while she rested her head on his shoulder—"God will avenge it. The monster shall pay the penalty! But come in. I must mount and away. The time is too precious for words. My dear friend," he continued, as the good Dr. Love joined them, "here is work for you among the living. Comfort this little flock, and pray for our poor country, whilst I am fighting for it!"

He then strode forth and mounted his steed, where several of his aides had been awaiting him. But before he put spurs to his horse, Captain Bim came up and begged to be permitted to accompany him, if he were going forth to battle. The President referred him to Alice and his major; and then sped away in the direction of the quarters of General Blount.

CHAPTER LXII.

BLOUNT'S HEAD-QUARTERS.

Randolph had not proceeded far before he encountered Captain Fink of the Scouts. The Captain brought the important intelligence that, although Sir Charles Hunt occupied an exposed position on the south side of the Potomac, he was nevertheless within reach of succor. The head of a heavy column of the enemy had passed over the bridge at Georgetown; and General Line, with his Western host, had ascended the river to the Little Falls, and would pass the bridge at that place early in the morning.

The President rode on, musing in silence.

When he reached the mansion occupied by Blount and Crook, he was met by the latter at the threshold.

"I have waited and watched for you," said Crook, in a half whisper. "We have terrible news from the city, brought by deserters and—"

"I suppose you refer to the bloody work of the guillotine?" said Randolph.

"But—but the—"

"Senator who was decapitated. You mean the elder Blount?"

"The same! It has been communicated to you then?"

"Yes, but where is the General?"

"He sleeps."

"Then he has not been informed of the butchery?"

"No. None had the heart to tell him, and I resolved not to communicate the news until your arrival."

"You have done well, General. Why should he be disturbed? Let him sleep on. Soon enough these evil tidings will pierce his ear. And it is not, perhaps, on the eve of battle that such an announcement should be made. Let us all seek repose."

"I have no objection," said Crook, "and, indeed, I have lost a great deal of rest lately, and will be the better for an hour's slumber. But you, they say, never sleep."

"It is a mistake; and even now a drowsiness weighs upon my eyelids. I will share your couch, with your permission."

"You shall have all of it. I have made a vow never to sleep in a feather bed again until after the expulsion of the enemy from the South. I shall sleep on the floor in my cloak. But come with me and see how calmly poor Blount is slumbering."

They entered the chamber. By the steady but diminutive rays of a lamp, they beheld the form of Blount steeped in profound slumber. He breathed as softly as an infant. His manly brow was unclouded, and a gentle smile rested on his lip. Randolph and Crook, the one on a bed, the other on the hard floor, reclined their weary limbs without disturbing the slumberer.

CHAPTER LXIII.

THE PROTECTOR IN HIS PALACE.

The Protector was now an early riser, having the affairs of State on his hands. He was sitting in the office on the second floor of the White House, where so many of the Presidents had been accustomed to meet their Cabinet Ministers, and whither his Secretaries had been summoned to assemble that morning.

Windvane was the first who made his appearance.

"Windvane," said the Despot, lifting his eyes from the document he had been reading, "I find there is much opposition to your appointment. They say you will betray me, and that you have betrayed others. Nay, man, don't turn pale at such an announcement."

"Will your Excellency be pleased to inform me who my enemies are?" asked Windvane, now red with anger.

"No matter, Windvane, since I am your friend. You shall be my Minister of Justice, and sign the death-warrants. You see at once, Windvane, I can have no fear of being betrayed by you, because when you shall have signed a few thousand death-warrants, there cannot possibly be any party for you to join after abandoning mine, but the party of the dead. That is my guarantee. For yourself, I need not indicate the advantages of the position, and the opportunities you will have to indemnify yourself for any little annoyances you may be subjected to."

"I fear very much—" stammered Windvane, and then paused, while a tremor agitated his frame.

"Fear nothing!" said Ruffleton. "You have only to guard against giving rise to a suspicion that you prefer the cause of Randolph to mine. And I shall fear nothing from my enemies, provided you keep the guillotines in motion. Terror, Windvane, the fear of death, is the most powerful lever with which to move mankind, or to keep them still."

"I did not mean to intimate," said Windvane, "that I feared my enemies. I shall not fear any one so long as you are my friend. But I fear very much that I am not competent to discharge the duties of the position you have named. I have a horror of blood—"

"Pooh! you will never see any, unless your curiosity, a thing not improbable, shall lead you to witness an execution. You will soon become accustomed to it. Nonsense! You are the very best man for the place. You have been a politician all your life, and will make a fortune; but beware that you do not jeopard mine in your dealings with the rich!"

They were now joined by Virus and several other members of the new Government.

"Ah, Virus!" said the Protector, "I see you have removed the mud from your boots."

"Yes, your Excellency," returned Virus, "or rather my shoes; and at the same time I have shaken the dust of the old United States Government from my feet for ever! I have now to announce joyful tidings to your Highness—"

"Highness!" said Ruffleton.

"Yes, sir, and Lord Protector! I bring sufficient returns of the elections, held in thirteen States, to warrant me in saying that, by the vote of the people, sovereign power has been conferred on your Highness. Therefore, I repeat, long live His Highness, our Lord Protector, General Ruffleton."

This was quite heartily responded to by those present.

"Gentlemen," said Ruffleton, rising to his feet, "I must confess to some surprise at the turn events have taken. But if the people have really done this, you may rely upon it that whatever benefits may flow from a change of Government, shall be liberally shared by my friends. I shall never forget those who stood by me through evil as well as good report. But sit down. Let there be no ceremony between us. Now, Virus, let us have the particulars. Was there a full vote? And what proportion voted against the proposition of the Convention?"

"In some counties nearly every voter went to the polls. None but the sick abstained from voting; and there were no disturbances—no riots—and everywhere the election was conducted with admirable propriety and silence—"

"Silence?"

"Yes; it must be confessed that no superfluous words were uttered, and it is said, very little drinking was indulged in; but having quietly deposited their ballots, the people returned immediately to their homes."

"Umph! But what were the majorities, generally?"

"In New York and New England, not a single vote was cast against you. In the West they were more divided, but your majority must be overwhelming!"

"It was the guillotine, gentlemen!" said Ruffleton, leaning back in his great chair. "They durst not stay away, and they feared to vote against me. Be it so! The charm shall be perpetuated! If the guillotine has been my friend and ally, I will cherish it! Let us not loosen the reins, gentlemen, until the work be complete. And you, Virus, will see that none but friends be returned to fill the vacancies in the Convention. And when they meet in the Capitol we must have a new Constitution in readiness to be submitted. But first we must beat all our enemies in the field."

During these transactions in the Cabinet, a scene of a different character was enacted at the opposite end of the Palace. A female of a rather robust stature, and quite gorgeously arrayed, strode to and fro before a large mirror. She was attended by a somewhat elderly, but certainly a very loquacious companion.

"It *is* a triumph, Flora Summers!" said Mrs. Punt, "and if your mother had only lived to see it, she would never have regretted—"

"No more of that, Mrs. Punt!" said Flora, hastily. "It is the future we have to do with. And we must play a skilful game to win!"

"If you don't win him the next time he sees you, my name's not Punt!" said Mrs. Punt.

"Oh, he has seen me thus long, long ago! But what does it signify? We were married, I know not by whom, nor what became of the witnesses—"

"I was one! The priest was an—but no matter—I tell you it was a legal wedding! He said he'd have you, and you said you'd have him."

"Peace! I agreed, likewise, never to mention our marriage to any one, until he gave me permission. And you were threatened with his vengeance if you disclosed the secret. He has never yet permitted me to proclaim it—and, I fear, he never will!"

"Did he not tell you—tell us both, to follow him here? What did that mean?"

"I know not—but will know, when he comes. You sent him my note?"

"Yes. And a very genteel man it was who took it. I said you was kin to the General, and that I was his housekeeper, and then he bowed to the very ground. He's a handsome fellow, and his name's Ready—Jim Ready—and he's to be the doorkeeper for the Protector."

"Are you setting your cap for him, already, Mrs. Punt? I thought you had news, not long since, from your husband."

"He's dead now, I'm sure. I wrote him I'd be here this very morning, and ordered him to meet me at the depot. But no Punt was there. Excuse me, and I'll run to Mr. Ready and hear what he says about the note—and what the General said—and how he looked."

Flora stood gazing at herself in the mirror, paying but little heed to Mrs. Punt. But when left alone she thus soliloquized:

"And why not be his acknowledged wife? Alas! one reason might be the recognition of the officers about his head-quarters! But might it not be attributed to my devotion to his cause? And what else was it? Nothing else! And must I be cast away in the hour of triumph, after adhering so faithfully to his fortunes? No! I am here in obedience to his command—and wherefore did he summon me——ah!" she exclaimed, as the door opened, and the General himself entered the room.

"Flora," said he, "I will tell you why I summoned you. It was to maintain the old mystery. Long since many busy gossips have been conjecturing the relation in which we stand to each other. Be discreet. Say nothing about it. Let them conjecture. But let us keep up the mystery."

"It is a mystery to *me*."

"To *you?* Is anything I do or require a mystery to you? You are not wont to murmur."

"I do not murmur. But it is a mystery to me why you would maintain the mystery."

"Is that all? Well, is not your sex addicted to mysteries? I know it will be a delightful idea. But—if any one should whisper a breath of scandal—should insult or injure—"

"I fear it not, sir. So long as I may have your approbation, your affection, I care not what the world may say or do. I have already braved its utmost enmity—"

"No more of that! But, I repeat, if any one shall dare to offend you, it will be at the expense of my anger—and the anger of the Master of an empire is not lightly to be provoked. Let them suppose you a relation, protegée, or what they will; and if they become inquisitive, change the subject; if persistent, turn away from them; and if they cease to frequent the Palace—remember this is a Palace henceforth—I shall be relieved of their importunities. But do not create disturbances. I shall be absent for weeks, perhaps; but messengers will come to me daily. You will be the mistress of the Palace, having influence. Exert your power as a spirited woman should—but always with a view to my advantage. Watch the Minister of Justice, Windvane, and Virus, and all. If I fall, you are nothing—if I stand, you shall share my greatness. Order breakfast—make Mrs. Punt bustle about! Here's my purse. Now I must return to the Council-board. Adieu for the present." And he hurried back, leaving Flora in a joyous delirium.

While Flora yet remained in this condition, Mrs. Punt came staggering in, and leaning her head first on one side and then the other, tottered across the room and sank down on a sofa.

"What in the name of all the gods at once, is the matter?" demanded Flora, staring at the panting woman.

"I was talking with Mr. Ready—standing in the vestibule, and he said the General smiled and rose on receiving your note—you will be a great lady—when some one rang the bell. He stepped forward and opened it—and La's a' mercy! What do you think?"

"What do I think? I don't believe the devil himself could have frightened you thus; and therefore it must have been your husband!"

"Punt! 'Twas Punt! You are right! Yes, my horrid Punt!" * * * * *

The gentlemen surrounding the council-board of the Protector were suddenly startled by the report of artillery.

"That is Randolph, gentlemen!" said Ruffleton, who retained his chair after the others had risen. "Balatrum, urge forward all our forces to the succor of Sir Charles Hunt. I warned him against exposing himself; but he insisted on encamping at the other end of the bridge."

"Your Excellency is quite right," said Lord Slysir. "The enemy has doubled and fallen upon Sir Charles. I hope the British troops will give a good account of themselves—but what can 50,000 do against five or six times their number?"

"Away, Balatrum!" exclaimed Ruffleton. "Drive the blusterers into their own negro quarters! But save our men as much as possible. If the bridge itself be assailed, open a fire from a thousand cannon from this bank of the river. I will send orders to Line to march down, and the column in Georgetown will also cross over and hasten to the scene of action. Virus, you will receive the foreign despatches. Remember that all our ministers abroad, who communicate with us, instead of Randolph, are to remain—for the present. Those who adhere to the old Government are to be summarily dismissed. Perfect the lists as soon as possible. Now, gentlemen, come with me to breakfast, and then those for the field to horse, and those for the pen to their offices. There is an immense amount of labor to

16*

be performed before the wheels of Government can run smoothly. But, my Lord," he added, in a low tone, as he led the way out, "you must lecture Sir Charles on his indiscretion. I will not yield to him again." His Lordship nodded assent, and intimated that Hunt would be sufficiently punished by the enemy.

CHAPTER LXIV.

AN ALARM AND A CAPTURE.

The inmates of Mount Vernon were roused by the same sounds which had startled the bogus Cabinet at Washington; and a few moments after all had risen from their couches and assembled in the parlor.

"It is the beginning of the battle," said Mr. Langdon, meeting Alice and Edith, and taking a hand of each.

"And when will there be an end of it!" exclaimed the Rev. Dr. Love. "He in Heaven must decide. And, my dear friends," he continued, opening a prayer-book that lay on the table, "let us address our petitions to Him, as the Church prescribes on such occasions."

This was done, and all united heartily in the supplication for victory. And when the service was over, a more cheerful expression rested on the faces of the group.

"Where is Charlotte?" asked Edith, looking round.

"She was here, and strangely calm and silent," said Alice, "during the prayer."

"And she responded punctually," said Dr. Love; "but at the final Amen I observed that she rose up quickly and glided out."

"I hope," said Edith, "she may return with good tidings."

"I rely upon Captains Bim and Fink," said Alice, "for early news."

"And where is Wiry Willy?" asked Mr. Langdon.

"I know not!" said Alice, with interest. "He was with us when we escaped the toils Virus and the treacherous

Windvane had prepared. We left him in a boat on the river, having those evil plotters in custody—but he was directed to release them on the island bar. Ever before Willy has been present in such critical times as the present; and if he lives, and is at liberty, I am sure he is now rendering valuable services somewhere. I hear the approach of a messenger. It may be Willy himself. It is!" she continued, a moment after, having gone to the door and returned on recognising the horseman.

"Your face is unclouded, Willy!" cried Edith, the first speaker upon the entrance of the messenger.

"It is neither sad nor joyful, Miss Edith," said he. "The President sends word that there will be no great battle; but that the enemy will be thrown into a panic, which will induce them to march in compact masses."

"And that," said Langdon, "will be equivalent to, if not better than a victory. The inhabitants will not suffer by a wide-spread devastation, while the enemy will have to transport from their own country the provisions they consume."

"But why, Willy," demanded Alice, "does he not think there will be a great battle? The thunders of the batteries would seem to indicate that all the forces were engaged."

"Ruffleton is firing nearly a thousand great guns across the river. Sir Charles Hunt, at the very onset, took refuge under the banks of the Potomac. And this is merely skirmishing, as I heard General Blount say."

"General Blount!" said Edith. "And had he heard the terrible news?"

"No," said Willy. "The President would not permit any one to tell him. I was with his father during his last moments, and he gave me his watch, and other valuable articles, and among them the portrait of the General's mother, to be delivered to his son; but—"

"But what, Willy?" asked Edith, her eyes suffused with tears.

"The executioner claimed them and snatched them away. I obtained an order from General Ruffleton himself for their restitution, and he likewise dispatched an officer for the execution of the miscreant—one of the friends of Windvane—"

"Was the executioner executed?" asked Alice.

"He was; but he had already disposed of the articles, and I was unable to find them. Nay, do not weep for him, sir," continued Willy, observing the tears rolling down the cheeks of Mr. Langdon. "He died happily, sir; and proudly, and patriotically. But hark! That's crazy Charlotte's voice!"

"Fly! fly!" cried she; and her startling warning became more distinct as she approached the mansion. "Away, away! Lamb of America! The shepherd is gone, the watch-dogs are at play, and the wolf approaches! Go, go! Don't ask me why—but go!" she continued, rushing in, and falling down in the midst of the amazed company from complete exhaustion.

"Charlotte!" said Alice, "what is the meaning of this?"

"Don't ask me! Fly! Your Blue Caps are not here! Away!" and, unable to utter another word, the panting woman motioned her hands towards the rear door, for them to make their escape in that direction.

"Fly!" cried Willy himself, returning from the lawn, whither he had gone to reconnoitre. "A fleet of British steamers is in the river, and the crew of one has been landed on this side!"

"Come—come with me!" cried Charlotte, springing up from the floor. "I will lead you to a place of safety! I know every inch of these grounds. Come!" and seizing the hand of Edith and of her father, she hastened away, not doubting that Alice and Willy would follow.

"I will remain!" said Alice.

"No, do not!" said Willy.

"They do not war against women! Nor will they dare molest the home of Washington," said Alice.

"Oh, do not trust either Ruffleton or Lord Slysir!"

"I trust not, but defy them."

"They come! It is yet time."

"Leave me! Provide for your own security. The daughter of the President will not fly from the home of Washington!"

"No; I will not leave you. I may serve you. I have no fear. If they take you away, I will accompany you."

"Surround the house, Buzzards!" said Lieutenant Junkins, the leader of some fifty men, just landed from the British steamer Buzzard.

Alice stood perfectly composed when Junkins entered.

"Good morning to your ladyship," said the burly purple-faced officer, advancing and extending his hand.

"I spurn your salutation, sir," said Alice, with indignation.

"I am Lieutenant Junkins, commander of Her Britannic Majesty's 'Buzzard!'"

"No matter. Seek your prey elsewhere," said Alice.

"By your leave, madam, we seek our prey wherever we can find it; and if I am not mistaken we have fallen upon a rich prize here. I cannot be mistaken. A few months ago I bore a despatch to Washington, where I am sure I had the honor of seeing your ladyship in the White House. It will do no good to deny it—and, of course, resistance will not be thought of."

"I deny nothing, sir, except your right to be impertinent. But if you venture still further, and indulge a brutal propensity for vulgarity, I shall spit upon you, and upon the flag disgraced by you."

"Pardon me, lady! I shall not, I hope, be either rude or brutal to the daughter of the late President of the United States. But if it be necessary, I must use sufficient constraint to conduct you on board my vessel, and to convey you to the Lord Protector, or to Lord Slysir. I grant you that we do not capture ladies, as a general rule—but I dare not decline making the daughter of ex-President Randolph an exception. If my conduct be not approved, I can repair the wrong in a few hours, by restoring you to your father."

"If there can be a doubt whether or not your conduct will be approved, why was the enterprise undertaken?"

"I had another duty to perform—and did not know that I would find you here."

"What other duty, sir?"

"One which several of my brother officers declined participating in—that much must be confessed. *The destruction of this house!*"

"Is it possible! No wonder the officers, being gentlemen, declined such a service. The man who applies the torch to this structure must reap an eternity of infamy, like the incendiary who fired the Ephesian dome! Let me beseech you, sir, to desist from such a diabolical purpose!"

"I should be deprived of my commission. No; I will

not consider what posterity may say, and I shall not live to hear it. The object is to render a reconciliation of the sections impossible. But my time has expired. Come; you need not behold it."

"Touch me not, sir," said Alice, starting back, when the officer extended his hand to lead her away. "I must needs obey, but will not be touched by the hand that fires the dwelling of Washington. Come, Willy, attend me to the ship."

"Willy! And pray who are you, sir?"

"These will show!" said Willy, exhibiting the passports and protections of both Ruffleton and Slysir.

"By St. George!" said Junkins, "you belong to our side. Suppose you fire the house?"

"No, sir, I—I have no such orders!" stammered Willy.

"Suppose I order you."

"Wiry Willy only obeys General Ruffleton and Lord Slysir."

"If they say so, I suppose it must be so."

"Besides, I couldn't do it, sir; I love Mount Vernon, and my tears would put the fire out."

"Come, Willy!" said Alice, leading the way out. "Millions will weep over the recollection of the dastardly profanation! Shall we proceed, sir?" she continued, addressing the officer.

"Yes! but in the right direction. And to insure that, I will go with you. Turn your eyes away a moment," said he, igniting a match, as several of his men came in bearing straw.

Alice needed not the suggestion. Her eyes were blinded with tears; and, taking Willy's arm, she urged him away in the direction indicated by the Lieutenant. They were overtaken in a few minutes by Junkins, who, with all the politeness of which he was capable, tendered his arm to the captive, and was again repulsed.

"I do not desire your assistance, sir," said Alice.

"I will not enforce it upon you, madam," said the piqued commander. "I have your word that you will go on board my ship, and you have mine that I will conduct you to the Palace for the decision of the Lord Protector and Lord Slysir."

"I will comply with my promise, sir," said she.

"And I with mine. But if that cannonading is kept up, I shall have to land you at the Navy Yard. And then we will go in a carriage."

Soon they were at the margin of the river, and passed on board the Buzzard, where they were joined by the men who had been left temporarily at the mansion. And Alice, with an aching heart, as the vessel started up the river, beheld a dark column of vapor ascending from Mount Vernon.

CHAPTER LXV.

THE ANNOUNCEMENT.

The heads of the columns of the invaders sent down the right bank of the Potomac to the relief of Sir Charles Hunt, were long kept in check by the skilful dispositions of Randolph and Blount, and the impetuosity of Crook.

"All is done that can be accomplished," observed Randolph, checking his horse at the side of Blount, in an elevated position whence they surveyed the entire field.

"Yes, sir," said Blount; "and although we must retire before irresistible numbers, it will not be without leaving traces of our work behind. Many thousands of the enemy have fallen, while our loss has been inconsiderable. The Scouts are terrible men! Why do they rush up to the dead? Surely they do not rifle them?"

"I have observed the same thing, and could not conjecture why it was done," said Randolph, with the glass to his eye. "They whoop like Indians—I hope they do not likewise scalp the enemy. General, call off Crook, or we shall lose him. It would be madness to encounter that hurricane!"

Blount dispatched the order, while Randolph sent one of his aides to Valiant and Carleton, with directions to retire slowly, but in order, towards the grounds they had occupied the preceding night, still keeping out of range of the batteries on the northern side of the Potomac.

Just after these orders had been dispatched, and the hoofs

of the horses of the aides-de-camp ceased to be heard, the steeds of both the President and General Blount snorted frantically and sprang apart, as an apparition rose up between them from the bushes obscuring an exhausted rivulet.

"Haste! haste to the eyrie! But the eaglet is gone! Gone! Oh, Genius of Liberty!" cried crazy Charlotte, now standing erect, while the hand that held the spear trembled violently. "Why sit ye here in idleness in the midst of the inundating flood, that must overflow the tips of the mountains? Strike your rowels deep into your war-horses, and fly upon the wings of the wind, oh, ye champions of the glorious South, made coruscant by the scintillations of the bright lights of the past!"

"What does all this mean, Charlotte?" demanded Randolph, convinced that the erratic being before him always mingled rational purposes with her extravagant ravings.

"Turn your eyes towards the Zion of the South, the holy Mount of Freedom, and look for yourselves."

"Where can that proceed from?" said Blount, quickly perceiving the dark column of smoke still ascending from the ruins of Mount Vernon.

"It is certainly in the direction of Mount Vernon," said the President; "but there is no enemy in our rear, and if there had been, they durst not fire that sacred pile! It must be the result of accident—"

"No—no!" said Charlotte, "I was there! My lips but utter what these eyes beheld! Oh, that my eyes had been cannon balls! It is Mount Vernon—now a heap of smouldering ruins! Fired by the hands of the British! They came up the river—a fleet of steamers! Oh, watchful Generals, where were your wits then? Why were the Blue Caps away from the presence of the President's daughter? Why? Why?"

"Ah, why, indeed?" exclaimed the President. "It was Alice's own order, that every available man might be in the field to resist the invader!"

"But, Charlotte," said Blount, "the inmates of the mansion must have had timely warning—had they not?"

"I warned them—who but Charlotte? But who heeds the warning of the lost Charlotte? Still they believed me. The Senator and his daughter fled to the woods—but the ministering vestal at the last fane of Liberty—"

"Alice!" exclaimed the President—"what became of her?"

"With folded arms, and the star of diamonds glittering on her Parian brow, she confronted the vile creatures of the tyrant!"

"Brave Alice!" said Randolph. "But what followed?" he continued, gathering up the reins, and bracing his nerves.

"They touched her not—they durst not pollute the last of the vestals by an unholy touch! But they led her away a captive, and the steamer proceeded up the river. Wiry Willy went with her."

"I breathe again!" said the President. "I fear nothing!"

"And we can do nothing!" said Blount. "We must bear the ills that are inevitable. And, really, Randolph, you do not seem to require commiseration!"

"No, Blount. Even now I am capable of condoling with you." And saying this, he motioned the General to accompany him, and they rode slowly away.

"But why do you utter such words to me, Randolph?" asked Blount, after they had proceeded some paces in silence. "Twice to-day, I have been on the eve of demanding an explanation from Crook, of his manner and speech—and now I observe the same mysterious bearing in you. Pray ex plain."

"We must bear the ills that are inevitable and irremediable, my friend," said Randolph.

"But what inevitable or irremediable ill has befallen me?"

"The appropriate time has arrived to make the disclosure. I have lost a daughter—not irrecoverably, I think—and the country has been bereft of one of its purest patriots and wisest statesmen."

"I do not fully comprehend," said Blount, checking his steed, and gazing steadfastly in the face of the President.

"You are prepared for the announcement—"

"Unquestionably!"

"Your father!"

"Has he fallen into the hands of the enemy?"

"Into the merciful hands of his God."

"Then it is over! Randolph, I know you are not mistaken. My father's father died before him, and in the service of the country. My father dies before his son—his son remains to die before his posterity. It is the fate of all. It is natural that these tears should flow—but they cannot unman me. No—fear it not! But the manner of his death? He was not ill when we parted."

"No, he was not ill when he died."

"Not ill? Ha! Then all has not yet been told! No matter! Death is the end of pain—and he was a hero! Proceed."

"He was the victim of Ruffleton."

"The guillotine—or assassination?"

"The former."

The chin of the General fell upon his breast. He remained perfectly silent—but the tears ceased to flow, Randolph gently grasped his hand, but did not break the silence. They proceeded thus until they were met by a messenger from Senator Langdon.

CHAPTER LXVI.

THE MYSTERY.

When the British steamer Buzzard landed at the Navy Yard the sun had set, and the first stars were twinkling in the East. The firing of the many batteries had ceased, and a comparative silence reigned where all had been so lately involved in the thunders and violences of furious war.

A carriage was procured, and the prisoner, still attended by Willy, whose passport and protection from Ruffleton yet served him, was driven into the city. Lieutenant Junkins sat outside with the driver; and knowing not what else to do with Alice, conducted her to the White House.

Jim Ready, at first, refused peremptorily to admit them. But upon learning that the officer had led the expedition against Mount Vernon, the destruction of which was already the subject of conversation in the city, and on seeing Willy's credentials, the doorkeeper gave way, and conducted the party into the Green Room, through which Flora Summers was just then gliding. She paused, and strove to penetrate the thick veil worn by Alice. Foiled in this, she retraced her steps, and accosted the maiden thus:

"Ah! the doorkeeper neglected to announce your name! Can I serve you—Is it possible?" she cried, as Alice threw aside the veil.

"Yes," said Alice, without the slightest evidence of perturbation, "we meet again. But it is not a voluntary act on my part. I am a prisoner. It was fitting that the one who applied the torch at Mount Vernon should be the one to make a captive of the President's daughter!"

"It was wrong! It was infamous!" said Flora, in a low tone, and gently seizing the hand of Alice, led her into the next room, saying, as she withdrew, to the Lieutenant and Willy, "Remain until I return, and hold no communication with any one."

"Flora," said Alice, "I cannot forget, neither of us can ever forget, the manner of your expulsion from the President's mansion but a short time ago. And now the daughter of the President is conducted into your presence a prisoner, and you are the mistress of the Presidential Mansion!"

"It is true!" said Flora, but not with an air of exultation. "Be seated—and deem me not your enemy."

"I do not think you are my enemy," responded Alice; "and although I could not approve your conduct, I could not avoid respecting your motive. There was a self-abnegation in the sacrifices you made, an abandonment of every consideration but devotion to the one you loved. I could not approbate your perfidy to my father; but I could not help admiring your fidelity to Ruffleton."

"Hush! speak lower!" said Flora, rising and tripping lightly back to the door, which she locked. Then resuming her seat near the sofa on which the weary Alice reclined, she continued:

"You have scanned the secrets of my soul! Ruffleton may be false, he may be wicked, he may be the vilest monster that ever existed: but he it was upon whom was centred my first young love! And, oh! Alice Randolph, I implore you not to interpose your high-born beauty and intellectual forehead between my love and me! Do not, in the hour of my triumph, snatch the prize from my grasp! I am more humble, or less polished than thou; but not less faithful than the highest-born maiden in the land! I look upon thy starry brow, thy femininely classical features, and perfect form, and admire them all. If I were a man I would worship at your shrine! But, being a woman, I would not have my love worship thee! Oh, Alice Randolph! was it fate or destiny that brought thee hither? Could you not have escaped?"

"My word was passed. I promised to obey the monster's orders, provided he touched me not with his polluted hand."

"And that word! Neither love, nor life, nor death, would suffice to violate the simple pledge of the high-born and high-bred maiden! And I, too, admire, although I have not practised such rigid virtue. But were there no means of rescue?"

"My guards were in the battle, and the arrival of these British steamers was not anticipated. But, Flora Summers, if my presence here is the occasion of such agonizing alarm, why not send me back again? Women are not usually made prisoners of war."

"I have thought of everything already. Thought, like lightning, has been flashing through my brain ever since we met. My first impulse was to kill you. And you do not start to hear it!"

"No; it would have been your love, not your nature."

"The next thought was instantaneous escape. But then he would have attributed it to my jealousy, and perhaps I should have atoned for it with my blood. But death would be preferable to desertion!"

"Then what was the next thought? What was the final conclusion?"

"You must see him. He will know of your capture and presence in the palace. I must dissemble, and seem to exult over your calamity, and then he will not suspect me of conniving at your escape."

"Escape?"

"Yes; and you must escape within an hour, or else we are both lost to all eternity! Promise me, Alice Randolph! Pledge me your word that you will leave this palace, leave this city, within the next sixty minutes!"

"I cannot promise anything without knowing I possess the ability to perform it. I will certainly make my escape if I can; and——"

"Oh, promise! Else my roused jealousy may cause me to strike you dead, before the expiration of the hour!"

"If you doubt my anxiety to depart, you do me great injustice. If you deem me capable of—of—remaining for the purpose of attracting the regards of Ruffleton——"

"No! no! Do not knit your brows. I do not fear anything of the sort! You do not love him, and never would or could love him! I would not kill you for any wilful injury done to me, or for any act or fault of yours; but for your beauty, for your perfections, your superiority in every respect, which would, however much he might contend against them, if inclined to do so at all, certainly weaken my hold upon him, and ultimately bereave me of his affection. You must understand me!"

"I do, Flora! And I have no hesitation in pledging my word to escape from this place at the very earliest moment possible. But I think you flatter me too much, in supposing that I might attract the regards of Ruffleton; on the contrary, I should certainly endeavor to be as repulsive as possible."

"Oh, but you know the more one is repulsed, in love, the more he will pursue! And yet you must see him! Use your own phraseology in a note announcing your captivity, and I will deliver it into his hand. There are the writing materials. I will return soon." Flora then hastened back to the green room, where Junkins and Willy awaited her.

"Lieutenant Junkins," said she, "I will, with your permission, take charge of your prisoner. It is not proper, you know, for a captive lady to remain in the custody of an officer."

"As for that matter, Miss," said Junkins, "I think she's all of a Tartar, and I'm glad to be rid of her. But I thought it my duty to bring her here; and if not, that the Protector would instruct me to deliver her over to Lord Slysir."

"Lord Slysir! By no means! He was once her father's guest, and then he conceived no partiality for her, nor she for him. But now—no! you have done right. I will inform his Highness of your meritorious conduct. His Highness is at the present moment engaged, and will receive no visitors at this hour. But to-morrow he will, himself, refer to this matter."

The Lieutenant, bowing, withdrew from the presence of one who seemed to exercise authority in the palace of the Protector.

"Now, Willy," said Flora, "I know you are a friend of Alice, of Randolph, and of the South——"

"Be pleased to look at this," said Willy, interrupting her, and presenting the passport and protection of Ruffleton.

"No! no! What do they signify? Put them away. You are in no danger here. But you must hide from the sight of Ruffleton. Come with me."

"Why must I hide, Miss Flora? And where would you lead me? he continued, inclined to extricate his arm from the grasp of the woman.

"You must assist Alice to escape!"

"Assist her to escape?"

"Yes. And it must not be known who fled with her. There is a boat yonder at the end of the lawn, where Virus and Windvane said they were taken. When I release you, you must repair thither with Alice, and lose no time in regaining the opposite shore, beyond the left wing of our army——"

"Oh, Miss Flora!" exclaimed Willy, now clasping her hand and kissing it, "how I have injured you in my thoughts! In gratitude for your generous conduct, I shall ever study how I may serve you!"

"It is not generous conduct, Willy! It is the reverse! But I have no time for explanations. Still it is a good service for your friend, and, possibly, some day you may have it in your power to serve me. Be quick; follow me. I hear Lord Slysir's voice. He approaches; and probably he met that thick-skulled Lieutenant. Step into this closet, and when I give the signal glide into the room, and away through the window with Alice!"

The closet was near the door, and as dark within as midnight; but Willy, the door being slightly open for the admission of air, had a partial view of the passage, then brilliantly illuminated, and might see into the room itself, when the door was open. He had not been long in concealment before he heard the heavy tread of some one, who he supposed might be Ruffleton, and held his breath in terror. But a moment afterwards he recognised the well remembered "Hem!" of Lord Slysir. His Lordship strode forward directly to the door of the room; but there he uttered his usual ejaculation again on being foiled in his attempt to enter. Flora had taken the precaution to lock the door. His Lordship strode back a few steps and paused to listen. He recognised the step of Ruffleton. Willy, peeping through the key-hole, having drawn the door quite close a moment before, saw his Lordship take a pinch of snuff, and then smile at a sudden conceit which occurred to him. But Willy's terror may be imagined when he beheld his Lordship approach the closet in which he was concealed! His Lordship pulled without, and Willy pulled within.

"Confound it!" said his Lordship. "Every place seems locked against me; and I have no diplomatic key to penetrate the mysteries of the palace! And here is Ruffleton himself, and I am discovered!"

"Ah, Slysir!" said Ruffleton. "I am rejoiced to see you. Come and assist me in deciphering the reports I have from the army. Randolph has taken to flight again, and I must follow him to morrow or the next day; and I think you had better accompany us. Diplomatic affairs of great magnitude have often been consummated in the field and on the water."

"Ay, and on the water," said Slysir. "I think I will go with the fleet, if we can recover our good Admiral Bang! And it was in relation to an exchange that I came hither."

"An exchange? What prisoner have we for whom Randolph would exchange Admiral Bang?"

"Ah! I am happy to inform you. One of her Britannic Majesty's officers has reported to me that an expedition, which he had the honor to command, most unexpectedly, and certainly most fortunately, made a prisoner which will enable us to offer an equivalent for the Admiral. This is good news, sir! And I trust you are prepared to congratulate your faithful ally on the joyful event."

"Most sincerely do I congratulate you! But what illustrious officer is this you have taken? I find none in the reports of Sir Charles, Balatrum, or Line."

"The capture being by one of Her Majesty's officers, the report was made to me."

"But that was irregular, and subversive of stipulations. I am the Commander-in-Chief of the British forces in this country as well as the American! I hope there is to be no interference—no misunderstanding——"

25

"No—nothing of the kind! But doubtless you will make every effort for the restitution of the Admiral."

"Unquestionably."

"Then you will permit me to open a negotiation for the exchange of prisoners—the President's daughter for Bang?"

"The President's daughter! You mean the smart American girl who humbugged Lieutenant Junkins?"

"Smart—humbugged! Was it not Alice Randolph?"

"Pooh! nonsense! Windvane says she's the daughter of an apothecary!"

"Then I have been mistaken, and grievously disappointed! But, Ruffleton, I have a great curiosity to see this specimen of an apothecary's daughter, so capable of personating Miss Randolph. And, now I remember, Junkins had seen Miss Randolph before, and it is very extraordinary that he should be humbugged so egregiously! The resemblance must be very great. At all events, this captive, he says, is quite beautiful. May I see her?"

"*I* can have no objection."

"*Allons!*" said Slysir, taking the Protector's arm.

"But she is not here. Flora thrust her out as soon as she discovered the cheat. Flora will have no pretty impostors in the palace! She is now in hysterics, and I am sent for to appease her. We will have a scene! Let go my arm. There must be no witness of our interview."

"By St. George!" exclaimed his Lordship, "your Highness is mistaken! I had a glimpse of Flora's hoops as I came hither. She is not in the green room."

"She *will* be there. She has no other means of access besides this entrance. Good-night, Slysir! I wish you happy dreams!"

And saying this, Ruffleton extricated himself from the grasp of his companion, and applying the key, entered the room and locked the door behind him. Slysir made one more ineffectual effort to open the door of the closet, and then turned away in despair. But he had not gone half-a-dozen paces before he was startled by the sneezing of Wiry Willy, who had imbibed some of his Lordship's snuff through the key-hole.

"What the devil's that?" said Slysir, pausing. And

when in the act of turning to investigate the matter, he was confronted by Flora herself, who glided in suddenly.

"Excuse me, my Lord," said she. "I am in great haste. A matter of importance——"

"Pooh! I know all about it. She is rightly *my* prisoner—not Ruffleton's. I want to exchange her for Admiral Bang, and you ought to aid me. If we put our heads together the thing can be accomplished."

"We cannot put our heads together, my Lord! I can do nothing without the countenance of his Highness. You are aware of that. And it would not be expedient for your Lordship to undertake to thwart any of the Lord Protector's plans. He could manage the affairs of the country now without foreign aid—"

"Nonsense, child! I have heard these intimations before. Let us not dabble in politics. But don't you see the danger to *yourself* in these protracted interviews between Ruffleton and the beautiful Alice?"

"I am not aware of any such interviews, my Lord!" said she, striving to stifle the agitation that tormented her. "I—I know nothing of this matter; and it will be well for neither of us to meddle——"

"Meddle? Not I. It is nothing, then. We were all mistaken. It was an apothecary's daughter, and not the daughter of the President, captured by Junkins. It is a mere counterfeit that Ruffleton is confronting in the green room—no one of any beauty, or pretensions—a mere bagatelle—and I shall go home and to bed. And I find lordly lodgings in the magnificent mansion of Langdon! Good-night—good-night."

Willy heard Slysir's departing steps, and soon after Flora glided softly past the closet and placed her ear near the door of the green room. After remaining in that attitude some time, she turned away and approached the closet in which Willy was concealed.

"Willy!" said she, in a low whisper. "Willy!" she repeated, for he seemed reluctant to reply for fear of discovery by Ruffleton. "Open the closet. Alice has demanded that the door of her room be thrown open, else she will respond to nothing he says."

"What do you want?" asked Willy, on hearing her words.

"I want to hide in the closet," said Flora, impatiently inserting her fingers in the slight opening.

"But where shall I go?" demanded Willy.

"Stay where you are!" said she, pushing in with some difficulty, destroying the shape of her crinoline, and crowding poor Willy without ceremony. This had hardly been accomplished before the door of the room was thrown wide open.

"Now," said Ruffleton, in a pretty distinct tone, "I have complied with your imperative, if not capricious demand. My proposition is made, and there is no constraint imposed upon you. It remains for you to decide. Peace and permanent power, or a bloody war and final subjugation. Your father shall exercise equal authority, and, if he survives me, shall be my successor."

"I answer no!" said Alice.

"But you do it faintly. Consider it well."

"It cannot be otherwise. My negative is calmly, not faintly uttered. And I am frank to say there is no suitor for my hand—and probably there never will be. Yet my refusal is deliberately considered, and will be firmly adhered to. If you would enjoy my respect, sir, you will lose no time in restoring me to my father."

"I am at war with your father, and you are a prisoner of war. I will not abuse my advantage, in having possession of the most charming woman in the world——"

"You dare not!" exclaimed Alice, her eyes flashing fire.

"Be not too fast!" said Ruffleton. "I might dare, *ad infinitum.* Hitherto my career has been a daring one—and you see how I have succeeded. Nevertheless, I confess my inclination to secure what I have gained, rather than to increase my gains. Randolph, you, and I, might have undisputed possession of the American world——"

"The Republic of Washington belongs to God!"

"Nonsense, maiden! The time has gone by for such patriotic exhibitions. Fancies have given place to things. Republics were always ephemeral, and now the whole brood is extinct. But I will not weary you now. Rest to-night in peace. I will write to Randolph that you are in safety, and pledge him my honor——"

"Do not, I beseech you!"

"Why not? Will not the consciousness that your father has such assurances from me be a relief, when you reflect on your captive condition? Will it not bring slumber to your eyelids?"

"No; I would depart without having the world know I was ever in captivity."

"That is plainly unreasonable and inadmissible. The very least advantage we can expect to reap from your capture would be the release of Admiral Bang."

"Release me, and he shall be liberated."

"It is easy for you to say so; but would your father ratify the agreement?"

"He will redeem the pledge of his daughter, made voluntarily, though in captivity."

"He might do so. But if he should not, what then? There would be no remedy; for he would violate no agreement."

"*My* word would be violated; and, rather than it should be so, I would return to your custody. General Ruffleton, you know I speak the truth. Why, then, do you hesitate?"

"I would do better. I would have you remain; but voluntarily, and share my power—be mistress of the world—"

"I would die first!"

"Knit not your brows so disdainfully; but even that expression becomes you. Oh, how I could adore her! and yet she spurns me."

"You promised not to insult me."

"And will keep my word. But when was woman insulted by the sincere homage of man?"

"A monster!—a murderer!"

"A murderer?"

"Ay; where is the aged Blount—the venerable Senator?"

"In heaven, I hope. But I am prepared to produce proof of his guilt."

"Of what was he guilty?"

"Of conspiring against my Government and my life."

"*Your* Government!"

"Yes, *my* Government; and all the nations and peoples shall respect it! Call it usurpation, if you please—subversion or revolution; nevertheless, it is *de facto*, and will become *de jure*. Farewell, till morning. Think of what I have said—dream on it, and perhaps your heart may relent, as your reason must teach you that the best policy—"

"I care nothing for policy! Never mention the subject again. *Your* best policy is to release me."

The last words were uttered in a loud tone, as the despot retired from the room.

"Not yet," whispered Flora, after Ruffleton strode past, and when Willy manifested an impatience to escape from his place of concealment. "Wait till he ascends the stairs. I can hear him. Oh, the perfidious man!"

"And may she escape, as you promised?"

"Escape! If she remains under this roof a single night, the next day she shall repose in the churchyard. Tell her so, Willy. Tell her that to accede to Ruffleton's proposition will be both dishonor and death. Now hasten—begone!"

"Oh, never fear us!" said Willy. "All we ask is an opportunity to get away."

He then glided into the room, and immediately after the prisoner escaped from the rear window, assisted by Willy.

CHAPTER LXVII.

NOCTURNAL ADVENTURES.

As the fugitives hurried past one of the lamps on the lawn, they were hailed by a drunken officer, and a moment after they were surrounded by a score of soldiers, with presented bayonets.

"Stand!" said the officer, staggering up in front of Alice and Willy. "You can't pass; his Royal Highness, the Grand Protector, will cut off your heads—eh! a petticoat? And where do you come from—and where are you going—and who are you?"

"Cast your eye on this!" said Willy, unfolding his passport, and stepping aside with the officer, where the rays of the lamp enabled him to decipher the autograph of Ruffleton.

"Your pardon! I beg your pardon, sir," said the officer, tottering backwards. "All right! And for heaven's sake," he continued, apparently sobered in a moment, "do not report this occurrence!"

Willy made no reply; but, with Alice clinging to his arm, strode onward, while the soldiers fell back, right and left, leaving a wide avenue.

"How did you obtain that, Willy?" asked Alice.

"Oh, it is the old passport given me in New York. I do not think that officer will be likely to make known our escape. Yonder is the skiff; and I hope the oars are not of the creaking sort, for we shall have to pass the British fleet at anchor, and no doubt many boats are plying constantly between the ships."

"Fortune favors the brave, Willy," said Alice, "and we have prospered so far. Can you row the boat?"

"Oh, yes; I am not very strong, but I am expert at it."

"I can aid you. I have often amused myself with the oars, until the blisters on my hands admonished me to desist. And more than that, Willy: if needs be, in a desperate case, *I can swim*—and the water is now warm and pleasant. So be of good cheer, for I do not mean to be retaken."

They were now at the brink of the water, and launching the boat, which had been left on dry land by the receding tide, they hastened to embark. All was quiet in the direction of the Palace, and they did not anticipate immediate pursuit. Flora, at all events, would not give the alarm. *She* could not desire the recapture of Alice, and would not report the fact of her flight, perhaps, till morning.

Such were the thoughts of both Alice and Willy as they both glided on silently, for the weather was calm and the river smooth, near the island of rushes, where Virus and Windvane had been landed on the night of the President's evacuation of the Capital. But, when emerging from behind the lower point of the island, the fugitives were terribly alarmed by the presence of more than twenty boats, propelled by muffled oars, which shot out from the rushes and spatterdocks, and completely surrounded them.

"What does this mean?" said Willy, and looking round

at the silent assemblage of boats, and yet perceiving no human beings in them.

"It is strange," said Alice. "Where are the rowers?"

"We'd squatted," said Captain Fink, rising, and placing his hand on the prow of the skiff in which the fugitives were seated. "I know your voice. Here, Captain Bim—here's good news! They have escaped!"

"By St. George and the Dragon!" cried Bim, rising in another boat. "I know that musical voice myself. Oh, Miss Alice! My heart is six ounces lighter than it was an hour ago."

"I am happy to hear you say so, Captain Bim," replied Alice. "And you were resolved to rescue me?"

"Or die!" said Bim.

"Never say die!" said Fink.

"And now, Willy," said Alice, "why are you so silent?"

"I have been thinking—"

"Is that you, Wiry Willy?" said Bim, interrupting him; "no wonder Miss Alice escaped! She never had a truer friend!"

"That is true, Captain Bim," said Alice.

"He's always ahead of me. When he's needed, he's there. When I'm needed, sometimes I'm away."

"Never mind, Captain Bim," said Alice. "Do not reproach yourself. No one blames you. It was my fault as much as yours, that you were absent. But what were you thinking about, Willy?"

"A scheme, Miss Alice, if it met your approbation, to cover the manner of your escape, and to embarrass Ruffleton." He then repeated the words he had heard when concealed in the closet, and suggested that if Lord Slysir were taken prisoner, without creating alarm, a feat quite practicable, since he had taken possession of Senator Langdon's mansion, the Protector would be very likely to couple his disappearance with the flight of Alice.

"It has my sanction," said Alice. "I give it my hearty approbation. I care not what Ruffleton and his army of traitors may say of me. I am delighted with the idea. Captain Bim, and you, Captain Fink, may distinguish yourselves, by capturing Lord Slysir."

"We'll do it or die," said Bim.

"Never say die!" said Fink—"but we'll do it! And

it's the best thing we could do to insure the escape of Miss Alice from the British. Let the boat go down the river by itself, having one of our pilots and two strong rowers in it. If they are likely to be observed, they can squat, and ride past on the tide."

"And if they board us," said Willy, "I have got a paper that will silence them. I believe you know which is Senator Langdon's house, Captain Bim?"

"As well as the fork knows the way to my mouth. But that reminds me that you don't know the way to the farm-house where Senator Langdon and President Randolph are now sleeping."

"Do you think they are sleeping, Bim?" asked Alice.

"May be not—it's not late—and we must wait some hours before we march into the city. Sleeping! no indeed! They're all thinking of you. Miss Edith has cried herself almost ugly. But the President bears up bravely, and tells them you have the wit to escape harm."

"I was in no danger of being harmed, Captain. But who will accompany us to the farm-house?"

"My silent lieutenant," said Fink. "Attention, Click!"

"I'm always attention," said the taciturn lieutenant.

"Get in there, and do your duty—what that is will be told you. You are under the orders of the President's daughter, and it's a great honor to you."

Click got in, and then the skiff was propelled forward with great rapidity by the muscular oarsmen, until they came in the vicinity of the British ship anchored highest up the river; when every possible precaution was used to elude observation.

CHAPTER LXVIII.

FURTHER ADVENTURES.

Bim and Fink led their party quietly up the canal, and awaited the flight of the hours, when the inhabitants of the city, not on duty, should be steeped in unconscious slumber. Fink, however, could not remain inactive; and although he had spent but two or three days in the Capital previous to its evacuation by the Federal army, yet his practised eye had indexed all its prominent landmarks, and now he was capable, even in the obscurity of night, of finding his way without difficulty to any remembered point. He wandered forth, therefore, to reconnoitre. Finding the street deserted and quiet in the vicinity of Lord Slysir's quarters, he contented himself for the present with extinguishing the lamp in front of the door, and then proceeded westward towards the White House, knowing very well that all the approaches to the Despot's Palace were strictly guarded by soldiers. But Fink had the faculty of creeping unperceived even into the camp of watchful Indians; and hence he did not doubt his ability to escape the observation of a regiment of half-drunken novices in the art of nocturnal perambulation. He had no difficulty in finding access to the Palace; every external portion of which he scrutinized with attention. In the rear, and near the western extremity of the building, one or two lights could be distinguished in the second story; and once he perceived Ruffleton himself, with a lamp in his hand, move across a window. He was in his night clothes, and doubtless just retiring to bed. Fink was constrained to abandon the hope, which had momentarily animated him, of capturing the Despot. But, as he was turning away, with an intention to escape in the direction of the canal from the lawn in the rear of the Palace, sounds from one of the basement rooms met his ear. He drew near the open window from which they seemed to proceed, and listened. Footsteps next attracted his attention, and soon after a man and woman entered the pantry, for such it was, the latter leading the way with a burning candle in her hand.

"Go! Be off!" said she, "and get your money, or I'll inform on you. I'll tell General Ruffleton that you are a Randolph man, and have been working on a ship at the Navy Yard!"

"You won't do any such foolish thing, Mrs. Punt!" was the reply.

"I will, I tell you! If I sacrifice my own husband in his cause, he'll be bound to reward me for it."

"You're an unnatural woman. President Randolph will pay me. He's an honorable man."

"Then go and get your money, and I'll be reconciled!"

"Yes, and if what the cook tells me is true, you'll be easily reconciled if I never return!"

"What do you mean?"

"Why, I'm getting suspicious you've been casting sheep's eyes at that Jim Ready at the door! If he don't take care I'll give him a black eye. He didn't want to let me in, and I had to get an order from the Colonel!"

"How did you get the order?"

"I told him you was my wife, and then he gave it quick enough!"

"You see I am a person of consequence!"

"I don't want my wife to be a person of consequence among the Colonels and doorkeepers! She don't belong to their circle."

"Don't talk about circles! I tell you many a rich lady would give her ears to occupy my place—and if I had a husband worth a cent, I could make a man of him."

"And that's what the cook said. Well, I'm worth a hundred dollars, for I know President Randolph will pay me."

"Where are you going now?"

"To Senator Langdon's."

"Senator Langdon's! Why he's gone."

"But his house has stayed, and Dick Clusky was left to take care of the things. I slept with him last night, and he invited me to come back to-night, if I couldn't find lodgings here."

"If you stayed here, we should all be guillotined for it. It's against positive orders. But aint Dick's mother, Maud, left behind?"

"Yes, she's now Lord Slysir's cook, and as proud as ever. She thinks his Lordship's going to marry Miss Edith, and then the fine house will belong to him."

"She must be a fool! And perhaps she thinks she's making a conquest of you—and perhaps she is——"

"What! that old wrinkled dishclout? Good night!" Saying this, Punt turned his back on his inappeasable wife, and passed through the window near which Fink was standing.

Coming out of a lighted room, Punt's vision was imperfect. He ran against a stone pillar, then stumbled among the flower pots, and fell to the earth.

"Let a friend help you up," said Fink, in a low tone, and at the same time assisting Punt to rise.

"I thank you, stranger," said Punt; "and you are a friend indeed. If you had been an enemy, you'd have been more likely to keep me down than to help me up."

"Yes, I'm your friend, because I've heard my friend Captain Bim speak about you. I know he wants to see you very much."

"Captain Bim! Where is he?"

"He's not far off. Would you like to see him?"

"Indeed I would, if he's not too far off, and if it wouldn't take me too long to go to him. Dick Clusky is waiting to let me in at Lord Slysir's."

"If you choose you can see Captain Bim in five minutes."

"That'll suit. Have you got a passport?"

"Yes—but it would be best for us to go singly. I'll meet you at the lower corner of the Treasury Building."

"Very well."

"Don't fail!"

"No danger of that. You helped me up when I was down!"

Punt then pursued his way out, passing through the brilliant gaslight from the tall lamps, and exhibiting his passport unsolicited to all the sleepy sentinels. And when he arrived at the place of rendezvous he was very much surprised to find Captain Fink awaiting him.

It was not long before Fink and Punt arrived at the boats in the canal.

"Captain Bim!" said Fink, standing directly over the boat containing the Captain.

"By George, I was napping!" said Bim.

"And if I had been an enemy," said Fink, "you would never have waked up in this world. But come out and see one of your old friends I have brought you."

"Captain Fink!" exclaimed Bim, scrambling up the wall, "if you've captured Lord Slysir by yourself, and without my assistance, you have perpetrated a very unfriendly and unofficer-like action, and I shall call you to an account for it, if you *have* a white eyebrow."

"Come and see for yourself," said Fink, laughing, and patting Punt on the shoulder.

"How are you, Captain Bim?" said Punt, seizing the Captain's hand.

"Very well, I thank you," said Bim, "but you are not Lord Slysir, I think."

"I should rather think not," said Punt. "I am a ship-carpenter by trade, and was once a sergeant in Captain Bim's company at the battle of Bladensburg."

"It's Punt! How are you, Punt? I'm glad to see you, Punt!" said Bim. "And, Punt, I'm glad you ain't Lord Slysir."

"Well," said Punt, "I can't say I'm glad, too, because his Lordship is in very comfortable quarters; and as he's a bachelor, he can't be harassed by a contrary wife. I'm going to his Lordship's house from here, and Dick Clusky is waiting to let me in."

"You are, are you?" exclaimed Bim. "So am I, and so are a dozen or so of us. And if you sleep there this night, it's more than Lord Slysir himself is fated to do."

"What do you mean, Captain?"

"I mean to take Lord Slysir prisoner, or die in the attempt."

"Never say die!" said Fink.

"Then I know you'll do it," said Punt; "for you never fail; and I can tell you it won't be a difficult thing to accomplish, particularly if I help you to get in."

"That's exactly the thing I intended you to do," said Fink.

"It's a capital idea," said Bim.

"It is, by jingo!" said Punt. "But if they found it out, the awful guillotine would be my lot. Will you take me with you? I want to go to President Randolph to get my wages, and if they believe I was made a prisoner with the great Lord, I can snap my fingers at the guillotine. And when I get my wages, and go back, the fearful Protector won't suspect anything."

"Go back?" asked Fink.

"What will you want to return for?" demanded Bim.

"Why, Mrs. Punt is now a great lady at the White House, and can make my fortune. The chances of promotion, by having access to the kitchen there, are not to be despised by anybody. That's what Mr. Windvane told me, and he's to guide me. He says immense influence may be gained through the kitchen, and he's to help me *engineer*, as he calls it."

"That's enough! It's about time now for us to be moving; you shall lead, Captain Fink, as we agreed."

Fink placed the men in single file, instructing them particularly to "tread" in each other's "tracks," so that the whole company would make but one sound at each step; and that this might be the more certainly done, he required every man to grasp the skirt of the coat of the one in front of him. Then placing himself at the head of the line, and putting the fringe of his hunting-shirt in the hand of Bim, he ordered every one to lift his right foot.

"Now, march!" said he, and away they strode.

But they had not gone twenty paces before Bim paused so abruptly that they all stumbled against each other, and several came near falling.

"What's the matter now?" demanded Fink.

"An idea just struck me," said Bim.

"An idea! And it struck so hard as to come nigh knocking us down! I hope such things aint going to hit us often!"

"But listen!" said Bim. "I haven't been so much about head-quarters for nothing. I've learned something of diplomacy—"

"What's that?" asked Fink.

"It's a weapon that sometimes kills without letting a person know what hurts him. It makes bargains and breaks them; and sometimes causes an enemy to kill himself—"

"Oh, that's nothing out in the prairies. It's not new to us. We do it every day—"

"Do what?"

"Why, when we catch a rattlesnake alive, we scratch his tail and make him bite himself. That's certain death."

"That's it! That's diplomacy! Now here's my idea, but Willy put it in my head. We'll make Dick Clusky say Lord Slysir ran off with Miss Alice, and that'll make Ruffleton bite himself! He'll fall out with the British, as sure as a gun! And then we'll tell his Lordship that Ruffleton gave us the wink to capture him, to get him out of his way—and that'll make him as mad as a hornet at Ruffleton."

"Captain!" said Fink, "that's a great idea. I don't wonder at its staggering us! But the latter end of it ain't perfect. How will we manage it when Lord Slysir sees the President's daughter at our head-quarters?"

"Hey! I didn't think of that! But we'll leave it for another idea, and it'll come. Yes! we aint to know anything about Miss Alice's escape. Remember that. And when he sees her, and learns all about it, of course he'll be all the better pleased!"

"That's natural, too!"

"But," said Punt, who was next behind Bim, "I rather think his Lordship has a hankering after Miss Edith—at least that's what Dick says."

"True, again!" said Bim. "Go ahead, Captain Fink. It's our duty to act, not think. I forgot that military maxim."

Fink led the way through the silent streets, until the party arrived in front of the mansion.

CHAPTER LXIX.

FEDERAL HEAD-QUARTERS.

As the skiff containing the fugitives glided past the British fleet, and when Alice and Willy began to breathe freer under the conviction that every obstacle had been surmounted, they were startled by a flash on the right, followed by the report of a cannon, and a terrible splash from the ball but a few fathoms ahead. Of course the rowers ceased their labor abruptly; and a few moments after they were confronted by a boat from the Styx, which lay below the Buzzard.

"Who have we here? And where are you going?" demanded the officer in command.

"Be bold, Willy," said Alice.

"Friends," said Willy, "on the service of the Lord Protector."

"If that be so," said the officer, in a lower tone, as he approached the stern of the skiff, "you shall pass."

"Come here," said Willy, "and you shall see." Then

striking a light with a match, he exhibited the signature of Ruffleton to his passport and protection.

"That will do!" said the officer, satisfied with a very brief examination of the papers, for before he could inspect them closely the light had gone out. Besides, while it lasted, he had caught a glimpse of the beautiful features of Alice, and could not avoid lifting his cap to her.

"Then work away, oarsmen!" said Willy, "for we have no time to lose."

"Can I render any assistance?" asked the young officer, addressing himself to Alice.

"No, sir," said she: "but I thank you."

The fugitives had now passed the last of the British cruisers, and the tide being with them, they rapidly approached the place of destination, as indicated by the guide.

An hour more, and the boat was near the spot where Bim and Fink had embarked. And there they were met by Major Milnor, and a number of the Blue Caps, who awaited intelligence from Washington, and hoped to be the first to announce to the President tidings of his daughter.

"What news have you?" demanded the Major. "What chance is there of a rescue?"

"None at all, Major," said Alice, "for the bird had flown."

"That voice!"

"Yes; it is my voice," said Alice. "And by your leave, Major, I would be the first to announce my escape to my father."

Upon hearing these words, the Major plunged into the water, some six or eight inches in depth, where the boat had grounded, and gallantly bore the maiden to land.

"Thank you, Major!" said she. "And now to horse. I hope the President's head-quarters are not far off."

"Not more than a mile, and we have your favorite Sir Archy yonder, awaiting you. I never saw him so restless; he really seems distressed at your absence, like all who have heard of your capture."

"I am sure I am obliged to them all. I see you are looking for the other boats with Captains Bim and Fink. We met them. But as I had escaped before their arrival, and as they had resolved upon a successful expedition, I gave them permission to bring off some prisoner of note, by way of retaliation. I think they will be successful; but they will not return immediately; even if they should succeed in eluding the vigilance of the British cruisers." Alice was soon mounted on her favorite charger, and accompanied by Major Milnor, galloped towards the ancient country-seat occupied as the head-quarters of the President.

But they were defeated in the purpose to present themselves unannounced before the weary watchers, who prayed for the enfranchisement of Alice. She was recognised by the Blue Caps surrounding the house, and it was impossible for them to repress the joyful feelings her return inspired. Deafening cheers announced the deliverance of the captive; and the enthusiasm, spreading with rapidity among the divisions of the army, the silence of midnight was startled by the thunders of their applause.

"My dear child!" said the President, upon rushing out on the lawn and folding his daughter to his heart, while a tear moistened his cheek.

"My father!" said she, "all is repaired. I have escaped unharmed; but henceforth I am the President's daughter, and not Marble!" She was next folded in the arms of Edith—then embraced by General Crook, who had wept like a child on hearing of her capture—by General Blount, pale and decked in the habiliments of mourning—by Senator Langdon—by the aged Doctors of divinity and medicine, Love and Durnell; and, indeed, hundreds of others would have shown their joy in the same manner. And as Alice, in reply to their congratulations, gave a large share of the merit to Wiry Willy, every one present grasped the young man's hand in token of their approbation.

"I cannot sleep, father," said Edith, who had been quite ill. "But I am well, now! Oh, Alice! I feared we should never meet again! How did you escape?"

"Answer me first!" said Randolph. "Where are Bim and Fink?"

"They resolved to make a prisoner of *importance*," said Alice, archly, "by way of retaliation."

"Now proceed with Edith," said Randolph, when they re-entered the house; "I am answered. I will say nothing about the egotism of camps or the vaulting ambition of heroines. Proceed."

"How did I escape?" continued Alice. "But how shall I escape the sarcasms of the Commander-in-Chief if I tell you?"

"Easily," said Randolph. "It shall be attributed exclusively to your address—your merit."

"It was not that—not that," she said.

"Not that!" iterated Edith.

"No; it was the jealousy of another."

"Jealousy?"

"Or fear—which, you know, is the same thing."

"I know nothing about it."

"How they do beat about the bush, General!" said Crook to Blount, whose sad expression of countenance had been momentarily relaxed.

"Don't interfere, Crook," said Randolph, "or the mystery will be prolonged indefinitely."

"It was the jealousy or fear—as she confessed herself—of Flora Summers."

"Flora Summers!" exclaimed Edith. "That fearful woman! The wonder is, that she did not assassinate you."

"She might have done so, if I had not escaped, and, indeed, she threatened it if I did not escape. She is the mistress, now, of his Highness's Palace; and wields immense power. She it was who furnished me the means of escaping. Let no one denounce Flora again. She is not vile by nature, but only loves the tyrant too well."

"No wonder, then," said Randolph, "that she could not be won by the President. However, since she served my daughter, I will serve her, if it be in my power."

"But who is the one of *importance* Jack Bim is to capture by way of retaliation?" demanded General Crook.

"Lord Slysir, I think," said Alice.

"Good! I do hope his Lordship will fall into our hands again," said Crook; "because I intimated that I had a presentiment we should capture him once more. But then the fellow said it would be no mortification——"

"I trust," said Edith, quickly, while a melancholy smile illumined the pale face of Blount, "that Bim will not bruise him again!"

At a late hour the company sought the repose of which they stood in great need after the fatigues and excitements of the day.

CHAPTER LXX.

DIPLOMATIC CATEGORIES.

"STOP there! Who are you?" cried Dick Clusky, seeing Bim, Fink, and a number of their men gliding in at the door which he had opened, on hearing Punt's signal.

"They are friends," said Punt.

"Friends? But there's too many of 'em. His Lordship will be in a rage!"

"That's true, Dick," said Bim, "but it can't be helped." He then proceeded very deliberately to station his men in the hall, while Dick looked on in amazement, ever and anon rubbing his eyes, as if doubtful whether it was a dream or reality. Bim next ignited the candle he always carried in his pocket, and then extinguished the gas. "Now, Dick," continued he, "you must not be astonished at anything. Lord Slysir will at least *pretend* to be in a great rage. He may swear a little. But it will be nothing but *sham.* You understand?"

"No, I don't!" said Dick.

"Well, I'll tell you. He's going to run away with a lady against the will of the Protector, and he wants the Protector to think we captured him, and dragged him off by force. Do you understand, now?"

"No, I don't! I know his Lordship is in love with my mistress—"

"Miss Edith? It was only pretence—and, besides, she wouldn't have him. I'll tell you a secret in your ear. Lord Slysir is going to marry Miss Alice, the President's daughter. He sent for us to come and take him prisoner. You know me, and you know Captain Fink?"

"Yes."

"Well. We are officers in the President's army, and it's not likely we'd be here without an invitation. You understand?"

"No, I don't: because you said he was going to run away with a lady."

"You are stupid! Don't you know General Ruffleton's got Miss Alice a prisoner at the White House?"

"No, I don't! Yes—yes, I do! I heard one of Lord Slysir's men say so, but I didn't believe it—for the British are most abominable liars about ladies."

"All you have to do is to keep quiet, Dick. We'll manage the rest."

Bim, then, candle in hand, led the way up-stairs, followed by Fink and ten of the men. He knocked at the door of Lord Slysir's chamber, through the key-hole of which he perceived all was darkness.

"Who's there? What do you want?"

"We have a message for Lord Slysir!" said Bim, entering, for the lock had given way under his gigantic pressure.

"A message! Who from?" demanded his Lordship, starting up in bed, and gazing at the intruders in astonishment.

"My Lord," said Bim, "perhaps I used the wrong word. We have no special message. It's a mission."

"A mission? What the deuce does this mean?" continued his Lordship, endeavoring to snatch a brace of pistols which lay on a table near his pillow.

"Pardon me, my Lord," said Bim, interposing and placing the pistols in his own belt, "but these tools are dangerous, and it's not our mission to let you commit suicide."

"Suicide! Mission!" repeated his Lordship. "Will you not oblige me by explaining all this."

"Well," said Bim, "our mission is to convey your Lordship down the river into the camp of the President. And the meaning is, I think, that without the permission of the Protector—or *rather I* think him a Traitor—it isn't likely we would have ventured into this city. Your Lordship must know who I am. It ain't possible your Lordship could have forgotten Captain Bim, already. Your Lordship's capture made me a captain—I hope it will now make me a major. But there is not a moment to be lost. The boats are waiting. Here is paper, pen, and ink. Please your Lordship write an order to the British cruisers to let the boats pass without question. Do this, and I promise not to bruise you this time." Saying this, Bim lifted Slysir from his couch and placed him on a chair beside the table.

His Lordship became suddenly aware of his helpless condition, and was stunned by the intimation that Ruffleton had been the contriver of the plot. Seeing no other alternative but submission and obedience, he wrote the lines dictated by Bim and affixed his signature to them.

"Now, your Lordship," continued Bim, again lifting Slysir in his herculean arms, "we will depart without delay."

"Stop!" cried his Lordship. "I must put on my clothes! You would not take me out in the street with nothing on but my nightcap and gown!"

"The air is pleasant," said Bim; "besides it's quite dark. We cannot gratify you, indeed, my Lord. We must hasten. And they say it takes a Lord two hours to dress. Bring his clothes along, Captain Fink. He can dress in the boat."

Silently the party descended the stairs, and returned to the boats. Then the oarsmen bent to their work and rapid progress was made.

In the meantime Lord Slysir proceeded to put on his clothes. But an indispensable garment was missing. He could find no breeches.

"My breeches!" cried he. "They are not here."

"I thought I had everything," said Fink. "What are these?" he continued, lifting up a light garment.

"They are my drawers!" said Slysir.

"I thought I got all the clothes in the room," said Fink. "Are you right sure, sir, you had any breeches?"

"Had any breeches! I will have none of your impudence!"

"You're safe!" said Fink; "but I'll give you a chance to fight on equal terms some day or other, perhaps. Still, I was perfectly serious in the question. Sometimes men wear leggings, and no breeches at all. However, I brought all the clothes that were in the room, for I never do anything by halves."

"My breeches were in the next room," said his Lordship.

"Then all I've got to say is," replied Fink, "they had no business to go in there by themselves, for now they're left behind. I peeped into that chamber—"

"You did?"

"And shut the door again—it was pitch dark. But

really I'm sorry for you—and I doubt whether any man has an extra pair of breeches to loan you."

"Loan me!"

Bim and Fink, who were in the same boat, held a protracted consultation in a low voice, which did not reach the ears of Lord Slysir.

"Captain Fink," said the former, "the moon will soon hinder us from giving 'em the slip in the 'snaking' way. I have got his Lordship's pass; but then we've got his Lordship himself, and he might revoke it! I want to hear what you've got to say—think well on it, for we've a high prize if we can only steer it into port."

"Captain Bim," said Fink, "I *have* thought the matter over. It's my opinion the boats ought to go all in a bunch, boldly and audaciously, to keep from being suspicioned. If we go in a bunch, right under their guns, and show 'em we don't want to hide, they won't suspicion us, I think, because the British are not half so smart as the Indians. We can gag his Lordship and make him lie down in the bottom of the boat, and pass him off for a sick man if any of the enemy should visit or search us."

"I like your plan, Captain Fink," said Bim. "There is only one thing I would add to it, which I hope you'll agree to, and the plan will be the joint production of two heads. To appear bold, and indifferent, and confident, I think our men should sing a boat song."

"A boat song? My men can sing a Western river boat song, ten miles long, if that'll do."

"And my men can sing any chorus that ever was invented. Now let us announce the result of our conference to his Lordship. Will you do it?"

"No; I'd rather not. I hav'n't been used to speaking to Lords, except one that came out to Missouri to hunt with us, and he could eat, and drink, and laugh, and joke, as well as any white man."

"Then I'll do it! My Lord Slysir," he continued, in a louder voice.

"I hear you, Bim. And, Bim, I don't blame you for what has occurred this night. But if my suspicions be well founded—no matter! If I see Randolph, or even if I escape, or am rescued by her Majesty's officers—"

"My Lord," said Bim, "it was concerning your rescue or escape, that we have been putting our heads together."

"I thought so. And no doubt Randolph will deem it meritorious conduct on the part of his officers in performing an act of courtesy to her Britannic Majesty's Plenipotentiary, when he had been betrayed by a perfidious ally. And I shall certainly regard it as a friendly service—"

"My Lord!" said Bim, "you're mightily out of it! We don't intend to do any such thing!"

"You don't!"

"No, sir—I mean your Lordship. We intend to conduct you to the President's head-quarters, breeches or no breeches!"

"The d—l you do! Then I am mistaken."

"Yes, sir—I mean your Lordship—you are mistaken in the men you have to deal with."

"But sure you don't reckon on being able to pass through the British fleet, with such a number of boats without being detected? Such a feat might be done of a dark night; but now the moon will reveal everything."

"But, sir—I mean your Lordship—you gave us a pass, and you wrote that we were not to be questioned."

"That was under compulsion. If they question me, they'll know my voice—"

"That's the point I've been steering for," said Bim. "On the matter of that, we have come to the conclusion to say a few plain words to your Lordship, and we hope your Lordship won't take any offence at 'em."

"Say on, Bim—never fear!"

"As for that, sir—I mean your Lordship—I never feared but once, and that was about a minute. I thought I saw a ghost. But to the matter in hand, and there's no time to spare. Captain Fink and I have come to the conclusion that you must not be heard or seen by any of the prying midshipmen or lieutenants."

"How will you prevent it, Bim," asked his Lordship. "Will you throw me overboard?"

"Lord! no, sir—I mean your Lordship. Throw you overboard, indeed! and lose our prize! No, sir—I mean your Lordship—we only intend to gag you and lay you down in the bottom of the boat—"

"What? What's that? Would you dare—"

"We're daredevils," said Fink, "when provoked."

"I must say you resemble them," added his Lordship, seeing they were entirely in earnest. "But I will have no violence. If you will not take my word, I will, myself, tie a handkerchief over my mouth, and conceal my face from recognition."

"I'm not afraid to trust your Lordship," said Bim—"and so the treaty's made. All I have to add, as a guarantee of its faithful performance, is that Captain Fink and myself are to sit at your elbows, with the understanding that rather than see the prize snatched out of our hands, we would sink it to the bottom."

"I agree," said his Lordship.

After this the boats were "bunched," as Fink expressed it, and the crews sang the western boat song. When they approached the first cruiser, Bim ordered his men to meet the boat rowed towards them. And striking a light and igniting his candle, he had his paper in readiness by the time the officer came alongside.

"That is good enough authority for me," said midshipman Slysir, a nephew of his Lordship. "But how is uncle Potbelly to-night?"

"Uncle who?" demanded Bim.

"Oh, his Lordship. He's my uncle, and sometimes I call him uncle Potbelly."

"He was quite well, I thank you," said Bim, "when I saw him last; and I think the pot was as great as ever. Good night, sir."

"The impudent rascal," said his Lordship, when the boats had glided some distance apart. "Uncle Potbelly! I'll send him home, to be put to school again! Thank you, Bim, for permitting me to express my dissatisfaction with my nephew. Now tie up my mouth again. You see I did not violate my word. My own nephew did not know me."

"If he had, he would have been more respectful, perhaps," said Bim.

"He shall not escape! But here comes another boat."

His Lordship's mouth was again bandaged, and by the time the man-of-war's boat was alongside, Bim had his light and his paper in readiness. The officer seeing the signature of Lord Slysir to the pass, did not pause to conjecture what might be the nature of the expedition; but, touching his cap very politely, ordered his men to row back to the ship. And soon after it was observed that signals were exhibited on the ships from one end of the fleet to the other.

"Now I may put the handkerchief in my pocket," said Lord Slysir, "for they have given orders not to visit us any more."

As they drew near the place of landing, Bim giving the signal, the solemn hour of early dawn was startled by three vociferous huzzas from the crews. The echoes and reverberations roused their comrades on the shore, and repeated cheers attested the hearty welcome which awaited the return of the adventurers. And when the boats touched the land, hundreds of gallant spirits crowded round Bim and Fink to hear the news. All was soon known, and many hearty bursts of laughter assailed the ears of his Lordship, as he walked between the two Captains in his white drawers.

"Where is President Randolph?" he asked. "Take me to his head-quarters immediately."

"As soon as our horses come," said Bim; "it's too far to walk without pantaloons."

"Pantaloons!" said his Lordship, glancing down at his nether garment. "Be careful, Bim," said he, in a less presumptuous tone, "not to lead me where the ladies or General Crook can see me."

"Well, sir," said Bim—"I mean your Lordship, you shall be obeyed. But I was thinking that none except General Crook's breeches would fit your Lordship. He's just about your size."

"And that's true, Bim. Lead me to him."

In the space of a few minutes they had galloped up to the mansion where the President and his Generals lodged. The sun was gilding the tops of the distant hills, the rosebushes on the lawn were bespangled with dew, and the fragrance of flowers filled the atmosphere.

Lord Slysir and Bim, who had approached the mansion, dismounted quietly in front of the wing of the house, where a sentinel said the General they were in quest of had his lodgings. They were met at the door by General Crook himself, who was an early riser.

"Well, Bim?" said he, "but what's that hiding behind

you? Stop!" he continued, pushing Bim aside and confronting his Lordship, at whom he gazed in silence. He looked at his Lordship's soiled hat and coat, and then cast his eyes down at his—drawers. He could restrain himself no longer. Clapping his hands, and laughing vociferously, nearly all the inmates of the mansion were roused from their slumber. The Venetian blinds of every window on that side of the building, above and below, seemed agitated.

"General Crook," said Slysir, "why do you keep me standing here exposed to the curious gaze of all who may choose to look at me?"

"What! Is it possible?" cried the General, in a very loud voice. "Pardon me! I didn't know your Lordship without your—breeches."

"Confound it, General!" said his Lordship, "speak lower, or everybody will hear you! Let me in, and lend me a pair of your breeches."

"Certainly," continued Crook, still very loudly. "Pardon me for keeping you standing here so long, in the dew, and without your breeches. John, you rascal, wake up, and get a pair of my breeches for Lord Slysir!"

"Why did you speak so loudly, General?" asked Slysir, when admitted within the chamber.

"I was not aware of it. But your Lordship must know that I have been bellowing so much in the field after the John Bulls, that my voice has become uncontrollable. But here are the breeches—put them on quickly, for I hear Randolph coming—and, for what I know, some of the petticoats may be with him. Bim has by this time reported everything, and Alice may claim you as her prisoner."

During these words his Lordship used the utmost dispatch with the breeches, and had only succeeded in adjusting them when Randolph entered.

"My Lord," said he, "you are right welcome! And I congratulate you on your exemption, this time, from the terrible bruises—"

"Bruises or breeches?" asked Crook.

"Ah, Crook," said Randolph—"you had better bridle your tongue before Ruffleton gets your head. He swears vengeance against you. But really, Bim informed me that your Lordship, in the hurry of departure, actually did leave one of your garments behind—"

"Yes—his breeches," said Crook.

"I hope your Lordship," continued Randolph, "will consider my wardrobe entirely at your service."

"I thank your Excellency," said Slysir, "and will avail myself of the generous offer."

"But," said Crook, "don't you see Randolph's legs are six inches longer than your Lordship's?"

"No matter," said Randolph, "come with me and examine the other garments; you may at least *change your coat!*"

"I recognise a diplomatic emphasis in that, your Excellency," said Slysir, "and will not neglect the intimation. But I hope there will be no danger of meeting the ladies?"

"None whatever," said Randolph, smiling. "They will fly before you like frightened fawns."

"And why? Have they been made acquainted with my condition on arriving hither?"

"Bless your life," said Crook, speaking at random, "did you not hear the rattling of Venetian blinds just over our heads when we were conversing in the yard? The young ladies occupy the chamber directly over mine."

"And it was for the purpose of attracting their attention, General," said Slysir, reproachfully, "that you spoke in such deafening tones! That was very unkind. I would not have been seen by the ladies for thousands."

"Nonsense, Slysir!" continued Crook, his eye gleaming with merriment; "you do not understand our American ladies at all."

Slysir, without uttering a word in reply, withdrew with the President. They proceeded directly to Randolph's private office.

"Now, my Lord," said the President, "if we have any business to transact, we will dispatch it immediately. But, my Lord, how can you treat? You have ceased to be a negotiator, and become—"

"What, your Excellency?"

"A prisoner. You let the opportunity slip of regaining Bang, when you held Senator Blount."

"I *protested* against his execution."

"I know it. But you should have prevented it."

"And I shall for ever protest against another, and a still more infamous act of Ruffleton's. They tell me, sir, that my capture, or rather abduction, was connived at, or instigated by him."

"They deceive you. It was the blundering idea of Bim, who supposed a rupture between you and Ruffleton would be of service to me. The honest Captain is no diplomatist, though he seems to have misled one."

"The unwashed ruffian! But then, your Excellency, all the world knows Ruffleton's weakness for the sex, and—"

"Yours, my Lord."

"Conceded. And, as I had no means of knowing that Miss Alice had escaped his clutches; and, as she had been captured by her Majesty's officer—"

"The one who applied the torch to Mount Vernon—the immortal Junkins."

"I protested against that, also. But, under all the circumstances, your Excellency may easily conceive why I might be, and any one might be, inspired with the belief that Ruffleton had yielded to the expediency of having me removed."

"Granted. But, my Lord, for either Ruffleton, or the Envoy of any nation on earth, to offend my daughter, would involve as serious consequences as befell the famous Trojan city. No more of that! Have you any proposition to make?"

"I believe my Government would not be averse to a renewal of the propositions I made your Excellency on the *status quo ante bellum;* for it never can and never will be *particeps criminis* in the sanguinary work of the guillotine."

"It is premature. *The pear is not yet ripe.* Ruffleton's alliance with England is a twofold necessity to me. Nay, start not, nor stare in surprise. If your Lordship had not been incapable, as all the British diplomats have been, of comprehending the public sentiment in this country—I mean the patriotism of our popular sovereigns—you would have withheld your co-operation from both sections, at least until the rupture and collision had progressed into more desperate stages. And now, my Lord, I not only decline forming any alliance with England myself, but will contribute all in my power to prevent a rupture between you and Ruffleton. Your Lordship may at any time return to your ally, on parole, to be honorably exchanged whenever an equivalent can be tendered. I will have your Lordship's breakfast served immediately, and, in the meantime, you will amuse yourself until I return from my morning's ride."

Saying this, Randolph withdrew, leaving his Lordship in a state of profound amazement.

During the interview between Randolph and Slysir, Blount and Edith met in the parlor. The General was promenading slowly to and fro, pale and haggard, having been unable to sleep during the night, for the vision of his father and the butchery of the guillotine frightened slumber from his pillow. But now he was composed, though very sad. Edith, who had been attracted by his measured step, was so overcome by his appearance, that her sympathy found expression in tears; and, upon beholding her bedewed eyelids, Blount advanced and silently folded her in his arms, and their tears were mingled together.

"Dearest Edith," said he—"and who else now remaining on earth can be so dear to me? I thank you for this! The vision is dispelled—the horrid picture of his humiliation and agony—and dispelled by an angel! The severed links that bound me to another earthly object, now for ever gone, only attach me the more indissolubly to you. Here and hereafter, now and for ever, we will exist for each other. Let us go to your father. Let us lose not a moment in consummating the union. You are silent," said he, gazing down at the fair maiden's face, half-hidden on his breast. "But you do not oppose?"

"No, Harry," said she.

"No? I have not misinterpreted? Then let us hasten to your father!"

Half-leading—half-bearing the precious burden, the General entered the room occupied by Senator Langdon. Blount briefly but explicitly made known the nature of his errand, and Edith was silent.

"My son!" said Langdon, while tears started in his eyes—"I will be your father in affection, as well as in law. I loved your father, though I often differed with him. I shall not differ with you, and therefore must love you more. Send for Dr. Love, and let us all repair to the little chapel in the grove which we attended last evening."

Blount, placing the blushing maiden in the arms of her father, hastened away to make the necessary preparations for the nuptials.

CHAPTER LXXI.

THE MINISTER OF JUSTICE.

Mr. Windvane, the Minister of Justice, or rather the head of the Police, was roused early in the morning by a tremendous knocking at the door of his dwelling. The stars being still faintly glimmering in the heavens, the great man ordered his library to be illuminated, and proceeded thither himself with as little delay as possible. The visitor, he felt assured, must be one of his secret agents, and he had already organized a corps of them in imitation of Fouché.

"Ah! it is you, Cuté!" said Windvane, on perceiving the visitor. Cuté was one of Lord Slysir's secretaries, whom Windvane had employed as a spy. He narrated the circumstances of Lord Slysir's abduction.

"This is important," said Windvane. "I thank you, Cuté, for this information—I mean for apprising me of the occurrence, for you——"

"True, your Excellency, the occurrence was all I could understand. It required your genius to unravel the tangled skein."

"I think I may lay claim to some sagacity, Mr. Cuté—but then I have the means of information possessed by no other man, and the power to defeat and destroy all false players——"

"I trust your Excellency will never have cause to suspect my fidelity," said Cuté.

"I trust so, too—because in the event—in that event—I should be under the disagreeable necessity—enough! Whither do you go now?"

"It was my purpose to report this matter to the Protector."

"No. Return to your couch. Go into that chamber and allow me to turn the key on this side of the door. I have reasons for it, perhaps involving your safety. The

Protector may order the executioner to decapitate all the household of Slysir, before I can appease him."

Cuté, trembling, for he was aware that Windvane's house was ever filled with the servitors of the guillotine, did not venture to hesitate.

And Windvane, left to his own reflections, promenaded his office a few moments, contemplating the web of intrigue which seemed to invite the control of a master-mind.

"Now, or perhaps never!" thought he, "the opportunity is presented for me to grasp the reins of power. The flight of Alice will exasperate the Protector, and the desertion of his British ally—but no! He cannot long avoid arriving at the conclusion that after the burning of Mount Vernon by the British, there can never be a reconciliation between Randolph and Slysir—never! But will that conviction come before he goes in pursuit of the enemy? I think not; and my point is to get him off, out of the way, until I can realize a fortune."

This result attained in his meditations, Windvane hastened to the Palace, and found ready admission. He was ushered into Ruffleton's bed-room.

"Windvane," said the Protector, "I have broken the thread of a most delightful dream. I hope your information may be of an agreeable nature; and quite sure am I that you would not have disturbed my slumber at this, the most unseasonable hour for one who perforce must be up late o'nights, were it not of great magnitude."

"It is of very great magnitude, your Excellency," said Windvane, "and I am sorry to say it must necessarily be very disagreeable to you."

"Pause there, Windvane," said Ruffleton, sitting upright in bed, "until I can consider the condition of affairs a moment. No. It was impossible for any serious calamity to occur. There has been no battle, of course, or I should have known it. What is the occurrence, Windvane, which has blown you hither?"

"There are two of them, your Excellency."

"Two of them? Nay, don't be alarmed—for I am as mild as a midsummer morning—I know the attitude of affairs immediately around me—and Randolph has more cause of distress than I have. One question. Is there any rebellion in the distant States?"

"No, sir. The guillotine secures permanent submission to your Highness's authority in all the free States, and in Delaware and Maryland!"

"Then, Windvane, I defy your worst! Out with it!" Saying this, he folded his arms and threw himself back on his pillow.

"Alice Randolph has escaped," said Windvane. Ruffleton stared a moment in silence, while his eyes revolved quickly and furiously in their sockets. Then he sprang to the floor, and seized the bell-string. So energetic was his action that the cord snapped in twain.

"But how do you know this?" he cried, turning to Windvane, and throwing the tassel to the floor.

"I have it from one of Lord Slysir's family."

"One of Lord Slysir's family! And how should one of Lord Slysir's family know anything about it?"

"His Lordship, himself—"

"Well? His Lordship, himself—"

"Is gone, likewise."

"Gone? Gone over to the enemy? What time is it? That clock was not wound up."

"He was seized by Captain Bim at the head of a detachment of the enemy; so your Excellency will see—"

"See d——n! Her own infernal Blue Caps. A pretty contrivance, indeed! That is the solution of Slysir's conduct last night. But none of them shall escape me. The guillotine shall make an inundation of blood—ah!"

The last exclamation was caused by the abrupt appearance of Flora Summers, who came running in, exhibiting marks of alarm. She was in her night-clothes, and paused suddenly on beholding Windvane.

"I feared you were ill, sir," said she, addressing Ruffleton. "I am sure you rang the bell. Did you not desire me to come?"

"Yes. What time is it? Look at your own clock and send me word."

Flora, astonished, withdrew, and instantly after sent word that daylight appeared in the East.

"That Bim!" said Ruffleton, as he proceeded to put on his clothes. "That is the whole secret in one word, and that word his name. My soldiers, excepting a few drunken or sleepy-headed loons, all over the river! But with the

Potomac between us and the enemy, who would have anticipated such a thing? The wonder is that they did not carry me off with the rest! But then I was not so palatable as his Lordship! Oh, no! I will rush like a tornado upon them all!"

"I must say, your Excellency, that it seemed as if Lord Slysir was not in the plot; for they hurried him away without his——"

"His what?"

"His breeches, your Excellency."

"A diplomatic *ruse*, a shallow diplomatic *ruse*, sir; I have known a pair of breeches to play an important part in politics—and why not in love, or perfidy, or treason?"

"His Lordship may have had another pair somewhere else—but Cuté declares the soldiers hurried him off in his drawers."

"His drawers! I'll soon have his legs, unless he can fly faster than I can pursue! It is broad daylight!" said he, turning to a window, and throwing open the shutters. "My horse! Ho, there! Rouse my aides," he continued, speaking to an officer below. "And, Windvane," he resumed, in a milder tone, "send Virus after me. Let my Ministers meet to-day as usual, and stay here all day. I will send messengers to you from the field of battle or the field of flight. In an hour you will hear my cannon."

The Despot withdrew hastily from the apartment by the door which Flora had opened, and Windvane retreated in another direction.

As the Protector passed through the next chamber, his hand was seized by Flora, who bathed it with tears.

"Listening! ever listening! When will you be done with it, foolish girl? Release my hand, I am in great haste."

"Hastening to the battle-field from which you may never return."

"I thrive nowhere else so well as in the field, Flora; and will try and preserve the life which seems not altogether worthless to you. I will not question you closely about this escape."

"What escape, sir?" asked Flora, in well counterfeited surprise.

"Oh, no matter—she was a woman, and you are a woman. She's gone—and that's an end of it, until the story be continued. Now, Flora, you remain without a rival in the Palace. Guard my interests well. From the secret closet you will hear every word my Ministers utter —and I can rely on *you*."

"You can, indeed."

"I know it. Now, farewell. Dry your eyes, and make a fortune. Make Windvane share his gains with you, or else defeat his projects."

The Protector, soon after, surrounded by many aides, was galloping over the intervening space between the Federal City and the Long Bridge.

CHAPTER LXXII.

A CONTRE TEMPS.

SHORTLY after Randolph left Slysir, his Lordship, happening to see Wiry Willy, beckoned him into the library.

"Willy," said his Lordship, "you see I am a prisoner again. I am not bruised, as before. Walk round behind me, Willy. Now do you observe anything odd in my dress?"

"I think your Lordship's pantaloons," said Willy, "may be a trifle too tight—but that defect is mainly concealed by the coat."

"That will do, sir. You speak like a costumer. But the letter, Willy—you remember the letter?"

"The letter? Oh, yes! Miss Edith gave it me, and I placed it—excuse me, and I will get it immediately."

"A letter from Edith!" said Slysir, when Willy had gone out. "By Jupiter! *Her Ladyship* and *her Grace*, may have their fascinations, after all! Ah, you have returned!" said he, on perceiving Wiry Willy standing at his elbow. "Now the letter, Willy!"

"Here it is, precisely as it came from her hand," said he, delivering it.

"Why, you rascal—"

"Rascal, sir?" said Willy.

"Why, this is my letter, sir!"

"I know it," said Willy, with imperturbable gravity "and have you it not in your possession?"

"In my possession? What does it mean, sir?"

"It means that when I delivered your letter, the one to whom it was addressed, seeing your Lordship's seal, returned it, unopened."

"That's not probable. The idea of any lady, and especially an American lady, returning a Lord's letter unopened! Why, feminine curiosity would be irresistible!"

"Nevertheless, your Lordship, if you will read the line in pencil mark and the initials below the seal, will discover that I have spoken the truth."

"By Jupiter," said his Lordship, with his glass to his eye, "this is most extraordinary."

"And if your Lordship be not yet satisfied," said Willy, "I am sure you will be very soon, for Miss Edith is to be married to General Blount within an hour from this time."

"Stupid fellow! Sure that such an occurrence will be satisfactory to me! Stay! Why are you in such great haste?"

"I am sent in quest of the good Dr. Love, to come to the chapel and marry them. I hope your Lordship will be present on the occasion." Willy then sped away without marking his Lordship's countenance.

"Come, Slysir," said General Crook, who entered and grasped his Lordship's arm—"come with me to the chapel. Blount is to be married. Why do you seem disconcerted?"

"Do I?"

"Crook, I am an unhappy man! But there is no remedy. Pray do not publish to all the world that I am in a borrowed garment. It may be the effect of habit; but the idea of being in any man's breeches but my own makes me very miserable."

"Will you accept them? Then they will be your own. But, really, you are too large for my breeches."

"Come—let us go to the chapel. I see the bridal party entering the President's carriage."

They repaired to the chapel. Senator Langdon stood by the altar in readiness to give away his daughter. Edith, arrayed in beauty, gazed through her veil alternately at

Blount and Alice. The former exhibited on his lofty forehead the calm majestic expression which had ever distinguished him, even in days of buoyant youth; the latter, veiled, seemed, indeed, like marble. The lips were not red like the bride's; and she stood as collected and motionless as a statue, her eyes fixed on the stained-glass window, whose variegated hues seemed concentrated on her head, and revealed the death-like pallor of her countenance.

After a considerable pause, the wonder felt at the absence of the minister and of President Randolph, began to be whispered from one to another.

"I hope the minister won't be—" said Lord Slysir, and then paused.

"Don't be uncharitable," said Crook; "Blount has waited, and watched, and fairly won her. He shall wear her. But, what's that? Look at him! What does he hear? His glance, for a moment, as his eyes were raised, reminded me of the animated expression which has distinguished him on the field of battle. But he saw nothing, heard nothing, and he is perfectly composed again. See, now, his smile! From the lion to the lamb, from the eagle to the dove, such are the characteristic transitions of the truly great! I, ass as I sometimes think myself, have observed it. But I bray whenever I please, and sometimes I kick like the devil! Yet Randolph and Blount understand me, and can control me. I love them both, and I have a universal love for womankind. How beautiful, but cold, is the President's daughter! And even Edith begins to hang her head, as if in fear the parson cannot be found! Gad, I'm determined there shall be no disappointment. I am a magistrate in my own country, and I'll marry them myself, in expiation of my offence. Did your Lordship know it was I who interrupted the ceremony at Washington, when the General first led that lovely creature to the altar? I have reproached myself for it ever since, and will make amends."

"Yes, she told me herself."

"And did she blame me?"

"No, General. She said you were not aware of what was going on at the church."

"That was true! By George! if I had known it, I should have delayed the attack on the President! And now I am one of Randolph's lieutenants! What changes in politics and in war!"

"And love!" said Slysir—"for here comes a disturbance!"

Crook turned his eyes towards the door, where a sudden commotion among the half-dozen slaves that were gazing in, had arisen.

"Go! scatter and conceal yourselves like partridges in the stubble!" cried crazy Charlotte, to the negroes that scampered away. "Where is the good shepherd?" she continued, striding towards the chancel, in her cuirass and painted helmet, and waving her spear. "Here are the lambs, but where is the good shepherd?"

"Sit down, Charlotte," said Mr. Langdon, "and be a witness of the marriage of my daughter. The minister has been sent for, and will arrive in a few minutes."

"A few minutes! Know you not what may happen in a few minutes? I saw him myself, a few minutes ago, holding up the head of a poor youth in a barn, who had received a fatal wound in his side. And a few minutes have sufficed to launch the noble boy into eternity! He was whispering a loving message for his mother! Could the Reverend man of God neglect the dying to wait upon the living? Then came Randolph like the rushing of a mighty wind—"

"Where is he, good Charlotte?" asked Alice, throwing aside her veil.

"Pale daughter of the President!" said she, "he was spurring towards the mansion to announce——"

At that moment a discharge of cannon and musketry startled the whole party, for it seemed in fearful proximity. Then the earth was shaken with a deep rumbling sound, as if all the cavalry were approaching.

"Blount!" exclaimed Crook, throwing aside the arm of Lord Slysir which had been thrust within his own. "It is a surprise! The enemy are upon us!"

"Away! Away!" cried Charlotte.

"To the carriage!" said Blount, leading the ladies out, and followed by Senator Langdon. "It is Ruffleton himself, no doubt," he continued, as he hurried them into the carriage.

The next moment Randolph dashed up to the chapel door. "Fly!" said he to the coachman, "to yonder house on the hill. Come, Blount—come, Crook—I have ordered Valiant and Carleton to converge in this direction. We shall check the enemy at this point until the ladies are beyond the reach of danger."

A moment after, all had disappeared, excepting Lord Slysir, who remained within the church, gazing at the place from which Alice and Edith had so suddenly vanished.

CHAPTER LXXIII.

THE MARCH TO RICHMOND.

THE enraged Despot, in contempt of the science of war, and in spite of the appeals of his Generals, who vainly declared that none of the necessary preparations for an advance had been completed, ordered all the cavalry and all the light artillery to follow him in a precipitate attack upon the rear guard of the enemy.

Lord Slysir, left to himself, remained undecided what step to take in such an emergency. In the game of diplomacy, he was ever ready; but in the actual incidents of war, he was, like other great negotiators, uncertain which course to pursue. Whilst he promenaded the nave of the chapel, along which the rays of a summer's sun were brightly streaming, one of the flat stones near the altar slowly rose from the floor. Upon this was inscribed the name of one of the rectors who had been buried a century before, and his Lordship started back involuntarily, as if the sheeted dead were about to come from their graves in his presence. But, when he looked again, he beheld the dusky features of a negro man who had selected that novel locality as a place of concealment for the living.

"Why are you there?" demanded Slysir.

"Pray, massa, don't tell anybody!" said the negro.

"I see how it is. You are a slave. I will not betray you. The Northern people and the British will make a free man of you."

"No, they won't! I'm gwine back to Alabama! I've

had 'nuff of 'em!" said the man, leaping out of the grave, and throwing back the slab with such violence that it was broken to pieces.

"What do you mean? Where are you going?" demanded his Lordship, seeing the negro striding towards the door.

"I'm gwine to massa Crook. But he musn't see me. I'm followin' him. He's my massa. I belong to him. I ran away in de under-ground railroad las year—and got sick ob de Norf. Dey starbed me, and wouldn't give me physic when I was sick—and now dey's got a gulleting dat chops off people's heads! Stan' aside, I say!"

The negro strode past his Lordship without molestation. And the next moment, with the noise of a hurricane, came the cavalry of Ruffleton. A yellow dust enveloped the earth as the host swept past, however, leaving here and there a horse or its rider stricken to the earth by a chance shot from the Federal batteries, now beginning to play on the intruders, and the Protector himself, at length reflecting on the impropriety of his conduct, paused suddenly in his career. He descended from his charger, surrounded by his staff, and rushed into the chapel, as he said, to get a mouthful of pure air, and to wipe the dust from his eyes.

"By Jupiter!" he exclaimed, on beholding Slysir, "here is one capital prize at all events. Your Lordship is my prisoner! If I cannot consign you to a deserter's doom—and we have overtaken and slaughtered a thousand this day—at all events I can prevent any further co-operation with the enemy."

"What does your Highness mean?" demanded his Lordship.

"Are you not a deserter? Answer me that!"

"Deserter? Whom have I deserted?"

"Have you not unceremoniously abandoned *me*, your ally?"

"By no means! I am gratified to find myself rescued from the hands of the enemy by your Highness. I was a prisoner—but now, I hope, I am free."

"You assert, then, that your flight was not a voluntary abandonment of my cause?"

"I do most positively assert it!"

"And that you did not escape with Alice Randolph?"

"Certainly not. She preceded me, and I knew nothing of her flight before my own seizure."

"Then I have made a grave mistake! Maller, sound a recall! Slysir, mount one of my horses—a number of them have lost their riders. Let us get back again before more mischief is done! Where's Col. Snare?"

"He pursued the carriage," said one of the aides.

"Send him word to return! Or they will cage him again where it will not be in my power to release him."

Col. Snare, promoted on the threshold of the prison door in Georgetown, dashed forward at the head of several hundred men, and surrounded the carriage as it ascended the hill pointed out by the President. But Bim was there. And Captain Fink, with his Wild Western Scouts, was likewise within striking distance. A most terrible conflict ensued. Bim on one side and Fink on the other, sprang upon the dragoons like tigers, and in a shorter space of time than it takes to record it, one half the horses of the enemy were galloping away without their riders. But two of the carriage horses being wounded, Alice, exposed to the shower of balls flying in every direction, descended to the ground, and induced the rest to follow. They took refuge in a deep ravine at the roadside without the slightest hindrance from Snare, whose attention was wholly occupied by his assailants. Bim charged at the head of about a hundred mounted Blue Caps, and Fink's men, throwing down their rifles, rushed upon the foe with their tomahawks, uttering horrible yells like wild savages. Snare fought pretty well, but in vain. Fruitless were his desperate efforts to retrieve his past mishaps. The notes of the bugle recalling him from the enterprise fell upon his ear, and he was under the necessity of relinquishing the prize which he supposed at one time had been secured. And it was full time. Five minutes more, and every one of this rash detachment would have been destroyed. When they overtook the Protector, himself in full retreat, Randolph, Blount, Crook, Valiant, and Carleton were launching their concentric thunders upon them.

In the meantime, however, the Generals of the Northern army had marshalled their mighty columns in battle array; and when the Protector, at the head of the cavalry, found shelter under their protection, the signal of battle was given. Randolph, from an eminence, surveyed the imposing attitude of the enemy, and knew it would be impossible to withstand such a multitude of combatants upon that ill-chosen field. Yielding to a necessity, apparent even to Crook, and contenting himself with the severe rebuke administered to the Northern Commander-in-Chief, he gave the order to retire along the line marked out for the retreat days and weeks before.

Save the occasional discharges from the batteries of the rearguard of the Federal army, as the enemy encroached too near upon them, there were no sounds of conflict during the remainder of the day. At night the two armies encamped some five miles apart; and at daylight the pursuit was resumed. And thus the invasion and the retreat continued for many days, during which no serious engagement occurred.

Scarcely a negro slave was seen by the invaders. This class of locomotive property had been previously removed out of the range of the Northern liberators. But the Southern and Federal forces in the field did not seem to increase, for Randolph was garrisoning all the forts, some eighty in number, which had been previously constructed by the labor of the slaves. These fortifications extended in a line five hundred miles in length, and from ten to fifty miles east and west of the track of the invaders. Every commanding position, every point, unassailable by nature, had been designated by the engineers, and were now occupied by the defenders of the soil. These were the depots for the arms, ammunition, and provisions, so that the main army in its retreat would be always accessible to supplies, and never under the necessity of transporting, like the enemy, excessive stores of articles indispensable for their subsistence.

Ruffleton marched directly to Richmond, declaring his purpose to spare the town, provided the bridges were not destroyed, and no resistance made to his entry into the Capital of Virginia. And Randolph evacuated the place without hesitation, followed by most of the inhabitants. The Protector, not yet seriously suffering for food, and not having sustained any losses of magnitude except from desertions, affected great state, and assumed an air of magnanimity in his intercourse with such of the Southern people as ventured in his presence. He issued here a lengthy Proclamation, in which he stated that the torch had been applied to Mount Vernon by a party who had misconstrued their orders. He announced that the Federal system was a failure—that the sovereignty of States and the National sovereignty constituted an absurdity—an *imperium in imperio*, which experience had proved a fallacy, and it was his mission to put a period to it. Like the Romans, we should henceforth be known only as Americans. State lines were to be obliterated. There were to be no Governors except in conquered provinces, and these were to be appointed by the head of the American Empire. The Senate should be composed of an hereditary order of nobles—the descendants of men who had won distinction. The Representatives were to be chosen as provided in the Constitution, and several other provisions in that instrument were to be preserved—its system of land offices—its post offices, etc., etc. And, although it would be necessary to have an Emperor—and for life, *or during good behavior*, still the Government would be a REPUBLIC, as that of Rome, with its Emperors. And, like Republican Rome, America would have its Patrician Order, to be chosen by the Emperor and the Senate; and the title of nobility would be conferred as the reward of existing merit, as well as on the descendants of illustrious men of former generations. *In regard to Slavery, the Proclamation amazed everybody by the distinct declaration that the institution should be perfectly lawful, as in Rome,* EVERYWHERE WITHIN THE LIMITS OF THE EMPIRE; that the agitations of anti-slavery fanatics should end, under pain of the death penalty. That sectional prejudices should cease, because, henceforth, there would be no distinctive sections at all, other than the points of the compass. That the navy should consist of 1,000 ships of war; and the army should number 500,000 men. That the entire Continent, and all the Islands adjacent, must submit to the sway of the American Empire. That religion, of all denominations, should be everywhere tolerated—but polygamy and free-love should be punished, as inconsistent with religion. Therefore the Protector, whose authority had been conferred by the millions of freemen who had changed the Government by the right of Revolution, called upon the people of the

South to rally under his standard, and aid him in the reconstruction of the Government on an enduring basis. The Proclamation asserted that Virginia, particularly, as well as several of the sea-board Southern States, contained many families entitled to the patrician distinction, and it was desirable that they should participate in the important public affairs of the Empire.

This document had been suggested, as a master-stroke, by Mr. Windvane, who affected to have the names of certain prominent Southern politicians, who, if the institution of slavery were conceded by the despot, would be willing to unite with him in overturning the Federal Government. But it turned out, when Ruffleton occupied the Governor's mansion, awaiting a responsive demonstration on the part of the aristocratic families of the Old Dominion, that none but a few old women had been captivated by his dazzling overtures. His Highness then resolved to penetrate still further, and with the utmost vigor. He seized all the flour found in the great mills in the vicinity of Richmond, the British fleet having failed to open a communication with the army by means of James river. The United States ships of war and the well-served batteries at Fortress Monroe, presented an insuperable barrier to the entrance of Hampton Roads. Therefore the Despot determined to pursue the invasion, assured that the British ships would be able to furnish the supplies he stood in need of in Albemarle Sound, North Carolina, and that the navigable portion of the Roanoke would be indefensible against his approaches.

CHAPTER LXXIV.

AMHERST CASTLE.

On one of the spurs of the Blue Ridge Mountain, on either side of which flowed the sparkling waters tributary to the great central river of Virginia, Randolph had caused to be erected one of the most stupendous fortifications on the American Continent. For months, no less than one hundred and fifty thousand negro laborers, under the direction of competent engineers and architects, had been employed in its construction.

It was in the vicinity of this pile, that a coach, escorted by a body of cavalry, entered the highway, whence there was an unobstructed view of the Castle. The party halted involuntarily.

"The Stars and Stripes!" exclaimed Alice, from the open window.

"Three of them," said Edith. "One over the dome in the centre, and one at each end of the noble Castle."

"That, indeed, is very grand!" said Senator Langdon.

"And he kept us all in ignorance of it," continued Alice. "But I observed a mysterious expression on my father's lip when you questioned him, Edith, in relation to the accommodations we would find in the garrison to which he was sending us."

"Ay, and I remember how he evaded my interrogatories. He said a soldier's daughter, and the affianced bride of a hero, would be contented with the fare and shelter which the Commander-in-Chief had provided. And, indeed, we are likely to be! I do believe he had us in view—an asylum in contemplation for us—when this magnificent Castle was built."

"No doubt—no doubt!" said Alice. "And, in truth, it is much better for us to await in a place of security the issue of this terrible campaign, than to follow the camp."

"Oh! I have grown sick of it."

"And I, too, my children!" said the aged Senator. "And I have a presentiment that I shall repose in Amherst Castle until the war be ended."

"Major Bim," said Alice, "why are you so melancholy?"

"Miss Alice," replied Bim, who had been sitting on his charger during the conversation, gazing in profound silence at the almost innumerable embrasures in the Castle walls, and the cannon on the turrets, "when I first saw that mighty work my heart sank within me; for it seemed that Jack Bim's fighting days were ended. But now I recollect hearing President Randolph say this was too important a fortress for an invading army to leave in its rear, and, therefore, I think there is reason to hope the Despot will send out a detachment to reduce us——"

"You *hope* he will do so, Major Bim?" demanded Dr. Love, who came pacing up from the rear on his gentle old brown mare.

"I will not lie, Rev. sir," said Bim, "and therefore I must confess the truth. I really did hope so; and if it was wrong, I pray you forgive me. But my motive was merely to contribute my share in the destruction of the enemy."

"Your motive is ever good," said Alice.

"And, therefore," said the Doctor, "we will forgive him. But what do I see yonder?" he continued, gazing through a spyglass; "a cross on a spire! Gothic windows, and—I believe, stained glass!"

"True," said Senator Langdon; "Randolph informed me there was a chapel. But let us not linger here!"

"On! on!" said both Alice and Edith. And the coachman drove forward without further delay.

Alice and Edith traversed the numerous and magnificent apartments of the Castle in joyful surprise. Everything had been thought of, everything provided, for their comfort and enjoyment, and all this during the incessant civil and military occupations of the President!

There were several regiments of volunteers within the Castle grounds, drilling for the service, and immense stores were daily arriving from the West. But the command of the citadel, and of the regular soldiers, had been assigned by courtesy to Alice. Two hundred of the Blue Caps, under Major Bim, had been detached as an escort.

At the time of the separation of Senator Langdon and the young ladies from the head-quarters of the President, the Federal army was in full retreat for Richmond, and followed steadily by Ruffleton. And since then nothing had been heard from the seat of war, excepting the vague and conflicting rumors of frightened fugitives. But Randolph had assured his daughter that if no unforeseen event occurred to change the plan of the campaign, there would be no great battle for many weeks. Every day the Northern host of invaders experienced serious diminution from desertions, and that was better than the destruction of so many lives on the battle-field. Hence the party, during their journey to the Castle, and after their arrival, were relieved of the many terrible apprehensions usually inseparable from a state of war. During the journey they had been exceedingly cheerful. The fine scenery, and the novelty of many objects and incidents, together with the sense of security, both for themselves and those dear to them retiring before the foe, sufficed, in a measure, to dispel the melancholy forebodings so painfully experienced in advance of the actual invasion. Major Bim, alone, seemed unhappy; and this arose, as we have seen, from the apprehension that he was to be immured within impregnable walls, beyond the reach of the enemy.

For several days the aged Senator and the ladies found sufficient divertisement within the walls of the Castle to prevent their thoughts from recurring unpleasantly to the probable events in the field, while Bim scoured the country for miles eastwardly and southwardly, industriously catching every straggler flying to the mountains. Yet the intelligence from the armies was always conflicting and uncertain. But even such items of news as these, reported at the eve of each day, at length created an anxiety in the breasts of Alice and Edith to receive tidings from those so dear to them, and whom, in their dreams, they now began to behold exposed to frightful dangers, and sometimes the victims of dire calamity.

It was a calm moonlight night. Senator Langdon and the young ladies were seated in one of the capacious balconies projecting from the eastern side of the Castle, and some seventy feet in height from the foundation of the structure. The summer air was dry, but cool and pleasant at that altitude. Within, a mellow light, radiating from a silver lamp, faintly illuminated the ample apartment, from which a few minutes before the sounds of music, under the magic touch of Edith, had issued, and where the Rev. Dr. Love and Major Bim still lingered, discussing the merits and moralities of bloody war. The tranquil scene for a long time seemed to impose a solemn silence on the party gazing into the obscure depths of the surrounding forest. They were mutely served with confections and refreshments by the several negresses that attended, as if they, too, and no doubt they did, partook of the inspiration of the hour.

"Father," said Edith, "can you point in the direction of Richmond?"

"Easily, my child," said the Senator. "It is almost due east from us."

"And how far?"

"Near one hundred miles."

"Oh," said Alice, after a pause, "if one could only with the same certainty point out the locality occupied by my father and his faithful Generals and followers!"

"Only ONE may do that," said the aged minister, abandoning Bim as incorrigible and joining the party: "and He can shield them from every harm."

"I think a military man," said Major Bim, following, "may indicate with some precision the relative positions of the head-quarters of the two armies."

"Then pray give us your opinion, Major Bim," said Edith.

"Do, Major," said Alice. "For instance, tell us where General Blount is at this moment, the condition of his health, the nature of his employment, and any other particulars which you may discover."

"No doubt such information would be particularly interesting to all concerned," said Bim; "but I am no seer, nor even a believer in Yankee spiritualism."

"I give you praise for that, Major Bim," said Dr. Love. "This modern ism of fruitful New England would really make the employments of the existence beyond the grave as frivolous, if not as absurd and sinful, as we behold them in this life. It is, I fear, the result of an excessive credulity, engendered by wicked persons for no good purpose."

"But according to my ideas, as a military man," said Bim, "there can be no difficulty in conjecturing the events since we left the camp to hide ourselves in this Castle. Napoleon could take a map and an almanac, and look at his watch, and foretell the place, the day, and hour, where and when a great battle would occur. Now, I don't pretend to be another Napoleon, but think it almost certain that President Randolph had a day's hard fighting at Richmond. And if he could not prevent the crossing of the British and Tory allies, I have no doubt, after slaughtering about 50,000 of them, he retired to the island, in the James river. That is what Napoleon did near Vienna. Unable to withstand superior numbers at Aspern and Essling, he took possession of the island Lobau, and defended Vienna. It was bloody business, though, and many brave Generals fell. And many of our brave Generals may have fallen ——"

"Which, do you think?" asked Edith; "Valiant, Crook, or ——"

"Which? Valiant is truly brave, and may have fallen. Crook! by George! it would be too bad to lose him! Blount? Never! Don't be alarmed!"

Senator Langdon and Dr. Love could not avoid giving vent to laughter, in which, a moment after, the young ladies joined right heartily, and their tones of merriment rang upon the moonlit scene.

"But what of the President, Major Bim?" said Alice; "you have omitted all mention of him."

"President Randolph?" said Bim, "his fall is altogether out of the question! I believe in crazy Charlotte. She says he will be preserved to regenerate the Union. And I have some faith in Captain Fink's rifle, after seeing him kill Ruffleton's horse a mile off. Well, I got the Captain to swear me an oath before I left the camp that he and his Scouts, or some of them, would never lose sight of the President, day or night, until I returned, or until they returned him safe to me. Therefore he's safe."

"Major Bim," said Alice, rising and placing her fair hand in that of the stalwart officer, "I thank you! Whatever else might be alleged, no one can question your noble fidelity. That quality is paramont to all others!"

"As well as I know my duty, Miss Alice," responded Bim, with an expanding heart, "I am always ready to perform it. In all things where I may be deficient in knowledge, I am willing to be instructed; and, right or wrong, I obey the orders of my superiors."

This speech checked the mirth at his expense, and all had some words of commendation to bestow on the Major.

"But now," said the Major, sighing, in response to the praises of his friends, "I fear my services are ended. Here am I, one hundred miles from the scene of war, and no—— What's that?" he exclaimed, leaning over the balcony and listening.

The clatter of hoofs was heard distinctly in the pebbled valley east of the Castle, where a road had been cut on the margin of the mountain stream.

"It is a horseman," said Alice; "a messenger I hope!"

"Heaven speed him, then," said Edith.

"But why does he come in such a terrible hurry?" remarked Bim, as the sounds approached. "Such a break neck gait as that is very strange. I will go down and see that he is admitted without delay."

The ladies strained their eyes to recognise the courier, that they might be assured of tidings from the army; but as he leaned heavily on the arm of the Major, and walked in the shadow of the gigantic soldier, the suspense was prolonged until the many flights of stairs which separated the balcony from the pavement could be traversed. At length, almost borne along by Bim, the ladies beheld the familiar face of Wiry Willy by the light of the silver lamp within the spacious apartment. Thither they ran to meet him. He was pale and haggard, and almost speechless from excessive fatigue and loss of rest.

"Let these speak for me," said he, placing on the table beside the lamp a number of letters, and then sinking into a chair.

"Some wine!" cried Alice to a slave. "Before I break the seal of the letter from my father, I vow to witness the resuscitation of his faithful friend and messenger."

"And you!" cried Edith to another obedient negress, "bring water and napkins! Willy, cool your parched lips, lave the dust from your eyes, and bathe your temples!"

In a brief time Willy seemed restored, and declined further ministrations from the fair hands of the young ladies.

"Huzza!" cried Bim, springing from his chair. Then sitting down, he indulged in such involuntary exclamations as these: "I like that! By George! let 'em come!" He rose a second time, and was about to hasten away, when a gesture from Willy arrested him.

"Major," said he, "I have later intelligence than is to be found in any of the letters. Do you not observe the date? I was taken on the road and detained several days."

"Hey! you were? On the road? Then they are coming now?"

"Close at hand!" responded Willy in a whisper. "But wait until Miss Alice finishes reading the President's letter."

CHAPTER LXXV.

AN EXCHANGE.

THE occupation of Richmond by Ruffleton, and the defeat of the British fleet in an attempt to enter Hampton Roads occurred on the same day; and immediately upon the reception of intelligence of the disaster, Ruffleton sent Virus, his negotiator, to the head-quarters of Randolph.

"Well, sir," said the President, when Virus entered his tent, "what are Ruffleton's demands?"

"Unconditional submission, of course," said General Crook.

"No," said Virus; "he *demands* nothing. He merely proposes an exchange."

"An exchange," continued the President. "What prisoners have you, excepting a few superannuated negroes, abandoned by their masters? And the owners of these poor creatures, it ought to be known the world over, were natives of the North. Ah, Virus, the most unmerciful slave-drivers in the South were once anti-slavery Yankees."

"That is true, sir!" said Virus, "and all such prisoners are made exceptions by his Highness. They are guillotined immediately."

"And yet your Highness proposes in his Proclamation to legalize slavery everywhere!"

"Therefore he punishes the inhuman masters who abandon the aged slaves to their fate."

"Pray give my compliments to General Ruffleton," said General Crook, "and say I have slightly modified my opinion of his character. He is not such a villain as I supposed him to be!"

"But what does he propose?" asked the President.

"He has taken possession of the two detached eastern counties of Virginia, Accomac and Northampton——"

"Ay," said Crook, "he holds the Oyster Fundum, but I doubt whether his men are expert at dredging."

"Well, what does he propose to do with Accomac and Northampton?" continued Randolph.

"To exchange them for Admiral Bang."

"For Admiral Bang! What a novelty! Did the counties make any resistance?"

"Every creek had its battery. We lost two thousand men!"

"But surely you have not made prisoners of the entire population?"

"No—but there is a question if the slaves be not a fair prize. If the project of his Highness to legalize slavery be carried into effect, the slaves of the eastern shore will bring a large sum of money."

"But," said Randolph, smiling, "in the meantime they will consume a vast quantity of provisions. At this season it will not do to eat the oysters."

"They have crabs and clams, your Excellency," said Crook, archly. "But here comes Blount, and I hope he will second the motion to exchange the Admiral for negroes."

And Blount did advocate the measure. Indeed, Randolph agreed to the proposition with cheerfulness, and the arrangement was consummated without delay.

"And now," said Crook, "I have an exchange to propose."

"Pray proceed," said Virus.

"Oh, you must understand that Lord Slysir is to be a principal in the negotiation. It is for an exchange of breeches."

"Pardon me, General," said Virus gravely, "but really I do not comprehend you. I am ignorant of the motive for this levity, and am wholly uninformed of the fact to which you allude."

"The motive of the levity," said Crook, "is to manifest our buoyant spirits under the calamity of an invasion, and to show you that we are not likely to despair. But as to the fact—I see how it is. His Lordship has endeavored to suppress the affair. I'll tell you all about it." He did so and then proceeded thus: "Now, Virus, you will much oblige me, when you return, by gazing steadily a moment at his Lordship's breeches, and then inquiring who's his tailor. If you don't divulge the secret to your people, I will send spies to whisper that Lord Slysir conquers both in the field and in the boudoir in my breeches."

"His Lordship," said Virus, "will no doubt be very much annoyed. But, nevertheless, I may as well inform you that he has not yet reached Richmond. Upon arriving at ——, his Lordship received certain information which induced him to pause in his travels."

"By George, Blount," said Crook, in a whisper, "it was at —— that the ladies left us! Can you put that and that together?"

Blount merely smiled, but made no remark, and Virus, having accomplished the object of his mission, embraced the opportunity to return to the head-quarters at Richmond.

"Gentlemen," said Randolph, who had been for some time perusing a report from Captain Fink of the Scouts, that had been despatched by a special messenger, "here is information of some importance. At ——, it appears, some 10,000 men, under General Maller, were detached, at the special instance of Lord Slysir, for the reduction of our Castle in Amherst."

"The deuce!" exclaimed Crook. "General," he continued, turning to Blount, "you are deeply interested in that movement. By George, the fat Lord, and in my breeches, too, has thrust himself between us and the ladies!"

"I own that I am deeply interested in this movement, General. Amherst Castle is an extremely important place. If it should fall into the hands of the enemy——"

"That is not probable," said Randolph. "The place is safe with 1000 men against 10,000. But Bim's Caps are the only disciplined troops there at present; however, there will soon be a division under Major General Toler. I think the Castle is safe. Still, the garrison must have warning of the menaced blow. Maller will employ every artifice for its reduction. Send for Wiry Willy."

A messenger brought in Willy, who readily undertook to perform the journey, not doubting his ability to notify the inmates of the Castle of the approaching danger in advance of the detachment's arrival before the walls.

CHAPTER LXXVI.

ARRIVAL OF THE ENEMY.

"ALAS!" exclaimed Senator Langdon, when he had completed the perusal of his letter, "we cannot escape the alarms and cruelties of war, fly whithersoever we will! And yet the brave Major Bim can give vent only to joyous exclamations."

"You look only at the alarms and cruelties of war, sir," said Bim; "while I shut my eyes to everything but its romantic adventures and glory. That's the difference between us. Miss Alice, I await your directions."

"Major Bim, you know I can but repeat the desires of my father. He says not less than 10,000 men, infantry, cavalry, and artillery, are marching against this Castle, and that messengers should be sent into Randolph, and the other counties beyond the mountains, where General Toler is organizing an army. The two or three regiments of militia now here, undisciplined as they are, may not be capable of withstanding so large a besieging force."

"Then we are to be besieged!" said Dr. Love.

"Until Major General Toler arrives," said Edith; "when that gifted and indomitable officer will doubtless put the enemy to flight. General Blount thinks we are in no danger. He says we are provisioned for 30,000 men a whole year."

"And father says it is a knowledge of that fact, in part," said Alice, "which has induced the enemy to march in this direction. They would fain capture our stores for their own consumption, as well as destroy a strong fort menacing their line of retreat. Retreat is the word he uses, and he never uses a superfluous word. Go, Major Bim, and send your fleetest couriers over the mountains to General Toler!"

Bim withdrew to execute the order, and to see that the men in garrison were properly posted and prepared to repel any sudden assault.

The next day being Sunday, there was a large congregation in the chapel. Dr. Love had once been the rector of the church in that neighborhood, and was highly reverenced by all the people in the vicinity. The venerable priest preached an impressive sermon, applicable to the condition of the country, demonstrating both the necessity of obedience to God, and submission to rulers exercising a rightful authority.

But the congregation had no sooner been dismissed than the people were thrown into great consternation by the arrival of several countrymen from the East, announcing the fearful proximity of General Maller's army. The visitors at the chapel, even the female portion of the congregation, departed immediately for their homes, notwithstanding Alice's pressing invitation for them to remain at the Castle, to remove their remaining personal effects beyond the mountains.

Major Bim made every preparation for defence, and Alice, accompanied by Dr. Love and Edith, exhorted the soldiers to stand up bravely in defence of the Castle.

In the dusk of evening, the little party again assembled on the high balcony, with their faces towards the East, the direction whence the arrival of the foe was momentarily expected. And, when the stars began to appear, a thousand camp-fires became visible a few miles distant in the valley.

"There they are at last!" exclaimed Alice, the first to discover the fires.

"And here are we ready for them!" said Major Bim.

"For my part," said Senator Langdon, "I should be well satisfied if they would keep at that distance. Still, Major Bim, I would not have you infer that I entertain any doubts of your disposition, and perhaps ability, to repel any attempts to storm the Castle."

"And, man of peace as I am," said Dr. Love, "I have more faith in God to defend the right, than in the strength of walls or the valor of the soldiery."

"The walls," said Bim, "around the grounds may possibly be battered down, or surmounted with ladders. And, indeed, if the attack is made before we receive succor from the West, we shall not have men enough to defend them. But let the enemy once get on this side of them, and ther you'll see them slaughtered by the thousand. The Castle walls are fifteen feet thick, and there are fifty guns pointed from each of the four sides, and loopholes for five thousand muskets. Believe me, ladies, we are secure in this Castle."

"But, Major Bim," said Edith, "cannot they assail us with their cannon from a distance?"

"Not easily. President Randolph, or whoever selected this site for a Castle, must have considered that. Our guns command every eminence within cannon shot, and no doubt General Maller must have been aware of that fact, or else he would not have encamped down in the valley in full view of us. He must intend to besiege us in the regular way; and a tedious process it is. I have just been reading an account of the siege of Sebastopol——"

"But, Major," said Alice, interrupting him, "that city was stormed and taken!"

"True; but recollect how long it held out! And how many assailants were slain! If this siege should only be as famous——"

"Bless my life, Major!" said Dr. Love, "I hope you do not anticipate anything of the sort!"

"In war, Dr. Love," said Major Bim, "it is hard to know what to anticipate. But of one thing I am certain. The defenders of this Castle will prove themselves as brave as the Russians did at Sebastopol. They may not be commanded by officers of equal skill; and neither may the enemy possess the same talents and experience as the French and English; indeed, I doubt whether the nigger-worshippers are equal to the Turks."

As the Major ceased speaking, a bugle was heard beyond the walls, sounding a parley; and Bim, leaning over the balustrade of the balcony, directed a Lieutenant to ascertain the nature of the summons. The officer soon returned with the information that one of the aides of General Maller demanded a conference.

"According to the rules of war," said Bim, "flags of truce, no matter who bear them, are always respected. Conduct the officer hither," he continued, addressing his subordinate, "but see that he be blindfolded."

The officer from the enemy's camp was led to the Castle, and appeared before the little party in the great saloon, then illuminated with many lamps.

"Unbind his eyes," said Bim.

"Monsieur Cuté!" exclaimed both Alice and Edith, upon recognising one of the Secretaries of Lord Slysir.

"I am very happy, ladies," said Cuté, bowing and affecting the fashionable foreign accent then so much in vogue by tufthunters, "to find myself in the presence of fair ladies, who are not altogether strangers to me."

"It would be strange, indeed, sir," said Alice, "if I were not to recognise one who has so often been the guest of my father in the Executive Mansion, now converted into a palace for the convenience of his enemy. But I had not been prepared to learn that the Secretary of the British Legation had embarked in the service of a traitor to my country!"

"Pardon me, Miss Alice," said Cuté, "but your inference is not strictly correct in regard to my position. I am still loyal to my Government, which is in alliance with the *de facto* head of the American Government. Although I have the honor of acting, on the present occasion, as an aide-de-camp of General Maller, I am still in the service and pay of my own Government."

"The explanation, sir, is quite sufficient," said Alice. "And now pray, what proposals do you bring from General Maller?"

"My message, Miss Alice," said Cuté, "is for the commander of the garrison and the Governor of the Castle; and I would not pain your ears, if it be avoidable, by announcing the purport of the General's demand."

"I am the commander of the garrison," said Bim; "and Miss Alice is the Governess——"

"*Governor*, Major Bim!" said Edith, smiling.

"Fear not to pain my ears, sir," said Alice; "they are quite familiar with unpleasant sounds, as my eyes are with frightful spectacles, since they beheld the destruction of Mount Vernon."

"Would to heaven that deed had never been done!" said Cuté. "But I have to deal with the business in hand; and I must say that it is not exactly a proposal I am charged to deliver, but rather a demand. General Maller demands the surrender of this Castle and fortress. He does this with a full knowledge, not only of his own irresistible means of capture, but of the weakness of the garrison, and of the impossibility of succor coming to its relief. You seem incredulous, and I am authorized to be more explicit. In the first place, then, the General is empowered to order, if necessary, men from the stream pouring into the country from the North, to his assistance. In the second place, he is credibly informed that Major-General Toler will have abundant employment in withstanding the growth and spread of the South-western insurrection."

"Insurrection! What insurrection?" demanded Senator Langdon.

"Oh, I see you are not aware of the great rising in the South-west, under General Fell."

"No. Are you, sir?"

"I am. We have means of intelligence of which you can have no knowledge. We have some of his proclamations in our camp. He is arming the slaves; and he says 250,000 negro soldiers, added to the white forces of the South, would have prevented the enemy from crossing the Susquehanna river. He is backed by the white population in the States alluded to, and is now marching in this direction."

"That is rebellion!" said Alice.

"It is infernal treason!" said Bim.

"No matter what it is," said Alice. "But say to General Maller that this Castle will never be surrendered to him. If he can storm it and overpower its defenders, he must use his pleasure; but until then I will use mine. Bear him our defiance; and say the stars and stripes shall float over the dome of Amherst Castle."

"Bravo!" exclaimed Dr. Love.

"It is the only answer," said Senator Langdon, "that could be returned by the daughter of the President."

"Or the daughter of a Senator of the United States!" said Edith, proudly.

"And God will prosper the parents who have such patriotic daughters!" said Dr. Love.

"That matter being disposed of," said Cuté, "I have next a request to make on behalf of Lord Slysir."

"A *request!*" iterated Alice.

"And from Lord Slysir!" ejaculated Edith.

"His Lordship," said Cuté, "has not been accustomed to the exposure of camps, and he is now suffering with ague and fever."

"Give him calomel!" said Alice.

"Quinine!" said Edith.

"Brandy!" said Major Bim.

"Oh, he has prescriptions enough from the surgeons," said Cuté. "But his complaint is against his quarters. The farm-house in the valley where he lies is damp, and there is a miasma from a pond—"

"No matter!" said Alice. "What is his request?"

"He begs to have lodgings in the Castle."

"Lodgings in the Castle!" said Alice.

"And would he not have boarding and washing also?" asked Edith.

"Upon my word, ladies," said Cuté, "I am unable to answer. I can only repeat his Lordship's language—that diplomatists are non-combatants, and that he throws himself on your mercy."

"Here is Wiry Willy," said Alice, "entering just in time to answer the question I was about to ask. Willy, was his Lordship very pale when you took leave of him a few days ago?"

"French leave!" said Cuté, aside.

"Pale? His face was as red as the sunny side of a Brandywine apple in October," said Willy.

"It is red when the fever is on," said Cuté. "But if I am to be the bearer of a denial, Miss Alice, in what language shall it be couched?"

"Say to his Lordship," responded Alice, after a pause, with averted face, "that we hold the request under consideration, and that it is not yet either granted or denied."

"And say to him also," added Edith, "that we have been enjoined in a communication from the brave General Crook, in any negotiations that may be conducted with the Envoy of her Britannic Majesty, to stipulate for the restitution of a certain article of property claimed by the said General as being exclusively his own, and not subject to legal detention or contraband—"

"Pray, lady," said Cuté, who had no knowledge of the matter alluded to, "be more explicit."

"Indeed I cannot be more explicit, sir," said Edith; "but doubtless his Lordship will comprehend it sufficiently."

"Oh, tell him all," said Alice, "else Lord Slysir will suppress the whole transaction."

"At all events," continued Edith, "if his Lordship persists in the negotiation for a diplomatic residence in the Castle, he must be prepared to make the surrender demanded by General Crook. It is our ultimatum. Major Bim, no doubt,. sir, will explain more fully the nature of the article—"

"Oh, the breeches?" said Bim, whose attention a moment before had been attracted by the challenges of the sentinel without.

"The breeches?" repeated Cuté, turning to the Major, while the ladies repaired to the balcony.

Bim, while conducting Cuté to the gate of the castle wall, made known everything concerning the capture and adventures of Lord Slysir.

CHAPTER LXXVII.

DESERTIONS TO RANDOLPH.

The Commander-in-chief of the Northern army, upon resuming his march from Richmond, strove in vain to bring Randolph to a decisive battle. The President's course had been taken after deliberate consideration. Futile then were the repeated stratagems of Ruffleton to precipitate a general engagement; and equally unsuccessful were the persuasions and remonstrances of many of the President's Southern friends. He knew that the preponderating physical force of the Despot must inevitably be diminished as he ventured farther into the country, and that he could, at the proper moment, concentrate all the patriotism and chivalry of the slave States against the invader. He went still further, and for every thousand men that joined his standard, he detached fifteen hundred from it, and stationed them in the garrisons on the right and left of the invaders, to be in readiness to fall upon their flanks, or to intercept their communications.

Thus for days and weeks Randolph retired and Ruffleton pursued. The former presented no serious obstacle to the passage of the Roanoke, or Cape Fear river, but fell back into South Carolina, much to the chagrin and disgust of the large planters, who were under the necessity of removing their dense population of slaves beyond the Catawba, and to witness, unnecessarily, as they believed or asserted, the destruction of the growing crop. But Randolph persisted in his plan, and Blount concurred in it heartily. Nevertheless there were dissensions in the camp as well as out of it, among divers ambitious political leaders; and the discontented chiefs in several States conspired together for the overthrow of the President. This conspiracy obtained consistency when it was ascertained that General Fell, the rival and competitor of Randolph for the Presidency, had levied an army in the valley of the Mississippi, consisting mostly of slaves, and was then approaching the Atlantic seaboard by way of Tennessee and Virginia.

Nevertheless Randolph remained steadfast in his plan of conducting the campaign. He sent couriers to Major-General Toler to oppose the passage of Fell across the mountains, and to render what aid he could to the beleaguered castle commanded by his daughter. But in the midst of these complications the President began to reap the fruits for which he had been laboring so long and so consistently. The seventh regiment from New York, the *élite* of Ruffleton's army, embraced the first opportunity, which occurred on the Pee Dee—for Ruffleton had been fearful of such an event—to go over in a body to the Federal army, with hearty huzzas for the Union. And Col. D—— was followed by twenty other Colonels, at the head of their respective regiments, bearing the National Flag, which had hitherto been concealed in their drums. The President embraced them all, and welcomed them as patriots, loyal to the Federal Government—and with whom he had been in secret correspondence for several weeks.

Even this accession to the Federal army gave rise to a new outburst on the part of Randolph's Southern enemies; and they made many credulous people believe that the President himself was in league with the Northern fanatics for the subjugation of the Slave States. They published depreciatory articles in the newspapers, asserting that the reason why Randolph did not fight the Despot, was because he intended to enlist his followers. And they insinuated that the seeming desertion of the Northern regiments was merely a preliminary to a more extensive union, for the purpose of abolishing slavery. And as Ruffleton, in one of his Proclamations, had offered to legalize slavery everywhere, he ought to be regarded as less an enemy to the South than the false and traitorous Southerner who had availed himself of the Federal sword and purse to destroy his native country.

Still Randolph remained unmoved. The approbation of his own conscience, the concurrence of his own head and heart, sustained him in the midst of the thickening shafts of calumny. And no other man could have risen above the cloud which enveloped the Federal cause. A return of the army exhibited the fact, that although there had been accessions to the ranks on southern ground, amounting in all to 250,000 men, yet, on the Pee Dee, the effective force in the field, retiring before the invaders, numbered 50,000 less than it did on the day that Washington City was abandoned. Moreover, Delaware, Maryland, Virginia (the eastern portion), half of North and South Carolina, with all their capitals and principal cities, had fallen into the hands of the enemy—and yet no blow had been struck, no battle had been fought, since the slight stand made on the banks of the Potomac.

But Randolph was aware of other facts not known to his Southern enemies. He knew that at least two-fifths of Ruffleton's army were on the sick list, and that the daily mortality was making terrible inroads upon his strength. Bilious fever, and the ague, were incapacitating the enemy in a greater ratio than the arrival of recruits from the North; so that if the retreating army was daily diminished by detachments sent off to healthy positions, the invaders were decimated by the departure of victims never to return to the theatre of mortal strife.

And, here, on the Pee Dee, Ruffleton paused in his career of invasion. Randolph, advised of the enemy's purpose to advance no further, sent General Carbon with a flag to Ruffleton, demanding an unconditional surrender. This, of course, was declined; and the long wished-for signal for battle was given.

Pale and debilitated by disease engendered in the miasmatic swamps through which they had been enticed by Randolph, and in a climate to which none of them, and particularly the English, had been accustomed, the Northern invaders were not prepared for the furious onset made by those whom they had so recently been chasing from river to river, and across so many plains, without encountering serious opposition. The battle raged furiously for several hours; when General Crook galloped through the dust and smoke up to Randolph, waving his hat, and announced that the enemy had given way at all points, and the victory was complete. Blount arrived soon after, and confirmed the good tidings. Then messengers came spurring from Valiant and Carlton.

"No!" said Randolph, on perusing the brief notes handed him in pencil-mark, "they are our fellow citizens. Keep back our cavalry. The war is over. Further effusion of blood would only be a national calamity. Arrest the leaders, and punish them according to law, but spare their followers. Gentlemen," he continued, as many of his principal officers rode up and surrounded him, "you have stood by me, and by the Constitution of our country, through evil report. None of you have abandoned me when I retired before the invaders, and when the almost universal cry was for battle. Now, that the battle has been fought and won, your fidelity is to be tested on the field of victory. With many it is harder to withstand prosperity than adversity. But I must announce to you that it is not my purpose to slay the Northern people who have invaded the territory of their Southern brethren. It was never my purpose to do so, and hence I have avoided as much as possible sanguinary engagements. Disease is mowing doing the ranks of Ruffleton's victims with sufficient rapidity. All we have to do is to confine them in as narrow limits as possible until they leave the country. This will be triumph enough for the Chief Magistrate of the Union."

"Sir," said Blount—the first to speak—"I am with you still. If the Union is to endure, no good could be accomplished by a sanguinary policy. By the frightful slaughter we might inflict, we should only exasperate the people of the opposite section, and enlist the sympathies of the world in their behalf."

"I must acknowledge I am very bloodthirsty," said Crook; "but, at the same time, I must own that the judgment of my superiors has always been superior to my own.

Randolph, I am with you to the end—and to the bitter end, if it must be so, against your old enemy, General Fell! I learn he has all my niggers with him and none of his own!"

This speech was followed by applause, and some merriment.

"I thank you, gentlemen," said Randolph. "And although we shall certainly have a reflux of the tide of invasion, from this point, and although it may be said from this moment there is a virtual termination of the war, we must expect strifes, executions, and, perhaps, bloody battles before the majesty of the law can be fully vindicated. The time has not yet expired named in my proclamation for the submission of the misguided rebels in arms against the Government. Those who lay down their arms must have mercy and assistance; while those who persist in their hostility must be tried and punished. For the leaders there is no pardon; and knowing this, they will make desperate efforts to prolong the civil dissensions. What General Fell may do, I have no means of determining. But he is acting quite as much in defiance of the authority of the United States as Ruffleton has been doing. And if it should be his purpose to subvert the Federal Government, he may possibly form a junction with the rebels, and turn his arms against the South, for which he has professed so much loyalty!"

"If so," said General Crook, "the South will be against him! And I should like to aim the first blow at the infernal traitor!"

"The first blow," said General Blount, "will be dealt by General Toler."

"Yes, sir," said Randolph, "for he will have several hundred miles the start of us. And the danger is that Toler will not have a sufficient force to withstand this motley army, numbering five or six to one. If Fell should succeed in taking Amherst Castle, in conjunction with Maller, and then unite with Ruffleton——"

"Can such a thing be possible?" exclaimed Crook, who had, until recently, been an admirer and partisan of Fell.

"General," said Randolph, "I have information that Windvane has been authorized, on the part of Ruffleton and Lord Slysir, to make certain propositions to Fell, which have been favorably entertained."

"Then —— him, say I!" was Crook's response.

"If this treasonable union be consummated," continued Randolph, "and a Revolution be proclaimed on the basis of a recognition of slavery everywhere, with the State lines obliterated, and the establishment of a consolidated empire, then the war will recommence in earnest. But the scene of its horrors will be shifted, and the despot will experience the bitterness of rebellion among his first advocates and followers. The North will rise up against him as the South has done, and then we must all make common cause with the North! And, you see, my friends, why it is I would spare the lives of the poor deluded creatures now flying from this field of victory."

"It is consummate wisdom and patriotic duty," said Blount. "But what becomes of Fell's black soldiers, when it is understood that negro slavery is to prevail everywhere?"

"We shall send them back to their masters," said Randolph.

"I am with you there, too, Randolph," said Crook, "and I shall claim my share of them. But who comes here?"

It was Virus, with a flag of truce. Orders had been issued to stop the pursuit.

"Well, Virus," said Randolph, "it has been some days since we had the pleasure of seeing you. Then you offered peace, with the Roanoke the dividing line between the North and the South. Is it now the Pee Dee?"

"I am not charged to offer peace, your Excellency," said Virus, with much gravity of countenance. "But I may say I would to God the war were ended!"

"Amen!" said the President. "But let us hear what you have to propose."

"I come merely to solicit a suspension of hostilities until we can bury the dead."

"Granted," said the President, "provided you agree to retrace your steps in the track of desolation you have made through the country."

"Perhaps I do not fully comprehend your Excellency," said Virus.

"I will be explicit. Your loss in this battle has not been very great, and more have fallen during the last month from disease than by the sword. The suspension is not for the purpose you name; for Ruffleton never stops to bury the dead. But he would 'steal a march' on us. His purpose is to retreat beyond the reach of our cavalry, if possible; but it is not possible. Say to him, however, whether he goes by day or by night, if his columns be confined within the limits I have named, I will not be the first to strike the next blow."

"I will faithfully report what your Excellency has charged me with," said Virus; "but I am quite sure his Highness the Protector has no purpose of retiring far from the scene of his last conflict. His army is suffering somewhat, however, with the enervating disease of ague and fever; and after a temporary cessation of marching, to restore the sick to health, and to incorporate his ample recruits and allies in the Grand Army, I know it is his intention to resume operations."

"No doubt you think so, Virus," said Randolph, smiling; "but it is probable the slaves will be quite as willing to live with their old masters as to die for their new ones."

Virus stared in astonishment, for he comprehended the significance of the allusion. But not venturing to reply, he returned to his principal, who readily agreed to the terms dictated by Randolph.

CHAPTER LXXVIII.

NOCTURNAL EXPEDITION.

During the fortnight which succeeded the arrival of General Maller before the Castle, several unsuccessful attempts to take it had been made. Breaches had been effected in the outer walls in several places, and the enemy had twice rushed in and filled the area in the centre of which the Castle was situated; but they had not been able to make any serious lodgment in the immense structure itself. They were driven out on these occasions by a destructive fire of grape and musketry, and were forced to return, foiled and bleeding, to their own camp.

It was night, clear and silent, but dark, for the moon had not risen. The two young ladies, the aged Senator, Dr. Love, and Major Bim, were seated on the eastern balcony. Though exposed to the aim of the cannoniers without, hitherto it had been observed that not one ball had struck that portion of the Castle where Cuté had been introduced into the presence of Alice. The exemption of that location from the missiles of the enemy, was owing to the interposition of Lord Slysir; and that fact had been made known by subsequent messengers from the hostile camp, who came with flags to adjust the terms of an exchange of prisoners taken by either party in the skirmishes which daily ensued. And it was quite obvious to Maller that nothing more than the destruction of furniture could have resulted from firing in that direction; for the balcony would have been instantly abandoned.

While gazing at the distant camp-fires with various emotions, for they were uncertain of the events transpiring at a distance, the party were startled by a full, manly voice beneath, in the Castle yard.

"Colonel Bim! Colonel Bim!" was repeated several times.

"He must be a stranger," said Bim; "and yet it seems like a familiar voice to me. But I have never heard of *Colonel* Bim, although I hope some day to make his acquaintance. What the deuce does he mean? And what is he doing there? How did he *get* there without being seen by the sentinels? I will go and unravel the mystery."

He descended the winding stairway hastily, and soon emerged in the yard before the stranger.

"Who are you?" he demanded, confronting the visitor, who was quite as tall as himself.

"You are Colonel Bim himself! How are you?"

"I am *not* Col. Bim!" said Bim, hesitating to take the hand held out. "But who the d—l are you?"

"I'm Major Fink."

"*Major* Fink? I don't know him. I used to be acquainted with one *Captain* Fink, and I also knew one Major Bim. Yes!" he continued; "it must be so! I understand now! We've been promoted. Give me your hand, Major!" A mighty shake ensued, for they were both giants in stature and strength.

"I'm the bearer of tidings from the President," said Fink.

"Then come with me, Major," said Bim, leading him by the arm. "But how the d—l did you pass the sentinels?" asked Bim, as they proceeded up the stairway.

"How, Colonel? Do *you* ask *me* that question? Why, I have just passed through the enemy's camp, and a more disorderly one I never beheld. I could put them to rout with half their number of men."

"I forgot your western skill, Major," said Bim; "but," he added, despondently, "we have not one fourth their number of men."

"Where's General Toler?"

"He's some fifty miles off yet; but he is hard pressed by General Fell and his negroes in the Shenandoah valley. Here we are," he continued, as they entered the large illuminated apartment, where they were met by the whole party, who had heard the words "from the President," and were impatient to receive their letters. "Ladies and gentlemen," said Bim, "permit me to introduce Major Fink."

Alice and Edith and the rest surrounded the Major with alacrity, regardless of the formal introduction; and after brief but hearty salutations, almost seized the sealed packets the faithful messenger produced. During the silence that ensued, the brave Scout, who had been really half famished, helped himself to the cold beef, and bread and wine he happened to espy on a side table.

"I have the great pleasure," said Alice to Bim, "of delivering the Colonel's commission. Here it is!" And she drew it forth from its envelope, and placed it in the hands of the delighted officer.

"I thank you—I thank him!" said Bim, with moistened eyes; "but there is one thing I must regret. There has been a great battle, and I had no hand in it!"

"A great victory!" said the aged Senator, lifting his eyes from his letter.

"And almost a bloodless one!" added Dr. Love, having perused his own letter from the President. "I thank heaven for it!"

"My father writes from the field of victory," said Alice.

"And does not doubt that the war is near its termination?"

"Yes," said Fink, joining them after his lunch, "they have taken the back-track, as we used to say in the backwoods, and it will soon be a run."

"And," said Edith, blushing and smiling, "our friends will probably be here at the expiration of ten days."

"Be here?" asked Alice. "The armies——"

"No; I don't mean that; but—but General——"

"Ah! I understand! The chapel! Yes; it must be so! God wills it!"

The little party were made very happy by the news from the Federal camp, and by the turn affairs had taken; and the only drawback to their felicity was the dark cloud in the West, directed by General Fell, who proclaimed everywhere his defiance of the Federal authority.

"It might be surprised!" said Colonel Bim, after a brief conversation in a low tone with Major Fink.

"What might be surprised?" asked Alice.

"The country house to the left of the enemy's encampment. Major Fink says he peeped in as he came——"

"Did you venture so near the enemy, Major?" asked Alice, in surprise.

"Oh, it was no venturing at all," said Fink. "I was merely acting the Scout, which is my second nature, and ran no risk at all. I even got near enough to see General Maller in his nightcap going to bed. But in the farm-house they were playing cards, and the sentinels were asleep."

"Playing cards? Who were they?"

"They were very high officers, I think, from the number of champagne bottles I saw on the table."

"And these officers, you think," continued Alice, "might be captured without risk to the assailants? If so, you have my permission to make the attempt. And they can resume their whist here, by way of divertisement."

"Away, then," said Bim, rising.

"And I'll guarantee that not a drop of blood shall be shed, if I may lead the expedition. And I want only twelve men," said Fink.

"You shall lead," said Bim, "and select your men, so I be one of them. I'll put off my officer's trappings, and go incog."

They set out immediately.

CHAPTER LXXIX.

GENERALS TOLER AND FELL.

General Fell had reached the head-quarters of the Shenandoah with his motley followers, and seemed to threaten Amherst Castle, for he was incessantly breathing vengeance against President Randolph, whom he charged with betraying the cause of the South. But General Toler had succeeded in interposing his comparatively diminutive army between Fell and Maller, for he did not doubt that the ambitious leader, notwithstanding his charges against the Southern President, meditated a junction with the enemy.

He granted the request of Fell, that they should hold a personal conference midway between the armies, attended by an equal number of officers, who were not to be within hearing. A small hut in the centre of a large field was the place selected for the meeting, and they proceeded thither on the morning of the day of Major Fink's arrival at the Castle.

"General Fell," said Toler, as the former approached, "before we clasp hands let us understand whether we are friends or enemies."

"Can I be mistaken?" exclaimed Fell. "General Toler, one of the most enthusiastic champions of Southern Rights, one whose pen and whose voice have been devoted to the cause of his native land, to ask the question whether General Fell is a friend or an enemy!"

"General Toler would hurl back the Northern invader from his native land: can General Fell say as much?"

"He can say," replied the other, quickly, "that he is resolved to hurl destruction on all the enemies of the South. But who is the worst enemy of the South? The one whom she has nurtured and trusted, and to whom she gave power and command, but who, nevertheless, permits her fair fields to be ravaged when he had the means to prevent the invasion; or the great leader of the North who proclaims, at the head of an army numbering nearly three-quarters of a million of men—an irresistible force—that slavery shall be legal everywhere?"

"Alas!" said Toler, "it is as I suspected! Sir, why utter such disingenuous words to me?"

"Disingenuous? Beware, sir!"

"Ay, disingenuous! for do you not assail Randolph because he did not sooner arrest the progress of this Northern Chieftain, who proclaims the universal legality of slavery, and whose interminable columns you admit are irresistible?"

"Irresistible without being opposed by the slaves."

"The slaves! And you would have had Randolph lead the slaves, and that too without the permission of their owners, as you have done, in the presence of an enemy which at first proclaimed their freedom!"

"At first. But now slavery is proclaimed everywhere. And the Federal Government no longer exists."

"Sir, I act under its authority," said Toler.

"Is that your determination?"

"It is."

"Then our conference is at an end. But you little dream of the great triumphs and achievements that would——"

"Dreams! All dreams, General!"

"No, by heaven! A month hence—and——"

"Randolph will again inhabit the Executive Mansion, and the rebellion will be at an end."

"No, sir! An hour hence, and you will think differently."

"Then be it so. I shall do my utmost to avert it. But beware of the announcement among your rabble of slaves, that Ruffleton, instead of setting them free, intends to close all the doors of freedom against them, in the North as well as in the South."

"Who can announce it?"

"Do you not intend to make your negroes unite with the enemy? And will they not learn it then?"

"That is my affair! But will you oppose my junction with Maller?"

"Unquestionably. I obey the orders of the President."

"The President! But are you not aware that I have two *white* men to your one?"

"I am. But I am thrice armed in a just quarrel!"

"Very well!"

And soon after the two Generals were mounted, and galloping away to the heads of their respective armies.

Fell led only his white soldiers against the strong position of Toler, and was defeated. Toler's superior artillery, furnished by the Federal garrisons, more than compensated for his inferiority in numbers; and after a bloody day of desperate conflict, the assailants fell back, and abandoned the field to the brave heroes who stood up in defence of the Constitution, which guaranteed liberty and equality (for white men) in all sections. Nevertheless, apprehending a demonstration in his rear by General Maller, for it had become apparent that Fell was in communication with the enemy against whom he had originally declared his purpose to fight, General Toler deemed it advisable, after burying the dead, to retire towards Amherst Castle.

CHAPTER LXXX.

THE PRISONERS.

"WHAT'S the matter, sentinel?" asked one of the officers, too intent at winning a trick with an ace to lift his eyes from the cards, when Fink and Bim entered the detached farmhouse.

"Nothing," said Bim, "only the honors are against you."

"And I'm a trump!" said Fink, seizing the pistols which lay conveniently beside the players.

"What does this mean?" exclaimed the players, springing to their feet.

"Oh, nothing serious!" said Bim. "Only the ladies have sent you an invitation to come to the Castle."

"The deuce!" exclaimed a Brigadier, gazing round at the muzzles of the menacing pistols.

"You've lost, General," said Fink, "and you must submit. If you resist, it is likely we may be prevented from having your company at the Castle; but you will surely die."

"I see it all!" said Lord Slysir. "There' Bim's face. We submit. He's the Sergeant, gentlemen, I was telling you about."

"No, your Lordship," said Bim, "I'm no Sergeant."

"True! He's a Captain now—promoted for capturing me."

"I'm not a Captain, either, your Lordship," said Bim.

"Oh! Major!"

"No, your Lordship."

"Higher still? A Colonel?"

"Colonel Bim, at your Lordship's service."

"I shouldn't have been surprised if it had been General, in this mutable country," said Slysir, seeing Bim's enjoyment of the enumeration of the steps he had taken. "Very well, then, we have the honor of surrendering to a Colonel."

"No, your Lordship," said Bim, "I'm only a volunteer, and Major Fink is the commander of the expedition."

"That tall white-eyed—"

"Scout," said Fink. "But we have no time for further parley."

"General," said Slysir, addressing the Brigadier (the others were British Captains on the sick list), "we should have won the rubber. You might as well take the money;" and he pointed to some fifty sovereigns lying on the table.

"Excuse me, sir," said Fink, interposing; "but it seems to my *my* partners and *myself* are the winners here."

"How is that, your Lordship?" asked Bim. "Is not the gold fair prize to the captors?"

"You an officer, and ask such a question!" exclaimed the balked Brigadier.

"I asked for information, sir. Take the gold, Major Fink, and when we arrive at the Castle we'll consult the books. Your Lordship must understand that there is a capital military library at the Castle."

"Come!" said Fink. "We have not a moment to lose."

"True, Major!" said Bim. "And his Lordship will excuse any little seeming rudeness in us newly promoted officers—"

"Oh, I hope your hard-trotting horse is dead, Bim!" said his Lordship. "After the great rudeness of being pummelled to a jelly on that infernal beast, we shall be happy to excuse any *little* rudeness on this occasion. But, Colonel Bim, I have a request to make, and I know I can rely on your honor—"

"I hope so, your Lordship," said Bim, somewhat flattered by the appeal.

"Then I entrust to you this packet of inestimable value. I will not attempt to conceal or destroy it; but boldly place it in your hands, relying on your honor as a man and an officer to see that the seals be not broken without my consent, and then only in the presence of President Randolph, and such other witnesses as he may select."

"My Lord," said Bim, in tones of solemn gravity, "I receive the deposit, and you may rely on my honor."

It was a parcel enveloped in paper, carefully wrapped with red tape, and sealed at both ends and in the centre with red wax, bearing the impression of his Lordship's arms.

This ceremony ended, the prisoners were led off without further delay to the Castle.

"Who are you? Halt, I say!" said Bim, as a man crossed his path, and then vanished in the bushes. "Gone! and he will give the alarm! Lead on, Major Fink—it will not do for us to be balked now. Take his Lordship's arm and run. I will keep the others close at your heels. Hey!" he continued, as the same person who had attracted his notice reappeared from the bushes and recrossed the path behind him. "Who the d—l are you? Speak, or I'll send a bullet after you, although I confess I would rather not make a report to any ears but my superior officer's."

"Don't shoot, Sergeant!" said the stranger.

"Sergeant? You're a fool!" said Bim. "But since you ask for mercy, you shall have it. Come out of the bushes, and let me scan your phiz as well as the darkness will permit."

"I'm not an enemy, Sergeant," said the other, gliding to his side.

"You'll make me your enemy if you call me Sergeant again!" said Bim.

"Oh, I forgot! I meant to say Captain Bim."

"Captain! I'm no Captain, either!" said Bim.

"Major, then. I shouldn't be surprised if you—"

"Nor Major, either."

"What then? A General?"

"Not yet. One step more first."

"Colonel Bim!"

"Now you've hit it. But, stranger, what are you?"

"Me? I'm a ship-carpenter by trade."

"Ship-carpenter?"

"Yes. Don't you know me? We were together in the deep ditch, after we lost all our men in the big battle at Bladensburg."

"What! Is this you, Sergeant Punt?"

"I'm not Sergeant Punt now."

"Not Sergeant. Have you been stepping up too, travelling the same road? Captain—Major?"

"No—nothing of the sort. I quit fighting from the day of our falling into the ditch. You know I went to work on the sloop at the Navy Yard. And so I'm now out on a collecting tour, hunting for President Randolph, or some of his men who have his money, to get my wages."

"Now I know all about you," said Bim. "But you can't get at the President, conveniently, just at this time, and I don't know how he's off for money. He's in arrears to me, or rather the country is—but I'll fight, you know, for the love of it."

"And hang me if I'll fight at all," said Punt, "because I don't see any use in it. I don't know who's right and who's wrong, and I'll let everybody alone if they'll let me alone. That's what I told General Maller this very night, when they had me up before him. And I showed him a pass, writ by Mrs. Punt, now in the White House, for me to go where I pleased, and so he discharged me."

"Here we are at the Castle gate, Punt," said Bim, "and you must excuse me, for I'm the chief officer. But you shall see Miss Alice, the President's daughter, and perhaps she'll pay her father's debt."

The Colonel hastened forward, and conducted the prisoners, accompanied by Major Fink, up to the great saloon where the ladies, and Senator Langdon, and Dr. Love, anxiously awaited the result of the expedition.

Lord Slysir stepped forward, and in the most friendly and cordial manner shook hands with his old acquaintances. Then, turning round, he introduced his fellow-prisoners.

"This is Brigadier General Gordon," said he; "this Captain Ponsonby, and this Captain Ashburton, all in Her Majesty's service, all in the line of the Peerage, ladies, and all on the sick list."

"Pray be seated, gentlemen," said Alice.

"Sick gentlemen," said Edith, "should not stand, and above all, should not be exposed to the night air. But I must say," she continued, addressing Slysir, "that the ague and fever have not left their usual marks on your Lordship's face; and I congratulate your Lordship on your speedy recovery."

"True," said Alice; "and I had forgotten that his Lordship's messenger, only the other day, alleged that his Lordship had been made a victim of that cruel disease of our unfortunate climate. But really the color has not all departed from his cheeks."

"Ah, Miss Alice!" said his Lordship, "if you could have seen me when the chill was on—"

"Oh, I am quite familiar with the phases of the terrible complaint," said Alice. "And I am aware of the change it makes in one's complexion when the fever succeeds. And, I must say, Colonel Bim—or rather Major Fink—that it was no proof of humanity to make his Lordship a prisoner, and rudely drag him from his couch when the fever was on—"

"I beg your pardon, madam," said Fink, not comprehending the drift—"but as I'm a man of honor and an officer of truth, though a Wild Western Scout, that red-faced man—and for that matter they are all red-faced enough—was sitting at a table and playing cards, and drinking liquor—"

"Hist, Major Fink!" said Bim, in a whisper, "she's only making fun of him."

"That's it, hey?" responded Fink, "then I'll not interfere."

"The color," said his Lordship, "is produced by the doctor's prescription. He advises brandy—and the abominable stuff they call brandy in the country, would make the devil blush!"

"It was hot whisky punch, Miss Alice!" said Bim, in a whisper, "for I drank some."

"So. But, Colonel," continued Alice, "what is it that

you grasp so carefully? A prize of value, or a file of his Lordship's secret instructions?"

"I know not what, Miss Alice," said he; "but his Lordship produced it himself, and received my word that it should be sacredly kept until the President demanded the breaking of the seals. It may be important papers, for what I know, or even diamonds and rubies, and I must say, upon reflection, that I regret it was entrusted to my care."

"Very well, Colonel," said Lord Slysir, rising and receiving the deposit from his hands: "I relieve you of the responsibility. Miss Alice, this packet contains what, if once lost, could never be replaced; and therefore, by your leave, I will entrust it to your keeping, relying wholly on your generosity to oblige me so far as not to break the seals—"

"I certainly will not break them," said she, "without your permission, or the orders of my father."

"Enough! I am content," said his Lordship.

"The packet seems to have been carefully prepared," said Senator Langdon, archly, "as if in anticipation of such an event as has just happened."

"Surely you do not mean to intimate that his Lordship exposed himself in the tempting farm-house for the purpose of being captured!" said Dr. Love, in a low tone.

"That is precisely what I meant," said the aged Senator.

"And now, our prisoners being rested," said Fink, "the next question is, what shall be done with them? Colonel Bim, I think you said there was a secure dungeon under the Castle?"

"Yes, Major, a dark and strong one! But it is a little damp. I went into it yesterday with a candle, and stumbled over some rats—"

"Rats!" said Brigadier Gordon.

"There was a great squeaking among them," continued Bim. "And on stepping down I found the cause of it. A tremendous rattlesnake had got in through the wall, and was swallowing them—"

"A rattlesnake!" said Captain Ponsonby.

"Oh, none of your dungeons, Colonel Bim!" said Lord Slysir. "A dark dungeon, under ground, for officers with the ague and fever!"

"My Lord," said Alice, "I cannot interfere with the

rules of the service. Whatever Colonel Bim and Major Fink may deem their duty, will, no doubt—"

"Heavens!" exclaimed Captain Ashburton, "a dungeon!"

"And is this to be the result of your Lordship's stratagem?" said General Gordon.

"Stratagem!" cried Edith, "what stratagem?"

"I will confess," said Lord Slysir, "that for several days, or rather nights, it was my confident expectation that we would be captured. The fare is infamous in Maller's camp. And now, after this confession, you *will* not, you *cannot*, consign us to a dungeon!"

"We will have your Lordship and companions," said Edith, with all the seriousness she could command, "provided with the best food our poor larder may furnish. You shall have calomel, jalap, quinine, and brandy; and then—"

"Oh, don't mention them!" said Slysir. "I know very well that we shall not be sent to the dungeon—"

"By your leave," said Bim, "that must be as the Commander of the garrison decides. You must not be at liberty, except on parole—"

"There you are right, Colonel," said Slysir; "and we are prepared to accede to the condition. We pledge ourselves not to escape, and to be present whenever and wherever our presence may be required. That being understood, I have to request a private interview with Miss Alice, on a matter of special importance—"

"A private interview!" exclaimed Alice.

"Or, if you desire it, Miss Edith may be present. Permit me to whisper a word in your ear before you refuse my request." Saying this, he did whisper something in the ear of Alice which seemed to interest her greatly.

"I will see you, sir," said she, "at once, and alone. Come with me into the library." And she led the way out, followed by his Lordship.

CHAPTER LXXXI.

STARTLING NEWS.

FLORA SUMMERS was the centre of attraction in the great saloon of the Executive Palace. She was surrounded by many courtiers, and seemed very happy during the absence of the Lord Protector; for hitherto all the bulletins which had been received, announced the uninterrupted progress of the invaders, and the probable subjugation of the country.

Windvane, knowing Flora's influence over the despot, had cultivated her good graces with so much success, that he attained a preponderating influence in the Cabinet. And the effects of this soon became apparent. He had the finest house, and coach, and horses, of any member of the Government; and as for Flora, she was a perfect blaze of jewels, and had, besides, near a million of dollars to her credit in the banks.

It was just when Flora was in the zenith of her glory, and surrounded by many flattering ladies, who, a year before, would have disdained to enter a room polluted by her presence, that Mrs. Punt, glittering with jewels in imitation of her mistress, glided into the saloon and whispered a message in her ear.

"Mr. Windvane wishes to see you immediately," said she.

"Wishes to see me immediately!" said Flora. "Then why don't he come to me?"

"The Cabinet is in session in the Lord Protector's office."

"Very well. I am not a member of the Cabinet."

"But Mr. Virus has come back."

"Ha! Has he letters for me? Has he news?"

"Mr. Windvane says he has; and not good news, either."

"I will see him immediately."

Flora arose, and making the necessary excuses to the company, proceeded with a quick, if not a tottering step, towards the door, still closely attended by Mrs. Punt.

"Punt's gone, madam!" said Mrs. P.

"Never mind, Punt! Where's Windvane?"

"In the green room, madam; and he wishes to see you before you meet with Mr. Virus. But I never expect to set eyes on Punt again. And Mr. Ready says you could have our marriage annulled."

"Nonsense! Why will you annoy me? Leave me. I will go alone."

Mrs. Punt, knowing the imperious will of Flora, paused, and turning aside, hastened away to Ready, to report the response to his sage suggestion. Flora, a moment after, confronted Windvane in the green room.

"What is it, Windvane? Say the very worst at once!" exclaimed Flora, with a flashing eye and contracted brow.

"His Highness," said Windvane, watching eagerly the effect of the announcement, "has been defeated."

"Defeated? Has he escaped death and wounds him self?"

"He was not injured, and his health is good."

"Enough! I can laugh at the rest!"

"But the defeat has arrested his progress in the South."

"So much the better! He will return the sooner. It is an unhealthy country. Witness the faces of all who return. Was he retreating?"

"He was."

"Why this is *good* news, instead of bad!"

"The Cabinet think differently. They do not *say* so; but, between us, they regard this retrograde movement as the beginning of Ruffleton's downfall. They fear henceforth his star will decline, and unless an amicable arrangement can be effected with Randolph, I think some of them will abandon their places."

"With Randolph! Let them go! Better and truer men can be found! But, Windvane, remember Ruffleton's last words——"

"Never fear me! Short shrift for traitors! I have my spies everywhere. But I wished to prepare you for the interview with the Cabinet. They despond; but I exult."

"Exult?"

"Yes. I have conjured up a new enemy against Randolph."

"You mean General Fell. Can he be relied on?"

"He is in the field in full march to join General Maller before Amherst Castle, and to fall upon the enemy's flank."

"Windvane, I thank you for this intelligence! I am now prepared to meet these faint-hearted gentlemen. Let us go to them at once."

Flora, taking the proffered arm of the consummate politician, they proceeded to the council-room, where the several Cabinet ministers were assembled, listening attentively, and with pallid countenances, to the narration of Virus.

"The letters! Virus, the letters!" exclaimed Flora.

"But one, madam," said Virus, "was all he had time to write. Here it is."

Flora, taking the letter, and breaking the seal as she strode rapidly to a distant table, over which a jet of gas was burning, threw herself into a chair, and plunged abstractedly into the contents.

"The Proclamation, Windvane," said one of the most timid members of the Cabinet, "has not proved the master-stroke you anticipated."

"We do not know that yet," said Windvane.

"Not one Southern man or woman of distinction has responded to it," replied the other.

"You are not well informed," said Windvane.

"Virus has just returned from the scene of action."

"Does he say no Southern leader has responded?"

"None has joined the Protector," said Virus.

"But one *will* join him," said Windvane.

"Who?" demanded Virus. "General Fell, I learned before leaving the camp, was marching eastward; but we could not ascertain exactly his purpose; and I know the Protector feared no reliance could be placed on his co-operation in the event of the retreat becoming a rout, which seemed inevitable."

"I have news from General Fell—a letter written with his own hand. He has fought a battle with General Toler and beaten him."

"I hope so," said Virus, evidently in doubt as to the accuracy of the intelligence, and his incredulity seemed shared by the others.

"Gentlemen!" said Flora, coming forward, "I am sorry you seem so much cast down!"

"Cast down!" said Virus. "You must not think so, madam, and above all, I trust you will not say so in your letters to the Protector. It is true, we have some slight apprehensions that the Proclamation, obliterating State lines, and declaring slavery legal throughout the Empire, may shock the prejudices of the Northern people; but still, the telegraphic intelligence received this morning does not indicate any serious opposition to the election of the General's friends."

"I am glad to learn such is the case, sir, and will write him fully on that point. But he will soon be here——"

"Soon be here?" exclaimed Virus, while the rest looked up in astonishment.

"I do not know—he does not say—how soon—but it is not to be supposed he will remain much longer with the army, after the junction of General Fell——"

"Junction of General Fell!" exclaimed several.

"Oh, yes! That is an event that will occur in Virginia, and then, with such an accession of Southern allies, Generals Balatrum and Fell will be enabled to prosecute the campaign in his absence. But he intimates, and no doubt his directions have been sufficiently explicit, that the guillotines will have to receive a new impetus——"

"The guillotines!" exclaimed the Postmaster-General, while a deathly pallor spread over his face. "There is no movement here against his authority."

"None openly made," said Flora; "but he has been informed that the Abolitionists have had secret conferences, and the object may be to organize a rebellion—"

"Rebellion!" exclaimed several.

"Never!" said Windvane.

"Oh, I assure you he writes me that overtures have been made to Randolph, even from Massachusetts, to revive the old Federal Government, on the terms of the Constitution, provided the former rights of the States be guaranteed, so that slavery shall not be re-established in the free States. Such propositions have been intercepted, gentlemen. They agree that slavery may be extended South and South-west, or in any new territory where the inhabitants desire it; and, moreover, the fugitive slaves are to be given up by the Northern States, and without trouble and expense to their owners; and even the decisions of the Supreme Court will

30

be respected and enforced by the free States, if Randolph will resume the Executive chair, and grant an amnesty—"

"Amnesty!" said several of the Cabinet Ministers.

"Yes, amnesty for the past, to all citizens who have not taken conspicuous parts—so you see *we* were not to be included."

"Nor General Fell," said Windvane. "And rely upon it, if there should be any defection in any portion of the North, it will be more than compensated in the South. I hope the Protector will soon give me the names of the Abolition conspirators. I'll make short work with them. Gentlemen!" he continued, rising and gesticulating with emphasis, "the thing we want is a *strong government on a stable basis.* There must be a master or nothing. We must be beyond the reach of the agitators, or they will bring us down. They call Ruffleton Dictator, and that is a far more abhorrent title than Emperor; let us make him EMPEROR!"

"Why not?" cried Flora, seeing the rest remained silent.

"We all propose it," said several.

"I am glad to hear you say so. And you will be his Dukes and Earls. Gentlemen, General Ruffleton shall be speedily apprised of your sentiments, for he has authorized me to dispatch special messengers.

Flora glided out of the council chamber in apparent exultation, and then the Cabinet Ministers resumed the consideration of the grave matters before them.

"For my part," said the Postmaster-General, "I am apprehensive General Fell's army will be seriously diminished when his sooty followers learn that we design establishing the institution everywhere."

"He will take precautions to prevent a knowledge of that fact being imparted to them," said Windvane. "The General himself would be involved in our destruction, if we failed to retain power."

"I have no doubt your calculations are all correct, gentlemen," said the Secretary of the Navy, "and that the Revolution will ultimate in the establishment of a great Empire. But I fear I am not destined to see it."

"Not destined to see it?" exclaimed Windvane.

"No; my health is failing. There is something in the

air of Washington fatal to certain constitutions, and I feel that my life is ebbing away—"

"I hope not," said Windvane. "A change of air, at this season—"

"I have been thinking of that," said the Secretary; "but my duties here, I fear, would be neglected."

"A few days could make no difference," said the Secretary of the Treasury. "We will remain, and if the Protector should return during your absence, we will explain everything to his satisfaction. Suppose you go to Philadelphia, or rather to Wilmington, and I will give you an order to the Collector there to sail with you on a visiting tour to the lighthouses. The fresh air on the water would be of service."

This was assented to; and indeed several other members of the Cabinet indicated a disposition to indulge in similar excursions for the benefit of their health; but they did not propose to join him. The Secretary of the Navy was indeed quite ill and restless of nights. He set out the next morning, and fell into the hands of Windvane's agents at the Baltimore depôt, and an hour afterwards was relieved of all his pains by the guillotine. It was proved that he intended to fly with a large sum of money; and his death struck a salutary terror among his surviving colleagues. They trembled in their places, but feared to fly.

CHAPTER LXXXII.

BALATRUM IN RANDOLPH'S CAMP.

It was after crossing Dan river, before its junction with the Roanoke, and after the army of invasion had retired more than one hundred miles from the scene of its last battle in South Carolina, that General Balatrum appeared with a flag of truce at the head-quarters of the Federal army.

"Well, General," said Randolph, who had been feasting sumptuously in the midst of his friends, "you find us in good health and spirits. We are disposed to be lenient, and if you will stipulate to lay down your arms and disperse your rabble before the day of grace expires, we'll send you physicians who know how to cure the ague and fever."

"And," said General Crook, with invincible gravity, "provided Lord Slysir agrees to return my breeches."

"Sit down, General," said Blount, "and eat some peaches. They were brought from beyond the mountain, where none of your stragglers could get them."

"We are not allowed to eat fruit," said Balatrum, whose cadaverous visage too plainly told that he, too, had been a victim.

"Your doctors are fools," said Crook. "Here are figs and watermelons, and we eat them every day. Why don't we suffer as you do?"

"It is your native climate," said Balatrum.

"That's true," said Crook. "And if you won't taste the fruits, take some brandy; that is the very best defence against the chills." In that opinion Balatrum concurred; and he frankly acknowledged that Ruffleton's store of liquors was nearly exhausted. Then turning to the President, he proceeded to deliver the proposals with which he had been charged. And these were by no means of a submissive character. They explained, however, the meaning of Ruffleton's slight divergence from his former line of march, and his inclination towards the mountain. A junction with General Fell was anticipated at the James River, where, Ruffleton's envoy intimated, offensive operations might be resumed.

"Ruffleton knows better!" said Randolph. "He cannot suppose the negroes will fight for him, after his Proclamation at Richmond. But say to him, once for all, that I do not recognise any decadence of the Constitution or overthrow of the Confederacy. My oath must be fulfilled. The insurgents must return to their homes and submit to the laws of the Federal Government, else no alternative remains but to deal with them as rebels and traitors. Balatrum, you must be aware that but for my forbearance your retreat ere this would have been a fatal rout. I might easily destroy three-fourths of Ruffleton's followers on Southern soil; but wherefore should I? Disease will punish them sufficiently. The best thing the leaders of this rebellion can do, is to decamp in the night, and fly to foreign countries. Their misguided followers may be forgiven. But I doubt whether their British allies will transport them from their native shores, since that Proclamation at Richmond."

"Such being the views of your excellency," said Balatrum, "of course there can be no agreement by which further bloodshed may be averted!"

"And, General," said Crook, as Balatrum rose to depart, "if you sail away in the British fleet, be sure and remind his Lordship of my breeches. I need them very much."

CHAPTER LXXXIII.

NEWS FROM THE CAPITAL.

"Now, my Lord," said Alice, when she accompanied his Lordship into the library, "pray be seated, and deliver frankly what you may have to say. But remember I can listen to matters pertaining only to the interests of the country. For better, for worse, in life and in death, with the exception of the affection due my parent and my friends, I am wholly devoted to the object of my patriotic solicitude. I need not be more explicit, and yet I might be. I might say there was a time—and another object—but it is past! When the last flickering ray of love goes out in the heart of a true woman —self-extinguished—it is gone for ever!"

Having uttered these words, Alice, who had reclined her brow for a moment on her hand, raised her pale face, and gazed with her tearless eyes at the now serious countenance of his Lordship.

"Fair lady!" said he, "far be it from me to desecrate the sacred shrine of the true and faithful heart of maiden! And if I have seemed to offend by any former levity, or by my politic suggestions, wherein, as is sometimes the habit in Europe, the heart might not be a party in an alliance subscribed with the hand—I humbly crave your pardon! And now, my words will surely convince you, I trust, that my motive in soliciting this interview may very properly merit your consideration."

"But, my Lord," said Alice, archly shaking her head, "it was really your design to be captured, when you persisted in occupying the farm-house!"

"It was—and I have confessed it. But it was for the purpose of announcing to you, and through you to the President, my purpose of rupturing the alliance of my Government with Ruffleton."

"Is it possible?" exclaimed Alice, gazing steadfastly at the diplomatist.

"It is not only possible," replied his Lordship, "but it became *inevitable*, when the Despot proclaimed his design to legalize slavery in all the States. After the adoption of such a measure as that, my Government has no alternative but to renounce the alliance. Every British Administration for years has been solemnly committed in favor of the abolition of slavery throughout the world. And yet this foolish man, yielding to the counsels of a mere weather-cock politician—"

"Windvane!" said Alice.

"Yes, lady—a mere wind-vane politician—has perpetrated an infamous absurdity, which, if it did not rupture our friendly relations, would justly subject us to the condemnation and contumely of all the civilized nations of the earth."

"Very true, my Lord! But, then, what does the world say in regard to the act which consigned the homestead of Washington to the flames!"

"It speaks but one voice! But we are prepared to prove it was not sanctioned by us. And we have dismissed Junkins from the service."

"I am glad to hear this. My Lord, we will confer again in relation to this matter. And in the meantime I will communicate with my father. An express starts for his head-quarters to-night."

"Adieu, then, till to-morrow," said Lord Slysir, rising and bowing profoundly. "I will not trespass further on your time to-night." And he rejoined his companions in the great saloon.

But he had no sooner retired than Edith glided into the library from another door, bearing a letter just brought to the Castle by one purporting to be a deserter.

"*Miss Alice Randolph, Amherst Castle*," repeated Edith, reading the superscription.

"Here am I, Edith," said Alice. "Did you call?"

"I but read the address of this letter—a love-letter, I hope, for our mutual diversion."

"A letter for me? Whom from? From whence?"

"Nay, that I am in agony to learn myself. But here let us sit and conjecture, before you break the seal," she continued, reclining in a great chair beside the one occupied by her friend, and placing the letter in her hand. "Our tête-à-tête will not be disturbed. Dr. Love has uttered his brief petition, and sent all the guests and inmates to their couches but ourselves and the nodding maids who await the tinkle of your bell. Gaze on—but do not break the seal yet; it was brought hither by one whom I have seen in Washington—I know not his name, but Willy says he is anxious to enter the service of the President."

"Then the letter may be from some one we left in Washington—but I will see!" Saying this, she broke the seal.

"Read on, while I close my eyes," said Edith. "I do not ask to know its contents. But if you should choose to read aloud, I may listen."

"Listen, Edith!" cried Alice. "It is good news! It is from ——"

"Whom?"

"Windvane."

"Windvane!"

"Ay, Windvane—and it is marked *confidential.*"

"Indeed! And does he possess your confidence?"

"The miscreant! But still he can be of infinite service. Listen—"

"You forget it is confidential."

"He has no right to impose any such restriction on me. But you will keep the secret until I absolve you. Listen."

The letter set out by saying that grass was growing in the streets of the Northern cities; the factories were idle; the ships rotting at the wharves, and most of the stores and shops closed and deserted—while everywhere the people were secretly pining for a restoration of the Government under which they had lived so long and prospered so much. In Boston the THREE had been assassinated, and half the guillotines had been destroyed by unknown parties in the night. In many places the obnoxious agents of Ruffleton had absconded in obedience to anonymous warnings; and more than five hundred of the three thousand fanatical political parsons had been hung by persons wearing masks. Windvane declared his purpose to overthrow the Tyrant, and to deliver him into the hands of justice. He said the Secretary of the Treasury was likewise disposed to abandon the enemy and serve the President, unless, indeed, he could succeed in shipping the $30,000,000 to Europe, and sailing in the same vessel. But that would be prevented, as his spies were ever watching the Secretary's motions. But the ladies were greatly startled at the next development of Windvane's sagacity. He said that by obtaining an interview with Lord Slysir, Alice could easily induce him to order the British fleet to guard the coast—and prevent both the escape of fugitives and the sending away of treasure—and that he—Windvane—*had induced Ruffleton to issue his famous Richmond Proclamation, for the express purpose of detaching England from his alliance!* The next announcement was a master-stroke of the politician. Supposing he was familiar with all the secret impulses of Alice's heart, he proposed, upon the reception of an affirmative intimation from the Castle, *to have Flora Summers seized and dragged to the guillotine!*

"Alice!" cried Edith, and at the same time throwing her arms round the neck of her friend, "a light is breaking from Heaven! The prayers of the good and great of the Union have ascended to the Throne of God! Peace will be restored, and the Republic preserved for ever!"

"For ever! For ever!" responded Alice, with uplifted and tearful eyes— "may HE who presides over the destinies of nations, and who vouchsafed his approbation of the work of Washington, grant that this great Republic may survive the crumbling of all other Governments, to the end of recorded time!"

"But, Alice!" continued Edith, "you will not permit the horrid executioner to guillotine the misguided but faithful Flora.

"No! No!" cried Alice, springing up, and ringing the bell violently. "Never! Never! She aided me in escaping, I care not what her motive was—I care not if she did meditate my death—I care not how much she loves the Despot. She is faithful in her love—true to the object of her love—and I will, at all hazards, fulfil my promise to her! Where's

Wiry Willy?" she demanded of the five or six female slaves that came running into the library in answer to the summons of the bell.

"La, missus," said the foremost, "he's done gone to bed long ago!"

"Wake him up! Tell him to come hither immediately!"

"Yes, missus!" said the maid, departing precipitately, while the rest remained awaiting further orders.

"Bring us some cake and wine," said Alice. "We shall not close our eyes to-night. Edith, you will aid me. Many letters must be written, and several messengers despatched before the dawn. Now," she continued, when she beheld a table covered with refreshments, and addressing the slaves, "you may go to your rest. Sleep while we labor, and be fresh in the morning. We labor for you as well as ourselves, for you are members of our families, and shall share our good as well as our evil fortunes."

"Miss Alice," said one of them, curtsying, "all de Abolitionists in de world couldn't make us desert you! And brother Pompey, who was wid General Fell, has stole away, and says none of de dark folks are gwine to fight agin de President."

"I hope they will not, Agnes. Good night!"

"I thought it was Pompey I saw talking to Agnes in one of the corridors," said Edith. "And why should any of Fell's army of slaves unite with Ruffleton, since his famous Proclamation consigns them to slavery? Not only so, but I am sure it is his intention to make slaves of all the free negroes in the North!"

"Nor is that all," said Alice, "he would make a nation of white freemen his slaves! But we are upon the eve of great events—events which will consign the enemies of the country to destruction! Ah, Willy!" she continued, as the faithful messenger appeared. "Come in. I am sorry to be under the necessity of disturbing your slumber. But, Willy, it *is* a necessity. It is a mission of the greatest importance—especially to me. It is for life or death—it is—"

"No matter what it is, Miss Alice!" said Willy. "I await your commands!"

"Willy, Windvane writes me—confidentially, he says, but from you no confidence is withheld—that the country—

all the North, is ready to rise against the Usurper and Tyrant, and—"

"Windvane too?" said Willy.

"Of course," said Edith, "if the wind is in that direction."

"Yes, Windvane, too," continued Alice smiling; "but he would go too far—he would seize and decapitate Flora Summers!"

"Flora Summers!" cried Willy, springing up from the chair he had occupied, in obedience to the injunction of Alice. "Do not permit it! She was your friend! She planned your escape and assisted—"

"I know it, Willy. And I promised my gratitude and protection, if it should ever be in my power to serve her."

"Let me go to Washington! I will set out immediately!"

"Can you pass in safety?"

"No doubt—no doubt! But I will procure a letter from Lord Slysir."

"True—it may be obtained. Go to him at once, Will," said Alice, "and say I sent you—say I desire as a special favor, that he will provide you with a passport, and any message in his own behalf that will facilitate your progress."

Willy hastened to the chamber of his Lordship, and Alice seized her pen and wrote with great rapidity; while Edith indited a letter to General Blount, to be borne by the messenger about setting out for the head-quarters of the President.

CHAPTER LXXXIV.

BATTLE AND STAMPEDE.

In pursuance of a previous agreement, Generals Toler and Fell again met midway between their armies, now encamped in full view of each other. The place selected for the interview was beneath a solitary sycamore, on the margin of a brook, in the centre of a plain chosen as the scene of conflict for the next day. The two generals had been accompanied by numerous officers to within a hundred paces of the tree, and from thence they had advanced alone.

"General," said Fell, after gazing a moment in silence at the tall form before him, and recognising the lineaments of the chieftain, "we meet again—may we not part as friends?"

"We may, if you will it so."

"By coinciding with your will? Is not that your meaning?"

"Rather say by yielding to the dictates of duty and patriotism."

"Duty and patriotism! General Toler, how often have I heard you say the first duty of Southern men was to the South? And that patriotism consisted in maintaining our equality and independence?"

"I know not how often—but I have said it repeatedly, General Fell. Equality *in* the Union, or independence *out* of it, has been my theme—and is so still. But neither equality nor independence is to be achieved by leading our slaves into the camp of the Northern enemy! I care not what Ruffleton may promise in his Proclamations. I will not trust him. I care not if it be his purpose to perform his promises—for I know the Northern people will not sanction his edicts. Nor would I desire to see slavery re-established against the people's will in the States where it has been abolished. Randolph is now hurling back the Northern invader—"

"How know you that?"

"I know it. I have intelligence of the fact. Let all the true sons of the South rally under Randolph's standard in this good work. There is no other course!"

"General," said Fell, in tones that evinced his feeling, "if this be so—if Randolph should succeed in driving the invader out of the South, after permitting him so long to ravage our fields with impunity—and should re-establish the Union and the Federal authority, what, then, will the South have gained?"

"It will gain security *in* the Union, or it will go *out* of it without further molestation."

"No—we shall have only the same old story! Randolph will be run for a *third* term of the Presidency, and of course the North must again be conciliated."

"General Fell," said Toler, with dignity, "we have not

20*

met to discuss the distant future. In regard to the past, when the portentous cloud appeared in the Northern horizon, I announced my readiness to follow your lead, and was then eager to strike for an immediate separation, but you failed me, and all your partisans shrank back, alleging that it would be better first to obtain possession of the sword and purse, by elevating you to the Presidency, a consummation then deemed practicable. I regarded the excuse as a mere pretext to obtain the Federal patronage, and so I abandoned your cause—but not the cause of the South. Aid me and Randolph in expelling the Northern invader from our native soil, and then I will unite with you, whether Randolph shall be with us or not, in demanding security *in* the Union, or Independence *out* of it. This is my ultimatum. Send back the slaves to their masters!"

"No. I shall go on. The ball of Revolution must roll to a final consummation. In the Union, or out of it, our safety will be best secured by the legal existence of slavery everywhere."

"The legal existence of slavery to be achieved by slaves! Fell, you are mad!"

"*You* are beside yourself!"

"Then to-morrow will be memorable as the day on which two madmen engaged in a pitched battle, for the security of the South. Southern men on Southern soil, with Southern armies!"

"You cannot withstand me! Why oppose my march?"

"I have no words to answer."

"Nothing but blows!"

"Nothing else."

"Then be it so! Good-night!" and the Generals separated and retired to their respective tents.

Every disposition had been made for a decisive battle the following day, and most of the officers retired early to their couches in quest of repose. General Toler alone was wakeful, and strode to and fro in his tent. On turning once he saw the canvas slightly agitated. He paused, and gazed steadily, and a moment after the following words reached his ear:

"Massa John! Massa John!"

"Who's there?" demanded the General.

"It's me, Massa John."

"And who the d—l's me? Let me see your face."

"Don't you know me, Massa John?" asked a very black negro, creeping under the canvas and rising in front of the astonished General.

"If it were not for the red flannel on your collar, and epaulette on your shoulder, with bright buttons and sword, I would say you were my slave Scipio."

"Dat's it! Dat's it, Massa John," said the negro. "I am so still, dough dey call me Captain Scip. I been belonging to de grand army under General Fell."

"And now you have deserted to your master, Scip."

"Not dzacly dat, Massa John—but dam if I fight, Massa John! And dat's de way all de niggers is thinking and talking too!"

"Ha! Is that so, Scipio?" asked the General, quickly, and at the same time advancing and cordially grasping the hand of his faithful slave.

"It's just so, Massa John!" replied Scipio, while great tears ran down his cheeks. "You know you learnt me how to read, Massa John? Well, I got one ob de Plocklamations of General Ruffleton, which says we's all to be slaves in de North as well as in de South. I had it and kep it for more dan a week, and read it ebery night by de pine knots to de colored Captains, till I got through wid 'em all—"

"You did, Scipio?"

"Sartin, Massa John! De niggers ain't 'lowed to be higher den Captain. But all de Captains is been 'splainin' de Plocklamation to de men—and now we's all ready."

"Ready for what, Scipio?"

"To break up and go home, Massa John, and 'tend to our work 'mong our wives and children."

"Is that so, Scipio? Why, it is understood Fell intends to lead you into battle to-morrow."

"I know dat, Massa John! We said he mus let us fight, or we'd desart. I put 'em all up to dat, Massa John; and now all's 'ranged. To-morrow all you'll have to do will be to jus' gallop your white horse right up to us and order us to throw down our arms and go about our business. Dat's all!"

"Scipio, I know you love me. We were boys together, almost like brothers—and indeed the slave in the South is more like a member of his master's family than the free negro of the North is like a freeman. Scipio, I shall trust you. If you deceive me, I shall perish, and my death will weigh upon your conscience—"

"Stop, Massa John—you're breaking my heart!" exclaimed Scipio, prostrating himself and embracing his master's knees. "But if Scipio's 'ceiving Massa John, dat he loves so much, may he roast in brimstone fires for eber and eber!"

"I will trust you, Scipio! You will know me by my white horse, which you trained from a colt! and I am sure he would know you if it were not for your military trappings. When you see me approach, contrive to be near the place where I shall address the men."

"I'll be dar, Massa John—nebber fear! And all de Captains, and all de men will know what's to be done. I've been preparing 'em! Dey all understand! De white horse'll be looked for! Ride right up to us. Nebber mine what the white soldiers say—dey'll think you're desartin'!"

"Scipio, your hand! If this scheme of yours succeeds—"

"Now, don't say so, Massa John. Don't say I shall hab my freedom, Massa John; I want to be wid you all your life, and I won't be free no how you can fix it!"

"Then farewell, Scipio, till to-morrow!" A moment after Scipio disappeared, and the General resumed his promenade, resolved to hazard everything on the fidelity of his slave.

Early in the morning General Fell put his army in motion, and General Toler awaited his approach behind the breastworks which had been constructed the day before. Not a shot was fired, except at the extreme left, where the white soldiers engaged—and these formed but an inconsiderable portion of Fell's army. On the black mass advanced, maintaining an ominous silence. The white officers were in the rear, urging the slaves before them, while Fell himself looked on in amazement from a neighboring hill. No smoke arose from the plain, no reports of fire-arms were heard, save from the most distant part of the field.

It was then that General Toler, in despite of remonstrances, galloped towards the interminable array of slaves. Nor did he pause until he was within a few paces of the foremost ranks, and not a shot had been fired at him.

"What are you doing here?" he exclaimed in a loud voice. "Why are you in arms against your masters? I tell you the Northern Abolitionists have deceived you. They are determined to be your masters themselves, and you all know what hard masters the Yankees make! Throw down your arms and go home, and I will forgive you! Go, I say!"

Then Scipio rushed out of the ranks and gave the preconcerted signal, and the sky was rent with cheers for General Toler and for the South. They threw down their arms, but a moment after snatched them up again, and demanded to be led against Fell, who had deceived them.

CHAPTER LXXXV.

FLORA'S INTREPIDITY.

The members of the Cabinet were assembled in Council, with pallid countenances and trembling joints. Flora sat apart, gazing in silence out of the window.

"It is bad news," said the Secretary of the Treasury.

"Bad enough!" said the Postmaster General.

"D—— bad!" said the Secretary of the Interior.

"My opinion," said the Attorney General—

"By your leave," said Virus, interrupting him, "I doubt whether a legal opinion, oral or written, can have much bearing upon the case. The country will not attach much importance, I fear, to the decision of an Attorney General in favor of an Administration of which he is a member. The question is, what should be done in the present exigency?"

"And the present exigency," said Windvane, "according to the dispatch received from Ruffleton himself—"

"*Ruffleton?*" said Flora, darting an indignant glance at the Minister of Justice.

"Certainly!" said Windvane. "Does his letter not lie before us on the table? Did you not receive one from him?"

"*Ruffleton!*" repeated Flora.

"Oh, I beg pardon!—the Lord Protector. According to the dispatch, then, from his Highness, the Lord Protector, we have intelligence that three-fourths of the army have been disabled by sickness, and that the remainder have not the physical ability or moral courage to contend against the President—"

"*The President!*" said Flora.

"Oh, by courtesy!" said Windvane; "or simply Randolph—that will do. But his Highness likewise reports the complete defeat and utter dispersion of Fell's army by General Toler."

"But the Protector," said Flora, "writes me that he would form a junction in a few days with General Maller, before Amherst Castle, and await fresh troops, which he expects the Secretary of War to send immediately."

"But will they *go*, when I send them?" said the Secretary. "There are only thirty thousand men remaining available for service; and if I order them to march away from the District, what security will we have here?"

"I am clearly of the opinion," said Virus, "that all idea of subjugating the South ought to be abandoned; else we shall have an ugly rising in the North. Why does not he —I mean the Protector"—he added, on beholding the reproachful gaze of Flora, "fall back with all his forces on this side of the Potomac? I am told the Castle in Amherst county is impregnable. On this side of the Potomac, he might still hold the reins. But the idea of sending more men to the South! Why, in less than two months we have sustained almost as great losses as Napoleon did in his disastrous Russian campaign."

"True!" said Windvane, with a sigh of impatience, and at the same time rising and promenading to and fro before his colleagues. "And he might have been utterly annihilated, but for the singular forbearance of Randolph. Do you not perceive that Randolph, for some politic purpose, hesitates to avail himself of the advantages fortune throws in his way?"

"*Fortune!*" said Flora.

"Yes; what else?" demanded Windvane.

"Treachery, I fear!" said Flora, returning with unflinching steadiness the surprised looks of the Cabinet ministers. "Gentlemen," she continued, "the Protector has sent for recruits, money, and medicine, and you are discussing the propriety of his conduct! You are deliberating instead of obeying."

"We are his Constitutional advisers," said Virus, "according to the form of Government we have been elaborating under his direction."

"That system has not yet been adopted," said Flora, "nor the advisers it provides for appointed. At present, the Protector is supreme or he is nothing. You must obey or oppose."

"We certainly do not intend to oppose," said Virus, "and we will obey to the utmost of our ability. But we may consider our ability, and unite in a representation of the condition of the country, and express our opinions frankly to our benefactor and friend. It is our duty, for instance, to apprise the Protector of the fact, that Admiral Bang declines co-operating with us, and that our recruiting agents have ceased to send us more men from the North and the West."

"And likewise make known to him," said the Secretary of the Treasury, "that all other sources of revenue, excepting duties on imports, have failed. The guillotine has lost its terror—"

"Because it has ceased its operations," said Flora, "except where it can victimize a friend of the Protector."

"A friend of the Protector!" exclaimed Windvane.

"Yes; a friend of the Protector. Who has been a more efficient friend than Dr. Blood?"

"Oh, that was a mistake of the clerk who copied the order," said Windvane. "Dr. Blood was the accuser in a case requiring prompt action, and my clerk, most negligently, in the order for execution, substituted the name of the accuser for the accused, and the blundering executioner beheaded the rich parson."

"You signed the order."

"I did not read it."

"Nor dictate it?"

"Dictate it! But yonder is a messenger! Perhaps we shall have further news from the Castle—I mean from the seat of war."

Windvane, in directing his eyes towards the window, had recognised Wiry Willy below.

"Excuse me a moment, gentlemen," he continued; "I will myself conduct him hither." He passed out into the hall, and seeing Willy ascending the stairway, awaited his approach.

"Your letter, Willy," said Windvane. He tore it open and perused its contents where he stood. And while his eye glanced eagerly down the page, a smile of triumph illuminated his features, for Alice had given him every encouragement in her power, to forward the project of counter-revolution. "Good!" said he. "All goes well. But, Willy," he continued, in a whisper, "did she not send me a verbal message regarding Flora?"

"No, sir."

"Are you quite sure?"

"Quite, sir. But she said she would send other messengers soon. She may have deferred it, if she intended any message in regard to her."

"I suppose so. Oh, yes, she will communicate with me frequently." And after some further conversation with Willy, he told him his general news had been anticipated by telegraph, and special expresses, and therefore he need not go into the Council Chamber. Then turning away, Windvane rejoined his colleagues.

"It is merely a messenger from Lord Slysir," said he, "with no tidings of public moment. His Lordship, you know, contrived to be taken prisoner to enjoy the society of the ladies and his whist. And now he sends for some articles of dress."

"His breeches, perhaps!" said the Secretary of the Interior. "But let us attend to our own affairs."

And during the discussion that ensued, Flora retired from the chamber, and sent for Willy, whom Mrs. Punt was questioning, in high excitement, in regard to the movements of her absent husband.

"Willy," said Flora, "why are you here?"

"I came, Miss Flora," said Willy, at the same time glancing round, that no one else might learn the nature of his mission, "expressly to bear a letter to you from Miss Alice."

"Ha! Alice Randolph! Where is it?" she cried, starting up and almost seizing Willy.

"One moment, Miss Flora, and you shall have it. I concealed it in a secure place, that it might not fall into improper hands. I knew it was a matter of importance to you," he continued, as he detached the false scalp from his head—"to you who have served Miss Alice so effectually when she most required assistance."

"Important to me! It must be so! Alice Randolph pledged me her word—and that, too, voluntarily—that she would serve me, if it should ever be in her power. Give me the letter! Ah! there it is! under your wig. Willy, I will never betray you!" Saying this, she threw herself on a cushion and tore open the envelope. The letter was as follows:—

"Flora:—My only motive, my only desire, in writing this, and in sending a special messenger, is to save your life. Ruffleton's career is nearly ended. But it was not the Usurper—it was the man—you loved. And I respect him for not abandoning you in the height of his power. I will save his life if possible. But yours is in the greatest danger. If you can rely upon Colonel Snare, who, I am told, commands the regiment at the President's Mansion, warn him that a conspiracy is in existence to arrest and drag you to execution. I cannot indicate the authors of this diabolical scheme—at present. But I declare to you that I know it exists. Lose not a moment in taking effectual measures to guarantee your safety. I know, however, that you cannot remain long in Washington—and I would advise you to leave the city and sojourn in some place of security where you may communicate with Ruffleton, who will soon be—I am certain, Flora—a fugitive. Fly with him to other lands. And that you may be happy is the sincere wish of ALICE."

"Happy!" exclaimed the almost frantic girl—"And why not? It is the only way! Alice Randolph is incapable of deception—she would perish rather than utter an untruth—it must be so! But where shall I fly?"

"Oh, believe it—take her advice!" said Willy.

"Ha!" cried Flora, lifting her face, which had been momentarily concealed in her hands, and having forgotten the presence of Willy. "But *you* are not my enemy."

"No! As God is my judge!" said Willy. "And if you desire to find a place of security, I will aid you, and faithfully deliver any message or note to General Ruffleton. I go now to my aged grandame's, where my Mary awaits me. If you would accompany me thither, I would answer for your safety."

"I thank you, Willy!" said Flora, rising and taking the hand of the young man between her own. "I have heard all about the little paradise you have on the Brandywine; the humble cottage—the peaceful grove—the sparkling brook, and the perennial flowers. But the most beautiful blossom is your Mary! Yes, happiness awaits you there, Willy! But for me—oh! would you have me conduct Ruffleton thither?"

"He should be concealed—"

"Alas! you speak as if he were already a fugitive! But if God spares us to meet again, he shall know how kind and forgiving you were! But, Willy, it has not come to that! Yet, were I compelled to fly, I know not where else I should go! Willy! I have riches! I have the command of the soldiers about the Palace, and I can rely on Colonel Snare! Go, Willy, to your happy Mary! As for me, I will battle it out bravely to the end! If we should meet no more—I charge you to say to Alice Randolph that I thanked her from my heart—and—what do you want?" she continued, addressing a messenger sent from the Council Chamber.

"Mr. Virus sent me to beg your attendance in the Cabinet Council. They have received fresh news."

"Fresh news! Good or bad?"

"I cannot say, madam—but—I think—"

"But you think what?"

"I'm afraid it ain't good news."

"Enough! Say I will be there presently. Go!" And when the messenger withdrew, Flora indited a few lines in pencil mark on a card, demanding Colonel Snare's presence immediately, and begged Willy to deliver it. Willy hastened away, and executed the trust without loss of time.

"Colonel Snare!" said Flora, who promenaded the room with composure, when the officer entered, "your fidelity has never been doubted by General Ruffleton or myself. Your own life, your own prosperity, must depend—"

"I owe everything to the Protector! And will serve him faithfully to my life's end," said Snare.

"In saving my life, you will serve him, Colonel Snare," said Flora.

"Saving your life? How is it endangered?"

"We are surrounded by traitors. There is a conspiracy to seize me to propitiate the enemy!"

"Is it possible! Give me the names of the traitors, and if Windvane don't cut off the heads of every one of them, I will have him shot!"

"It must not be! I cannot do it! But, Colonel Snare, I am menaced, here, in the Palace. You will be responsible for my safety. Be vigilant—that is all you can do at present, and until you have my signal to arrest the traitors. If charges be made against me—if an attempt be made to arrest me, even by any legal process—"

"I'll shoot every civil officer in the District, from the Executioner up to the Minister of Justice!"

"Enough! Go, Colonel, and charge your sentinels to be vigilant—it is all we can do until we know our enemies."

"I obey. The Protector said your command over the troops stationed here, was unqualified. If you should at any time order me to seize and shoot the traitors, it will be done. But without any order, I will shoot any one who ventures to molest you!"

Flora wrote some specific instructions for the Colonel, and then ascended to the Council Chamber, where she found the members of the bogus Government in great dismay, occasioned by the reception of despatches both from the South and the North. From the North, the ocean telegraphic intelligence induced the belief that England would at once withdraw from the alliance with Ruffleton, in consequence, at least it served as a pretext, of his famous Richmond Proclamation. But Russia and France were arming—and it was believed that Randolph's Plenipotentiaries had succeeded in consummating treaties with both nations. It was further rumored that France had agreed that Russia should have Constantinople, and that the former would receive an aggrandizing equivalent on the American continent. At all events, a combined fleet of unprecedented magnitude, would soon sail towards the West. From the South, the despatches and messengers not only confirmed the news of the defeat of General Fell, and the utter dispersion of his army, but indicated that the day of grace named in the President's Proclamation, beyond which every insurgent would be out of the pale of Executive clemency, was to be made memorable by the submission of the greater portion, if not all, of the followers of Ruffleton in the field. An express stated that the guillotine had already been destroyed within sight of the Despot's tent; and that instrument of terror removed, all subordination was at an end.

"Let us cut the wires!" said Virus.

"Wherefore?" asked Flora.

"It would do no good now," said Windvane, "for I learn that the news reached Boston simultaneously with its reception here. And the intelligence from Europe is already on the bulletin boards in New Orleans!"

"Then what is to be done?" asked the Attorney-General.

"What is your *opinion?*" asked the Secretary of the Treasury.

"Gentlemen," said the Secretary of the Interior, rising, "I will give you my opinion; and whether it be according to the Attorney General's construction of law, or not, I shall act in pursuance of it, and others may do as they please. Randolph, or rather the Union, is the victor, and I submit. I resign. I will not fly. I will face my fate, and I shall oppose the seizure of the public treasure."

"I will follow your example!" said Windvane.

"I will put my seal on the treasure," said the Secretary of the Treasury. "It is in specie, and in Washington."

"And I will defend it!" said the Secretary of War, "for the use of the Federal Government."

"Let us unite in an address to Randolph," said Windvane, "and he will save us; it is the only course. What says the Postmaster General?"

"He's gone!" said the Secretary of the Interior.

"Ah! I know the reason!" said Windvane. "He has

been appointing partisans of his own, and aspired to the Chief Magistracy himself!"

"And what is to become of the Protector?" demanded Flora, with flashing eyes.

"The game is played out," said Windvane, "and *sauve qui peut!* Let him protect himself!"

"Ingrate! Traitor!" said Flora.

"Miss—or Madame!" said Windvane, "you forget that while the guillotine has been demolished at head-quarters, it is still in operation here!"

Flora rose with dignity, and, turning her back on the ex-Cabinet Ministers, approached the open window. She gazed in silence for several moments at the lawn and at the barracks, as if in profound meditation. Then taking from her pocket a silver whistle, she sounded what seemed a preconcerted signal, for a moment after the roll of the drum was heard without, and in unusual proximity to the Palace during the sessions of the Cabinet.

"What does that mean?" asked the Secretary of War.

"In my opinion the Secretary of War ought to know exactly what it means," said the Attorney General.

"D— opinions now!" said the Secretary of the Interior; "we have to deal with facts; and I am not afraid to face the music."

The roll of the drum continued, and was heard the more distinctly every moment, as a body of troops, headed by Colonel Snare, ascended the great stairway of the Palace. And soon the door was thrown open, and a score of bayonets were precipitated into the room.

"What means this, Col.?" demanded the Secretary of War.

"She commands here," said the Colonel, bowing deferentially to Flora.

"Then," said Flora, "arrest that traitor!" pointing to Windvane, who shrank aghast in his great chair.

"Arrest me?"

"No words, sir!" said Colonel Snare. "I obey—and you must be silent. Soldiers, conduct the prisoner away, and keep him securely."

He was led out, pale and trembling at every joint.

"Do you want any more of us, Colonel?" asked the Secretary of the Interior. "If so, just call the roll."

"I await the order of Flora Summers," said Snare.

"You may retire," said Flora, and the next moment the chamber was cleared of the military.

"By George!" said the Secretary of the Interior, "that was bravely done, and well done, and not undeserved. He threatened to cut off your head, Flora, and you have caged him. It is a lesson for the rest of us! And for my part, I declare that I shall do nothing to injure you; but as for the cause—"

"Gentlemen," said Flora, "what I have done was in self-defence. It was Windvane's purpose to send my head as a peace-offering to Alice Randolph. But she, appreciating his villany, warned me of the danger. He shall not die by my hands, but will be dealt with according to law. And, believe me, I have no intention to molest any one of his colleagues; for I do not think any other member of the Protector's late Cabinet meditated my death."

"No!" said Virus. "Windvane enjoyed a monopoly of that conception; and I am glad you have not doomed him to death, because it was not ill-will, or malignity, but a mere trump-card in politics—"

"Why did Ruffleton appoint the rascal?" demanded the Secretary of the Interior.

"No matter, gentlemen!" said Flora. "You have all resigned; and from the tenor of the despatches, the Government of the Protector is at an end. What next?"

"We have only to consult the means of safety," said Virus; "for we know not what another day may bring forth."

"For my part," said Flora, "I shall provide for my own security. I have resolved what to do. Let each one pursue his own course. I fear not for myself. I see other couriers approaching!" And fresh despatches were laid on the table, which only increased the consternation.

CHAPTER LXXXVI.

SCENES AT THE CASTLE.

THERE was a succession of excitements in the Castle after Wiry Willy had been sent to Washington. The agents of Lord Slysir had found access to him with despatches from his Government, transmitted by the Ocean Telegraph. These seemed to confirm his Lordship in his policy, and now he denounced Ruffleton openly.

General Toler, after sending off the negroes to their respective masters, and seeing that the white followers of Fell, consisting in great part of natives of the North who had become citizens of the South, were hopelessly demoralized and dispersed, encamped his army, now swollen to 70,000 men by desertions from the enemy, outside the Castle walls, and in front of Maller, to whom he offered battle. Disappointed in not being assailed in the position he had selected, it was his purpose to become the assailant, when a messenger arrived from President Randolph with orders to act only on the defensive, and await events. But instead of a hostile disposition being manifested by Maller, that General, after the second day of the presence of General Toler, fell back further down the valley, abandoning his sick and wounded, amounting to several thousand men.

The Castle was illuminated very brilliantly, and there was a festival in its capacious hall, in celebration of the prospect of a speedy re-establishment of law and order throughout the vast Confederacy. The aged Senator occupied one end of the ample board, between the young ladies, while the aged Dr. Love pronounced a benediction from the other. Lord Slysir, with his captive companions, General Toler, Colonel Bim, Major Fink, and other officers and gentlemen were present. But in the midst of the repast the company were startled by the shrill voice of one at once recognised by Alice and Edith.

"Ha! ha! ha! Laugh! laugh! All ye sons and daughters of America! The night is far spent, and the day is dawning! I come, the herald of glad tidings! Who shall stay me? Let me pass, I say!"

"Charlotte!" said Alice. "That is her voice! Let her enter!"

"I knew it!" said the demented woman, rushing in with the same helmet, cuirass, and spear, with which she had appeared at the White House before its abandonment by the President. "I knew the virgin of the starry brow would have the door thrown open to Charlotte! Fair Maid of the Morning, let me kiss the hem of your garment!"

"No, Charlotte!" said Alice, rising and kissing the pallid cheek of the poor woman.

"And I, too," said Edith, "claim the privilege of saluting with a kiss the harbinger of glad tidings!"

"Glad tidings?" said Charlotte. "Yes! He comes! The conquering hero comes! Hail to the chief who in triumph advances! The Bridegroom approaches! The President returns! I am the *avant courier*."

"But sit down and eat and drink, Charlotte," said Alice. "You would not tarry and partake of the feast at Washington—do not decline the invitation at the Castle."

"No! brave and bonny lassie! I am hungry as a shark, and thirsty too. Some wine! Never fear, but I will eat and drink with you now! And I have earned my wages!" And she did devour the viands with a voracity which attested her need of refreshment.

"Now tell us where you have been, Charlotte," said Edith, when the poor creature had finished eating and drinking.

"Where have I been? I have been to all the State Capitals distributing the Proclamations, both the President's and Ruffleton's."

"And that was really good service!" said Senator Langdon.

"Was it not?" said she. "But before doing that I spent a week in the camp of Ruffleton, reading the future to his deluded followers. And now the future has dawned, and my predictions have been verified!"

"But, Charlotte," continued Edith, "did you not say the President was coming hither?"

"I did! And I said the bridegroom was approaching. Let your dear heart leap with joy, blushing daughter of the

North! And why are you so pale, thou heroine of destiny?" said she, gazing at Alice.

"Am I pale, Charlotte? If so, it is with joy. Have you not heard of joy having its victims as well as grief? But I will restrain my heart from breaking with gladness. I *am* glad—Heaven knows how truly glad I am to witness the triumph of the Republic of Washington! But go on with your narrative."

"Two days ago I left the head-quarters of the President, and, with Randolph's permission, plunged again into the camp of the enemy. Ha! ha! ha! I *will* laugh! Did you not hear my laughter at the door? Well, it is a farce. There were the tents and the sick, but no army——"

"No army!" cried Colonel Bim.

"And who are you?" demanded Charlotte, gazing at the gigantic form of the faithful officer. "Oh, I remember! Alas for you! Your sword will be converted into a sickle! No army—I say no army, but the army of the sick. All who could run away had taken to their legs, and they will be swarming *here*, ay, *here*, and everywhere, to-morrow——"

"Here?" asked General Toler.

"Yes, here, General—but not with arms in their hands. Fugitives and mendicants, your foes will crave a little food and water for charity! Nor was Ruffleton there——"

"Ruffleton not there?" demanded Alice.

"No—not there! Fled! no one knew whither. His men, by hundreds of thousands, swarming like locusts, had thrown away their arms and spread out in all directions in quest of magistrates, before whom to swear allegiance to the Federal Government, and to crave a little food for charity!"

"This is most extraordinary intelligence!" said Langdon.

"You may rely on it implicitly!" said Edith.

"Charlotte never gives false information!" said Alice.

"How could she? Why should she?" she exclaimed. "You have dungeons! If my news be not confirmed in an hour, let me suffer—There! There! Hear you not the rattle of hoofs? List to the bugle! Prepare all your throats to shout for your country! God, and your native land!"

These words had hardly been uttered before the huzzas

of a great multitude were heard in the distance; and soon after the enthusiasm spread among the soldiers within the Castle walls, and the sounds were echoed and re-echoed in every direction.

"Huzza!" cried Colonel Bim, springing from his chair and waving his hand over his head. "Excuse me, ladies and gentlemen," said he, a moment after, "but I never could hear the hearty cheers of Young America without flapping my wings and crowing!"

"For one," said Senator Langdon, "I can pardon you right heartily for that!"

"Colonel Bim!" said the Rev. Dr. Love, "there is not only patriotism, but religion in huzzaing for the Union, framed by Washington, under the auspices of God!"

"May God preserve it, then!" said General Toler; "but, at the same time, may He preserve the honor and equality of the South!"

"General!" said Alice, "believe He will preserve both. My father is a native of the South. Confide in him."

"I have drawn my sword at his bidding," said the General.

"And not only drawn it," said Alice, "but flashed it on the field of victory in behalf of the Great Republic!"

"The Great Republic!" said Lord Slysir, standing up; "I propose the Great Republic of Washington!"

This sentiment was applauded heartily, but the clapping of hands was interrupted by Charlotte, who rose hastily and rushed out. A moment after, her shrill laughter rang through the hall, and was succeeded by another deafening burst of applause.

"The soldiers," said General Toler, "have heard Charlotte's news of the dispersion of Ruffleton's army."

"General!" exclaimed Bim, springing to his feet again, "that is Carleton's band! I know every bugle of the Blue Caps! They are here! Behold the torches through the loop-holes! The parade ground is filled with cavalry—and here we are feasting and toasting——"

"The President!" exclaimed Alice. "Did you not hear that! He comes! he comes! I heard his voice, Edith! Let us haste to welcome those who thus announce themselves. Let us bid our hearts be still—but give our arms to the heroes."

At that moment Randolph, Blount, and Crook appeared at the entrance of the hall, having galloped up to the door and dismounted before any one could announce their arrival.

We will not attempt to describe the scene that ensued. The rapturous embraces—the joyful tears! But one incident ought not, perhaps, to be omitted. General Crook, dashing ahead of Blount, snatched up Edith in his arms, and running away with her, was pursued with celerity by his superior officer, to whom, at last, he was compelled to resign the blushing maiden.

"That is my last act of nonsense," said the humorous General, with a sober countenance, as he rejoined the President, and received Alice from her parent's arms.

"General!" said Alice, when the greetings were over, "you have fought a good fight, but Edith has conquered!"

"How is that? I don't understand it!"

"Come!" said the President, "we have not leisure for explanations. Let us dine."

"Ay," said Blount, "here's good cheer, and we have keen appetites after a gallop of forty miles."

"Fire away, then," said Crook, suiting the action to the word.

And during the repast, the President confirmed the news brought by Charlotte. Ruffleton was a fugitive, and his army had submitted to the Federal authority. More than seven hundred thousand muskets and other small arms had been given up or strewn along the roads. And while these details were being narrated, General Toler was informed by an officer that Maller had fled, and that his troops had signed a submission in accordance with the President's Proclamation.

"Charlotte," said the President, "has labored diligently in distributing the Proclamations in the camps of the rebels."

"And, father," said Alice, "is not this the day named in the Proclamation, beyond which no indulgence would be extended?"

"It is, my daughter," said the President, "or rather the night—and," he continued, looking up at the clock, "several hours yet remain before the beginning of another day. But the work of submission will be complete! The wires, repaired by my friends, have brought me intelligence of the public sentiment in the North and the West. Our troubles are over. Gentlemen!" he continued, rising, "the rebellion is at an end. Let us repair to the chapel. Come, Alice. Take my arm, Langdon. Let us follow Dr. Love to the holy altar, and give thanks to God!"

It was done. And God was present!

* * * * * *

Long after the principal personages of this drama had retired to their couches that night, the sounds of innocent and patriotic revelry rang through the halls of the Castle, and reverberated from the peaks of the mountains, where bonfires had been lighted in celebration of the great event. And thousands of stragglers from the deserted camps of Ruffleton and Maller came in and partook of the bountiful fare of the Federal quarters. Men, from different sections, who had been recently armed for each other's destruction, now embraced like brothers. The hungry were fed, and the sick were ministered to.

CHAPTER LXXXVII.

THE FUGITIVE.

Willy, and Mary, and the grandame, were seated at the breakfast table, as the early sun of the morning threw its rosy tints on the peaceful valley of the Brandywine.

"Yes," said Willy, "we shall have peace, now, and a lasting peace, I have no doubt. Both sections have found that nothing is to be gained by civil war; and as for Disunion, what is that but war?"

"True, Willy," said Mary, who had always sympathized with the South, "*such* Disunion as was attempted by Ruffleton and General Crook. But if either section were to seek to deprive the other of its constitutional rights, so that the people of the opposing sections were unanimous, then separation would be quite a different thing—it would be the same as the separation of the Colonies from Great Britain, which Washington approved, and which his Maker seemed to sanction."

"His Maker *did* sanction it!" said the grandame, "or it would not have succeeded. And, be assured, my children, that this Union will continue, until the Lord, which sanctioned it, shall consent to its destruction. And I pray that he may not be made angry by the guilt and ingratitude of the people, so as to permit them to become the victims of anarchy and despotism! But who is that?" This inquiry was occasioned by the barking of Bruce, the watchdog, and a moment after the latch of the door was raised, and a woman in tattered garments, but whose face was enveloped in a thick green veil, entered hurriedly, and tottered to a chair, seemingly exhausted by fatigue.

"Begone, Bruce!" said Mary, interposing between the dog and the visitor.

"Poor thing!" said the grandame. "How she pants! Lift up your head, child—you are among friends here. Come, sit at the table and eat with us."

"Yes, you must be the friends of the houseless wanderer!" said the stranger. And throwing aside her veil, Willy and Mary recognised her face, though pale and careworn.

"Flora Summers!" they exclaimed.

"Yes—it is Flora!" said she. "I am now a fugitive, and crave a little food for charity! I have wandered on foot all night long, in quest of—no matter!"

"All night!" said the grandame—"and no sleep—no food—no rest!"

"No—no rest! No rest for me!" said Flora, swallowing some coffee, which had been brought by Willy. "Thank you, Willy! That will do. Now let me read this paper which I obtained from a boy at the depot." It was one of the Philadelphia journals, printed that morning, and contained telegraphic news from all directions. A copy had likewise been received at the cottage, and Willy and Mary were already familiar with its contents, and they maintained a respectful silence while Flora glanced at the exciting items.

"It is as I supposed!" said Flora. "President Randolph has arrived at Washington, and is re-established at the White House. All the members of the late government have signified their adhesion. All abandoned Ruffleton in the hour of adverse fortune! None—none, true to him! None but me! And here I see that it is the same in the

East, the North, and the West. And even in England. They are rejoicing in France over his downfall, and call him another Robespierre! But I—yes, I will share his fate!"

"Where is he?" asked Mary.

"Where is he? If I knew, think you I would tell—and above all, tell *you*, who hate him?"

"I hate no one," said Mary. "I feared him—and he sought to do me injury—but that is forgiven—for he has since been kind to Willy."

"To Willy—yes! I would trust Willy. But there is no necessity. He will meet me at the place appointed, if not taken—and if he had been taken, would not the news have been in the paper? And yet I have waited and watched in vain, I will return to the place appointed. Willy, you must not go with me! I believe you would serve me—but it is not necessary, and it might put you in trouble, for he is charged with the death of General Hudson. I have provided a vessel, and if we escape, we shall leave the country for ever. A morsel of bread to carry with me, and then I must leave your blessed cottage—with many thanks for your kindness. And now—pray do not reply—farewell—and may God bless you!"

Flora, being revived, hurried away, without heeding the menacing eyes of the dog. But the animal was awed by her indifference, and did not dare to molest her. She proceeded to the place appointed for the meeting, and seeing a portly man in a harvester's blouse, she rushed forward and threw herself in his arms. It was Ruffleton. He bore her to a homely cart a few paces distant, and drove away towards the river, where a schooner lay at anchor. They were soon on board, and were never heard of afterwards.

CHAPTER LXXXVIII.

THE UNDERGROUND BRIDAL CHAMBER.

Colonel Bim arrived in Philadelphia in time to witness the grand illumination. Not only the public edifices, but private dwellings and shops, were in a blaze of light. Every city, and almost every town and village in the Union was illuminated. Peace was restored, and the Federal Government had once more resumed its sway.

"This is the place," said Bim, to the four policemen who attended him.

"Here?" said one of them in surprise, as they halted in Sixth street, opposite Independence Square.

"Yes," said Bim, "here we will find them, dead or alive. But if they were not economical of their fish and crackers, no doubt they starved to death."

"They deserved such a fate," said one of the officers.

"No doubt," said Bim, leading the way, and igniting a candle by means of a lucifer match when they passed into the chamber. "But yet, gentlemen, I would rather have them hung according to law than their blood should be on my hands."

"That's strange," said one of the officers.

"Not so," said Bim. "In fair fight I have killed my share. But I do not fancy being an executioner of common culprits. Here we are! and now we'll see what has been their fate." Saying this, he descended, followed, not without some hesitation, by the ministers of the law. A great accumulation of rust on the iron door of the dungeon attested that it had not been disturbed.

"Cardini! Popoli!" said Bim, in a loud voice, "if you live, answer me. I have come to release you from this dungeon."

"Yes!" cried they, after a momentary pause. "We live—but are nearly famished. Are you General Ruffleton?"

"No," said Bim, hurling back the door on its creaking hinges, "I am only a Colonel!"

"Captain Bim!" said the pale and haggard Cardini, starting back, and falling into the arms of Popoli.

"No such thing," said Bim. "I am a Colonel! But no matter. The war is over—the Union saved—and Ruffleton is nowhere. I surrender you into the hands of justice, to be tried for murder. Officers, do your duty. Take them to the legal prison, until the day of trial. This is the prison for offenders when there is no law to punish criminals; and I think even an assassin has reason to prefer the lawful one. Now, gentlemen, I must leave you. I have some private business to transact."

The Colonel hastened to the attic where his gold had been left in the keeping of Solomon Mouser.

"Aha! Old Tuppenny!" said he, as he stalked in, and beheld the Jew seated at a table figuring away on paper, before a lighted tallow candle stuck in a porter bottle.

"Captain—it is Captain Bim," exclaimed Solomon.

"No—I'm not Captain Bim. You are mistaken."

"Mistaken? Not Captain Bim!" said Solomon, lifting the candle and scanning the features of the officer.

"I'm Colonel Bim, at your service."

"Ah! A Colonel! Good! But the higher the rank the greater the expenditure. And it has been long since you drew any money."

"I have not drawn any, Solomon, since I was here in person. So, if you have been paying drafts, they were forgeries, and you must be the loser."

"No—no! You don't understand me. They were no drafts or checks; but I heard several creditors abusing you in your absence, and I thought you would thank me for paying the debts."

"Debts?"

"Yes, debts of honor—*honor*, Colonel. I O Us."

"Gambling debts. They were not large. I don't care —for, between us, Solomon, I had some misgivings about finding you this time. But since my money is safe, I won't quarrel about a few disbursements to the swindlers that used to cheat me. What did they amount to?"

"About $2,000."

"Hardly. Have you the vouchers?"

"Here they are."

"By George, that was signed when I was drunk," said

Bim, gazing at the principal one—" but it's my signature—I can't deny it."

"It's a debt of *honor*, Colonel," said the Jew, who had purchased it for five cents on the dollar.

"Well," said Bim, "charge me with it—but the rascal offered to take half the amount—I recollect that—if I would pay the next day—but I forgot it. The rest is safe?"

"Safe? Certainly! But it has brought me no interest, no commission! Now, having got your commission, I hope there will be some operations."

"Commission? Oh, I understand. Yes, you'll make money fast enough now. Why, you'll make your fortune, Old Mouser. Haven't you heard the news?"

"I don't meddle with politics. But I see they are wasting light everywhere, and the boys are selling extra papers in the streets. I hope real estate and stocks will rise."

"Rise? They'll go up like balloons, and you'll be rich! Have you any stocks?"

"I've got *some!*" said Solomon.

"And I shall invest my money in them. Have you any Pennsylvania Railroad shares?"

"I have one thousand shares!"

"And what did they cost you?"

"Ten dollars a share."

"I'll give you fifteen."

"Fifteen! Five thousand profit! And commission."

"I don't care—I suppose it would be right."

"Good! I'll do it!" And Mouser, who really had not been well posted in recent events, hastily pulled from under his vest the number of shares he had named, and with incredible rapidity made the transfer.

"So far so good!" said Bim. "Now shell out the balance, after deducting the commission for keeping my money according to agreement."

This Solomon did with alacrity, as if in fear the terrible Colonel might change his mind; and then proceeded to deduct a *broker's* commission for the purchase of the stocks.

"What's that?" demanded Bim, on seeing one-fourth of one per cent. added to the $15,000.

"Nothing—only the customary broker's commission—you said you didn't care. It's all right, you know."

"I meant the commission on the money drawn out of your custody. But let it go!" said Bim, taking possession of the remainder of the gold after all reductions. "The speculation on the shares will satisfy me. I've got you, Mouser! Mr. Corcoran advised me, just as I left Washington, to buy Pennsylvania Railroad shares, and—"

"Mr. Corcoran! Did *he* say that? Are you sure? What did he say you ought to give?"

"He didn't tell me the price I ought to pay," said Bim, having pocketed his shares and his cash; "but he said he would buy all I could get—"

"He buy all! He? And how much will he give?"

"He said he would pay me twenty-five dollars for every share I could produce."

"Ah! I'm robbed! I'm cheated!" cried the miserable man, and fainted.

"Hello, Old Jew!" said Bim, turning over Solomon's body after it fell to the floor, "don't go to dying in my presence! Wake up! Or they'll say I killed you! It was a fair bargain, Solomon!" he added, stooping down and bellowing in the Jew's ear. This produced signs of returning animation, and the Colonel abandoned his banker, and hurried away.

CHAPTER LXXXIX.

THE RESTORATION.

At Washington the excitement was intense. On the morning succeeding the arrival of the President—which had occurred in the night—the whole population of the city appeared to be hastening to the White House for the purpose of uttering their congratulations. Randolph stood in the great East-room, calm and self-possessed, precisely as he did immediately after the rupture of the Government. But a slight smile of the satisfaction he felt was perceptible on his lip.

And Alice stood, pale and proudly, at his side—proud of the Republic, and pale from the subsidence of the violent emotions which had so long agitated her. Edith, clinging to the arm of her honored father, was radiant with smiles and blushes, for Blount was presently to lead her to the altar, and her imagination could not now summon even the shadow of a phantom to mar the ceremony. And Crook was present, all glee and exultation—for he was immediately to be made Secretary of War, and had sent a message to his family to repair without delay to the Capital.

The Diplomatic representatives of all the nations were there, in their stars and ribbons; and Lord Slysir seemed as well contented at the turn affairs had taken as any of them.

Never before had there been so much enthusiasm at the Executive Mansion. The multitude was so great it was impossible to keep open the avenues for the visitors, and hundreds might have been seen passing through the windows. For hours the President did nothing but submit his hand to be shaken by his friends; and then, embracing the first good opportunity, Alice having preceded him, he made his escape into the green-room, where he found the wedding party awaiting his presence. Soon after his appearance, a side door opened, and Mrs. Punt appeared, leading her husband. All eyes were turned upon the intruders.

"Well? Who are you?" demanded the President, gazing at Punt.

"I'm a ship-carpenter by trade," said he, "and—and—you owe me a hundred dollars!"

"I do? Yes—I remember!" said Randolph, smiling, and thrusting his hand in his pocket. "But, my friend," he continued, a moment after, "I have not so much money about me at this moment, and you must call again to-morrow, or the next day, and the account shall be audited and paid."

"That'll do—come out, Punt!" said Mrs. P., and he obeyed.

"And that reminds me," said Alice, "of a deposit in my keeping. It is in the next room. I will fetch it in a moment." She withdrew, and returned instantly, bearing the sealed packet belonging to Lord Slysir, which had been placed in her keeping at the Castle.

"Will your Excellency," said his Lordship, "break the seals?"

"If you desire it," said Randolph, tearing away the paper. "But what have we here?" he continued, gazing at the contents, while the rest looked on with interest.

"My breeches!" exclaimed Crook.

"Your breeches!" said Slysir; "and I am much obliged for the loan of them."

"Never mind the breeches!" said Crook. "Let us have the wedding!"

* * * * * * * *

It was with great difficulty that the lines of carriages passed to the church through the dense crowd, constantly increasing in magnitude, as train after train arrived every hour, both from the North and the South, filled with patriotic citizens.

"Father," said Alice, when the carriages halted temporarily, while a procession of young girls, dressed in white, with garlands, obstructed the way, "I hope your clemency will be extended to all. I trust no more blood will be shed, and that the rejoicing will be universal."

"Never fear, Alice," said he, "that *I* shall become MARBLE, since you are flesh and blood again. But, really, my child, I would be glad to see more color in your face."

"Fear not for me, father! The good Doctor Durnell need not be so particular in his attentions. It is not consumption nor the ague. But let me plead for the late offenders—"

"I must except Windvane. The fellow begged a private interview this morning, and had the impudence to claim great merit for his secret correspondence with you. I told him that was subsequent to the change of the wind, and that I should have no use for him. But I will not pursue him, or any of his colleagues, with my vengeance. But Slysir's case is the most difficult. He says he is really in love with you—"

"Father! if he refers to the subject again, pray rebuke him, effectually and finally."

* * * * * * * *

The ceremony was performed by the Rev. Dr. Love, in the presence of as many witnesses as the church could contain. And when the bridal party returned to the Presidential Mansion, the signal was given, and a thousand guns were fired in honor of the Restoration. All the flags, bearing the stars and stripes, floated once more on the breeze; and Generals Valiant and Carleton ordered the hands to play "The Star-Spangled Banner," "Hail, Columbia, Happy Land," and, finally, "Yankee Doodle." Then followed the waving of hats, and thunders of spontaneous huzzas!

* * * * * * * *

CONCLUSION.

The author sat on his pillow, with his right hand uplifted over his head. His wife, with dishevelled hair, and in great astonishment, confronting him.

Wife. Give me my night-cap!

Author. Night-cap? It is not night.

Wife. Day is breaking. But why have you been huzzaing so? And why did you snatch my cap and hurl it round and round?

Author. Have I been huzzaing?

Wife. Certainly—and you have alarmed the house.

Author. Nonsense! But has not President Randolph returned to the Capital?

Wife. President Randolph? There is no such President. There never was a President of that name.

Author. No such President as Randolph? Where are we?

Wife. We are in our own poor house in this quiet village.

Author. (*Rubbing his eyes and looking round.*) These fractured chairs, and that broken glass, do seem familiar.

Wife. Then give me my night-cap, and behave yourself.

Author. (*Lowering his hand and gazing at the cap.*) And this is your night-cap in my hand! Wife, I have had a singular dream!

Wife. A dream! You have been dreaming all your life! And all your fine fancies fade away when your eyes are opened.

Author. But, wife, if one sleeps half his life and is happy in his dreams, and miserable by day—what is the difference between his enjoyment and that of the one who is happy all day and miserable in his dreams?

Wife. That may be a very comfortable philosophy for *you*—but for *my* part I do not dream at all. Suppose you publish this singular dream, and let all the world and your wife read it.

Author. I WILL.

THE END.

MRS. CAROLINE LEE HENTZ'S WORKS.

The Lost Daughter; and Other Stories of the Heart. (Just published.) Two volumes, paper cover. Price One Dollar; or in one vol., cloth, for $1.25.

Planter's Northern Bride. Beautifully Illustrated. Two volumes, paper cover, 600 pages. Price One Dollar; or in one volume, cloth, for $1.25.

Linda. The Young Pilot of the Belle Creole. Two volumes, paper cover. Price One Dollar; or bound in one volume, cloth, for $1.25.

Robert Graham. The Sequel to, and Continuation of Linda. Two vols., paper cover. Price One Dollar; or bound in one volume, cloth, for $1.25.

Courtship and Marriage. Two volumes, paper cover. Price One Dollar; or one volume, cloth, for $1.25.

Rena; or, The Snow Bird. Two vols, paper cover. Price One Dollar; or in one vol., cloth, for $1.25.

Marcus Warland. Two volumes, paper cover. Price One Dollar; or bound in one volume, cloth, for $1 25.

Love after Marriage. Two vols., paper cover. Price One Dollar; or bound in one vol., cloth, for $1.25.

Eoline; or, Magnolia Vale. Two vols., paper cover. Price One Dollar; or in one vol., cloth, for $1.25.

The Banished Son. Two vols., paper cover. Price One Dollar; or bound in one vol., cloth, for $1.25.

Helen and Arthur. Two vols., paper cover. Price One Dollar; or bound in one vol., cloth, for $1.25.

The whole of the above are also published in a very fine style, bound in full Crimson, with gilt edges, full gilt sides, gilt backs, etc., making them the best books for presentation, at the price, published. Price of either one in this style, $2.00 a copy.

MISS PARDOE'S WORKS.

Confessions of a Pretty Woman. By Miss Pardoe. Complete in one large octavo volume. Price 50 cents.

The Jealous Wife. By Miss Pardoe. Complete in one large octavo volume. Price Fifty cents.

The Wife's Trials. By Miss Pardoe. Complete in one large octavo volume. Price Fifty cents.

The Rival Beauties. By Miss Pardoe. Complete in one large octavo volume. Price Fifty cents.

Romance of the Harem. By Miss Pardoe. Complete in one large octavo volume. Price Fifty cents.

The whole of the above Five works are also bound in cloth, gilt, in one large octavo volume. Price $2.50.

The Adopted Heir. By Miss Pardoe. Two vols., paper cover. Price $1.00; or in cloth, $1.25. (*In Press.*)

MRS. ANN S. STEPHENS' WORKS.

Mary Derwent. This is Mrs. Ann S. Stephens' last new work. Complete in two volumes, paper cover. Price One Dollar; or in one vol., cloth, $1.25.

Fashion and Famine. Two volumes, paper cover. Price One Dollar; or in one volume, cloth, for $1.25.

The Old Homestead. Two volumes, paper cover. Price One Dollar; or in one volume, cloth, for $1.25.

The Gipsy's Legacy; or, the Heiress of Greenhurst. Two volumes, paper cover. Price One Dollar; or in one volume, cloth, for $1.25.

COOK BOOKS. BEST IN THE WORLD.

Miss Leslie's New Cookery Book. Being the largest, best, and most complete Cook Book ever got up by Miss Leslie. Now first published. One volume. Price $1.25.

Mrs. Hale's New Cook Book. By Mrs. Sarah J. Hale. One volume, bound. Price One Dollar.

Miss Leslie's New Receipts for Cooking. Complete in one large volume, bound. Price One Dollar.

Widdifield's New Cook Book; or, Practical Receipts for the Housewife. Recommended by all. One volume, cloth. Price One Dollar.

MRS. HALE'S RECEIPTS.

Mrs. Hale's Receipts for the Million. Containing Four Thousand Five Hundred and Forty-five Receipts, Facts, Directions, and Knowledge for All, in the Useful, Ornamental, and Domestic Arts. Being a complete Family Directory and Household Guide for the Million. By Mrs Sarah J. Hale. One volume, 800 pages strongly bound Price, $1.25

CHARLES LEVER'S WORKS.

All neatly done up in paper covers.

Charles O'Malley, *Price* 50 cents.
Harry Lorrequer,..... 50 "
Horace Templeton,... 50 "
Tom Burke of Ours, 50 "
Jack Hinton, the Guardsman,.............. 50 "
Arthur O'Leary,...*Price* 50 cents
Knight of Gwynne,.. 50 "
Kate O'Donoghue,.... 50 "
Con Cregan, the Irish Gil Blas,...................... 50 "
Davenport Dunn, a Man of our Day,...... 50 "

A complete sett of the above will be sold, or sent to any one, to any place, *free of postage*, for $4.00.

LIBRARY EDITION.

THIS EDITION is complete in FOUR large octavo volumes, containing Charles O'Malley, Harry Lorrequer, Horace Templeton, Tom Burke of Ours, Arthur O'Leary, Jack Hinton the Guardsman, The Knight of Gwynne, Kate O'Donoghue, etc., handsomely printed, and bound in various styles, as follows:

Price of a sett in Black cloth, ... $6.00
" " Scarlet cloth,.. 6.50
" " Law Library sheep,.. 7.00
" " Half Calf,.. 9.00
" " Half Calf, marbled edges, French,......................... 10.00
" " Half Calf, antique,.. 12.00

FINER EDITIONS.

Charles O'Malley, fine edition, one volume, cloth,.......................... $1.50
" " Half calf,.. 2.00

Harry Lorrequer, fine edition, one volume, cloth,.......................... 1.50
" " Half calf,.. 2.00

Jack Hinton, fine edition, one volume, cloth.................................. 1.50
" " Half calf,.. 2.00

Valentine Vox, fine edition, one volume, cloth,................................ 1.50
" " Half calf,.. 2.00
" " cheap edition, paper cover,.................................. 50

Ten Thousand a Year, fine edition, one volume, cloth,...................... 1.50
" " Half calf, ... 2.00
" " cheap edition, paper cover. Two volumes, ... 1.00

Diary of a Medical Student. By S. C. Warren, author of "Ten Thousand a Year." One volume, octavo,.. 50

HUMOROUS ILLUSTRATED WORKS.

Major Jones' Courtship and Travels. Beautifully illustrated. One volume, cloth. Price $1.25.

Major Jones' Scenes in Georgia. Full of beautiful illustrations. One volume, cloth. Price $1.25.

Sam Slick, the Clockmaker. By Judge Haliburton. Illustrated. Being the best funny work ever written by any one in this vein. Two vols., paper cover. Price One Dollar; or bound in one volume, cloth, for $1.25.

Simon Suggs' Adventures and Travels. Illustrated. One volume, cloth Price $1.25.

Humors of Falconbridge. Two volumes, paper cover. Price One Dollar; or one vol., cloth, for $1.25.

Frank Forester's Sporting Scenes & Characters. Illustrated. Two vols., cloth. Price $2.50.

Dow's Short Patent Sermons. First Series. By **Dow, Jr.** Containing 128 Sermons. Complete in one volume, cloth, for One Dollar or paper cover, 75 cents.

Dow's Short Patent Sermons. Second Series. By **Dow, Jr.** Containing 144 Sermons. Complete in one volume, cloth, for One Dollar; or paper cover, 75 cents.

Dow's Short Patent Sermons. Third Series. By **Dow, Jr.** Containing 116 Sermons. Complete in one volume, cloth, for One Dollar; or paper cover, 75 cents.

American Joe Miller. With 100 Illustrations One of the most humorous books in the world Price 25 cents

CHARLES DICKENS' WORKS.

Fourteen Different Editions in Octavo Form.

"PETERSON'S" are the only complete and uniform editions of Charles Dickens' Works ever published in the world; they are printed from the original London Editions, and are the only editions published in this country. No library either public or private, can be complete without having in it a complete sett of the works of this, the greatest of all living authors. Every family should possess a sett of one of the editions. The cheap edition is complete in Sixteen Volumes paper cover; either or all of which can be had separately, as follows:

Little Dorrit,.........	*Price* 50	cents.
Pickwick Papers,........	50	"
Dickens' New Stories,	50	"
Bleak House,.................	50	"
David Copperfield,......	50	"
Dombey and Son,........	50	"
Nicholas Nickleby,......	50	"
Christmas Stories,......	50	"
Martin Chuzzlewit,....	50	"
Barnaby Rudge,...	*Price* 50	cents
Old Curiosity Shop,....	50	"
Sketches by "Boz,".....	50	"
Oliver Twist,................	50	"
The Two Apprentices,	25	"
Wreck of the Golden Mary,............................	25	"
Perils of certain English Prisoners,.........	25	"

A complete sett of the above Sixteen books, will be sold, or sent to any one, to any place, *free of postage*, for $6.00.

LIBRARY OCTAVO EDITION.

Published in Seven Different Styles.

This Edition is complete in SIX very large octavo volumes, with a Portrait on steel of Charles Dickens, containing the whole of the above works, handsomely printed and bound in various styles.

Vol. 1 contains **Pickwick Papers** and **Curiosity Shop.**
" **2** do. **Oliver Twist, Sketches by "Boz,"** and **Barnaby Rudge.**
" **3** do. **Nicholas Nickleby,** and **Martin Chuzzlewit.**
" **4** do. **David Copperfield, Dombey and Son,** and **Christmas Stories.**
" **5** do. **Bleak House,** and **Dickens' New Stories.**
" **6** do. **Little Dorrit.** In two books—Poverty and Riches.

Price of a sett, in Black cloth,	$9 00
" Scarlet cloth, extra,	10.00
" Law Library style,	11.00
" Half Turkey, or Half Calf,	13.00
" Half calf, marbled edges, French,	14.50
" Half calf, real ancient antique,	18.00
" Half calf, full gilt backs, etc.	18.00

ILLUSTRATED OCTAVO EDITION.

THIS EDITION IS IN THIRTEEN VOLUMES, and is printed on very thick and fine white paper, and is profusely illustrated with all the original Illustrations by Cruikshank, Alfred Crowquill, Phiz, etc., from the original London editions, on copper, steel, and wood. Each volume contains a novel complete, and may be had in complete setts, beautifully bound in cloth, for Nineteen Dollars a sett: or any volume will be sold separately at One Dollar and Fifty cents each. The following are their respective names:

Little Dorrit.	**Nicholas Nickleby.**
Pickwick Papers.	**Christmas Stories.**
Barnaby Rudge.	**Martin Chuzzlewit.**
Old Curiosity Shop.	**Sketches by "Boz."**
Bleak House.	**Oliver Twist.**
David Copperfield.	**Dickens' New Stories.**
Dombey and Son.	

Price of a sett, in Black cloth, in Thirteen volumes,........$19.00
" Full Law Library style,........26.00
" Half calf, or half Turkey,........29.00
" Half calf, marbled edges, French,........32.50
" Half calf, ancient antique,........39.00
" Half calf, full gilt backs, etc........39.00

DUODECIMO ILLUSTRATED EDITION.

Complete in Twenty-Five Volumes.

The Editions in Duodecimo form are beautifully Illustrated with over *Five Hundred Steel and Wood Illustrations*, from designs by Cruikshank, Phiz, Leech, Browne, Maclise, etc., illustrative of the best scenes in each work, making it the most beautiful and perfect edition in the world; and each work is also reprinted from the first original London editions that were issued by subscription in monthly numbers, and the volumes will be found, on examination, to be published on the finest and best of white paper.

This edition of Dickens' Works is now published complete, entire, and unabridged, in Twenty-five beautiful volumes, and supplies what has long been wanted, an edition that shall combine the advantages of portable size, large and readable type, and uniformity with other standard English authors.

This Duodecimo edition has been gotten up at an expense of *over Forty-Five Thousand Dollars*, but the publishers trust that an appreciative public will repay them for the outlay, by a generous purchase of the volumes. All they ask is for the public to examine them, and they are confident they will exclaim, with one voice, that they are the handsomest and cheapest, and best illustrated Sett of Works ever published. This edition is sold in setts, in various styles of binding, or any work can be had separately, handsomely bound in cloth, in two volumes each, Price $2.50 a sett, as follows:

Pickwick Papers.	**Sketches by "Boz."**
Nicholas Nickleby.	**Barnaby Rudge.**
David Copperfield.	**Martin Chuzzlewit.**
Oliver Twist.	**Old Curiosity Shop.**
Bleak House.	**Christmas Stories.**
Little Dorrit.	**Dickens' New Stories.**
Dombey and Son.	

Price of a sett in Twenty-Five volumes, bound in Black cloth, gilt backs,....$30.00
" " Full Law Library style,........40.00
" " Scarlet, full gilt, sides, edges, etc.,........45.00
" " Half calf, ancient antique,........60.00
" " Half calf, full gilt back,........60.00
" " Full calf, ancient antique,........75.00
" " Full calf, gilt edges, backs, etc.,........75.00

PEOPLE'S DUODECIMO EDITION.

Published in Eight Different Styles.

This Duodecimo edition is complete in Thirteen volumes, of near One Thousand pages each, with two illustrations to each volume, but is not printed on as thick or as fine paper as the Illustrated Edition, but contains all the *reading* matter that is in the Illustrated Edition, printed from large type, leaded. The volumes are sold separately or together, price One Dollar and Fifty cents each, neatly bound in cloth; or a complete sett of Thirteen volumes in this style will be sold for $19.00. following are their names:

Little Dorrit.
Pickwick Papers.
Martin Chuzzlewit.
Barnaby Rudge.
Bleak House.
David Copperfield.
Dombey and Son.
Nicholas Nickleby.
Christmas Stories.
Old Curiosity Shop.
Sketches by "Boz."
Oliver Twist.
Dickens' New Stories.

Price of a sett, in Black cloth,	$19.00
" " Full Law Library style,	24.00
" " Half calf, or half Turkey,	26.00
" " Half calf, marbled edges, French,	28.00
" " Half calf, ancient antique,	32.00
" " Half calf, full gilt backs,	32.00
" " Full calf, ancient antique,	40.00
" " Full calf, gilt edges, backs, etc.	40.00

ADVENTURES AND TRAVELS.

Harris's Explorations in South Africa. By Major Cornwallis Harris. This book is a rich treat. Two volumes, paper cover. Price $1.00; or in cloth, $1.25.

Wild Oats Sown Abroad; or, On and Off Soundings. Price 50 cents in paper cover; or cloth, gilt, 75 cents.

Don Quixotte.—Life and Adventures of Don Quixotte; and his Squire, Sancho Panza. Complete in two volumes, paper cover Price $1.00.

Life and Adventures of Paul Periwinkle. Full of Illustrations. Price 50 cents.

EUGENE SUE'S GREAT NOVELS.

Illustrated Wandering Jew. With Eighty-seven large Illustrations. Two volumes. Price $1.00.

Mysteries of Paris; and Gerolstein, the Sequel to it. Two volumes, paper cover. Price $1.00.

First Love. A Story of the Heart. Price 25 cents.

Woman's Love. Illustrated. Price 25 cents.

Martin the Foundling. Beautifully Illustrated. Two volumes, paper cover. Price One Dollar.

The Man-of-War's-Man. Complete in one large octavo volume. Price 25 cents.

The Female Bluebeard. One volume. Price 25 cents.

Raoul de Surville. One volume. Price 25 cents. (*In Press.*)

GEORGE LIPPARD'S WORKS.

Legends of the American Revolution; or, Washington and his Generals. Two vols. Price $1.00.

The Quaker City; or, The Monks of Monk Hall Two volumes, paper cover. Price One Dollar.

Paul Ardenheim; the Monk of Wissahikon. Two volumes, paper cover. Price One Dollar.

Blanche of Brandywine. A Revolutionary Romance. Two volumes, paper cover. Price One Dollar.

The Nazarene. One vol. Price 50 cents.

Legends of Mexico. One volume. Price 25 cents.

The Lady of Albarone; or, The Poison Goblet. Two volumes, paper cover. Price One Dollar; or bound in one volume, cloth, for $1.25. (*In Press.*)

New York: Its Upper Ten and Lower Million. One volume. Price 50 cents.

HUMOROUS AMERICAN WORKS.
With Original Illustrations by Darley and Others.
Done up in Illuminated Covers.

Major Jones' Courtship. With Thirteen Illustrations, from designs by Darley. Price 50 cents.

Drama in Pokerville. By J. M. Field. With Illustrations by Darley. Price Fifty cents.

Louisiana Swamp Doctor. By author of "Cupping on the Sternum." Illustrated by Darley. 50 cents.

Charcoal Sketches. By Joseph C. Neal. With Illustrations. 50 cents.

Yankee Amongst the Mermaids. By W. E. Burton. With Illustrations by Darley. Price 50 cents.

Misfortunes of Peter Faber. By Joseph C. Neal. With Illustrations. by Darley. Price Fifty cents.

Major Jones' Sketches of Travel. With Eight Illustrations, from designs by Darley. Price Fifty cents.

Western Scenes; or, Life on the Prairie. By the author of "Major Jones' Courtship." 50 cents.

Quarter Race in Kentucky. By W. T. Porter, Esq. With Illustrations by Darley. Price Fifty cents.

Sol. Smith's Theatrical Apprenticeship. Illustrated by Darley. Price Fifty Cents.

Yankee Yarns and Yankee Letters. By Sam Slick, alias Judge Haliburton. Price 50 cents.

Life and Adventures of Col. Vanderbomb. By author "Wild Western Scenes," etc. Price 50 cents.

Big Bear of Arkansas. Edited by Wm. T. Porter. With Illustrations by Darley. Price Fifty cents.

Major Jones' Chronicles of Pineville. With Illustrations by Darley. Price Fifty cents.

Life and Adventures of Percival Maberry. By J. H. Ingraham. Price Fifty cents.

Frank Forester's Quorndon Hounds. By H. W. Herbert, Esq. With Illustrations. Price 50 cents.

Pickings from the "Picayune." With Illustrations by Darley Price Fifty cents.

Frank Forester's Shooting Box. With Illustrations by Darley. Price Fifty cents

Peter Ploddy. By author of "Charcoal Sketches." With Illustrations by Darley. Price Fifty cents.

Streaks of Squatter Life. By the author "Major Jones' Courtship." Illustrated by Darley. 50 cents.

Simon Suggs.—Adventures of Captain Simon Suggs. Illustrated by Darley. Price 50 cents.

Stray Subjects Arrested and Bound Over. With Illustrations by Darley. Price Fifty cents.

Frank Forester's Deer Stalkers. With Illustrations. 50 cents.

Adventures of Captain Farrago. By Hon. H. H. Brackenridge. With Illustrations. Price Fifty cents.

Widow Rugby's Husband. By author of "Simon Suggs." With Illustrations. Price Fifty cents.

Major O'Regan's Adventures. By Hon. H. H. Brackenridge. With Illustrations by Darley. 50 cents.

Theatrical Journey-Work & Anecdotal Recollections of Sol. Smith, Esq. 50 cents.

Polly Peablossom's Wedding. By the author of "Major Jones' Courtship." Price Fifty cents.

Frank Forester's Warwick Woodlands. With beautiful Illustrations, illuminated. 50 cents.

New Orleans Sketch Book. By "Stahl." With Illustrations by Darley. Price Fifty cents.

The Charms of Paris; or, Sketches of Travel and Adventures by Night and Day. 50 cents. (*In Press.*)

C. J. PETERSON'S WORKS.

Kate Aylesford. A Love Story. Two vols., paper cover. Price One Dollar; or bound in one vol., cloth, for $1.25

Cruising in the Last War. First and Second Series. Being the complete work. By Charles J. Peterson. Price 50 cents

The Valley Farm; or, The Autobiography of an Orphan. A Companion to Jane Eyre. Price 25 cents.

Grace Dudley; or, Arnold at Saratoga. Price 25 cents.

Mabel; or, Darkness and Dawn. Two vols., paper cover. Price One Dollar or bound in cloth, $1.25. (*In Press.*)

www.ingramcontent.com/pod-product-compliance
Lightning Source LLC
LaVergne TN
LVHW021315110826
845150LV00003B/582